Breakout at Stalingrad

HEINRICH GERLACH served as a lieutenant in the 14th Panzer Division at Stalingrad. Wounded and then captured by the Soviets, he wrote *Breakout at Stalingrad* while being held in captivity in the USSR. He died in 1991.

CARSTEN GANSEL (b. 1955), who discovered the manuscript of *Breakout at Stalingrad* in a Moscow archive in 2012, is a professor of contemporary German Literature at Giessen University. He is a member of the German PEN Centre and president of the jury for the Uwe Johnson Advancement Award. He is the author of numerous books on literature from the eighteenth to the twenty-first centuries, including the work of Hans Fallada, Christa Wolf and Johannes R. Becher.

PETER LEWIS (b. 1958) is a writer, editor and translator of both fiction and non-fiction. He studied German at St Edmund Hall, Oxford and Albert-Ludwigs-Universität, Freiburg, graduating with first-class honours in 1981. His translation of Jonas Lüscher's *Barbarian Spring* (2014) was described as 'brilliant' by *The New York Times*.

Heinrich Gerlach

Breakout at Stalingrad

With an Appendix by
CARSTEN GANSEL

Translated from the German by
PETER LEWIS

APOLLO

an imprint of Head of Zeus

First published in Germany as *Durchbruch bei Stalingrad*
in 2016 by Kiepenheuer & Witsch

This translation first published in the UK in 2018 by Apollo,
an imprint of Head of Zeus Ltd

The translation of this work was supported by a grant from the Goethe-Institut
which is funded by the German Ministry of Foreign Affairs.

A catalogue record for this book is available from
the British Library.

ISBN (HB): 9781786690623
ISBN (E): 9781786690616

Typeset by Adrian McLaughlin

Printed and bound in Germany by CPI Books GmbH

Head of Zeus Ltd
First Floor East
5–8 Hardwick Street
London EC1R 4RG

WWW.HEADOFZEUS.COM

Mortuis et Vivis

To the Dead and the Living

Contents

Translator's note

First, a word about the novel's title: although the German 'Durch-bruch' most commonly translates into English as 'Breakthrough', I have instead chosen to render it as 'Breakout'. Heinrich Gerlach tells his story almost exclusively from the perspective of the officers and men of a German Wehrmacht unit trapped in the 'cauldron' or 'pocket' of Stalingrad in the winter of 1942–43, and much is made of the fear that the Red Army might 'break through' the German perimeter and annihilate them (a fear that is never actually borne out). It was to avoid any suggestion that this potential Russian breakthrough was the main focus of the novel that I opted for the less obvious translation; 'Breakout' alludes to a suicidal plan mooted by some of the Wehrmacht unit (but again, never realized) to try to burst out through the Russian encirclement and reach the safety of the main German front hundreds of kilometres to the west.

One way in which Gerlach puts across the desperate plight of his 'band of brothers' at Stalingrad is through an abrupt switching in his narrative from the past to the present tense – an effective method of conveying the raw immediacy of events, in particular the terrifying suddenness and confusion of combat. I was keen to retain these tense changes, both in order to do justice to the power of the author's original text and because they are a key feature distinguishing Gerlach's Ur-manuscript from the one he recon-structed after hypnotherapy, which formed the basis of his 1957 bestseller *The Forsaken Army*. Another touch of verisimilitude is the author's liberal use of *Landserdeutsch* – German infantrymen's slang; to try to capture the flavour of this argot, I have used corresponding words and phrases that would have been common among British troops of the same period ('the Real McCoy', 'skedaddle', 'Elsan gen', 'lah-di-dah', 'swanning about', etc.).

The flow of the narrative is all-important, so I was concerned not to overburden the text with explanatory annotations. Much of the terminology of the Second World War and the Third Reich is already common currency in the Anglophone world thanks to oft-repeated documentary series and war films. I therefore confined myself to glossing only abstruse references to military hardware or to aspects of German culture that would otherwise have eluded English readers.

PETER LEWIS
Oxford, November 2017

Breakout At
Stalingrad

PART 1

The Gathering Storm

I

Back Home to the Reich?

WINTER HAD SENT OUT its reconnaissance parties into the brown steppe between the Volga and the Don. The unseasonal warmth of the first days of November had, by the sixth, given way to a snowless frost that froze the mud on the endless tracks as hard as asphalt. Along this pleasingly smooth, firm new surface sped a small grey car, lively as a colt that had bolted from its stable. It was coming from the great depression to the south, where the general staffs and the supply trains for the German units fighting to take Stalingrad had dug in, and heading for the railway station at Kotluban. The driver, so heavily muffled in winter clothing that all one could see of him were a pair of crafty eyes gazing out at the world and a red snub nose, gave the little vehicle free rein. Despite having a very poor view of the road ahead through the iced-up windscreen, he'd even occasionally take his hands off the wheel and quickly tug off his thick hopsack mittens to rub his cramped fingers. In peacetime, he'd been a long-distance lorry driver, adept at handling six- or eight-tonners, so he felt entitled to take liberties with this dinky little Volkswagen saloon.

The officer in the front passenger seat was also feeling the cold, even through his padded greatcoat and two rugs. He drummed his feet in alternating rhythms on the floor of the car and against the metal door panel.

'Christ, it's cold!' he muttered through his teeth, which were clenched on a cigar. 'You could freeze to death in this crate.'

'That's the fault of the rear engine, Lieutenant,' the driver replied through his woollen balaclava. 'The civilian version's much better. The exhaust gases warm it up inside.'

'Ha, that's cold comfort right now!' laughed his passenger. 'Try lighting up this nose-warmer, then,' he said, fishing a cigar from the recesses of his multiple layers of clothes and shoving it into his travelling companion's mouth. 'Its exhaust gases aren't to be sneezed at either! Besides, we shouldn't be so ungrateful. At least, I don't know how I'd have made it through the quagmire of the Ukraine or the Kalmyk Desert if I hadn't been bucketing about in this friendly old jalopy. Bet its manufacturers couldn't have imagined we'd still be needing it in the Russian winter, that's for sure.'

'Them and us both, Lieutenant – and this is the second winter already.'

'And hopefully the last, Lakosch! Even Ivan's bound to run out of steam sometime.'

The driver, Lakosch, took a long drag on his cigar and squinted at the officer sitting beside him, sizing him up. First Lieutenant Breuer, a reservist and third general staff officer who had only come to head up Section Ic – the Intelligence Unit – a few weeks ago, was certainly more approachable than his predecessor, a regular army captain who'd been a stickler for non-fraternization between officers and men. Even so, they still barely knew one another, so best tread carefully. Lakosch liked what he saw; the man had a pleasant air about him. So he hazarded a question that had been bothering him for days:

'Is it really true, Lieutenant, that the division's about to be stood down?'

If you're cooped up in the same car day after day, bumbling through enemy territory avoiding any pitfalls, and if you're sharing the same filthy dugout and eating from the same mess tin, then there's not much room for secrets any more, even those officially stamped 'confidential'. The officer looked at Lakosch out of the corner of his eye for a while and then burst out laughing.

'Trust you to get wind of that, you smart alec! Yeah, it's true all right. As soon as we've completed our new assignment up in the Don River elbow, we're off to winter quarters in Millerovo. But don't go shooting your mouth off about it beforehand, d'you hear?'

'Then surely we'll get some more home leave too?'

Breuer tightened the scarf round his neck and said nothing. Leave… He hadn't seen his wife and children in over a year. The field hospital where he'd spent more than six weeks fasting while recovering from dysentery had put in an urgent request that he be granted a spell of home leave to recuperate.

'No chance, Breuer!' the general had told him. 'Right now we need every last man, maybe even over Christmas. Go and lie down in your bunker and try to take it easy!'

As if taking it easy was even an option around Stalingrad! After a long series of battles in which they sustained heavy casualties, the two grenadier regiments had finally managed to capture the tractor factory and had pushed forward almost to the banks of the Volga. Now the companies, which by this time were uniformly only eight to fifteen men strong and bereft of almost all their officers, were strung out in a thin line along the crest of the steep riverbank. Crawling with lice and caked with filth, freezing and utterly exhausted, they'd already waited for weeks to be relieved, exposed to constant bombardment by Russian artillery and mortars. And the few poorly trained replacements they'd been sent were picked off like flies by snipers. Down at the foot of the bluffs, the Russians were clinging on like barnacles; not even repeated dive-bombing by Stukas could dislodge them. Night after night, they received reinforcements from across the river and kept launching counter-attacks, which inflicted even more losses on the crippled German division. What was it Hitler had once said? 'I'd rather hold Stalin-grad with a few small combat patrols!' Yeah, small combat patrols – that was about all that was left now! Take it easy, pah! And where was he supposed to do that? In Stalingrad, which was daily being steadily reduced to a pile of rubble by a hail of bombs and artillery salvos, or maybe at the POW assembly points behind the lines, or among the regimental and battalion staffs who were holed up in some basement or other, never seeing the light of day? Only the incessant nights of bombing in that foxhole in Gorodishche had been worse… Well, at least that was now in the past. The division had been withdrawn from there. The tank regiment, artillery and other units were already on the move, and the grenadier regi-ments were shortly due to follow. Off to winter quarters! Then, and only then, might there be some point in speculating about home leave.

But there still remained this new assignment up in the Don River elbow… A short-term operation, by all accounts. It wouldn't be long before he got some more gen about it.

A sudden jerk as the car's brakes were slammed on jolted Breuer from his reverie. Lakosch opened his door and looked out.

'A crossroads!' he announced. 'Should we carry straight on?'

'I think this is where we have to turn left. Wait here a mo, though, and wipe some petrol over the windscreen so we can see where we're going at last!'

The first lieutenant clambered out of the car and, after shaking and stretching his frozen legs a few times, walked over to the weather-beaten signpost. With some difficulty, he was finally able to decipher, on the arm pointing west, Russian letters spelling out the name 'Vertyachi'.

'Left it is!' he called out to the driver. 'Still twenty-five kilometres to the Don!'

The well-worn track to Vertyachi was as smooth as a properly metalled road, and with virtually no traffic. The small car shot westward like an arrow, away from the Volga and Stalingrad and towards the Don.

'Seems like you're in a real hurry to get away from the place,' Breuer remarked jovially.

'Oh, you know, Lieutenant – bloody Stalingrad!'

'Now, now, Lakosch. We should be happy that we're actually in the city. And hopefully we can dig in there. Capturing it could decide the outcome of the war. You can't go counting the sacrifices in those circumstances, especially not your personal ones.'

Lakosch had his own thoughts on that subject, but kept them to himself. Breuer fell silent too. After the relentless monotony of the last few days and weeks, their sudden departure today had profoundly agitated him and he couldn't stop his mind from churning. He felt that his last words had not been entirely honest. Didn't he also increasingly feel the urge to just get away from Stalingrad? And hadn't he found himself thinking much more of late about leave and his wife and children at home than about the poor devils up at the front on the Volga? How egotistical people had become over these three years of war! It took a Herculean effort to suppress the selfish bastard that lurked inside everybody. Breuer felt duty-bound to feel sick to the stomach that they'd left Stalingrad, but he couldn't help but experience a feeling of liberation all the same. Sure, Stalingrad had to be held at all costs, and so it would be: no question. Hitler's words from the speech he'd delivered at the opening of the fourth annual Winter War Relief Programme, which he'd heard broadcast over the tannoy at the hospital, were still ringing in his ears.

'No ships come up the Volga any more. Our key objective must now be to take Stalingrad… And once we've achieved that goal you can be sure no one will ever dislodge us.'

The wounded men crowded into the hospital vestibule that day, crouching or sitting packed like sardines on the floor, listened in silence and stared dull-eyed into the middle distance. Of course they all recognized full well the military importance of the battle for Stalingrad. But the sheer crushing difficulty of the struggle weighed down on them, and everyone present in that room felt that *they*, at least, had now sacrificed enough for that miserable heap of ruins on the Volga, and that others should now be brought in to do their bit. That was why they kept quiet – Breuer's own division had suffered enough too. They deserved to be relieved. They should be happy!

'There it is!'

The lieutenant gave a start.

'Who, what?'

'There: the Don!'

They both leaned forward to get a better view. The road dropped away gradually and at the foot of the slope stood a small settlement, behind which the silver-grey ribbon of the river lay spread out. Small, dark patches of woodland, the like of which they'd only seen in their dreams the past few months, stood large as life on the far bank. The car rolled slowly through the almost deserted village, then turned onto a corduroy road that ended in the bare wooden planks of a pontoon bridge.

They could clearly hear machine-gun fire now, interspersed with occasional more powerful explosions. The fortified line to the north sealing off this area from Stalingrad was not that far away. Near the bridge there was clear water, but in the distance they could see broken floes of matt-grey ice. Flat meadows and sparse scrubland surrounded the river at this point.

The Don! Breuer couldn't help but recall the day he'd crossed it for the first time. It had been at the end of July, far to the south of here. The sun was blazing down, and thick clouds of dust were being kicked up on the roads along which the army was advancing, turning foliage and grass, vehicles and men alike a yellowish brown. Back then he'd still been a company commander in a motorized infantry division. In a rapid thrust, the unit had forced its way across the river at the wine-growing village of Zymlyanskaya. A brief rest stop there had given the sweat-caked, dust-covered troops an opportunity to take a dip in the fast-flowing waters of the river, which lay there peacefully before them like some sleeping giant from mythology. The Cossacks called it the 'quiet' Don. Certainly, an aura of silence and secrecy lay over the wooded banks there, and over the vineyards and the shabby wooden shacks poking up here and there out of the verdant landscape. Even the dead Russian pilot lying prone, with one waxen hand pointing skyward, on a shining sandbank midstream, next to the wreckage of his plane (half of which had already been carried away by the wind), couldn't disturb the peace of the scene. But the strong current, against which the swimming soldiers could make no headway, hinted at the restrained power that lay dormant in this giant.

A few days later, all the hopes they had nurtured of pushing on to the Caucasus and seeing the palm groves on the shores of the Black Sea had run into the sand. The division was ordered to swing northeast, and that was when Breuer heard for the first time the name that to him had an uneasy, ominous ring about it right from the start – Stalingrad. There ensued a rapid march across the desolate Kalmyk steppe, whose fine-grained sand penetrated every crack and joint and destroyed the engines of vehicles, followed by a series of expensive and fruitless battles in the south, until they finally managed to execute a flanking manoeuvre and enter the city from the west. And that was just the beginning! There followed intense street battles, in which possession of every house, every cellar, every wall and every heap of rubble was bitterly contested, hand-to-hand fighting that cost the lives of untold numbers and caused the German divisions to melt away like April snow in the sun. Throughout the whole course of the war, there had never been anything like it. And even though three months had passed, this struggle was still going on…

But for him, at least, it was all over now. With a feeling of quiet elation, he took in the view of the hilly landscape with its copses and villages, a sight he had not seen for so long. It was like emerging from a nightmare. And now the Don was behind him. He would not be crossing it for a third time. Next spring, once the division was refreshed and rested and had entered the fray once more, the battle for Stalingrad would be decided once and for all.

The village of Verchnaya-Businovka is situated in the northern part of the great elbow of the Don River. A narrow strip of wooden houses runs for several kilometres along the flat valley floor, broken only by small clumps of trees, a grey wooden church and a brick house of several storeys in the urban style, where the German occupation forces had set up a hospital. The whole place was now heaving with supply units. The divisional staff had established its headquarters here.

Sonderführer* Fröhlich was strutting through the rooms of a wooden farm cottage, issuing orders. Now that he found himself within the four walls of a proper house again, all his bourgeois pretensions to a civilized life had resurfaced. His beak of a nose poked into all corners of the bare room and lighted with satisfaction on the shining icons reflecting the flames of two candles. Within a few hours, the building would be lit with electric light; the generator had already been installed. But it would still take a lot of work to make this place into suitable quarters for Division Ic.

'I want these windowpanes spick and span and a table and five chairs in here by first thing tomorrow, understood?'

The pallid woman following him at a distance nodded. She stroked the hair of the small boy clinging to her skirts and gazing wide-eyed at the stranger in their house. They were now living in the

---

* *Sonderführer* – literally 'special leader'. A rank in the German Army (Wehrmacht) and SS assigned to specialists without any military training who were drafted in for their expertise in certain areas, such as interpreting, civil engineering, archaeology, and finance and administration.

tiny stable and had to sleep between the hooves of the one horse of theirs that hadn't been requisitioned.

'Will they come?' the woman asked.

'Who?' Whenever the interpreter Fröhlich spoke to Russians, he had an unpleasant habit of half-closing his eyes and looking past the person he was addressing.

'Our lot – the Bolsheviks, I mean.' The woman was afraid because her husband was collaborating with the Germans.

'The Reds?' Fröhlich gave a curt laugh. His Russian was hard, like beaten metal. He was a Baltic German. 'Listen, if German soldiers are occupying somewhere, no Bolshevik's coming near the place, get it?'

Stupid bitch, he thought to himself. Still pinning her hopes on *Batyushka** Stalin!

Private Geibel came in, clutching a bundle of clean straw under his arm ready to make up a bed against the long wall of the cottage. His face, round as a pumpkin, was flushed with a calm, contented glow. For months on end, they'd known nothing but steppe, foxholes and ruins. And now this little hamlet with the unpronounceable name seemed almost like home. There wasn't even any danger here from enemy aircraft if the German troops' stories were to be believed. He spread out the straw, put some blankets on top of it and carefully smoothed them flat. He felt happy.

In the room next door, Corporal Herbert was tinkering with a large cooking range in which a wood fire was already crackling. He was fishing potatoes out of a bowl of water with his long fingers, peeling and slicing them in the twinkling of an eye and dropping the honey-yellow slices into a huge iron frying pan. He was the unit's clerk, very fair-haired and blue-eyed, and did all the domestic chores. He was one of those tender flowers that can only thrive in the forces in the rarefied atmosphere of an office.

---

* *Batyushka* – 'Little Father', a term of endearment traditionally used by Russians of their leaders, and dating from tsarist times, when it was held up as the complementary quality to the epithet '*Grozny*' ('awe-inspiring/terrible').

By the time the potatoes were sizzling in the pan, Lakosch had joined them and watched as they went about their business. He had just driven up in the staff car after dropping off the first lieutenant at Division Ia to submit his report. His shock of ginger hair glowed like flames in the flickering light cast by the range.

'Wow, Herbert, fried potatoes! It's three months since I last tasted those, maybe even four. Reckon I could eat the whole panful single-handed?'

'Like you aren't already famous enough for your gluttony!' replied Herbert drily as he lifted a pan of boiling milk off the heat. Lakosch took the opportunity to pop a particularly crispy slice of potato into his mouth. When Herbert turned back round, Lakosch's face was still contorted with pain from the piping-hot morsel he'd just consumed.

'Keep your fingers off my frying pan, you pig! At least wash your grubby mitts first!'

'Ooh, get him!' rejoined Lakosch. 'Barely five minutes out of the shit and already acting like he's Lord Muck! Plenty of time for that sort of thing later, it's not like you're going home tomorrow! Anyhow, frying pan – that reminds me, have you heard the one about the frying pan? As the actress said to the bishop…'

'Put a sock in it!' cried Herbert, covering his ears. Lakosch rarely hit the mark with his jokes; he told them too often. On the other hand, he was never offended by rejection.

'Come on, Herbie, old son,' wheedled Lakosch. 'Why don't you bake us a cake tomorrow? You know, one of those nice yellow ones of yours. The lieutenant's still got some baking powder left, and we'll get Panje to issue us some flour.'

'You'll get sod all from me!' replied Herbert, though he was flattered by this open acknowledgement of his culinary skills. Lakosch sidled up to him and winked.

'Hey, I know something you don't – some really big news! You'll be gobsmacked when you hear it. But I'll only tell you if you bake us a cake.'

'Don't talk crap!' Herbert said. 'Here, pass those potatoes – no, on second thoughts, get the milk pan, and I'll carry the spuds.'

Once Breuer had arrived too, they sat by candlelight round the big potato pan, slicing off large hunks of army bread, drinking milk and swapping stories about the journey.

'By the by, your colleague at Corps HQ sends his best,' Breuer told Fröhlich. 'He's living like a king there, isn't he, Lakosch? Got his own place, with a Russian housekeeper and two volunteer servants. The staff officers there live the life of Riley, I tell you… it's like some luxury casino. They've even got their own cinema, just like in peacetime!'

'I don't understand why they've sent us here, then,' said Fröhlich, poking around with his knife in a tin tube of processed cheese, which as usual refused to yield up its contents. Breuer shrugged.

'A few new Russian divisions have appeared at the front over there, and it's put the wind up the Romanians. So we're here to put our shoulder to the wheel and settle their nerves.'

'What does Lieutenant Colonel Unold have to say about that?'

'Moral support, he calls it. "Give them moral support round the clock!" We're supposed to supply them with gramophones, games and boxes of books. He says we've been lying around in the shit for long enough. He even wants me to get hold of the Rembrandt film to show here in three days' time.'

The Sonderführer chuckled: a mirthless, self-satisfied laugh. So, not for the first time, he'd been right all along: this supposedly big-deal 'mission' was nothing but an interlude, an assignment that could be measured in days. Like a passenger getting off a train during a brief station stop to stretch his legs and cast a quick glance backwards before setting off once more, never to see the place again. Fröhlich didn't live up to the meaning of his surname – he wasn't a happy person at all. Sure, he was optimistic, but his optimism wasn't of the bright and breezy kind that others find appealing. Rather, his outlook was stubborn, dogged, unshakeable as an air-raid shelter, and constantly on the defensive.

'Unold's been going on about that Rembrandt film* for weeks,' Breuer went on. 'He's dead keen to see it. I don't know what to do. If I can get hold of it he's promised me I can finally have an orderly officer.'

Section Ic had had an orderly officer, an '03', assigned to it, but the post had been unoccupied since the last incumbent was killed in a bombing raid.

'What do we need another 03 for, Lieutenant, sir?' interjected Herbert. 'I mean, now we're about to go into winter quarters…'

Breuer looked at the girlish face of the NCO, which became suffused with red flushes, fleeting as clouds in April, whenever he spoke. There they sat, fretting over rest and recreation, and all of them already with their thoughts on time away from the front. Finally, he said:

'If you promise not to breathe a word about this, I'll let you into a secret. Do you know what the general told me over at Corps HQ? "You'll just need to honour us with your presence for a few days more," he said, "then it's home leave for you lot."'

'Back on home leave to Germany? But how—' Fröhlich stopped midway through sinking his equine teeth into a slice of bread and gaped in astonishment at Breuer. 'So, we're not going to Millerovo, then?'

'Apparently not. Seems like we're heading back to Germany!'

A look of sheer astonishment crossed Geibel's pasty face, like a full moon rising over a wheat field. Herbert looked at Lakosch, who grimaced ironically in response.

'What did I say?' cried Fröhlich, slapping his thigh in triumph. 'Home for Christmas. And the war'll be over by the spring!'

'That's right, Fröhlich,' laughed Breuer. 'Then you can open your fishmonger's shop again and set up a branch on the Volga dealing in salmon and caviar.' Saying this, he pulled a key from his pocket.

---

* Rembrandt film – *Rembrandt* was a 1942 feature film directed by Hans Steinhoff depicting the life of the seventeenth-century Dutch painter.

'Lakosch, fetch me the little brown bottle from my trunk, will you? I reckon we've got good reason to raise a glass. Plus, from midday today, we're part of the Tank Corps again. So if things ever get dicey for us here, General Heinz will bail us out somehow.'

The men nodded. They all knew the young general, whose rise through the military firmament had been nothing short of meteoric. Not long ago, he'd been at the head of their division, first as a colonel, then as a major general, and had been a very popular figure because he pushed himself hard too. Since the first of November he'd been leading the Tank Corps with the rank of lieutenant general. Lakosch put the bottle down on the table and leaned over to Herbert.

'So, are you going to bake me that cake now, loser?'

Corporal Herbert nodded and smiled, his thoughts far away as he stared blankly into the middle distance.

Lieutenant Colonel Unold, the division's first general staff officer, leaned across the wide table, studying the campaign map. On it, the blue, winding ribbon of the Don twisted its way through green- and brown-coloured expanses as it flowed in a wide arc on its eastward course. The hieroglyphic script of chalk annotations, comprising symbols and numbers, was divided into a red group and a blue group. The front ran along the river, the huge northern flank of the wedge that thrust towards Stalingrad. Relying on the natural barrier formed by the river and on the weakness of the Russian forces, the German Army High Command had manned this section of the front with relatively thinly spread-out Italian and Romanian divisions. As a result, these units had been unable to prevent the enemy from establishing a number of bridgeheads, which were being defended with grim determination. It was to one of these Russian bridgeheads that the mobile elements of their division – led for the time being by Unold after the division commander had been transferred – had now been ordered. For security reasons, they'd been told…

The lieutenant colonel's narrow face displayed nervous irritation. From time to time, he'd grab a piece of chalk and make a few imperious corrections. The situation here wasn't to his liking, not in the slightest.

It wasn't the two or three new divisions the enemy had committed to the bridgehead at Kletskaya that bothered him. The reports on this painted a familiar picture: the troops were all either boys or old men, bad morale, poorly equipped and armed (some even had Model 41 muskets with unrifled barrels). Unold was a specialist. As a young captain on the general staff he had been active in the department 'Foreign Forces/East' at the Army High Command when the invasion of Czechoslovakia was being planned. He spoke Russian and liked to interrogate prisoners himself. He knew the Russians weren't planning to launch any serious assault with divisions like this. But other things were troubling him. For instance, there were the two new bridges across the Don, constructed clandestinely, almost unnoticed. What were the Russians up to building these bridges, if not…?

At an adjacent table, Captain Engelhard, the division's first orderly officer, was sorting through a pile of dispatches. He was young and had an elegance about him that was quite out of keeping with these surroundings. He had ended up at the divisional staff thanks to a bullet lodged in his lungs.

Now he stood up and placed a slip of paper on the desk in front of Unold. The lieutenant colonel skim-read the dispatch out of the corner of his eye and then, taking a sudden interest, picked it up. As he reread it, his lips widened into a thin line. His grey eyes cast a swift glance at the captain, who had remained standing by the table; then his hand, clutching the chalk, suddenly moved rapidly over the pale green wooded area north of the Don. He looked through narrowed eyes at the red circle he'd drawn there for a moment, and the muscles around his cheekbones twitched. Then, studiedly and almost lovingly, he drew a large number 5 inside the circle and below it the lozenge symbol denoting a tank.

'Does the Lieutenant Colonel really believe they have a tank force there?'

Unold did not respond. He walked over to the low-silled window and looked out. His gaunt face shimmered like a death mask in the bluish light of the badly made windowpanes. Skating over the rough cobblestones of the empty village street, his blurred vision raced back through time and space…

Poltava, 1941. The windows of the administrative building that was home to Army Group South looked out on the monument commemorating the victory of Tsar Peter the Great over the Swedes. The Army High Command had dispatched General Staff Major Unold – as he then was – there in lieu of the third general staff officer, who was ill. However, he had recovered sooner than expected and Unold, suddenly finding himself at a loose end, had immersed himself more and more in the great work that the Imperial Russian general staff had compiled about the battle of 1709 outside this Ukrainian city, a volume he'd come across by chance. Excursions to the plains outside the city, whose blood-soaked earth yielded up to his digging an old helmet here or a rusty weapon there, brought what he had read vividly to life, and the lectures he delivered in the mess hall to an audience of staff officers and others soon earned the eloquent major the reputation of an authoritative expert on Russia's great battle of liberation. In December 1941 – shortly after the failure to take Moscow – Field Marshal von Brauchitsch, the army's commander-in-chief, appeared one day at Army Group South. One evening in the mess, he expressed a wish to see the historic battlefield, and the next morning they were all driven out to the site in an open-topped Volkswagen *Kübelwagen*,* muffled in furs and blankets: the field

---

* *Kübelwagen* – literally 'bucket car'. The German equivalent of the Jeep, manufactured by Volkswagen. Its official designation was the Typ 82 light field car, and the nickname referred to the unglamorous appearance of this open-topped utility vehicle. VW also produced a military variant of its familiar 'Beetle' saloon car.

marshal, the CO of Army Group South General Field Marshal von Rundstedt, and Unold. Unold spoke for almost an hour. On the icy winter plain, he conjured up the rich hues of summer, peopled the place with colourful army columns and filled the frost-clear air with the tumult of battle, the roar of cannon and the cries of the wounded. It seemed to him that he'd never before spoken so well. The commander-in-chief only interrupted him with an occasional polite question. In the silence that followed his presentation, as the present once again settled over the scene, Brauchitsch uttered a sentence that hung – as the only enduring thing to emerge from this incident – like an inscription on a gravestone over these flat fields:

'A would-be conqueror came to grief here too. There's no defeating the Russians on home soil…'

They walked back to the jeep and started on the return journey in silence. And it was then that Major Unold was witness to a conversation that for him was like suddenly looking from broad daylight into a black, bottomless pit.

'The operative objective for this year', to paraphrase what the two generals discussed on the ride back, 'has not been achieved. After mobilization of the Second and Third Wave, four hundred Russian divisions will be facing one hundred and seventy-five German. It's not feasible to overcome this enemy with the resources at our disposal. We've got to fall back to the defensive line running from Lake Peipus through Beresina and along the Dnieper, possibly even further, right back to the Neman and the Vistula, and then we could build an eastern defensive wall there that the Russians can knock themselves out trying to breach. Our main task now is to preserve the army as an effective fighting force.'

Unold inhaled deeply and audibly and drummed his fingers against the windows. That conversation had dogged him even in his dreams, straining at his nerves from his subconscious. He was too good a general staff officer to be able to ignore the logic of such deliberations. And yet he was too great an admirer of Hitler not to invoke his faith in the Führer to help allay his perfectly rational fears.

So had anything happened to justify the experts' gloomy pessimism? As Unold pondered this question, his eyes grew bright and clear once more. Nothing, absolutely nothing! Brauchitsch and Rundstedt were history, cast off into oblivion as unbelieving doubters, and other, more faithful followers had been promoted in their place. Hitler himself had assumed supreme command of the army. A year had passed, and here they were outside Stalingrad. A genius, unfathomable in his autonomy, had swept away all theory and book learning. A genius, whom the faith of millions – the faith that can move mountains – had made strong and capable of working miracles. Who would ever have thought that a single division could hold a sector fifty kilometres wide? Any officer cadet who'd dared to suggest such an idea at training school would have been sent home for hopeless incompetence. And yet today such a thing was common practice here on the Eastern Front. The unshakeable faith of all had made this possible, and it guaranteed victory. Doubting was tantamount to desertion.

'We must all believe!' Unold announced involuntarily to the room. Only Engelhard's startled look made him realize the ambiguity of what he'd just said. He gave a brief, hollow laugh, went back to the table and picked up the dispatch again.

'OK, as you were,' he said with relief. 'Look, they even say themselves right here: "Deliberate disinformation can't be ruled out!" It's clearly another case of the Russian signals intelligence trying to pull a fast one.'

After all, hadn't the Corps also dismissed the possibility of a major Russian offensive as absurd? And even if the Russians displayed the same kind of sheer obstinacy they'd shown last winter and *did* attempt an assault, the Corps' battle deployment plans showed three hundred tanks ready and waiting to repel them, including the brand-new armour that the First Romanian Tank Division had just taken delivery of. And this time they had the reserves that they'd been lacking in 1941. So what did they have to fear?

Unold picked up an eraser and wiped out the ominous symbol he'd just drawn; all that remained of it was a faint mark against the green background of the forest. With its disappearance, all his nagging fears and doubts were dispelled too.

'It's a bluff,' he declared, turning on Engelhard a look of such clear resolve as to make his captain's heart jump for joy. 'A cheap bluff! The Russians aren't coming. They're finished.'

In the days that followed, the weather changed. It turned dank and foggy, and a fine drizzle covered the cobblestones of the village street with a thin layer of ice that made every step taken out of doors treacherous. Even in Lakosch's sure hands, the Volkswagen that First Lieutenant Breuer used to visit neighbouring units slithered about on the slippery surface. They found it difficult making any progress.

The mood was clearly sombre at the Second Division of the Fifth Romanian Corps, which was billeted in the little wooden shacks of the village of Kalmykov. A captain sporting an elegant khaki uniform, and who was as swarthy and spirited as a bullfighter, presented his German colleague with some pristine maps of enemy positions, drawn up in the last few days.

'Look here, comrade, sir,' he explained in his drawling Balkan German. 'These three infantry divisions are new. We only found out about the last one a few days ago. Anyway, we're not bothered about them. But behind them there's the Third Russian Cavalry Corps! I ask you, what do you need a cavalry regiment for unless you're planning an attack? And we've no idea what might be hiding in this large forest behind the town of Kletskaya. We don't have any planes of our own, and no German reconnaissance aircraft were available. And with the weather like it is now, we've got no chance of finding anything out. But Russian prisoners have told us about a tank force that's supposedly positioned there. That may or may not be true. But if it is, that's very bad news for us, comrade, sir! We've got no heavy weapons, as you know, and our soldiers are exhausted…'

His dark eyes flitted across the wall, where portraits of the young Romanian King Michael and the country's dictator, Marshal Antonescu, gazed down self-consciously from heavy frames.

'That's what we're here for, Captain,' answered Breuer, taking one of the Turkish cigarettes the Romanian proffered him from a silver case. 'We've brought plenty of heavy weapons and tanks with us.'

'I'm aware of that, comrade, sir. But when will your men be available?'

'Well, within a few days, come what may!' The captain poured the contents of a bottle into a couple of thin-stemmed liqueur glasses.

'Your health, comrade, sir. Here's something to warm the cockles! It's Tuica,* the real McCoy.'

He held his glass up to the light and emptied it in small sips.

'It'd be good,' he announced, 'if your units could get a move on. We were already expecting the Russians to attack on the ninth of November. But it never happened.'

'You just wait and see, Captain,' replied Breuer. 'It won't ever happen!'

'Let's hope you're right, comrade, sir!'

On the way back, Breuer made a detour across the high ground south of Kletskaya. At a crossroads where a road led down to the Don, a Romanian sentry was pacing up and down in the freezing rain, his rifle held at the ready, and casting an occasional glance to the north. His steel helmet was perched on top of a tall, dirty-white sheepskin

---

* Tuica – a traditional Romanian spirit produced by fermenting and distilling plums.

cap like a protective roof, and the rain was running off it in small rivulets that trickled onto his shoulders and back. The colourful piece of tarpaulin that he'd draped over his greatcoat gave him the appearance of a particularly lovingly dressed scarecrow. When he caught sight of their car, he started gesticulating wildly that there was no access down this road. Breuer got out of the car and walked a short way up the hill until he could get a clear view over the area to the north. A few hundred metres ahead, the Romanian trenches cut across the bare land. Everything was quiet, drowned in rain. The hill sloped down gently to a hollow, where a few tiny houses could be made out: Kletskaya. Behind it, barely visible in the grey gloom of the rainy day, was the pale ribbon of a river: the Don. Turning round in silence, he stretched out both arms; he still felt stiff and sluggish. The dark shadow way off in the distance, though – that was the dreaded forest. The range of hills here seemed to be ideal defensive terrain. It dominated the whole of the Don Basin; in clear weather it would afford a good view far behind enemy lines. God only knew how the Russians managed to supply their forces on the southern bank of the Don and even to build bridges under such conditions!

Around the same time, the new divisional commander was just arriving at Businovka. He immediately let it be known that he wanted to meet the staff officers, and those attached to the subsidiary units, at an informal gathering in the mess. Captain Fackelmann, the commandant of the headquarters, was instructed to lay on a substantial dinner for around forty people. The little reserve captain, though not terribly au fait in military matters, was adept at producing a hearty style of cooking and performed the task keenly and skilfully, ably assisted by three orderlies who were eager to keep their positions. On the appointed evening, the village church vestry, which had been designated as the officers' mess, was resplendent in the festive glow of many candelabra and spotless white tablecloths. The general, a bulky figure with a rubicund, pudgy face, made his entrance in the company of Lieutenant Colonel Unold, who, in honour of the occasion, had put on his stylish black tank commander's uniform. The general greeted all the assembled officers individually, enquired after their name and rank, and fixed each of them with a brief stare from his watery blue eyes, into which he tried in vain to inject some ardour. Then he asked the higher ranks to join him at the head of the long table, while the more junior officers took their places at the remaining seats. One striking feature was the large number of young captains present. The straw-blond, freckled Captain Siebel – who had sacrificed his left arm for the Fatherland at Volkhov and had in the interim resignedly accepted a clacking prosthesis, the award of the Knight's Cross, a quartermaster's position on the divisional staff, and the prospect of the nation's gratitude in the glorious time that was coming – was twenty-seven years old. The first orderly officer, Captain Engelhard, and the divisional adjutant Captain Gedig, a jolly Berliner with brown squirrel's eyes, weren't even in their mid-twenties yet.

Under the influence of the white Bordeaux, the conversation soon became animated. It turned primarily on the dishes that Captain Fackelmann had surprised them with. The main course had been liver dumplings with boiled potatoes.

'Quite exquisite, my dear Fackelmann,' said Captain Siebel patronizingly.

'Truly the crème de la crème, eh?'

'Steady on now, gentlemen. I wouldn't go that far,' the chubby Fackelmann was quick to interject.

'You treated us to a real speciality there, though. Didn't you know that horses' livers are considered a great delicacy? One of the main ingredients for the famous Brunswick liver sausage is foals' livers.'

Uncertain, amused glances were cast in the speaker's direction. His tendency to boast was well-known. Captain Endrigkeit, the head of the military police, a burly East Prussian with a thick moustache, passed the orderly his plate for a second helping of potatoes, and turned to the paymaster across the table.

'So, if you're going into Tchir tomorrow to get provisions, Herr Zimmermann, don't forget to bring back half a dozen steppe ponies with you! Then we can have a real sausage-fest here.'

The dinner guests' discussion of further culinary possibilities was abruptly curtailed. The general clinked his knife on his glass, rose with some effort to his feet, cleared his throat and addressed them in his tinny bleat of a voice.

'Gentlemen! The Führer in his wisdom has entrusted me with command of this division, which under the experienced leadership of my predecessor gained a host of battle honours. I shall endeavour to live up to the trust that has been placed in me and to the traditions of the division. I expect each and every one of you to display obedience, to fulfil your duty with the utmost loyalty, and to come down hard on yourself, on your men, and on the enemy. The name of our division must become the epitome of absolute terror to the global Bolshevist foe. In this holy war against the Asiatic race of subhumans, victory must and will be ours! No sacrifice is too great to secure it, and failure to do so would make life no longer worth living. Let's set to our task in this spirit! I ask you to raise your glasses to our beloved German Fatherland and to Adolf Hitler, our supreme commander and peerless Führer!'

The toast was followed by an awkward silence. Breuer glanced at the officer opposite him, the pale Lieutenant Wiese, who was sitting there with tensed lips, shaking his head almost imperceptibly.

'Cheers, then!' Captain Siebel chimed in, then added under his breath, so that only his immediate neighbour could hear it. 'No doubt great times are just around the corner.'

First Lieutenant von Horn, the tank regiment's adjutant, flashed a look towards the top end of the table with his monocle.

'I bet a case of champagne,' he proclaimed in his nasal voice, 'that he's never seen the inside of a tank.'

'Tank?' butted in Captain Eichert, commander of the tank destroyer battalion and an old stager who'd signed up for twelve years' service. 'I'll eat my hat if he's even seen anything of Russia before. Smells like an SS man or a policeman to me!'

Captain Fackelmann tittered softly to himself and mopped his shining bald pate with a napkin.

'If I'm honest with you, gentlemen,' he whispered, 'I'd like that head of his better if it was nicely roasted on a silver platter with a lemon in its mouth!'

This was greeted with a gale of raucous laughter, which attracted disconcerted looks from some of the other guests. Captain Engelhard was embarrassed.

'Gentlemen, I really must object! The general was in command of an artillery regiment from early '42 on and has been commanding a division here in Russia for the past few months!'

'Keep your hair on, Engelhard,' said Fackelmann soothingly. 'We'll see how he fares… and besides, he'll be good enough for France.'

The others pricked up their ears at this. *France?*

'Yes, didn't you know, gentlemen?' Fackelmann beamed at them, puffed up with self-importance. 'Have you really not heard yet? The division's being sent to France after all. To the Le Havre region, just a stone's throw from Paris!'

'To France?'

'I'd love to know,' growled Captain Eichert, 'what latrine you dug that shit up from.'

Fackelmann splayed his plump hands disarmingly.

'No, honestly, gentlemen. I swear it's true! I've got my contacts. I have it from a totally reliable source.'

'Hasn't operational headquarters got something to say about it?' Captain Engelhard asked, still sceptical. 'Mind you, I suppose nothing's impossible,' he continued. Old Endrigkeit stretched his legs under the table and puffed like a walrus.

'Heigh-ho, Gedig,' he said to the adjutant, who was due to go off on a course the next day, 'you'd better get the destination on your return ticket changed pronto, then! And don't forget to ask Unold what his favourite brothel in Paris is, ha ha! Otherwise you might never find any of us again!'

The young captain laughed. Sonderführer Fröhlich, meanwhile, turned to his right-hand neighbour to celebrate the news.

'See, Padre, what did I say? The big attack on England's coming! How strong must we be if Hitler can afford to withdraw a whole division from Stalingrad and send it to the West? You mark my words, the war'll be over by the spring!'

Johannes Peters, the Protestant chaplain to the division, smiled indulgently; his peaceable demeanour was at variance with the Iron Cross First Class that adorned his chest.

'The opposite could just as well be the case, Herr Fröhlich. Perhaps Hitler's been forced to withdraw the division to try to counter the threat of a Second Front.' The Sonderführer reached for the cigars and, without responding, shrouded himself in a thick cloud of smoke. He was mightily put out.

At the far end of the table, the general was busy expounding his views on the situation.

'Naturally, one of the first things I did was ask for a full report on the current state of the division,' he said, his watery eyes surveying the faces of those around him. 'And it's clear to me that we need to rest and regroup. I spoke to Keitel about it before I left and he's in complete agreement. And we'll get it too, you'll see! It's just scandalous that we're being held up here by the hysteria of these bloody Romanian horse thieves. They should be grateful that we're granting them the honour of making a sacrifice for the freedom of Europe in the first place. But these people know nothing about heroism or ideals. Well, I just hope that after the Final Victory, the Führer will have a thorough clear-out among his so-called Axis allies.'

The gathering broke up early. The general wanted some time alone with his senior officers.

The two officers made their way back through the darkness, past the dilapidated cemetery to the open fields. A fresh northeasterly wind was blowing and a light frost had dried up the wet paths. Now and then a star appeared through the broken clouds. Snatches of a familiar song drifted over from the distant village:

> My Lili of the lamplight,
> My own Lili Marlene…

'What do you think about the situation here, Breuer?' Captain Engelhard suddenly asked. Breuer, taken aback, stopped in his tracks. The captain sounded alarmed.

'Captain, do you seriously think we have anything to worry about here?' he replied.

The captain said nothing for a while. 'You know,' he announced finally, 'I sometimes have my doubts whether things will turn out well here. You can't talk to Unold about such things; he gets really tetchy. And the less said about our new general, the better. I just don't understand the army's personnel office any more. And then there's the Corps – I don't want to say anything bad about Heinz, but I do wonder if he's the right man for the job…'

'At least he's got an old hand in Colonel Fieberg as his superior.'

'Ah yes, Fieberg, the heart and soul of the Corps! He's a cool customer all right – an outstanding tactician. And that's precisely why I'm finding it so hard to understand why nothing's going right at the moment. What's happening? No cooperation with the Romanians, no proper intelligence. And we still haven't completed our deployment…'

All of a sudden, in the far distance, a parachute flare lit up the sky, spreading a yellowish light. Red and green tracer fire shot up from the ground, spiralling around it. After a long pause, a faint patter of gunshots reached them.

'Then there's the Russians,' the captain continued. 'I think our early successes have misled us into underestimating them. How often have we written off the Red Army, yet it's still alive and kicking – in fact, it's grown even stronger! The way they quickly switched over to using grenade launchers and "Stalin organs"* was a huge achievement. And there's no comparison between their air force now and the way it was in 1941! There's the evidence right now, over there… And their top brass is getting smarter by the day. Let's not fool ourselves, Breuer, those tactical withdrawals by Timoshenko last summer were a master stroke! We hardly took any prisoners in that campaign. But you try telling anyone that! No one wants to hear it.'

Later, Breuer lay awake for a long time on his straw mattress. A welter of thoughts kept churning in his mind. If even Captain Engelhard was starting to complain, then… He eventually drifted off to sleep with the thought that the captain must have been having a bad day and seeing things in a particularly bleak light. Engelhard's fiancée lived in Essen, which had just taken another heavy pounding by Allied bombers.

Against all expectation, the business with the film turned out well. Breuer's polite request to a neighbouring corps yielded an offer to put the cinema van that toured their units at the other division's disposal on a regular basis for two performances a week. And by happy coincidence, they also had the Rembrandt film that Unold had been asking for, which was released for screening on two consecutive days in Businovka.

The main body of the wooden church was transformed into a makeshift cinema, and Breuer drew up a plan for spreading the performances as fairly as possible across the individual units. Unit Ia

---

* Stalin organs – Russian BM-13 *Katyusha* multiple-rocket launchers. Mounted on trucks, this fearsome artillery weapons system was less accurate than conventional shelling, but could saturate an area extremely effectively.

was duly informed that it would attend the inaugural showing at the Businovka Movie Theatre on Thursday the nineteenth of November, at 17:00 hours, with the Rembrandt film as the main feature and a newsreel as the supporting programme.

Lieutenant Colonel Unold was uncharacteristically full of praise.

'When I make a promise, I keep it. You'll get your orderly officer, Breuer! Got anyone in mind?'

'I was thinking of Lieutenant Wiese, sir.'

'The platoon leader from the Information Section? Fair enough – if Mühlmann agrees to release him, I've no objection.'

The same day, two gaudily coloured posters, painted by the draughtsman at the mapping unit and pasted outside the regional military command and on the church door, announced the forthcoming event to the astonished inhabitants.

Lakosch had especially high hopes of the occasion, which he shared with Geibel when they were both detailed to wash the car pool vehicles.

'The film'll be brilliant, I'm telling you! This Rembrandt was a painter in the Middle Ages, see, and even then he was drawing aircraft and submarines and things like that. And they chopped off his head because he knew too much… Hey, don't stand there gawping at me like that, you idiot! At least you're in no danger of having your noggin cut off for that!'

2

Nasty Weather on the Don

THE NINETEENTH OF NOVEMBER dawned grey. Private Geibel tossed and turned on his bed. He was being tormented by a horrible dream. He was sitting in his shop in Chemnitz, which looked remarkably similar to the last bunker outside Stalingrad, busily sifting out dried peas from a sack and putting them into an enamel pan, and sweating all the while. Every pea he dropped into the pan made a noise like a bomb falling and exploded with a loud bang into nothing as it hit the base of the receptacle. And Geibel kept wondering why the pan wasn't getting full, despite the sack already being half empty. Suddenly, he noticed a man standing in front of him, wearing a gold-coloured steel helmet on his head, from which tumbled a strand of black hair, and fixing him with a wide-eyed, penetrating stare. Geibel immediately recognized him as Rembrandt. 'I've got aircraft and submarines,' the stranger said menacingly, 'but I still don't have any herrings!' 'Be my guest, dear sir!' Geibel quickly offered. 'We've got some excellent pickled herrings, tender as butter.' He pointed at a large barrel over whose rim herrings were anxiously poking their heads. 'I'll take the whole barrel!' said the man with the golden helmet, dipping into the barrel with both hands. The herrings, which all of a sudden had taken on a very human appearance, screamed out in horror but the stranger crammed a vast mountain of fish into his gaping hippopotamus' maw and devoured them. A hot stab of pain shot through Geibel. 'That'll be fifty-seven Reichsmarks and thirty pfennigs,' he said sadly. 'Are all those fish herrings?' the stranger asked, glancing greedily around the shop. 'All the herrings in Germany!' Geibel replied firmly. 'But that's not enough for me!' shouted Rembrandt. 'There must be plenty more herrings in Europe!' His face swelled to enormous proportions and distorted into a ghastly grimace. 'You know too much!' he said mockingly. 'I must have your pumpkin!' Geibel was gripped by mad fear. 'The pumpkin's not for sale,' he told the stranger, trembling. 'It's a display item. We've got some others, very nice pumpkins they are too, thirty-five pfennigs a pound!' 'But I want this one!' shrieked the stranger, clutching at Geibel's throat with his long, greenish fingers. 'Nobody must hear anything about this, get it? Not a soul!' Geibel flailed about in desperation. He knew that it was the end for him if he lost his pumpkin. He clawed with the fingers of his left hand at the looming face's puffy eyes, while with his right he groped to pick up the telephone receiver to call the riot squad. 'Help!' he yelled in sheer panic. 'Help!!!'

Woken by a searing pain in his side, caused by an elbow jabbed into his ribs, Geibel gave a start.

'I'll give you "Help!", you bastard!' Lakosch thundered at him. 'Your bloody raving's got the rest of us wide awake now – and that damned phone's been ringing itself off the hook, too!'

On cue, the ringing began again. It was coming from the telephone that Geibel always placed next to his bed overnight. He noticed with astonishment that he was already holding the receiver in his hand.

'Division Ic office, Private Rembrandt here!' he announced, still all in a fluster. Lakosch was seized by a fit of laughter, at which Corporal Herbert, who was still trying to sleep, angrily shushed him.

'Good evening, you halfwit!' replied the voice at the other end of the line. 'Sergeant Schmalfuß here, from Staff HQ. First Lieutenant

Breuer is to report to this division forthwith, and to be ready to decamp straight away! Without his staff car!'

'First Lieutenant Breuer to report immediately to "Ia", no staff car!' Geibel repeated mechanically. 'What, in the middle of the night?' he added, perplexed. 'How come? What's up then?'

'Stop talking such drivel!' the voice snapped at him. 'Firstly, it's eight in the morning. And secondly, I'll tell you what's up. The Russians are attacking, that's what!'

Geibel was wide awake in an instant. Without more ado, he slammed the receiver back on the cradle, leaped up and ran into the adjoining room.

'Get up!' he shouted, 'Get up, Lieutenant, sir! The Russians are attacking!'

'Okay, okay,' yawned First Lieutenant Breuer. 'I got the message. No need to go yelling it like that.'

So, it's happened, he thought to himself in his semi-conscious state. One-nil to the Romanians! He dressed with more than usual haste and, without pausing to sit, gulped down a cup of cold tea, while Lakosch quickly spread a couple of slices of bread with tinned liver sausage for them to take with them.

'Just our luck that it's kicking off today, of all days!' Breuer called out as he was leaving. 'Try to get hold of that film again, Herr Fröhlich! We'll probably be back long before five.'

The morning light slowly ate its way through the dense patches of fog lying over the Don and the range of hills around Kletskaya. The broad expanse of snow shone white, cut through at many points by the black-brown tracks and ribbons of road and the poorly constructed Romanian trenches. From under their tarpaulins the lookouts in the machine-gun nests peered out with bored expressions across the barbed-wire entanglements at the shifting, milky-white fog banks. In this half-light, their view towards the Don only extended barely a hundred metres. The night had passed off quietly. Even now, a deep silence lay over the enemy lines. No shots, no voices, no sound of engines. After all, who in their right mind would want to wage war in weather like this?

Chilled to the bone and glad of the freedom of movement that the blanket of fog afforded them, the first infantrymen crept out of their bunkers and foxholes, clapped their arms around their bodies like coachmen and ran up and down the field for a stretch, taking short steps on the snowy ground. Before long, little clusters of them were standing around outside the trenches, smoking and chatting. Letting off steam, getting their annoyance off their chests.

The situation was this: the Romanian divisions were only sent on six-monthly tours of duty to the Eastern Front. The Romanian Army High Command could not expect their soldiers, who were less than enthusiastic about fighting here anyhow, to put up with a longer deployment. For quite some time now, it had been intended that the infantry division manning the central section of the front at Kletskaya should be relieved on the eighteenth of November. For weeks, the troops had been longing for that day to come. Their thoughts were no longer in the dreadful here and now, far from home, but were already flying back home to their wives and children, to the fertile lowlands of the Dobruja region, the wild Carpathian forests, or the joys of easy-going Bucharest. Due to some problem or other with transport, however, the division that was supposed to relieve them had not yet arrived. But as the result of an error on the part of German supply points, all the provisions that were destined to go to the troops waiting to be relieved had instead been sent to the new division. No wonder, then, that the men here were swearing the whole time, cursing the miserable food, the appalling Russian winter – which they were now going to have to endure part of, after all – and about this lousy war, which they hadn't wanted to happen and which wasn't their fight.

There! Suddenly the air fills with a sinister and eerie hissing and whizzing sound. Cries of fear and shouts of alarm ring out. And then, in an instant, the storm is upon them. All of a sudden, a forest of flames erupts from the rumbling ground, and a hailstorm of shrapnel comes whistling towards them, as clouds of sulphurous smoke billow across the plain. So sudden is this attack, and so unexpected in the sluggish stillness of the morning, that even the front-line troops' keen antennae for trouble are of no use. Only a handful of the men, standing around with no inkling of what's about to happen, heed the threatening hum and dive for cover in time. The rest are scythed down even before they realize what's happening.

The bombardment grows in intensity, with the countless Stalin organs being joined by weapons of every calibre. Fountains of earth burst upwards, forming a wall that then comes crashing down on the minefield in front of their position, setting off the charges, shredding the barbed-wire entanglements, burying trenches and machine-gun nests, and whipping up a maelstrom of pieces of wood, weapons and human body parts, before rolling on to the rearward artillery positions. All to the accompaniment of a terrible seething, roaring, howling and cracking sound… The very ground on which they are standing, torn and lacerated, flinches under the hellish onslaught of material. What a piece of work is man…!

The artillery barrage lasts for about an hour and a half before breaking off just as abruptly as it began. A few stray shells still occasionally putter across the sky and explode somewhere further behind the lines. When the clouds of smoke disperse, the landscape lies there, torn open like a field ploughed up by a giant's hands. There's not much left of the Romanians' positions. Dead bodies are strewn around everywhere, and the silence that suddenly ensues is filled with the sound of the wounded shrieking and moaning.

The survivors in their foxholes claw their hands into the damp earth, press their contorted faces into the clay, conscious that hell could break loose again at any moment. Their brains start working again, and to a man they all have just the one thought: We'd already put all of that behind us, our homeland was already beckoning! And now, right at the very last, we're supposed to die a miserable death for these puffed-up swastika lovers? And in a flash, with no words being spoken, this thought generates an equally snap decision: Let's get out of this hellhole right now! Let's save our own lives at all costs! And they leap to their feet, one by one at first, then in groups. Chuck away our weapons and any other encumbrances! Fall back! And like rabbits, off they hop across the plain, between the brown heaps of earth thrown up by the shelling, falling over, struggling to their feet again and disappearing in the fog. Here and there, an officer shouts and gesticulates wildly at them, shooting in the direction of the fleeing men with his pistol. But what can you do when faced with people's will to live? So, ultimately, the officers are reduced to doing something they've never done before, but that remains the only thing to be done in these circumstances: follow their men.

When the Russian infantry subsequently stormed the position, they encountered virtually no resistance at this sector of the front. A scattered handful of troops who still put up a fight were quickly wiped out. While all this was happening, the massed Russian tanks, which left their forward assembly positions in the woods and, rumbling past their own lines, went straight on to the attack, managed to penetrate deep into enemy territory.

Lieutenant Colonel Unold was woken by an urgent radio message from the Panzer Corps. The telephone connection to the Corps, which ran for the best part of forty kilometres, had been cut again.

'Enemy attacking along whole length of the Romanian front since first light, with strong support from artillery and tank units,' he read. 'Situation unclear at present. Isolated tank breakthroughs are to be expected. Division taking up assigned initial position in the rear of First Romanian Cavalry division, centred on Hill 218, ready to launch counter-thrust against enemy incursions.'

'What did I tell you!' said Unold, handing the message to Captain Engelhard. 'We need to get our skates on now, though! Give Kallweit and Lunitz their orders to go into action!' (Major Kallweit led the division's remaining thirty tanks, while Colonel Lunitz was the commander of the artillery regiment.) 'Really outstanding intelligence they've provided us with, mind!' he added angrily. '"Situation unclear!" What are we supposed to do with that! Try and get hold of the Romanian Corps again, will you?'

'The line's been down for the last two hours,' the captain replied laconically, stepping into his tank-crew trousers.

'Radio them, then!'

'Radio? The Romanians?' Engelhard gave a pitying smile. 'We don't have a radio connection with the Romanians!'

'Christ Almighty, it's enough to drive you crazy!' the lieutenant colonel exploded. 'What are we doing sitting around here, then? Schmalfuß, get me my car, and be quick about it!'

'What, does the Lieutenant Colonel intend to go—?' Engelhard started to ask in amazement. This would be the first time that a chief of staff had ever left the command post during an engagement.

'Yes, I'll drive myself over there!' Unold shouted at him before he could finish. 'I want to see for myself what's going on. Or do you think the general's about to give us the intelligence we need?'

Captain Engelhard thought nothing of the sort. But since he could hardly respond to that effect, he thought it better to keep quiet. As he was leaving, Unold ran into First Lieutenant Breuer.

'You're to accompany the general!' Unold called out in passing. 'Make sure that you— Oh, you know what to do!'

The two staff cars, with the commanding officer's black, white and red pennants on the bonnet, drove first to the Romanian staff headquarters at Platonov. The general, wearing an elegant fur coat and his peaked cap with gold braid, sat up front next to the driver of the large, grey Horch limousine and, wreathed in the smoke of a fat Brazilian cigar, said nothing throughout the trip. Breuer, whom the general had not even deigned to acknowledge, had made himself comfortable on the leather upholstery of the back seat. The briefing given by the staff of the First Romanian Cavalry Division had been pretty sketchy.

'It's astonishing,' the German liaison officer explained during the meeting, 'how the Russians managed to bring up all those artillery pieces completely unnoticed. In front of our sector, all the attacks they've attempted so far without tank support have been repulsed. But on the sector on our left, which it appears bore the brunt of this assault, the enemy seems to have succeeded in breaking through. We don't know anything more at present. We don't have a direct telephone link to that sector, and the line to our Corps has been down since this morning.'

'Of course it has,' grumbled the general angrily.

'Besides, it's of no concern to us.'

They continued driving. The two staff cars overtook a few small columns of motorized units with lorries and artillery that were slowly making their way towards the battle zone, and headed on towards point 218.

Sonderführer Fröhlich had gone to a great deal of trouble arranging the film show. A large canvas screen had been stretched across the nave of the church, and they'd run the accompanying newsreel as a test to get the picture sharp and the sound balanced to perfection. Now Fröhlich was sitting in his quarters waiting for Breuer and Unold to return. With him was Captain Endrigkeit, whose military police unit was there to keep order among the crowd that was massing outside the makeshift cinema. He had undone his coat and was busy puffing away on his lidded pipe, smoking the Russian green wild tobacco called *makhorka*, whose spicy aroma he'd developed quite a taste for. He poured himself a fifth cup of coffee from the steaming pot. And, to Herbert's dismay, the golden-yellow sponge cake – the most accomplished of miracles that had ever been performed on the lid of a mess tin – kept dwindling. To add insult to injury, the captain was so engrossed in his discussion with Fröhlich that he hadn't even praised Herbert's baking skills. They'd chatted about home and their last spell on leave, and now they'd got on to talking about the war.

'Look here,' Endrigkeit said in measured tones, 'I'm not saying anything against the war. There's always been wars in the past and there'll continue to be wars in the future…'

With a slight sense of unease, he recalled that, many long years ago, he'd argued quite the opposite. Back then, in 1918, when he returned home still feeling the artillery barrage at Saint-Mihiel in his bones, he – like everyone else at the time – had only one thought in his head: Never again. No more war. And now, despite themselves, they'd slipped back into fighting another one.

Slipped right back into it, despite all their good intentions. It had begun quite slowly, harmlessly and amiably. A revision of the Treaty of Versailles? That seemed fair and peaceable. The other nations were forthcoming, and Austria, the Sudetenland, and the Klaipeda region fell into Germany's lap like ripe apples from a tree. How about teaching the Poles a lesson? Granted! If one were to believe Goebbels, they really had grown far too impertinent. And when everything was said and done, all it had been was a 'police action'. The other nations were on high alert, after all! It could all have ended after the fall of Warsaw and the fortress at Modlin. People took no notice of declarations of war on paper. Still, they were at war now and so it was to remain. Yet when France – that same France they'd once sweated blood over for four years, attempting, in vain, to conquer – collapsed in an instant like it had been hit by lightning, this had calmed their nerves. That Hitler really was a force of nature! He'd wangled victory over France without a repeat of Verdun or the Battle of the Somme or a winter of hardship and hunger like they'd suffered in 1916–17. It had all come so easily, almost without casualties. The handful of dead, whose numbers he'd sometimes tot up, nice and neatly, hardly counted. At the beginning, it was hard to take seriously what they were so grandiosely calling 'war'. Until this business with Russia flared up, that is... Endrigkeit could still vividly recall his shock when he'd heard the radio broadcasting the unthinkable news. There was something uncanny about this campaign from day one. Though there had been lightning successes at first in Russia, too, the advance still moved too slowly for the vastness of the space there. Where were they going to call a halt? At Stalingrad? At the Urals? Or only when they reached Vladivostok? Then they suffered some setbacks, like the dreadful winter of 1941, and that unholy mess outside Moscow... No more fanfares rang out, and for some time now the German news had given up reporting casualty figures. Quite unexpectedly, God damn it, they'd gone from a smooth succession of breezy 'campaigns' to being bogged down in the most unwieldy of world wars, and no one knew quite how and why.

'This business with Russia,' said Endrigkeit, puffing thick clouds of pipe smoke across the table, 'really goes against the grain where I'm concerned. It was just sheer stupidity to get involved!'

In saying this, he was simply voicing an insight that many a German soldier on the Eastern Front had arrived at through bitter experience. Fröhlich, though, had a different take on things.

Piqued, Fröhlich rose to the challenge. 'And what was so stupid about it, might I ask? Should we just have waited until we were overrun by Bolshevism? We know the Russians have had just one goal in mind for ever and a day – world domination.'

'Do you really know that for sure, old man?' asked Endrigkeit. 'Now,' he continued, without waiting for an answer, 'I know that your lot up there on the Baltic are naturally a bit jittery about the Reds. They haven't exactly treated you with kid gloves, have they? But look at the Russians' preparations for war. What have they actually done? Built a couple of bunkers, like they were perfectly entitled to do. But all the things they needed for a war of aggression, like modern tanks and a proper air force, well, they only began building those once the war had started! No, my dear fellow, things really aren't that simple!'

Endrigkeit produced a grey checked handkerchief, gave his nose a loud, long blow, and then carefully wiped his beard.

'And then there's that whole story about our war aims,' he went on. 'First they were telling us it was about "wiping out Bolshevism", and then suddenly all the talk is of "Lebensraum". All of a sudden, it turns out the German people can't survive unless our frontier's at the Urals!'

'"The German spirit will heal the world!"' rejoined Fröhlich, quoting an old nationalist slogan.

'But what if the patient isn't ill in the first place? The doctor only goes where he's called to… And are you really saying that if you were a German farmer or a tenant landholder or a forester, you'd want to be living here, with the woods teeming with partisans?'

'We Balts have always been pioneers of civilization,' Fröhlich replied vehemently. 'If Russia's worth anything at all, then it's ultimately thanks to us!'

'And in recompense for your evidently totally selfless services, they threw you out,' laughed the captain. 'No, no, my dear chap, it's surely not as simple as that! And you can tell that old Adolf wasn't exactly sure what he was up to from the fact that he kept us in the dark right up to the last minute with his so-called "Eastern Campaign". Just look at all the fibs they told us: Stalin was joining a Triple Alliance with Germany and Italy! Molotov was supposedly planning a "national revolution" and had offered us a couple of divisions as a friendly gesture of support! The Russians were allowing our forces safe passage through to Iran, and German military transport trains had already been on the move through the Ukraine for weeks! And who was it who was peddling all this nonsense? Some really serious people, local National Socialist group leaders, heads of the SA, railway chiefs! I got a letter from my niece Emma from Berlin at the time, telling me that the paper mill she worked at had received an order from the Party for two thousand red paper flags with the Soviet Red Star on them for people to wave when Stalin came on an official visit to Berlin! That's right: direct from the Party, an order slip with a genuine stamp of the regional propaganda department on it! What was all that about, do you suppose? It was because they knew no one was really willing to go along with this war, and that there'd be an almighty stink if it went ahead!'

'The Captain will excuse me,' Fröhlich responded very formally, 'if I take a fundamentally different view of the matter. But it's all a moot point now, anyhow. The Führer has deemed this war necessary, in order to rid the world once and for all of the Bolshevik pestilence, and it's our duty to prosecute it to its victorious conclusion!'

'There you go, my dear Fröhlich,' said Endrigkeit in a spirit of good-natured mockery. 'We're completely in accord on that score. We've made our own bed and now we must lie in it. It's clear that we need to win the war, even if it costs us our shirts. And I also believe that we'll achieve a halfway decent peace. I can tell you one thing for sure, though: time was when I'd sit in my old wood at Johannisberg and not give a fig for politics. Perhaps that was a mistake. But when we get back home again, we're going to need to clear the stable out a bit… Don't look so glum there, pour me another cup of coffee, why don't you?'

Saying this, he pulled a large fob watch from his trouser pocket. 'Oh, hell and damnation!' he exclaimed in alarm. 'It's half-seven already! We've wasted almost two hours gassing away here!'

From outside came the sound of a door slamming, then voices growing louder in the anteroom. First Lieutenant Breuer came in. He looked exhausted and angry.

'Thank goodness you've finally turned up, Lieutenant, sir!' said Fröhlich, who was relieved to see Breuer for various reasons. 'We've been waiting here for hours to show the film. There's still time, though. After dinner we can have a nice evening showing.'

'Film? Film?' groaned Breuer, who by this time had shed his outer garments. He flung himself down on the straw mattress and stared at the ceiling. 'I'm afraid you can forget the film, matey!'

'How's that then?' enquired Endrigkeit, shocked. 'What's up?'

'Oh, there's not much up, truth to tell. But Unold's completely hacked off. If you start pestering him now about the film, he'll turf you out with a flea in your ear.'

'So couldn't we just go ahead without—?' Fröhlich began.

'No!' the first lieutenant cut him off brusquely. 'If the division's about to go into action – and it's possible that there's some heavy fighting on the horizon – then we can't just swan about here having fun.'

'Right, so I'd better tell my lads to disperse that crowd in front of the cinema and tell them to go home,' said Endrigkeit glumly. 'The shit'll really hit the fan, I tell you! They've been pushing and shoving out there for the past three hours.'

He went outside briefly and ordered one of his men to go over to the church. Breuer stood up and poured himself a cup of coffee. Presently, the two slices of cake that Corporal Herbert had had the foresight to save for him loosened his tongue.

'So there wasn't anything much special to report,' he said, picking up his thread once more. 'The Romanians were right to worry. The Russians have attacked like they feared they would. The Romanian cavalry in front of our position behaved impeccably, though they came under some pretty heavy shelling. But Christ only knows what went wrong in the section to their left. It was suspiciously quiet over there. Kallweit spent the whole of the afternoon patrolling around with his tanks in the surrounding area: no sign whatsoever of the German combat group that was supposed to be there, but instead some wide tank tracks running north–south! And what does the general have to say to that? "Don't talk such rot!" So, ahead of us in the mist we spot a squadron of tanks, around thirty or forty of them. And they loose off a couple of rounds across our bows. "Russians!" I take the liberty of remarking. And what does the general have to say to that? "Don't talk such rot!" In fact, it's the only response he seems capable of uttering: "Such rot!" You should have heard how Unold ranted and raved once he'd cleared off. "I can't work with lunatics!" he hollered in front of everyone.'

'Do you reckon the situation up there could get out of hand, then?' asked Captain Endrigkeit. Breuer shrugged his shoulders.

'Unold's really worried, especially because there's no proper liaison with the Romanians or the Panzer Corps. Our combat group on Hill 218 is prepared for anything, at any rate. Colonel Lunitz put up a hedgehog defence overnight using 8.8-centimetre flak with lighter flak in between. No tank's going to come near that, even under cover of darkness.'

'Come along, my dear Lieutenant, a couple of tanks breaking through our lines is nothing new for us. They'll trundle about there for a few days, causing trouble. Then their fuel will run out and we'll smoke 'em out.'

Breuer took off his jacket.

'Please don't hold this against me, Captain,' he said, turning to Endrigkeit, shaking his hand as the latter was on his way out, 'but I'm dog-tired.'

'Oh well, have some sweet dreams about the Rembrandt film, then,' the captain replied as he pulled on his sheepskin jerkin. 'That'll at least make up a bit for not being able to show it!'

It's dead of night and pitch-black. A motorbike roars into the village on the road from Manoylin. Its headlamp rakes the fences and cottage walls with its bright glare.

'Halt! Password!'

The bike skids to an abrupt halt, topples over, and its headlight goes out. The rider picks himself up and dashes up to the sentry.

'Is this where the Staff HQ is?' he pants, out of breath.

'This is where operational headquarters are,' the sentry answers mistrustfully. 'Who are you, then?' He can't make anything out in the sudden darkness. But the unknown rider has already rushed past him and disappeared into the house he's guarding. The duty clerk leaps up from his chair and stares at this late interloper, who stands propped against the door frame gasping for breath and seemingly in danger of collapsing at any moment. He's a young sergeant, with no coat or helmet, dishevelled and caked in filth. His lank hair is plastered to his forehead, and he is bleeding from a gaping head wound.

'The chief of staff,' he wheezes, 'I must speak to the chief of staff!'

Captain Engelhard, who is still up and working at that hour, sticks his head round the door of his office.

'What's going on here?'

'The Russians, Lieutenant, sir, the Russians!' the man puffs, and at this point he really does collapse. Engelhard is just quick enough to catch him as he falls and help him over to a chair.

'Just sit there and catch your breath for a minute, man,' he says, pouring the exhausted man a cognac. Weakly, the man lifts the glass to his lips with trembling hands and, replenished, downs a second glassful straight after. Slowly he calms down to the point where he's able to impart some intelligible news. By this time, they have been joined by Unold, who has thrown on a greatcoat over his silk pyjamas.

'Where have you come from, then?' he asks the man.

'From Manoylin, Lieutenant Colonel, sir. The Russians are already in Manoylin!' Engelhard and Unold exchange glances.

'In Manoylin?' the lieutenant colonel exclaims. 'But surely that's just not possible!'

Captain Engelhard gestures that everyone should try to remain calm and collected.

'Just tell us what happened, step by step,' he says.

Still groping for words, the sergeant begins to tell his story.

'We're lying in bed, totally unsuspecting... Suddenly, there's a massive bang, and the whole roof comes crashing down on our heads... and the place is on fire... First thing I do is run to the window and climb out into the open! There, all hell has broken loose. Half the village in flames. Explosions all around, everyone running about like crazy. In the midst of all this, Russian tanks... they were firing into the houses... Our horses from the veterinary hospital were racing past in blind terror... some of them hadn't made it out of the blazing stables. They were screaming... literally screaming... It was terrible.'

Then the man shrinks back into his shell again. A third cognac helps him rally once more.

'Roughly how many tanks were there?' asks Unold. The sergeant thinks for a while before answering.

'Six, eight maybe... possibly as many as twenty,' he replies uncertainly. 'Those I could make out were all T-34s.'

'With infantry support?'

'Yes, infantry too!'

'About how many?'

'I couldn't say. They all had machine-pistols, at any rate.'

'So there we have it,' says the lieutenant colonel resignedly. Engelhard takes the sergeant – who by this stage is barely conscious, his head wound beginning to bleed heavily again – into a side room.

'Try and get some shut-eye. You can stay here tonight, we might still need your help. I'll have a doctor come over and bind that wound for you. And then tomorrow we'll see how things stand.'

Unold, meanwhile, has unrolled a map and is leaning over it. He is very pale and his eyes are darting uneasily this way and that. Only now is the full enormity of what he has just heard sinking in.

'Good God, just look at this! Manoylin's almost thirty kilometres behind our front line. That's a terrible breach they've made in our defensive line! How could something like that have happened? We won't ever be able to plug a gap like that!'

'The man's clearly suffering from a panic attack,' Engelhard chips in. 'Besides, people's senses are always exaggerated at night.

It's probably only a handful of tanks that have broken through with a few machine-gunners riding shotgun on them, and they're just out to stir up trouble behind our lines.'

The lieutenant colonel shakes his head. 'No, I don't buy that, Engelhard. No, no, some dreadful cock-up's happened here.' He reaches for a ruler.

'It's about fifteen kilometres from Manoylin to here. And a clear road… With nothing between here and there!' He looks up, pallid as death. 'If they swing to the east, they'll be here within half an hour. And here in the western sector, we'd be first in the line of fire! Alert all the staff officers immediately, and tell regional military command what's going on. It's imperative we organize a makeshift local defence as soon as we can!'

The general alarm woke Breuer from a deep sleep. He had no idea what was happening, but guessed that something major must be going down at Staff HQ and knew from experience that it was best to give Unold a wide berth in such circumstances. So he decided to go over to the communications hut. There was always something new to be learned there, and besides it would give him the chance to ascertain at first hand whether the intelligence staff officer's report from the previous evening had already been sent to the Corps.

In the room of the head of communications, he ran across Lieutenant Wiese.

'Wiese – good heavens, what are you doing here?' he asked, delighted and surprised at the same time, as he shook his colleague warmly by the hand.

'Why the surprise, Breuer?' smiled the lieutenant. 'I was made head of this department as of yesterday! Didn't you know?'

'So, you're the new HOC? said Breuer regretfully 'That's a pity… a real pity… Please don't get me wrong, my dear fellow,' he added quickly when he saw the wounded expression on Wiese's face, 'of course, I'm very happy for you. Thing is, I'd been working on Unold and had got him to the stage where he was ready and willing to transfer you to the general staff as an intelligence officer. That role would have been right up your street, too… But now nothing'll come of it. Shame, a real shame!'

'Ah well, you know what they say: "the best-laid plans of mice and men…",' replied the lieutenant.

'And who knows,' he went on, 'the chief of staff might not have given his approval anyhow. The way things stand…'

'Yes, very true!' mused Breuer. 'On which subject, what's going on? What's the point of this alarm?'

'I still haven't heard anything. Maybe it's just a dummy run. Yesterday evening, all we got was a brief radio message from the Panzer Corps, telling us that as of twelve midnight today, the division's under the command of the Eleventh Army Corps again.'

'Strange,' said the first lieutenant.

'Coming back to the business about the intelligence officer position, though,' continued Breuer, 'I'm really sorry that nothing will come of it now in all likelihood. You know, I often find myself thinking of that glorious summer's day in your bunker at Gorodishche, when you read us those poems by Hofmannsthal and Rilke.'

Hearing this, the lieutenant's pale face took on a curious glow. Putting on a wistful smile that was not without a hint of self-parody, he recited:

> What profits us all this and such contending,
> Since lifelong loneliness our manhood grips,
> And to no goal our erring feet are wending?

'You're right,' he went on. 'It was a lovely day. I've just got a new volume of Rilke, as it happens. My fiancée sent it to me: *Stories of God*. Some of the poems are set in Russia. There's a wonderful simple piety about them that reminds me of Tolstoy. It's the kind of book that could make you very fond of the Russians. When we get a moment's peace again, you should read it.'

'That's kind of you,' said Breuer, happy to have completely forgotten by now his original reason for visiting the communications hut. 'I know what you mean about Russia, my friend! As a boy I dreamed of the vast, virgin territory of this country. I always thought the only colours that could possibly be in the landscape here would be green and violet. How often back then I'd sit and imagine myself on the banks of the Volga…'

'What a difference between our dreams and reality,' replied the lieutenant, sadly. 'Now we're seeing the real Russia. And we'd give anything not to.'

Time was when the divisional HQ had had a proper infantry unit attached to it for its protection, which went by the proud name of 'Staff Company'. The siege of Stalingrad, which didn't allow for such luxuries, had rung the death knell for this institution. Since then, a rapid-response unit had been formed, comprising various clerks, foragers and orderlies who weren't wholly 'indispensable' and who could therefore be called to arms in an emergency. That emergency had now come to pass for the first time. The unit of around eighty men had taken up position a couple of hundred metres outside the western exit of the village, on both sides of the road to Manoylin. The men, most of whom had only a nodding acquaintance with Prussian military discipline and a general aversion to handling weapons, had cursed long and loud at first about being roused from their night-time slumbers to engage in this stupid exercise, but soon fell silent when Sergeant Major Harras issued them with twenty live rounds per person and told them that the time had now finally come when even the 'old pen-pushers' would get a chance to show if they had the slightest element of the real soldier about them.

Captain Fackelmann, who had been a reserve lieutenant in the final months of the First World War and was the proprietor of a furniture shop in Wismar, had found neither the time nor the inclination to indulge in any further war games in the course of his peacetime profession, and so, at the outbreak of the current war, had found himself assigned to the third-class and little-respected class of 'Officers Available for Deployment'. Extremely relieved that this categorization to some extent officially sanctioned his cluelessness regarding infantry warfare, the captain readily devolved all matters of military service to his 'Master Sergeant in attendance'. The man who bore this inspired coinage of the Army High Command as his official designation of rank was none other than Sergeant Major Harras. Having left secondary school at seventh grade, he had signed up for a long spell of army service in the hope of becoming an officer. Although the peroxide-blond young man with an impressive athletic physique appeared to fulfil all the requirements to do so, he had twice failed the officers' exam.

Nobody really knew why. When the war came, he counted on attaining the goal that he had long hankered after by virtue of his service at the front. Yet his attachment to Staff HQ had thwarted that plan too for the time being. All the same, Sergeant Major Harras still endeavoured to do what he could to approximate to his ideal. Accordingly, he sported elegant top boots, a pair of his own trousers with a suede trim and an officer's peaked cap, from which he'd removed the silver braid. He had also taken to speaking in the clipped, somewhat nasal manner he thought was typical of officers. His constant cry of 'Right, listen up, everyone!', which he delivered in an affected drawl, had become something of a catchphrase at Staff HQ, and had earned him the nickname of 'Lissnup' among the lower ranks.

Harras now felt that his big moment had come. The opportunity he had long yearned for to distinguish himself through his courage and leadership had finally arrived. And so he appeared decked out in a polished steel helmet, a pair of field glasses, two hand grenades hitched to his belt, and clutching a machine-pistol. In a state of high excitement, he went up and down the rows of men, shining his torch and dispensing last-minute words of advice.

'Listen up! No one opens fire without an order, right? Sit tight and let the enemy come on to us, till they're about twenty, thirty metres away, and then give them everything you've got! And when they start running, then it's time to fix bayonets and get after 'em!'

All of a sudden, he stopped dead, his eyes growing wide in astonishment.

'Where's your bayonet, you waste of space?' Lakosch – who up till then had been crouching down, seemingly totally absorbed in tinkering with his machine gun – looked up vacantly and then got slowly to his feet. Looking completely swamped in his oversized greatcoat, with a thick woollen scarf wrapped round his head, he blinked at the sergeant's torch with the stupidest of looks on his face.

'I, I…,' he began, before being overcome by a coughing fit. 'I, that is to say… it's in the car, Sergeant, sir!'

'Oh, right, in the car, is it?' said Harras, drawing out every word. 'Of course, you're one of the lah-di-dah chauffeurs from the motor pool, aren't you? Well, you sad specimen, you're in the infantry now, do you hear?' he suddenly roared at Lakosch. 'An infantryman – any idea what that means? The infantry is the spearhead of the army! An infantryman without a bayonet – unheard of! Report to me tomorrow morning in the orderlies' office. You can reckon on three days' fatigue duties for this!'

He noted the misdemeanour in his dreaded notebook, a reddish-brown calfskin pad he always kept wedged between the breast buttons of his greatcoat, and moved on down the line. Lakosch, sinking back down into the snow, muttered an audible 'Bonehead!' and went back to testing the bolt on his machine gun. He was one of the few men in the unit who had done a crash course on this weapon, and so Harras had entrusted him with one of two MG 34 light machine guns issued to the Staff HQ. The 'second gunner', who fed in the gun's ammo belt, was Geibel. He'd only been conscripted ten weeks ago from his shop in Chemnitz and, following eight days of basic training at the relief battalion, he'd been transferred straight to the divisional Staff HQ. Geibel didn't know one end of a machine gun from the other.

'What do we do if tanks come?' he asked in great anxiety. 'Does this thing make any kind of impression on them?'

'Yeah, course it does!' said Lakosch. 'You've just got to aim at the observation slit.'

Geibel only had a vague idea of what an observation slit was.

'Surely you can't make out where they are at night, though?' he said doubtfully.

'Well,' replied Lakosch with the lofty disdain of the expert, 'if that doesn't work, just climb on top, open the hatch and chuck in a grenade.'

'But we don't have any grenades!' said Geibel, growing ever more alarmed.

'Then chuck in anything that comes to hand, a brick or something. That'll confuse them, and they'll come out of the hatch. Or you could try jamming your bayonet in the tank tracks. Then the tank'll go round and round in circles till it runs out of petrol.' Geibel gave Lakosch a distrustful sideways glance. He could never tell if he was being serious or not.

Hours passed without anything happening. By this time, it was probably already after 4 a.m. The fogs from earlier in this confusing day had given way to flurries of snow. Staying out in the open in these conditions half the night was anything but pleasant. The men had not been issued with winter vests and long johns, or warm felt boots. As a result, in no time they began to freeze piteously in the slushy snow, whose dampness seeped through even their padded topcoats, and their mood sank to rock-bottom. Sergeant Major Harras stood out on the road and strained to peer into the darkness through his binoculars. Suddenly, he thought he heard voices in the distance. He listened intently, his heart beating fast. There it was again! Definitely voices. And now he could make out the other unmistakeable sounds of a column of marching men. No doubt about it, they were on their way! How many of them might there be? A company, a battalion?

'Take up your positions!' he ordered quietly. Hoarse voices, thick with tension, murmured the command down the line. 'Take aim!' Harras was determined to let the enemy (even if they were an entire battalion) get so close he could see the whites of their eyes before unleashing a sudden volley of gunfire on them. The sounds of the approaching column grew more distinct. And now, in among the voices, he could hear the clatter of mess tins and shouldered weapons knocking together. Marching along without a care in the world, it seemed. The tension was unbearable... There they were! For a few brief moments, a gap opened up in the light flurry of snow, revealing a dark mass of troops. They were already very close! Harras's hands were trembling so much he could barely hold the field glasses still.

'Get ready!' he hissed, raising his hand... Then, abruptly, he lowered his binoculars and yelled, 'Don't shoot! Lower your weapons!' Through his field glasses he had spotted tall white fur hats. They were Romanians.

Sergeant Major Harras, suddenly brought back down from the lofty heights of dreams of heroism to an all too prosaic reality, could not afford to lose face in front of his men. So, behaving as if this was what he'd been expecting all along, he called on the pitiable, leaderless gaggle of Romanians to halt and subjected them to a grilling. They hadn't come from Manoylin, as it turned out, but from the front sector held by the First Romanian Cavalry Division. The unit had disintegrated after the Russians had launched their surprise assault the previous evening, attacking quite unexpectedly from the flank as well as from the rear. But what about on their way here? No, came the answer, they hadn't encountered any Russians.

The rest of the night passed without further incident. As morning approached, the rapid-response force was relieved by other units, which HQ had cobbled together from various supply columns in the region. Weary and downcast, the men staggered back to their quarters. Even Sergeant Major Harras had lost some of his customary stiffness. Once more, he was forced to put his aspirations on hold. He'd also come to realize that thin leather top boots, however elegant, were not the ideal footwear in which to spend a night out in the cold and damp, and that this war had some distinct downsides.

Heavy snow had been falling since early morning. From daybreak on, Romanian troops had been wending their way through the village. The fat snowflakes piled up on their black and yellowy-white lambskin hats, clung to their earthy-brown greatcoats, and stuck, wet and cold, to their unkempt beards and wild eyebrows. The troops passed through one by one, or in smaller or larger clusters, looking exhausted and miserable and not speaking. Here, a rifle dangled from a slumped shoulder, and there a machine gun mounted on wheels was being dragged behind a pair of stumbling feet, but for the most part they had divested themselves of everything that was of no use in protecting them from cold and hunger. Either freshly discarded and fully visible or already half-covered by the white blanket of snow, a litter of weapons, gas masks and steel helmets lined the road, along with metal boxes crammed with full ammunition belts. The wounded, with injured feet wrapped in rags and sackcloth, crept slowly past, or limped along on crutches, dragging their shot-up limbs bound in grime-caked field dressings. The lucky ones had managed to get hold of horses and swayed along, perched singly or in pairs on their bony backs. Some even more fortunate individuals had found places on creaking horse-drawn carts; driven on with yells and blows, the wretched draught horses inched painfully forward, pulling the massively overladen wagons behind them. As the hours passed, the stream of humanity grew ever more dense and unstoppable, increasingly unreal, improbable and ghostly in the grotesque forms it took as the situation unfolded. It was as if Napoleon's *Grande Armée* on its retreat from Moscow had risen from the dead.

Corporal Herbert stood at the window with Fröhlich and watched dumbfounded as the dismal procession filed past.

'It's just awful,' he said, 'that this has happened to us!'

'Us?' bristled Fröhlich. 'What do you mean, "us"? Can't you see it's the Romanians? This sort of thing could never happen to us!'

The army of refugees had just one aim in mind: to find food and rest. Like a plague of vermin, the wretched horde swarmed into farmhouses, outbuildings and stables. But like a saturated sponge, the village wasn't remotely in a position to absorb this unforeseen flood of human beings. Crowds massed in front of the field hospital and the mess hall. Anyone whose legs could still support them moved on, making for the south and the east, ever onward, to anywhere that was out of range of the Russian tanks and Stalin organs.

The straw hut in the courtyard of the house requisitioned by the Intelligence Section, where the house's former occupants, the Russian family, now lived, was overrun with Romanians. Breuer had also turned over the entrance hall of his billet to them. He was hoping to glean some information about developments at the front. But it was fruitless. They didn't even listen to his questions. They just fell to the ground where they stood, utterly exhausted, collapsed on top of one another and started snoring. Latecomers trying to get into the house had to clamber over a mountain of arms and legs; those they trampled on didn't raise a peep. As they warmed up and thawed, their filthy clothes, boots and bandages gave off an animal stench. Lakosch and Geibel stood outside by the fence to prevent any more people from entering.

'Nix, nix! Komplett, komplett!' they called out, using the curious lingua franca that had evolved on the Eastern Front from the constant commingling of Russians, Romanians, Germans, Italians and other nationalities, as they pushed the crush of people pressing forward back on to the street.

'All guest rooms taken!' Lakosch added, by way of explanation.

'You see,' he told Geibel, 'this lot are sick to death of the war. They're all heading back home.'

'Back home, my arse!' replied Geibel. 'And we're never going to make it back home ourselves, either,' he added, visibly upset. He thought of his wife, who was now having to look after the shop all on her own. And little Ernst was only one month old!

'Why ever not?' enquired Lakosch in astonishment.

'Well, if this lot here all clear off, someone's got to plug the gaping hole they leave in the front. And because we've only just arrived, they'll be bound to stick us there!'

'Blimey!' said Lakosch. 'You've obviously got the makings of a strategist! Watch out, next thing you know they'll make you a general! … Hey, look at the jockey there!' he said, suddenly changing tack and pointing at a Romanian riding by on a cow, barefoot and with his steel helmet set at a jaunty angle. Geibel tore loose a half-rotten sack that had frozen hard on the icy ground and tossed it towards the man, who adeptly caught it in mid-air and bowed chivalrously to them. From the main street below there came the sound of a great disturbance. A string of riderless horses, harnessed together in teams of four or six, led by a stable-hand, came charging down into the crowded village from the north. Hitting the obstruction, the first phalanx of oncoming horses reared up, their eyes wide open in sheer terror, sliding around and smashing car windows with their flailing hooves and dragging the rest along behind them. A knot of animals' and men's bodies were left writhing on the ground. The air was filled with the sounds of piercing whinnying, screaming and moaning; then, losing their heads, a group of military policemen started firing their machine-pistols into the air, making the pandemonium complete. The men in their fur hats pressed forward into the building housing the Regional Staff HQ, which exuded a smell of good order and warm food. A sign on the door, in both German and French, read 'Only limited groups under the command of an officer will get fed!' But who among this new group could understand that? The plump regional commander was at his wits' end. He was already completely hoarse from constant shouting.

'Nix *kuschait*! Nix *manger*!' he croaked. 'Orderly columns with an officer *kuschait*! Otherwise nix *kuschait*!' A short, dark-skinned officer in a fur jacket, and with highly polished Russian leather boots on his bow legs and his cap set askew on his glossy black hair, beat his way through the gaggle of men with his riding crop.

Reaching the front, he thrust his gloved right hand across the table at the fat captain and announced: 'My salutations, Cavalry Captain Popescu, if I may be making so bold! I urgently require stabling and oats and hay for my five hundred horses from the First Cavalry Division!'

The captain was rendered speechless. He'd been fed up to the back teeth for some while. Now all he needed was some clown like this waving a riding crop!

'My dear sir, how do you imagine I'm going to get you that?' he sputtered. 'You can see with your own eyes what's going on here! You think I give two hoots for your nags?'

The cavalry captain waved his crop around and gave vent to a string of Romanian expletives, the gist of which was: 'So much for our fine upstanding allies: they can talk the talk all right, but when the chips are down, suddenly it's no business of theirs! He too was long since sick and tired of the whole affair! Yesterday was the final straw!' Eventually his fury found an outlet in a German of sorts:

'My horses have fighted! And for whom have they fighted? For Hitler! For Germany! And now they is supposed to starve and freeze to death?'

By now the captain had lost his temper as well.

'I am the regional commander here, sir! Not some circus manager!' he barked with all the power his voice could still muster. 'You'd do better to slaughter your bloody beasts and give your men something to eat!'

The captain could not have known quite how prophetic he was being at that moment. The little cavalry officer's face turned puce with rage. His valuable horses, those miracles of the bloodstock business – 'beasts'? Feed these noble creatures, every one of them a thoroughbred, to those grubby peasants of soldiers! The very idea was worse than cannibalism – it was blasphemy, from the mouth of an utter barbarian!

'Outrageous, sir!' he shrieked back. 'Outrageous! I am now using force, you understand? I will requisition everything… everything!' And with that, he vanished, still cursing, back into the heaving throng.

'Good luck with that!' the captain called after him. Like Fröhlich, he was thinking: why are we even dealing with these swineherds?

The general was pacing up and down the office of the chief of staff with long strides. Lieutenant Colonel Unold stood, propping himself up with his fists on the table with the large map, and stared out of the window into the middle distance. His face was even paler than usual, while the deep creases at the corners of his mouth appeared to have grown even more pronounced. Coming to a sudden decision, he swung round to face the room.

'In my view, the General simply *must* give the order to retreat, sir!' he said firmly. 'The anti-aircraft battery's up there on the ridge without any infantry support. Before long they'll have used up all their ammunition and then it's game over. The ridge is already surrounded on three sides. In half an hour it could all be too late. In fact, it may already be too late,' he added, nervously.

'I'm not about to take lessons in soldiering from you, Unold!'

replied the general angrily. 'I've already told you several times that I
won't issue any such order! The ridge must be defended and will be
defended. You know what the Führer's standing orders are!'

'The order that makes the withdrawal of even the smallest units
subject to the Führer's approval – if that's the order the General is
referring to – came about as a result of the special circumstances of
the past winter. We have no reason to feel bound by it any longer.'

'Is that intended as a criticism?' the general flared up. 'For me,
every order given by the Führer is Holy Writ, understood? Holy
Writ!' Yet in his realm of authority, Unold, trusting the great generals
of history, only acknowledged the iron laws of military tactics. As
far as he was concerned, he recognized only the slide rule and good,
rational judgement. His lips trembled as he responded: 'It is my duty
as head of operations to state in the strongest possible terms that
this pig-headed – yes, pig-headed! – insistence on defending Hill
218 at all costs is militarily insane! It won't help halt the Russian
advance one iota.'

The general stopped his pacing and squared up to Unold, waving
his clenched fists in his face.

'So, do you want to see me court-martialled, Lieutenant Colonel?'
Unold's face remained as impassive as a slab of granite, but his eyes
flashed dangerously.

'What happens to the General is not the point at issue here, sir,'
he replied sharply, 'any more than it's about what happens to me or
to any of my men. It's all about how we carry out the military task
that's been assigned to us. There's no sacrifice too great for me in
fulfilling that, believe you me. But this short-sighted order of yours,
General, not only places our ability to do so in jeopardy, it also has the
potential to put us in a disastrous position. The General is sacrificing
an entire artillery unit with valuable equipment, particularly its eight
88-millimetre anti-aircraft guns, which we're sorely in need of right
now, and condemning it to complete annihilation! And for what?
Nothing! For absolutely nothing!'

'Absolutely nothing, you say? The heroic fight of the unit to the very last man and to the very last bullet will be a shining example to the division for all time!'

At this, the lieutenant colonel lost all self-control. He couldn't take hearing such sentiments come out of the mouth of this pompous windbag, this charlatan arrogating to himself the sacred rights of some military genius! His reply burst forth in a storm of fury. Slamming his fist down on the table so hard that the pencils leaped up into the air and landed in disarray, he roared:

'I can't be a part of this monstrous hoax a moment longer! Either we exercise leadership here responsibly, like proper military commanders, or we go on making these grand, futile gestures and churning out claptrap! But if we go down that route, Herr General, we're going to lose this war!'

The general's face turned deep crimson and then violet, his ugly bloodshot eyes bulged, and his mouth gaped like a fish gasping for air. He's about to have an apoplectic fit, thought Unold. Followed immediately by the unspoken wish: I do hope so. But all of a sudden, the blood drained from the general's cheeks, leaving behind a slack, jaundiced sack of a face, and he sank down into a chair, doubled over and buried his head in his hands. After a long while, he glanced up. He looked like a wrung-out dishcloth. In a voice now changed beyond recognition, he asked: 'Do you by any chance have a cognac, Unold? My nerves have been shot to pieces something awful recently. I really think I should take it easy for a bit.'

He stood up slowly, wiped his eyes and reached for his cap. 'Tell Lunitz,' he said over his shoulder on his way out of the door, 'that he can do what he likes. There's no point in anything any more—'

The lieutenant colonel shot a look of cold contempt at the general's retreating back. Then he lifted up the receiver to phone through the order to the artillery commander, Colonel Lunitz, to abandon his position on Hill 218 immediately. The line was down.

3

In Retreat – to the East!

THE DIVISIONAL HQ WAS in headlong retreat. At least, it was hard to find any other way of describing their hasty departure from Businovka. In the early hours of the morning, after the first Russian artillery salvos, Lieutenant Colonel Unold gave the order to all sections of the Staff HQ to withdraw by whatever route they saw fit and to regroup in a village a few kilometres to the east. Some motorized units had already reached the appointed location and were parked beside the road leading into the village.

A hard frost and a biting easterly wind had set in overnight, coating the windows of the farmhouses with thick patterns of ice. The officers and men stood around their vehicles in a state of bewilderment. Up till then, the division had only known successful advances or hard-fought defensive actions that had cost many casualties but always ultimately ended in victory. And now here they were – on the run? It was just inconceivable! Only yesterday, they'd been making fun of the Romanians… and now they were confronted with a shocking reality that they could see, feel and experience at first hand, but found quite impossible to comprehend all the same. And if all that wasn't bad enough already, there was that seemingly inconsequential little word 'eastward'. It lurked there in the background, buried deep like some landmine with a time fuse – even Sonderführer Fröhlich's otherwise unshakeable confidence was momentarily dented. His mouth was half agape and his slightly bulging eyes darted about restlessly in his gaunt, angular face. Endrigkeit's ubiquitous pipe was sticking out from beneath his ice-encrusted moustache, but it wasn't lit. The captain took no notice.

Unold was dashing up and down the line of parked vehicles, clearly agitated. He was unshaven and his face was almost as grey as his weather-beaten leather jacket.

'Christ in heaven!' he shouted. 'Where the hell's Fackelmann? And Siebel, with the stores? And Harras isn't here yet with the field kitchen either! I'm sick to the back teeth! We've got to press on; the Russians could catch us at any moment!'

At the end of the line stood Breuer's little staff car, behind the unit's bus. Corporal Herbert had disappeared with Geibel into one of the cottages to warm themselves up a bit. Breuer was standing by the car, shivering and stamping his feet to try to keep his legs warm. A consignment of felt boots had finally turned up the previous evening. But the ones he'd been issued with – a nice pair with leather toe caps and soles – were too tight. He hadn't been able to get into them. He too was very disturbed by the overnight calamity, which had hit them like a bolt from the blue. The images from earlier that morning were still replaying in his mind's eye: the wildly gesticulating troops running down screaming from the high ground after the first salvo of rockets from the Stalin organ hit; the hideously mutilated Romanian lying in the courtyard, the victim of a direct hit on the straw hut; the crying woman with the child cradled in her arms; the expression on the face of the Russian prisoner clutching his bundle of belongings and getting ready to make a run for it – a look that seemed to say 'See, old chum, I told you so!' The burning village, the confusion of people rushing about and vehicles roaring by on the road, which was obscured by clouds of smoke and churned up by the impact of shells; the horse that galloped past with its stomach torn open, dragging its entrails behind it… Suddenly, he couldn't help but burst out laughing, as he called to mind the sight of the lieutenant colonel lying on the floor of his room covered in plaster dust and shards of glass, with the window frame, which had been blown into the room, wedged firmly over his buttocks, and recalled the incredulous surprise in Unold's voice as he announced: 'Good grief! I think it's time we were moving on!'

Good that some humour could still be extracted from this dire situation…

'Breuer – you're looking fighting fit!' A young man's voice close by jolted him from his reverie.

'Oh, hello there, Dierk!' he replied to the officer in the white winter camouflage suit who had sidled up to him silently on felt boots. 'Real heap of shit we're in, eh? Did you manage to get all your guns out of there in one piece, at least?'

'Certainly did!' answered Lieutenant Dierk, who commanded the detachment of four-barrelled anti-aircraft guns. 'But I nearly got stuck fast myself in these bloody new boots!'

He pointed at the new felt boots on his feet, which were clearly far too big for him.

'Here, chuck us those things!' said Breuer. 'Perhaps we can swap.'

There was a sudden commotion up front, with someone shouting 'The general – where's the general! Has anyone seen the general?' It was Unold, running along the line of vehicles once more. Breuer was still hopping about on the road with one bare foot when the lieutenant colonel approached.

'You'll have to go back again, Breuer! The general must still be stuck in Businovka. Tell him we're moving on to Verchnaya-Golubaya, and bring him with you if you can!'

Breuer tugged on the second felt boot. He slapped Lieutenant Dierk, who was happy with the transaction, on the back and climbed into his car. As he was leaving the village, he ran into Captain Fackelmann.

His face was deathly white and large beads of nervous sweat covered his brow.

'Strike a light!' he gasped at Breuer. 'That was a barrel of laughs, I can tell you! I only went and drove slap into the middle of a bunch of Ivans, didn't I? Suddenly there was this cavalry unit about thirty metres ahead! Jesus!' He pointed at the bullet holes in the bonnet of his car. Up on the ridge, the wind was whistling, whipping up little eddies of powdery snow. In the hollow down on the right lay Businovka. Several buildings in the village were ablaze. On the road leading down to the settlement, an 88-millimetre anti-aircraft gun was unlimbered and in position to fire. Seemingly unconcerned by the small-arms fire whizzing down at them from the hillside opp-osite, the gun crew were standing around, with their collars turned up against the wind and their hands buried deep in their greatcoat pockets. Lakosch stopped and stuck his head out of the window.

'Has a car with a divisional pennant come by here? With an escort of two armoured cars?'

'Nope,' answered the crew leader, without taking the lit cigarette from the corner of his mouth. 'Could be we just didn't notice, though. We've got other things on our mind right now.'

Breuer stepped out of the car. He was following the gaze of the crew leader, whose eyes were suddenly trained on the horizon.

'Oh Christ,' Breuer exclaimed, 'that looks like trouble!'

A dark mass was flowing like syrup over the snow-covered ridge on the far side of the village. A dense swarm of Russian cavalry!

'It's not as bad as it looks, Lieutenant,' said the artilleryman. 'That's the third time they've done that today already.'

'Don't you want to fire a couple of rounds at them?'

'We'll wait until they're all over the ridge. Then it might be worth it.'

Meanwhile, Lakosch, who was far less perturbed by the incident than the first lieutenant, had been searching about elsewhere.

'There they are!' he exclaimed, pointing at the burning supply depot at the entrance to the village. Breuer immediately recognized the two armoured scout cars. A little further away, parked beside the wall of a house, stood the general's limousine. Lakosch put the car into neutral and coasted down to the village. The general was standing in the middle of the road in his field-grey inner fur coat with its wide cuffs, and with the beaver collar turned up. The abandoned vehicles, the agitated soldiers dashing past, the Russian POWs wandering about aimlessly – none of this bothered him in the slightest. He also seemed oblivious to the flying bullets and to the flak rounds that now came arcing high in the air above him and, landing on the far side of the village, tore terrible gaping holes in the massed ranks of riders there. He only had eyes for the tank crewmen, who were busy dragging a crate bound with steel bands from the smoking ruins of the supply depot.

'No, no, it's claret again!' he shouted furiously after reading the label on the side. 'Get back in there! There must be a crate of cognac somewhere!'

He scrutinized the cases of cigars that one of the men had just turned up with.

'Hmmm, Charles V!' he said rather despondently. 'Oh well, smokable in an emergency, I suppose. See if you can't find a couple of cases of Brazilians, though! They're always good.'

Breuer stood observing the scene for some while, dumbstruck by what he was witnessing.

'General, sir!' he said finally, pulling himself together. 'Lieutenant Colonel Unold has sent me to inform you—'

The general spun round to face him.

'What are you doing here?' he asked.

'The divisional staff is relocating to Golubaya, and I've been ordered to—'

'I don't give a damn where the staff is going!' roared the general, his face beetroot-red with fury. 'Go to hell!'

Although Breuer knew there was little chance of him being able to carry out the general's final order to the letter, he considered his duty discharged, and so walked back to his car without another word. No sign of Lakosch – where had that bloody rogue got to again? 'Lakosch!' he yelled. 'Lakosch!'

Then he spotted a figure emerging through the smoke of the smouldering warehouse, its face blackened with soot, the pockets of its greatcoat stuffed, and clutching two cases of cigars under its arms. Breuer couldn't help but guffaw at the sight.

'The heat hasn't affected the crispbreads,' said Lakosch, putting the cigar cases down on the running board of the car, 'but I'm afraid the chocolate's a bit cremated.' From his trouser pockets, he also produced a bottle of Martell and three tins of canned meat. 'Oh, and the cigars are Brazilian,' he added. 'After all, the general says they're always good!'

The billet to which Sergeant Major Harras assigned the Intelligence Section was one of the so-called 'Finnish tents', which had been pitched a little way outside the village of Verchnaya-Golubaya in the middle of a copse of stunted conifers. These circular dwellings with conical roofs comprised a wooden frame with panels of weatherproofed cardboard nailed onto it. They only warmed up if you half-buried them in the ground. But no one had taken the trouble to do so here. From a distance the group of tents looked like a kraal.

Corporal Herbert and Private Geibel had gathered firewood and got the small field stove glowing red-hot, but an icy wind was still blowing through the thin walls, instantly dissipating any heat. Sonderführer Fröhlich, wrapped up in his entire stock of coats and blankets, was lying on the sparse bedding of straw left by the tent's previous occupants and snoring. Today, he'd found nowhere where he could deploy his customary optimism, and so he'd resolved to sleep through the critical period if he possibly could. Breuer, who'd spent his day frantically running around doing adjutant duties for Unold, only arrived at their new quarters after dark.

'What a shithole!' he announced. 'Five hundred metres from the rest of the staff sections and no 'phone line. Right, that's fine by me! At least it means they'll leave us in peace now.'

He put his boots near the oven to dry. Then, without more ado, he flaked out fully clothed on the rank-smelling straw, with his cap still on his head, and dropped off to sleep instantly. Lakosch covered him solicitously with all the blankets he could muster and then enquired what was for supper.

'Bon appetit!' replied Herbert grimly. 'We're on half rations as of today. And the canteen van hasn't even been round yet.'

'Great, that's all we need,' grumbled Lakosch. 'In that case,' he continued, reaching into his jacket, pulling out one of the tins he'd purloined and passing it to Herbert, 'magic us a roast veal dinner with all the trimmings out of this!' He sat down on the woodpile near the stove, pushed his cap back and rubbed his hands together. Geibel was sitting on a sawhorse he'd found somewhere and flicking idly through a frayed synthetic leather wallet.

'By the way, you're on sentry duty tonight from midnight to two,' he said casually.

'What, me?' exclaimed Lakosch, outraged. 'Lissnup must be off his rocker! I've been driving round the whole day, and then I'm expected to keep watch half the night as well? Not a bloody chance!'

'Maybe it's in lieu of those "three days' work details" he threatened you with that time,' said Geibel. He held up a photograph in the glow cast by the oven. 'Get a load of this, though,' he announced proudly. 'It's my wife!'

But Lakosch wasn't in the mood any more. He cast a desultory glance at the picture. It showed a buxom young woman who was passably pretty.

'Shame she's shacked up with such a halfwit,' he muttered.

Geibel took that as a mark of respect from Lakosch, and as a mark of his gratitude, he asked, 'No photos of your own to show us, then?'

'What am I, some kind of photo album?' grumbled Lakosch, but he still pulled a dog-eared passport photograph from his pay-book and passed it over to Geibel.

'But this is a picture of you!'

'Well spotted!'

'So, you were a storm trooper, eh?' said Herbert in astonishment, looking over Geibel's shoulder. 'No, wait a minute – the National Socialist Motor Corps,' Herbert corrected himself, 'and a squad leader, what's more!'

'You don't miss a trick, do you?' remarked Lakosch drily.

'I'm a Party member, too, you know,' said Geibel, somewhat peevishly, as he handed the photo back to Lakosch. 'I really didn't want to join at first, but my wife kept on at me. And it's actually better now that I am, given that all my customers...'

'Well, I don't have to worry about all that crap, thank God!' Herbert interrupted. In the interim, he'd cut up the sausage from the tin into small pieces and was stewing it in a mess tin on the top of the oven. 'No one bothers asking a dentist whether he's a Party member or not.'

'I can see you have a pretty low opinion of me!' snapped Lakosch, leafing through his pay-book. Herbert took exception to this.

'Are you trying to tell us that you cheerfully go and ruin your Sundays by playing those war games out of sheer conviction?'

Lakosch put his papers away and looked up, incensed.

'Yes, I am, as a matter of fact! You obviously can't imagine how anyone might possibly be interested in improving the lot of the ordinary working man, can you?'

'You've got nothing to complain about! You earned plenty as a long-distance lorry driver!'

'I'm not talking about me. Take the miners in Upper Silesia, for example! My dad was a coal miner, you— Hey, it's no laughing matter!'

'Oh right! So everything's got better and better for him since 1933, has it?'

'No, not for him. He's dead,' conceded Lakosch, momentarily put off his stride. 'But it has for other people, no question!' he continued, growing more animated again. 'Loads of things have changed, I can tell you! And if they hadn't foisted this war on us, we'd already have socialism in Germany!'

'If, if…,' Herbert said mockingly. 'And if you hadn't brought the tin of sausage with you, we wouldn't have anything to eat now! So, why don't you get stuck in and pipe down, you old socialist?'

Saying this, he pushed the mess tin over to Lakosch; a smell of burned fat wafted up from it. Lakosch took an aluminium spoon and a piece of crispbread from his pocket and began eating.

'That's the thing about this war,' he resumed, busily chewing. 'Why did they go and start it? I'll tell you – it's because they envied us our socialism! That was all it was about! But just you wait: when we've won the war, then you'll see some changes all right! Adolf will abolish the banks and the trust funds, and do away with big business altogether. Everything'll be nationalized.'

'Nationalized?' asked Geibel in alarm. 'What, the little shops and all?'

'No, of course not all small businesses, you clod!' Lakosch replied dismissively. 'We're not communists!'

'And he won't nationalize the big concerns either,' Herbert chipped in. 'Do you imagine Hitler'll allow them to profiteer from this war just in order to snatch it all back from them once it's over?'

'You know nothing!' spluttered Lakosch. 'Do you think the words "National Socialist" and "Workers' Party" are there just for show? Adolf was a working man himself. I'm telling you, he won't do the dirty on ordinary people!'

At that moment, the sentry stuck his head through the flap of the tent.

'How about relieving me, then? It's ten past twelve already!'

Lakosch got to his feet, cursing, jammed on his steel helmet, picked up his rifle and went out into the cold. He'd been fired up by the discussion and was irritated at being interrupted. He paced slowly up and down between the tents, from which came the faint sounds of the sleeping men. Memories of the distant past, suppressed in the frenzy of war, had been stirred up in him once more. He thought of his father, who'd been dead six years now. His memory of him was quite hazy, as he hadn't seen him that often. Either he was on the day shift at the colliery, or when he was on night shift he spent the day asleep. But on Sundays, he'd sometimes take little Karl by the hand and walk past the pithead with him. He'd show him the dark sheds where they washed the coal, the tall winding tower with its wheels and cables, the huge spoil tips, the confusion of railway lines, with coal slack piled up between them, and he'd tell Karl about the back-breaking work down at the coal-face. But he also spoke about the future, about a time when the pit would belong to the miners and they'd work freely in humane conditions. And he'd talk about Lenin, whose ambition was to liberate working men around the world. And so the young boy, who grew up in a sooty tenement block, had an ideal image of the future implanted deep within him at that time, an image that for him was associated with the open air and sunlight and bright colours and a loaf of white bread on the table every day. Together with the other lads from the neighbourhood back then, he'd go around the streets chanting 'Long live Moscow!', chuck stones at policemen from a safe distance and draw Soviet stars on the walls of houses in chalk. And he'd always be at the forefront of the procession, shouting and singing and clapping his hands to the beat of the music, when the 'Red Front' marched through their part of town in their green shirts, with the shawm pipe band at their head…

Then came 1933 – he was fourteen at that time, but still looked like a ten-year-old – and the 'National Revolution', and he'd found himself enrolled in the Hitler Youth. Both there and at school, he was taught that the Führer was going to create a 'community of the German people', and that once the 'bonds of interest slavery' had been broken, workers would be freed and they would see the dawning of a great, powerful empire of social justice. Full of enthusiasm, he'd gone home and told his parents about this. And his father, who'd been aged prematurely by his job, and who could only summon up a contemptuous laugh for such stuff, or smack him roughly round the chops, struck him for ever after as a misfit, a strange relic of a bygone era. He couldn't understand how people could get worked up over such abstract things as that Lenin, who'd been dead for ages after all, while at the same time being unable or unwilling to see the great miracle that was occurring before their very eyes in Germany. Well, the old man could think what he liked as far as he was concerned. If only he hadn't gone around shooting his mouth off! But he would keep saying things in public like 'Hitler – that means war, you mark my words!' and other such nonsense. So one day they picked him up and stuck him in a concentration camp. And after a few weeks the family received the briefest of messages: 'Shot while attempting to escape.' That dreadful day came back to him like it was only yesterday. While his mother, pale and silent but not crying, held the card in her hands and stared at it, he bawled his eyes out in grief and fury. How could the old man have been so stupid as to try and do a runner! What would have happened if he'd just sat tight? A couple of months' hard labour in the camp and a bit of political re-education, which would have done him no harm. And for *that* he tries to escape? Well, it had happened now, and his dad would never get to see the new social order that he would surely, in time, have come round to.

Two years later, when Karl joined the Motor Corps, he had had the most almighty bust-up with his mother. This haggard woman, who had become withdrawn and a bit batty after his father's death, flew into a rage the like of which he'd never seen. She called him a 'class traitor' and screamed at him that he'd betrayed his dead father. Angrily, he'd left the house, never to return. Since then, he regularly wrote his mother short, awkward letters full of embarrassed expressions of love, and sent her money every month, even from the Eastern Front. He never got a reply. It was the cross he had to bear. If he hadn't had Erna back at home, and their little dark-haired tearaway, things would have been really unbearable...

Lakosch pricked up his ears. From somewhere behind him came the sound of gunfire. Suddenly, lights came on in the village, and a hubbub of noise and voices drifted over. A motorbike dispatch rider roared up.

'Sound the alarm!' he called from a distance. 'There are Russian tanks in the village!'

Lakosch bounded along the line of tents, rousing everybody. 'General alarm!' he yelled through the flaps. 'General alarm!'

All around, sleepy figures began to emerge and make their way at the double to the assembly point in front of the chief of staff's bunker. First Lieutenant Breuer, a machine-pistol hanging round his neck and his eyes still bleary from sleep, Sonderführer Fröhlich, Herbert and Geibel were all on the move too. The area in front of the bunker was a wild melee of vehicles, tanks and people gesticulating and shouting. Sergeant Major Harras was trying and failing to impose some sort of order on the chaos. Unold, bare-headed and with tousled hair, was flitting around the assembled crowd.

'Where's Kallweit?' he yelled 'Kallweit!' His voice rose to an uncontrolled shriek.

'Here!' answered a basso profundo voice.

'Right, Kallweit, get going immediately! I hear Russian tanks have broken through in the southern sector!'

Major Kallweit rumbled off with his squadron of three tanks. After a quarter of an hour of nervous waiting, he returned.

'Nothing!' he reported 'Must have been Elsan gen!'*

---

* The German word *Latrinenparole* that Gerlach uses here literally means 'latrine password', soldiers' slang for an unsubstantiated rumour. The exact English equivalent term in the Second World War was 'Elsan gen'. An 'Elsan' (a trademark name formed from the initials of its inventor, Ephraim Louis Jackson and the beginning of the word 'sanitation') was a portable toilet; the pejorative phrase derived from the fact that latrines were places where soldiers congregated and hence hotbeds of gossip.

'For Christ's sake!' shouted Unold, on the verge of tears. 'I'm at my wits' end! Three more days of this and you'll be carting me off to the loony bin!'

After the false alarm, no one felt like going back to bed. A group of officers gathered in the spacious bunker that a signals unit had vacated for the staff. They stood or sat around in the dim candlelight in the hope of learning something new about the situation. Lieutenant Colonel Unold had a bottle of cognac in front of him, which he was drinking in long draughts. It calmed him down visibly, though shudders of abating agitation passed across his pallid face from time to time.

'Well,' he said, rubbing his forehead, 'what's to be said about the situation? You can see for yourselves. Come on, have a slug of this!' Immediately, the mood in the bunker lightened.

'At least the general left a case for us.'

Major Kallweit sat at the table, his legs splayed. He held his glass of cognac up to the light and inspected it.

'Right,' he said, 'I heard all sorts of rumours out in the field. What's up with the general exactly?'

'He's done a bunk!'

'What!?'

'Yes, cleared off! Just like that – took the Horch limo with him, plus half the contents of the officers' mess!' There was a murmur of alarmed voices.

'How can he have just done a bunk like that?' asked a flustered young officer. 'That's... that's nothing short of desertion!'

Captain Engelhard shot him a look that warned him to watch his tongue. Unold's disrespectful utterance had embarrassed him.

'The general is suffering from nervous exhaustion,' he said in carefully measured tones. 'He urgently needed a rest cure at a sanatorium near Vienna. The army granted him leave to quit the front immediately.'

'That explains a lot, then!' Breuer, who had been leaning against the back wall, suddenly blurted out. He proceeded to tell them about his encounter with the general at the food depot.

'And get this,' Unold chipped in, 'he wanted me to give him a truck to carry all the stuff he was taking with him. At least he came to the right person!'

'Disgraceful!' exclaimed Captain Siebel. 'To just up and vanish in a situation like this. Makes you ashamed to be a German officer!'

'Who knows whether he'll even make it?' someone called out.

'Oh, his sort always gets through,' grumbled Captain Endrigkeit.

'Are you talking about me, by any chance?' came a voice from the bunker entrance. Everyone gave a start and swung round to stare at a white-clad figure standing in the doorway. Unold had leaped up. 'My God! Colonel Lunitz!' he said in an almost toneless voice. 'Is it really you? We'd almost put up a war hero's monument to you on Hill 218 in our thoughts!'

Colonel Lunitz knocked the snow off his winter camouflage, pushed the white hood back off his grizzled, weather-beaten head and came into the room.

'Your celebrations were a bit premature, old chap!' he said glumly. 'Anyhow, I don't mean to interrupt your little party here for long,' he continued, casting a glance over the table strewn with bottles and glasses. 'I just wanted to drop in and say hello. As far as your monument is concerned, Unold, be my guest and go ahead and build it. I didn't manage to bring much back with me. About twenty men and a couple of artillery pieces… When we'd fired our last shell, they rode us down and cut us to ribbons.'

A deathly silence, pregnant with unspoken questions.

'OK, then,' said the colonel through clenched teeth, a reply that spoke volumes. 'OK, then,' he repeated, this time with a hint of false jollity, 'then I'll just get my head down for a couple of hours. You've almost drunk all the wine anyhow. Night, all!'

Lunitz trudged out. Opening the door to let him out, Breuer was seized by the sense of an oppressive weight bearing down, the kind of feeling one gets before a thunderstorm. It wasn't just the demise of the flak battery, or the increasingly obvious disintegration of the division, it was also this strange evening with wine and conversation, the shameful desertion of their commanding officer, the scornful insubordination that had burst forth from Unold, quite uncharacteristically, and Engelhard's phony insistence on propriety. What was going on? All at once, the clear, firmly entrenched world of soldiering, disempowering but also somehow reassuring, which up to now had allowed him to move as if in a daze through the countries of Europe, unthinkingly losing himself in the here and now, took on new, more terrifying contours. Was it this single failure that was shaking at hitherto firmly locked doors? For several moments, Breuer felt like he was standing on volcanic ground, whose deceptive solidity might give way without warning to reveal the fiery abyss beneath.

'So how long is this glorious withdrawal supposed to last?' said Captain Siebel, who was finding the silence unbearable. 'Surely something's got to happen sooner or later!' As he spoke, he fiddled nervously with his false arm, which never worked properly.

Lieutenant Colonel Unold poured himself another cognac. He was drinking purely in order to get drunk.

'It's pointless sounding off like that, Siebel,' he said. 'The Russians have broken through and they're trying to widen the breach they've made. Of course, our Army High Command will bring up operational reserves. It'll only be a matter of a few days before they arrive. But until then, we're facing a serious situation and we must prepare ourselves for anything. In any event, there's no chance of us withdrawing now. We've got orders to hold the Golubaya Valley down here at all costs. To help us, the Eleventh Corps have placed Group Steigmann, which is fighting in Businovka right now, under our command, along with some other units. The key thing now is that the Russians give us just enough breathing space until tomorrow at least and above all don't start attacking us on our exposed southern flank.'

'How far have they penetrated by now, then?' asked Breuer, suddenly realizing that he had heard absolutely nothing more about the enemy's position since yesterday.

The lieutenant colonel shrugged his shoulders.

'The Corps doesn't know, or at least it isn't saying precisely. I reckon it must be about fifty or sixty kilometres. Ivan won't risk pushing forward any further, even if he doesn't encounter any opposition. The Russians haven't got a good enough command structure or supply lines to pull that off. We know as much from last winter. And they're running scared about us attacking their flanks if they push on too far.'

Meanwhile, Captain Engelhard had been called to the phone. When he returned, his usual professionally composed demeanour could not conceal his pleasure and excitement.

'We've had word from the Corps!' he called over to Unold. 'The army has released the Sixteenth and Twenty-Fourth tank divisions from the front. They're on their way here already!'

The mood in the room lightened in an instant. A hubbub of animated chatter broke forth.

'The Twenty-Fourth has been newly equipped in the interim!'

'And it was the Sixteenth that made the breakthrough to the Volga in the summer!'

'Now we can really give them hell, gentlemen!'

'Well, it was a bloody cheek of them to attempt this breakthrough in the first place!'

'And don't forget, Heinz is waiting in the west with two more intact tank divisions!' Major Kallweit interjected. 'If he turns up with them, they'll cut off the neck of the whole salient within a day. Then the Russians'll really be in a fix!'

'I'll drink to that, Kallweit! Let's raise a glass to Heinz!' shouted Unold, pushing a full glass of brandy across to the tank commander.

'I reckon the whole scare's going to be over in a few days, anyhow. By which time the Russians'll be a couple of tank divisions lighter, and they'll have learned a lesson they won't forget in a hurry.'

Their faces became flushed under the influence of the alcohol as they wallowed in memories and dreams of future glory. Unold, too, progressively slipped into a state of desperate, forced hilarity. Major Kallweit, who'd partaken very liberally of the drink on offer, was telling off-colour jokes in his typically dry way, eliciting roars of laughter from his listeners. By the time Captain Engelhard, remarking on the difficult day ahead of them tomorrow, discreetly hinted that they should call it a night, the case of wine was completely empty.

Breuer walked back to his quarters through the brightly moonlit night. The sound of military columns on the move drifted over from the far bank of the Golubaya River. Lieutenant Dierk trudged through the snow beside him. He was silent, and the moonlight cast strange shadows across his young, still unformed face.

'That piece of filth! That miserable piece of filth!' he exploded without warning. 'How can someone like that call himself… or even dare to utter the Führer's name?'

Breuer shot him an astonished look, and saw that his eyes were flaming with fury and welling up with tears. My God, he thought to himself, they've really got him hook, line and sinker – Dierk had been a Hitler Youth leader. With the natural enthusiasm of his twenty years, he had pressed and pressed until the powers that be finally allowed him to go to the Eastern Front. Breuer had spent a lot of time chatting with him, even sometimes attempting a circumspect discussion about shortcomings and weaknesses within the 'movement'. These had usually ended with the lieutenant getting very aerated; yes, he conceded, there may have been certain regrettable occurrences, you encountered those everywhere after all, but one shouldn't keep 'whingeing' about them and most importantly it was imperative not to lose sight of the greater goal.

But an outburst of the kind he'd just witnessed concerning their deserting divisional commander was something Breuer had never seen before. 'The worst of it is,' he remarked almost flippantly, 'people like him are by no means uncommon – at least outside the army!'

'Yes, they are!' the lieutenant flared up. 'They're exceptions. Complete anomalies, thank God! But the thing is, scum like him can destroy something in an instant that it took ten proper soldiers years to build up. That's the real tragedy of it!'

'Look, please don't misunderstand me, Dierk,' said Breuer hesitantly. 'You know I don't harp on about such things in the normal run of events – but back home we've got this regional Party chief, right? Not only is he the county commissioner, he's also the owner of a sawmill. Now, wearing his county commissioner's hat, this "old Party lag" proceeds to award all the region's contracts to himself, the same "old Party lag", but this time in his guise as the sawmill boss. It's also apparently quite OK for him, in view of the services that he's rendered the Party, to charge higher prices than other timber yards, and as a regional Party chief who isn't bound by any fixed pay scale for his staff, to exploit the men who work for him quite shamelessly, and to get the regional administration to grant him a grace-and-favour country house, and so on. Recently, a regular court convicted him of perjury. But in the event it was the president of the district court who was forced to stand down, while he remained in post. Since that incident, he hasn't been able to look any decent person in the eye again. Yet despite all the legal actions and complaints against him, the Gauleiter stands by him and the Führer stands by him too! You see, that's what I don't get. Are things like that really just irrelevances?'

By this time, the two of them had reached the camp and were standing outside the Finnish tents. Only the soft tread of the sentry broke the silence. Lieutenant Dierk looked up at the disc of the moon, mourning pale and distant behind a veil of clouds.

'I've no reason to doubt the truth of what you say, Breuer,' he said quietly. 'We've known each other too long for that. But what you've just recounted to me is an isolated instance, believe me! And why would the Führer stand by such a man, you ask? I'll tell you – it's because this man must have stood by Hitler when the movement was still small and insignificant. He fought with him, believed in him, and probably bled for him as well. You see, it's one of the Führer's guiding principles to reward loyalty with loyalty. That's the whole ethos of the movement, it's the secret of its success.'

As he spoke, the young officer's eyes shone with an unnatural brilliance, as if under the influence of a drug.

'And it's that unswerving loyalty,' he went on, 'that makes me love the Führer. My life belongs to him, and I'd follow him to the ends of the Earth! Because I know that he'll always keep faith with me, and with us all.'

Breuer refrained from saying anything more. It's fortunate, he thought, that such young men still exist. Very few people in the Party – all too few – had such a pure heart. As he himself frankly admitted, he too had joined the Party back in 1933 for ulterior motives. Back then, he'd been a trainee teacher looking for a job, as well as being married with the first child on the way. How else could he have ever hoped to secure a post? He hadn't exactly been overjoyed at being so craven. But these days he bore his burden more lightly.

A lorry bumped down the road leading from the railway station at Tchir to Kalach. The white cones cast by its headlights waved around in front of it, clutching clumsily at the grass steppeland that formed the verge of the carriageway. Here, in the back of beyond behind the lines, you could drive around on full beam with no qualms on a night like tonight, since no enemy pilot would venture out in such poor visibility. The clock on the truck's dashboard stood at 2.25 a.m.

'Isn't it the twenty-second today already?' asked the man in the fur coat sitting next to the driver.

'Since a couple of hours or so ago, Chief Paymaster, sir!'

'Damn, that means we're going to arrive almost two days late. And then we went and lost another three hours, thanks to that stupid breakdown!'

'Oh well, Chief Paymaster. If people at Staff have only had to tighten their belts for a couple of days, we like as not won't hear any complaints,' replied the driver.

'Especially not when they see what we've brought for them! Ten days' worth of rations for a hundred and seventy-four men, though since the seventeenth we only have to claim for a hundred and fifty-three,' the Paymaster chuckled smugly to himself, 'plus two hundred bars of chocolate, and three pigs and ten geese – I'm looking forward to seeing the look on Captain Fackelmann's face!'

Chief Paymaster Zimmermann smiled and listened with contentment to the sounds coming from the back of the lorry, clearly audible over the rumble of the diesel engine: the cackling of geese, alarmed by the bumpy ride they were having to endure in their wooden crate. It was a stroke of amazing good fortune that he'd still managed to get hold of the birds from that remote collective farm, particularly at this time of year, when every last German foot soldier was scouring the countryside for any sort of poultry for the Christmas table.

'Even so, there'd be no harm in stepping on it,' he said to the corporal at the wheel. 'Let's take the direct route to Kletskaya this time. If the road stays as clear as this, we'll be in Businovka in just under three hours. Let's hope that's where Staff HQ still is!'

He sat back and pondered for a moment. In Tchir, there'd been talk of some heavy fighting going on in the north over the past few days.

From the darkness, the headlights picked out an approaching crossroads. This was where their route diverged and descended to the crossing over the Don just below Kalach. A sentry, heavily swaddled against the cold and his rifle slung beneath his arm, stepped forward and waved them down. The driver switched his lights to half-beam, stopped and opened the cab door.

The sentry asked him for his travel papers and driver's licence.

'So, you're heading for Kletskaya, are you?' he asked. 'Well, take care! The Russians have broken through! In any event, we're setting up a defensive position here. It'd be safer to take the road up the eastern bank via Kalach.'

'Stuff and nonsense, man!' growled Chief Paymaster Zimmermann. 'We're taking the direct route. Let's get going! Funny thing, isn't it,' he added once the lorry was underway again, 'that the people behind the lines are always the most jumpy. Let's say a couple of Russian tanks break through somewhere – at the front-line regiment they take emergency action, at divisional Staff HQ they get the wind up, at the Corps they start packing their bags, and a hundred and fifty kilometres behind the lines they're already razing supply depots to the ground to stop the enemy capturing them!' Zimmermann was an old squad paymaster who'd won the Iron Cross Second Class for bravery in the face of the enemy.

The new road was in good condition, and they made swift progress. The dashboard clock was showing a few minutes past three when, ahead, a row of headlights came into view from an oncoming column of vehicles.

'See?' said the paymaster. 'Looks like a nice steady flow of traffic! Besides, we can ask them if there are any problems ahead. Slow down a bit!'

The column drew nearer. It appeared to consist of tracked vehicles. The lorry driver changed down to second, and Zimmermann wound down his window. Were they tanks? he wondered fleetingly. Heading north–south? No sooner had the thought crossed his mind than the first colossus was rumbling past; it was a German 'Panzer IV' with figures in white winter camouflage sitting on top. So, they really are retreating, thought the paymaster. Things don't look so good after all!

'Everything OK up ahead?' he called out as the second tank loomed up, quite a way behind the first. No answer at first. Then a voice shouted:

'All goot, yes!'

Zimmermann did a double-take. The man had said 'goot'. 'Stupid idiot!' he muttered.

'Any Russians up ahead?' he called out to the men perched on the third tank. No answer. Suddenly a hot flush of terror shot through him. In the hands of one of the soldiers, he thought he caught a glimpse of a Russian machine gun, that all-too-familiar weapon with its wooden stock and big, circular cartridge drum. There was something desperately wrong here.

'Faster, drive faster!' he told the corporal. But in the next instant, his alarm gave way to annoyance with himself. Laughable how jittery everyone had become after three years of war! The lorry was almost past the whole column by this time; the final tank was just coming into view. The paymaster breathed a sigh of relief. Even so, he couldn't rid himself of an eerie feeling... Suddenly there was a flash up ahead, the windscreen shattered and a bullet whistled past Zimmermann's head.

'Step on it! Step on it!' he yelled, ducking down in his seat as far as he could. The driver stepped hard on the accelerator, causing the truck to lurch forward. It sped past the last tank. Thank God, they'd done it! Just then, a sharp crackling sound penetrated the cab from behind, and the corporal slumped forward with a gurgling sound. Out of control, the lorry veered wildly across the road. Zimmermann tore open the passenger door and leaped out. Something slammed heavily into his back as he fell. He tumbled head over heels, blood pouring from his mouth and chest and forming an expanding blackish pool on the icy roadway. The lorry staggered on for a few more metres before slewing round and toppling over with a loud crash, disgorging barrels and crates across the road. The wooden crate was smashed to pieces, and with a loud screeching and a frantic flapping of wings, the geese flew off across the steppe into the darkness.

Lieutenant Wiese had been ordered to report to the chief of staff's office. He walked over to the hut with very mixed feelings. During the first days in his new role, he had come to realize that the post of Head of Communications at a divisional headquarters was anything but an easy ride. Whenever Unold clapped eyes on him, he laid into him and bawled him out, because this or that line of communication was down yet again, called him 'the biggest idiot of the century' and shouted that he'd have him locked up or cashiered for gross incompetence. Although, in the light of the current situation, Wiese could understand to some extent why he was being treated like this, he still tried to avoid the highly strung first lieutenant as far as he was able. Who could say what he was going to find fault with next? And yet miraculously, though he was clearly suffering from exhaustion, Unold was all sweetness and light this morning.

'Ah, there you are, my dear fellow! Have you got a lot on right now?'

Lieutenant Wiese did not know what to make of this curious greeting. He lapsed into an embarrassed silence.

'What I mean to say is,' Unold continued, 'can you find someone to stand in for you today?'

'Well, there's Lieutenant Oster,' Wiese deliberated, 'the head of radio communications. Radio communication is virtually all we get nowadays, after all. All the phone lines are out of action again at the moment...' He cast a guilty look at the first lieutenant but the expected outburst never came.

'I'm aware that we can't count on telephone connections in our current situation,' Unold began. 'Well, as you know, the new commander of the division has arrived this morning. He wants to go to the front straight away. Gedig is off on a training course, and I can't spare any of the others. And besides, I can't just send any old person along on this first tour of inspection, can I? We've got to make a good impression!' His attempted smile at this point turned out, as always, to be more of a sinister leer. 'And that's why, my dear Wiese, I thought of you. Get yourself ready to leave and report to the colonel!'

'Yes, sir, Lieutenant Colonel!' Wiese replied with all the martial zeal he could muster. I know why you're acting so friendly all of a sudden, you old bastard, he thought to himself. It's because you know you can't give me an order to deploy without my CO's direct say-so! Even so, he was actually delighted to be given such a golden opportunity to heap burning coals on Unold's head.

A few minutes later, when, kitted out with his greatcoat, bayonet and machine-pistol, he entered the nearby bunker, he came face to face with a colonel who appeared somehow familiar. He was probably around forty-five years old, and was sitting at a desk and writing. His clean-shaven face was tilted slightly and his dark, well-groomed hair was combed back to reveal a domed and shiny forehead. His slim hand, on which he wore a signet ring with a reddish stone engraved with a coat of arms, calmly traced tall, well-formed letters onto the page in front of him. The lieutenant was struck by the comforting thought that, even after experiencing a month in the filth of the trenches here, this bloke would still look every bit as unruffled and pristine as he did right now. He announced himself.

'Nice to make your acquaintance, dear chap!' said the colonel. The warm timbre of his voice instantly forged a human link with his interlocutor. 'So, you're to accompany me today! We must go to Businovka again. I'll be with you in just a moment!'

He began writing again. Wiese took the opportunity to look round the room. On the desk, neatly arranged, lay a few books, a sponge bag and a pile of freshly laundered hand towels. Next to them was a photograph in a matt silver frame, a head-and-shoulders portrait of a young serviceman in a pilot's uniform. The lieutenant leaned forward to take a closer look.

'But that... that's old Ferdi! Ferdi Hermann!' he blurted out in astonishment. The colonel looked up.

'My son, Ferdinand!' he said, equally surprised. 'You know him, then?'

Now it dawned on Wiese why the colonel had seemed so familiar to him. In his delight, he forgot all military protocol.

'Of course I do, he was my old school friend! He was a couple of years below me, but we used to go walking a lot together and became great friends – though we were like chalk and cheese. Even back then, he was mad keen on soldiering!'

'Well, I very much hope you are too!' laughed the colonel.

Wiese was embarrassed by his gaffe. 'I make every effort to fulfil my duty as an officer in wartime, Colonel, sir,' he said, 'but it wouldn't be a lifetime's calling for me.'

'Ah well,' replied the colonel, 'not everyone can be a soldier, it's true. But you're quite right: Ferdi was obsessed with the military even as a small boy, and with flying in particular.' He gazed fondly at the framed picture. 'His only concern was that he hadn't been assigned to a fighter squadron. In his last letter home, he wrote indignantly that they were going to make him fly transports. Oh well, he'll just have to learn that they need able people in that role too, and that a good soldier needs to do his duty no matter where he's sent.'

He's even got a slight lisp, Wiese thought to himself, just like Ferdi! A lisping colonel seemed something of a miracle to him, but it was a miracle that pleased him.

'Right, then, let's be on our way!' said the colonel, getting to his feet.

The faint scent of some brand of cologne wafted over to Wiese. He helped his new divisional commander into his greatcoat, which was still missing the proper epaulettes.

Already waiting outside were the half-tracked troop carrier, which the colonel had requested they drive in, and the two armoured scout cars escorting them. The road to Businovka, whose snowy surface had been packed hard by the columns of vehicles travelling along it overnight, was almost empty. They encountered a handful of stragglers, mostly on foot, while here and there they passed the odd driver tinkering with his vehicle's engine or motorbikes roaring past. Because contact with the enemy couldn't be ruled out, the scout cars ranged far ahead and kept a lookout for trouble from the high points along the route. The colonel stopped a group of wounded soldiers, enquired about the nature and extent of their injuries and asked them what unit they belonged to. The troops, mistrustful of this unknown officer, hesitated before replying.

'You can tell me,' the colonel reassured them. 'I'm your new divisional CO, Colonel Hermann.'

On learning this, the men grew animated. How were things in Businovka? All in very good order there, sir, no chance of the Russians taking it! The colonel had a pensive look about him as they moved on.

'It's no picnic having to assume command of a division that's in such a shambles,' he confided to the lieutenant. 'But things will improve, believe me.' As they proceeded, he pointed to the scores of burned-out Russian tanks covered in mantles of snow that littered the flat land beside the road like so many mushrooms.

'See those? They're the remnants of our advance last summer. My regiment and I accounted for most of them. I'd never have dreamed then that I'd be passing this same way again, but in very different circumstances…'

While all this was going on, Lieutenant Colonel Unold was pacing up and down in his bunker. His unkempt hair, the stubble on his ashen-grey face and his unbuttoned, grimy uniform jacket all hinted depressingly at the man's impending mental disintegration.

'Appointing a greenhorn like that over my head… Disgraceful!' he muttered, partly to himself and partly for the benefit of Captain Engelhard, who served as a lightning rod for Unold's chronic anger.

'Ahead of me, a man with years of service in the Army High Command! Like I wouldn't be capable of leading this miserable rump of a division on my own! Who's led them up to now, then? I'll tell you: me and me alone! It's all just petty jealousy, that's what it is! Schmidt's having his revenge against me for stymieing his nephew's chances of promotion that time. I know what's going on all right! It's down to him that my commendation to receive the "German Cross" was blocked, too. I'm telling you, I'm going to chuck this whole thing in! A man of my calibre doesn't belong here anyhow!'

Engelhard maintained a worried silence. He alone among the staff officers had gained an insight into the cruel fate of this man. An ethnic German born in Russia, Unold had lost his family as a young boy and been forced to flee his homeland; as an orphan he'd worked his way up from the poorest of circumstances. How could a man like that let himself go so badly to pieces now?

Colonel Hermann's small column reached Businovka without incident. Despite incurring some heavy damage, the village, which just the day before had still been in the grip of panic, had by now returned to a semblance of orderly calm. The level of traffic on the streets was light once more, with people driving sensibly. The ongoing artillery barrage, which started new fires here and there, was no longer causing much alarm and had become part of the fabric of the place. A work detachment was busy cleaning up the burned-out supply depot.

The crews of the two armoured scout cars, the special nature of whose missions had made them accustomed to fending for themselves, requested and received permission from the colonel to forage in the charred ruins for provisions. They soon fell into conversation with the clearance squad.

'What bollocks,' said the corporal supervising the operation, 'to go and burn down the depot when our own troops were still occupying this area for days. Goes without saying that this stunt was the handiwork of one of those little pipsqueaks whose business it is to prolong this war. Can you imagine, the man stood right here holding a checklist to make sure that everything went up in flames! And brandishing a revolver to stop the ordinary troops from salvaging anything. If I could just get my hands on the little shithead…'

The colonel, meanwhile, went off in search of the Steigmann task force's staff officers. On the road through the village, their car was flagged down by a sergeant standing beside a petrol drum and clutching a filling hose.

'Still got plenty of petrol in your tank?' The driver told him yes, he had.

'Take some anyway,' said the sergeant. 'I've got orders not to let anyone drive by without filling up. We've still got quite a few drums of gasoline lying around,' he continued, on spotting the two officers in the back, 'and we can't go leaving it to the Ivans!'

The staff headquarters they were looking for was situated in a house in the north of the village. In a low-ceilinged room, the new divisional commander came across a group of officers all in the best of spirits.

'We can safely say the Russians won't be capturing this area, Colonel!' announced Colonel Steigmann, a giant of a man who towered easily head and shoulders over the slight figure of the divisional commander. 'We've given them a bloody nose now five times in a row!'

'I'm sorry to have to begin my new assignment with an unpopular order,' began Colonel von Hermann, 'but we have to abandon this position. We're in serious danger of being encircled. And we need you to throw your weight behind us in the Golubaya Valley, which will be our new line of defence.' General consternation gripped the room.

Colonel Steigmann was breathing heavily.

'Jesus Christ!' he exclaimed at length, his voice hoarse with emotion. 'That's a real body blow! How am I going to break it to my men?'

During the return journey, on the high ground outside the village, von Hermann's column came under fire from a Russian battery. Splinters of wood and clods of earth rained down on the vehicles. A number of wounded men were staggering along the road in a bewildered state. The colonel ordered the column to stop and pick them up, personally helping the desperate troops clamber aboard.

'Easy does it, lads,' he told them. 'You know what they say: more haste, less speed.'

He pulled a packet of sandwiches from the pocket of his coat and divided them up among the men.

A detour to another unit to inform it to pull back as well took them past a forward airfield. The place was as quiet as the grave. About thirty aircraft, a mixture of fighters and reconnaissance planes, were parked on the apron, all of them wrecked.

'We had to destroy them,' explained a solitary anti-aircraft gunner standing guard on the road. 'They couldn't take off in the fog. The ground crews, and the pilots and radio operators who didn't make it out, are up front there with the infantry unit.' The colonel stared pensively at this sorry scene of self-inflicted destruction. Was he thanking his lucky stars that his son wasn't with a front-line fighter squadron? Lieutenant Wiese would never have dared broach the subject out loud, and the inscrutable expression on the colonel's face was giving nothing away.

4

Caught in a Trap

THE HECTIC DAY FULL of bustle and aggravation means that Breuer is only able to snatch a few hours' worth of restless sleep. In the morning, when he goes over to see Unold, he encounters Captain Engelhard outside the door of the chief of staff's bunker. He hardly recognizes him. Engelhard's face is like a tattered curtain behind which a huge conflagration is raging.

'The Russians have advanced to Kalach!' whispers the captain. 'Our new orders are to withdraw to the far bank of the Don!'

Breuer is shocked by what he sees. His first thought, on the spur of the moment, is that Engelhard has gone mad. 'The far bank of the Don?' he repeats cautiously. 'But we're already on the far bank of the Don!'

'Good God, man, don't you get it? To the eastern bank of the Don, I mean – towards Stalingrad! The whole of the Sixth Army's been encircled. Hitler's ordered it to take up a defensive position in the city!'

The first lieutenant's face is a frozen mask of horror. A feeling of constriction rises up in him and takes a stranglehold grip around his throat. 'Encircled?' he asks stupidly.

'You can't have heard the news yet, evidently! It's the same bloody mess in the south too, around Beketovka. And in the Romanian sector. The Russian units linked up at Kalach yesterday!'

'But that can't be right,' Breuer stammers, then shouts out loud: 'It's just not possible!' Engelhard hands him a slip of paper.

'Look at this, we just received it! Order of the day from Paulus.'

With a trembling hand, Breuer takes the note. He reads the message as though he's peering through a veil.

'Soldiers of the Sixth Army! The army has been encircled! That is not through any fault of yours. As always, you have fought hard and courageously, until the enemy was breathing down your necks... The Führer promised us help, and the Führer has been true to his word... Now it's imperative that we hold on until the outside help that's been promised finally brings us relief!'

His hands fall to his sides.

'The far bank of the Don...,' he repeats dully, still far from grasping the enormity of the situation. 'Can we manage that, then? We've hardly any fuel left!'

The captain shrugs his shoulders; his eyes are moist with tears.

'Anything that can't move must be abandoned. Kallweit's already been ordered to blow up the tanks if need be.'

Breuer continues on his way, in a daze. Reality keeps ambushing him in fragments of thoughts: Encircled... Blow up the tanks... The Führer has kept his word... To Stalingrad!... Daddy, when are you coming home next?... Encircled... Encircled.

Captain Fackelmann comes rushing up. All his former youthfulness has drained from his face. He seems to have aged by years.

'Have you heard? Have you heard?'

Breuer nods.

'It's terrible, though, just awful! More than a whole army suddenly encircled... And what do you think of that surprise attack at Kalach? Apparently they used captured German tanks and floodlights... A real act of bravado!'

A few hours later, a change of occupancy takes place at a command post a few kilometres to the northeast. On the map the place is marked with the legend 'dairy' but there's no house in evidence anywhere nearby. In a gorge, well hidden by dense bushes, is a row of well-appointed bunkers. Electric light, built-in beds with mattresses, and a toilet block with a proper sink. The former occupants (infantry staff officers, who in the meantime have marched east) had, it seemed, got themselves settled here like they were planning to stay for an eternity.

The men of the Intelligence Section squeeze themselves into one of the bunkers here, alongside the filing department and the cartographic division – thirteen men all told, in a room that was meant for three. No matter, it's warm here, and the brick oven allows you to cook up something really fast. Unold, still a bundle of nerves, hounds Breuer out once more, sending him down to the local village. There are rumours that Russian tanks have broken through there. The snowbound lane is choked with traffic – trucks, assault guns and long lines of horse-drawn carts. German foot soldiers, on their own or in groups, and little isolated gaggles of Romanian troops shamble along, shivering and lethargic. It's nigh-on impossible to find a way through the crush. Machine-gun teams have taken up position along the ridge. These men with their white winter camouflage, scanning the surrounding countryside with a steady, alert gaze, are points of fixity in the maelstrom of disorder.

In the middle of the village, Breuer finds Colonel Steigmann, standing in the back of an open-topped half-track. 'What's that? Russian tanks?' he says with a dry chuckle. 'Nothing of that sort here! You're obviously all a bit frazzled in your unit! A few of our own self-propelled guns drove through here a while back. Some idiot clearly mistook them for Russians!'

As the half-track clatters on, he can still hear Steigmann's grim, hollow laugh ringing out.

It's already dark by the time Breuer gets back. The glow of a fire shines out from the area above the gorge where the staff's vehicles are parked. As he draws closer, a ghostly scene unfolds: smashed crates, stacks of files, boots, tarpaulins, underwear, oddments of uniforms and books have all been heaped up into a huge pile, out of which tall flames are leaping. All around the bonfire, men are engaged in a whirling frenzy of destruction. A constant round, fetching more and more 'fuel' from the lorries. Crockery, commendations for awards, appointment books lie strewn on the ground, all just impediments on this path to annihilation, to oblivion! Chuck the lot! Sergeant Major Harras, bathed in the red glow of the blaze, is the devil orchestrating this witches' dance.

'Don't let me catch anyone trying to hide anything from me!' he bellows. 'Everyone only gets to keep the clothes he's standing up in, understood?' Unold is also mooning about amid the pandemonium. His head looks like a skull.

'Get rid of it all!' he shouts hysterically. 'Everything off the trucks! Only ammunition goes in the lorries – troops, food and ammo! Just the bare necessities!'

Lakosch watches as a staff clerk drags a crate off into the darkness. He jumps over to lend a hand lugging it to the bonfire, where he breaks it open. Two silk shirts are consigned to the flames, followed by a hood hairdryer… Sergeant Major Harras suddenly swoops down on him like a hawk.

'What are you thinking of, man! Have you gone mad?'

'What?' asks Lakosch in amazement. 'Didn't you just tell us, Sergeant Major…'

'On your bike, you! I'll sort this myself!' But Lakosch ignores him and goes on rummaging through the crate.

'But surely the Sergeant Major wouldn't want to get his hands dirty!' he says, feigning friendly solicitude. He hurls Harras's top boots into the fire, along with his elegant peaked cap, a pair of soft leather gloves and a manicure set… Hullo, what's that down there? Yes, indeed, it's an officer's dagger! Into the fire it goes! By now, a group of men has gathered round to watch the entertainment, grinning with Schadenfreude. The sergeant major stands there with clenched fists, his eyes bulging from their sockets, but says nothing. All at once, he turns on his heel and melts into the night.

Breuer goes to his car. He catches Lakosch in the act of loading a crate into the boot. 'For Christ's sake, Lakosch!' the first lieutenant shouts at him.

'Well, Lieutenant, sir, I thought…,' his driver stammers sheepishly. 'I… I can easily fit it in!'

'Not there, you don't!' Breuer says. 'Grab hold of the other end!' Together, they carry the crate over to the funeral pyre of the unit's belongings and empty the contents into the fire. Breuer stares into the flames, watching letters and photos turn to ashes before his eyes… Inside, he's on fire as well. Bonfire of the vanities, he muses ruefully. All the things that have a thousand happy memories attached to them, everything that connected him to home, the flames consume the lot, erase it for ever. Farewell to his homeland, farewell to peace, farewell to his past! The thread of life back to that world is cut for all time… Is there any going back now?

In the bunker, Breuer cracks open the last bottle of Cointreau. He'd bought it from a sutler last August, intending to take it home with him on his next leave. An aluminium cup is handed round and a delicate, exquisite aroma fills the room, a throwback to past times. Leave – My God! Would they ever get leave again?

Suddenly the door opens. It's the clerk from the registry. He gazes wildly round the room before lighting upon Breuer.

'Lieutenant, sir! What about the operational orders? I… that is, you don't want me to burn all of them, surely? Do you have any room in your car?'

Breuer can't believe his ears. 'What, you want me to… for heaven's sake, man! Here we are ditching the last of our stuff and you want me to save your stupid files… Burn all that rubbish as fast as you can! No operational orders are any good for the situation we're in!'

The man appears not to understand. With a vacant expression, he drains the cup as it's passed to him. As he's leaving, he mumbles under his breath, 'But they're the operational orders… classified papers!'

The telephone rings. Breuer is summoned to the chief of staff's office again. There, he finds Unold poring over a map with the divisional commander.

'I want you to get on the move straight away, Breuer,' says Unold in his customary state of alarm. 'Look, this road here… it runs for thirty kilometres to the Don. We don't know if it's passable or if the Russians have already cut it. You need to find out immediately! Endrigkeit will go with you! Be thorough, mind! There a lot riding on this – everything, in fact.'

It's half-past midnight. The landscape is shimmering white in the moonlight. It's bitterly cold. Breuer waits beside his car, ready for the off. He pulls on a woollen balaclava while Lakosch helps him on with his greatcoat. Corporal Herbert suddenly rushes up, his eyes filled with horror.

'Lieutenant, sir! In the squad bus… he's lying there! Oh God!'

'What's happened? Who's lying where? Get a grip, man!'

'On the bus… the registry clerk… he's just shot himself.'

On the western perimeter of the snow-covered aerodrome at Gumrak, the chimneys of a row of earth bunkers built by the Russians were still smoking. The staff headquarters of the Second Army Corps, the division spearheading the siege of Stalingrad, was situated in the northern sector of this subterranean settlement. On the twenty-second of November, after being driven from its previous command post on the Don by Russian tanks, the High Command of the Sixth Army had moved into a bunker complex just south of here.

In one of the northern bunkers, lit by a small skylight in the roof, sat an officer of the general staff, absorbed in his work. On the trestle table in front of him lay a map on a scale of 1:100,000 showing the region between the Volga and the Don. It was covered with black lines, arrows and symbols. This was the army's plan for a breakout to the southwest. The officer diligently put the finishing touches to the plan with a few strokes of his charcoal pencil. 'It must work,' he murmured to himself. 'Of course it'll work!'

Behind him, his batman smoothed down a straw bedding sack on a rough earth bench and laid a brown army-issue blanket over it. He put another couple of logs into the field oven and then began fiddling with a metal implement in the corner.

'So, Müller, another catch, eh?' enquired the officer in passing, without glancing up from his work.

'Three in one fell swoop this time, Colonel!' replied the batman. His red-cheeked face cracked into a sly smile, as he proudly brandished a knapsack emitting a faint squeaking noise. 'That's seven all told in three days!'

'Now we're on half rations, the mice'll be feeling the pinch pretty soon, too,' grumbled the colonel, adding a new arrow to the map.

'The little creatures even had a go at the general's boots yesterday,' said the batman as he was leaving the room. From the staircase outside came the sound of steps and a large figure eased through the narrow doorway, bringing with it a blast of cold air. It was General von Seydlitz, the commander of the Second Corps. Taking off his cap, he ran his hand over his grizzled white hair, cut short on the sides. Then he took off his camouflage jacket, revealing a tunic bearing a Knight's Cross with oak leaves. To judge from his lined face, the general was about fifty, though his upright horseman's bearing, the fruit of a long, binding family tradition of equestrianism, made him appear considerably younger.

'The reply's come back from the Führer's HQ!' he announced. 'Paulus has just received it. It's a flat refusal!' The colonel put down his pencil and looked up. General von Seydlitz warmed his cold hands with the glow from the oven, his forehead lined with deep furrows.

'You're familiar with Paulus's report, right?' he continued. 'You saw how he tried time and again to water it down and soften the blow and how we had to fight tooth and nail for any clear, decisive formulation to be included. But in general he didn't shy away from presenting a vivid picture of the real situation – and now we get this reply! No cognizance of our deep misgivings, no acknowledgement of my suggestions. Nothing, absolutely nothing! Just the curt instruction: "The army is to take up a defensive position as ordered within the specified boundaries!"'

The colonel took a deep breath.

'That's rich!' he said quietly. 'I really wouldn't have expected that. After all, the unanimous opinion of an army commander and five generals ought to carry more weight than that! You know, sir, that I'm not usually one to criticize the High Command, but this business, it's… well, it can't end well!'

'It's sheer madness!' erupted the general, slamming his hand down on the table. 'Complete and utter insanity! To voluntarily bottle up twenty-two divisions – who ever heard of such a thing? It's the act of a total madman! And Hitler's demanding an immediate explanation of why Paulus has already pulled back the right wing of the northern fortified position without his express permission. Can you imagine?'

Von Seydlitz strode across the room and stared blankly at the wall, where an old copy of Der Angriff* was pinned up. 'Final Victory Looms in the East!' read its banner headline. The colonel propped his head in his hands.

'So what does the C-in-C have to say?' he asked after a while. The general swung round to face him.

'Just what you'd expect Paulus to say,' he said in exasperation. 'Nothing, absolutely nothing, of course! He just made that usual gesture of his with his hands and shrugged his shoulders… An army

---

* Der Angriff – 'The Attack'. A daily newspaper founded by the future Nazi propaganda minister Joseph Goebbels in Berlin in 1927.

commander letting himself be treated like some stupid schoolboy. It's scandalous!'

The colonel shook his head. General von Seydlitz leaned on the table and looked at his chief of staff. A nervous twitch spasmed across his face.

'I'll tell you one thing for sure,' he rasped, 'I for one won't take this lying down. Not me!'

He began pacing up and down the room once more.

'Paulus must act independently,' he began again at length, now calmer. 'In extremis he'll have to be compelled to do so.'

'We've tried coaxing him along like a sick horse,' said the chief of staff resignedly. 'But nothing we said did any good. He's like putty in the hands of his superior – and Schmidt is the army's evil spirit.'

'You know what we should do?' the general said all of a sudden, stopping in his tracks. 'We should send a written statement of our position to the High Command, with the express request it be passed on! I'll set out my views to them again in it, plain and simple. Maybe it'll do some good... Yes, I think that would be the right course of action. Let's draft it right now!'

The colonel looked dubious. He knew these outbursts of anger and their often embarrassing consequences; even so, he said nothing and picked up a pencil and paper. The general had resumed his pacing. His clear eyes ranged restlessly around the room.

'To the commander-in-chief of the Sixth Army and general of the tank divisions Paulus!' he dictated. His voice vibrated like a tautened wire. Correcting himself frequently, he recounted his experiences on the Valdai Hills and in the successful breaking of the encirclement at Ternovaya near Kharkov, outlined the impossibility of the western line of defence that they had been ordered to hold (a line that ran right across the middle of the Russian steppe, lacking in any natural obstacles, let alone strongholds or trenches), explained the unfeasibility of being resupplied from the air, and gave an extensive résumé of the current state of the army on the Eastern Front, whose men were exhausted by the heavy fighting they'd endured. With the aid of the colonel, he searched for new and ever more trenchant ways to put across his point. He finally drew the letter to a close.

'In the eventuality that the Führer nevertheless insists that his will be obeyed,' he dictated succinctly, 'I would emphatically urge the General to break out to the southwest on his own initiative in direct contravention of Hitler's orders, and answer for his actions solely to the German people! Right, end of paragraph, full stop! Let's get this typed out straight away. Then I can circulate it among the other commanders.'

The colonel skim-read the pages one more time.

'Do you really think, sir,' he asked apprehensively, 'that we'll achieve anything by this… and that the other generals will go along with it?'

'God alone knows. But I sincerely hope so. Something's got to be done, after all!'

The colonel gave the general a searching look. 'If the C-in-C passes on this communiqué,' he said, choosing his words carefully, 'you'll be court-martialled, General. The Führer won't tolerate being contradicted like that. It could end up costing you your head, General, sir!'

General von Seydlitz stopped pacing, seemingly unsettled for an instant.

'Oh, what nonsense!' he exclaimed, snapping out of it. 'That's not what's at issue here, anyhow. It's about the lives of three hundred thousand German soldiers.'

The moon shone down, huge and full, from the midnight sky. Its milky-white brightness obscured the stars and cast a cruel light on the bleeding Earth, which would rather have hidden under cover of darkness. The lorry moved swiftly along the ice-hard road. All around, the horizon was suffused with a red glow; there too, no doubt, things that had been vitally important yesterday were today being incinerated as worthless. Up above, red and green points moved across the sky, the navigation lights of Russian aircraft on the prowl, untroubled by German fighters. Now and then, the truck overtook lines of carts laden with belongings. The small shaggy ponies pulling them plodded their way wearily through the night. A grey mass of humanity was making its way eastward – Russian POWs from some camp that had been cleared, herded on at a leisurely pace by a handful of shabbily dressed guards; a sense of a shared fate seemed to render them more easy-going.

Captain Endrigkeit sat in the back of the lorry in a black mood, incessantly grinding his lower jaw beneath his dense moustache. He felt incomplete somehow; during the upheavals of the previous day, his pipe had gone missing. Finally, with a sigh, he lit a cigar and proceeded to sullenly push it from one corner of his mouth to the other. Just an unsatisfactory stopgap.

Breuer still found himself totally bemused by the day's frantic events. What had possessed the man to shoot himself? He kept turning this thought over in his mind. Was it simply due to the stupid standing orders, or was there something else? Maybe he just wanted to have done with the war, and found a way out for himself. But what kind of solution was that? And what could you write to his wife, at home with several young children? 'Fallen in battle for the Führer and the Reich?' No, that wasn't an option. Suicide was tantamount to desertion, and the dependants of soldiers who'd taken their own life didn't receive any widow's pension... No, that was no way out, it was nothing but cowardice and egotism!

Via a series of hairpin bends, the road wound its way down a gorge to a river crossing. When they got there, they found the area choked with vehicles. With the aid of a divisional pennant repurposed into a traffic paddle, which Breuer – with no official authorization – carried with him in the car to deal with traffic problems, they nosed their way amid much yelling and cursing to the front of the queue.

'What day is it today?' enquired Breuer absent-mindedly when they were underway once more. In all the confusion of the past few days, he'd lost all sense of time. Lakosch glanced at his watch.

'It's the twenty-fourth since about an hour ago,' he replied.

The twenty-fourth... Breuer felt his mouth go dry and a tightening sensation in his throat. He had an irrational, superstitious fear of this day. It was a curious story, whose origins went back to his schooldays during the Weimar Republic. At the grammar school he'd attended in his home town, the seat of a knightly order in medieval times, there'd been this master who taught them German and gymnastics. Herr Strackwitz was a man of medium build in his forties with a carefully groomed centre parting, a pince-nez perched in front of his cold blue eyes and an old duelling scar on his left cheek, which turned a livid scarlet when he got angry. He usually came to school dressed in a suit of green Loden cloth, sometimes – in defiance of a ban on political symbols – with the brightly polished badge of the 'Stahlhelm' organization in the lapel, and with woollen gaiters and walking boots on his slightly bandy legs. Strackwitz was quite popular among the boys, despite – or perhaps precisely because of – his regime of strict discipline. At the beginning of every gymnastics lesson, he would get the class to form up in single file and march around the schoolyard a couple of times.

The courtyard would ring with the sound of high boys' voices belting out the words of 'We're off to conquer France...', or an old Austrian nationalist song adapted for the current political situation:

> And if the Poles invade our land,
> We'll drive them back with gun in hand,
> We'd give our lives to set you free,
> Our Fatherland, dear Germany!

The other teachers at the school would shake their heads and close their classroom windows.

Every year, the boys celebrated the emperor's birthday 'in secret' in their classroom in front of a lectern decorated with the old imperial naval ensign. This was, after all, an old, long-established grammar school, which saw its principal role as bringing to bear all the patience and indulgence it possibly could to getting the ignorant and arrogant offspring of the East Prussian landed aristocracy to pass their school-leaving exams. As the son of a middle-ranking civil servant, Breuer was on the very bottom rung of the school's social ladder. Strackwitz was always present on these occasions, as the guest of honour. As a state official, he was careful not to take a leading role in the festivities, but it was well known that the pupils who put themselves forward to deliver speeches at these parties could count on at least a grade 2 for German in their next reports. Sometimes, Senior Master Strackwitz, who was rather too fond of a drink, would arrive at school considerably the worse for wear, and then the boys would have a field day. His customary strictness evaporated and he would let them take all kinds of liberties during the lesson. Only when the boys became too boisterous would he wag his finger benignly and warn them he'd 'have to keep a tighter rein on them' next time. On such days, he'd give them some truly inspirational talks, recounting his experiences in the First World War.

'So, boys,' he would customarily end his addresses on these occasions, 'I hope I'll see you all again in my machine-gun company when the next war comes!' Saying this, he'd shake everyone's hand firmly and give them a penetrating stare through his pince-nez.

Several years then elapsed. Breuer was already a student by this time. One night he had a terrible nightmare. He and the boys from his year were gathered together in a dimly lit room; at the front of the classroom, notebook in hand, stood Senior Master Strackwitz.

'The examinations are over. Now you're off to war!' he announced curtly. 'And so as to leave you in no doubt, I'm now going to tell each of you which day you're due to die.'

Breuer was gripped with horror. He wanted to scream, but his throat felt like it had been sewn shut. Strackwitz opened his note-book and began, calmly and methodically, as if he were announcing the results of a test, to read out the boys' names, with a date attached to each of them.

'Abel… Arnold… Von Batocki… Brandes…' This was it, here it came! Breuer felt the urge to run away, to close his ears, but some powerful force kept him rooted to the spot. 'Breuer…,' – a searching look struck him through the lenses of the teacher's pince-nez – 'the twenty-fourth of…' Breuer let out a dreadful, piercing scream. He woke up, bathed in sweat.

Ever since then, Breuer was on tenterhooks every time the twenty-fourth of the month approached. He tried to suppress the feeling, but in vain. He cursed himself for being a fool, no better than a superstitious old washerwoman, but all to no avail. When the day came around, though he was normally anything but cowardly, he'd instinctively go out of his way to avoid placing himself in any particular danger. And most likely as a natural consequence of precisely this lack of self-confidence, something unpleasant would generally befall him on the twenty-fourth of the month. Breuer had always been extremely careful not to reveal this curious weakness to anyone else.

So, today was the twenty-fourth once more! Today, the Eleventh Corps would be withdrawing east across the Don through a narrow corridor. The Russians would do their utmost to hamper this retreat and make life as difficult as they could for them. Weather-wise, the day promised to be clear and bright. The Soviet Air Force would fly sorties round the clock, bombing and strafing the German columns as they tried to pull back, and attempt to destroy the two bridges over the river. Would this be the day his number came up? A debilitating sense of fear took hold of him. No, it couldn't be the end today, he couldn't go now. He still had things to do… His life wasn't complete yet! From somewhere deep within he was assailed by a feeling of guilt, an intangible, indefinable guilt that had not been assuaged.

'Look, there's an air raid happening up ahead!' said Captain Endrigkeit. 'They must have a forward base behind the ridge.'

Parachute flares lit up the road in the far distance. On the ground there was a red glow, interspersed with flashes of bright yellow. The dull thud of bombs drowned out the sound of their engine. Ahead, the road descended into a valley bottom, where they could see a village burning. Just in front of it was a fork in the road. Breuer and the captain stepped out of the car. An almost completely burned-out car stood a few metres away on the verge. Parts of the engine were still glowing red-hot, while small flames flickered along the charred skeleton of the bodywork. Beside the vehicle lay the body of the driver, burned to a cinder. Its teeth and glazed eyeballs shone out ghastly white against the shrunken skin of the face. Its black, shrivelled arms were stretched up to heaven. A group of Russian POWs loitered around the scene of the conflagration, holding their mess tins over the guttering flames. One of them had propped his foot on the chest of the dead man. They were chatting and laughing, pleased to have found this little oasis of warmth.

Breuer consulted the map.

'Unold marked the right fork here as the one to take,' he said. 'No question that's the better road, but it does loop a long way down to the south. Who knows if it's even passable still? I reckon we should see what the road to the left's like first! It's far shorter by the look of it. Maybe it'll be wide enough for troop columns to drive down it.'

Captain Endrigkeit signalled his assent. 'Don't give a damn either way,' he muttered indistinctly.

The road soon turned out to be very bad. It was narrow and criss-crossed with deep tracks worn by previous vehicles, between which their little car lurched about uncontrollably. If that wasn't bad enough, a series of hairpins presently came into view, winding steeply down to a gorge covered in dense undergrowth. This clearly wasn't a viable route. Breuer was all for turning around.

'Wait a minute!' said Captain Endrigkeit suddenly. His keen hunter's eye had spotted something.

'There's someone up ahead! Maybe he can put us right.' He clambered out of the car. Breuer looked on impassively as the captain, his hands in the pockets of his sheepskin, went up to the figure in a white camouflage suit who was standing in the middle of the road about thirty metres ahead. All of a sudden, he gave a start. The man had made a movement of some kind and Captain Endrigkeit had fallen backwards to the ground. In the same instant, gunfire erupted from the bushes by the side of the road, and a bullet pierced the canvas roof of the car. In a flash, Lakosch snatched a hand grenade from the rifle rack and jumped out of the vehicle. He pulled the pin and hurled the grenade into the bushes. There was a loud detonation, followed by a burst of flame and thick smoke. A couple of white-clad figures disappeared into the darkness of the gorge. Breuer, who by this time had got over his initial paralysing shock, loosed off a couple of rounds from his machine-pistol at them as they fled. On the road up ahead, two figures were locked together in a deadly embrace, writhing around in the snow and grunting and groaning with exertion. Endrigkeit had managed to grab his adversary by the legs and bring him down and was now wrestling desperately with the man's right hand, which clutched a revolver. The man was hell-bent on fighting to the death, and had already fired off two shots. Lakosch bounded up to them in long strides. He looked around for a weapon, before remembering the bayonet on his belt under his greatcoat. The image of Harras tearing him off a strip that time for not carrying it flashed across his mind. He whipped out the blade and plunged it into the back of the man in white, who in the meantime had fired another shot. Lakosch's gorge rose as he felt the cold steel meet some bony resistance and then drive deep into soft tissue. The Russian's grip on Endrigkeit loosened, his heavy frame jerked spasmodically, then his body went limp and gave no further signs of life. Panting heavily, Captain Endrigkeit got to his feet. He looked in a bad way.

His snowy-white sheepskin jacket hung in tatters, his face was bruised and his moustache had been tugged in all directions like a twig broom. There was a fresh bloodstain on his left sleeve.

'Hell's bells!' he gasped, still out of breath. 'I thought I was a goner there. Cheeky fucker!'

He pulled out his brightly patterned handkerchief and wiped the dirt off his face. 'Lakosch – Karl... thanks so much, mate!' he exclaimed, slapping the little driver so heartily on the shoulder with his big, meaty hand that he almost fell over. 'If it weren't for you, I'd be pushing up daisies... I won't forget that in a hurry, lad! If you ever need anything, now or when the war's over, don't you dare go asking anyone else – you come straight to old Endrigkeit, understood?'

'Yes, sir, Captain!' answered Lakosch, cautiously shaking the huge paw that Endrigkeit proffered him; he still couldn't rid himself of the queasy feeling in his throat.

Breuer, who meanwhile had scouted round the immediate vicinity, joined them once more.

'There are some ski tracks back there,' he said. 'Must have been a Russian patrol on snowshoes. Four or five men at most. If there'd been more of them, they wouldn't have tried ambushing us like that. They obviously thought they could polish us off no problem in our little jalopy out here in the middle of nowhere!'

They frisked the dead man, who was lying in a pool of blood. Beneath his winter camouflage suit, he was wearing a normal ochre-brown Russian army shirt. He had no papers on him.

'Well then, Lakosch,' said the first lieutenant a while later, after they'd tentatively investigated the other road and, having found it free of Russians and even quite busy with Wehrmacht traffic, were now on their way back to base again, 'but for you, we'd all have been in a hell of a fix today. I'm sure you know that Iron Crosses for men on the divisional staff have to be run by the High Command for approval, and how reluctant the chief of staff is to do that – but this time I'll get you an Iron Cross if it's the last thing I do!'

★

Endless columns of troops march through the night, heading for the Don, whose crossing points are being kept open against attacks from advancing rapid-deployment units of the Red Army by elements of the Sixteenth and Twenty-Fourth Panzer divisions. The Eleventh Corps, meanwhile, on High Command's orders, on Hitler's orders, withdraws towards Stalingrad. Retreating to the east – an utter absurdity!

Draped with blankets and tarpaulins, exhausted figures slowly make their way, shuffling and stumbling on painfully blistered feet, along the furrows worn by tyres in the snowy road. Pushed to the limits of their endurance by two summers of relentless 'lightning warfare', and in between an icy winter without pause or rest, shackled to a grinding treadmill from which only death or serious maiming could free them, with no hope of being relieved and only very infrequent spells of leave, they finally found themselves dug into foxholes here on the Don, hoping for a period of trench warfare in which to catch their breath – a prospect that seemed almost as alluring as home leave.

Yesterday, they'd been busy shoring up their fortified winter positions, with the enemy already threatening their flanks and rear. They were told to pay no attention to the sounds of battle they could clearly hear – it meant nothing and would all quickly calm down again. And then all of a sudden, the word was: 'Quick! Abandon your positions!' And they'd had to hastily quit the little patch of threatened homeland that they'd created on the banks of the Don and were determined to defend. Driven out into the hostile night, into the unknown! Out there, there was no farmhouse, no bunker, not even a bale of straw behind which they could take refuge. That kind of thing undermines morale and discipline.

Gradually, rumours begin to percolate through the half-asleep columns of marching men.

'I've heard the Russians captured the entire staff corps in Ossinovskoye.'

'Exactly the same shit as last winter! It began just like this outside Moscow, too!'

'So where are we going now?' – 'Across the Don, supposedly.'

'That time outside Moscow – at least back then the word was we'd be heading home…'

The top brass give orders and the little infantryman has to keep his trap shut and march on. This last, unexpected forced march has been dreadful, nothing short of a catastrophe, with the men's feet rubbed raw by ice-hardened winter paths. It's easier issuing orders than marching. Endless columns of troops march through the night…

Group Steigmann is one of the last to withdraw. The colonel drives past the long lines of men in his VW *Kübelwagen*. He's worn out and embittered. That he should live to see a day like this! They'd held Businovka and taken heavy losses in the process. But it was like a lone rock in a raging sea. All for nothing! They'd defended the Golubaya Valley and could still hold on to it today if called to. But it had all been in vain, and they'd been ordered to pull back.

And to what end? No one could say. Somewhere out there, far in the distance, lay Germany. The colonel, though, gives no outward sign of his irritable mood. He gives his troops pep talks, gees them up, and prevents any rash and senseless actions by giving clear orders.

The route is lined with silent reminders of those who have gone before them: abandoned vehicles, dying horses, discarded equipment, smashed crates, scattered papers; signs of coercion, of defeat. 'A trial of endurance,' muses the colonel, 'physical and psychological. It's vital we get through it.'

As night falls, fires of destruction flicker in the surrounding fields, beacons of impending victory for the enemy! The colonel has forbidden his men from indulging in this pointless torching.

He knows only too well the corrosive effect of an orgy of destruction sanctioned by military order. Horses plod by, breathing heavily, with long white needles of ice hanging from their mouths and nostrils. The carts are loaded with the wounded, as the proper ambulances are already full to bursting. Behind them come the infantry's field guns, drawn by teams of men, twenty harnessed to each gun. With cries of 'Heave… ho!' the men strain to pick up the slack on the ropes. In their wake, the heavy artillery rumbles slowly along, the white-caked steel of the wheels squeaking as it cuts into the drifts of snow. Slave labour! Spurring them on is their belief that this senseless task has some sense, their blind faith in their commanders.

'So far so good, Colonel!' shouts the sergeant. 'If only those gun tractors would turn up soon!' The gun tractors from the quarter-master's unit – they were supposed to be here ages ago!

The colonel drives on, past other vehicles and squads of march-ing men. From somewhere in the darkness, a Stalin organ fires rockets in a high arc, shooting with a venomous hiss across the night sky and trailing comet tails behind them. The distant noise of a firefight from behind, the rearguard defending the column. A faint rumbling is also coming from up front, somewhere to the left. The northern fortified position! A bicycle company wheels its machines past through the snow; the exhaled breath of the panting men hangs over them like a cloud of steam. Medical orderlies come by with stretchers, or drag travois behind them carrying wounded men. Infantrymen drag along heavy machine guns and cases of ammunition, clinging on to them for grim death. As long as they've still got guns and equipment, order will prevail. Their heavy burden is sheer torment for the body, but a psychological crutch for the soul. Ahead, a lorry has slewed across the road, blocking the way. A jam starts to form. The lorry's axle is broken, and the driver's lying drunk in the cab. The troops swarm over the truck like ants, rummaging through its load with furtive glances. Nobody makes any move to clear the obstruction. A bottle starts to circulate among a group of men standing off to one side. An officer steps in, his young voice rising to a shrill pitch.

'Get rid of that alcohol this instant! Do you want to catch hypothermia? Lend a hand here! Put your shoulders into it, you shitheads!' The colonel has stepped out of his car.

'Calm down, Schneider, calm down!' he tells the young lieutenant. He knows that the men will see sense. They'll rally round all right. But this isn't the way to deal with them, not tonight.

'Okay, lads, let's shift this thing, right?' he calls out, grabbing hold of the back of the truck and bracing himself. 'There'll be plenty of time for a drink later, when we've got to where we're going!'

His words break the spell. The lorry is manhandled off the road, leaving the way clear again. The colonel takes the driver with him into the Volkswagen and wraps him up in blankets. He's a young man who's tried to drink himself into oblivion and has no idea how close he came to death. His nose and cheeks are already showing signs of frostbite. Presently, the road starts to descend a steep hill. Another of those damned *balkas*!* The slope down the gorge is covered in ice. The men slip and slide down it in long chains. The vehicles have to be winched down on ropes. While this is going on, a high-pitched voice rises above the general hubbub:

'Hold it… Hold it, will you! Over to the right a bit! And put the brakes on, man, for Christ's sake!'

It's the company commander of the First. He's got a bullet wound through his shoulder. He didn't manage to get airlifted out in time, so the unit's become his home and hospital. Without warning, a gun breaks loose and, tumbling over with a thunderous roar, cartwheels down into a knot of men, a steel avalanche. The air is filled with screams and moans… The night has claimed its first victims. And then they spot them – the two gun tractors they've been hoping to

---

* *Balkas* – the *balka*, an eroded valley forming a steep-sided gorge or gully, was a characteristic feature of the terrain around the River Volga near Stalingrad.

see all along! One of them has broken through the weak bridge at the bottom of the gorge. It's firmly wedged there, blocking their path. The other one's marooned helplessly on the far bank. The frozen surface of the river won't bear such a huge weight. Sergeant Strack jumps up on the running board of the colonel's car. He gives Steigmann an imploring look, but his voice fails him. He's at his wits' end.

'Blow up the lot!' the colonel snaps. Suddenly he looks old and haggard. The sergeant stays rooted to the spot in seeming incomprehension. So was all this in vain, all this superhuman effort? He can see himself having to file loss reports, and face court-martial proceedings for losing a gun… Is he supposed to just destroy his own artillery, and the world will carry on as normal?

'Blow it up?' he asks in disbelief. 'Our guns? What, all of them?'

In his six years of service, he's never questioned an order in this way. But extraordinary events change people. The colonel understands.

'No questions, Strack!' he says, in an almost fatherly tone. 'Even I can't question orders.'

Finally, they make it to a larger road.

'Stop! Sto-op!'

Are they at their destination? No, not yet, not by a long chalk. It's just a rest stop. The glowing remains of a burned village in the first light of dawn. Amid the smoke of the ruined houses, on the verge between fire and ice, they drift into sleep, men and horses all packed together, showered with crackling sparks from the flames.

A message comes in from the rearguard. 'The enemy are still in pursuit, but keeping their distance. We've taken out two of their tanks!'

Two T-34s destroyed! A murmur ripples through the ranks. They haven't got us yet! We're still in the game, we're still up for a scrap! After a few minutes' pause, the column sets off again. They've got everything with them, including the wounded and even the dead. Only their heavy guns are missing, and their armoured ammunition tractor, which is trying to find a passable way through across the fields.

They've made it through the first terrible night, they've survived their trial of endurance. They're still managing to keep it all together.

The colonel motors slowly past the tightly packed column. His face now no longer conceals his grave concern or the immense strain he's under. Sergeant Strack approaches him again.

'We've made it through after all, Colonel!' he calls. 'It was hard, mind… And our beautiful guns! Oh well, couldn't be helped. Things like that don't happen for nothing, I suppose!'

The colonel doesn't reply; his face has taken on a stony expression. No, he thinks, not for nothing. Hopefully not for nothing.

The crossing over the Don. The line of marching men, baggage trucks, tanks and guns snaked endlessly over the high ground, wound its way down to the wide river, traversed the wooden bridge, passed through the village of Peskovatka on the east bank and was swallowed up in the vast steppe leading to the city of Stalingrad. Their worst fears had not been realized. Spared by the Russian artillery (which had kept the northern river crossing at Vertyachi under constant bombardment) and largely untroubled by the occasional bombing by Soviet planes, the task of getting the army across the Don was accomplished in a calm and collected way and without major incident. This regained sense of order also brought with it a new-found confidence that the crisis had been overcome.

Major Kallweit, who had managed to get his tank squadron to the Don after all, fought alongside the other armoured formations at the bridgehead to ensure that the route remained open for the evacuation of the remaining units of the Sixth Army. By rapidly withdrawing the divisions fighting around Beketovka and with the aid of forces that had been quickly pulled back from elsewhere, it had been possible to establish a new southern front utilizing the old Russian positions in the Karpovka Valley. Despite their lack of strength in numbers, the German forces proved themselves capable of holding this defensive line – at least initially. The future boundaries of the 'Stalingrad Cauldron' began to take shape.

Accompanied by Unold and Breuer, Colonel von Hermann went in search of the Corps HQ in Peskovatka in order to receive new orders. Bombproof and extremely comfortable, this headquarters was situated in a series of sumptuous living and office quarters excavated by the Pioneer Corps at the foot of a steep hillside. During the meeting in the holy of holies of the headquarters' commanding officer, Breuer sat in a wicker chair in the anteroom and flicked through a pile of illustrated magazines on a side table. Oh, look – a photo report from Russia, with the headline 'A Young Lady Out and About in Kiev'! There she is in her smart outfit, gloves in hand, and holding her head with its pretty tumbling locks high as she strolls through 'the ruined capital', while a young 'native Ukrainian' pulls her large suitcase along beside her in a handcart. And in another shot, she's shown wearing a chic bathing costume for 'a spot of sunbathing on the banks of the Dnieper' and flashing the photographer a friendly and carefree smile. In the background, people can be seen playing with a beach ball…

Breuer put the magazine down. What a picnic this war was for some people, he thought. He wondered if they had any idea how many sacrifices or deaths it took to enable starlets like Lilo Schulze or Jutta Mayer to swan around cities in Eastern Europe playing the role of a squeaky-clean figurehead of the new 'master race'? He wasn't at all bitter about it; he just felt a world apart from these people, from their lifestyles and way of thinking – decades ahead of them, in fact. So, was that what they were fighting for – for those kinds of people and their superficial world of selfish indulgence? No, it damn well wasn't! For what, then? Maybe in the end they were all just fighting for themselves, in order that this trial by war might make them more mature, more rounded and better individuals. He for one knew he could never pick up from where he had left off and resume his former life, would never be able to lie on the beach in the sun like he had before, devoid of all thoughts and desires and without a care in the world. He'd never be able to rid himself of memories of this war. It had got under his skin and become an indissoluble, unforgettable part of his very being.

The elegantly dressed officers who briskly went about their business, passing through the anteroom, cast astonished and rather worried glances at the pallid, unshaven stranger in the mud-spattered greatcoat sitting there and staring vacantly into space.

Towards the end of the serious discussion that took place between colonels Hermann and Unold and the ageing general who was the Corps HQ commandant, the latter asked:

'By the by, didn't your division used to be part of Heinz's Tank Corps?'

'Yes, indeed, sir,' replied Unold, 'until quite recently, in fact. General Heinz is our former divisional CO.'

'Ah yes, that's quite right, as I recall. Then it might well interest you to learn that Heinz and his chief of staff have just been placed under arrest.'

Hermann and Unold looked at the commandant in sheer disbelief.

'Things have been happening thick and fast, gentlemen!' the general went on. 'The Russians, who pushed forward not just from Kletskaya but also further west, from Serafimovich, caught Heinz and his two Panzer divisions in a pincer movement. So Heinz took the perfectly natural decision to break out to the west, with the result that he brought the two divisions through virtually without loss. But apparently that went down very badly at High Command. They evidently took the view that he should have tried to break out to the east and join us in the Cauldron!' Here, he gave a hollow laugh. 'As if a man with orthodox general staff training should have anticipated the utterly brilliant plan of voluntarily allowing an entire army to become encircled! Well… In any event, he's been arrested and demoted.'

Unold, deeply upset by this news, made as if to speak, but words failed him. Heinz had been one of the few men whose military skills he admired without envy or reserve, and it was shameful that this first-rate soldier should have been treated in such a disgraceful manner – he simply couldn't fathom it. Colonel von Hermann, meanwhile, seemed to have turned even paler than usual, though his face betrayed no emotion.

'You're a divisional commander too now, Hermann,' said the general, his eyes twinkling at the colonel from behind his spectacles. 'Take care not to get yourself promoted to general too soon. It's no fun at all these days!'

The vehicles of the divisional Staff HQ were parked up, far apart from one another, on a treeless expanse not far from the Don. Whereas on the other side of the river they'd had to struggle through thick drifts of winter snow, here there was only a light dusting that barely covered the short steppe grass. First Lieutenant Breuer stood alone, away from the vehicles, and looked out over the river to the west. The sharp wind cut into his face, ballooned out his capacious greatcoat and piled up the dry, powdery snow around his feet. Atop the bluffs on the far side of the Don, the launch rails of an enemy rocket battery that had taken up position there were silhouetted against the evening sky like a grille. Through his field glasses he could make out on the road that ran along the top of the cliffs long columns of Russian cavalry arriving from the north. Breuer looked at the dying sunset. The sun would still be shining down on his home town, but here it had already set… Yet along with this setting sun, the spectre of the twenty-fourth had also faded, for another month at least. A great feeling of calm washed over him. He recalled the day when he'd crossed the river down there heading from east to west, confident that he'd never have to return here again. When had that been? Just a few days ago? No, surely some years had passed since then… You won't ever let us leave, will you, you terrible city on the Volga? No pangs of sentimental self-pity accompanied this thought, just a sober acknowledgement of reality. Stalingrad – you are our destiny!

PART 2

Between Night and Morning

I

Manstein's Coming!

IT WAS THE BEGINNING of December. A keen east wind blew across the frozen white surface of the Volga. It whipped lacerating ice crystals into the frost-reddened faces of the soldiers up on the bluffs and got caught up in the ruins of the devastated city, where it rattled furiously at exposed rafters and sheets of corrugated iron. Suddenly breaking free, it raced on, out into the steppe, with even greater violence than before. Clouds of powdery snow hissed through the leaves of the wormwood growing there, piled up against the ice-bound vehicles and formed lines of drifts against the humped roofs of bunkers. The blizzard tore down the bare ravines, whipping its long white streamers over the soldiers who were cowering under tarpaulins in their shallow foxholes, defending the western front of the Stalingrad Cauldron. Nothing had resulted from General von Seydlitz's letter of protest, not even a reprimand. In all likelihood, at the army group that High Command forwarded it to, without adding any comment of its own, it had simply found its way into the waste bin. General Paulus had withdrawn the encircled German forces to the line ordered by Hitler and, effective from the first of December, had been promoted to the rank of four-star general. Since the end of November, the Stalingrad Cauldron had assumed the definitive

form it would take thereafter until its anticipated relief – 'definitive',
that is, only in so far as the Russians were prepared to collude in this
state of affairs. Thus far, that did indeed pretty much appear to be
the case. In the various military commands, officers huddled round
to study the map showing the current positions of forces.

'Extraordinary shape, isn't it? Looks like the Crimea!'

'More like the Free City of Danzig if you ask me! About the same
size too!'

'Well, I measured it just for the fun of it. It's roughly sixty kilometres long by thirty-five wide, takes in an area of about thirteen
hundred square kilometres and has a front totalling a hundred and
fifty kilometres in length.'

'And just a tiny speck in the vast Russian wasteland… Don't know
about you, but I'd rather be in Danzig right now!'

'Now, now, gentlemen! No need to go losing our nerve quite yet!
We've got twenty-two divisions and three hundred thousand men…
what do we imagine is going to happen? We could break out from
here any time we liked if we had to. But why would we want to do
that! Think of it as a game! At this rate we'll beat the endurance
record of the Cholm Cauldron; then we'll be the ones with bragging
rights.'

Soon enough, though, it became anything but a game.

The short winter days were equally bleak for the men trapped in
the Cauldron, no matter whether the sun rose like a glowing ball
of fire in the east and, after a brief transit across the frost-spangled
aluminium dome of the firmament, sank once more below rose-
tinted snowfields, or whether the sky and the Earth merged together
in a dirty grey. And the agonizing nights stretched on interminably,
filled with the monotonous drone of aircraft engines, the chatter of
machine guns and the dull rumble of artillery fire. Its bottomless
blackness was rent time and again by the yellow flashes of gunfire,
perforated by the bright pearl strings of tracer bullets and erased for
minutes on end by the limelight of star shells and parachute flares.

There was talk of 'days of rest'. But the fighting never took time off. And hope bled to death on the frost-hard ground of real life.

A few kilometres west of the village of Pitomnik, on the road to Novo Alexeyevsky, stood a hamlet of three or four tumbledown houses, with a group of vehicles clustered around them like a herd of sheep. Above the door of one of the houses hung a rough-hewn wooden board bearing the legend 'Regional Command'. Just at that moment, a man emerged, cast an anxious glance up at the sky (which, now it was three o'clock in the afternoon German time, was almost completely dark), turned up his coat collar and walked briskly away, adeptly picking his way down the treacherously icy road. The strong wind lifted the hem of his short, waisted fur jacket like a ballerina's tutu. Sergeant Major Harras was immensely proud of his new wardrobe, particularly the white leather peaked cap with a lambswool lining, which the Staff HQ tailor, following Harras's own instructions, had run up for him. Only today, a soldier from another unit had addressed him as 'Captain'. Harras was in a hurry to get back to his bunker. It got a little spooky around the houses here once darkness fell. Captain Fackelmann, who had recently been appointed regional CO of Dubininsky ('really prime location, don't you think, this handful of hovels!'), had just shown him the place where the two bombs had landed last night, immediately behind the commander's house. 'Honestly, I ask you! A lorry and an armoured scout car completely destroyed, one wall of the house almost flattened, half the tiles blown off the roof, and of course all the windows shattered!' Now they had to sit behind the boarded-up windows in candlelight, even during the daytime. The sergeant major turned off on to a side path that went north. There, a few hundred metres from the main road, an entire city of sizeable proportions had sprung up. Row upon row of snow-dusted dugouts, densely packed, with blackish smoke rising from them, and in between several rough-looking shacks, antenna masts, steaming field kitchens, and vehicles hastily camouflaged with limewash, either half-buried in the ground or with banks of snow built up around them to protect them from bomb splinters. In among this confused mess ran a spider's web of driveable tracks and footpaths. Looking at this wintry army camp, Harras was always reminded of the polar research station he'd once seen in a documentary film. Even the infantrymen, swaddled in their winter gear and their felt boots, didn't look much different from Eskimos. The only things missing were polar bears and dog sleds. Sergeant Major Harras pinned back his ears. He could clearly hear a noise somewhere between a rattle and a drone. Their first 'sewing machine'! – that was the name the German troops gave the Russian 'U2' trainers, small biplanes that were sent out under cover of darkness to harass German positions. Towards the airfield at Pitomnik, a parachute flare suddenly lit up the night sky. It floated there virtually motionless, flooding the snowy landscape with a yellowish-red light. The dull thump of bombs drifted over. The remarkable thing was that the Russian pilots were leaving the polar settlement here almost unscathed. They'd probably mistaken the huge collection of lorries and other vehicles for some sort of junkyard. Besides, the nearby aerodrome acted as a lightning rod. In actual fact, it was pretty cosy here. They were right in the middle of the Cauldron, out of range of the Soviet artillery. It would surely be far more uncomfortable to be with the units fighting on the southern front.

'Damn and blast it!' Harras had tripped over something hard, lying directly across the path. It was a human body, pressed into the mud, still just about recognizable from the tatters of frozen-stiff brown cloth it was dressed in. Some Romanian or Russian who'd starved to death, or been run over or shot – who could say? Its bare feet, a sickly greenish hue, protruded from the snow, and its head had been flattened by the wheels of vehicles. The acting sergeant major's sense of order was outraged at the sight. Incredible to leave a body lying around like this! When the thaw came, it'd stink to high heaven round here. He gave the corpse another kick. But it had merged with the frozen mud to become one inseparable unit, and refused to budge. Harras cast his eyes around. Was he even on the right path still? You were forever getting lost in this labyrinth. They really ought to put up some signs to help people find their way! But no sooner did these go up than they were stolen for firewood. He trudged on angrily. Ah, at least things were thinning out a bit now! He appeared to have reached the western fringe of the foxhole city. He stopped to get his bearings again. That black box shape over there, surely that was their unit's bus, and that might well be the CO's car behind it, and where the old jalopy was, the intelligence officer's bunker couldn't be far off… All of a sudden, Harras tensed, his head straining forward like a predator waiting to pounce. No doubt about it, a figure was squatting right next to the low roof of the bunker! A naked backside, turned to the wind, stood out palely against a dark frame of clothing. Just you wait, you pig, I'll have you! Like a stooping hawk, Harras shot towards the crouching lump of humanity.

'Are you out of your tiny mind?' he shouted. The figure rose, holding up his trousers with his left hand, and trying with his right to cover as best he could the place where, on a respectable soldier, the rear seam of his trouser seat would be.

'Well, well, what a surprise!' drawled Harras, relishing every word. 'Herr Lakosch – of course, it had to be you! Don't you know it's against regulations to defecate within fifty metres of the bunker?'

'Yes, sir, Sar'nt-Major, sir!'

'So what do you think you're playing at?' By now, the biting easterly wind had chilled Lakosch to the marrow, and his teeth were chattering violently. Harras took it to be the effect of his commanding personality. But the little driver's response soon put him wise on that score.

'It's just so perishing cold, Sergeant Major! And besides, with the kind of food we've been getting, I wouldn't make it fifty metres!'

Harras took a deep breath and prepared to bawl out Lakosch for

his impudence. But at the last minute, he checked himself. He was
due to leave the staff shortly, and everyone knew it. That sort of thing
could compromise your authority. It'd be more sensible to quit on
a positive note. So he changed tack and adopted an avuncular tone.

'Look, lad, it's really not on! Just think about it: we might still be
stuck here in the spring. And when the little offerings you've laid
start thawing out, imagine the pong! Have a care!'

Lakosch responded in kind to Harras's banter.

'Yes, sir! On the other hand, though, has the Sergeant Major
considered that it's actually fertilizing the steppe? Who knows, we
might end up growing potatoes here… Shame you're going to be
leaving us and miss all that, Sar'nt Major!'

Speechless with rage, Harras uttered something incoherent, before
turning on his heels and striding off. Lakosch buckled up his belt.
After just eight days, he could already pull it two notches tighter, he
noted with alarm, and walked over to the Volkswagen, which stood
alone and unprotected in the cold. It too would be for the knacker's
yard soon. The clutch and transmission had pretty much had it, and
it took hours to get it started in the morning. 'You've served us well,
old girl!' muttered Lakosch, gently stroking the car's whitewashed
door panel. 'Twelve thousand kilometres on Russian roads, that's
no mean feat. Manstein ought to get a move on; otherwise he won't
find you still alive!' With a practised movement, he unclipped the
two bucket seats from the front of the car and, whistling, carried
them down into the dugout.

Lakosch dubbed it the 'trunk', plain and simple. It was clear what
he meant by it. With the ribbed patterns on its rough clay walls,
pickaxed out of the frozen ground, the shallow dugout bunker
occupied by unit Ic resembled nothing so much as the inside of a
steamer trunk. Just above the head height of a standing man, its
lid comprised a layer of planks covered with soil. Admittedly, you

couldn't open this lid, so in order to exit the bunker you had to clamber up five slippery steps hewn out of the clay and heave open the corrugated-iron entry hatch with sufficient force to stop the fierce wind blowing it back down on your head. The fact that you were surrounded on all four sides by earth meant you were perfectly safe from shrapnel, and also ensured that the little trench heater had an easy job keeping the place warm and snug. Initially, when the entire Staff HQ had had to make do with only four bunkers, they'd had to share this space of about eight square metres with the mess orderlies and the men from the signals unit. During the day, it was just about tolerable, at a pinch, so long as everybody squatted on the ground and didn't move around too much. But at night the thirteen men had been packed in like sardines in a tin, jammed against, and even on top of, one another. And woe betide anyone who dared to shift position or start scratching himself when the lice embarked on their nightly round through the pile of bodies! Later, when they got more space, just two of their former bunker-mates remained: Lieutenant Wiese, the head of communications, and Senta.

'Well,' Breuer ribbed Wiese, 'as an intelligence officer *manqué*, so to speak, you're already part of the family! Your people'll be glad to be shot of you for a while – and we're delighted to have you here with us!'

Wiese was only too happy to stay. Senta was part of the family, too. Senta was a small yellow-haired bulldog bitch, which Lakosch had saved from being shot by a pilot officer somewhere down on the Don. Since then, he'd become besotted with the animal, flying off the handle one time when Herbert referred to it as an 'ugly beast'. Once there was a bit more room, a table was cobbled together. Breuer and Wiese invariably bunked down together on top of this at night, top to tail. Sonderführer Fröhlich, meanwhile, slept underneath, where there was no danger of suddenly plummeting to earth. On the other hand, he'd sometimes crack his head painfully against the boards when explosions in the night woke him and made him sit up with a start. Also, this arrangement ensured that there was plenty of room for the others to bed down on the – fortunately boarded – floor of the bunker.

The daylight that penetrated the bunker through a narrow glass window along the top edge of the long wall was opaque. Even dimmer was the light at night from a small oil-lit storm lantern. Yet they were proud of this precious item, which Lakosch had purloined from another unit's bunker. Every three days, he scrounged a little diesel oil from the sergeant in charge of the motor pool. When Geibel broke the lamp glass one day while cleaning it, the others could have lynched him. But they managed to fashion a new glass out of a conserve jar, and the lamp continued to cast its meagre light on the few pictures that had been put up on the walls to try to make the place seem a bit more like home. One of these was a photograph, set in a frame made from the golden-yellow cardboard of a file cover, showing Breuer's wife and their two boys. Next to Wiese's bunk was a colour reproduction on a postcard of Matthias Grünewald's *Stuppach Madonna*. But the principal ornament in the bunker was a poster produced by a soldiers' magazine, printed in red and black ornate lettering on yellow paper and bearing a famous quotation by the sixteenth-century humanist Ulrich von Hutten:

> I do not dream of past happiness,
> I break on through and never look back!

'Doesn't sit well with me at all,' said Lieutenant Wiese. 'Dreaming of past happiness is the only thing that keeps me going.'

Fröhlich took quite a different view. It was he who had hung up the poster, and felt himself inspired anew by it every day.

'Hutten was a truly great man,' he told Geibel, who never failed to lend a willing ear to his lectures. 'It's almost like he wrote that specifically with us in mind. If only he was here with us now… But just you wait and see; we're going to send them packing. Watch how the Russians turn tail and start running for their lives once we get started! – "I break on through." What a brilliant rallying cry, eh?'

Little homilies like that were generally followed by long disquisitions on the current military situation. Fröhlich went on to explain how the Russians might soon be facing encirclement and annihilation themselves, if only… Corporal Herbert, whose temper had become very frayed of late, couldn't bear to listen to Fröhlich's drivel. He either threw in snide interjections or left the bunker for the duration. Breuer often found himself staring pensively at the quotation on the wall. He found these sentiments from a former age deeply moving.

The surviving elements of Colonel von Hermann's Panzer division were also based at Dubininsky, almost exactly in the centre of the Cauldron. Its role there was to act as a reserve intervention force for the army. If the Russians happened to 'kick up a stink' anywhere – if they broke through the main line of defence ordered by Hitler, that is – von Hermann's unit was required to 'iron out' the problem. Rather more accurately, Major Kallweit described their task as 'playing fireman'. The remains of the artillery regiment under Colonel Lunitz, the twenty tanks of the tank regiment that the mechanics had somehow made serviceable again, and the newly formed 'Eichert Battalion', comprising former gunners, men from the logistics and signals units and the remains of the defunct tank destroyer detachment, were run off their feet. For, unfortunately, a stink arose all too frequently, especially on the northwestern section of the front, where divisions that had been seriously depleted during the withdrawal found themselves in very unfavourable terrain. Much to the chagrin of the divisional CO, every time the battalion's units returned from their rotating sorties to this section, they did so pretty badly mauled. One morning, the rumbling sounds of fighting in the northwestern sector seemed to go on for ever. There seemed to be one hell of a stink over there. When Colonel von Hermann came back from a conference at the Corps in the afternoon, Unold, his composure now restored somewhat by the fact that the situation had stabilized – at least for the time being – since the terrible days of the withdrawal, handed him their mobilization orders, which he'd just received from High Command.

'There's been a major breakthrough,' he explained. 'They've advanced up to the artillery positions at the Vienna division's sector. This time we have to throw everything we've got at them. You've been tasked with leading the counter-attack, Colonel, sir. The Welfe Regiment from the next division down the line's going to support us.'

The colonel nodded. He remembered Lieutenant Colonel Welfe very well from the days of the withdrawal. With the help of his regiment, he felt sure they'd pull it off.

They duly set to work devising their plan of attack. That same evening the Eichert Battalion, which represented almost the entire infantry strength of the division, was dispatched on lorries, to be placed at the immediate disposal of the division that was so hard-pressed.

Breuer and Padre Peters were passengers in the small car that Lakosch was struggling to steer through the slushy snow. The division's padre, who was bosom buddies with Lieutenant Wiese, was always a welcome guest in the Intelligence Section's bunker. He would sit there in the corner, smiling serenely and listening to the others' conversations. He rarely spoke himself, but when he did it carried real weight and made the men sit up and listen. His face wore an expression of calm assurance that remained unshaken by the changing fortunes of war from one day to the next.

'Tell me, Padre,' Breuer asked one day, his eye caught by the Iron Cross First Class pinned to the pastor's coat, 'as a military chaplain you're still a soldier, right? But how can you square the business of war with your duties of pastoral care? As a devout Christian, you ought by rights… Well…'

The padre smiled. 'What, be a pacifist, you mean? Turn my back on the wicked world so as to remain pure? And stop giving succour and spiritual comfort to men who look death in the face every day – just because I have a moral objection to war? No, Lieutenant, that would be a sin – not just against the men, but the German people as well, whom we're bound to through thick and thin. The world's an imperfect place, unfortunately. But you can't make it better by adhering to some rigid theoretical programme. No, my task is to bear witness to my Christian faith in a hostile environment, to lead by example and hopefully change people and the world in the process.'

That was Padre Peters all over. His words were anything but empty rhetoric. He acted on his pronouncements. Because the medical orderlies who had once been attached to the division had been scattered to the four winds, he no longer had much in the way of official duties. But he made work for himself. He accompanied units on operations or went on foot with his sacristan – since Breuer couldn't let him have a car – to visit other divisions' field hospitals and dressing stations. So it was only natural that he should be present when his own division launched this major operation.

In Baburkin, an unpleasant dump of a place, pandemonium had broken out. Filthy, unkempt soldiers, some of them without weapons, were standing or lying around, yelling at one another, brawling with Romanian troops in front of a house, or dragging crates, bundles and sacks out of huts and bunkers. Now and then the mayhem was punctuated by a loud crack of gunfire, which made horses rear up, while all the time heavily laden trucks and sleds raced down the road, splashing through thawed puddles. At the edge of the village, the area around the medical bunker, whose entrance faced the front, was peppered with craters where anti-tank shells had exploded, while sulphurous smoke wafted in yellowy streamers across the snowy expanse. They got the wounded men out quickly. Just then, Kallweit's tanks rumbled into the village. Padre Peters took his leave. He wanted to get over to the field hospital. Because the road was jammed, Lakosch drove the car behind a house to give it some cover. 'I reckon you must be short of men over at your division,' Breuer said to an officer who was loitering there, "cos the place is teeming here!'

'What's to be done?' he said disconsolately, casting a jaded eye over the unruly goings-on. 'They're all displaced men, remnants of units that don't exist any more. They're running wild! We can't do anything to stop them. When we tried clearing the rabble out of a couple of the houses, see, a firefight almost broke out! If the army doesn't step in…'

The staff headquarters of the Vienna division was situated north-west of the village of Baburkin in bunkers clinging high up to the side of a gorge, like swallows' nests. They could only be reached by a treacherous cliff path, protected by railings. When the army's emissaries arrived in the grey light of dawn, the site was under fire from some Russian tanks that had broken through. The divisional CO – clearly somewhat relieved, though the cares of the previous day were still etched in his face – bade them welcome to his mountain fortress with a piece of good news: during the night, the Eichert Battalion had succeeded in pushing the enemy back on the left flank and capturing the commanding position on Hill 124.5.

'Great stuff, that's our job almost done!' crowed Unold. 'Welfe can mop up the rest… And I'm sure you can polish off the last few Russian tanks that are roaming around here, Kallweit!'

Major Kallweit, who had driven on ahead of his unit, nodded sullenly. They hadn't needed to dispatch his entire force just for that! Colonel von Hermann, who was embarrassed by his chief of operation's high-handed way of going about things, turned to address the commander of the Austrian division, who, feeling redundant in the midst of this sudden burst of activity, had withdrawn in irritation into the corner. 'Eichert has carried out his mission by taking the heights, General!' he told him. 'I suggest your division take over from the battalion without more ado.'

The general muttered something incomprehensible and turned to leave. He seemed less than overjoyed at the prospect of assuming responsibility.

Breuer found the head of the Austrian intelligence section, a portly, asthmatic captain, in a foul mood. He'd been moved out of his bunker to make room for the staff of Colonel von Hermann. Muttering under his breath, he took his plate of sauerkraut and dumplings and went to sit in a corner. He left it to his adjutant, a first lieutenant with the weather-beaten, strong-boned face of a Tyrolean lumberjack, to bring his visitor up to speed on their current position. Breuer was happy to let him give a long-winded account of what was going on.

'Our position is… how can I put it? Well, we don't have a position any more! When we arrived here, our general just pointed out over the snowy fields there, see, and told us: "This is where our new defensive line will be, gentlemen!" So, there and then we just banked the snow up into walls and ramparts… and then, when we got hold of some entrenching tools, we dug ourselves some foxholes, one every ten metres, each for two men – up to chest height, right – and we chucked some rags of clothing from dead Russians in for extra warmth, and later we even managed to construct a couple of small bunkers for the battalion and company staff. So then the Russians launched a rolling attack, shouting through loudspeakers that we as Austrians shouldn't be letting ourselves get killed for the criminal Hitler. We just laughed at that and let them have it, right? Until they bombarded the hell out of us yesterday with their artillery and those damned Stalin organs, that is… And then their infantry stormed us, wave after wave, and they overran us with tanks… and today, we have to find a way of pushing them back again.'

★

Up to midday, the Welfe Regiment's attack made excellent progress. The battalion on the right flank had overrun the Russian positions, destroyed a heavy mortar detachment and almost reached their final objective. The men of the Eichert Battalion were still occupying the high ground. The Austrian general kept putting off the moment when his forces would relieve them. During the afternoon, Captain Eichert stumbled into the bunker, with blood seeping through a fresh dressing round his right arm.

'Colonel… General, sir! We can't go on like this! They're laying down heavy artillery and mortar fire on us up on the hill… it's never-ending! We've taken twenty per cent casualties already. If we stay up there for another two hours, the whole battalion'll be wiped out!'

'I thought as much. I knew we'd have no joy trying to hold that position,' the general replied, not without a hint of schadenfreude. 'No one can hold out for long up on that bleak hill. First the Russians take it, then we do. And every time the enterprise costs unsustainable losses – but there's no telling the army that, oh no!' he added, finally remembering that they were all in this together. 'I've lost count of the number of times I've tried suggesting – and the Corps backs me up on this – that the front line should be moved back down to the bottom of the hill. Nothing doing! comes the answer. Hitler's orders! I can hardly go to the High Command and make the same request.'

'Look, Eichert, I'll get on to the army right away and see what can be done,' Colonel von Hermann, himself very shocked, told the captain, before ordering him back to his post. But before he could deliver on his promise, a message arrived from the combat group: 'Hill 124.5 has had to be abandoned in the face of overwhelming enemy infantry forces. Unable to evacuate all of our wounded!'

Unold's hands started shaking, all his sense of superiority suddenly dissipated and his composure blown away like chaff in the wind. He telephoned the Wehrmacht and asked to speak to the chief of staff. He gave a detailed account of the situation and proposed moving the front line back down to the base of the hill.

Then he put the general on the line: '...No, the Russians won't gain any advantage from it! They couldn't hold it either... Any time we like we can just blow them off it with artillery, just like they did to us... Yes, we've still got plenty of ammunition for that!'

He then handed back to Colonel Unold. Presently, on the other end of the line, it was none other than General Schmidt, the army's chief of staff, to whom Unold found himself speaking.

'Yes, sir,' the colonel said, and the others in the room saw the colour slowly drain from his face, 'Yes, sir, General!' He reinforced this last 'Yes, sir' with a brief, tense bow as he stood there holding the phone. After a few minutes, he put down the receiver. Taking a deep breath, he turned to Major Kallweit, who had just come in to report that they'd taken out the last of the Russian tanks that had broken through.

'So, Kallweit,' he announced breezily, 'new orders for you straight from the top! At nightfall, your tanks are to take Hill 124.5 and hold it until the infantry arrives at first light.'

For an instant, the major stood there as if thunderstruck. And then Kallweit, the imperturbable Kallweit of all people, found his nerves failing him for the very first time.

'What!?' he roared. 'That's sheer bloody madness! At *night*? We're not bloody cats; we can't see in the dark! And when the morning comes, they'll pick us off before we even realize what's happening!'

The colonel shrugged his shoulders.

'It's no use getting upset,' he said. 'Orders are orders.'

By now, though, the major was in full flight.

'Fuck orders!' he screamed, abandoning all propriety. 'The top brass has no idea about tank ops! Letting a bunch of infantry tossers wank around with tanks is like... Look, you could afford to do that on manoeuvres, maybe, but not here in this shitstorm!'

He stormed out without saluting and slammed the door behind him.

By nightfall, First Lieutenant Welfe, who had been with the

battalion on his left flank during the attack, was able to report that he'd reached the former main defensive line. Flushed with this success, he immediately called the commander of his division to inform him. 'Yes, General, sir, a complete success! The First Battalion was particularly brave. The battalion commander led the charge, holding his baton... He was killed, unfortunately... Shot through the hand, then when he was being transported back on a tank, they got him in the stomach too. He died at the dressing station. Yes, indeed, a great shame... Otherwise? Around six per cent dead, ten per cent wounded. Yes, sir, thank you! Why's that, General? Oh, right! Right... Very well, then... All the best... General, sir!'

The lieutenant replaced the receiver and, removing the monocle from his eye, polished it absent-mindedly and blinked as he stared into space. His face was pale. Colonel von Hermann was keen to learn the latest.

'So, Welfe – what does your CO have to say? Is he happy?'

'Yes, very,' replied the lieutenant in a deadpan voice. 'He said how much he appreciated all we've done, and wished us farewell and all the best.'

'Farewell?'

'Yes, he's leaving. The staff's being flown out! On the eighth – for redeployment elsewhere!'

During the night, the tanks captured the high ground. And by the morning of the following day it was back in Russian hands again. The Panzer regiment had five total losses, while eight more tanks were severely damaged but capable of being salvaged. The Eichert Battalion suffered forty per cent losses, either dead or wounded, and another fifteen per cent disabled by frostbite. The only success of the day was that the army top brass now adopted the division's suggestion and moved the front line down to the base of the hill. The Austrian general expressed his heartfelt thanks to Colonel von Hermann for having achieved that.

Mission accomplished for von Hermann's division.

★

Lakosch sat agonizing over a letter. In front of him lay a pile of banknotes. This time, he'd decided to send his mother all his ready cash. After all, what was he supposed to do with money out here? There wasn't anything to buy. Lieutenant Wiese, meanwhile, had his nose in a book that Padre Peters had brought him. It was Tolstoy's *Resurrection*. First Lieutenant Breuer was playing the mouth organ. Every time he picked up the little instrument, he remembered his leave-taking that time, during his last spell of leave, at the blackout-darkened station in the small town in East Prussia he called home. His young son, Joachim, seven years old, had shyly pressed the little brown cardboard box into his hand at the last minute. 'Take it with you, Daddy, so you can play music in Russia and make the soldiers happy. I can't play it!' 'Go on, take it!' his wife whispered to him. 'Otherwise he'll cry his eyes out.' Smiling, Breuer had taken the box and slipped it into his greatcoat pocket. And there it had lain, forgotten, until now, the dark days leading up to Christmas. One evening, he'd pulled it out and tried playing it. And now nothing on earth could have persuaded him to part with the shiny little instrument.

He was playing an étude by Chopin. He only knew it by the title 'Tristesse'. It was a favourite of his. He had it at home on a record, sung by a tenor in French:

> *Tout est fini*
> *la terre se meurt,*
> *la nature entière*
> *subit l'hiver…*

The wartime winter of 1940–41 in Paris. From every café and bar came the sound of chanteuses singing this melancholic air and weeping. But for German soldiers back then, life was still a bed of roses. All past now, gone for ever… Lieutenant Wiese hummed along softly with the melody. The lamp swayed gently on its thin wire. Its flickering glow flitted over the decorations on the bunker wall, momentarily illuminating the golden light radiating down from joyous heaven onto the tranquil Madonna in Grünewald's picture. The run-up to Christmas…

> *Les oiseaux heureux se taisent.*
> *La nature est en deuil…*
> *tout est fini…*
> *tout est fini.*

Herbert and Fröhlich were marking crosses on scraps of paper they kept shielded from one another's view with their hands; they were playing the game 'battleships', which only required a pencil and a piece of paper. You could while away whole days like this. Herbert fired a new salvo: 'A3… D7… G5' and Fröhlich announced the result: 'Miss… Miss… Hit on a battleship.'

'Aha,' growled Herbert, 'so that's where the beast's lurking! Right, next go I'll finish him off!'

From outside came a droning sound, growing in intensity. Fröhlich sat up and listened. 'Great – they've got the supply flights up and running again! That means tomorrow's food in the bag!'

Herbert, too, raised his head for an instant. 'Nah, it's a sewing machine!' he said.

'Crap,' replied Fröhlich dismissively. 'They're Ju 52s,* no question! You're always hearing sewing machines, Mr Misery-Guts!'

---

* Ju 52s – the Junkers 52, a large tri-motored monoplane, was originally designed as a passenger plane for Lufthansa but at the outbreak of war became the Luftwaffe's standard transport workhorse, deployed in all theatres of the conflict. Dating from 1931, it was already an obsolescent type by the 1940s and its rather quaint appearance, with its three engines and its corrugated metal skin, earned it the affectionate nickname *Tante Ju* ('Auntie Ju') among troops.

'I'm telling you it's a sewing machine!' shouted Herbert. 'Even a child could tell that! Why do you always have to be such a smart-arse?'

He threw down his pencil and stood up. As if to prove him right, from the distance came two thuds, in quick succession. The bunker walls shook slightly and bits of clay showered down from the roof.

'Calm down now, gents!' Breuer intervened. 'What's up with you two?'

'It's true though, Lieutenant! He always has to have the last word. You can't say anything now without being gainsaid and insulted. It's getting on my wick, it really is!'

Herbert was on the verge of tears.

'Pull yourself together, for heaven's sake!' said Breuer. 'Do you think it's easy for any of us, just sitting around here and waiting?'

In his heart of hearts, he had to concede the corporal was right. With his desperate optimism, which he'd wrapped around himself like protective armour, Fröhlich could sometimes be truly insufferable. And his absurd air of superiority even managed to rile people far less touchy than Herbert.

When the argument began, Lieutenant Wiese had clapped his book shut and left the bunker. Breuer now followed suit. These incessant little tiffs were very wearing. Outside, he found the lieutenant gazing up at the black sky, which was filled with the steady drone of transport planes. Breuer went up to him but did not disturb his reverie. Above the airfield, a flare went up, showering a cluster of red stars to earth as it burst.

Suddenly Wiese spoke, as if to himself. 'It's so desolate. This wilderness… no trees, no bushes, not a house or a hill, just this endless white expanse… it's like a shroud. The only thing for your eye to light on is a horse's cadaver here and there… We're imprisoned in a coffin of ice and snow, surrounded by the unknown… I can't take it any more. The stench of death about this place will be the end of me.'

'Not you as well, Wiese, surely?'

Breuer was genuinely shocked. Time and again, it had been his much younger comrade's aura of calm, cheerful equanimity that had pulled him out of the slough of despond.

'Wiese!' he said. 'You can't go giving up on us now, lad! What'll become of the rest of us if even you lose heart? Why do you think old Endrigkeit likes to come and smoke his pipe around us? And the same goes for Fackelmann, and Engelhard and Peters... Even Dierk, who makes out he can't stand you, eh? It's because they're looking for a bit of home in our company. Because they want to forget the war for a few minutes, that's why! In this whole sorry mess, our bunker's become a haven of peace. And that – you can take my word for it – that's all down to you. You're our keeper of the flame, Wiese. It mustn't go out.'

Wiese threw up his hands in despair.

'The flame, hmm…,' he said sadly. 'It's the last glowing ember of coal, about to go out. We're dying, Breuer, slowly but surely. The war, this primitive existence, is devouring us. The filth, the lice, our pitiful scratching around for a bite of food – and then there's the homesickness, Breuer! We're two thousand kilometres from home. We can't cope with it any more – psychologically, I mean. This fighting's pointless. Just go and take a look down in the bunker at how everything's slowly falling apart on your wonderful "island of peace" – comradeship, altruism… More and more we're ceasing to behave like human beings, whether we want to or not.' His voice grew bitter. 'Schiller called war a gift, you know? A beautiful gift! What's the use of a test if you know right from the outset that you're going to fail? Christ, if only we knew what the point of it all was!'

Breuer laid his hand on his friend's shoulder.

'You know when you read to us recently,' he told him, 'that passage out of Goethe's *Faust*: "He serves me, but still serves me in confusion/ I will soon lead him into clarity". That was really well chosen. It gave us new heart. One day we'll know what the point was, too.'

The lieutenant suddenly swung round to face Breuer.

'Do you think we'll ever get out of here?'

His voice was choked with emotion.

'Of course we will, Wiese! No doubt about it! Just now, Unold was talking about the major relief operation that the High Command's set in motion.'

The lieutenant shook his head.

'No, we won't get out of here; I know it. Even if we're relieved one day – and I really believe it might happen – we won't be the same people. We'll never bring our best side home with us. That's fallen victim to this war. It's lying dead and buried under the snowy fields of Stalingrad.'

Stalingrad… the name fluttered out into the night, and the two men stood pondering it. From the far northwest came a dull rumble, and faint yellow flashes momentarily lit up the sky.

Then Wiese spoke again, this time clearly and calmly. 'You're right, Breuer. We mustn't give up as long as we're still able to fight. We should tend that glowing ember; maybe one day it'll burst into flame again…'

They heard the sound of shuffling steps approaching. It was Geibel, who'd gone to fetch the next day's provisions. The forager doled out rations as soon as he received them now; otherwise too much food got stolen overnight. The two officers followed Geibel into the bunker. By the time they got down there, he was already being mobbed by the others.

'What delights do you have for us today, then?'

'Cold dandruff with artificial honey, right?'

'It's not great,' Geibel conceded glumly. 'Two hundred and fifty grams of crispbread, thirty grams of tinned meat and three cigarettes each. There weren't any supply drops today.'

The men's faces had grown long. Less bread yet again… and the pathetic number of smokes, too! Even yesterday, they'd still had five, and the company sergeant major had assured them that would continue. Geibel put the little ration packets on the table, while Lieutenant Wiese glanced through the bundle of mail.

'Newspapers, nothing but newspapers!' he announced. 'All dating back to October and November. Not a single letter, I'm afraid.'

'What's this lot here, then?' asked Herbert, pointing at a pile of boxes and tins.

'Oh, yeah,' said Geibel, 'forgot about them. There's a tin of boot polish and a tube of toothpaste per person!'

'Toothpaste? When we don't even have any water to wash with?'

'And what's this I see?' cried Herbert, holding up two large rolls against the light. Printed on the packaging were the words 'Premium toilet tissue'. The men stood and gawped in disbelief at one another.

'Oh, that's really bloody priceless!' Breuer exploded. 'They send us fuck-all to eat, but they manage to fly us in bog paper – bog paper, for Christ's sake! Maybe they'll follow it up tomorrow with a collapsible flushing toilet!'

In his fury, he grabbed the rolls of tissue and booted them into the corner.

'The forager told me,' Geibel went on, 'that the Corps got a load of other stuff, too. Toothbrushes, combs, razor blades and… and…'

Realizing he'd said too much, his face was flushed with embarrassment. Once more, it was plain to see he hadn't been a soldier for very long. 'No doubt some nice galoshes too,' Lakosch said in a stage whisper to Herbert, 'as winter wear so they don't go catching a nasty cold.'

Herbert kicked his shin to shut him up.

'They've lost their minds,' said Breuer, perfectly calmly. 'Don't you reckon, Wiese? Well, either it's the case that the top brass has gone crazy, or—'

Fröhlich broke into a nervous laugh.

'Come, come, Lieutenant,' he giggled hysterically. 'Don't you see that's fantastic, wonderful news? It's the best possible indication that the encirclement's about to be broken!'

The phone rang. Breuer snatched up the receiver and gestured for everyone to pipe down. On the other end of the line was Cavalry Captain Willms, the tank regiment's intelligence officer. The men caught the sound of his nasal, always rather sleepy-sounding voice buzzing faintly from the earpiece.

'Hello, Breuer. Yes... Just wanted to give you a quick update. Thing is... Manstein started his push to relieve the Cauldron two days ago... No, no, not from the west! From the south... What's that? Yes, absolutely... so far it's going well, he's made good progress...'

At a stroke, the mood in the bunker changed. All their cares were suddenly forgotten. There was a hubbub of excited chatter. Even Senta emerged from under the table and dashed about whimpering and barking from one person to the next, celebrating the news in her own doggy way.

'See? What did I tell you!' crowed Fröhlich. 'It was absurd to think that the Führer could have just left us to rot here, just absurd! We'll be out of here within a week or so, and they'll give us a Stalingrad campaign flash to sew on our shoulders, and then it's off home to mother to celebrate Christmas!'

And this time, even Herbert said nothing and did nothing to signal his disagreement.

When the Russians broke through in November, what remained of the two grenadier regiments from the tank division had been withdrawn from Stalingrad and placed under the command of one of the two regimental COs to form a combat group. This new unit was ordered south with all dispatch to close the breach in the defensive line there. And that was where they still remained, having in the meantime been incorporated into a motorized infantry division. Sergeant Major Harras had been with this 'Combat Group Riedel' for the past eight days. When, dressed in his stylish fur jacket, he reported to the CO and clicked his heels, the lieutenant colonel had peered down his long nose and looked Harras up and down.

'Hmm… so, you're Harras from the divisional HQ, are you? You can start by taking off that ballet costume and getting hold of a camouflage suit! Then at least you'll look halfway like a soldier!'

Together with the ten men from all the other sections of Staff HQ who had been 'sifted out' as superfluous to requirements, Harras was assigned to a company. Up to now, he'd had no reason to regret his change of unit. The southern sector was now quiet. The front line ran along the high railway embankment, an effective barrier above all against tanks. Behind this, flanked along parts of its course by water meadows, elms and scrub, wound the Karpovka River. Their positions were well developed and protected by minefields. The Russians showed little desire to attack here. Through the binocular periscope, they could observe them doing square-bashing and field training. When Harras walked through the bunkers here for the first time, he couldn't believe his eyes. Wooden shuttering, lamps, tables, proper doors and windows! And the blokes here were loafing about on beds with spring mattresses.

'Pah, this place looks like a brothel!' he said resentfully, though when he called to mind the wooden shack that had been his billet in Dubininsky, he rejoiced inwardly at his good fortune. 'Where did you conjure all this stuff up from?' he enquired.

'From Stalingrad,' the private who was showing him round said proudly. 'We brought it down the railway line on a handcar. If we're all going to hell in a handbasket, better do it in style, eh, Sergeant Major?'

Harras seethed. Next thing you knew, the bloke would be slapping him on the back! Harras hadn't really got the measure of the men here yet. At first, he'd tried taking the authoritarian approach he'd employed hitherto. 'Click your heels together properly, you shithead! Are you off your rocker, you sad specimen? You've no idea who you're dealing with here!' First the men looked at him stupidly, then later took to grinning slyly at one another, and finally played a couple of practical jokes on him so as to make it crystal clear to him, the newcomer, that he was dependent upon them here – not the opposite. Thereafter, Harras tried now and then to mimic the crude, blokeish tone that the company commander had adopted to get in with the men. The result was a crass, patently insincere familiarity, and this only reinforced the somewhat contemptuous reticence with which the men in the trenches customarily regarded a superior whose only decoration was the ribbon of the war service cross. As a result, he was really happy when he picked up a minor head wound during an air raid, which entitled him to pin the official black-metal medal worn by wounded soldiers on his chest. At a suitable opportunity he exchanged it for an old, worn one that shone like dull gold from a distance. But even this didn't help much.

On the other hand, after a few initial clashes that helped clear the air, Harras now got on much better with the leader of the company. The first lieutenant was in his thirties. He had a rather brutal face, furrowed with deep duelling scars, and the protruding backside of a prize stallion, which had earned him the nickname 'the Arse' among the troops. During the fighting around the tractor factory in Stalingrad, he had been awarded the Knight's Cross. Skilled in ingratiating himself with superiors who might be useful to him, Harras soon discovered this officer's weaknesses and learned how best to exploit them. He often made up the third in marathon games of Skat in the CO's bunker; he eagerly helped drain the bottles of wine and cognac, listened intently and patiently as the Arse regaled them with his tales of drinking and womanizing in France or during his brief spell as a student, and knew the right moment at which to crack a subtly racy joke. In this way, he earned himself a kind of condescending tolerance on the part of his CO. Yet Sergeant Major Harras was particularly pleasantly surprised by the favourable state of the food supplies at his new unit. Here there was four hundred grams of bread per person each day, while the CO also got fried potatoes and chicken. The first time they were served cabbage soup with plenty of meat in it, Harras remarked:

'Strange how horsemeat tastes different here!'

'Horsemeat?' asked the others in horror.

'Yes, horsemeat!' Harras replied indignantly. 'What else could it be?' At the divisional Staff HQ, it had invariably been horsemeat, and even that had become scarcer over time.

'Look here, sunshine!' exclaimed the lieutenant colonel. 'If you think you can come here and start taking the piss…'

It took a lot of persuading to convince the CO that horse flesh was the only thing soldiers at other units got to eat; he looked at the sergeant major like he was a leper.

'Listen, old son,' the quartermaster told Harras cheerfully, 'nothing comes from nothing! The division here planned ahead. We were on the move the whole summer, down to Kharkov and Dnepropetrovsk. And in September we got hold of five truckloads of canteen provisions that had been in storage in Vienna. Still all the good stuff from France! And if you think we were about to let High Command know, you must be off your rocker. What, so we could waste away here on basic rations while someone else scoffed our sardines and potatoes? Not bloody likely, mate – "finders, keepers" more like!'

Harras thought that was fair enough. He couldn't help but call to mind the bloke who'd succeeded Senior Quartermaster Zimmermann, who'd gone missing. The man was a hopeless idiot, who'd sit for hours poring over his lists and totting things up. He told them about him: 'Can you imagine, one time he got twenty loaves of bread too many delivered from the Corps – by mistake, of course! A total stroke of luck, the sort of thing that only occurs once a century… so what does the twat go and do? He only sends them back, and apologizes into the bargain for not having paid more attention!'

The others laughed uproariously.

Slowly but surely, Sergeant Major Harras got used to life at the front. When the bunker began to shake from the impact of shells landing ever closer during artillery barrages, he still occasionally caught the lieutenant colonel, whose nerves were dulled by alcohol, giving him a mocking look, seeing if he'd crack. But by now Harras had managed to control the facial twitch that betrayed the trembling fear he was experiencing inside. Gradually he came to understand the language of the front. He'd learned to tell the difference between the insistent clacking noise of the Russian machine guns and the nervous chattering noise of their German counterparts, and during artillery bombardments he was easily able now to distinguish the report of a howitzer from the sound of a shell hitting home, and the whiplash crack of anti-tank shells from the dull, harsh thump of mortar rounds. From the sound and the duration of the whistling noise that projectiles made as they flew through the air, he could also guess roughly how long it would be before they exploded. His instincts became sharper, and began to react automatically to a variety of different noises. From day to day, Harras felt more and more like an old hand at the front. One time, the Arse told him about the 'shabby dress code' that existed among some of the very traditional student duelling societies. Harras was enthralled by the idea of this code, in so far as he understood it. Looking in his little hand mirror, he noted with satisfaction his mud-streaked face, with the stubble of his beard poking through like corn stalks in a field. He decided he'd grow a beard.

Thus far, then, Sergeant Major Harras was pretty pleased with the way things had turned out. Even so, some things still troubled him deeply. There was talk of them being relieved. The nervous tension increased palpably among the men as the days passed.

'Listen, Sar'nt Major… Can't you hear it? Shelling… to the south!'

'No, it's further to the right, in the direction of Kalach!'

'Look out, lads, they're coming!'

They'd get him out of bed in the middle of the night, convinced they'd seen white flares go up in the far distance. One day, Colonel von Hermann and Lieutenant Colonel Unold turned up at their positions in the company of the divisional commander, and completed a thorough tour of inspection. Although they didn't say much, they seemed to be making preparations for a breakout.

'You've really got to get a grip on yourself now, Harras,' Unold told him as he was leaving, 'so you can come back and join us as soon as possible!'

The Russians, too, had clearly grown restless of late. At night you could hear the sound of engines behind their front line, and one day they launched an attack in strength on the right-hand neighbouring sector of the front around Marinovka, evidently with the sole intention of disrupting any potential attempt to break out.

'It's a good thing that this nonsense, this laughable encirclement business, is coming to an end here!' Harras told himself. Then again, he didn't relish the prospect of being in the vanguard when they broke out and dying a hero's death. Accordingly, he made a point of monitoring his heart rate and listening to his breathing, trying to determine if there was any irregularity there that might offer the possibility of an honourable withdrawal from the field of combat. But it'd be even better, he thought, if they'd just finally make him an officer. Then he'd be posted back to divisional Staff HQ – Unold had promised him in as many words. And so he kept a keen eye out for any opportunity to distinguish himself, if possible without placing himself in any danger. And the opportunity duly arrived.

'Manstein's coming!' The relief that the three hundred thousand men trapped in the Cauldron had been longing for with every fibre of their bodies was now close at hand. The great hope that, time and again, had sustained their fighting spirit and their will to hold on through the dark nights and the cold and hunger was now about to be realized.

Hitler had appointed Field Marshal Erich von Manstein Supreme Commander of Operations in the Stalingrad region. Goebbels's propaganda machine had trumpeted Manstein as the conqueror of the Crimea and the man who had captured the hitherto impregnable fortress of Sevastopol. Since then, he'd been widely seen as some kind of military miracle-worker. His name hung in the air in bunkers and trenches, at food distribution centres, field kitchens and latrines. 'Have you heard? Manstein's started his push!' 'Lads, I really think Manstein's going to do it! I tell you, he'll have us free within a week!' 'I've heard he's got new tanks, amazing things they are, they just shrug off anti-tank fire!' 'That's right! I've seen them myself... someone in Pitomnik told me... he's just taken delivery of five hundred of them!' 'Manstein, now, he's the one who...' Manstein, nothing but Manstein! None of the troops had ever seen the field marshal in person, and hardly anyone even recognized his photograph. The besieged men of Stalingrad were investing all their heartfelt hopes in a name.

But there was another man whose name almost no one mentioned, and only the various staffs knew that he was playing a key part in the rescue operation that had just got underway. This was General Hermann Hoth, former commander-in-chief of the Fourth Panzer Army, some elements of which had been caught along with Paulus's Sixth Army in the Stalingrad Cauldron. Many men of the Tank Corps still had a vivid image of the small, hyperactive general, who was in the habit of turning up unannounced at the spearhead of armoured thrusts, and whose sarcastic severity had earned him the nickname 'the Poison Dwarf'. Hoth had been given overall command of the newly formed Army Group Don, made up of three German tank divisions and a number of Romanian infantry and cavalry formations. On the twelfth of December, he pushed up from the south, from the area around the railway station at Chir and from Kotelnikovo, to try to break the encirclement. And the miracle happened – despite the harsh Russian winter, which up until then had thwarted all attempts by German commanders to undertake major offensives, Hoth's advance was a complete success. In the face of intense cold and snow and fierce enemy resistance, the tank formations crept ever closer to the Cauldron. The spirits of the trapped men rose with every passing day. The talk was of relief, rest, recreation and leave. The staffs of the Sixth Army awoke from the slumber they'd lapsed into after receiving Hitler's order to let themselves be encircled. While Hoth stormed forward, the plan was for the troops in the Cauldron to hit the Russians from behind like a 'Thunderclap'. At least, that was the auspicious code name given to the operation that was being planned inside the Cauldron. The intention was for the army's mobile forces, primarily the flak batteries, tanks and assault guns, to form into combat groups and break out to link up with the vanguard of the advancing Army Group Don.

A period of feverish activity ensued. Field commanders and general staff officers sat in bunkers, hunched over maps; quarter-masters worked out the available transport capacity and the munitions and fuel required; tanks and lorries were overhauled, units were dissolved and new ones formed, columns assembled to shuttle provisions to the front, and military police detachments were deployed to guard the roads, lest anyone took it into their head, once the Cauldron was opened, to escape from it under their own steam, never to be seen again.

The Tank Corps was charged with the tactical leadership of Operation Thunderclap. Colonel von Hermann was chosen to lead the first shockwave of the tank thrust. He was adamant that the operation should begin as soon as possible.

'Even if we don't manage to break through on the first day, we can still regroup into a tight defensive formation,' he explained. 'I don't see what the big deal is. We've done it often enough before, after all! Anyhow, it'd be a great relief to Hoth if we really put the cat among the pigeons by attacking the Russians from the rear!'

Though the Corps approved von Hermann's suggestion, High Command did not act on it. They insisted on a guarantee that the operation could be completed in the hours between dawn and dusk.

'We only have sufficient fuel to push forward eighty kilometres,' was the official explanation. 'We might well run into difficulties, and then we'd be stranded. We need to wait until Hoth has advanced to at least thirty kilometres away.'

However, the matter seemed about to resolve itself when it became clear that Hoth's task force had already advanced to a point only around fifty kilometres away. It wouldn't be such a problem to wait for a couple of days.

First Lieutenant Breuer rang his opposite number at the Corps on a daily basis, and Count Willms was very forthcoming with his reports. His apathetic attitude had largely dissipated in the interim.

'Yes, right. What's that? Yes, they're making slow but steady progress… yes, steady … Yes, and huge supply camps are already in place for them, it's absolutely phenomenal! Yes, and behind the tanks are long columns of trucks carrying ersatz honey…'

Even Corporal Herbert had become less of a pain. He jotted down recipes in his notebook for a whole new range of cakes that he planned to try out as soon as they were relieved, and waxed lyrical about the order of the menu for the banquet that would be held to commemorate the breakout from the Cauldron.

Fröhlich spent the whole day in the bunker, rubbing his bony hands together and delivering interminable lectures on the long-term military outlook. Lakosch caught sight of him 'unburdening' himself out in the open one time, and noticed how he waved his arms about like a grand orator as he rehearsed his speeches while squatting in the snow. More often than not, he could be found standing in front of the campaign map and explaining the current position to Geibel. 'Look here, lad! Now here comes the big push from the west and – it stands to reason, doesn't it? – that leaves the Russians right up shit creek! The result is that we bottle up at least three armies – that's right, isn't it, Lieutenant Breuer? – at least three Russian armies! And that means the war's over, lad, don't you see? The Bolsheviks are on their last legs anyhow, so this'll spell the end for them.'

Geibel was only too eager to believe these predictions. He was thinking of his shop, and his wife, and that it was high time they had some more leave. His only worry was that there wouldn't be enough room for all of them in the staff vehicles for the long journey back west. Some more cars had bitten the dust in the last few days. This worry had turned him into something of an expert on cars. Every day, he'd hang around the motor pool, lying under the cars in the snow with the unit's drivers as they worked with cramped fingers on the vehicles' ice-cold engines. Only Lieutenant Wiese remained the same as he had always been. When he wasn't busy with his signals unit, which now had more work to do once again, he could be found immersed in his books, seemingly untroubled by the frantic activity going on around him. Lakosch, for his part, had largely lost interest in his vehicle. It had definitely had it, grinding to a halt every five minutes. Lakosch had resolved to leave it behind here as a memento. The task force would no doubt be bringing new vehicles with them. So he spent his time mooching round the camp with Senta, watching the aerial battles unfold above the airfield at Pitomnik, collecting bones and kitchen scraps for the dog and humming or singing to himself, to a tune of his own devising and with the words changed to reflect current events, the verses of an old soldiers' ditty that he'd recently found in a book about the Thirty Years' War:

> Manstein is coming,
> Manstein's on his way,
> Manstein's already here,
> And we all shout Hooray!

2

Hunger and Morale

IN ROSTOV-ON-DON, FOUR HUNDRED kilometres from Stalingrad, a group of men, wearing a variety of field-grey and slate-coloured uniforms embellished with gold and red and white and rows of glittering medals, were seated round a table. Some twenty heads whispering to one another, poring over documents and staring in deep concentration into the middle distance. These heads, moreover, belonged to the leading figures of the German army and air force. Their number included both forces' quartermasters-general, the Luftwaffe generals Milch and Jeschonnek, the army group leaders von Manstein and Baron von Weichs and their respective staff officers. Also present – having been obliged to host this conference – was Colonel General Wolfram von Richthofen, head of the Fourth Air Fleet. And finally there were the opposite poles round which this whole martial world revolved. Sitting at one of the long sides of the table was the voluble and (albeit warily) blustering Hermann Göring, the white-and-gold-bedecked Reichsmarschall, while alone and aloof at the head of the table sat the silent, commanding presence of the Führer himself, Adolf Hitler – an extraordinary meeting of the Board of Directors. Dandified adjutants scurried about without a sound, assiduously whispering into reluctant ears. The oppressive spectre of dreadful events to come weighed heavily on the twenty heads gathered here. The lives of hundreds of thousands of people were at stake. The principal item on the agenda was how to supply the encircled Sixth Army.

The meeting began with a report by Baron von Richthofen on the Luftwaffe's previous experiences in supplying German ground forces from the air. The colonel general, blond and clear-eyed, spoke softly and succinctly, though he found it impossible to fully conceal his irritation. The problem of air supply hung like a millstone around his neck. Because the supply canisters could only be dropped from the bomb bays of aircraft, pretty much all his bomber force had been doing of late was making supply runs. His offensive operations had been effectively paralysed. Nor had this just been the case since the start of the encirclement; it had been going on for months already, ever since September. The intention had been for German forces to press on to Astrakhan and Tbilisi and God knows where else, but no sooner had they set off than these advance forces found themselves running out of food and munitions and fuel. Small wonder, when everything was going awry here! And now they expected him to fly in three hundred tons of supplies to Stalingrad every day. Naturally, no one had told him how such a feat might be achieved.

'Since the construction of forward airfields, at least we can fly in and land with Ju 52s,' Richthofen explained, choking back his anger. 'However, this has given rise to various new problems that clearly weren't fully anticipated in forward planning. At this time of year, the weather conditions in the Stalingrad region are about as bad as can be. Most days we can only fly a limited number of sorties, and often none at all. That means we have to try to concentrate our efforts into limited windows, and we simply don't have the aircraft numbers available for that. Plus, flying over the bare steppe the Ju 52s are sitting ducks for fighters. Our losses are appallingly high. We've lost—'

'Yes, yes, we know all about that!' Göring interrupted, nervously drumming his gold-ringed fingers on the table. 'That's why we're here! We need to tackle the problem from a totally different angle. – Morzik, let's hear from you, please!'

Leafing through a pile of papers, Colonel Morzik, Head of Air Transport Operations (East), launched into his presentation on the condition, operational strength, stationing and potential for concentration of transport units. His forehead was beaded with sweat, and the slightest interruption seemed to throw him. Sitting diagonally opposite him was the quartermaster-general of the army, General Wagner. With his hands clasped in front of him on the table, he sat there without saying a word or moving a muscle. Every so often, he'd close his eyes and tilt his head up to the ceiling. A suppressed smile played around the corners of his mouth. The Luftwaffe – typical! It damn well served the air force right, and its fat C-in-C sitting over there! He could still recall every detail of the meeting that had taken place about a month ago around this very table and with almost the same cast list present. No punches had been pulled on that occasion, for it had long since become clear that the two fronts in the Caucasus and on the Don could not be properly supplied simultaneously. The barren nature of the land around the Don elbow meant that there was no chance of getting supplies by foraging there. Everything had to be brought in, including fodder for the horses. But they just didn't have enough transport capacity at their disposal for that. Those in charge of operations had been told about this unequivocally, and shown the relevant figures. And at the same time, the only possible solution to the problem had been raised: shorten the supply lines – in other words, abandon Stalingrad, withdraw from the Don elbow and pull the front back to a line running, say, through Zemlyansk, Morozovsk and Veshenskaya.

'If we don't bite the bullet on this,' the quartermaster-general responsible had said at the time, 'then I see disaster looming for the Sixth Army.'

And everyone present had agreed, even Manstein, who always wanted to go at things like a bull in a china shop. For adopting this solution would mean that the threat of being outflanked in the north would also evaporate, without having to abandon the Caucasus. Even Hitler seemed to be in agreement. Then Göring had intervened, blithely guaranteeing that the Luftwaffe would be able to fly in ample supplies, and assuming full responsibility.

'Then the front stays where it is!' Hitler had cried triumphantly.

'As of right now,' Morzik was saying meanwhile, 'the bulk of the transport units are under the command of the Director of Mediterranean Transport Operations. Of course, we could withdraw a few units from that theatre. Then again, the fuel situation is very touch-and-go for Rommel... I honestly don't know how far we can go without causing a negative impact on the Africa front...'

'That's it: just keep twisting and turning, my friends!' thought General Wagner. 'Serves you right. You've really made fools of your-selves! If you hadn't stuck your noses in, the Sixth Army wouldn't be up shit creek now. And as usual it's going to be the army that has to put things right.'

Hoth was due to launch his rescue mission within a few days. He'd dig the Sixth Army out of their hole. And then, having learned from bitter experience, they'd withdraw at last from the Don elbow and see out the rest of the winter without any further scares.

By now, Colonel Morzik had finished his presentation. An embar-rassed silence fell over the room. The report had shown pretty conclusively that the necessary transport capacity didn't exist for supplying the Sixth by air.

'The forthcoming operation by Army Group Don,' the chief of staff of the Luftwaffe, Colonel General Jeschonnek, declared in a cold, aloof tone, 'will settle the matter once and for all.'

'Nonsense!' Göring interjected brusquely. 'Let's not count our chickens before they're hatched. If Hoth manages to break through, it'll bring some relief at best, nothing more. And who knows how long he can keep the pocket open? Come what may, the army will remain in Stalingrad. The Führer has not altered his decision.'

That wiped the smile off General Wagner's face. The army's staying in Stalingrad? He could feel himself being rudely jolted out of his preferred role of indifferent bystander. For Christ's sake, it wasn't just about inter-service rivalry any more – the whole shooting match was at stake here! Back in September, when all the lines of communication were still open, they'd all agreed that an army would starve to death there come winter. Yet now, now that things had turned out even worse than the gloomiest predications, they were still planning to…? The army needed six hundred tons of supplies every day to live and fight effectively, not the three hundred they'd all so glibly taken to be the bottom line. But it was undeniably the case that even that figure was out of the question. Uneasily, he scanned the others' faces: Jeschonnek's cold death mask, the piggy eyes of Field Marshal Milch. These were people who could see the situation for what it was, surely. No, reason must prevail, and would prevail.

At that moment, Milch stood up. He didn't need to consult any papers. His head, pink and smooth and as harmless and genial-looking as that of a suckling pig, contained the production figures and capacities of the aircraft manufacturing industry of the whole of Europe. He could rattle off long calculations and statistics by heart. The list of all the official positions and titles he held, which was as long as the string of titles of a medieval prince – among other posts, he was Secretary of State for German Aviation, Head of the Air Ministry Planning Department, Chairman of the Board of Lufthansa, Inspector-General of the Air Force and Head of the Air Force Administration Office – underlined the breadth of his technical and commercial know-how. The bare minimum for the encircled army – in other words, what they needed in order to keep ticking over with no possibility of resupply or replacement of men and materiel – was, Milch explained, two hundred and eighty tons daily, of which one hundred and twenty tons would be ammunition, one hundred tons food and sixty tons fuel. On the basis that each Junkers Ju 52 could carry two tons, this would require an average of a hundred and fifty flights per day. His soft, sensuous mouth struggled to make these stark facts sound clipped and to the point. As he spoke, his pudgy hands described curiously jagged motions through the air. Only his little round eyes kept moving restlessly and ceaselessly around in circles. Milch played at being a military man. And did so very badly; he simply wasn't cut out for the role. His uniform made him look like a character from light opera. He was less a general than a director-general. And the military honours that had been bestowed upon him (Knight's Cross and the rank of Field Marshal) reeked of inauthenticity. In the Luftwaffe, people still laughed about Milch's one and only spell of 'front-line service' during the Norway campaign. As commander of the Fifth Air Fleet, he had bombed the French expeditionary force out of Åndalsnes. With great success, apparently; for after the bombardment, not a single Frenchman could be found in the little town, which had taken a terrible pounding. But that, it turned out, was because the French had never been in Åndalsnes in the first place; instead, they had landed in a nearby fjord. In one respect, then, Milch most decidedly was a soldier – though in this instance it would have been better had this not been so – namely, even as a specialist, he obeyed orders from above unquestioningly.

'Taking all these factors into consideration, therefore,' Milch concluded, 'we need a transport fleet of some two hundred and fifty to three hundred aircraft. If the air supply operation were to last longer than anticipated – earlier, there'd been talk of the spring of 1943 – the fleet would have to be resupplied with new planes on a running basis to make up for the losses. And so, for the reasons already mentioned, it is currently not possible to prepare and muster such a large number of transport aircraft.'

'Thank God for that!' thought General Wagner. But the next utterance from around the table caused him visibly to wince.

'It *must* be possible!' said a harsh, guttural voice. All faces turned to the figure at the head of the table. These were the first words that

Hitler had spoken in this meeting. The officers present who had not seen the Führer for some time noted with alarm that he was no longer the great magician he had once been. His face was grey, while his permanently slightly stooped back looked positively deformed today. White hairs had begun to appear in his Charlie Chaplin moustache, and his temples were greying noticeably too. Never before had this deity seemed so pathetically human to them. Only the eyes, which bespoke a dangerous fixation, gleamed as brightly as ever from beneath his bushy brows. Even Field Marshal Milch, whose frequent contact with the godlike figure had made him immune to any sensation of mystical awe, flinched at the sound of this voice and fell silent. For several months, aircraft production in the Reich had been unable to keep pace with the losses, and it was he who'd had to shoulder the blame. He was desperate to make amends. Had he taken his eye off the ball? Had he said too much? He cowered like a frightened rabbit beneath the gaze of a snake. Others in the room took up the baton. Manstein spoke briefly and to the point, while the old-fashioned Baron von Weichs beat about the bush with any number of ifs and buts. But to a man they all, some in carefully guarded terms, others plainly and soberly, concurred that it would be an impossible undertaking.

'I managed to supply six divisions in the Demyansk Pocket,' rasped the feared voice once more, this time more ominously. 'That was in the face of opposition from my so-called experts, too. Yet we pulled it off all the same. There's no such thing as "impossible" for us!'

General Wagner was not a religious man; he was an everyday kind of person who believed in reason. But at this point even he clasped his hands together in prayer under the table and repeated the words under his breath: 'Dear Lord, deliver us from evil!' The Sixth Army was lost, and with it the war. They were running with eyes wide open headlong to destruction. 'Retreat!' he wanted to scream. 'Pull the army out and withdraw to Donetsk! It's our only hope! It's still not too late!' But he didn't open his mouth and shout it.

Why not? Instead, he looked across the table at the wan, inscrutable face of Jeschonnek, as if some salvation might still come from that quarter. General Jeschonnek sat there motionless, with his thin line of a mouth drawn together even tighter than before. He was tapping a pencil gently on the table. He was remembering the pocket at Demyansk. Six divisions had been encircled there, not twenty-two like now. To get enough transport capacity to supply even that force, they'd had to close the flying schools. In addition, the Luftwaffe was now hamstrung by a shortage of newly qualified pilots. Sure, they'd succeeded in freeing the bottled-up forces then – but at the cost of more troops killed than the number of those trapped.

'How about you, Jeschonnek?'

The colonel general raised his eyes slowly. His gaze passed over Göring, who was glaring at him like a furious sergeant major, and came to rest, earnestly and calmly, on the glowering face of Hitler. The Führer's anger knew no bounds if anyone ever dared to contradict him. He tore down curtains and dashed inkwells to the ground. Jeschonnek was all too familiar with these outbursts, and was perhaps the only person who did not go in fear of them.

'The best will in the world can't help if the material wherewithal is lacking,' he said, barely moving his lips. 'Weighing up all the various factors, it's clear that dropping enough supplies to the Sixth Army by air just isn't feasible. I for one am not in a position where I could take responsibility for that.'

You could have heard a pin drop. Only General Wagner, normally a model of composure, shifted uneasily in his chair. Now was the time for him to speak up, surely! He still hadn't uttered a word, nor had anyone asked his opinion. Why didn't he just say something? Hitler's grey face, to which everyone's eyes were glued once more, flushed momentarily, and an evil gleam appeared in his watery blue eyes.

'Is that all that my generals have to tell me, then?'

It was indeed. The generals had come out in opposition to Hitler, tentatively for sure, but unanimously all the same. Hitler, the all-powerful, had been deposed. A new, stronger force had overcome all feelings of dependency and now held sway over the room, where a heavy atmosphere prevailed, like someone had poured lead into the space – the force of circumstances. Suddenly, Göring sprang to his feet. He stood there, a monstrous mountain of flesh with the gold-bordered Grand Cross of the Iron Cross dangling from the collar of his buttoned-up white dress jacket.

'My Führer!' he barked, his puffy, jowly face turning puce. 'My Führer, there is no such thing as "impossible" for us! We'll build... in fact, Willy Messerschmitt is already building giant gliders and powered transport aircraft! Milch, this is your department! You're building us giant planes, you'll show what we can do! At night... we'll fly huge air convoys in to Stalingrad by moonlight! We'll... my Führer, I can guarantee that the Sixth Army will be resupplied!'

It's late at night. Sergeant Major Harras is back in the company CO's bunker again, playing Skat. The Arse has just declared a 'Grand' with all four jacks in his hand. Suddenly, footsteps are heard clumping down the ladder and the door is thrown open. The sentry stands in the doorway.

'Lieutenant, sir! Come quickly! Something's not right out here!

And with that he disappears again.

'I don't get it,' mutters the Arse. 'It's all quiet out there. I propose we carry on with the game after I've seen what's up!'

He puts down his cards and, with an irritated sigh, hitches up the belt of his grey-brown corduroy trousers, drapes his fur coat round his shoulders, clambers out of the bunker and climbs to the top of the railway embankment. Sergeant Major Harras follows him. The night is bitterly cold. The stars are shining in the pitch-black sky, and low on the horizon is the reddish disc of the waxing moon. The front is quiet, uncannily quiet. Only the sound of transport planes coming and going fills the frost-tingling air.

'There's nothing going on. Quiet as the grave.' says the first lieutenant, and turns to leave.

At that moment, over on the enemy front line, a flare goes up. The
bright point of light pirouettes up into the darkness and bursts into
a cascade of individual red stars, which for a second or two bathe
the landscape in the dull red light of a photographer's darkroom
before falling slowly to earth and fizzling out, one after the other.

'That's one of our flares, though,' says Harras in astonishment.
'Since when have the Russians been using those?'

'Dunno,' replies the Arse, who's bored and thinking of his game
of Skat. 'Some new trick of theirs, no doubt.'

Then a searchlight is switched on over at the enemy lines. Slowly,
it arcs in a semicircle across the snowy expanse. For an instant, the
light tries to pick out the two men standing on the embankment, who
quickly throw themselves to the ground. But everything remains
quiet. Harras hesitates... Then the whole performance begins anew.
He's seen something like this before from his bunker overlooking the
aerodrome at Pitomnik! A sudden hot flush of shock passes through
him. Ignoring all protocol, he grabs his commanding officer's arm
and shakes him violently.

'Lieutenant, sir – they want to... they're trying to get our planes!
They're trying to dupe them so they crash-land over there!'

'God damn it!' exclaims the first lieutenant. 'You're right, man!
We've got to... that is, what can we do?'

'Fire into the air!'

'Don't be stupid! They won't hear it up there. And we can't get the
artillery to do that...'

'How about some flares of our own?'

'Do you know what signals the air force uses? Well, then! What
do you want to fire off?'

In the meantime, the drone of approaching aircraft has grown
louder. One of the planes is circling, steadily losing height. The
searchlight goes on again over there. This time it stays still, casting a

broad cone of light over the snow. The lieutenant fires his pistol into the air, a futile gesture. Somewhere, a machine gun starts rattling away. All to no avail! The plane roars low over the heads of the two men, a huge dark shape, heading for the wide beam of light. And then it touches down, bounces a couple of times along the ground and rolls to a stop. It comes to a halt a few hundred metres in front of the railway embankment. A handful of white-clad figures emerge from the darkness and run towards the plane. The machine gun opens up again.

'Hold your fire!' bellows the Arse. 'You'll hit your own men!'

Several men clamber out of the aircraft, and are surrounded by the others. It all happens very calmly. Suddenly, the spotlight goes out. Soon after, a Russian artillery barrage forces the men on the embankment to retreat to their bunker.

The daily-worsening food situation began to sap the men's morale. Despite the fact that the transport planes, even in the face of heavy losses, kept flying whenever the weather permitted, barely a quarter of the three hundred tons of vital supplies required made it into the Cauldron each day. Latterly, the horse carcasses lying by the sides of the roads had started to stand out blood-red from the snowdrifts, like predators had been gnawing at them. In actual fact, roving bands of Romanian soldiers or Russian auxiliary volunteers, crazed with hunger, had been eating them. All the stray dogs and cats that had once roamed around the camp gradually vanished; Lakosch didn't let the portly Senta – whose belly grew larger by the day, attracting hungry looks – out of his sight for even a moment. He was ashamed of himself for having grown so foolishly fond of the dog, and for sharing his thin broth, which wasn't remotely filling, with it, and for spending hours trying to find it a bone to gnaw on.

When Lakosch was alone, he'd often say to himself: 'Right, that's it! I'm going to get rid of that mutt!' But when he gazed into the animal's brown eyes, so full of grateful trust in him, his heart would melt; he'd stroke the dog's ugly head, pat its brown flanks and tell himself and Senta: 'That's right, old girl, we're going to stick together! Who else have we got, after all? Yes, yes, don't you worry now! You can't help it that you got mixed up in all this war business! None of this is your fault, that's for sure!'

The divisional Staff HQ had been particularly hard hit by the general lack of food supplies, since it didn't have any reserve stocks. First, it was one loaf of bread for six men… then one loaf between fourteen – and then twenty… a hundred grams of bread per man, a single slice as their daily ration. Add to that thirty grams of potted meat and every lunchtime, sometimes evenings too, a thin, watery soup with a bit of buckwheat semolina thrown in.

'Christ Almighty!' said Geibel, 'I'd never have thought a person could live on so little.'

Secretly he speculated with horror on what would become of his business if this kind of subsistence food should ever become the norm in Germany. Up to now, his meaty face had lost little of its healthy vigour. But almost every night he dreamed he got into terrible arguments with his wife, who used force to stop him from devouring the entire stock of their delicatessen.

Sonderführer Fröhlich had become a dab hand at dividing the daily loaf among the men. Every morning witnessed a solemn ceremony, with all the occupants of the bunker looking on with rapt attention as he closed his left eye and, sighting with his right down the blade of the carefully sharpened knife, began to cut off slices with the precision of a surgeon wielding a scalpel. At the end of the process, Geibel would hold the results of Fröhlich's artistry in his hand and marvel at what he saw. 'Truly amazing, Sonderführer, five complete slices! I can't manage that even with a piece of Edam.'

Fröhlich would then carefully toast the millimetre-thin slices on the little stove, filling the bunker with a heavenly smell. He'd proceed to spread them thinly with fat, and could spend hours nibbling with his long teeth at his own portion. The others weren't nearly so patient, wolfing down their slices in the twinkling of an eye. It was only fortunate that they still had plenty of coffee, a good blend of beans, sweetened with saccharin from Geibel's supplies.

One day Private Krüger, one of the mess orderlies, took Lakosch aside and pointed at the herd of shaggy ponies outside the camp, grazing on a few impertinent stems of steppe herb that had dared to poke their way up through the mantle of snow. He spoke quietly to the driver, reinforcing his words with extravagant hand gestures. Lakosch nodded thoughtfully and disappeared into the bunker. Soon after, he could be seen wandering aimlessly out over the plain. Senta ran ahead of him, snuffling round the half-eroded foxholes dating from the time when the Russians were here. Seemingly quite innocently, Lakosch sidled up to the sentry, who was standing, his rifle under his arm, on the small knoll that he used as a convenient vantage point to survey the herd in his charge, which belonged to an infantry division from the northern sector. A little further on, three Russian prisoners sat chatting around a campfire. They appeared to be *Hilfswillige* (or '*Hiwis*' for short, as the German troops called them),* who'd been sent out there to help the sentry. They didn't seem to be taking their task very seriously. Anyhow, the half-starved ponies, barely able to keep themselves from falling over, certainly wouldn't run away.

'Mornin',' Lakosch greeted the sentry. 'Pretty brassy today, eh?'

The man shot him a mistrustful sideways glance and muttered something under his breath. Lakosch tried to act indifferent. He took out his cigarette case, which he'd just taken the precaution of filling with the daily tobacco rations of all the mess orderlies, and

---

* *Hilfswillige* – 'Auxiliary Volunteers'. After the early successes of Operation Barbarossa, the German invasion of the Soviet Union, thousands of captured Ukrainian and Russian soldiers volunteered to fight against Stalin's regime by providing assistance to the German forces in non-combat roles, especially engineering and logistics.

made great play of lighting one up for himself. The sentry looked over at him, his interest rekindled.

'Still so many fags?' he asked, astonished. 'You're in clover all right!'

'S'pose so,' answered Lakosch. 'Ten cigarettes a day, that just about does at a pinch. Sometimes there's even cigars. You get more of them.'

He nonchalantly offered the guard the open cigarette case. The man dipped in eagerly.

'Ten smokes a day, you say?' he marvelled. 'We've only been getting three for the past week or so… And to think I was a twenty-a-day man before that!'

He dragged greedily on his cigarette.

'In fact, it's pretty shitty in general for us, I don't mind telling you. We've even taken to eating our own horses!'

Lakosch pulled a face.

'What, those old nags there? No thank you! Haven't you got anything else, then? No tinned meat? We've still got two lorryloads of the stuff, just for the Staff HQ! Herrings in gravy, and goulash and tuna and sardines in oil and grade-A pork, all the stuff from France still!'

He grew quite drunk on his own eloquence. The sentry licked his lips. His hand started trembling so much that he dropped his cigarette butt into the snow. Lakosch handed him the case again. The two of them sat down on the rim of a snow hole.

'Tell me, mate,' the sentry began, 'what are the chances of you getting… I mean, a tin of that tuna, for instance… I'm not expecting to get it for nothing, mind!'

From the depths of his greatcoat, he fished out a pocket knife with a mother-of-pearl handle. 'There you go, it's got two blades, a screwdriver and a tin opener, it's really something! All genuine stainless steel.'

Lakosch, feigning real interest, opened and closed the various blades. 'Hmm,' he pondered, 'it's not that simple! Our sergeant major, see…'

The sentry shifted about uncomfortably, his eyes now blank and staring. He rummaged through his pockets to try to find anything else to swap. In the process, he failed to notice that a lorry had stopped about two hundred metres along the road. He also didn't spot that two soldiers had jumped down and were grappling with one of the ponies. Only the shouts of alarm from the auxiliaries caused him to look up. Cursing, he sprang to his feet and levelled his rifle at the rustlers. But he was already too late. The two men were jumping back onto the moving lorry. The pony, which had had a tow rope lashed around its hind legs, was pulled to the ground. The truck picked up speed, dragging the pony behind it. It lifted its head a couple of times and opened its mouth to utter a pitiful cry. The sentry fired two shots in vain at the disappearing lorry. Their report did not even startle the grazing ponies, who hardly even pinned back their ears. 'God damn it!' cursed the soldier. 'That's the second time that's happened on my watch… now I'll really cop it from my CO!—'

All of a sudden, he paused and directed a curious look at Lakosch, who now thought it prudent to beat as hasty a retreat as possible, and not to pause to offer the guard his condolences. He whistled to Senta to follow him, and wandered off in the direction of the camp. As he departed, the sentry shot him an impotent look of growing realization…

By the time Lakosch got back to the kitchen, the pony had already been eviscerated.

That evening, roasted horse's liver was served in the Intelligence Section's bunker. Everyone was amazed at how generous the cook had been. Lakosch had chosen not to divulge that this was the payoff for the part he'd played in the rustling escapade. For three days, the whole Staff HQ indulged in horse goulash and horse rissoles, while Unold even had a horse schnitzel. Then all that was left of the scrawny pony was the skeleton. The bared teeth in the beast's mangy rotting head kept grinning up from the rubbish pit for many days thereafter.

The great grey bird stands alone on the white expanse of snow. It's a Junkers Ju 52, the good old 'Auntie Ju'. It must have come down just short of the Russian lines. When the regiment gets word of the forced landing, people are beside themselves with frustration. We could have… should have… It's amazing how wise everyone is after the event about what they might have done to prevent this catastrophe. Two tons of food, or ammunition, or fuel lost to the encircled army! But at least the Russians won't get to enjoy their ill-gotten gains. Two tons of cargo aren't exactly easy to unload, when you're forced to work within range of enemy artillery. During the day, there's no Russian to be seen anywhere near the aircraft. Most of the cargo might well still be inside! The heavy machine guns fire a couple of bursts into the fuselage – and nothing happens. So, it's definitely not fuel. After much deliberation, the division allows the artillery three rounds to try to blow the plane to smithereens. The third shell lands quite close, but it will take a direct hit to destroy such a large aircraft. Ultimately, the order comes from the regiment that a commando squad will be sent in to blow up the plane. Sergeant Major Harras goes to see the Arse.

'Lieutenant, sir, I'd like to volunteer to be part of the commando unit!'

The company commander looks him up and down.

'You? Okay, then! But think what you're letting yourself in for! The operation won't be without its dangers. If anything goes wrong, we can't give you covering fire!'

'I've weighed up all the dangers!' replies Harras. And that was certainly true; he had considered things carefully: in a few days, the whole hullabaloo of the attempted breakout would erupt.

Compared with that, this business here, executed under cover of darkness, would be a picnic. After all, the aircraft wasn't behind enemy lines. This was just the opportunity he'd been waiting for.

'Fine – as you wish,' says the Arse. 'I'm putting you in charge of the squad, then. I can spare you four men. And make sure you get the job done!'

The operation gets underway that same night. Overcast skies shroud the scene in total darkness. The men are carrying hand grenades, machine-pistols and an explosive charge with a time fuse. They are wearing white camouflage suits, with their faces, weapons and equipment all whitewashed, too. After only a few metres, the uniform grey of the landscape has swallowed them up. Crawling, separated from one another by some distance, they inch their way forward. Sergeant Major Harras is at the head, while a few metres behind him is the man with the explosives. The front is quiet. Every so often some yellowish flares are sent up over the enemy lines, forcing the men to lie motionless, face-down in the snow. In these enforced pauses, they can clearly make out their target, which looms ever larger out of the snow. Crawling along like this is tiring. Snow gets into their boots and their sleeves; their hands are cramped and the coarse steppe grass scratches their faces; hoar frost forms around their mouths and noses from their hot exhalations. Suddenly, a machine gun opens up somewhere in front of them and to the right, and is answered by another further to the left. The burst of fire buzzes over their heads. They've been spotted! Damn it – what now? An uninterrupted cascade of flares suddenly goes up, bathing the open expanse of ground in glaring brightness. And then, from the dark curtain of the enemy lines, come three or four brief flashes in quick succession, and shells burble over, tearing up the ground with an ear-splitting boom. Chunks of frozen earth, big as children's heads, fly through the air. They've no shortage of ammunition over there, that's for sure! They can afford to bombard a party of five men with artillery! A second salvo drones towards them, landing almost plumb in the area where the demolition squad is lying prone. Someone behind Harras screams. The piercing, drawn-out shriek drowns out the sound of the shells exploding, and chills the others to the bone. Harras has pressed his face into the snow and clasped his hands to his ears. His back is heaving and sinking with wild gasps of breath, and he is trembling in the last fibres of his being. Escape! Enough! Make it stop... somehow... is his only thought. But he cannot move a muscle. His supine body is racked by a terrible shaking that lifts it momentarily from the ground. Then Harras takes a violent blow to the head, and everything goes black.

After several hours, two men from the demolition squad make it back to their own lines. They are dropping from exhaustion and completely unresponsive. The dreadful screaming of the wounded man slowly ebbs to an increasingly intermittent whimpering groan, which lasts for the rest of the night and the whole of the following day. As darkness falls once more, stretcher-bearers manage to make it to the man. But after many arduous hours spent getting him back to their own lines, he is found to be dead. The bodies of Sergeant Major Harras and Private Seliger, formerly a mess orderly at divisional HQ, are not found.

During this period, Lakosch found another opportunity to improve the food situation. Admittedly, however, this time the enterprise did not pass off without repercussions for him in many regards. Lieutenant Colonel Unold had insisted that a new bunker be built for himself and the commander. Grumbling, the starving troops of the divisional staff set about the backbreaking task of digging – work they thought was utterly pointless. They only made very slow progress in the hard, frozen ground; sometimes they even had to resort to explosives. It was highly doubtful whether the building would be finished before Christmas. One day, Lakosch was assigned to a work party that was ordered to fetch timber for building and window glass from Stalingrad. Gearbox damage to their lorry forced them to spend an uncomfortable few days in the bomb- and artillery-ravaged city. While the others holed up in the deep cellar of a derelict house, Lakosch roamed around the ruins. On his travels, he ran across an NCO he knew from before, who had an interesting tale to tell. Food? They had some top-notch stuff to eat in their unit, claimed the NCO. There was a half-sunken barge full of flour and grain frozen fast into the Volga, which they'd been helping themselves to for a while. This wasn't a simple task, though. It was in direct contravention of a ban imposed by the division, and because the Russians kept the barge under constant fire, a few men had already bought it. Also, there was an ongoing feud with the neighbouring division, in whose sector the barge was located. The lily-livered bastards didn't have the guts to raid the barge themselves, Lakosch's friend told him, but they were determined no one else should get at the spoils either. 'Anyhow, we're going out there again tonight,' concluded the NCO. 'It's my turn again. I've got some good lads in my group, too. If we pull it off, that's a fortnight's supply of white bread in the bag!'

Lakosch was raring to go. He could see all kinds of possibilities for such provisions.

'Hey, count me in!' he said. 'If anything goes wrong, just say I was someone from the other division, and you had nothing to do with me!'

After a protracted spell of bargaining, the NCO eventually agreed, given that he and Lakosch were old mates. But the undertaking proved more tricky than they'd anticipated. To reach the barge, you had to traverse about three hundred metres of ground, crawling on your stomach and picking your way over ice floes and around holes in the ice. The Russians soon spotted that something was afoot, and before they knew it the raiding party had come under heavy mortar fire. The cracking river ice swayed and shuddered like in an earthquake. One of the men was hit, and lay there whimpering in pain. But eventually the rest made it to the barge, which had been peppered with bomb splinters and machine-gun rounds. It took all the effort they could muster to work their way back with their haul of grain and their wounded comrade. When Lakosch finally collapsed in a bunker, drenched in sweat despite the intense cold, he was the proud owner of a sack of wheat flour and a can of syrup.

But a nasty shock lay in store for him when he got back to divisional HQ. Senta was nowhere to be seen! Geibel, in whose care Lakosch had entrusted the dog on pain of death, was a gibbering wreck. He'd searched high and low and asked everyone he met, but all to no avail. In a fit of rage, Lakosch punched the big private hard in the face; conscious that it was all his fault, Geibel forebore to retaliate. He accompanied Geibel around the camp searching tirelessly for the dog, rooting around in other units' bunkers under all sorts of pretences – but all in vain! Senta had vanished for good.

With the addition of saccharin, a pinch of bicarbonate of soda and some of the syrup, plus all the coffee grounds he could lay his hands on, Herbert used the fine white flour to bake wonderful cookies in the mess tin. Geibel, with his usual penchant for trying to brighten up his life with illusions, went so far as to compare them to macaroons. Another time, Herbert appeared beaming from ear to ear and clutching three round loaves of bread, which a Russian woman from one of the houses below the camp had baked for him in return for a portion of the white flour. For two days they dined sumptuously on this bread, spread liberally with the contents of Lakosch's pilfered can. The 'syrup' turned out to be an engineering lubricant, based on benzine or petroleum. They all contracted terrible diarrhoea, which not only used up the two rolls of toilet paper they'd been issued with but also expended the few extra calories they'd eaten. Their raging hunger also thwarted the good intentions they'd had of saving some of the flour for Christmas.

★

Lieutenant Dierk had positioned his two 20-millimetre, four-barrelled anti-aircraft guns in some old Russian machine-gun nests a few hundred yards away from the Staff HQ bunkers. He was only permitted to fire in the event that the bunkers came under a low-level attack by Russian planes. Up until now, the enemy hadn't obliged him in this, so he and his men idly sat out the long days and nights frustratedly observing the high-altitude aerial dogfights they were unable to take part in. It was an engrossing spectacle when the long lines of transport planes, escorted by a handful of fighters, would circle above the airfield, gradually gaining height until, one by one, the aircraft were swallowed up in the protecting blanket of cloud, or when Russian fighters suddenly burst out of the grey shroud and, twisting and turning around one another with siren-like howls from their engines, began mixing it with the German Messerschmitts. The soldiers on the ground craned their necks to follow every move of the dogfights like they were some sporting contest.

'There, over there! See how he's getting stuck in! You wait, he's going to get him!'

'You've turned too sharply. Told you, you pulled out of that far too early! You'll never hit him like that!'

'Look at that bastard! He's bottled it, the coward!'

'Yes, now… now… oh, so close! He's got some guts, that guy! Want to bet he downs another one?'

'Look, they're hightailing it out of here now. Yeah, see, Franz? They've gone! Vanished into the clouds! Nah, that's our lot, they won't be coming out of there again. What shitty luck!'

No sooner had the paltry German force of three fighters, which flew sorties round the clock, touched down to refuel and re-arm than the Russian bombers were overhead. They moved steadily across the skies, gleaming silver, and those watching from below could clearly see small shapes dropping from their bellies. Soon after, the dark mushroom clouds of explosions rose up from the ground; a thick black column of smoke indicated that a fuel dump had taken a hit.

One time, though, they arrive prematurely, while two German fighters are still in the air. The Russian planes weave about uncertainly, firing wildly with all guns blazing. But the two Messerschmitts stick doggedly to their task, attacking the formation time and again. There – a thick plume of smoke trails from one of the bombers, it's on fire! Two small objects detach themselves from the stricken aircraft; one plummets to earth, gaining in velocity as it falls, while above the other a white ball suddenly blossoms. Swaying gently to and fro, it drifts straight towards Dierk's flak position. Soldiers rush from all sides. The parachute is dropping faster and faster, and now they can clearly make out the head and limbs of the man dangling beneath it. As they look up, without warning several flashes appear in rapid succession.

'Hey, the bloke's taking potshots at us!' The soldiers reach for their rifles.

'No! don't shoot!' shouts Lieutenant Dierk. 'He's scared, that's all.'

By now the parachute has touched down. It billows out one more time, dragging the man attached to it over the snow a short distance before collapsing on top of him. The infantrymen approach the white bundle with caution. But the Russian fires no more shots. Either he dropped his pistol when he landed or he's out of bullets. They unravel the parachute and free the man, who has got caught up in the lines. He stands up slowly and looks at the men surrounding him, uncertain what to expect. He is short and slender in build. His youthful face is bruised and swollen. When one of the soldiers tugs off his cap, a tousle of blond hair falls across his forehead. Lieutenant Dierk hands him a cigarette and lights it for him. The Russian smokes it in short, quick puffs, his hand trembling slightly. In the meantime, Captain Endrigkeit has also appeared on the scene.

'Tough luck, fella,' he laughs. 'You've picked a bad time to become a prisoner of war.'

The two officers escort the man to the bunker. The crowd of onlookers disperses, avidly discussing whether the Russian is going to be executed.

'Executed?'

'Yeah, absolutely, we've either got to kill him or let him go. After all, we haven't even got enough to feed ourselves!'

'You know what, I'm more in favour of letting him go.'

'You cretin! You want to release this Bolshevik. He could be a political commissar for all we know, you blockhead!'

'Here, Breuer, we've caught a rare bird for you,' Endrigkeit announces on entering the Intelligence Section's bunker. 'He just fell from the sky. At last, you'll be able to carry out your proper duties again now!'

Sonderführer Fröhlich asks the captured Russian the standard questions about name, rank and serial number. On opening his flying suit and examining the insignia on his collar, the young man turns out to be a flight lieutenant. He sits slumped on a wooden bench, and doesn't answer. Breuer attempts some more questions. What's his official position? His unit? Which airfield did he fly from? Nothing, no response! Was he wounded or in pain? Everyone's watching the Russian's face with rapt attention. He doesn't move a muscle, and says nothing. His pale grey eyes look past his questioner. Lieutenant Dierk is the first to lose patience.

'Come on, let's beat this bloke to a pulp! Then maybe he'll open his mouth!'

'Dierk, please!' Breuer upbraids him. 'You're an officer, aren't you? Well then, remember your position! This man's got the right, and from his perspective even the duty, to keep silent when questioned. Or do you think you'd act any differently if you were in his shoes?'

Dierk is chastened and annoyed at the same time.

'So, we have to behave honourably as officers when we get hold of this red scum, have we?' he mutters. 'I'd like to see if they'd worry about an officer's honour if we fell into their hands. Kick the shit out of us, more like!'

'And even if they did so a thousand times over,' Breuer answered sharply, 'it wouldn't absolve us of our responsibility to act like people from a civilized nation. We're German soldiers, not mercenaries and freebooters!'

The lieutenant holds his peace.

'Right, get him out of here!' says Breuer, concluding the interrogation. 'After all, in our position it makes no odds whether we know how many bombs the Russians have or where their airfields are. Have we still got anything for him to eat, Geibel?'

'There's still your ration of bread and lard left, Lieutenant.'

'What, nothing else? Oh well, give him that then, and warm up some coffee too! The man's half-frozen!'

They turn their attention to discussing the military position. Nobody pays any further attention to the prisoner, whose face had betrayed a faint hint of involvement during the altercation between the two officers. Out of the blue, he suddenly pipes up, speaking calmly and in fluent, almost accent-free German.

'Finish me off, please! I'm begging you… shoot me!'

Everyone's heads suddenly swivel round, looking at the airman as if he were some exotic animal.

'What do you take us for?' Breuer replies angrily. 'No one's planning to shoot you! Maybe you'll die of starvation alongside us here. I can't say. But shoot you? We're not murderers, we're not criminals!'

The Russian doesn't reply. In the look he gives the German officers, coolly appraising them, there is more than a trace of contempt. He shrugs his shoulders.

'Ya nye znayu,'* he says slowly. 'Maybe you're not a criminal,' he continues in German. 'You're an upstanding German citizen' – he rolls his German 'r's – 'you've given me your food. No doubt you'd give me wine and chocolate if you had any. Yes, you're all…' Here his gaze sweeps quickly over the assembled German officers once more, and comes to rest for a split-second on the defiant features of Lieutenant Dierk. 'None of you are criminals… perhaps. You're

---

* *Ya nye znayu* – 'I don't know.'

all just – now, what's your word for it? – henchmen, right? No, you won't shoot me…'

There is a pause. The eyes of those seated around the airman are glued to the pale face that's now looking through the bunker walls and fixing on somewhere out in the far distance.

'…more's the pity,' the young man quietly continues. 'That's not good for me, see. Now I'm a prisoner, I'm lost to my compatriots. My life's at an end. I'll cheerfully starve or freeze to death with all of you here, or be killed by your desperate soldiers, just in the hope that, tomorrow, all of you will get your comeuppance. That's how I see things.'

The silence grows ever more oppressive.

'Ha ha ha!' The silence is suddenly broken by Fröhlich's forced laughter. 'You're very much mistaken there, my friend! You obviously think because we're in a bit of a fix right now that we're finished?' He purses his lips contemptuously. 'Well, we've beaten you so far and we'll go on beating you, yes sir! Till there's nothing left of your wonderful Soviet Union! You clearly don't know us Germans, friend!'

The Russian prisoner gives Fröhlich an almost pitying look.

'On the contrary, I know the Germans only too well,' he says. 'There's peace between our countries and then suddenly you invade us. You go on a rampage of pillage and murder. You began by killing the Jews, now you're murdering Soviet citizens. You hang people on gallows. And for what, exactly?' He casts a look round the assembled faces. When he gets no reply, he goes on: 'When I was younger I read Heine, and Goethe and Hegel. But now I know that Germans are criminals.'

Someone awkwardly clears their throat.

'But the people of the Soviet Union will take a dreadful revenge on the German occupiers. Our war is in a just cause. Every man, every woman, the entire populace is engaged in fighting the Great Patriotic War. We're defending freedom, the Rights of Man and the achievements of the great Socialist Revolution. And that's why we'll win.'

The young airman's voice is calm and measured and so uncannily matter-of-fact that it holds everyone in the room spellbound.

'You see, the German Sixth Army, which planned to capture Stalin's city, is on the brink of defeat. Not one of its troops will escape… and that's just the beginning. Before long, our sacred Soviet soil will be swept clear of the German Fascist aggressor.'

No one says a word. Breuer can feel the blood pumping in his temples. Forcibly suppressing his agitation, he pushes the plate of bread and lard over to the Russian.

'Better keep your strength up first,' he says. 'Tomorrow you'll be sent to a POW camp, and hopefully you'll come to think better of the Germans before the war's over.'

While the Russian was eating, the first lieutenant arranged with Captain Endrigkeit that the prisoner should spend the night at the military police headquarters and be transferred to the Corps' POW collection point in the morning. Presently, Endrigkeit set off with the Russian airman. Breuer gave the captain a note addressed to the camp commandant, entrusting the prisoner to his special care.

He then sat around for some time chatting with Wiese and Dierk. Their sole topic of conversation was this unexpected event.

'Strange thing is,' Breuer told them, 'I've interrogated any number of Russian officers in my time. You name it, staff officers of all ranks, even generals, but I've never had an experience like that before. Nor have you, Wiese, I'll wager, right? A completely different caste of person. Truly inscrutable!'

'That's right,' agreed Lieutenant Wiese. 'The others before, they were just – prisoners. But this guy was one of those we only normally find dead on the battlefields. He stood in front of us like… well, almost like a victor. Maybe that explains the oddness.'

Fröhlich, meanwhile, had looked through the papers and letters the airman had been carrying. 'Aha!' he exclaimed. 'Look here: in Civvy Street, he was a literary critic on some kind of international journal. Means he must have been a full-blown card-carrying commie. That explains everything.'

'Still, hats off to the man, I say.'

Dierk could contain himself no longer.

'I just don't get what you all find so fascinating about this bloke! He's a cheap little agitator, stuffed with Bolshevik propaganda slogans!'

'I really think you're doing him a disservice there,' Breuer replied. 'He knew full well he wasn't going to make communists of us. What we witnessed was the simple and rational settling of accounts by someone who'd drawn a line under his life. Sure, he sees things through the filter of Soviet propaganda, like he's been taught to, but even so, some of what he said… In my opinion, we'd do well to take heed of it. In any event, meeting someone like him puts a fair few things into perspective. For one thing, it makes you disinclined to believe that old one about commissars having to drive men into battle at the point of a gun.'

'And all that about a just and an unjust war,' Wiese chipped in. 'I wouldn't have expected a Bolshevik of all people to come out with that.'

'That's just typical of you, Wiese!' Dierk pounced on the lieutenant. 'You and your Christianity – that stuff was guaranteed to play well with you! Let me tell you, there's no such thing as justice in politics. There, might is right and that's that!'

'You don't say, my dear Dierk,' countered Wiese with gentle irony. 'Well, just for a moment, let's try applying that marvellous little principle of yours to the personal relationships between people. The logical consequence of that is that you could beat out the brains of your weaker neighbour and steal his possessions any time you liked. I presume even you would think that was naked barbarism! We've got beyond that stage since we stopped being cavemen. Yet your law of the jungle is supposed to be the governing principle in the relations between peoples and states? God forbid that the German people should ever be on the receiving end of what you're proposing… but I'm sure you can't really mean it, Dierk. I've always taken you to be an idealist. But if you truly believe what you just said, that makes you nothing but a mean little egotist… how shall I put it, a nationalist egotist.'

Dierk's face reddened.

'Yes – that's exactly what I am!' he shouted. 'Guilty as charged, a nationalist egotist! And that's what we should all be! The superiority of our race gives us the right to – indeed, it obliges us to be just that. Our people are a chosen people! I believe implicitly in that; it's what I live for and what I'm prepared to lay my life on the line for at any time. The magnificent qualities of the German people, their honesty and diligence, their talent for organization, their creativity… it's our duty to liberate that from all constraints, from all external coercion… and to open up the world as a place where our people can live and work. That kind of egotism – I'm telling you this, Wiese, as you set so much store by religion – is nothing short of sacred! That's right, it's holy, God-ordained! And a holy egotism like that will ultimately be the salvation of mankind too! And… and if our nation isn't strong enough to assert this egotism, then – well, it might just as well go under. It deserves nothing better!

'It almost seems to me, Dierk,' said Wiese with a faint smile, 'that you're the cheap agitator now. "The salvation of mankind", you say? As you can see with your own eyes, the Russians don't consider what you're bringing them as salvation, but damnation. And they're right to see the kind of "salvation" that you're proposing as "ultimately" being just crumbs off the master's table… Just let people find their own salvation in their own way, Dierk! What you're advocating here is a morality of naked, brutal force, a law of the jungle. But man was put on Earth to raise himself up from the depths of bestiality… (No, they're not my words, it's a quotation from Fichte.) "Love They Neighbour as Thy Self", that's the secret of humanity. Take a look inside yourself just for once, Dierk, into your heart of hearts. Can't you feel that I'm right? Sure, the war's brutalized a lot of things in us.

But hidden somewhere deep inside us all is this miraculous treasure. Dig it out, Dierk, so you can become a human being again!'

Lieutenant Dierk rubbed his hands nervously on his thighs, as a gamut of conflicting emotions passed across his young face. Then he forced his features to assume a mask of resolute severity. 'I really don't know why you're always talking about *me*,' he said sharply. 'And in terms of *my* morality. What we're talking about here is the principle of "What is right is what serves the German people", and that's the guiding principle of the movement we're all part of. When all's said and done, you, gentlemen, are National Socialists too!'

The room suddenly fell silent. Their faces froze as if hit by an icy blast. Breuer felt like a curtain had been pulled back in front of him for a few moments. Slowly, and with a shaky-sounding voice, he heard himself saying:

'Yes, of course… we're all… National Socialists.'

Lakosch had of late lapsed into a state of rather sad introspection. Nor, it seemed, was Senta's disappearance the sole cause of this. He never spoke about the dog, and appeared to have forgotten about her. He'd followed the surprising interrogation of the Russian airman with more interest than he let on. The evening of that same day, he approached Breuer.

'Lieutenant, sir, I wanted to ask you, sir… That business about socialism and freedom in Russia that the prisoner mentioned, that's all a load of hogwash, right, Lieutenant?'

Breuer hesitated for a moment before replying.

'Yes, Lakosch,' he said finally, and with the very first word he uttered, he knew he was speaking against his own convictions but that he was duty-bound, as a German officer – as a National Socialist – to lie. 'Of course it's hogwash. You know that, surely! You've read that in any number of places and heard how the people here are oppressed and tortured! You know all this yourself, man!'

As he spoke his words came out ever faster, as he worked himself up into a convulsive frenzy.

'Of course it's all a con, a lowdown, dirty con trick! Fairy tales, opium for the people! It's... it's a complete...'

He broke off and left the room. Lakosch stared after him in astonishment.

The following day, when Breuer asked Endrigkeit how the Russian airman was getting on, he found the old officer in an unusually emotional state.

'He's dead,' Endrigkeit told him, his small eyes beneath his bushy brows revealing a suspicious gleam. 'That's right – dead! Here's what happened: so, this morning, I sent my two lads, Emil and Krause, off with him to the collection point, and on the way there, right in the middle of the street, the sodding bloke gets it into his head to do a runner, and hares off across country like an idiot! My lads can't believe their eyes. Sheer bloody suicide! They call out to him not to be so damned stupid, and start chasing him. But there's nothing for it, he refuses to stop and just keeps on running. Zigzagging all over the place, like a hare, they said. He'd gone completely crazy. Anyway, Emil's finally forced to open fire. First shot, straight through the head. Stone dead on the spot.'

The captain wiped his hand across his face. Momentarily, a surge of suspicion welled up in Breuer.

'Captain,' he asked uneasily, 'your men – they didn't... I mean, they haven't gone and...' His words tailed off; the captain looked up at him in surprise.

'What, you're thinking they might have... just for the hell of it? Now listen here, lad, this is my lads you're talking about! I told them all about you interrogating him. Dead impressed with him, they were. No, no, it's out of the question, Breuer – the bloke had a death wish.'

★

Meanwhile, all the hoo-ha about Manstein had died down. Some people maintained they could still hear the sounds of artillery fire and battle in the south, and someone claimed to have sighted from the western front German armour moving once more along the road above the Don escarpment; even so, the rallying cry, repeated time and again by the Army High Command, of 'Hang in there – Manstein will get us out!' had by now lost much of its impact. Even Count Willms had become positively monosyllabic with the information he divulged latterly. He pointed to the great difficulties in launching such an attack, especially during winter, and urged everyone to remain calm and be patient.

One day the mess orderlies to whom Lakosch had given some of the white flour he'd purloined sent him a dinner invitation, which hinted at some great treats in store. The rather draughty wooden bunker next to the kitchen was set out for a banquet. The table was laid with an old general staff map for a tablecloth and three candles. A wonderful smell of roasting pervaded the space. It grew even more intense when Krämer came in with a tray and set down in front of each of them an aluminium plate carefully covered with a piece of paper. Lieutenant Colonel Unold was accustomed to having his breakfast served in this way. The NCO in charge of the mess rose from his chair, arranged his permanently grinning face into a semblance of gravitas, and opened the banquet by saying grace:

> Come, Robert Ley,* and be our guest,
> And bring along the very best!

---

* Dr Robert Ley was, for the entire duration of the Second World War, head of the *Deutsche Arbeitsfront* (German Labour Front), a Nazi organization established to take the place of trade unions. The DAF was responsible for administering the *Kraft Durch Freude* ('Strength Through Joy') programme of organized mass leisure activities for the nation's workforce, including holidays, cruises and 'cultural' visits to approved galleries and concerts.

Not herrings and spuds – that ain't no treat,
We want what Göring and Goebbels eat!

'I won't hear a word said against jacket potatoes and herring!' laughed Lakosch. 'If you could magic that up, that'd do me just fine.'

Cautiously he uncovered his plate. The others kept a close, expectant watch on his eyes, which grew steadily larger and rounder. Before him lay a huge schnitzel, framed by two large Thuringian dumplings in a fragrant caramelized onion gravy. Lakosch had been prepared for a big surprise, but this went beyond his wildest dreams. Almost in reverence, he sliced into the juicy, wonderfully tender meat.

'Oh, lads,' he enthused, 'what a feast! I haven't eaten anything this good in years. It tastes just like veal. Now, don't you try telling me this is horsemeat, no way! I'd give anything to know where you got hold of it, though!'

'Don't ask, just eat!' the NCO told him, while the rest sat around with sly grins on their faces.

'There's more where that came from if you're still hungry,' the NCO reassured him. He felt like a millionaire who was treating some poor wretch to the time of his life just for once. Lakosch felt very comfortable in that role – he loosened his belt and devoured the schnitzel like a ravening beast. The others got stuck in to their food with almost as much gusto, while the mess chief regaled the company with jokes. The atmosphere grew appreciably livelier, especially after Lance-Corporal Wendelin produced a bottle of cherries steeped in rum of dubious provenance. Lakosch, too, felt moved to treat his fellow diners to some gems from his inexhaustible supply of witticisms and anecdotes.

'Have you heard the one about the walking stick?' he asked, his mouth still half-full of schnitzel and dumplings. 'No? Well, there's these two friends from Silesia, Antek and Franzek. One day, Antek runs into Franzek on the street, and he's carrying a new walking stick that's much too tall for him. So Antek says to Franzek: "You don't look too comfortable with that – where'd you get it?" "Inherited it from my uncle!" replies Franzek proudly. "Well, if I was you," suggests Antek, ever the practical one, "I'd shorten it a bit." "Nah, that's no good," says Franzek, "then I'd have nothing to hold on to." "No, not at the top – at the bottom!" his friend replies. "How come?" asks Franzek, baffled. "It's the top bit that's too tall!"'

Gales of uproarious laughter. The portly NCO laughed so hard he found it hard to catch his breath. His face turned alarmingly red, and his large protruding ears waggled about like an elephant's.

'It's the top bit… ha ha ha, priceless!' he spluttered, with tears running down his cheeks.

Lakosch was frankly a bit surprised at the rip-roaring success of his joke, which he'd already tried out on a few people at Staff HQ. During the outbreak of laughter, he'd glanced aimlessly a couple of times at a heap of clothes lying in a corner of the bunker. All of a sudden, his gaze froze to that same spot and his body tensed. In among the greatcoats and camouflage jackets, there was a tawny patch of something that looked like a foal-fur pelt. Lakosch got up slowly and crossed the room like he was sleepwalking… A silence fell over the room.

'Wait for it, lads,' whispered the NCO, 'he's twigged! Now we'll have some fun!'

Lakosch thrust his hands into the clothes pile. They came out holding the neatly flayed coat of his dog, Senta. For a moment he stood there, rooted to the spot. Then, all at once, he felt a warm sensation rising in his gorge and he vomited all over the heap of clothes. When he'd finished, he turned around and strode stiffly back to the table. A feeling of apprehension gripped the others. Lakosch stopped in front of the corpulent NCO. His hands gripped the table edge, and his upper body swayed slightly to and fro. His bloodshot eyes bulged from his greenish-white face, where his freckles stood out like flecks of mustard. Then he raised his fist and smashed it as hard as he could square into the fat man's face, which had frozen in terror – once, twice... before the others dragged him off.

Over the next few days, Lakosch didn't utter a word. His jollity and his penchant for tricks and practical jokes had vanished. An alien, angry flicker now inhabited the depths of his once-gentle eyes. Geibel, puzzled by this sudden and inexplicable change of character – for obvious reasons, the kitchen orderlies had kept quiet about the incident – gave his comrade a wide berth whenever he could. Breuer felt sorry for the little driver. He supposed Lakosch had heard something about the deterioration of their situation, and so made some futile attempts to cheer him up.

On the sixteenth of December, a few days after Army Group Don had begun its push towards the Cauldron, the Red Army resumed its attack on the middle section of the Don in numbers. This time, the fighting took place west of the sector from Kletskaya to Serafimovich. Mobile units broke through the positions held by the Eighth Italian and Third Romanian armies, and within just a few days had formed a salient of up to two hundred kilometres in depth. They penetrated as far forward as the gates of the important supply centre at Millerovo and, after taking control of the airfield at Tazinskaya, two hundred and fifty kilometres west of Stalingrad, once again severed the crucial supply line to the Cauldron. This breakthrough had disastrous consequences for the German military leadership. Six German, six Italian and two Romanian divisions had been smashed. They had to be replaced by forces that had been earmarked for the siege of Stalingrad. With the help of such contingents and of new units hastily assembled from troops who had either been due to go on leave or who'd been assigned to the baggage train, the Germans finally managed to fight the Russian shock armies to a standstill in the depression of the great Don elbow.

While these operations were still going on, the Russians, unhampered by any attempts to break out of the Cauldron, suddenly launched a surprise and well-supported attack on the flanks of the wedge that Colonel General Hoth had driven forward. Hoth found himself in danger of being cut off. Shortly before Christmas, he was forced to turn back. His detachments were driven back beyond Kotelnikovo, the point from which they had begun their thrust, incurring heavy losses in the process.

Colonel von Hermann had just returned from a discussion of the situation at the Corps. He sat in front of the campaign map, which showed broad red lines slicing through the black arrows that pointed in the direction of the Cauldron. His fingers drummed on the tabletop.

Then he looked up at Unold, who was leaning against the wall opposite him, staring at the ceiling.

'So, Unold,' he said, 'that's the end of the dream, I'm afraid. High Command has told us that we're in it now potentially for the long haul... Nice Christmas present, eh? Plus they've also let it be known that under no circumstances should we tell the men about the business with Hoth.'

'Very wise move, too, I should say!' replied the lieutenant colonel. 'Your average foot soldier exists on a diet of food and booze and illusions. If we start coming clean with them, the whole house of cards would come crashing down within a fortnight.'

'I don't share your jaded view of the German soldier,' the colonel rejoined after a moment's thought. 'The prerequisite for any military success is trust. How can we expect our troops to put their trust in us if we don't reciprocate? I've been through thick and thin alongside my men, even when we've been in some really tight spots, and I've never had cause to regret that. Nowadays, smoke and mirrors seems to be the thing, but it's a dangerous game. When the scales drop from people's eyes, deception can come back to bite you big time. But really there's no point in discussing it. Orders are orders.'

The colonel's gaze came to rest, pensively, on the photograph of his son in front of him on his desk. Ferdinand lived in a world of illusions, too. But he was allowed to; he was still young, after all. You needed such things at that age. He'd learn soon enough that the soldiering profession was a bit like the life of a monk – a constant state of renunciation, even to the point of renouncing one's better judgement.

'Yes, Unold,' he said, picking up the thread of their conversation, 'that puts paid to any idea of a breakout. Shame, I'd have really relished that! Now we have to sit around here twiddling our thumbs and wait for better weather, while the others are fighting... I'm not stuck on the title of "Tank Commander" – it's only a rank on paper, when all's said and done. I put in a request today to be transferred to a front-line division.'

Unold became animated. 'I completely understand and sympathize with your position, Colonel, sir! It's just the same for me. I feel like a spare part here. Right now, the German people can't afford to let people with my kind of education stagnate in a posting like this. And so I've taken the liberty' – here, he handed the colonel a piece of paper – 'of putting down in writing a formal request for my own transfer.'

Colonel von Hermann cast his eye over the sheet, which was covered in large letters, then looked up. 'What's the meaning of this, Unold?' he enquired, visibly taken aback. 'You're asking to join the SS? There aren't any SS units here in the Cauldron. Does that mean you want to leave the Cauldron?'

The lieutenant colonel bit his lip. His cheekbones, which always looked like they had thin parchment stretched over them, appeared even more prominent than usual. He avoided the colonel's searching look and didn't reply. Von Hermann passed the letter back to him. 'I strongly advise you,' he said icily, 'not to submit this request. At the very least, you'd be laying yourself open to – hmm, how shall I put it? – misunderstandings regarding your motives.'

Unold screwed up the piece of paper in his hand. Red flushes appeared on his face. He seemed to be searching for a suitable rejoinder. But when none came, he turned on his heel and left the room.

3

Black Christmas

CHRISTMAS WAS DRAWING NEAR. But no guiding star appeared to the men fighting in the Stalingrad Cauldron. The firmament of their hopes and yearnings was overcast with a dense veil of gloom. Battle, frost and hunger came riding over the remote foreign wasteland that was now their home like three Horsemen of the Apocalypse, and found ever richer pickings among anything living. In the graveyards at Karpovskaya and Pestshanka, and at Gorodishche and Gumrak, where those who had fallen in the bloody fighting during the autumn lay buried, the rows of hummocks of brown earth multiplied, mercifully cloaked overnight by a mantle of snow, while the bare coppice of wooden crosses with names and dates written on them in black kept growing by the day. The Place of the Skull – the Golgotha of the three hundred thousand! The crucifix of Stalingrad! In time, the wooden crosses will rot to nothing, and new life will blossom once more on the neglected graves. But the invisible crucifix of Stalingrad will go on looming over space and time, standing for ever as an admonishment and a warning.

Lakosch, too, had his own cross to bear. Increasingly he would lapse into dark brooding, for which the endless days of aimless waiting afforded him ample time. For one thing, there was the demise of his Senta, which upset him more than the death of many a comrade; and for another, the military situation, which – this much he had gathered from the telephone conversations he'd overheard in the bunker – was pretty dire; and last, but by no means least, the business with the captured pilot. All that stuff the bloke had said about revolution and socialism – that was all one big con, of course. He for one wasn't taken in by it for a moment! After all, he'd seen a thing or two with his own eyes in the Soviets' 'Promised Land'. The peasants' hovels with their straw roofs and earth floors, and so much filth and squalor inside that you'd rather sleep out in the open. The Russian peasants didn't even own a hammer and nails, let alone a spanner. Was that supposed to be socialism's great 'achievement', then?

It was with such thoughts as this that Lakosch tried to reassure himself. But he didn't have much joy. Other images kept obtruding: schools and polyclinics with dentistry facilities, even in the smallest villages; the large, modern housing and administration blocks nestling between the wooden shacks in Russian towns; the neat model estates in the southern part of the Don elbow, with their combine harvesters and tractor stations; the huge industrial plants in the Donetsk region and the massive hydroelectric dam at Zaporozhye.

So maybe there was something to this talk about the achievements of socialism after all. And then there was the thing with the Jews. Whenever Lakosch hit upon this subject, he vividly recalled an incident from the summer of '41.

It had been a hot July day. After driving along dust-choked roads, they'd arrived at the Ukrainian village of Talnoye, at the northeastern corner of the Uman Pocket. Just the previous day, the Russians had attempted a breakout here. In the village streets, which still showed signs of the fighting, Lakosch came across a jeering crowd of soldiers, who were herding a bunch of small figures dressed in strange black garb ahead of them down the street.

'What's going on here then?' he asked.

'They were firing at us from a basement!'

'What, this lot here?'

'No idea! Someone was, at any rate!'

'So what now?'

'What now? We're gonna do 'em in, that's what! It's all their fault, the swine!'

Lakosch joined the procession. A sick feeling began to rise in his gorge, but at the same time he was gripped by a wild urge to witness the impending slaughter. Amid a tumult of shouts and blows, the Jews – he estimated there were around fifty of them, all men of middle age, with black beards, ragged clothes, and very poor, too, by the look of it – were driven into a courtyard, where they were pushed up against a wall. Boys who were there on fatigue duty, anti-aircraft gunners and men from every conceivable unit were jostling and shoving and yelling all at once and waving rifles and pistols in the air.

A stocky NCO from a flak battalion had appointed himself the ringleader of the mob. His bloodshot eyes were bulging out of his puffy face, and there were flecks of frothy yellow spittle in the corners of his mouth. Lakosch had seen this sort of thing in a rabid dog once, but never before in a human being. The Jews huddled in front of the whitewashed brick wall and clung fast to one another, forming an indissoluble entity of both abject misery and a black, piercing hatred that seemed to well up from the innermost core of their being. Though fear and loathing flickered over this group like a living flame, not one of them cried out or made the slightest sound whatsoever. Indeed, if anyone so much as opened his mouth, blows immediately rained down upon him. Here and there, trickles of blood appeared, which only seemed to whip the lynch mob into an even greater frenzy. Efforts were already being made to clear a space in front of the wall. Someone called out:

'Who's going to bury these pigs afterwards?'

Of course, how the devil were they to bury them? There was a momentary pause.

'This filth can dig their own graves!'

'Yeah, dead right! Let's have some spades!'

Some of the crowd broke off to fetch the necessary tools. While they were gone, the NCO from the flak battery continued to lay into the defenceless victims. His rage knew no bounds. His voice, hoarse from shouting, now produced only an animal-like bellow. Out of the blue, an officer suddenly appeared on the scene.

'What's the meaning of this?'

The troops flinched, instantly brought to their senses. The NCO approached, swearing and gesticulating wildly.

'Get a grip on yourself, man!' the officer barked at him. 'Who gave you orders to do this?'

Suddenly waking from his frenzy, the NCO stood there silently gaping before slumping down, a broken man. Taking a furious swing, the officer batted the pistol out of his hand.

'Get out of my sight, you animal!' The NCO slunk off there and then, without a word. 'And the rest of you, disperse this instant!'

Muttering among themselves, the soldiers retreated, but stayed loitering around the scene. An elderly man detached himself from the group of Jews. The lobe of his left ear was badly torn, and blood was running from his broken nose into his matted beard. Bowing deeply and clutching his greasy hat in his hands, he thanked the officer for saving them.

'Oy too, moy dear sir, velcome from ze bottom of my heart ze noo Churman goffernment!'

An impotent loathing shone through the mask of slavish sub-jugation imposed by centuries of serfdom. The officer turned his back on the man.

'Just piss off,' he said curtly 'and don't show your faces here again!'

Lakosch also found himself seized with rage at the time, because the officer's intervention had deprived him of a ghoulish spectacle.

Even so, he could never rid himself of the memory of this incident. And this recollection changed his outlook. Now, whenever he thought of the faces of the seventeen-year-old boys on fatigue duty – predatory children's faces distorted with bloodlust – all he felt was disgust and shame.

'That isn't war any more,' he would recall with a shudder, 'it's…'

But he couldn't even find the words to express what was troubling him.

Lakosch had been hugely nonplussed one time when he discovered that Lenin and Stalin weren't Jewish. He had no idea where he'd picked up this curious bit of information, but it had been an article of faith with him. His disappointment on learning the truth shocked him and shook his confidence in Joseph Goebbels's propaganda. Who on earth had ever come up with such a bunch of shit in the first place? Rosenberg* most likely, that Baltic German whose arse the Russians had given a good kicking. He'd probably bamboozled Adolf, too, with his fabrications and horror stories about Russia! After all, for a while Germany had rubbed along just fine with Soviet Russia, when they'd signed the Non-Aggression Pact that everyone had been so pleased about. And then along comes this snake-oil salesman from the Baltics, who gets Hitler all worked up over absolutely nothing! Maybe Stalin wanted just the same thing as Hitler, maybe he wanted socialism as well – and this entire war was nothing but a stupid misunderstanding? If only the two of them could get their heads together, in private. Hadn't there been some rumour recently about Stalin and Hitler possibly meeting in Turkey?

That would sort things out all right – for the troops trapped at

---

* Alfred Rosenberg (1893–1946) was one of the principal theorists of the Nazi movement. A Baltic German, Rosenberg was instrumental in devising Nazism's racial policies and advocated a new mystical 'religion of the blood' to replace Christianity. He was sentenced to death at the Nuremberg trials and hanged.

Stalingrad, too. It would mean the end of this war! He was at a loss to think how it might otherwise come to a sensible conclusion.

The little ginger-haired driver would ruminate long and hard on such hopes and deliberations while picking lice out of his clay-caked shirt, and would lie awake at night cogitating on these matters while planes droned overhead and the bunker shook gently from the shockwaves of distant bomb blasts. His freckled face took on a tortured expression from the effort of thinking.

'I dunno what's the matter with you! Are you hungry or something?' asked Geibel anxiously, offering Lakosch a bit of crispbread.

'Don't talk such utter crap, you simpleton!' Lakosch spat back venomously. Casting a pitying glance at Geibel, he added: 'It's all right for you, mate. You've got the consolation of being a moron!'

And now, it seemed, Private Lakosch would get to wear his Iron Cross.

Some time ago, the sergeant at the Adjutant's Office had hinted that the application that divisional Staff HQ had submitted for Lakosch to receive his decoration had been approved by the Army High Command. On the day before Christmas Eve, the little driver was ordered to report to Lieutenant Colonel Unold. Before setting off, Lakosch spent quite some time trying to get the worst of the dirt off his battledress tunic, picking off the most obvious lice from his collar and washing his face and hands in the snow outside the bunker. Geibel observed his ablutions with positive reverence.

'Here, Lanky,' said Lakosch with good-natured condescension, 'you know the story about the old dear who asks the soldier on leave: "Where's your Iron Cross, you young hero?" And he replies: "My platoon leader's wearing it for me!" That's the way it is in the army, see. You've still got a lot to learn! Chin up, lad! I'll put the thing on for your benefit soon as I get back! Anyhow, there's another "Order of the Frost" being awarded this winter, an extra-thick medal with two gilded icicles hanging off it. You'll get one of those as well, for fearless teeth-chattering in the face of the enemy!'

He slapped Geibel, who was relieved to see the driver in a good mood again, on the shoulder and sauntered over to the chief of staff's bunker with a spring in his step. One of the principal didactic aims of the Prussian parade ground is to instil respect for more senior ranks. And this respect does not even desert a common soldier who has been at Staff HQ long enough to observe all the human failings of his superiors at close quarters. So it was that Lakosch tiptoed down the steps leading to Unold's bunker and listened apprehensively outside the wooden door to check that he wasn't interrupting anyone. The sound of conversation came from within. That cold, impersonal voice was Lieutenant Colonel Unold's, without a doubt, while the other seemed to belong to Captain Engelhard. Lakosch resolved to go in. He was just raising his hand to knock when something suddenly made him pause.

'… saving the world from Bolshevism,' said a voice, clearly audible through the badly fitting slats of the door. 'Don't pay any attention to that nonsense, Engelhard! It's just old wives' tales told to frighten children. We can tell that sort of thing to our men here. You see, I was here once before, before the war; I was in Lipetsk helping the Russians organize their fledgling air force. I know these people. They're not after world domination. They'd have been jolly glad to have avoided this war, believe you me!'

Lakosch held his breath. What was going on? He strained to listen. Up above, a sentry's footsteps clumped past, drowning out the captain's reply. Now Unold was speaking again.

'Why us? Simple! We have to conquer land in the east, create *Lebensraum*! That was all there already in *Mein Kampf*. Or do you think big business gave Hitler the money to found his party and churn out propaganda year after year for nothing? Their payoff is factories in southern Russia, and the wheat fields of Ukraine and Kuban.'

Lakosch propped himself with his hand against the damp mud wall of the bunker entrance. Unold's sharp voice jabbed at him like knives.

The captain's answer was more impassioned than was customary for him. He spoke of Hitler's plans, the Nazi Party programme, and German socialism. Lakosch was swept up by Engelhard's words and found himself unconsciously nodding in agreement with every sentence. 'Yes, yes! Quite right! Let's see what he has to say to that!'

'But Engelhard!' Unold interrupted, and Lakosch saw in his mind's eye the lieutenant colonel's pallid face and the crooked smile that was never reflected in his grey eyes. 'I do believe Christmas is making you sentimental. You need to take a sober view of these things. "National Socialism" – what is that, exactly? It was a bluff, a propaganda bluff of the kind that only Hitler can pull off. It effectively took the wind out of the Reds' sails… Sure, after the war, they'll settle a few farmers here in the east, why not? But it's other people who'll be making the big money. Look what's happened in Dnepropetrovsk, and in Kiev! They're all there already: Allianz, Deutsche Bank, Krupp, Rheinmetall-Borsig, Reichswerke Hermann Göring, etcetera, etcetera, with all their branches and head offices. Didn't you read what Goebbels had to say in Gdynia recently… No? Hang on a mo – now, where did I put…? Oh yes, here it is, you really ought to read this! It's all there in black and white: "We're fighting for oil and iron, for swaying wheat fields. That's what inspires our soldiers, and that's what they give their lives for!" – and he goes on: "Let no one imagine that we Germans have suddenly been gripped by a new morality. No, our first priority is to make a pile!" See, right there! What do you say to that?'

Lakosch could feel little beads of sweat forming on his brow. His breathing was becoming more laboured, preventing him from hearing properly. He was only just able to make out what the captain said in response.

'So what you're saying, then, is that we were spoiling for this war and we're to blame for it!' was the gist of Engelhard's reply. 'I refuse to believe that, it's simply untrue! Sure, it may well be the case that, during the war, some… Look, appetite comes with eating. But how did it all start? We had an agreement with Russia. Russia broke it and stabbed us in the back by signing a mutual assistance pact with Yugoslavia. That meant war! We couldn't have done things any differently even if we'd wanted to.'

'Yugoslavia!' scoffed Unold. 'You know, Engelhard, I really rate you. You'll make a first-rate staff officer one day. But sometimes, and please don't take this amiss, you're just like a child. If you go after a particular goal in politics, you can find a thousand ways and means of justifying it. But listen here, will you! What I'm about to say to you is for your ears only, and you must promise never to repeat it to anyone else. Hitler gave the order to prepare for war against Russia way back, on the twenty-second of October 1940! Yes, that's right, 1940, just a few months after we'd conquered France – in other words, long before the business with Yugoslavia! How do I know that? I was attached to Army High Command at the time. We played a key role in drawing up the plans. We were pretty much the only people in the know. Even the C-in-Cs were out of the loop back then. They were blindsided by that pantomime about "Operation Sealion" – you know, the famous invasion of England that was actually never seriously contemplated at the time.'

A pregnant silence filled the room next to where Lakosch stood waiting. The bunker oven crackled and spat noisily. His heart was thumping away like the piston of a steam engine. Outside, a plane droned past, and somewhere a shot was fired.

Then the lieutenant colonel was speaking again, and this time his cold voice had a metallic edge. 'Don't go living in a dream world, Engelhard! That's no way for people like us to behave. You must learn to see Hitler for what he is. The thing to remember about him is that his urge for power knows no bounds. He's absolutely ruthless and unerringly consistent in his pursuit of power. He couldn't give a damn about the "great stupid flock of sheep, the patient but mutton-headed German people" – those are Hitler's own words. He doesn't have any compunction about exploiting or discarding his financial backers, his old comrades and friends as it suits him. He's got no sentimental or moral inhibitions – and that, Engelhard, is what makes him great! There's something of the Nietzschean "superman" about him; he truly is "beyond good and evil". That sentimental-sounding stuff he trots out about "national community" and "socialism" and so forth, and if need be shedding the odd tear, are just bait to lure in women and chancers when he needs their support. Otherwise, he wouldn't have any followers, since your average person couldn't bear the sight of this genius unfiltered; they'd go insane at the sight of him, in just the same way that Nietzsche's ideas drove him mad. You really ought to read some Nietzsche, Engelhard! He's the only philosopher worth reading. Then you'll understand Hitler. And only then will you be a true National Socialist! Hitler's the only statesman – in fact the only person full-stop – for whom I have any respect.'

After the event, Lakosch was at a loss to explain how he entered the room, what the lieutenant colonel said to him when he pinned the medal with its black, white and red ribbon to his chest, or how he found his way back to his own bunker. In a state of dazed unease, his let his comrades' congratulations wash over him. His father's face loomed up before him, that tired, embittered face, whose lines and creases were deeply ingrained with coal dust even on his days off. What would his old man have said? 'Hitler – that means war!' Lakosch began to understand at last…

A short while later, Lance Corporal Lakosch removed the ribbon from his tunic and put it in his pocket. When Breuer, with a shake of his head, informed him that, according to army regulations, he was required to wear the decoration for twenty-four hours after receiving it, he mumbled something about 'too bad' and refused to put the ribbon back on in the days that followed. And because Sergeant Major Harras no longer had his beady eye on the men of the Staff HQ, nobody noticed its absence.

In the Intelligence Section's bunker, all the preparations had been made for Christmas Eve. Granted, no one had even thought about trying to put up a tree; no doubt, such a thing couldn't be had for love nor money throughout the entire Cauldron. Instead, they'd hung a barrel hoop from the low plank roof and wound strips of green paper and pine twigs around it; dangling from it were the shiny dog tags and wristbands that Corporal Herbert used as currency when trading with the civilian population, along with shiny silver and gold tinsel made from the foil from inside old cigarette packets. But the most valuable things on the makeshift Christmas wreath, which they'd been keeping safe for ages, were four solitary little wax candles. A more substantial candle, which Lakosch had acquired from somewhere in exchange for tobacco, had been carefully dissected into three bits and used to make wall lights, set in wooden holders artistically whittled over many days by the skilful hands of Sonderführer Fröhlich.

Since early morning, a festive and reflective atmosphere had reigned in the bunker. Everyone was making a special effort to be friendly and helpful. Lanky Geibel, with his round, doll-like eyes set in a guileless child's face, sat daydreaming. Herbert, as fussy and bustling as a housewife, busied himself with trying to improve the look of the place. The main thing preying on his mind was that he hadn't had a chance to bake anything. Sadly, he contemplated his stock of flavourings and essences, and went off on flights of fancy, dreaming up audacious recipes for artificial marzipan and all manner of honey cakes. Today, even Fröhlich resisted talking about the military and political situation, and instead told tales of Yuletide celebrations past at his father's parsonage near Riga, and the little

'Adler Trumpf' saloon car he'd surprised his wife with four years ago at Christmas. Only Lakosch mooned about the bunker, glowering and taciturn. Towards midday, Captain Fackelmann put in an appearance; after Harras's departure, he'd assumed responsibility once more for supervising the staff's troops.

'Sad to report, lads,' he declared glumly, 'there's nothing extra today. Half a pack of crispbread and three ciggies each: that's your lot. I wish I could treat you, but there's nothing to be had – absolutely nothing, believe me!'

They believed him. They knew he'd give his eye teeth to be able to present the men with a slap-up five-course meal today. But they could clearly see that he wasn't getting enough to eat himself. His appearance had changed alarmingly over the past few weeks. His face was as yellow as a quince and heavily lined, and the skin hung down from his cheeks in limp bags. 'Just a touch of jaundice,' he'd reply to concerned enquiries after his health, and with a lame attempt at humour would go on: 'In years to come, if anyone asks me if I was one of those who came back from Stalingrad, I can say: "Yes, in part! When I went there I weighed a hundred and ninety-three pounds, now I'm only a hundred and thirty. The rest of me stayed there."'

But the poor fellow looked so thoroughly wretched it was really difficult raising a laugh in response.

'Incidentally,' the captain said as he was leaving, 'the CO's given us leave to dip into the iron rations for Christmas. Dunno if that's of any use to you…?'

They smiled sheepishly at one another. Yeah, right, the iron rations – they'd been used up weeks ago, for Christ's sake! When it grew dark outside, Breuer lit the candles. An unfamiliar warm glow suffused the cramped space and was reflected in the silver tinsel on the wreath and the bright eyes of the six men who sat silently watching the flickering flames. And as the smell of melting candle wax and crackling pine twigs spread, a breath of home wafted through the bunker. Breuer picked up his mouth organ and began softly playing the old tunes of Christmas Eve.

> O joyous, o blessed
> Grace-bringing Christmas time!

One after the other, the men joined in: Herbert's light, fresh tenor, Lieutenant Wiese's rather quavery baritone and Fröhlich's booming bass, which threatened to drown out everyone else.

> The world was lost, Christ is born...

The men's souls, hardened by more than three years of war, unfolded like buds in the warm sun.

> Silent night, Holy night...
> Heavenly hosts sing Alleluja:
> Christ the Saviour is born!

The carols sounded odd coming from throats coarsened by war, but the sweet resonance of them crossed the thousands of kilometres that separated the men from their homeland and permeated the bunker. The invisible hands of a loving wife, an anxious mother, stroked their hair, their foreheads, and the joyful voices of their children joined in inaudibly with their singing, Christmas, Christmas! You most sacred of all festivals, you eternally flowing spring of everything that is good within the human spirit!

Then Lieutenant Wiese opened the black book with the golden cross on its cover, and proceeded to read the simple words of the Christmas story. The men listened with rapt attention. They were the shepherds abiding in the fields, to whom, in their painful awareness of the dreadful present, a new revelation of something long buried was now being imparted.

Glory to God in the highest
And on Earth peace,
Good will toward men!
Peace on Earth… yes, peace on Earth.

Their fervent hopes of receiving Christmas mail came to nothing. No letters or packages had arrived; no tangible greeting from home for the men. But now, one after the other, they started to fish out little gifts, presents that each of them had secretly collected for his comrades. They didn't amount to much: a couple of cigarettes, carefully wrapped in paper, a carved pipe, a glued photograph frame. Fröhlich had drawn a little picture of the bunker for everyone, with the legend 'A Souvenir of Christmas in the Cauldron, 1942'. Breuer gave Geibel, who was an avid smoker, two cigarillos he'd saved from more plentiful times. It turned out that Geibel had had much the same thought. Smiling in embarrassment, he produced a little packet of three cigarettes for the lieutenant, which he'd sacrificed with a heavy heart from the last five remaining in his iron rations. Lakosch, meanwhile, had disappeared outside. After a while, he came back in and put something on the table. It was his entire iron ration: a tin of 'Scho-Ka-Kola' chocolate and a bag of crispbreads.

'Good job that at least someone didn't eat all their rations!' he growled. But his words were drowned out by the eruption of sheer delight that greeted his revelation. Breuer tipped the crispbreads into the lid of a billycan – a heap of broken bits mixed with mouse droppings.

'You're a star, Lakosch, lad! You really sure you want to donate this for general consumption? Well, if you change your mind, you'd better pipe up quick! We can't afford to turn our noses up at such generosity!'

Breuer divided up the two bars of chocolate in the tin and the crispbread pieces into six portions, so everyone had something to nibble on – almost like old times. But as it transpired, this wasn't the only surprise of the day. All of a sudden, they heard someone slowly clumping down the bunker steps, and in came Wendelin, the mess orderly, lugging with him a steaming stockpot and a stack of tin plates.

'Captain Fackelmann sends his warmest Christmas greetings… and says that he managed to rustle up another horse from somewhere!' he announced, puffed but flushed with the bonhomie of the gift-giver, and proceeded to ladle out two large meat dumplings swimming in a yellow broth for each of them. So, they were to enjoy a Christmas dinner after all… 'Cement balls,' sighed Herbert, not by way of criticism, but in reverential appreciation of the captain and his magical, philanthropic powers.

After the meal, Breuer got to his feet and, after slowly rubbing the bridge of his nose with his thumb and forefinger, addressed them:

'Comrades…' he began, but then, finding this familiar word actually too formal for a day like this, corrected himself in slight embarrassment. 'Dear friends… Dear friends!' he repeated, this time clearly and resolutely, 'I'll be brief. Our thoughts today are far away, with our loved ones. So anything someone like me has to say might well sound superfluous. All I will say, though, my friends, is that this particular Christmas celebration of ours today has a very special significance. We've been used to celebrating Christmas since we were children, and when we look back at all those times, our memories merge into one big picture of happiness and joy and brotherly love around the Christmas tree. But we've never marked the birth of Our Saviour in quite the way we're doing here today: far, far away and cut off from our homeland, suffering from hunger and the cold, and surrounded by doom and gloom. But nowhere more than in this sea of hatred, I believe, have we felt the power of the Gospel of Love, which brings us a message of peace, that inner spiritual tranquillity that alone is the source of all true and lasting peace between peoples and nations. And never before has it been clearer to us that we will lose ourselves, that all that's good within us will wither and die, if we should fail to heed the call and the warning of that message. But the fact that this is in our hands, that the way has been shown to us so clearly, and that we may celebrate our Christmas in this spirit once more as Germans – all this fills us with profound joy, with a calm, unquenchable cheerfulness despite everything, despite the dark place in which we currently find ourselves. I don't know if we will ever get to celebrate another Christmas. But I do know this: even if he lives to be a hundred and no matter where he might find himself on Christmas Eve, any of us who survives this ordeal will find his thoughts returning time and again to the friends he had in hard times and to this moment in our little bunker outside Stalingrad.'

As Breuer's words died away, all that could be heard was the soft crackling of the candles. He then shook each of his comrades by the hand. When he got to Lakosch, he kept hold of his hand for a moment longer.

'Chin up, Lakosch!' he said warmly. 'There'll be peace on Earth again!'

Two large tears ran down the little soldier's cheeks.

'Not just like that there won't be!' a voice inside him shouted. 'Not if we don't do something!' But he said nothing. Slowly, the candles burned down. Just before guttering out, they flared up brightly, one after another. The pale dribbles of wax solidified to yellowish icicles on the candle sconces. Outside, though, no angel flew by; only death swept over the land, beating its black wings.

The candles on the Christmas tree in the living room of Bailiff Helgers in Gotha were also gradually going out. The quiet celebration and the present-giving were finished, and the family were sitting peaceful and relaxed around the circular mahogany table, over which a nickel-plated standard lamp cast its soft light. From a record-player cabinet came the high voices of the Boys' Choir of the St Thomas Church in Leipzig:

> Holy Night, come pour your
> Heavenly peace into this heart…
> The stars are shining bright,
> Beckoning from the blue distance…

Captain Gedig had slumped down deep in the wide armchair. He was wearing stirrup pants and had crossed his legs. The breast pocket of his short tunic was bedecked with medals. He was gazing absent-mindedly at a large map of Europe on the wall and listening to the happy voices of the children, which were just fading away. His young face displayed an uncharacteristic earnestness. He had just completed the Senior Adjutants' Training Course at the army staff college in Berlin, after which he had come to see his fiancée for two days and spend Christmas Eve with her. His train was due to leave at three o'clock in the morning. He carried in his pocket the special certification from the leader of the training course authorizing him to fly into the Stalingrad Cauldron. Bailiff Helgers, an elderly pensioner who, as befitted a civil servant of the old school, was a stickler for doing things by the book, was leafing through the latest edition of *Meyers Encyclopaedia*, a Christmas present from his wife. Frau Helgers, visibly touched by the sufferings of the war and already somewhat matronly, sat bent over her knitting frame, working with nimble fingers on the flower pattern of a cushion cover. Eva Helgers, her daughter, had been observing her fiancé's abstracted face with hidden anxiety. Now she got up and went over to the gramophone to put on a new record. Aged just twenty, she was already a popular and successful teacher at a sport and gymnastics school. Her platinum blonde hair, oddly at variance with her dark eyes, lent her small, lightly tanned face a unique allure. 'You've hardly eaten a thing, young man,' said the old lady, looking up from her knitting to cast a worried eye at the captain. 'Have a bit of this chocolate. Kurt sent us it from Holland for Christmas. I'm sure you won't find anything as tasty as this in Russia in a hurry. Yes, if our boy didn't give us a bit of a helping hand every now and then, we wouldn't have had much to offer in the way of Christmas treats this year. It's hard trying to get by just on our ration cards…'

The old gentleman passed one of the weighty tomes of the encyclopaedia over to Captain Gedig.

'Have a look at this, why don't you? It's a magnificent work. Colour plates incorporated into the text, that's a real novelty! And they've completely re-edited it according to National Socialist principles. The publishers went beyond the call of duty there.'

'Just so long as it gives you pleasure, Father,' Frau Helgers beamed at her husband. Eva had gone to lean over the captain's chair. She put her arm round his shoulders and craned over him to look at the book. Her fingers played coquettishly over the two gold stars on his epaulette. She hummed along with the tender melody coming from the gramophone. A strand of her hair dangled down and brushed her fiancé's cheek. He looked up at her with a smile.

'Werner, Darling, you're going back today,' she whispered. 'When will we see one another again?'

Her eyes welled up, wet with tears.

'Next summer, children! At the latest!' blustered Herr Helgers, breaking in. 'If there's a spring offensive like the one last year, the war'll be over in no time! So, tell us a bit about Russia, young man. It's not like you to be so withdrawn.'

'Leave him be, Father! Not on Christmas Eve, of all days, please!' Frau Helgers interjected.

'So, what about the Russian girls?' Eva teased him, sitting on the arm of his chair. 'Come on, tell me how many hearts you've already broken, you rascal! Who's prettier: the peasant girls in the Ukraine or Cherkessian girls? Or maybe the young Communist girls with their "free love", hmm? Maybe they're more to your taste?'

She playfully tugged the captain's ear. He turned red, like a schoolboy.

'Evi, please!' he stammered, half-indignant and half in embarrassment. 'I… I haven't… that is, I didn't… Besides, you've got quite the wrong impression. That stuff about "free love" is way off the mark! Russian girls are much shyer than German girls. They don't even know how to bat their eyelashes at a man!'

'Oho, so you tried it on, did you, you philanderer, and got the brush-off, eh?'

Saying this, she dug her sharp fingernails into the captain's ear lobe. His future father-in-law smiled knowingly at the captain from over his pince-nez.

'Come, come, my friend, that's not quite true now, is it? This entry here on Bolshevism's got some quite interesting things to say about love and marriage in the Soviet Union. I reckon I might have to chuck that particular volume away! Eva'll be having sleepless nights if she reads that.'

'Ach, that's all a load of nonsense!' muttered the captain indignantly. 'Believe me, I know what I'm talking about! Besides, there are no girls left in Stalingrad anyhow.'

Eva removed her hand from her fiancé's shoulder and sat up. A shadow flitted across her face.

'In Stalingrad?' she said in a flat tone of voice. 'I thought you said you weren't in Stalingrad any more!' Captain Gedig bit his lip.

'No, of course not,' he hastened to reassure her. 'We left there ages ago. I was just using it as an example.'

'When the war's over, they're going to have to rework the entry on Russia from top to bottom, in any event,' said the old man, still fixated on his pet subject of the encyclopaedia. 'It'll look quite a bit different then. The regional party leader here gave a talk recently about the plans for a New Order in the east. That was really fascinating, I can tell you! They're aiming to set up four great Imperial Commissariats. Ukraine and the Eastern Territories, they exist already, and in addition to those, there'll be the Caucasus and Russia. Moscow will be razed to the ground. It'll simply be wiped off the map.'

He'd stood up and walked over to the map on the wall, where a forest of little paper swastika flags marked the line of the front.

'That's probably the best way to go about things, too – cut out this running sore once and for all, root and branch! And then there's the Crimea; that's going to be made an integral part of the empire, a *Reichsgau*. Bet that surprised you, eh? Herr Ley's got plans to site a huge "Strength Through Joy" camp there!'

The captain found himself becoming increasingly angry at the smug, presumptuous and clueless complacency of their bourgeois outlook.

'I really wish,' he said, more vehemently than he intended, 'you could come to Russia one time and see things for yourself. Then you wouldn't get such stupid ideas in your heads! There are a hundred and eighty million people there who know exactly what they want, so you can't just go treating them like they're some negro tribe! At the very least they've got the right to self-determination. You need to win people's hearts and minds, not oppress them. But thus far we haven't made the slightest effort to make any friends there. And what's the upshot of that, I ask you? We're hated wherever we go, and we're forced to deal with passive resistance and a partisan movement that makes our lives more difficult by the day.'

'So, do you think the Russians are even capable of governing themselves?' the old man flared up. 'We've had plenty of opportunity to see what happens when you let them do that!'

'There you two go, at each other's throats again!' wailed Frau Helgers. 'Always the same old song. Just let it lie for once – you'll never agree.'

'Very well, whatever you say,' Bailiff Helgers mumbled appeasingly. 'But just explain one thing for me if you would, Werner. I'm not sure where to put my flag down here around Stalingrad any more.

Whereabouts does the front run now? One moment the Army High Command report mentions defensive battles in Stalingrad and then in the next breath talks about heavy fighting in the Don elbow… but that's a long way west of the city! What's going on?'

The captain shrugged his shoulders uneasily.

'Well, I don't know for certain myself,' he said finally. 'There appear to be some breaches in the front at places… you'd best leave this sector open until the situation becomes clearer.'

'I do think,' replied the old man, 'that the Wehrmacht reports ought to be more accurate. Confusing statements like that just put people on edge. Why, just the day before yesterday, Mother came back all in a tizz from the baker's, where someone had said that an entire army had been encircled at Stalingrad! People are very susceptible to such rubbish.'

'Turn the wireless on, would you, Eva dear?' Frau Helgers said. 'Maybe there's something sensible on by now. Goebbels will have stopped handing out Christmas presents to children.'

The radio was broadcasting the Christmas hook-up with German forces on various fronts. From the loudspeaker came the sounds of singing and accordion playing. Reporters at the fronts gave colourful accounts of how the troops were spending Christmas: on Crete, in Narvik and North Africa and on the high seas. The same happy festive mood came across from all these far-flung locations. But all of a sudden, the presenter announced in sombre tones:

'Attention, attention – we're now going over to Stalingrad!'

Then came the sound of someone talking. His voice sounded distant and muffled, like he was speaking from a cellar.

'There's no Christmas spirit or Christmas tree in evidence here. The only things lighting up the sky are the glow of flares and the flash of shell bursts. There's no lull or relief for the men here, just relentless, intense fighting that places an enormous strain on our hard-pressed troops…'

'That's quite enough of that, thank you – Eva, turn it off, would you please?' Frau Helgers said quietly. 'It's so awful. Those poor, poor men... Ah, this dreadful war! When will it ever end?'

Eva went up to her fiancé and took his head in her hands. Her eyes scanned his face intently.

'Tell me honestly, my love,' she implored him, 'you're not really going back to Stalingrad, are you?'

Captain Gedig gently removed her hands. He avoided looking directly at her.

'Absolutely not, Eva,' he replied tensely. 'I've already told you. Whatever gave you that idea?'

Eva Helgers and Werner Gedig stood on the station platform under the dim bluish light cast by a few cowled blackout lamps. Dressed in his flowing greatcoat and officer's peaked cap, he once more exuded the atmosphere of the front. The two of them remained silent. They still had much to talk about – so much, in fact, that words alone were not enough. Acting on a sudden whim, the captain felt in the inner pocket of his coat.

'It's just occurred to me... Here, Evi, take this cash. There's eight hundred marks there. I was going to pay it into the bank, but I forgot.'

Eva hesitantly took the banknotes.

'Why don't you take them with you?' she asked in surprise. 'You can pay the money into your account from there.'

'No, no, please just take the money... I might lose it.'

The train snorted its way into the station. Brakes screeched, doors slammed and the darkened platform was filled with rushing people.

'Werner,' the girl said, and her voice sounded strangely muted. 'Werner, I'm begging you, please don't lie to me... not now, just when we're about to part. You... you're going to Stalingrad, I know it!'

The captain took her hands in his. He said nothing. He gazed deep into her desperate eyes. The look he gave her was full of hurt. And of love. And of parting: a painful, painful parting. He bent down and tenderly kissed away two shining tears that had appeared on her cheeks. There was a sharp blast of a whistle, and the train began to pull slowly out of the station. The captain swung round, leaped up on to the running board and gave her one last wave.

'Werner!' the girl cried, her voice choked with tears, and she stretched out her hands to him. Then, whispering, she uttered his name once more before letting her arms drop, forlornly. The train rumbled off into the darkness.

'To Stalingrad,' she thought, and felt the blood surge to her heart. 'To Stalingrad – I'll never see him again.'

A figure tramps with long strides through the bright, moonlit night. The mammoth's footprints he leaves behind in the encrusted blanket of snow, from the heavy felt boots he is wearing, are instantly filled in again by the biting east wind. It assails the solitary traveller time and again, its incessant gusts tugging at his heavy overcoat and trapping it between his legs, and piercing his clothes and balaclava with its icy needle-jabs. The glimmer of the stars has been extinguished by the milky light of the moon, but an invisible star is guiding the traveller. The figure is Padre Peters. Behind him, he is dragging a little sled with equipment. He is making for the head of the remote gorge where the main field dressing station is located. Since the order came through that the wounded and sick could only be flown out with the express permission of the chief medical officer, field dressing stations and hospitals have become full to bursting. The number of men dying of cold and hunger grows by the day. But still the big transport planes, each of which can evacuate around thirty-five wounded, regularly return to the airfields they set out from with empty spaces. The padre has been working his way up the long gorge for several minutes now. He knows the way; he has been here many times before. But today he appears to have gone astray, despite it being almost as bright as day. Then, momentarily, a strip of light flashes somewhere off to the side. Ah, yes, there it is at last! That must be the mobile operating theatre. From the large vehicle, parked in a hollow excavated from the slope of the ravine as if in a garage, a medical NCO emerges and walks towards him. He is carrying a large pail, from which something naked and bloody is protruding, surrounded by stained bandages and torn scraps of uniform – a freshly amputated leg.

'Good evening to you, Padre,' the man greets him, his voice trembling from the cold. 'It's been all go here today again… what a great Christmas!'

Padre Peters climbs the steps up into the lorry, pulls aside the tarpaulin, and opens the wide door. For a few seconds, he's dazzled by the bright reflection of the creamy white walls inside. The acrid smell of disinfectant stings his nostrils. The head doctor, identifiable by the peaked cap he's wearing, is just completing the final stitches under the intense glare of the operating lamp.

'Evening all!' says the padre. 'You ought to signpost your dressing station better, doctor! It would have been a shame if I'd missed you today.'

'Signpost!' With a hollow laugh, the surgeon chokes back the reproach he was about to utter, and instead repeats the padre's word. 'That's all we need! So we can become even more overrun than we are now, eh? As it is, I've no idea how we'll ever manage to treat all these patients. The place is jam-packed. Fifteen to twenty deaths on the operating table and, if we're lucky, thirty to forty men evacuated is all we can get through in any one day – yet a hundred new patients show up daily! Day and night, it goes on. We're barely getting any sleep nowadays…'

He passes his surgical assistant the instruments and wipes his damp brow with the back of his hand.

'It's a bottomless pit, I tell you. It can't go on like this.'

His face is grey and haggard. The assistant drapes his fur jacket round his shoulders and goes outside, with the padre following.

In the middle of the gorge is a large marquee housing the wounded. It has not, as is customary elsewhere, been sunk into the ground as protection against the cold and flying shrapnel. The fierce wind is shaking at its canvas sides and blowing drifts of snow in through the gaps at the bottom. Inside lie the injured men, tightly packed together. Even the narrow passageways are crammed with stretchers. A little trench oven in the middle of the marquee is crackling away busily, but it only manages to warm those in its immediate vicinity. Two storm lanterns, hung from the tent poles, emit a guttering light that doesn't reach the far corners. Next to one of the lamps stands a construction of wooden battens roughly nailed together, which is meant to represent a Christmas tree. Three candle stubs are burning on it.

As Peters walks in, a few of the men lift their heads. A whisper goes around the tent: 'It's the padre, the padre!' – 'You see, didn't I tell you? I said he wouldn't forget about us on Christmas Eve!'

'Thanks for coming, Padre!'

'What news is there, Padre? Tell us! Is it true our tanks are still in Kalach?' In front of one of the lamps, Padre Peters hangs a colourful poster showing the infant Jesus in the manger. Next to it he sets up the record player he's brought with him. What should he say to the men? He knows how things stand.

'Let us put our faith in God,' he says solemnly. 'His Will be done!' Saying this, he sits down under one of the lamps and starts reading them the Christmas story. His voice, pure as freshly fallen snow, fills the tent. Silence descends. Only the steady, rambling delirium of a severely wounded soldier and the uneasy drone of aircraft overhead form a backdrop to words lost in the mists of time, but which now bring childhood memories flooding back:

> And she brought forth her firstborn son, and wrapped him
> in swaddling clothes, and laid him in a manger; because there
> was no room for them in the inn…

Silent tears run down grime-encrusted, frostbitten faces. For a few minutes, the men who are lying here in abject misery forget the pain, the hunger and the cold. And now from the gramophone comes the sound of Johann Sebastian Bach's Toccata and Fugue in D Minor. The soaring notes of the organ resonate around the marquee. The padre has put the loudest needle he can find on the playing arm to try to drown out the din of aircraft engines, which is increasing by the minute. Suddenly a roaring sound rushes through the air, and their hearts stop beating for several moments. *Wummmmp!* The earth shudders, the tent poles shake and the lamps flicker wildly. And once again – *ssischschsch… wummp!* That was a close one! And now the noise reaches a terrible crescendo of howling intensity. Bomb splinters tear and hum through the canvas at the top of the tent, which pitches and shakes like it's caught in the eye of a storm. There follow moments of fearful, helpless tension… then a collective sigh of relief. So, they've got away with it again! The aeroplane engines die away, and the powerful notes of the organ soar upwards in triumph. Padre Peters goes along the lines of wounded men. Here and there he squats down, asking questions and offering words of encouragement and consolation. An NCO who had had both of his feet amputated just the day before is keen to tell his story.

He stopped being a churchgoer many years ago, he confides, clutching the padre's hand in his frost-cramped hands. 'Thank you,' he stammers, 'thank you so much… for coming to visit us.' After a long pause, he begins again: 'The thing with me and religion, that's going to change after this war is over, let me tell you. My God, we've come to understand the value of it here, right enough. Maybe it's a lesson we could only learn here. And we've only come to appreciate the true meaning of home here, as well.'

The padre packs up his things and prepares to do his rounds of the bunkers. That's where the really seriously wounded have been put, the men with inoperable head and stomach injuries who will be dead by tomorrow or the next day, and finally relieved of the burden of human suffering. It's bitterly cold down in the bunkers. The medics can ill afford to waste the scarce fuel available, which is vital for sustaining the living, on those already marked for death. Under the gaze of their knowing eyes, the padre finds it impossible to offer any easy words of solace. He listens to the last wishes, and promises to convey the last greetings, of those who are still conscious and lucid – and there are many, very many of them – before joining them in prayer and giving them communion. The wine keeps threatening to freeze, so he warms the chalice in his hands. He cradles the head of a recruit from the last detachment of replacement troops in his hand as he offers him the Host and wine. He's still a boy, flung straight from school into this living hell. His body is swollen tight as a drum skin. Shrapnel from an exploding shell ripped through his abdominal wall. The beatific, omniscient smile he bestows on Peters renders the padre small and immeasurably humble.

'It's good that I don't have to go on the attack any more, Padre!'

For a moment, his shadowed, sunken eyes blaze in triumph. Then they grow large, and in a clear, cold, already unearthly voice, which only serves to remind the padre of his own mortality, the patient's waxen face joins the cleric in intoning the words of the Lord's Prayer:

'For thine is the kingdom, the power and the glory…'

Then veils fall over the young man's eyes; he goes rigid and his disfigured body weighs heavily in Padre Peters's arms… A short distance away from the marquee, a smaller tent has been erected. It is dark inside. The padre stumbles over men's bodies. He strikes a match – corpses! They're being stored here until the ground thaws again and is ready to claim what rightfully belongs to it. Peters is about to turn and go when a quiet voice from the corner says, 'Padre, please!'

The padre spins round and lights another match. In the corner, surrounded on all sides by cadavers, sits a slightly built little man, shivering with cold beneath multiple layers of coats and blankets. Stretched out in front of him is a heavily bandaged leg.

'Padre, please… a cigarette!'

Peters lights a candle stub and sits down by the solitary watchman over the dead.

'What are you doing here, then?' the padre asks.

The young man swallows nervously a couple of times before replying, 'I'm here because I… because of self-mutilation! But…' – by this stage he is almost shouting – 'it's not true. I didn't do it!'

'Now look here, lad,' the padre says earnestly. 'Today's Christmas. Think on that… and think of your mother. Don't lie, now. You shot yourself in the leg, didn't you?'

The young soldier looks fearfully at the padre; his mouth is half-open and his lips are trembling. And then his face crumples and he buries his head in his arm and starts weeping uncontrollably, whimpering and keening like a child. The padre gently strokes his hair.

'I can't take it any more!' the boy sobs. 'Can't go on like this… It's terrible… I don't want to die… I want to go home! Mum… oh, Mum!'

His halting speech dissolves once more into whimpering sobs. Abruptly, he lifts his head and brings his face up close to the padre's, his hand digging into his shoulder.

'They're going to shoot me, aren't they? They're going to shoot me!'

The padre feels an icy grip seize his heart. What should he say? Yes, that's what they're going to do…

'We're all in God's hands, my boy,' he answers. 'Everything that He does is for the good of mankind. None of know if we'll survive this ordeal. But we've been shown one certain way to escape all our suffering: the way to heaven.'

And the padre begins to pray with the physically and mentally damaged individual. The young man keeps staring at his lips, and he repeats the words haltingly. Does he know what he's promising?

The padre walks on through the night. From the battalion command post to the front line closest to the enemy is a distance of seven hundred metres. During the day it's impossible to traverse this area, which is as flat as a billiard table, because it's in the enemy's sights. But at night it's feasible. Just a single machine gun sends the odd staccato burst of fire over the open land. He finally makes it to the shelter of the trenches, and warms himself in the first of the bunkers. In the rough clay wall here, someone has hacked a hole, where a couple of logs are ablaze. The acrid smoke is unbearable. The men have had to crouch down close to the floor just in order to breathe. On the wall, cut from a piece of green tarpaulin, is the silhouette of a Christmas tree. The gramophone is cranked up and from it comes the sound of the Dresdner Kreuzchor singing German Christmas carols. The padre squats in front of the fire and opens a book. His eyes are watering from the thick smoke, and large embers fall on the pages. He reads them Selma Lagerlöf's *Legends of Christ*.* The men's eyes shine white in their soot-blackened faces.

After that he goes and stands outside in the trench next to the sentry manning the machine gun. Quiet singing drifts up out of the bunker. The sentry keeps his eyes fixed ahead, looking across the snowfield at the Russian trenches. The padre shivers.

'Brrr, it's cold!' he says. 'When will you be relieved?'

'In two hours,' the man replies, without looking round. Then, after a longish pause, he continues: 'I volunteered for this watch, you know,' before adding, almost in a whisper, 'I can't celebrate Christmas any more. As far as I'm concerned, God died outside Stalingrad.'

The padre says nothing. The Russian machine gunner opens up again. A star shell briefly bathes the scene in a brilliant white glare. Finally, Peters gives his response: 'You're right, God did die outside Stalingrad... a thousand times over. He suffered every one of our sufferings and died every death with us – and it's outside Stalingrad that He will rise again.'

Now it's late at night. Padre Peters is sitting in his own bunker again, writing letters to the relatives of the wounded and dead by the light of a candle stump. He racks his brain for simple, humane

---

* Selma Lagerlöf (1858–1940) was a Swedish writer and the first woman to win the Nobel Prize in Literature (1909). Her short-story collection *Kristuslegender* was published in 1904.

expressions of solace. But his mind keeps wandering from the task in hand. There was that order issued during the early days of the war, for instance, that prohibited army padres from writing to families about the fate of their men, their fathers and sons, unless it was their express wish that their loved ones should be informed. Peters smiles bitterly. Strictly speaking, then, what he ought to have said to the dying boy in the marquee was: 'Listen, you're going to die soon. If you want me to send your old mum one final word of greeting from your deathbed, you have to give me specific instructions to that effect.' Peters struggles to decide whether that order was born of bureaucratic stupidity or satanic wickedness.

And once more he picks up the secret decree that came to him a few days ago. It is a list of the names of military chaplains who have violated the military code 'regarding distributing books, writing to relatives, etc'. To deter others, notice is given of the severe punishments meted out to them for such transgressions.

'No,' the padre says out loud, 'I won't be banned from being a Christian or living my life in a Christian way! And if they punish me for it, that will be the cross I have to bear!'

Christmas 1942. His pen glides over the paper. Peters's hand shakes; the incredible stress of the day just past threatens to overwhelm him. He finds it hard to order his thoughts. He thinks of the doctors who have come to see their life-saving occupation as a mere manual skill in which their hearts play no part. And the thought fills him with a nightmarish dread. Is that happening to you now, as well? Faced with all this appalling suffering, are you growing a thicker skin? Fervently, from the bottom of his heart, he starts to pray:

'Dear Lord, support me in my frailty! May Your spirit light my way and fortify me! God, give me strength!'

On the second day of Christmas, quite unexpectedly, the mail turned up after all. A handful of letters buried under a mountain of newspapers. Corporal Herbert, who was tasked with sorting through the pile, pushed over to Breuer an envelope the size of a cigarette packet, almost a quarter of which was covered with a blue airmail sticker. The lieutenant recognized the spidery child's handwriting of his elder son, who had been attending school for a year now. With a smile, he unfolded the little sheet of children's writing paper and read:

DEAR DADDY

Lots of happiness and blessings to you at Christmas. I like going to school. Our teacher's name is Herr Kräkel. I haven't been given the cane or the slipper. So that you can be happy too in Russia, I am sending you a picture. I painted it for you myself with love. Mummy says you are coming home on leave soon. Hannes is still too stupid to understand, but I get very scared sometimes. Hello from,

JOCHEN

Breuer put down the letter and picked up the drawing, which had slipped out of the envelope on to the table. Drawn in crayon, it showed a collection of wonky little houses, green trees with crowns like balls of cotton wool and a brown path, and looming above all this a yellow church with barred windows and a huge tower. Above this church, a red sun with broad yellow beams radiating from it was just about to be swallowed by a thick grey cloud. But, as if by some miracle, a second, even larger sun still shone down on the small houses.

Breuer folded the drawing and placed it carefully inside his pay-book.

'You're quite right, my boy,' he thought to himself, moved by what he'd seen. 'One sun really isn't enough to illuminate this gloomy old world of ours.'

Lakosch received a letter too. When he caught sight of the envelope, he turned as white as a sheet. The letter was from his mother. She was writing to him for the first time since that massive bust-up, years ago. He stood up and left the bunker. Out in the open, he tore open the envelope. The frost made his eyes water as he struggled to decipher the crooked lines painstakingly scrawled by an unpractised hand on a sheet of graph paper.

DEAR SON

I got your letters and your money safely. You wrote that you are in Stalingrad, and Frau Ebertsche told me that you're encircled there and will probably all die, so now maybe you'll see at last that your late father was right, and understand who's really to blame for all of this. And now that you're having to learn this at first hand, perhaps it'll set you back on the right track. This is your mother telling you this, and I know that when you read it you'll feel like murdering me like you did your father. But I don't care, I'm an old woman, and so many young people are dying right now. The Müllers' eldest has been killed in North Africa, and Frieda Kalubzig's lost her right hand at the factory. Life's just too hard and my back's given up the ghost too. They came and took your old suit for the rag-and-bone collection yesterday. Erna says hello, she can't write herself, she's going out with a sergeant from a flak battery now. Try to make it back in one piece if you can. All the best, dear Karl, from your Mother.

Lakosch's small hands were turning blue from the cold, and the wind was driving stinging ice crystals into his face, but he didn't notice. He couldn't tear his eyes away from the lines on the paper, which brought back a powerful surge of past memories.

That afternoon, Breuer and Wiese found themselves alone in the bunker. Sonderführer Fröhlich had sought leave to go and visit the quartermaster, Captain Siebel, in one of the neighbouring gorges, and the men were off doing the rounds of their comrades in their foxholes nearby to wish them season's greetings. Breuer was leafing through one of the newspapers that had just come, while Lieutenant Wiese was reading a small volume of poetry. The Christmas wreath was still hanging from the ceiling, though all the shine had faded from the candles.

'That was a fine speech you gave on Christmas Eve, Breuer,' Wiese said without warning. He put his book down and looked at the first lieutenant.

'How on earth did you ever become a National Socialist?'

Breuer looked up at him, taken aback by his tone.

'I mean,' Wiese explained, 'anyone who really believes in Christmas can't possibly be a National Socialist.'

Breuer was visibly rattled by this ambush. To buy himself time, he deliberately made a meal out of cutting and lighting one of the Christmas cigars before replying.

'I don't understand you, Wiese. What's National Socialism got to do with Christmas? Christmas, well… it's the fixed point in the onward rush of time. It's an opportunity for quiet contemplation and reflection. It's precisely at Christmas that I'm reminded how much of a Christian I am, despite the fact that I don't go to church every Sunday. That all has to do with faith, and with your outlook on the world, not with politics. The NSDAP is a political party. I don't see how the two things can't coexist.' Wiese smiled sceptically at this; irritated, Breuer went on, now speaking even faster.

'How did I become a National Socialist? Well, after the thirtieth of January 1933, when I realized Hitler wasn't only a superb propagandist but a statesman of real stature too, I joined the party, as one of the "March hares",* so to speak. It seemed to me fate had

---

* 'March Hares' – a disparaging term (German: *Märzhasen*) used by old Nazis who had been in the party since its inception in the early 1920s to refer to new party members who rushed to join after Hitler's accession to power in early 1933.

brought us the NSDAP to free us from the shackles of the Versailles treaty and to create a Greater Germany once more. And it achieved that, too, without any bloodshed. So that's why I'm a National Socialist, see – and a staunch one at that.'

'No, you're not, Breuer, not really,' said Wiese, still training his unsettling gaze on the first lieutenant. 'Not nowadays, anyhow. The thing is, National Socialism wasn't content with being just a political party. It wanted to become a "movement": a world view that reached into every aspect of the way people lived their lives. Are you really telling me that's somehow passed you by, Breuer? Or saying that they haven't come round to check on where you hang your portrait of Hitler… or "suggested" that you take out a subscription to the party newspaper? Haven't you been lectured about "God" being simply the law of cause and effect, and urgently advised to turn your back on the Church? Has nobody ever interfered in your family's private business or the way you bring up your children? Or tried to make you hate other peoples, or swallow that arrogant shit about the superiority of your own race, or preached you the gospel of brute force?

'But let's assume, shall we, that you really haven't noticed all this and that you've been jogging along quite happily in the belief that you're free to think what you like. You wouldn't be the only one. Plenty of others fancied that by giving up their Sundays to go out campaigning with the Brownshirts, they'd buy themselves a free pass for the rest of the time, and failed to notice how the poison kept on drip-dripping into every other bit of their lives all the same and how, little by little, they were turning into different people.'

Breuer had let his cigar go out. He knew that there were hidden, securely sealed corners of his psyche full of dangerously incendiary frustration and dissatisfaction at what had been going on over the past few years. Even he was deeply alarmed whenever he found his thoughts straying towards these explosive no-go areas, yet here, to his mounting horror, came someone riding at full tilt towards them, intent on breaking down all barriers.

'Come, come, Wiese, you're exaggerating,' he said with calculatedly cool disapproval. 'It isn't as bad as all that! Okay, certain things could be better; I'll concede you may have a point there. There are a few crazies out there who overstep the mark, for sure. Those things you mention are either the last hangovers from the time when the party was fighting to establish itself, or exceptions, or isolated instances…'

As he spoke, he recalled with unease that, not so long ago, someone had tried to assuage him using almost exactly the same words.

'Remember, wherever there's light, there's also shadow,' he continued. 'But now's not the time to be troubling ourselves with this. It only undermines our ability to resist. We should be thinking instead about all the greatness the Führer has brought us in just a few years: we're a unified nation, an empire of all the Germans, which provides its people with work and puts bread in their mouths. We're the envy of the world! And it's appalling that all this is being jeopardized by this war, which no German wanted, that's for sure. It's a terrible thought that this war might never be won if everything comes unstuck here in Stalingrad.'

'You're right there, Breuer,' replied the lieutenant. 'It can't be won. And what's more it *mustn't* be won!'

First Lieutenant Breuer sat bolt upright; the cigar dropped from his hand. He felt a cold and clammy sensation clutching at his heart.

'Mustn't…? What are you saying?' he stammered. 'Just think for a moment what you're saying, man! You… You can't be serious!'

'I mean it. It's vital that Germany doesn't triumph in this war.' Wiese repeated, unperturbed. 'Have you any idea what'll happen if this war ends with the victory on Hitler's terms? Then he'll have unlimited power. He won't have to hide his true intentions from anyone after that. He can tear aside the last flimsy mask that's still barely concealing the grinning face of Satan! I'm telling you, then the world will witness a spectacle that will make Nero's ravings seem like mere child's play in comparison. Lawlessness and immorality on a grand scale... selective racial breeding like we're on a stud farm... absolute respect for force and brutality and exploitation of the weak as the overriding principle! Entire peoples will be exterminated or condemned to slavery just because they don't have blond hair and their skin isn't white. And what will become of our Germany, the "nation of poets and thinkers", the embodiment of rectitude and legality? They'll turn us into a nation of barbarians: a horde of rapacious savages, freeloaders and parasites! We're halfway there already. Can't you see that we're all being turned into animals by this war – a war, let me remind you, that *we* started?'

Painfully aware of his inability to contradict Wiese's audacious logic, Breuer was seized with rage.

'I feel I don't know you any more, Wiese,' he said finally, fighting to maintain an appearance of calm. 'The monstrous things that are coming out of your mouth... the German people aren't just anybody! The German people and you and me and countless others, all human beings like us... Take our Dierk, for instance. He's a thoroughly decent young man with a passionate enthusiasm for the cause. Do you think for one moment that he could ever fight for something he knew to be wrong? Germany's made up of people like him! In those circumstances, how could the appalling picture you paint of the future ever come to pass? And besides, do you imagine the Führer would ever allow such a thing? He's got a firmer grip on power than anyone in history. And you're saying he can't bring to heel the handful of animals that any mass movement inevitably washes to the surface? No, don't go shaking your head at that, Wiese! When all's said and done, the Führer is just a human being too, I know it for a fact. He has his faults, and can make mistakes like the rest of us. But the sufferings of this war will be a process of cleansing by fire for him, just as it will for our entire nation. We'll come out of it purer and wiser.'

'Hitler!' the lieutenant guffawed bitterly. 'Propaganda sets him up as this great, unapproachable graven image! All you see in him is a man who loves children, a warm-hearted public orator overflowing with love for his people. Try seeing him how he really is just for once! How does he appear then? Nothing but the product of one long string of crafty lies and extreme violence! First off, he breaks the Concordat with the Catholic Church. Then he gives a solemn pledge to respect the sovereignty of Czechoslovakia minus the Sudetenland – and promptly proceeds to invade and annex it. The Naval Treaty he signs with Britain – terminated because of German violations! The ten-year Non-Aggression Pact with Poland – broken! The pact with Stalin – shamefully violated! In the Night of the Long Knives in '34, he murders his political opponents, including some of his oldest comrades-in-arms – simply slaughtered with no judicial process! Then he goes and signs a truce with the Church for the duration of the war, to great applause and fanfares! And what happens? Before you know it, the concentration camps and gaols are full of priests, the monasteries plundered and dispossessed! Here, have a read of this: it came first thing this morning. It's a letter from my cousin in Eibingen – she's a nun in the St Hildegard Convent there. Within the space of two hours, they'd turned all the sisters out onto the street and only let them pack small suitcases with personal belongings. Everything else was stolen, and the convent turned into a Nazi training college. Go ahead, read it! That's Hitler for you! Anyone who hasn't been cretinized by propaganda, anyone with eyes to see, can see him for what he is. But for many people nowadays, this man isn't a person any more, no; they worship him as a god, as a second Christ, this—'

'That's enough!' shouted Breuer, leaping to his feet. All his self-control was gone. 'You're forgetting yourself! You can insult who you like, but leave Hitler out of it! The Führer is far too important a figure to be touched by your pathetic criticism! I won't stand for it, Wiese, do you hear? I won't stand for it!'

When he gave his reply, Wiese's voice sounded quite calm again, almost sad.

'Fine, you get on your high horse if you want, Breuer. You're only doing it because you know I'm telling the truth. It's become crystal clear to me over the past few weeks here what the score is, so I have to call it as I see it. We're not in Germany any more, in our nice, comfortable, peaceful bourgeois world, where there's all sorts of ways of dodging unpalatable truths. We're in a life-and-death situation here. We could all be wiped out tomorrow. There's a premium on truth in such circumstances. You speak of Hitler's successes. They've all been achieved through deceit and foul play. The German people aren't any happier as a result. All that's happened is that they've lost their sense of decency and honesty and sacrificed their good name. And what kind of successes were they anyway? Smoke and mirrors, nothing more. Promises of jam tomorrow! And now we're picking up the tab for them with rivers of blood and tears. War, that was the answer to everything where National Socialism was concerned. The fact that we're sitting here today up to our necks in shit is the clear and logical result of Nazi policies and ideology. And not just us, either, the whole of Germany's in the same predicament – surrounded by enemies who want us dead. The whole world's at war with us and hates us as the worst enemy of humanity!'

'So knowing that,' said Breuer, shocked, 'how can you say that you want Germany to lose this war? No, Wiese, you can't mean that!'

'I know what you're going to say,' answered the lieutenant. 'That the consequences of losing the war will be dreadful. The Allies will make us pay a terrible price, so bad even our children and grand-children will still be paying it. But there's no other way. Our people won't be cleansed by fire by winning this war, only by losing it, with all that that entails. Only through that most awful of experiences will they come to realize the disastrous consequences of taking the wrong path, and rediscover how to behave decently and honestly. I hope with all my heart that the German nation will be able to save its soul from these darkest of times, but this is the only way I see that happening.'

Breuer was more moved than he was prepared to admit by his comrade's profound sincerity. After a while, he spoke again. 'I think we should leave things where they are, Wiese. I know that you're a fundamentally decent person. You only want the best for your country. But the things you've just said are completely beyond the pale for a German, and still more so for a German officer! Just tell me one thing, if you will: if you really and truly believe everything you've said, how can you still wear the Wehrmacht uniform with the symbol of the Reich on your chest? How can you even bring yourself to fight in this war?'

A look of dismay crossed the young officer's face. He groped about for the right words. 'That's a question,' he said at length, 'that I ask myself over and over. You're absolutely right: I oughtn't to be fighting this war any longer. But...,' he gave a tortured smile, 'which of us is ever totally consistent? Life demands so many concessions from us – and, you see, I'm a believer in divine guidance. Fate has been kind to me so far. Over three years of fighting, I haven't been called upon to shoot another person. And I'm determined that I won't ever point a gun at anyone for the duration of this war – even if it costs me my life. But let's draw a line under this conversation. It's all so remote from what we're up against now. We're all in the same predicament here, so it's vital we stick together. I'd hate to think this discussion of ours might cast a shadow over our friendship. It won't, will it, Breuer? Please say you're not angry with me.'

Giving Breuer a look of friendly candour, he proffered his hand. Breuer shook it with genuine warmth and sincerity.

As evening fell, the men returned in dribs and drabs to the bunker. Fröhlich was in buoyant mood.

'That lot over in the quartermaster's section,' he announced, 'are living the life of Riley – their mess is groaning with food! You name it: buckwheat blinis with ersatz honey, proper coffee, and a fantastic cognac... By the by, I spoke to Namarov as well, the Cossack leader. He's from Sevastopol, an officer in the sappers. A really nice bloke!

Hasn't got any time whatsoever for Bolshevism – you should hear him! Not bothered in the slightest about being bottled up here. And he's a real fan of Germany. He sent Captain Siebel Christmas greetings with a note praising the "German talent for organization" and saying how the camaraderie between officers and men in the Wehrmacht will ensure us victory! Yeah, that's what it's come to now, when a Russian has to bolster our faith in the unshakeable power of the German military, while there's people in our own ranks who don't believe we can win.'

Fröhlich cast a reproachful eye around his comrades. He was puffed up with self-importance after his encounter.

'Captain Siebel's convinced there's going to be another relief operation soon. The army's chief quartermaster told him that some major preparations were afoot. Apparently huge tank formations are assembling in Morosovskaya. What's more, Captain Siebel reckons we can easily hold out to the spring if need be, given the current weakness of the Russian forces.'

While all this was going on, Herbert had arrived with the latest batch of dispatches from the divisional office. Breuer glanced through the pile. 'Aha!' he exclaimed. 'It's our regular dose of pick-me-ups from the Corps! Let's see what gripping stuff they've got to report today… Three more German prisoners bestially murdered by the Russians; I'd love to know where they claim to have discovered the bodies… The Russians have deployed a Kazakh division on the northwestern sector of the front; they're all illiterate – apparently that's a sure sign the Soviets are running out of fighting men. I see, how interesting! A medical company has destroyed twelve Russian tanks with Teller mines,* a heroic instance of the German will to fight triumphing against all odds, which should be held up as an example to the fighting units… hmm: Oh, get this, this is a good one:

---

* Teller mines were German anti-tank mines commonly used in the Second World War. Their name derives from the German word *Teller* meaning 'dinner plate', a reference to their shape.

On 22.12, two Russian deserters appeared in the sector of a division on the southern front of the Cauldron. They explained that they were well aware that German forces were encircled, but that the rations and treatment on the Russian side were so bad and the outlook for Russia in the war so hopeless that they preferred to desert.

'You see!' cried Fröhlich triumphantly. 'That's what I'm always saying!' A chorus of derisive laughter silenced him. Offended, he slunk away to sulk in the corner.

'And here's another,' continued Breuer. 'This one's not bad either.'

A sergeant and a private, both members of a motorized division, who spent over a week undetected behind enemy lines, have returned with some valuable intelligence. Among other things, they claim that the Russian forces encircling the Cauldron are actually very weak. According to them, there is a palpable shortage of tanks and heavy weapons, and the Russian soldiers' morale is poor. Complaints about war-weariness and inadequate food are rife. These two brave men were personally decorated by the commanding general.

'So, what do you say to that?'

'There is just one thing, First Lieutenant, sir,' Corporal Herbert piped up. 'How do they explain how those two managed to chat with the Russian troops over there about all this stuff?'

'I've no intention of passing on any of this crap to the men,' Breuer told Herbert by way of reply. 'As far as I'm concerned, you can cut up all this bumph right now for bog paper! Just don't go using it right outside the entrance to the bunker, d'you hear, Lakosch?'

And with that, the men of the Intelligence Section got down to the humdrum business of everyday life in the Cauldron once more.

4

Faint Outlines in the Fog

EVER MORE FREQUENTLY, SPELLS of unrelenting gloom with flurries of snow were beginning to alternate with the clear, silent, frosty days of the depths of winter. On days like these, the Russian morning dawned in a riot of colour like virtually nowhere else. In the east stood a deep-violet wall of cloud. Above it, in the most delicate shade of sea-green, a narrow band of the clear vault of heaven gradually appeared as the sun rose; the shafts of light it radiated danced in the bright white smoke wafting up from the bunkers, made the myriad ice crystals of the snowfield sparkle and glitter like diamonds, and finally spilled out like a string of tiny purple lanterns across the endless white expanse of snow, where it seemed the fleeting wave pattern of a gentle sea swell had taken on a frozen permanence. The soldiers trapped in the Cauldron watched awestruck as these beautiful mirages played out over the pitiless icy wasteland, as if in mockery of their plight – a spectacle of frozen splendour concealing death a thousand times over. This cruel play of nature seemed positively to encourage that self-deception, that mystical faith in miracles to which the men abandoned themselves ever more freely the more hopeless and desperate their situation became. The military leadership, in deference to the official line of optimism, kept stoking this belief in miracles despite knowing better, until they too fell prey to their own delusion. No one wanted to recognize the truth any more, so they simply refused to see it. Like a person freezing to death who knows full well he is in the grip of an icy demise yet who persists in entertaining paralysing fantasies of good fortune, so the three hundred thousand – emaciated, gnawed at by the cold, betrayed and abandoned – grew drunk on fanciful overestimates of their own might and options and clung on in the hope that the magician of Berchtesgaden might perform new signs and wonders. A spectral otherworld of dazzling dreams, hopes and wishes settled over the grisly reality of Stalingrad, sapping everyone's vitality.

One of those who did not fall victim to this dream world was Lance Corporal Lakosch. The experiences of the past few weeks had rained down on him like an artillery barrage, destroying the edifice that his upbringing and propaganda had built within him. Yet beneath the ruins of this structure something long suppressed was now stirring, impelling him to action.

In the days following Christmas, another link to his former life had been severed. His beloved little Volkswagen, his faithful companion through the long, arduous years of war, finally gave up the ghost. On the orders of the NCO in charge of the motor pool, Lakosch had taken it to the division's workshops, where they'd promised to get it back to him within three weeks. Lakosch knew only too well what that meant. Three weeks… who could say what might have happened within three weeks? He was sure he was saying goodbye to his car for good. Sunk in melancholy, he trudged his way back through the *balka*. The snow crunched and squeaked beneath his feet, and behind him the hissing sound of welding and the thumping and hammering noises from the workshop gradually died away. From a cloudless sky, a feeble sun cast its rays across the shimmering snow and threw blue wedges of shade into the jagged-sided gorge. Thin ribbons of smoke snaked up from the black oven chimneys on top of the bunkers. Ragged Romanians were shovelling soil into the reddish-brown bomb craters that pockmarked the road. A group of heavily muffled German infantrymen were jostling and stamping their feet in dirty grey puddles around a steaming field kitchen. Outside a bunker entrance curtained with sacking, a soldier was hastily shovelling snow into various cooking utensils. As Lakosch passed by, he lifted his head.

'Hey, Karl! What brings you here, mate?'

Lakosch stopped in his tracks. He knew that voice! He peered over towards the speaker. Yes, indeed, it really was him – Seliger, the old mess orderly.

'Well, blow me down,' said Lakosch in a deadpan voice, 'and there was me thinking you were a goner.'

Seliger came over to the little driver, swinging the clanking cooking pots.

'Oh, you think so!' he laughed. 'No way, old son, you know what they say – "bad weeds grow tall"! Come inside for a bit, why don't you! It's cold enough to freeze the balls off a brass monkey out here.'

Lakosch hesitated, but Seliger took him by the arm and steered him towards the bunker.

'We've got a bottle on the go! Our CO's off somewhere and won't be back for another couple of hours. I'm Captain Korn's batman for the time being here, see, while I recuperate.'

Down in the cramped, frowsty bunker, he produced a bottle of vodka from underneath a camp bed and placed two mugs on the table. Lakosch's gaze wandered to the Iron Cross ribbon that shone spick and span from Seliger's tattered battledress jacket. His thoughts were still on his car.

'How's things with you, then?' he enquired somewhat indifferently. 'At ours they told us you'd bought it.'

Seliger looked at him in amazement. He was clearly put out.

'Don't you know anything, mate? Me and Harras gave the Russians a run for their money! Haven't you read about us in dispatches, then?'

'What! – that was you?' exclaimed Lakosch, suddenly shaken from his torpor. 'You're the two who went roaming around behind Russian lines? Come on then, spill the beans!'

Seliger was duly assuaged, so he didn't need much prompting to start telling his story. Boy, oh boy – all the things they'd seen and done! After their way back had been cut off by a Russian reconnaissance unit, they'd taken their courage in their hands and decided to work their way through enemy lines. They'd spent two nights hiding in an abandoned bunker. Then, under cover of darkness, they'd nicked bread and jam from a food truck, killed two lone Russian sentries, taken their coats and weapons, and thus equipped had moved undetected through villages and Red Army encampments. Lakosch, who had started by interposing questions now and then, had grown increasingly quiet. He knew Seliger of old: all mouth and trousers! And here he was trying to tell him… what tosh!

'You know what?' he said at length, interrupting the torrent of words issuing from Seliger, who by now was noticeably a bit tipsy, 'You can tell that to the Marines! You reckon you can pull a fast one on me after just a little tot of vodka, eh? I could believe it of old Lissnup, maybe… but you, of all people? You shit your pants at the slightest bang!'

Seliger swallowed a couple of times. His bragging bonhomie instantly switched to angry resentment. The drink was clearly disagreeing with him; his eyes were already looking glazed.

'You just watch it!' he slurred indignantly. 'You won' b'lieve me, but iss okay comin' from the bloody high-and-mighty sar'nt-major, yeah? Course, no one believes the li-little private, right! But ol' Lissnup – he can tell you anything he likes, that puffed-up sack of shit! I tell you, over there, he was sucking up to me like there was no tomorrow – yeah, Seliger here, his dear old comrade Seliger! And now he won't even look me in the eye, the pig.' He gave a loud belch. 'But I'm telling you, sunshine, if I ever spill the beans, he's finished… finished, d'you hear!'

Lakosch pricked up his ears. The whole business was starting to smell a bit fishy. 'Hey, hey,' he said, trying to mollify the orderly, 'what have you got against him, then? I thought you and him were thick as thieves after your escapades? You're a big noise now!'

'Big noise – what shit!'

Seliger slammed his fist down on the table.

'The only big noise round here is Lissnup – made him a lieutenant with the Iron Cross First Class! And what do I get? This scrap of ribbon here!' He slapped his chest. 'So I can just sit here in this bunker and die!'

'You're off your head!' said Lakosch. 'If things go wrong here, we're all done for, every man jack of us. Do you think they'll make some exception in your case?'

'Yes, that's exactly what I thought! D'ya think I'd have bothered coming back otherwise? I didn't... I didn't need to... But he wouldn't let up, the bastard! Kept going on about being flown out to the Führer's HQ, and about the home leave we'd get and so on. What an idiot I've been! Karl, I'm an i-idiot!'

Unsteadily, he got to his feet, propped himself against the table and put his arm round Lakosch's shoulders. His face puckered into a tearful grimace.

'Karl, tell me that I'm an idiot!'

'Yeah, yeah, you're an idiot,' Lakosch replied impatiently. 'But what makes you realize that now all of a sudden?'

Seliger downed another slug of vodka. He was sobbing uncontrollably now, overcome by emotion and world-weariness.

'Karl, you – you've always been my mate, you've al... always understood me. I'll tell you why I'm an idiot. I wan' – I wanna – hic! – confess something to you... the last request of a – hic! – dying man. When I'm six feet under, I want you to avenge me... take revenge for me against that bastard, that piece of crap... promise me that.'

'Yeah, yeah, right you are! Just get on with it!'

Seliger stared vacantly, his eyes wandering. The emotional picture he'd conjured up of his tragic end had sidetracked him. He started to sing: 'When I'm go–o–ne put roses on my gra–a–a–ve…'

Spittle ran down his chin; this particular hero didn't exactly cut an inspiring figure. His hand groped for the bottle. Lakosch grabbed the drunk Seliger by the shoulders and shook him. 'Come on, mate, your last request! Tell me!'

Seliger's head lolled to and fro, and his eyes were closed.

'My laaa – My lasht requesch,' he mumbled, 'you, you've always been… roses on my…'

His head slumped forward, his hair flopped over his forehead and his slurred babble turned into a wheezing snore. He'd checked out. In vain, Lakosch tried to rouse him once more, but eventually gave up. Disgruntled, he set off home again, but not before pocketing a couple of cigars he spotted lying on a bench next to the camp bed. When the captain returned, his esteemed batman would have quite some explaining to do about the vodka. A couple of cigars here or there wouldn't make much odds.

The command bunker at the Eighth Corps was thick with smoke. A group of some ten to fifteen officers, belonging to the General Staff for the most part, had assembled here. No one knew the reason for this meeting, which the Army High Command had scheduled for the morning of the thirtieth of December. It must be something extraordinary. Colonel von Hermann, the only divisional commander among COs from various corps headquarters, had already speculated on what it might be about during the drive here with Unold. He reckoned it could only concern the new plan for a breakout, rumours of which had even reached his isolated position at Dubininsky. This conjecture of his, shared by several others, was all but confirmed by what the commander of the Fifty-First Corps had to report about the eastern front of the Cauldron. Everything had been made ready there, he told them, with sectors clearly demarcated and daily objectives set. The balloon was due to go up on the third!

'It's very simple,' the Fifty-First's commander reassured them in response to the storm of questions that ensued. 'In the north and east, we'll disengage ourselves from the enemy gradually, while on the other parts of the front we'll punch our way forward. In this way, the whole Cauldron will slowly start slipping – like a jellyfish, don't you know! A kind of mobile Cauldron. And we'll steadily move with it, heading for home.'

'Mobile Cauldron, Mobile Cauldron,' cantankerously muttered the only general present – an old corps commander with a head like a tiger – as he cast a disparaging eye around the walls of the new command bunker, which a pioneer company had only just completed after weeks of work. 'Has the High Command approved this bloody nonsense, then?'

'That's what we're about to find out, General!'

From outside came the sound of a car drawing up and the engine being switched off, and in the doorway there suddenly appeared – very tall and thin, with a slight stoop and clearly somewhat hesitant in his movements – General Paulus, Supreme Commander of the Sixth Army. The room fell silent, as the officers stood to attention. For a moment, their eyes rested on the general's refined, ethereal features, which seemed somehow out of keeping with his uniform, appearing more at home above a lectern or in an academic's study. This was the man who held all of their fates in his hand. Yet as each of them in turn stepped forward to shake this hand, which was proffered listlessly and limply, he was confronted anew with a realization that had been weighing down on the Sixth Army for some time now, like a nightmare – namely that he was not a rock that one could cling to in these desperate times. Embarrassed and not without a certain shameful feeling of pity, the officers averted their gaze from his face, once so handsome but now scarred by deep furrows and disfigured by a constant nervous twitching and blinking; and, as if drawn by some secret magic, lighted instead upon a large pair of steel-blue eyes spraying out their cold fire from behind the sloping shoulders of the supreme commander. These piercing, domineering eyes, the striking centrepiece of an energetic face beneath hair that had already greyed, belonged to the man who had entered the bunker at the same time as the general – General Arthur Schmidt, Chief of the Sixth Army's General Staff.

'Please, gentlemen, let's take a seat,' Paulus invited the officers in his muted, mellifluous voice. They took their places at a long table piled with dossiers and maps.

'It's a serious, a very serious matter that has prompted us to summon you here. The High Command has... It's a matter of... Schmidt, perhaps you'd better explain the situation.'

Schmidt did not acknowledge this invitation with so much as a flicker of his eyelids. While Paulus bowed his head, looked at his folded hands and lapsed into silence and reverie, Schmidt's compelling gaze spoke an altogether more unequivocal language. This look, which had a dangerous gleam about it, said clearly: 'Look at *me* – I am the Sixth Army!'

General Schmidt began speaking. In terse sentences, laden with imperatives, he set forth the situation they were in once more – one that could not, for the time being, count on any outside assistance. The play of light in his strange blue eyes, which he somehow contrived to make flash in a constant variety of ways, held those attending the meeting in thrall. Even Unold, for whom this was nothing new, found himself – much to his annoyance – falling again for this deception. Adopting the cool and attentive expression of the professionally interested listener, he pretended to follow Schmidt's address, but his thoughts wandered. He knew Schmidt from the days when he'd been an officer cadet, and he loathed the man with every fibre of his being. He hated everything about him: the exaggerated elegance of the pampered bachelor, his ostentatious fitness, and his whole paradoxical nature, in which an above-average intelligence was coupled with an utterly shameless deceitfulness, personable amiability could quite unexpectedly switch to cutting chilliness, and a self-indulgent capriciousness could co-exist with a pitiless severity towards others. 'That smarmy fucker!' Unold would spit in his bunker whenever the general, for the umpteenth time, had countermanded one of his orders. 'Careerist poser! How that peacock loves to display his feathers!' Among friends, he referred to Schmidt simply as 'Lying Arthur'. Yet, time and time again, this loathing would collapse into impotent acquiescence whenever he came face to face with Schmidt. The simple truth was that Unold hated the man because he admired him. It was the hatred of unfulfilled love for an unattainable idol. In General Schmidt, fate's spoilt golden boy, whose every move (at least on a personal level) met with success, Unold saw embodied something of the Nietzschean 'superman', such as he yearned to be. Hadn't Schmidt told him only recently about a compensation claim of seventy-five thousand Reichsmarks that he'd submitted for a bombed-out bachelor pad he owned – and that he'd duly been granted it? 'Bear in mind the wine cellar I had there!' he'd said laughingly when he saw the stunned expression on Unold's face.

Wait, what was that he just said? The lieutenant colonel was brought back to reality with a bump.

'So you see,' General Schmidt was saying, 'we need infantry reserves. We requested that fresh forces be dispatched to us by air in good time. But by the middle of this month, High Command had already turned us down. Insufficient transport capacity. Even then we were forced to draw on reserves that we cobbled together from our logistics and staff units, and so on...'

Damn and blast, that didn't sound like planning for a breakout! A ripple of unease passed through the room. Unold's suddenly alert gaze lighted upon the divisional commander, who was sitting next to him. Colonel von Hermann had turned pale, and could feel the blood pulsing through his veins right to his fingertips. The news had hit him like an electric shock. So, the High Command had recommended the 'combing out' – for which read 'winding up' – of all the non-front-line occupations as early as mid-December, had it? At a time when Hoth's rescue mission was still in full swing, then, they'd ordered a clearance sale of the entire army? Pure and simple, that was tantamount to saying, 'We can't help you, help yourselves as best you can...' Had the top brass already written off the Sixth Army, in that case? Well then, if that was so, an immediate breakout using their own forces was the only thing that could save them! What were they waiting for?

'So what about the "jellyfish"? The "Mobile Cauldron"?' he asked, interrupting the general's dazzling stream of verbiage and looking imploringly at the C-in-C for support. 'I mean to say, a breakout was in planning, right?'

Shocked at this intemperate show of dissent, Schmidt stopped talking. Paulus looked up and blinked like he was looking into too bright a light. His hand lifted slightly from the table, as if by itself, before dropping back again.

'The plan was turned down,' he said quietly. General Schmidt, disregarding the interruption, immediately carried on with his presentation. 'As long as we could entertain the possibility of breaking out under our own steam, we didn't go along with the High Command's suggestion. But as you will all now appreciate, the situation is different. Only the ruthless exploitation of our own manpower reserves at the front will afford us the possibility of holding out here for the duration.'

Holding out here for the duration... so *that* was the name of the game! Hungry and cold, stuck in this barbaric wilderness, where people dropped like flies in autumn. For the sake of this dubious attempt at 'holding out' they were going to forego the last opportunity to save the army? By implementing the planned 'combing out' exercise, the army would render itself permanently immobile, condemn itself to inaction, and throw itself, for better or worse, on the unreliable mercy of an external rescuer. When the general stopped speaking, the only sound in the room was the officers' heavy breathing.

'But this is all a load of nonsense!' the old general with the face like a tiger blurted out at length. 'We pressed rear-area troops into the front line ages ago. Anyone who can shoot a rifle's already at the front. We don't need the High Command's orders for that!'

The grizzled old soldier was the only one present who didn't fear the Sixth Army's 'evil spirit'. As an ensign, he'd been an effete and sickly young man, but almost forty years of service in the Prussian military had taught him what toughness meant. In the process, he had lost his heart. As president of the Imperial Military Court, he had also developed a cruel streak of misanthropy, and the whole package was rounded off by a splenetic, temperamental maliciousness born of old age and constant stomach complaints. He feared neither the Devil nor his acolytes. He was a match for them.

Schmidt's eyes flashed like steel blades. 'Oh yes, we know your "combing out" all right!' he countered angrily. 'Listen, if you had enough men spare to build grandiose bunkers like this—'

The tiger slammed his fist down on the table; the tips of his moustache trembled.

'Utterly outrageous!'

Paulus raised his hands imploringly. 'Gentlemen, gentlemen, I beg you! The gravity of the current situation…,' he began in pained tones. It was clear he found the whole affair embarrassing, deeply embarrassing. Did no one care what he thought?

'The High Command has worked out for us,' General Schmidt calmly continued, 'that of the more than three hundred thousand men under our command, some two hundred and seventy thousand can be deployed on the front line. According to my calculations, there are still at least fifty thousand men here in the Cauldron who are hanging around to no useful purpose. That's fifty thousand infantrymen!'

Infantrymen? Those drivers, ammunition-luggers, bakers and trench-diggers, all of them ailing and half-starved – infantrymen? What a joke! Was the top brass really that stupid, or just doing a very good impression of idiocy? Under the compelling glare of Schmidt the conjurer, with his incredible figure-juggling, no one dared give vent to their ridicule or indignation. For his part, Colonel von Hermann was only half listening. All this stuff no longer concerned him. He'd been summoned here only to learn that the breakout to the west, which he'd been hoping for all along and which he was to have spearheaded, had now been cancelled for good. He was a man of action, used to going on the offensive. Whatever might happen now was none of his business. He also felt paralysed by the stifling miasma of resignation emanating from the silent C-in-C over there, an aura that the breezy bumptiousness of the chief of staff could not dispel.

'Fifty thousand men,' Schmidt repeated, still juggling his imaginary figures. 'Fifty thousand men: that makes eighty battalions, eighty new battalions! All we need to do is come at this problem from the proper angle, with a centralized administration. Register people by issuing special orders, give them eight days' training and then pack them off to the front...'

Colonel von Hermann gave a sudden start. Was that his name he heard mentioned? He looked up to see General Schmidt's gaze turned on him, full of barely concealed mockery.

'So, Colonel von Hermann, that'll be your responsibility, you and your staff officers. You're forever requesting a responsible and important assignment – well, here it is! As of today, you'll be Inspector for the Provision of Replacements in the Sixth Army!'

The colonel was in a state of profound shock. He was being entrusted with making this ridiculous numbers game they were fooling themselves with a reality? *He*, of all people? Contrary to his normal practice, he found the courage to object.

'I'm grateful for your vote of confidence in me, General,' he said, with much effort, 'but I can't pretend not to have deep misgivings about the whole enterprise. We simply don't have what we require: winter clothing, field kitchens, enough officers and NCOs. Plus, in the present circumstances, these men would be of no use whatsoever in combat, nothing but cannon fodder. Eight days' training won't do anything to change that – that's even assuming that we still have eight days to play with! The major Russian offensive—'

Schmidt flung down the pencil he'd been nervously tapping the table with. 'Difficulties are there to be overcome, Colonel!' he said frostily. 'Key personnel will be flown in, weapons too. The niceties of training aren't really of much relevance in our current situation. Even so, there'll be enough time for all that anyhow, rest assured! And as far as the Russian offensive is concerned that everyone here keeps harping on about, the Russians just aren't up to it! Not before the end of January, in any event – we have reports clearly demonstrating that.'

Though inwardly seething with indignation, Colonel von Hermann refrained from raising any further objections. Weapons would be brought in – pah! When they couldn't even get hold of a few provisions any more? Recently, they'd moved heaven and earth to have twenty MG42 machine guns – the so-called 'buzz saws', with their rapid rate of fire – flown in. When they arrived, they were all missing a vital component and so were unusable. The colonel pursed his lips and gave a small bow. Any further discussion here was pointless.

The officers turned to discussing details. After much toing and froing, in which the tiger found several more opportunities to lose his temper, they finally agreed on the formation of ten battalions in the first instance. They spent a long time mulling over how these new units should be designated. Unold suggested the name 'fortress battalions', but this met with fierce opposition. It falsely implied, the others objected, that these were detachments specially trained in defending strongholds! They had every reason not to conceal the gravity of their situation from the High Command and the German public back home with such hokum. What with all that stupid talk going around already about 'Fortress Stalingrad'… Some fortress, this bunch of foxholes dug in the snow!

On the drive back, Unold kept glancing across at the taciturn von Hermann, who seemed not to have noticed the smug look of 'told-you-so!' satisfaction on the lieutenant colonel's face. The colonel hadn't exactly covered himself in glory at the meeting. On the other hand, he, Unold, had earned himself some brownie points. Despite everything, the top brass had ultimately accepted his suggestion and opted for the designation 'fortress battalions'.

Colonel von Hermann, though, wasn't a man to duck an assignment just because it displeased him. He duly set about assembling the fortress battalions with his customary diligence. He found himself constantly on the move and the telephone was forever ringing off the hook in Unold's office. Their prime concern was to try to exploit the manpower resources of the signals sections. They were then to be joined by the numerous logistics units who were holed up in remote *balkas* somewhere, leading a nomadic existence. The disbandment of all the artillery formations that could no longer be supplied with munitions was also authorized, while the sole rocket regiment was subsumed almost in its entirety, including its staff officers, into the organizational structure of the fortress battalions.

Yet it took some time for all these measures to take effect. In order to put something in place immediately, however, their own division was scoured once more for infantry reinforcements. Unold was in a hurry to get this done. It seemed as if he couldn't expedite the breakup of the division quickly enough. In the first instance the 'Eichert Battalion' was revived, with the addition of drivers and artillerymen, and rechristened 'Fortress Battalion I'. This unit, to which Lieutenant Dierk was also assigned, with his two quadruple flak guns, cut a very sorry figure where its leadership and equipment were concerned. As early as the first days of January, it was dispatched to the western front of the Cauldron. Almost simultaneously, Fortress Battalion II was formed from elements of the tank division's signals section.

This restructuring of the Staff HQ condemned the Intelligence Section to complete inactivity. Breuer felt sure that Unold would wind up the section, but nothing of the sort occurred. Ultimately, Breuer was forced to go and see the lieutenant colonel to request a transfer to one of the new battalions. He was driven not by ambition or a sense of duty; rather, it was an act of sheer desperation. Since his discussions with Wiese he had become scared of his own thoughts. He found all this sitting around, this grinding monotony, intolerable. He had to do something! Work, slave away till he dropped from exhaustion, fight, shoot, freeze and fall in battle – it was all the same to him. Just so long as he didn't have to think any more!

Unold received him with uncommon friendliness.

'No, Breuer,' he said, clapping him on the shoulder, 'it's not going to happen. You can forget that right now! The division's pretty much on its last legs, I know, but the few of us left here on the staff should at least stick together for as long as we can. We've always got along well, I think, so we shouldn't just scatter to the four winds like a pack of dogs!'

He smiled but avoided Breuer's gaze.

'The thing is, when we've finished assembling the fortress battalions here – and that'll be the case in about a fortnight – we'll be surplus to requirements. A complete divisional staff full of valuable professionals – just think what that means! The 384th have already shipped out, and the 94th, and there are rumours that the 79th will soon be on its way too… so we'd better stick together, old boy!'

A roll call of all the remaining members of the Staff HQ took place on the afternoon of New Year's Eve outside the chief of operations' bunker. The little band of men formed up in line, with the officers on the right. A bitter northeasterly wind was blowing. It cut through the men's clothes and gnawed through the frozen flesh right down to their bones. Most of them were wearing balaclavas or earmuffs. Shivering, Breuer stamped his feet to try to stave off the cold. 'Hope this doesn't take long,' he thought to himself, 'otherwise I can kiss my ears and nose goodbye!' After a few minutes, Colonel von Hermann appeared. Captain Engelhard stepped forward and saluted. With his woollen balaclava, which also had a section protecting his nose, he looked like a knight of old in chain mail. The colonel had no coat or cap, but seemed oblivious to the cold. He told the men to stand at ease and then addressed them. The wind tore the words from his mouth, making them sound curt and jerky.

'Comrades! The new year is almost upon us. We've no idea what it holds in store for us – liberation or defeat. We stand alone here, far from home, fighting what seems like a losing battle. The worst is yet to come. We're facing a dark future. But there's one thing we do know: there's a Western Front in this war too, and it's keeping the war at bay from Germany. And the fact that it's there and holding firm is due in no small part to our efforts. We're tying down powerful enemy forces here in Stalingrad. If not for that, the enemy might already have broken through the hard-pressed Eastern Front. If we're fated to die, then our sacrifice will not have been for nothing... we have to believe that this sacrifice has not been in vain. Firm in that belief, let's go forward into the new year. Long live Germany!'

Fated to die? Our sacrifice not in vain?

The men looked at one another. What was up with the colonel today? It wasn't like him to talk in such an illogical way! After all, Hitler had sent the men at Stalingrad a New Year's greeting (it had just been announced that same afternoon) in which he said: 'You can rely on me with rock-like confidence!' The Führer had given his word, loud and clear. There was no room for doubt or interpretation there!

At twenty-two-hundred hours, a protracted rumbling noise drove the men out of their bunkers. A ghostly yet magnificent spectacle was unfolding against the night sky. Flares of all colours, pearl strings of tracer bullets and the brief flashes of artillery rounds, Stalin organs and mortars engulfed the whole area in a ring of fire. Never before had the limits of the Cauldron been so graphically demonstrated to them, and never before had they felt the reality of this prison they were trapped in so keenly.

'So, there are the borders of our little domain!' said Breuer to Lieutenant Wiese. 'The Russians are welcoming the new year. They have good reason to celebrate.'

'What were the names of those two Roman consuls who were defeated at the Battle of Cannae that time?' asked Wiese. The question was so odd that Breuer could only turn and look at him in astonishment.

'Wasn't one of them called Aemilius Paulus?' said Wiese, then quite out of the blue he asked, 'Do you really think we saved the Eastern Front?'

'How do you mean?'

'Well, the reports you get from the Corps every day have been consistently telling us since mid-December that the Russians are withdrawing significant forces from the Cauldron front. They've hardly any tanks left here! And it's clear that, for the time being at least, they can afford to throw everything they've got against Rostov and the Don elbow. Or do you think the Russian top brass hasn't been kept closely informed of Hitler's order banning us from attempting a breakout? And that we couldn't break out any longer even if we wanted to? Even if there wasn't a single Russian soldier facing us any more, we couldn't move an inch!'

Breuer gave a deep sigh. 'Dear God, Wiese, you're truly abominable!' he said in an agonized voice. 'The colonel told us that we *have* to believe! And he's right. How can you even bear to go on if you've lost all faith?'

★

Lakosch couldn't get the encounter with Seliger out of his head. A thick curtain, which Nazi propaganda kept painting with lurid images of horror, stood between him and the mysterious 'opposing side'. The little driver had been granted a fleeting glimpse behind this curtain just the once, that time when they'd interrogated the Russian airman. Ever since, Lakosch had been longing for the curtain to drop. He wanted clarity, and the truth. There wasn't a scintilla of doubt in his mind any longer that everything that Harras and the private had reported about their time behind the Russian lines was a pack of lies.

One morning he went over to see the former mess orderly again. Seliger was sullen and stand-offish. He appeared to have bad memories of the driver's first visit and its aftermath. Only when Lakosch openly threatened to report the whole incident did Seliger start to talk, though not before swearing Lakosch to absolute secrecy. What Lakosch ultimately managed to extract from the orderly was basically this: Seliger and Harras, who'd been knocked out for several minutes by a clod of earth thrown up by the explosion, had been surprised by the Russians ('This is it, now they're going to kill us!'). In the event, all they suffered were a few blows from rifle butts to force them to their feet. They were taken to a staff headquarters in a village further behind the Russian lines, where they were subjected to a thorough interrogation on conditions in the Cauldron. Their treatment there was remarkably friendly and they were given plenty to eat.

Seliger waxed lyrical on this last point: 'Oh, mate, I'm telling you – we had lovely white bread with butter and bacon and sausage! And fags and chocolate that they'd filched from the Junkers! That perked up old Lissnup pretty sharpish.'

Lakosch wasn't interested in all that, so he urged Seliger to tell him more. The following day, it seems, they were left alone with two men who, to their amazement, turned out to be German. These men, writers who had emigrated to the Soviet Union, engaged them in very earnest conversation.

They described the hopeless position the encircled army was in and painted a terrifying picture of the consequences of the massive Russian assault that would soon be unleashed. It would undoubtedly mean the death of the three hundred thousand men unless they surrendered in time. One of the men then touched on the subject of the war being Hitler's fault, which prompted Harras to claim that he'd always been opposed to Hitler. But Harras turned down the invitation to address their German comrades over the tannoy from the Russian trenches by saying that no one would believe him, and suggested instead that he and Seliger should be sent back into the Cauldron so that they could argue there for a cessation of hostilities. At first, they didn't receive an answer on this score. But after a few days, they were given sheaves of propaganda material and taken back to the front, where they were spirited through the lines under cover of darkness. Harras was extremely worked up on the return journey. He told Seliger that this was a really big opportunity for them. If they played their cards right, they might not just be in line for a promotion and decorations, but could even get out of the Cauldron. Seliger let Harras talk him round, and Harras then discussed with him in the minutest detail the report that they duly submitted on their return. This account of their escapade, which Seliger divulged only very reluctantly, threw Lakosch into a state of great agitation. He kept on pressing for more details. 'So, they didn't shoot you?'

'No, Karl, see for yourself! Never crossed their minds.'

'And they were German communists, the people you spoke to?'

'Yeah, one was a lanky bloke with a grey quiff, and the other one was short, really twitchy and on edge all the time, came from Hamburg I think… Their names? Wait a mo… No, it's gone, sorry. But they'd already written loads of pamphlets. Lissnup knew them all right. And get this: there are officers over there too! German officers, fighting against Hitler… and all the German POWs have come out against Hitler as well!'

Lakosch found it hard taking this all in.

'Making out that you'd escaped was a really dirty trick, though, mate! Our commanders ought to hear about what you've just told me! If Paulus knew… well, he might act quite differently!'

Seliger was appalled.

'Are you out of your tiny mind?' he cried. 'You think the top brass don't already know all that? They know a bloody sight more than we do, chum! So just keep your mouth shut if you don't want to end up getting hanged. I bloody knew it – it's not safe telling you anything! I couldn't give a shit about Lissnup, the bastard! But they'll have my head too if this all comes out!'

Lakosch stood up. In response to Seliger's fearful entreaties, he hastily repeated his promise not to say anything. In his thoughts, he was already miles away. An urgent resolution had taken root in his mind, born of his experiences over the last few days.

The next morning, Lakosch was gone. The men of the Intelligence Section were faced with a conundrum. They feared at first that something untoward had happened to him. But the fact that his rifle and his other effects were nowhere to be seen either left them in no doubt that he had deliberately taken flight. Breuer, who in retrospect recalled several things about his driver's recent behaviour that had struck him as odd, reproached himself for not having taken greater care of the lad. Maybe he'd tried to do away with himself? With a heavy heart, he decided to report the incident to Unold. The lieutenant colonel was apoplectic with fury when he heard the news.

'No question!' he shouted. 'The bloke's done a bunk – deserted! We've never had a deserter in our division before, let alone from Staff HQ. What a ghastly bloody mess! The bloke always seemed a bit rum to me, I must say. But naturally you didn't notice a thing, did you, you dumb bleeding-heart liberal? Don't you dare breathe a word to the High Command about this! All we need now is to piss away the little bit of credit we have in that quarter with crap like this!'

Everyone in the section was hit hard by the disappearance of their comrade. It sometimes looked as though Geibel had been secretly crying. But for whatever reason – be it the inhibitions that, despite their common fate, still attached to the uniform, or some veiled mistrust of one another or a fear of the abyss that any mention of the event might open up – everyone kept their thoughts to themselves. No one said a thing.

5

The Bone Road

LIEUTENANT DR BONTE, THE battalion adjutant, a short, dark-haired officer of that unobtrusive yet robust kind that is so beloved of the infantry, walked with short steps towards the bunker where the commanding officer had taken up residence. Bonte was out of sorts. His men were billeted in an unheated horse stable, and despite being crammed together like sardines, were still frozen stiff. Yet all around were paymasters and other desk-jockeys who were holed up in nice warm bunkers. But wasn't this always the way when you were placed under the command of another unit? God helps those who help themselves! The captain, his CO, would need to raise hell about it at divisional level. Things couldn't go on like this. His men, who weren't up to much at the moment anyhow, would go completely to the dogs even before they went into action if they kept on being treated in such a shabby way.

Captain Eichert, the commander of Fortress Battalion I, was studying a map. When the lieutenant came in, he raised his head and combed his wispy hair back from his forehead.

'See, Bonte, what did I tell you?' he said. 'It's "do this one minute and do that the next"! But at last, here's our order to go into action!' The lieutenant was taken aback. The battalion had only been formed two days ago, with seventy per cent of the men seconded from other units and with no infantry experience. And as of yesterday it had been placed, as a reserve detachment, under the command of the hard-pressed infantry division that was defending a difficult sector of the western front of the Cauldron. And today they were expected to deploy?

'Where are we headed, then, Captain?' he enquired apprehensively. The captain's lacklustre eyes shot him a searching look.

'Kazatchi Hill,' came the reply. 'But don't tell the men just yet.'

A shock ran through the lieutenant. Kazatchi Hill! Almost every foot soldier in the Cauldron knew and feared that name. It virtually amounted to a death sentence.

'So, I want the battalion ready to move within the hour,' the captain went on. 'And send the company leaders to me straight away.'

On his way back to the stables, the lieutenant came across two soldiers who were using their sidearms to try to detach the swollen joints from the legs of a horse carcass. As the officer walked by, one of them got to his feet. He approached the lieutenant sheepishly, nervously fingering his camouflage jacket.

'Begging your pardon, Lieutenant, sir,' he muttered. 'We've... that is, we'd like to... Could you give us a bite to eat by any chance?'

'What are you doing here, then?' asked Bonte suspiciously.

'We're all on our tod here. Our captain left us behind with his stores.' The other soldier now stood up too.

'It's been a fortnight since we heard anything from the battalion. Who knows what might have happened to them? And our rations have run out...'

Bonte felt a pang of sympathy. Anyone who became detached from their unit here was a goner.

'Yes, that's bad news, guys. Let's see if we can't rustle up something for you. Where was your battalion headed?'

Two pairs of hooded eyes flashed at the lieutenant.

'To the front, Lieutenant, sir. To Kazatchi Hill.'

★

An hour later, the battalion, loaded onto lorries, is bumping along towards the front, passing shot-up vehicles and the wrecks of downed planes. Sections of the broad, well-used track are obscured by drifting snow. When the trucks are forced to swing round the lips of bomb craters, they wallow about wildly, causing their cargoes to clatter and crash about in the back. The men, wrapped in blankets, sway to and fro on the bench seats; the cold and hunger have made them oblivious to the discomfort. The wind whistles through the lorries' tarpaulin sides. Clasped in frozen hands, the troops' rifles sway between their knees. Occasionally, one of them is woken from drowsy semi-consciousness by the muffled bang of one of the trucks backfiring. Extraordinary sights loom up on both sides of the road: severed horses' legs sticking upright out of the earth, bleached ribs, curved as Turkish scimitars, and horses' heads arranged in a neat pyramid. And over there... my God, what's that? Yes, it really is: a person, a dead person – to judge from the brownish uniform, either a Russian or a Romanian. Like a tin soldier, the man's corpse, frozen stiff, has been rammed head-first into the ground with its legs in the air. There is a light dusting of snow on the dirty grey soles of its feet.

'The Bone Road!' the driver tells Captain Eichert. 'We had to mark where the roadway went somehow, 'cos it's always getting covered by snowdrifts. And there was no wood to hand; people keep nicking it.'

The captain is an old stager. But a shiver runs down even his spine at the sight.

The lorries struggle up an incline. From the top, a small cluster of wooden huts comes into view. That must be the place where they're hoping to find the regimental Staff HQ. The column stops by the first of the shacks, and the men climb out, stiff-legged. Light disruptive enemy artillery fire is being directed at the northern exit to the village. The 'greenhorns' huddle together like sheep and cast nervous glances at the sky when they hear a mortar burbling towards them. Some throw themselves to the ground, only to get to their feet again shamefacedly when the round explodes some way off. Lieutenant Dierk, commanding the second company, is at his wits' end. He really wants to give them a rocket, but faced with this abject helplessness, clearly not meant maliciously, he hasn't the heart to. His gaze wanders over to the eight men from his former unit, who are busy unhitching the four-barrelled flak guns from the trucks. Corporal Härtel is issuing orders as calmly as ever. Everything's running like clockwork. He's fortunate to have these guys on board still. They can provide some stability for the greenhorns until they've got over their first few days of stage fright.

The bunker on the edge of the village housing the regimental Staff HQ is full of officers. Captain Eichert reports for duty. A giant of a man detaches himself from the group and comes over. It's Colonel Steigmann. His face looks tired, but his gaze radiates energy and determination.

'Good that you're here,' he says, giving the captain's hand a forceful shake. 'We've been eagerly anticipating your arrival.' He goes over to the map, laid out on the table. 'The battalion here is… it's taken heavy losses, so we're replacing it. So, this area here will be your sector. It's an exposed, windy corner right on the border between divisions. The Russians like to try to exploit that… Where are you from, incidentally?'

'Pomerania, Colonel, sir!'

'Oh right, a Pomeranian, eh? That means we have pretty much the whole of Germany represented here. I'm mostly surrounded by totally unfamiliar faces now; there's hardly anyone left from my old regiment. The heavy fighting during the retreat and then trying to defend this position here have taken their toll. The Russians keep shooting us to pieces with their artillery and rocket launchers in this open terrain. Not to mention the frostbite… yes, it's fair to say the attrition's been high. What kind of signals equipment have you brought with you, by the way?'

'Very little, Colonel – in fact, nothing! We're a "fortress battalion" and we've only just been assembled recently on a shoestring.'

'That's bad news, very bad,' the colonel replies gloomily. 'Our entire ability to fend off the Russians here depends first and foremost on a smoothly functioning intelligence network.'

He turns to the map once more. 'Look, see these here, that's "Max" and "Moritz": two large hulks of knocked-out tanks. You'll recognize them straight away out in the field. They mark where the Russian line runs. Then there's the depression over here, and after that some fields we can cover with curtain fire – we've called them "Platinum", "Silver" and "Gold" – and then the areas with flower code names. And up here are the infantry's observation posts. See – it's a really tight network. And all the positions are connected by 'phone, so everyone knows what's going on across the entire sector. And if a single Russian dares to show his head anywhere, he gets the whole of the division's artillery down on his head like a ton of bricks.'

Eichert finds himself delighted and terrified at the same time by this masterly mechanism, which can only operate if every cog turns exactly as it should. And here he is with his men, this bunch of hopeless bumblers… He feels like a stable boy who's been sent to service a steam locomotive.

'I can see you're surprised, right?' laughed the colonel. 'Without all this, the Russians would long since have broken through and overwhelmed our little force here!'

But as the captain proceeds to give him more information about the composition, equipment and combat readiness of his battalion, the colonel's face takes on a very grave expression again.

'You know,' he says finally, 'two hundred and seventy extra men in the trenches, that's all well and good, of course it is. But if I'm honest with you, I'd rather you'd brought me ten canny old infantrymen. One time, a while ago, they sent us three hundred Luftwaffe personnel. Within two days, they'd all been wiped out, every last one! The shit really hit the fan over that, I can tell you. But it's not sheer numbers that count.'

He paces up and down a few times before stopping in front of the captain.

'It's a disgrace,' he says, 'to deploy your battalion here in the state it's in. I'll have another word with divisional HQ presently. But in the meantime, you'd better take up position in the trenches. There's nothing else for it.'

Padre Peters makes his way through the village to the dressing station. He has accompanied Fortress Battalion I and intends to stay in this sector for the duration of the unit's deployment. All of a sudden, he stands stock still. In front of him, carefully stacked up against the side wall of a house, is a heap of bodies. They are clad only in shirts and long johns; some of them are completely naked. The greenish-yellow, rigidly frozen corpses are covered in brown spots of dried blood. Their faces are frozen in either a rictus of death throes or an expression of apathy. At that moment, a new consignment of bodies is being unloaded from a sled. Troops are busy undressing them and sorting through uniforms and pieces of equipment. One soldier is kneeling and using both hands to hold one of the bodies by the head, which consists only of a forehead with a ruddy mess of flesh below, while another soldier attempts to tug a felt boot off its foot. They are chatting loudly and unconcernedly and are treating the task they are engaged in like some workaday activity. Padre Peters has encountered death in a thousand different forms. He has seen it often enough to know that constant contact with it has a way of desensitizing a person. But even among medical orderlies and work parties detailed to bury or rebury corpses, he is used to seeing a vestige of reverence, which at least helps maintain a semblance of dignity. This is the first time he's seen men handling their fallen comrades like they're logs of wood.

He goes over to have a word with the old sergeant who is there to collect up the dead men's dog tags. The man lifts his head and looks at the person addressing him. Without more ado he flares up, his hoar-frost-covered moustache trembling with anger. 'So what are we supposed to do?' he asks, his voice quick and hoarse. 'There's no way we can transport them out of here any more! Almost every day, there's another mountain of them. This lot here are just the ones from yesterday, from Kazatchi Hill, and this isn't all of 'em either. What's that – you want to know if we have a cemetery?' He gives a hollow laugh. 'Oh yeah, we'd have our work cut out there all right! And some nice crosses on the graves too, perhaps? Ha ha ha, crosses!' He shoves his face close to the padre's, who recoils in alarm from the dangerously unstable look in the man's eyes. And now the sergeant barks at Peters: 'You should have thought of that beforehand! We chuck 'em in the gravel pit back there, right? Shovel a bit of snow on top, and then some more bodies, and then more snow, that's the way it goes! What are you looking at me like that for? We didn't want it to be like that. It's not our fault!'

The padre turns away. He's lost for words. Around his chest, it feels like he's wearing a breastplate of ice, beneath which his heart is burning and trembling.

In the so-called 'reception bunker' of the main dressing station, he is met by a blast of smoke-laden fug. The room is full of soldiers with dirty field dressings round their heads and limbs. They are sitting on the narrow wooden bench along the back wall or squatting on the ground and quietly enjoying the modicum of warmth in the bunker. Somewhere beyond them, another soldier is moaning in pain. His muted cry of 'aah... aah... aah' punctuates the passing moments like a time signal.

The young assistant doctor gives the padre – by now a familiar face – a brief nod. He is in the process of unwinding a grubby strip of rag from the hand that a thin and worried-looking soldier is holding out to him. The smell of carbolic mingles with a sweetish, putrid stench. As the doctor unravels the final bit of the dressing, a blackish, gelatinous mass comes away with it. The doctor is holding the skeleton of the young man's five fingers, now stripped clean of all their flesh. He gazes in silence at the white bones.

'Disgraceful!' he suddenly snaps at his patient, whose whole body is shaking like a leaf. 'It's a bloody disgrace that you've been going around with it like this for so long, d'you hear? Don't imagine for one moment that this'll get you a free pass home!'

The man's mouth gapes helplessly. His gaze wanders in uncomprehending horror from his mutilated hand to the surgeon's furious face and back again. The doctor regains some of his composure.

'Well, don't gawp at me like an idiot, man!' he barks. 'It's no big deal, anyhow! They'll snip off the bones, and in a week or so you'll be able to shoot again. Off you go, get yourself over to the operation bunker!'

He turns to his next patient, who extends a filthy foot to him. The toes are a midnight-blue colour.

'I'm bloody sick of these endless cases of frostbite!' shouts the doctor. 'They should lock up the lot of you! You know what this is, don't you? It's self-mutilation! I know you lot! You know how to play the system all right, don't you? Well, you've come to the wrong person here!'

The soldier's eyes grow moist.

'What are we supposed to do then, Assistant Surgeon, sir?' he asks, on the verge of tears. 'We never get to take off our boots! We're on sentry duty day and night, and when we aren't we're building defences. And all of us are stuck in foxholes the whole time!'

'Right, get some ointment rubbed into that and then be off with you! And don't show your face here again!'

Things go on in the same vein for almost an hour. Eventually, peace descends. The doctor emits a heavy sigh, mops his sweaty brow and sits down on an upturned crate. The padre looks at his harried face, trying to guess his age. Twenty-six, twenty-seven maybe? Yet he looks like he's wasting away from the strain of a century's worth of suffering.

'My God, Doctor!' he says quietly, 'I hardly recognize you! What's got into you?'

The doctor leans forward and looks wide-eyed at the chaplain. He waves his hand in the air, in an undecipherable gesture.

'Save your breath, Padre!' he exclaims. 'I know precisely what you're going to say, every word. Hold your tongue, I beg you!'

He slumps back against the wall and lights a cigarette with shaking hands. He inhales the smoke in long drags and blows it out up to the ceiling. Slowly he grows calmer. Then he begins to speak, quietly, as if talking to himself.

'I'm from an old medical family. I studied medicine out of a love for mankind… to reduce the suffering in the world and to try to conquer death.' He gives a short, cynical laugh. 'What grand dreams we have when we're young! Now I'm not a doctor any more. It's not possible. The men here with second- and third-degree frostbite, see, they turn up in their hundreds every day. As a doctor I ought to be sending them home.'

He pauses to light another cigarette from the stub of the previous one.

'And that's not the worst of it either. About a week or so ago, they started bringing us the first cases of consumption, men who were emaciated down to the bone and completely exhausted, and who'd given up eating and even speaking. You'll get to see them by and by. There was nothing we could do to help; they just wasted away and died. We've already had more than twenty cases in the division. Recently, we had one of them on the autopsy table, he was one metre eighty tall and weighed just forty kilos. His skin tissue was like it had been desiccated, not an ounce of fat on his entire lanky frame. We reported this case to the High Command. You know what response we got back? "Quite impossible!" was what they replied. "It must be some new, unknown form of disease." They'd send a specialist, they told us.'

The doctor gets to his feet. He paces up and down the bunker in long strides, a red flush of agitation marking his sallow cheeks.

'A specialist for the dead of Stalingrad, Padre! A specialist who can peddle a suitable lie to the folks back home about the great charnel house here. No, Padre, anyone who planned on remaining a doctor here would spend all day and night howling with impotence and shame and rage at the fact that all of this is even possible!'

Padre Peters is devastated by what he's hearing.

'Doctor,' he says earnestly and imploringly, 'please don't give up on yourself! Think how much more dreadful it would be if you and your colleagues weren't here! Day after day I see what you all do for our sick and wounded men here. Your readiness to help and make sacrifices is beyond measure! I refuse to believe your work is all in vain, Doctor. And even when you can't give any medical help, a kind word or a friendly look at the right moment can work wonders. Don't give up on yourself and your profession, I beg you!'

The doctor stopped in front of Peters and looked at him, his eyes ablaze.

'What do you know?' he yelled. 'Am I even *allowed* to be a doctor any more? Even if I still had the will and the capacity to be one, I'm not permitted to practise my profession any longer. A few days ago, the Corps' chief physician was here, and kicked up one hell of a stink. Far too many men being signed off sick, he said! We shouldn't be making a great big song and dance about every stupid case of frostbite... the men were nothing but malingerers... we needed to be hard, ruthless... we oughtn't to forget that we were army officers first and foremost, and that we should keep the requirements of the Wehrmacht uppermost in our minds. The army needed every man that could still carry a rifle... So that's the way things are here, dear sir! We're required not to give a rat's arse about suffering, starving, freezing human beings. Our sole focus should be on the man who can shoot. You've got it easy, Padre. You're only called upon to help people when they're dying. I have to bellow at them to make them go on living. All that's expected of me is to harangue sick people back to health! Do you imagine I can still grant myself the luxury of a heart, or feelings of pity? Who takes any pity on *me*? Your God, maybe, who's letting us all die in misery here? You've still got it so easy, for the present at least. But just you wait: you can see which way the wind's blowing here! Watch out, 'cos tomorrow you're just as likely to get an order to raise the dead so they can die one more time for the Führer and the Reich!'

The doctor flings himself down on his camp bed in utter exhaustion. Padre Peters senses that he ought to say something, but words fail him. 'Waking the dead, yes, that's it!' he thinks to himself, and feels the full weight of his own impotence. It strikes him that he couldn't awaken anyone any more, not even this young doctor, who's still alive and yet already dead – dead inside from the sickness of Stalingrad.

The long column of the fortress battalion marches towards its forward positions. As they proceed, the front grows ever more lively and more threatening. Bizarre silhouettes of ruined houses, wrecked vehicles and shot-up tanks line their route. The harsh rattle of machine-gun fire drifts over to them, and every so often the fierce explosion of a round from an anti-tank gun splits the air. Yellow and red flares shoot up in a shower of light and sway slowly back to earth. Their evil glow and flicker paints ghostly dancing shadows on the snow. An atmosphere of great tension hangs over the line of marching men. All of their lassitude has been swept away. The agitated thudding and stumbling of their stamping feet mingles with low whispers, terse shouts and commands and the tinny jangle of equipment hanging from their packs, which they try in vain to muffle somehow. The pathfinders at the head of the column warn them in hushed tones to keep quiet and be careful. A little further on, the path divides. This is the fork where the individual companies have to split up. All of a sudden, there are three bright, reddish flashes in swift succession, and three explosions blend into a single dull thud. Mortars – they've been spotted! The men have scattered and flung themselves to the ground.

'Forward! Get to your positions fast before the next salvo comes!' shouts Captain Eichert. The lines of men vanish quickly into the darkness in single file. Eichert hurries with his adjutant and the battalion doctor to the bunker where the command post is supposed to be. A small stretcher sled is standing in the way, with two wounded men lying on it swaddled in blankets, moaning; the two medical orderlies pulling it have been hit by the mortar rounds. One of them is showing no sign of movement; a piece of shrapnel has pierced his head. The other is crouching on the ground, propping himself up on his hands. He is moaning and can't get up unassisted. Bonte and the doctor lift the man, who screams in pain, and carry him into the bunker, while the captain drags the sled. Behind them, another salvo of mortar rounds hits home; bomb splinters buzz past them like malevolent insects. A figure approaches from the bunker entrance, an officer. He dispenses with any greeting and bends down to look at the wounded man.

'Oh Christ, now they've got Knippke too!' he whispers as he helps the others pull the groaning man into the bunker.

'Poor Knippke!' he says, clearly distressed. 'That's all we need! An old warhorse like you!' Eichert's doctor examines the injured soldier.

'It's a small splinter in his lower back,' he says reassuringly. 'Nothing too serious! You'll be right as rain again in a fortnight!'

The man's face has taken on a deadly white pallor, but now he bites his lip stoically. The whites of his eyes are showing prominently.

'Quick, get moving!' the officer calls to a dark corner of the bunker. 'Put Knippke on the stretcher sled! But watch out!'

In the corner two figures stand up, barely still recognizable as soldiers. Their faces and uniforms are caked with filth. They put on their kit without a word and carry their comrade out. Finally now, the officer, a first lieutenant, finds the time to deal with the new arrivals, who are hanging around the bunker, barely tall enough for a man to stand up in, rather self-consciously. The lieutenant's face, too, is sunken and hollow-eyed. His black hair droops over his forehead; it's evident that he hasn't washed or shaved for several days.

'Those two men I've just dispatched were the last survivors of the staff battalion,' he says. 'Yes, that's right, not many of us left now! They pretty much finished us off yesterday. The CO dead, the adjutant seriously wounded... There's just a couple of sentries out in the forward positions.'

The tall captain, weary of standing hunched over in the cramped space, sits down on an ammo box and takes off his cap.

'Well, things'll be different from now on!' he says.

Attached to a board on the wall is a radio receiver. The daily army bulletin is being broadcast on it, sounding distant and fuzzy – bland reports of successful defensive actions somewhere or other. From time to time the programme is drowned out by the mocking voice of a jamming station repeating over and over again the same intrusive message, uttered in drawling tones:

'Death to Hitler! What's – going on – at Stalingrad? – German Army High Command – is lying – to the people!'

'How many bunkers are there in this sector, as a matter of fact?' asks the captain.

'Four in all. Old Russian bunkers,' replies the lieutenant. Giving an irritated grunt, he turns off the radio, puts its cover back on and puts the field-grey-coloured box with his other possessions, which he's already gathered together ready to leave. Eichert shakes his head pensively.

'We can't build anything here, see?' the lieutenant continues.

'There's no wood. Plus you daren't show yourself above ground in daylight. One of those men you just saw on the sled there got hit straight after stepping out of the bunker. They got the corporal who went out to try to retrieve him as well. It's sheer bloody hell here!'

'Is that really all?' Eichert asks, playing with a hand grenade he's picked up from the floor. 'I mean, the four bunkers...'

'Yes, that's it. Otherwise we've only got foxholes in the snow, with tarpaulins over them.'

In parting, the captain does a tour of inspection around the sector with the first lieutenant. Cautiously, sometimes crawling on their stomachs for long sections, they pick their way from one foxhole to the next, and are often forced by the glare of flares or machine-gun fire to press themselves flat to the ground for minutes on end. The Russians are very lively; they seem to sense that a changeover is happening. From somewhere comes a flickering reddish glow. In a small dip, four men are sitting round an open fire, including the sentry from the B-position, code name 'Erich'.

'What the devil?' Eichert hisses at them indignantly. 'Are you out of your tiny minds? You've lit a fire out here, where the enemy can hear every word? The Russians'll pick you off in the blink of an eye!'

The soldiers stare at the captain uncomprehendingly and reproach-fully. Surprise, surprise – it's a bunch of greenhorns!

'But there's another sentry up front, Captain, sir! Surely nothing can happen if he's there?'

Eichert soon whips them into shape with some short, sharp com-mands. It is with very mixed feelings that he returns to the bunker. The first lieutenant, on the other hand, is extremely animated.

'It's really great to see all the foxholes occupied again!' he exclaims. Momentarily overcome by sad memories, he quietly adds: 'You know, just three days ago it looked the same, exactly the same...'

But his melancholy passes. He nervously rummages in all corners of the bunker to check he hasn't left anything behind. He no longer even bothers to conceal his delight at being able to get away from this place at last.

'Break a leg, then, as they say, Captain!' he says in parting, shaking Eichert's hand repeatedly like he's thanking him for something. 'I hope you have better luck than we did!'

The captain and his adjutant look at one another in silence. The inevitable, the inescapable envelops them in its eerie embrace.

Lieutenant Dierk personally marshals the men of his company into their foxholes, which have been lined with some mouldy straw and old rags. As a flak officer, he's unused to infantry combat, but in comparison with these poor little wretches with their helpless questions he sounds to himself like an old hand at trench warfare. The men cannot grasp what's being asked of them. It was bad enough beforehand, but at least then they had a roof over their heads and a bit of warmth. And now they're supposed to crawl into these holes in the ground, in their half-starved and weak condition, with no winter clothing, and lie here throughout the freezing nights and the days without budging, and not even able to lift their heads? They're expected to lie here with no end in sight, even if that's being wounded or killed? This just can't be right! It's sheer madness! This isn't war any more; it's nothing but murder: futile mass murder!

A short and slight artilleryman clutches at the company leader's arm in a very unmilitary fashion and whispers: 'Lieutenant, Hitler wouldn't leave us in the lurch here, would he, sir? Does he even know what it's like here? Someone really ought to let him know, Lieutenant! He wouldn't allow this, surely, Lieutenant!'

Lieutenant Dierk feels like there's a lump in his throat stifling his words. Back in the day, when he'd still been a Hitler Youth leader, rousing pep talks had tripped off his lips so easily. But now he finds himself tongue-tied. Inform the Führer – yeah, if only it were that easy! Not long ago that commanding general, the one with only one arm* who'd fought his way to the banks of the Volga north of Stalingrad the previous autumn, had flown to the Führer's headquarters in a towering rage, determined to tell Hitler some home truths for once. The man was fearless when confronting the enemy, no question. But when he came face-to-face with Hitler, his courage failed him. Meekly he let himself be decorated with swords to add to his Knight's Cross and was granted special leave to attend his daughter's wedding.

What has become of the ideal of speaking truth to power? wonders the lieutenant. Frederick the Great's officers had thrown their daggers down at the king's feet. How come their modern counterparts were so craven? How had that happened?

He finds no answer to this puzzle.

The artilleryman is still lying right beside him, seemingly waiting for an answer. Should he tell him what he's just been thinking? It wouldn't exactly be consoling.

'Chin up, man!' he forces himself to respond. 'We just need to hold out here for a couple of days. Then things'll get better, for sure! The division's promised us some winter togs… and the Führer's thinking of us; he won't forget us. What was that he told us? "You can rely on me with rock-like confidence!" Well, you can bet your life on that!'

★

---

* 'only one arm' – an allusion to General Hans-Valentin Hube, who had lost his right arm at the Battle of Verdun in 1916. Hube commanded the 16th Panzer Division during Operation Barbarossa and *Fall Blau* ('Case Blue'), the German army's summer offensive in southern Russia in the summer of 1942. He was later given command of the XIV Panzer Corps. Hube, an extremely able and widely respected commander among both fellow officers and men, was ordered by Hitler to fly out of the Stalingrad Cauldron in January 1943 but refused; in response, Hitler ordered members of the SS to fly in and force him to leave at gunpoint.

Captain Eichert lies on an earth bench cut out of the back wall of the bunker. Someone has thrown a coat over him; he's asleep. The dim glow of the flickering candle flits across his grey face, casting a sharp profile of his backward-sloping head onto the clay wall. From his open mouth, in fits and starts, comes a stertorous snore, which changes now and then into a deep moan that seems to emanate from his chest. The captain is dreaming. He's standing alone on a dead-straight road receding to a vanishing point in the far distance. This road is lined on both sides with dead soldiers sticking rigidly out of the ground like telegraph poles, their heads buried in snow. It's Victory Boulevard, and the Führer is due to drive down it. Captain Eichert takes a sighting down the row of soldiers to check that they're all correctly aligned. Suddenly he feels invisible hands take hold of him and try to shove his head down into the snow. 'Stop!' he cries out in horror. 'The war isn't over yet! I'm not dead yet!' He struggles in vain to free himself, but the strange arms grasping him are impossible to shake off. 'Not dead yet?' a voice laughs. 'Ha ha ha! The whole army has to form a guard of honour! You too, Captain!'

Eichert wakes with a start of terror. Looming over him he sees the face of his adjutant, who is shaking him by the shoulders.

'Captain!' he shouts in alarm. 'Captain, sir!'

'Yes… what… how… yes? What's the matter?'

'Captain, sir, there's a sound of fighting coming from the left sector, and it's growing louder! Seems like it's all kicked off down there!'

The battalion commander is already on his feet, cursing.

'On the left, you say? Dierk's sector?'

The field telephone rings and he picks up the receiver. It's Lieutenant Dierk on the line and he's very het up.

'I wanted to call you straight away, Captain! It's a real mess down here… the Russians have broken through, they caught us with our pants down…No, I haven't got a clear overview of the situation yet… The anti-tank gun on the left isn't firing any more. And on the right? We've locked that down as best we can, sir.'

'I'll be down there myself right away, Dierk!' says the captain. He hangs up and calls the regiment. The answer he receives isn't encouraging. The battalion must deal with the breakthrough as quickly as they can with their own resources.

The captain manages to secure the services of a handful of older, more experienced troops from one of the other two companies. With their help, Lieutenant Dierk is to drive the Russians back from their positions at daybreak the next day. The lieutenant, though, is in total despair.

'That won't do any good, Captain!' he declares. 'The Russians have made a really major breakthrough. And they appear to be constantly reinforcing as we speak. There's no hope of us plugging the gap without some stronger forces of our own!'

The captain shrugs his shoulders. He too has little faith that the operation will succeed. But in the event, the planned counter-attack never takes place. The next morning – with a fifth of the battalion already incapacitated by frostbite – the Russians launch a large-scale assault of the kind the division has become increasingly accustomed to in the last few weeks across the entire sector controlled by the regiment. The attack is executed with extensive armoured and artillery support. Colonel Steigmann's curtain-fire system inflicts heavy losses on the enemy. Four waves of attacking troops are beaten back. Only the fifth wave finally succeeds, as evening falls, in widening and deepening the area that has been breached. Several Russian tanks break through and cause havoc in the artillery emplacements.

All that Captain Eichert can salvage from his battalion the following morning is a group of around forty men and two officers. For the third time, the 'Eichert Battalion' has ceased to exist.

6

Is There Really No Way Out?

GÖRING HAD DONE WHAT he could. It wasn't what he had promised. No convoys of heavy transport gliders flew to Stalingrad by moonlight; but alongside the old 'corrugated-iron' Ju 52s, which suffered heavy losses, a few of the more modern Heinkel He 111 bombers put in an appearance. In addition to the cargo they carried in their fuselages, they could also transport food in their bomb bays and petrol in their tanks. A few obsolete Ju 86s – a type now consigned to a training role in Germany – were even pressed into service. Now and then, the troops trapped in the Stalingrad pocket would lift their heads and stare in wonder as a large, four-engined machine approached and circled majestically over the aerodrome at Pitomnik. These were either Focke-Wulf Condors, hastily redeployed from the south of France, or Ju 90s, which came straight from Sicily and were still being flown by the factory's own pilots. Although these heavy transports had a payload of around five tons apiece, their principal effect was on morale, for only a handful of these showpiece aircraft were sent on the Stalingrad run at any one time, and even these presently came to grief while attempting to land on or take off from the snow-swept airfield. The food situation had by now become critical. Two hundred grams of bread a day for an infantryman in the trenches, and one hundred grams for everyone else. The horses were all skin and bone, and the cavalry captain from the First Romanian Cavalry Division who had been so concerned about his equine charges back in Businovka could surely never have dreamed that every last one of them would one day end up in the pots of German field kitchens. All that now remained of their carcasses were the bleached white bones protruding from the snow beside every road. Russian prisoners, starving Romanian soldiers and the hordes of wounded men who drifted from hospital to hospital in hope of admission had picked them clean in their desperation.

Hunger was also rife in the Intelligence Section's bunker. Fröhlich's head steadily shrivelled and began to take on the unappealing look of a vulture, Herbert had lost all interest in the business of cooking and flew off the handle if anyone quizzed him about it, and even the well-padded Geibel started to become visibly more emaciated. Breuer, though, who had never fully recovered from his bout of dysentery, observed with alarm how day by day not only his physical strength appeared to wane but also that his mental powers were increasingly deserting him. It was only with the greatest of effort that he was able to concentrate on his work.

To make matters worse, a real stinker had been lying in his in-tray for the past few days. In the confusion at the time of the Russian breakthrough, some secret documents had gone missing from the supply train of the Tank Destroyer Division, and Captain Eichert, who had an insuperable aversion to all forms of paperwork, had asked Breuer to draft the necessary reports on the matter. In the meantime, the Tank Destroyer Division had long since ceased to exist. Despite this, he had just received the fourth itemized request from Corps HQ asking him to explain:

a) Why the papers were being stored in the supply train in the first place.

b) Whether, and if so by whom, the driver of the lorry in question had been informed about the confidentiality provisions concerning his load.
c) How it came to be that, among the secret orders, there were still certain papers dating from the time of the French campaign, notwithstanding the fact that, in compliance with Army Ordinance XY HV sheet number so-and-so, these should have been destroyed by the summer of 1942.
d) Why the driver, assuming that he had, as noted under query b), been apprised of the situation, had not made every effort to defend the truck containing the secret documents or, if this had not proved possible, why he had not destroyed it.

'Oh, for Christ's sake!' Breuer swore as he read the message. 'Seems like the old nag of Prussian bureaucracy keeps on galloping even when all its riders have already kicked the bucket. Do you know what I feel like writing back to them, Wiese? I'll tell them to—'

'Just say: "The driver is dead. There are strong indications that he was driven to suicide by incessant questioning on the part of the army!"' suggested Wiese.

Wiese is just in the process of buckling up his belt. His company commander has ordered him to report to him on official business. Just as he's about to set off, Geibel, who has been washing his hands in the snow outside, sticks his head into the bunker.

'Quick, Lieutenant Breuer!' he calls excitedly. 'Come quickly! Something's going on out here!'

The two officers rush out into the glaring light of day. It's one of those clear, frosty days on which the super-chilled air shimmers with tiny ice crystals when it is caught in the rays of the sun. 'There, there!' hollers Geibel, pointing ahead. 'Now he really has got him… bugger it!' A few hundred metres away, where the plain begins to rise to the north, a large transport aircraft, a Ju 52, is skimming close to the ground, trailing a plume of blackish-brown smoke behind it.

It staggers like a bird with an injured wing, and the frantic drone of its engines cuts out intermittently. There is a sudden flash of silver-white above. A nimble Russian fighter dives one more time like a hawk on the stricken plane, delivering the coup de grâce with a short burst of machine-gun fire. The Junkers pancakes onto the uneven ground, smashing its undercarriage with a loud crunch, and the large grey-green fuselage buckets across the snow for a short distance before finally coming to rest heeled over in a dip. The fighter banks steeply over the crash site to make sure of its 'kill' and then disappears with a flash of white into the blue yonder.

From all sides, soldiers come stumbling as fast as they can through the deep, ice-crusted snow towards the blazing aircraft, shouting and waving their arms. A crash like this is a red-letter day, a welcome change from the bleak monotony of their daily lives; and besides, who can say what treasures the 'Ju' might be carrying?

'Come on, lads! Maybe it's a cargo of Scho-Ka-Kola!' 'Or salami!' 'Hope it's not fuel or ammo!'

Lieutenant Wiese dashes round the burning plane. It's in a bad way. One of its engines has embedded itself deep in the wing and is on fire. Thick smoke is also billowing from the middle of the fuselage. Soldiers are crowding around the cockpit, pressing their faces to the windows. Oblivious to the flames, two men have clambered up on to the side of the plane.

'Get down from there!' Breuer shouts at them. 'Do you want to get burned alive, or what?'

'But the crew's still trapped inside, Lieutenant!'

Lieutenant Wiese rushes up to lend a helping hand. The pilot and co-pilot are trapped in the front part of the aircraft. It appears the access door into the cockpit from the cabin has got jammed after the hard landing. The heat of the fire has roused the two men, who must initially have been stunned by the impact of the crash. They are screaming and hammering wildly at the plane's corrugated skin. Every now and then, their heads appear at the smoke-blackened windows. One of them seems to be wounded; his face is smeared with blood. The seamless aluminium sides of the plane and the smooth windows offer nowhere for the rescuers to gain purchase.

'A hatchet! Someone fetch a hatchet!' shouts Wiese. A couple of men head off towards the bunkers. The side loading-door of the aircraft is swinging loose on its hinges. Cubes of dried, compressed pea flour have poured from the opening, forming a huge pile. The flames are already licking around them. The troops have pounced on the heap, eagerly filling their pockets, forage caps and balaclavas with the goods. After running around the plane to try to gain access, Breuer and Geibel drag a body out from the tail section. It is the rear gunner. He isn't moving but is still just about breathing. His face and hands are blistered from the intense heat. He is wrapped in a coat and carried away. All attempts to break into the cockpit prove fruitless. By this time, the metal skin of the aircraft is too hot to touch. Fierce flames now erupt from the engines and the cockpit, spraying burning fuel around, and the aluminium ignites, emitting a blinding bluish-white light that hisses and splutters. The heat is becoming unbearable and the smoke ever more acrid. All at once, there is a loud bang. Someone shouts:

'Watch out! Get back! Take cover! The machine-gun belts are going up!'

There follows an erratic patter of small detonations. Burst cartridges buzz through the air with a metallic hum. The rescuers eventually manage to smash through the toughened glass of the cockpit windows, but the opening is too narrow to pull the pilots through. The sudden influx of air prevents them from suffocating, but that only makes their predicament all the more awful. The piercing screams of the men don't sound human any more. Their piteous shrieks drown out the spitting, crackling sound of the voracious blaze.

'Hee-ee-ee-lp!! … Shoot me! Shoo-oot me! … Eeeaurghh… aaaiiieeee… hee-ee-ee-lp… Mo–oother… Mo– aaaaaiih…'

Every so often, when the smoke clears, they catch glimpses through the window openings of the men's faces contorted in their death agonies and framed with tongues of leaping flame.

'Oh, Jesus Christ Almighty,' gasps Breuer. 'We've got to put them out of their misery!... Doesn't anyone have a gun? This is ghastly!'

Lieutenant Wiese stands there staring at the inferno in helpless horror. A thought is hammering away in his brain with painful insistence: Dear God, we have to do something! We can't just look on helplessly and impotently while two people are burned alive in front of us! We just can't! His head threatens to explode.

He shields his eyes with his hand, as if hoping that this will efface the reality of these dreadful minutes. He feels the urge to run away, to bury his burning head in the snow, and to see and hear nothing more. But he doesn't act on it. Instead, he does something else... All of a sudden, he feels as though his dislocated self has parted company with his body. He has a sense of floating, light as a feather, free and formless. He's looking down on his body like it belongs to someone else, and sees himself straighten up, reach into the leather satchel at his side, pull out a pistol, release the safety catch and slowly, ever so slowly and without trembling, raise it to eye level and take aim. He sees the finger tense on the trigger, hears from afar the report of the shots, and watches the bullets fly straight into the terrible grimacing faces there in the fiery cage. And with an ardent rush of sympathy, he senses that the person down there has done something good and charitable but at the same time something terrible; and a warm feeling of contentment washes over him. That's not me, no, that's not me! Fate has spared me from having to make this dreadful decision. It's not me!

The blood-curdling screams have ceased, and the faces have vanished from the windows. The nose of the aircraft is now one vast sea of flame, forcing the onlookers to retreat to a safer distance. Only Lieutenant Wiese stays rooted to the spot. His cap has fallen into the snow and the searing heat is scorching his face. He doesn't notice it.

He stands there like a statue. Slowly, his arm sinks to his side and the pistol drops from his hand. Then he turns around and walks stiffly and with hesitant steps towards the circle of men. His gait is that of a sleepwalker. His staring eyes look as if they are sightless. Silently, the men move aside to let him pass. Breuer stretches out his hand. 'Wiese,' he says quietly, 'come here.'

The lieutenant's vacant gaze passes straight through him. He staggers past them through the snow with weary steps. Meanwhile, at the rear of the aircraft, disregarding the flames, the soldiers keep returning to fall upon the cremated cubes of dried pea, jostling and fighting with one another and scraping up handfuls of pea-flour mixed with dirty snow into mess tins and cooking pots. One man's clothes have caught fire. He runs across the field waving his arms and yelling. No one pays him any attention. He hurls himself into a deep snow bank and rolls around in it like a dog, whimpering.

Even after several hours, the wreck of the burned-out plane is still smouldering. Soldiers continue to poke around with sticks in the smoking debris; here and there, men are nibbling on charcoal-crusted lumps of pea-flour that have been welded together. The two dead men have been recovered from the wreckage. They lie in the snow, blackened and unrecognizable, shrivelled by the heat to the size of dwarves, and with a few strips of charred clothing still clinging to their grotesquely twisted limbs. Standing over them is Colonel von Hermann, who has driven out to the crash site with Captain Engelhard. He stares in silence at their desiccated, shrunken faces, which look for all the world like wizened apples. Then he slowly takes off his greatcoat and lays it over the bodies.

Colonel von Hermann sits in his bunker in front of the small trestle table. He rubs his hand a couple of times across his eyes, which he has screwed up like something is dazzling him. There is a knock at the door. The colonel wakes with a start from his reverie.

'Come in!'

The sergeant from the adjutant's office enters and gives a brisk salute.

'Begging your pardon, Colonel, sir,' he stammers, 'I wanted… I thought… Lieutenant Colonel Unold isn't here, is he, sir?'

'No, he isn't back from Corps HQ yet. What did you want to speak to him about?'

'Nothing special, Colonel. It's to do with the dead pilots' belongings. I just wanted to know what we should do with them, seeing that their identity papers were burned with them.'

He places a few small objects on the table: the melted remains of a propelling pencil, a charred cigarette lighter, a handful of coins and various other items.

'Well, Sergeant,' says the colonel, pensively weighing one of the objects in his hand, a little lump of gold that must once have been a ring. Embedded in this shiny lump is a stone, a burgundy-red, polished stone… and engraved in the stone is a coat of arms.

'Oh, sweet Jesus, Colonel!' the sergeant whispers when he catches sight of it.

The colonel himself has gone as white as a sheet. He grips the corner of the table with one hand, and his body is trembling right down to the tiniest muscles in his face, from which all semblance of composure has vanished.

'Colonel, aren't you feeling well, sir? Should I…?'

A brusque, dismissive wave of the hand shoos the sergeant from the bunker. He departs, shaking his head and full of unease.

When Lieutenant Colonel Unold returns from his meeting at the Corps, he recoils in shock at the sight of the colonel's deathly white, mask-like face. He doesn't dare ask what the matter is, though. This alien countenance seems just too forbidding to him.

'So, my friend,' he thinks to himself, 'it's finally got to you as well, has it?' In his own steadily worsening state of nervous exhaustion, it's something of a pleasant surprise to discover that even people he'd thought were as solid as a rock have their Achilles' heel. Besides, as the day progresses, the colonel is as calm and matter-of-fact as ever. Only his voice has become harsh and brittle, and his eyes, once so lively, now seem somehow to have turned inwards. Yet Unold is far too wrapped up in his own woes to give much thought to the change in his CO's demeanour. Nor does he notice that the photograph in the silver frame that has always stood on the desk in front of the colonel's chair is no longer there.

For several days on the trot, the occupants of the Intelligence Section bunker are treated to a thick pea porridge. It tastes divine. Sonderführer Fröhlich is full of praise, and offers the opinion as he wolfs down the tasty stew that, as far as he's concerned, a Junkers could crash-land nearby every week. The faint aftertaste of charcoal and smoke seems scarcely to bother the men. Geibel even thinks it adds a certain something. And Corporal Herbert, who has prepared the dish with the utmost care, finds his culinary pride wounded by Lieutenant Wiese's point-blank refusal to eat so much as a mouthful.

A dense pall of grey hangs over the white wasteland of Stalingrad. The four-wheel-drive staff car makes heavy weather as it ploughs its way through the deep snow covering the roads. Up front, next to the driver, sits Colonel von Hermann, and on the back seat First Lieutenant Breuer and Captain Gedig have hunkered down and made themselves tolerably snug in a cocoon of coats and blankets.

The captain returned from his training course yesterday. On the way back, he was interviewed at Army High Command regarding a request he had put in for promotion some time before. When they learned that he was flying back to Stalingrad, they began to take an interest in him and detained him for an entire day. Gedig's impressions of the place were not very encouraging. He soon noticed that the attitude of fatherly and condescending optimism that they displayed towards him, a young and inexperienced officer, simply didn't ring true and that the generals and officials among the top brass who were responsible for the Eastern Front treated the topic of Stalingrad with undisguised scepticism. And he found the atmosphere at Army Group Manstein even more disconcerting. Growing confusion reigned there as a result of the front being pulled ever further back and the rapid Russian advance on Rostov-on-Don. Every moment brought new, urgent and totally insoluble demands, which left scarcely any room for considering the fate of the Sixth Army, let alone for a serious attempt at relieving the Cauldron. Gedig realized with horror that they had clearly already written off the Sixth Army here, once and for all. However, the captain was careful not to recount all this when he got back to his unit. It was essential to display optimism, optimism at all costs, even when you were up to your neck in it. His brief visit to the High Command and the Army Group had taught him that at least. And what would be the point of alarming one's comrades anyway? Besides, he took the view that things actually weren't as bad as some people were making out. After all, Hitler must have had good grounds for broadcasting his message: 'You can rely on me with rock-like confidence!' Consequently, even now Gedig is perfectly happy to chat away cheerfully about his experiences back home.

'Yes, it was marvellous. Not much sign of the war there at all. The theatres and cafés and bars were all heaving, just like before the war. What was the mood like? Well, news has certainly trickled through that things aren't going so well in Stalingrad. But they're confident nothing too serious is going to happen here. Anyhow, you should have seen the Winter Gardens…'

Colonel von Hermann pays no attention to his officers' conversation. Silent and lost in thought, he looks out at the snow-covered road. He is making a conscious effort to focus all his thoughts on this new assignment. Since yesterday, some very worrying developments have been afoot down in Zybenko.

Yet again the car gets stuck in a snowdrift. Everyone out and push! It's bitterly cold this January morning. Their breath rises like smoke into the biting air. A squad of Romanian soldiers who are busy clearing the road here help get their car moving again. They are half-frozen, starved-looking creatures, grateful for the handful of cigarettes that the colonel gives them.

It is already dark by the time they reach their destination: a row of small earth bunkers in a *balka*, with a faint glow of light coming from their entrances. They are the staff headquarters for an infantry division.

The general's bunker is lit by two electric lamps. A young general staff officer, a first lieutenant, is sitting at a table strewn with maps. With a charcoal pencil in his right hand, he's busily adding arrows and symbols, while holding a telephone receiver to his ear with his left. The general is pacing up and down the small room. He is wearing a tattered battledress top, open at the neck; underneath, the wide roll-neck of a brownish woollen pullover makes it look like he's got a scarf on. With his thinning, almost completely white hair and dense grey stubble, he resembles the skipper of a fishing boat. Colonel von Hermann salutes him. A glimmer of happiness lights up the general's eyes. He shakes the colonel warmly by both hands and claps him on the shoulder.

'Thank goodness you're here, thank God! What have you brought for me?'

The colonel looks at him in astonishment. He hesitates before replying.

'Brought for you? Ah, well… my two officers here, General.'

'What's that? But… that's just not possible! Where are your tanks?'

'We don't have any tanks left, General.'

The general slowly raises his hand to his throat like there's something constricting it.

'What am I to do, then?'

And now tears are running down his tormented, furrowed face.

His hand drops helplessly. Once more, barely audibly, his trembling lips murmur: 'What am I to do, then?'

Gripped by a sudden, desperate urge to do something, he lunges towards the map table.

'Look at this, the Russians broke through at both these places, here and here, first thing this morning. We've managed to plug this breach here, after a fashion... but we had to use all the reserves in the regiment that we could scrape together. Now I've committed some supply-train troops and men from the signals section to this second gap. And just now the regiment defending the sector on the far left reported that the Russians have broken through there as well. They're now marching north, roughly battalion strength. Marching! There's nothing to stop them there now. And I can't spare a single man, do you understand? Not a single man!'

Virtually unnoticed by the others, Gedig and Breuer have sat down on a bench along the wall. The captain gives Breuer a wide-eyed look, but says nothing. Only now does it appear to dawn on him exactly what he has returned to.

The telephone keeps ringing almost non-stop. An endless stream of bad news. No sooner has the lively general staff officer despondently hung up than another call comes in. Then he's over to the map once more with his charcoal pencil, drawing in new lines to try to get on top of the rapidly changing position. His chirpy voice is oddly at variance with the gravity of the situation.

'What's that, Colonel, sir? You say you can't...? But it *has* to be that way! It must be possible to take two more platoons out of the battalion. Station a man every thirty metres! You'll have to rake the ridge with machine-gun fire from a flanking position, then... No! I can't send you any more men. It *has* to be done that way! What's that? Yes, those are the general's orders, and that's that! '

Eventually, the general turns to Hermann in exasperation. 'Look, Colonel, you're an experienced tank commander. You're familiar with these kinds of situations! Help me, please. Tell me honestly if there's any way out of this sort of predicament? Is there anything we can do now?'

Colonel von Hermann shrugs his shoulders and says nothing. Suddenly, his mission here strikes him as totally pointless. On the orders of the High Command, he is expected to assume command here of the regiment on the right flank as well as the one on the far left of the neighbouring division. Does the top brass seriously think they can restore this desperate situation by simply shoe-horning a new, unfamiliar and untrained command post into the well-established system operating here? What utter madness! It's men who are missing here: men! And more especially, a well-rested and battle-ready force.

The general breaks the oppressive silence. 'The Corps promised me two hundred extra men. We could have used them to... But where have you been all this time, anyhow? We've been waiting for you since midday.'

Again, several minutes pass in silence. The general paces up and down restlessly. A feeling of impotence weighs heavily upon every-one. Suddenly, the low door to the bunker creaks and the tarpaulin curtain twitches. Two officers edge their way into the bunker. One is dressed in a white camouflage suit with a machine-pistol slung over his shoulder. He walks doubled over and evidently finds it hard putting one foot in front of the other. With an effort, he raises a hand in salute and announces in a weary voice: 'Captain Lemke reporting for duty with two hundred men, sir!'

'At last! We've been waiting for you. But just look at the state of you, man! What's up with you? Are you ill?'

'General, I'm only just back on my feet. I've been in hospital for the last six weeks with rheumatoid arthritis.'

'God in heaven, man, what are you doing here then? I need soldiers, not cripples!'

The captain's expression remains impassive.

'General, sir,' he says quietly and evenly, 'my men are in much the same state as well. They're all either wounded or sick. Most have come straight from hospital like me.'

The general stares aghast at the officers, one after the other, before launching into a gratuitous and unfocused diatribe, which he directs at the captain.

'What the devil were you thinking of, eh? The situation here is deadly serious! I can't help you, man! Like as not we're all going to die like dogs here. So look, see this ridge here? That's your sector. You've got to hold it at all costs, to the last man, understood? Tell your men that the fate of the entire Sixth Army depends on them, and them alone!'

The captain doesn't budge from the spot and simply stares wide-eyed at the general. Slowly, and with visible discomfort, he starts to speak: 'General... we haven't eaten... since early this morning. Might we perhaps...?'

'But of course, that goes without saying! You, Paymaster: issue your two hundred men with marching rations immediately! At the double, though, there's no time to lose!'

The paymaster, the officer who had entered the bunker with the captain, breathes a heavy sigh. 'That's not possible, I'm afraid, General.'

'What? Not possible? It must be! That's what you're there for!'

'I don't *have* any more rations, General! For weeks now, all we've been handing out are the hundred and fifty grams of bread a day per man that we're given. I really don't have anything more than that – no extra bread, no tinned meat. I could provision three or four men now at a pinch, but two hundred...'

The general lapses into a sudden state of apathy. His hands make a helpless gesture. Quietly, he says, 'Oh well, they'll just have to deploy as they are, then.'

He comes up to the silent captain and takes both of his hands in his. There are tears in his eyes again. He whispers, 'It's dreadful, I know. But there's nothing I can do to help you.'

After a considerable wait, in response to an appeal by the Corps, the High Command revokes the order given to Colonel von Hermann. The general can scarcely find the time to take his leave of the visitors; he has long since returned to poring over the maps with his adjutant.

Under cover of the pitch-black night, the staff car jolts its way back to the old command post. An icy wind howls through the gaps in the bodywork and gnaws at the men's limbs even through the blankets and greatcoats. The three officers travel in silence. Captain Gedig can feel his teeth chattering uncontrollably from the fierce cold. He was prepared for a lot of things, but hadn't envisaged his return would be remotely like *this*. What had become of the happy times in Berlin, and the Christmas he'd spent in Gotha? What had once been a shining reality was suddenly submerged, extinguished. Through his feverish brain, like a film, rolls a sequence of images of that procession of the dead, setting out from somewhere beyond the Cauldron perimeter to liberate the Sixth Army.

There they go, dragging themselves through the darkness in their thin coats, their field caps perched on their heads. Some of them have wrapped rags around their ears to protect them from the frost. Their rifles are carelessly slung over their backs, and rattling in their greatcoat pockets are the ten bullets they've each been issued with. Hungry and shivering from cold, they trudge on through the knee-deep snow. Every so often, one of them keels over with a loud groan, picks himself up and then, after staggering on for a few more steps, finally collapses, never to rise again.

Their leader's hand motions indistinctly forward. Up there is the hill, the position they've been ordered to take. Their faces, emaciated by illness and hunger, stare into the distant darkness illuminated only by the muzzle flare of the Russian guns. There are no trenches or bunkers up there. Before them, the white expanse stretches out endlessly, with flurries of powdered snow sweeping across it. There is no going back on the road they have come by. Anyone who is spared from being killed by enemy bullets will surely succumb to the biting cold of this icy January night.

The column disperses and fans out across the plain. One after another, they slip to the ground and are slowly enveloped by the white shroud as tracer bullets from Russian machine guns whistle over their heads. There's no shouting, no questions, no noise at all. That kind of deathly hush can only come from people who have given up on everything. But this terrible silence rises up to the heavens like a single painfully pressing question, to which no answer comes: 'What is the point of these sacrifices, what are they for?'

In a blinding insight born of all that he has experienced over the past few days, the truth now dawns on Captain Gedig: the High Command... Army Group Manstein... No, these two hundred sacrificial lambs won't save the Sixth Army. No one can save it now. It too is going to be put to the sword, pointlessly, senselessly. It is all over.

'It's nothing short of criminal!'

The two officers sitting at the back of the bunker give a start. What was that? Did someone speak? Or are some thoughts so distressing and urgent that they can miraculously express themselves? The colonel up front there can't possibly have said anything so outrageous. It's just not possible! But then the two of them hear quite clearly what Colonel von Hermann says next:

'And the worst thing is, there's no way out now... and woe betide anyone who tries to save his own skin after he's had to demand this of his men!'

'So, there's no escape from here?' thinks Breuer desperately. 'Is there such a thing as a "must"? Is there really and truly no way out?'

And he is at a loss to explain why the image of Lance Corporal Lakosch pops into his head.

★

When Colonel von Hermann got back to his bunker, Unold pushed a note under his nose.

'High Command just called,' he said. 'You're to be transferred with immediate effect, as per your wish.'

The colonel glanced at the note, giving a couple of thoughtful nods.

'But that's Calmus's division they want me to take command of! What's happened to Calmus?'

'Nervous breakdown… apparently!'

'My, my! Is that division in the northern sector of our eastern front?'

The lieutenant colonel cast an eye over the map.

'It covers the sector from the tractor factory to Rynok,' he replied briefly.

'And what's going to happen about the formation of fortress battalions?'

'The CO of the rocket regiment will take over responsibility for that.'

'Hmm,' said the colonel, casting a searching look at his chief of operation's inscrutable face. 'So that now makes you and the rest of the divisional staff redundant, so to speak?'

Unold did not reply; at the corners of his mouth, little creases started to form.

'Well, my dear Unold,' the colonel went on, and his choice of words came across like he was trying to expunge the man from his life once and for all: 'then I wish you all the very best for your life hereafter and for your career!'

Breuer found his men in a state of considerable uproar.

'Is it true, Lieutenant, that we're shifting command posts this evening already?'

'People are saying that the planned breakthrough is going to happen after all!'

'Are our advance Panzer units really just outside Kalach already?'

'Gentlemen, please!' Breuer told them irritably. 'That's all a load of rubbish. We're staying put, and everything stays the same – for the time being, anyhow.'

The men sat back down, deflated. Corporal Herbert handed the first lieutenant a small pile of filled-out telephone message forms.

'It's the communiqués from the Corps,' he said eagerly. 'I've put them all together.' Breuer skimmed through the slips. Their content was the same as that of all reports over the past few days: the Russians were reinforcing along the whole of the Cauldron front. And a report of an enemy breakthrough at Zybenko? Well, he'd just experienced that at first hand. Suddenly, something in the pile caught his eye and made him pause.

'What's this nonsense! "At one location, one hundred and twenty Stalin organs are believed to be massed." That's got to be an error! They must mean twelve!'

He reached for a pencil to strike out the zero. But Herbert assured him, 'No, no, Lieutenant, sir, that's right. It struck me as odd, too, so I queried it straight away. Eighty have been reported at another site!'

Breuer blanched. He did some quick mental arithmetic: a hundred and twenty multiple rocket launchers, each mounted on a simple lorry with an operating crew of four or five men, 8-centimetre calibre… that made a total of three thousand, eight hundred and forty rounds. Or maybe they had some of the heavier-calibre launchers too, the 13-centimetre ones – that would mean almost two thousand rounds in a single salvo. Two thousand 13-centimetre rockets landing on a single spot, on this open plain, which offered no cover or protection whatsoever for the men. Every living thing would be wiped out in an instant! He continued with his calculations: one German unit of heavy field howitzers of 10-centimetre calibre, which required a complement of more than six hundred soldiers and the same number of horses, could fire just forty-eight rounds in any one salvo…

You can rely on me with rock-like confidence! Pah!

'That's all just bluff, of course,' said Sonderführer Fröhlich calmly. 'They've probably parked up a few trucks with tree trunks on the back to fool our reconnaissance. They used those kinds of tricks in East Prussia back in 1914. But no one with half a brain's taken in by that nowadays!'

'Herr Fröhlich,' replied Breuer, 'if you caught a bullet in the ribs, it really wouldn't surprise me to hear you say "No worries; it's all a sham – most likely just a pamphlet"!'

A man climbed down into the bunker, out of breath. It was the corporal from the mess.

'Finally!' cried Herbert. 'There was us thinking we weren't going to get anything else to eat today.'

'No, the soup isn't ready yet,' said the corporal with a grin. 'I'm just bringing you one of the ingredients for the time being!'

With this, he handed Breuer a sodden piece of blue paper and launched into a rambling account.

'So, I look at my watch, right, and it's half-four already! So I say to my two *Hiwis*: "*Dawai* – get a move on, lads! I need some water for tonight's soup!" Back they come with a huge pile of snow in their arms. In it goes into the pot, with six of the pea cubes and the horse's leg. Well, I'm busy stirrin' it round and round, nice and careful like, so it doesn't get too thin... an' all of a sudden there's this piece of paper here sticking to the ladle!'

Breuer carefully spreads the soggy scrap of paper out on the table.

'Probably another one of Paulus's Epistles to the Cauldronians,' he jokes.

'Nah, Lieutenant,' replies the cook, 'this one's from the comrades over there! I'm on tenterhooks to hear what you reckon to it. Me and the lads over at the mess have already had a long discussion about it. So, anyhow, that's the reason the soup's still going to take a bit longer.'

Breuer, meanwhile, had a quick read of the note.

'Well, well… that's very interesting! Listen to this: it's an ultimatum to Paulus!' He read:

> To the commander of the German Sixth Army, General Paulus, or his deputy, and to all the officers and men of the encircled force…

The men crowded round the first lieutenant, who had gone to stand under the light so he could read the note more easily. Only Lieutenant Wiese carried on reading. Since the incident with the burning Ju 52, he took hardly any interest in what was going on around him. If someone spoke to him, his response was friendly enough, but he was distant and indifferent, and he frequently alarmed his comrades with the meaninglessness of his responses. But even he pricked up his ears as Breuer continued:

> The German Sixth Army, the units of the Fourth Tank Army and their reinforcements have been completely encircled since 23 November 1942… All hopes of rescue by means of a German offensive from the south and southwest have proved unfounded: The forces that were rushed to your aid have been destroyed by the Red Army, and the remnants of these forces are falling back towards Rostov. The German transport planes that have been supplying you with starvation rations of food, ammunition and fuel are being forced by the victorious and swift advance of the Red Army to move airfields, and to fly from great distances to reach your positions. Moreover, the Russian air force is inflicting huge losses on German transport planes and their crews. Air transport is unlikely to continue for much longer.

'That actually sounds quite… quite civilized!' said Geibel in surprise.
'And it's all true, what's more!' muttered the cook.

'What?' Fröhlich butted in. 'You think that's the truth? These absurd exaggerations?'

'Pipe down, damn you!' shouted Breuer. 'Either let me read, or you can prattle among yourselves!'

He resumed reading:

> Your encircled troops are in a grave situation. They are suffering from hunger, sickness and cold. The harsh Russian winter is only just beginning: hard frosts, cold winds and snowstorms are still to come, but your soldiers do not have winter uniforms and are living in unsanitary conditions. You, as commander, and all the officers of the surrounded troops know very well that there is no longer any realistic possibility of breaking through the encirclement. Your position is hopeless and further resistance is useless.

'Ha ha,' scoffed Fröhlich, 'they've got a surprise coming!'

'Will you just hold your bloody tongue for once?' Herbert interrupted. 'What they're saying there isn't so very wide of the mark. Seems to me like they're pretty well informed about our situation.'

> Given the inescapable position that your forces now find themselves in, and in order to avoid unnecessary bloodshed, we propose that you accept the following terms of surrender:
>
> 1. All surrounded German troops, with you and your staff, are to cease any further resistance.
> 2. You are to hand over to us, in an orderly fashion and intact, all men, arms, weaponry and army property.
>
> We guarantee the lives and the safety of all officers, non-commissioned officers and men who lay down their arms.

We also guarantee that at the end of the war they will be returned to Germany, or to any other country of their choice. All surrendering forces will be allowed to keep their uniforms, insignia and medals, along with their personal belongings and valuables. High-ranking officers will be permitted to retain their service daggers. All officers, non-commissioned officers and men who surrender will immediately be issued with normal rations. All those suffering from wounds, illness or frostbite will receive medical attention.

Now it was Herbert who could contain himself no longer.

'Well, blow me down, that's really decent of them! You'd never have believed that was written by Bolsheviks!'

'That's just the problem!' sputtered the mess corporal. 'If it was the British rather than the Bolsheviks, then fair enough. But you can't trust that lot!'

'And all that stuff about providing us with food, I'm not so sure about that either,' Geibel chipped in apprehensively. 'I doubt whether they'll actually be able to cater for all of us. Three hundred thousand men – that's like feeding a whole city!'

'It's all a complete swindle!' shouted Fröhlich furiously. 'A cheap con trick! Leaving the officers their daggers – when they know full well that no one here even carries a dagger! And of course they won't be able to feed us. They haven't got anything to eat themselves! As soon as we've laid down our arms, they'll chuck us all into the Volga.'

With some difficulty, Breuer got them all to quieten down again.

'Don't you want to hear how it ends first?' he asked, before continuing:

We expect your written reply on 9 January 1943, at 10.00 hours, Moscow time. It should be brought by a representative whom you have personally appointed, and who should proceed in a car flying a white flag along the road from the Konny railway halt to Kotluban station. Your representative will be met by Russian officers in Region 'B' 0.5 kilometres southeast of the railway halt at 10.00 hours precisely.

If you choose to reject our proposal for your capitulation, be warned that the forces of the Red Army and the Red Air Force will be compelled to take steps to destroy the encircled German troops, and that you will bear the responsibility for their annihilation.

Breuer's hand holding the sheet fell limply to his side; it felt like a lump of lead. His glance met that of Lieutenant Wiese, who was staring intently at him.

'We all bear the responsibility,' Wiese murmured, 'all of us!'

'Well…,' Corporal Herbert began. The feeling of anxiety that was now weighing down on them all made him very uneasy.

'And what do you reckon to all this, Lieutenant Breuer, sir?' enquired the cook presently. Before he could answer, Fröhlich erupted once more: 'There's no question of reckoning anything! Even if all that were true… a German soldier never surrenders, do you hear? It has never happened in the whole of German history!'

'Nonsense!' shouted Breuer. In his excitement, he completely forgot that, as an officer, he should not even have allowed a discussion of this sort to take place in front of the other ranks.

'Even Blücher surrendered! He was forced to surrender at Radkau when he ran out of bread and ammunition. A capitulation in honourable circumstances, after putting up a brave fight, isn't a disgrace – it can even be a soldier's duty! And what do I think in general?' he went on, more calmly. 'I think that we don't have a clear picture of the situation we're in here, and don't know whether the Russians are able or even willing to keep their promises. But I do believe that Army High Command is perfectly capable of evaluating these things. And if there's even the faintest guarantee that the Russians mean what they say, then – well, I think that Paulus will accept their ultimatum. In a situation like this, he can't take responsibility for what might happen if he refuses.'

'Yessir, Lieutenant,' the mess corporal agreed, 'that's just what I was thinking too while I was stirring my soup and the old horse bone kept floating up to the top. No one's taking responsibility for this business any more!'

Breuer quickly read through the ultimatum one more time. What had Colonel von Hermann said? There's no way out now? This, *this* was the way out! If only they could know what awaited them in Russian captivity, if only anyone knew anything, for that matter…

'Well, I still reckon, Lieutenant,' said Geibel timidly, 'that the top brass – I don't mean our colonel, of course, but the officers in the Corps and High Command – don't think twice about us little foot soldiers when they're drawing up their war plans. Their minds are on far bigger things, on honour and heroism and such like… but those generals have no idea of what that might cost us ordinary soldiers.'

'You're a stupid idiot, Geibel!' Breuer replied angrily. 'General Paulus thinks and cares just as much about the plight of the ordinary soldier here in the Cauldron as the rest of us, perhaps even more. And that's why I'm convinced he'll accept the ultimatum.'

'Chuck that pamphlet away, Breuer!' said Wiese, looking up from his book. 'Paulus won't accept it.'

'Absolutely, quite right!' cried Fröhlich. 'The ultimatum must have been rejected already! What's written there? Answer by the ninth of January at ten o'clock? Well, it's the ninth today! If it had been accepted, they'd already have declared a ceasefire long since!'

'What's that, where…?' Breuer snatched up the slip of paper again. 'the ninth of the first, 10.00 hours, you're right! I must go and speak to the chief of staff this instant!'

Over in the CO's bunker he found Colonel von Hermann busy packing his things.

'Good that you've dropped by, Breuer,' von Hermann greeted him. 'That means I can say my goodbyes right now. And please inform Lieutenant Wiese he should get ready to leave straight away! He's coming with me to the new division as my adjutant.'

Breuer stood there, thunderstruck. The CO was leaving, and Wiese was going with him. Their little circle was breaking up. Everything was falling apart…

'What have you got there for me?' asked the colonel, reaching for the slip that Breuer still clutched in his hand. 'Oh right, the leaflet with the Russian ultimatum! Yes, please destroy that! And make sure the men don't get to learn about its contents.'

Von Hermann went over to his desk and started searching through some papers.

'Here, this concerns the Intelligence Section.' He handed Breuer a typewritten form, which read:

TO THE GENERAL COMMANDING, 14TH PANZER CORPS.
SECTION IC.
COMMUNIQUÉ TO BE READ TO THE RANKS.

On 8.1.43, at Makeyevka, Russian peace envoys delivered a sealed letter addressed to the Supreme Commander of the Sixth Army containing a call to surrender. German representatives refused to take delivery of the letter, and the Russian officers were immediately dismissed.

Now the enemy has realized that he cannot conquer the Cauldron by force of arms, he is trying to undermine our resistance with transparent propaganda tricks. He will not succeed! The Sixth Army will hold Stalingrad until the hour of liberation approaches.

In future, if any enemy peace negotiators attempt to approach our lines, they should be fired upon.

PART 3

The Moment of Truth

I

The Die is Cast

BREUER WOKE FROM SLEEP with a start. He looked about in confusion. His heart was thumping wildly and his chest felt like it was being held fast by bands of iron. What the hell was going on? Had he been having a bad dream? The room was filled with the steady breathing of other sleepers. From beneath the table he was sleeping on came the monotonous sawing sound of Fröhlich's snoring. The first light of dawn was breaking through the small window. The lamp hanging from the ceiling, whose wick had been turned down to just a pinprick of flame, flickered gently and the grey half-shadows in the room were heavy with foreboding. And all of a sudden Breuer knew what had woken him from his slumbers.

'Hey, Fröhlich!'

A reluctant grunt came from below.

'Hey, wake up, will you man? Just listen!'

Fröhlich's sleepy face appeared from beneath the tabletop, gazing up questioningly at the first lieutenant, who was listening intently. And now Fröhlich heard it too as it drifted over to them, a persistent dull rumble that sounded like a far-off drum roll.

'Artillery fire!'

'Yeah, that's right, artillery fire,' Breuer replied. Gingerly, the two of them picked their way over their sleeping comrades and emerged into the biting cold of the early morning. Out here, the noise, only faintly audible down in the bunker, filled the entire expanse of the landscape: an incessant rumbling punctuated with muffled thuds, which appeared to be bursting forth from the skies and the earth simultaneously and making the ground tremble like it was suffering a shivering fit. The western sky, though, where the shadows of the fast-vanishing night still hung, was bathed in a blood-red glow, into which tongues of yellow flame kept shooting all along the horizon. The two men stood and held their breath. Breuer placed a heavy hand on the shoulder of the Sonderführer.

'It's the main Russian offensive,' he said hoarsely. 'It's beginning.'

A main field dressing station on the edge of the Rossoshka Valley, just one of many. It had been set up to deal with two hundred casualties at most, though now there were more than six hundred men lying there. They lay packed in like sardines in the semi-darkness of the old stable block, those torn, mutilated, frost-disfigured human bodies that still harboured a glimmer of life. And they sat in the long corridors, every man sitting between the legs of the man behind him, their ragged clothes teeming with lice as dense as a coating of mould. And when one of them moved, a ripple of pained groans ran through their ranks. The stench of a wild animal's cage, rank enough to make you catch your breath, filled the building. Lumps of peat were burning in two empty petrol drums, sending clouds of acrid smoke billowing up to the wooden-boarded roof of the stables, which was holed in many places. But the cold also seeped into the room through the small glassless windows and the crumbling clay walls, creeping into the men's faces and hands and freezing solid the contents of drug vials.

This house of misery, which frequently shook from the impact of artillery shells nearby or bombs dropped in the night by planes, had cast its spell over Padre Peters and refused to let him go. The images of this horrific world followed him into the spells of fitful sleep he managed to snatch at dead of night. There was that trench beside the shed, for instance, full to the brim with amputated limbs… and the untold number of new 'admissions' every day, who lay outside in the snow and were forced to wait until space was made for them inside. The medical orderlies sullenly weaved their way between them, here and there dragging to one side the stiff cadaver of someone who had lost too much blood and had not survived the severe frost. Padre Peters had to witness all of this. Then there was the field surgeon here, a tall, gaunt fellow who wore a permanent hangdog expression and who barely slept, keeping himself awake with coffee and other stimulants. In the light cast by an oil lamp, he would stand over the simple trestle table that served as an operating table and worked with cramped hands on opened-up bodies that steamed in the chill air like a washing tub. He was in the habit of weighing up the seriousness of the men's injuries with curt dispassion: 'Stomach wound – that'll take an hour. Can't do anything about that… not now, anyhow.' Not now; that meant never. But in an hour, he and his team here could perform three amputations; if they immediately wrote off one hopeless case, then there was a slim chance they could save the lives of three other men. It was a simple calculation, dreadful in its sober logic.

Padre Peters saw all this, day in, day out. And he saw assistants and orderlies keel over during operations from lack of sleep; he saw wounded men lying there apathetically, sunk in profound hopelessness and waiting silently for the end to come; he saw those who, out of sheer desperation, tried to help themselves and, either by using subterfuge or by summoning up their last remaining strength, somehow managed to get themselves as far as the operating table. When they were rebuffed and told to get lost, they begged the medical staff to be merciful and put a bullet through their heads or give them a lethal injection. He saw the feverish waves of renewed hope swell up over the lines of men whenever the surgeon major managed to flag down a couple of empty lorries and dispatch thirty to forty men, primarily those with brain or eye injuries, to the airfield at Pitomnik, or when a rumour frequently spread and given credence – namely that German tanks were approaching – was revived and did the rounds once more.

And he saw starving men, emaciated by dysentery and bouts of diarrhoea – not the countless men in this condition who perished of sheer weakness in snow holes out in the open somewhere, but the few who still had sufficient strength to drag their hopes to this field hospital. He looked into their mask-like, twisted faces, which had a bluish pallor to them, and their wide, staring eyes that glowed feverishly in dark hollowed-out sockets, and watched them wolf down the food that was handed them like wild animals, only to double up on the floor, wracked by violent stomach cramps, just a few minutes later. The doctor would shrug his shoulders: 'Nothing to be done; their bodies just won't accept solids any more. What they need is two months' worth of glucose injections.' And for a few seconds, Peters would see a fleeting mirage of white hospital beds, light, sun, and nurses in crisp white uniforms with kindly eyes and soft, gentle hands…

Peters saw day by day how the stretcher-bearers would stumble in unfeeling monotony with their loads to the place behind the shed, where the Russian *Hiwis* scraped out makeshift graves in the snow to bury the long line of corpses. And he stood in attendance while this was going on and noticed how one of the Russians pointed at the pile of bodies that had just been unloaded and announced in broken German: 'Lives! Still lives!' And he was right, there was a man among the corpses who was still alive! His mouth opened and closed in grinding motions in his frozen face, while the fingers of one hand, lying listlessly in the snow, tightened and unclenched again in the same rhythm. Without a word and with a studied air of indifference, the bearers heaved their burden back up onto their shoulders and trudged back to the stables.

Padre Peters saw all of this, and he saw it as a human being whose gaze was fixed not on the husk of the body but on the kernel of the soul. The men who were suffering so anonymously here, dying in his arms, in agony or with curses on their lips or in harrowingly dumb submissiveness, were not in Peters's eyes simply soldiers, serial numbers or cannon fodder. Each of them revealed himself – often in deeply moving last testaments – to be a profound and multi-faceted individual blessed by God. They had all worked and loved and hoped and gone astray; they were the loved ones of women and children or the object of a mother's anxious concern. As he looked on, this misery multiplied into a penitential procession by a whole people, and suddenly all the suffering and death broke over Padre Peters with unchecked force. He agonized and prayed to God to give him strength. And the inner strength he gained from these prayers he channelled into the services he conducted in rotation with his young colleague from the other denomination. Here he found words that, for a few brief moments, filled the dismal room with light and warmth and provided succour to the soul when the hand of the doctor could no longer help the body. It was in moments such as these that he truly felt his career to be a vocation.

But the situation went beyond all human endurance. The tide of misery threatened to engulf him. At that point, the part of his being that remained untainted triggered a kind of automatic self-preservation mechanism. Like in a leaking ship, the bulkheads within him shut fast against the overpowering swell of suffering, only letting through what his soul was able to deal with. This meant that, at times, he was totally abstracted, carelessly stumbling over the rows of wounded soldiers and oblivious to the groans of the men he trod on. Utterly unaware of what he was doing – if he'd realized the full extent of his actions, he would have been horrified at himself – he gradually learned, just as the surgeon standing there at his blood-soaked operating table had done, to apply a kind of triage system to his pastoral care. His brain would automatically register when a person was in dire need of spiritual comfort or could forego it, and he would only deploy the valuable psychological forces of empathy and sympathy in priority cases, dismissing anything that fell outside this category. Accordingly, he had begun by offering up a short prayer for the dead who were being buried outside. Now he gave that up. Every prayer for the dead was one less he could expend on men who, for the time being at least, were still clinging on to life. For all his active involvement at the dressing station, Padre Peters knew full well that everyone who came here was already marked for death and that the only question remaining was in what precise manner they would depart this life.

When the division had been relieved by a motorized division from the south at the start of January, Colonel Steigmann was the only one among his comrades who did not greet this switch with unalloyed delight. Sure, this relief was fully deserved, and the fact that the best-equipped unit in the Cauldron was now taking over the defence of its most difficult sector seemed to be in everyone's best interests. But the self-confident, supercilious way in which the officers of the relief unit had looked at his tried-and-tested defensive system... he hoped these gentlemen wouldn't have any nasty surprises! But everyone else was over the moon at being transferred to the quiet and well-secured southern sector. They really had been saved by the skin of their teeth; this was almost like a holiday! And there had been no envy or annoyance when the advance parties of the new unit came to cast a condescending eye over their pitiful defensive positions. 'So this is where you've been living, eh? Oh well, no matter, no matter. We'll build everything ourselves! We've brought whole columns of lorries along with building timber and T-beams!' Fine then, so much the better! Good luck with that! Their own division at least were sick to the back teeth with this miserable sector, which they'd defended at such a high cost in blood.

The self-confidence of the 'new boys' didn't always ring true. Another person who followed the changeover between the two divisions with very mixed feelings was Harras, recently promoted to the rank of lieutenant. His hopes had once more deceived him: Unold had refused his request for a transfer, and the supposedly imminent breakout from the Cauldron had come to nothing as well. Now he found himself embroiled in this unholy mess as a company leader. That trick he'd pulled a while back hadn't paid off, despite being awarded the Iron Cross First Class and getting himself promoted. Quite the opposite, in fact: it would have been better to have stayed with the Russians. But the way back to the enemy lines was now barred too.

Besides, despite being relatively well equipped with winter clothing, it turned out that the men from the motorized unit, who were used to warm bunkers, could not cope with this snowy, shelterless wasteland. They were often found frozen to death in the morning in their foxholes, their rifles still in the firing position. From the very first day, the losses as a result of the severe cold were shockingly high, but there was no question of engineering work to improve the forward positions even though piles of railway sleepers lay ready behind the lines. You couldn't raise your head above the parapet by either day or night now. With growing alarm, the unit leaders observed movements on the other side, which indicated that new forces were being brought into position. Had that always been the case here, or were they preparing for something special? The new division's unfamiliarity with this sector contributed to a general sense of nervousness.

And so it came to the ninth of January. The preceding two days had passed off unusually quietly, so that evening in the battalion bunker a game of Skat was organized, something they hadn't done for a while. The Arse – who had been made a captain on the first of January – was also less than overjoyed about the division's relocation to another sector. His unhappiness manifested itself firstly in an increased intake of alcohol and secondly in him cursing about anything and everything – the lousy bunker, the feeble new troops and their endless complaints about the cold, the rations, the smoking stove, the dog-eared playing cards, and the top brass from the regimental staff upwards, who were solely responsible for the shit they were in. Yet none of this prevented him from being tirelessly active on behalf of his battalion from morning to night.

The fact that he showed his face at the forward front line on an almost daily basis and wasn't afraid of contradicting the divisional commander if he felt it necessary had earned him the respect of the ordinary soldiers, though he did ask a lot of them. He was one of those eternal mercenaries for whom war and fighting at the front had become a way of life and who in peacetime generally go to the dogs for lack of any suitable job opportunities.

Lieutenant Harras suppressed a yawn while the captain was shuffling the cards. Once again, the Skat game seemed never-ending. If the Arse found himself on a losing streak, he refused to throw in his hand until he'd won everything he'd lost back again. He had undone the top buttons of his uniform jacket – a stylishly cut garment, though it was already badly faded and patched at the elbows – and his Knight's Cross was dangling in a rather melancholy way from one of the hooks on the jacket collar. Harras stole a glance at his watch. Hell, it was almost six already! It must be light outside by now. Blinking, he looked at the little junior doctor sitting opposite him, whose eyes were also drooping from tiredness. The two messengers were snoring on the bench behind him. The only person who wasn't wilting was the Arse. As he nonchalantly shuffled the pack, he regaled them with a story.

'So, this brunette whore just sidles right up to the general, bold as brass, and pats his bald head and says, "Ooh, là là, Fatty!" and plonks herself down on his lap! "Fatty" she calls him, in German too! You should have seen the look on the old man's face!'

'Ha ha,' Harras laughed mechanically. He'd heard this story, the pièce de résistance from the captain's posting to Paris, at least ten times already and knew at what points he was expected to show his appreciation. Not a peep from the doctor, though. He was staring glassy-eyed at the hand he'd been dealt. 'Pass,' he murmured, and closed his eyes.

Suddenly, all three of them leap up from their seats with a start. The silence is abruptly shattered by an ear-splitting explosion. The small bunker trembles and shakes like it has been hit by an earthquake. Sand showers down from the roof, pieces of dried clay fall off the walls, and the flame in the storm lantern bends and flickers nervously. The two messengers in the corner have been rudely roused from their sleep and are bracing their backs against the earth wall, their arms spread wide as if they're looking for something to cling fast to. The blast seems to go on for ever. It continues as a deep, incessant booming and roaring, like the sound of breaking surf amplified a thousand times over. The Arse shoots the others a crazed look, his hand reaching automatically for the bottle dancing around on the rocking table. He says something, the words disintegrating as they leave his mouth. But already he's got a grip of himself; he's a man of action once more. He jams his helmet on his head, throws on his fleece overjacket and springs over to the entrance. Harras can feel beads of cold sweat breaking out on his forehead; he gropes for his camouflage jacket, only managing to get hold of it at the third attempt.

Outside, all hell has broken loose. A few hundred metres in front of the bunker, where the forward positions are, the earth seems to have been turned inside out. The entire breadth of the sector controlled by the division, and doubtless extending far beyond it, is engulfed in a wall of fire, a living, blazing forest out of which new bright peaks of flame keep shooting skywards. And as they watch, this wall staggers in fitful leaps ever closer to the men, billowing out clouds of sulphurous smoke as it advances. The captain turns around, his face a ghastly grimace. He shouts something, but the roaring din swallows his voice. With a single leap, he propels himself back into the bunker, which suddenly seems to be seized by giant hands and shaken violently. A single sharp explosion rises above the backcloth of thunderous roars. Harras is hurled into a corner. As he is falling, he sees wooden beams splintering, and the ceiling and the walls shifting towards one another and appearing to dissolve. Then stifling dust fills the room, pouring into the lungs like lead. The light goes out. Harras buries his head in his coat and presses his fists to his ears; his teeth are chattering uncontrollably and his whole body is shaking like he's caught a fever. He has a vague sense of someone pushing up against him and grabbing hold of him. Something warm flows over his hands.

By the time he dares to look up again, the room has grown light. Bent double, legs akimbo, the Arse is standing over the upended table; his helmet is sitting lopsidedly on his head, covered with what looks like flour. The side wall is half collapsed, and up above there is a gaping hole, through which Harras can see, alongside daylight, clouds scudding by and powdery snow falling. The planks of the roof have been exposed and a steady trickle of soil is pouring down from it. The floor of the bunker is a rubbish tip. A figure levers itself out of the mountain of clods of earth, clothes, boards and telephone equipment, clutching wildly at the air, and slowly staggers to its feet. It's one of the two messengers.

Harras works himself free of the body lying on top of him. It yields like rubber, slips back and slumps over. It is the junior doctor. He's dead.

Meanwhile, the infernal concert thunders on. Harras sinks back into his corner. His senses start to fail him. He's lost all sense of feeling, and all his willpower. He has become insubstantial, and his body is being absorbed into the shaking and humming vibrations of the earth. His bottom jaw goes slack and his head lolls back and forth, banging at regular intervals against the clay wall.

The three men have no idea how long they have been sitting there like this. Ten minutes, an hour, two hours? It seems like an eternity... All of a sudden, they lift their heads. Something has changed. Their ears are still ringing and buzzing, and their nerves are vibrating like taut musical strings. Outside, though, it's fallen quiet, unbearably quiet...

Then there's the sound of running steps. 'Get out!' a hoarse voice yells through the entrance. 'Get out now! They're coming!' The captain grabs his machine-pistol, staggers on stiff knees to the exit and ascends the stairs, stepping over a lifeless body as he does so. Bounding out into the open and drawing himself up to his full height, he stands as if thunderstruck at the sight that meets his eyes. Churned-up earth as far as the eye can see – clay-coloured soil with patches of black in it, in the midst of a snowy winter, a ploughed-up, turned-over wasteland, a landscape of craters. Harras has followed him. He peers cautiously over the edge of the top step. The messenger is cowering behind him. High above them, the last remnants of the heavy artillery barrage go droning overhead to land somewhere far behind the lines. But up ahead there, they're advancing, in dense white lines across the brown landscape, slowly and bolt upright like they're on the parade ground. Between them manoeuvre the white rumps of tanks, with fur-coated figures perched on them, stopping briefly before moving on another short stretch. Hardly a shot is fired. The only sound of gunfire comes from a machine gun hammering away to one side. A single, solitary machine gun, in forlorn, asthmatic bursts. Up ahead, there's a sudden flash, and at the same time a metallic blast whips through the air around him. Harras feels it like a punch in the face; suddenly, he's wiping something sticky and soft from his eyes. And then he sees it: up front, where the captain had been standing a moment ago, just six metres away, all that's now left is a half-person, a pair of legs up to the waist. As he looks on, the legs slowly topple forward...

Harras bellows like a wounded steer. He jumps up and makes

a run for it, leaping and bounding in long strides over craters and shell holes. Another shockwave blasts past his head; the air pressure knocks him off his feet, momentarily dazing him. But immediately he's up and running again, dashing on in a crazy zigzag, still yelling his head off. His hammering heart clings to this screaming; it reassures him that he's still alive. He rushes past the wrecks of vehicles, past destroyed field guns, over the dead bodies that are lying all around. His eyes take in none of this. All they can see is a pair of legs, tipping slowly forward, over and over again...

He tumbles down a slope. A pair of fists grab hold of him. 'What's up, then?' asks a calm voice. 'Looks like someone's gone crackers!' And in the grip of these strong hands, Harras loses consciousness. Blackness swims before his eyes.

The pale red traffic light of the sun, which pushed itself up out of the grey layer of mist, brought with it a cold, clear winter's day. The atmosphere was fraught with tension. The sound of fighting drifted over from the west. On the road leading from Novo Alexeyevka to Dubininsky, which was normally almost empty, motorbikes and lorries were speeding back and forth, and squads of marching soldiers and small columns of trucks were heading east. In the city of bunkers, things were humming and buzzing like a beehive.

First Lieutenant Breuer was profoundly shocked at what had happened over the past two days. His thoughts were plagued by dark doubts and bitter questions. Yet the pace of events, which came thick and fast, left him no time for reflection. He was buffeted by the whirlwind like a ship that had lost both its mast and rudder. He telephoned the Corps early this morning. The orderly officer picked up the phone. The man was clearly in a foul temper and gave monosyllabic answers to Breuer's questions: Yes, the Russians were attacking... Nobody knew for certain, no clear general picture had emerged yet... No, he didn't have any more information at present. Breuer lost his temper and demanded to speak to the captain in person.

'Who, Count Willms?' came the response. 'He's not here any more!'

'How come?! What do you mean?'

'Flew out a few days ago. He's an army messenger now!'

Breuer hung up. That told him all he needed to know. So that was how things stood!

Around midday, a call came through from the chief of staff: 'Get yourself over here right away!' Lieutenant Colonel Unold had finally been able to occupy his new bunker. When Breuer arrived, Unold, Engelhard and old Endrigkeit were already assembled in the panelled room with wide map tables, while in the corner there stood a small figure in a greatcoat that was far too large for him and was torn and caked with mud. The balaclava he was wearing framed a grey face covered with several days' growth of stubble. Breuer gave a start. It was his driver, Lakosch.

'So, we've caught the little bastard!' said Unold, giving the first lieutenant's outstretched hand a perfunctory shake. 'What did I tell you? The bloke deserted, tried to go over to the enemy. Clear-cut case. He's confessed to everything.'

Breuer stared at the lieutenant colonel.

'But that's just not possible!' he stammered.

Unold's pale face was a mask of mocking scorn.

'Go ahead, ask him yourself!'

Breuer turned his gaze on Lakosch. How utterly worn out the poor lad looked! He couldn't have eaten anything for days.

'Is that true, Lakosch? Were you planning to desert and go over to the enemy?'

The little driver's eyes shot Breuer a sad but unabashed look. 'Yes, Lieutenant, sir,' he replied calmly.

'You're saying you wanted to save your own skin by betraying us all here? I can't believe it!'

Lakosch couldn't meet the lieutenant's gaze. He said nothing.

'No, Lieutenant Colonel, sir.' Breuer swung round, agitated, and faced Unold again. 'It simply isn't possible! The man's clearly taken leave of his senses. I know him! You know yourself, sir, what a good soldier he was. He's just had a nervous breakdown. It happens… After all, we're all…'

Suddenly, words failed him. Unold narrowed his eyes slightly and, stroking the corners of his mouth, gave Breuer a searching look. Then he turned to Endrigkeit, who had been sucking silently on his pipe the whole time.

'Put him in the old bunker,' he said. 'And keep him in the dark there. Lock the place securely and post a sentry outside. And no one is to speak to him! Make sure that all metal objects are removed from the room. A bloke like him is capable of anything.'

Straight after supper, a drumhead court martial was convened. It consisted of Lieutenant Colonel Unold, Captain Engelhard, and Unold's batman as a representative of the other ranks. Lakosch refused to explain to the court why he had acted as he did, but the fact that he clearly reiterated his intention to defect to the enemy made the verdict a foregone conclusion: death by firing squad. Unold confirmed the verdict in his capacity as acting divisional commander and immediately after passing sentence summoned Captain Endrigkeit once more. 'I want to draw a line under this business as quickly as possible and with the minimum of fuss,' he told him. 'God knows, we've got plenty of other things to worry about right now. So I'm ordering that the judgement should be executed at first light tomorrow. The firing squad will be made up of military police. I'm putting you in charge of carrying out the execution!'

Up to now, the captain hadn't uttered a word about the whole affair. Now he broke his silence.

'You want me to shoot the lad?' His broad East Prussian accent rose from the depths of his beard as if it were coming out of a dense forest. 'No, Lieutenant Colonel, sir, I can't. I just can't do it.'

For a moment, Unold was speechless. Nothing like this had ever happened to him before. Had everyone here gone mad? He pulled himself together and decided to overlook this act of insubordination. After all, the old captain was only a reservist, and he wasn't from high up the social ladder either. There was no point taking such people very seriously.

'What kind of nonsense is that, Endrigkeit?' he said with forced joviality. 'There's no one else I can entrust this task to, see. You've got experience in these matters! I mean, this won't be the first time you've executed someone.'

'No, it's just not on,' the captain replied. 'I can't do it.'

Unold's frayed nerves finally snapped.

'For Christ's sake!' he shouted. 'Have you gone completely crazy, or what? I'm giving you a direct order, and that's an end of it! Tomorrow morning at nine sharp you'll come and report to me that the sentence has been carried out. And you haven't heard the last of this, either!'

Captain Endrigkeit walked out across the open steppe. He felt the need to clear his head and straighten things out in his own mind. The lacework patterns of the frost-encrusted snow crunched beneath his feet. The rolling attack by the Russians had even forced its way into the silence of this desolate winter landscape. The air was humming with the drone and howl of aircraft engines. Up above, agile fighters pulled breathtaking turns. Over to the west, at low altitude, ground-attack aircraft skimmed over the Rossoshka Valley, unleashing fiery-tailed rockets from beneath their wings with an evil hissing sound onto unseen enemy forces below. High up in the sky, reflecting in the afterglow of the sun, which had already sunk below the horizon, were the tiny fuselages of a squadron of bombers. Black mushroom clouds erupting on the ground marked their progress.

The captain, though, took no notice of any of this. His gaze was turned inwards. They were expecting him to shoot Lakosch, the very lad who had saved him from a real fix that time by the skin of his teeth? Endrigkeit was a tough nut. He'd had to carry out many an execution and hadn't been greatly concerned about the whys and wherefores. But this business was beyond a joke. To go and do such a thing to a bloody rascal just because of an act of sheer stupidity! If only he'd been a thug, or a real criminal…

Suddenly making up his mind, he turned around and trudged over to the bunker. The sergeant standing guard there opened the door and lit a candle for him. Lakosch sat huddled in the corner of the unheated room. When the captain entered, he got to his feet. Endrigkeit was irritated at the feeling of pity he felt welling up inside him.

'What were you thinking of, you miserable wretch?' he blustered. 'Thought you'd just do a runner, eh? And leave your mates in the shit, right? And now they can shoot anyone who does that! So how does that make you feel, eh?'

All of a sudden, when confronted by this bear of a man, Lakosch felt very small. It was like when he was a kid and was about to get a thrashing from his dad for doing something stupid.

'I… I'm very sorry, Captain, sir,' he stuttered, 'for causing you all this trouble. And the thing about my mates, well, I hated doing that, I really did – but I'm at my wits' end. I just can't take any more of this!'

And then it all spilled out of Lakosch. Everything that had been seething inside of him for weeks and tormenting him to the point where he took his final desperate step now erupted from him like a stream that had been long dammed up. He spoke about his youth, about his father, who had been murdered in a concentration camp, about his belief in the Führer and a 'German socialism', about the war and his experiences in Russia, and finally about how his whole world had collapsed after overhearing a conversation quite by chance. And he went on to explain about Seliger and Harras and the German communists who were over there behind Russian lines working to try to save the men of the Sixth Army…

In the meantime, Endrigkeit had sat himself down on the bench next to Lakosch and lit his pipe. His anger had subsided. He sat in silence and listened to the little driver, who was sometimes halting in his delivery, while at other times he tripped over his words in his haste to get them out. Endrigkeit blew out dense clouds of smoke. So that was how things stood, then. Unold really ought to hear this. However, no sooner had this thought occurred to him than he immediately rejected it. He knew it would be pointless. The Prussian army wasn't interested in people's motivations.

'So you see, I didn't do it out of cowardice, Captain, sir,' Lakosch said disconsolately. 'And I was actually thinking of my comrades… given that there are Germans over on the other side. So I started thinking that maybe the Russians aren't like they're painted and wouldn't go slaughtering everybody … and that there might be a truce and the army might be saved if one of them from over there explained how things really are with the Russians.'

Lakosch waited in vain for an answer. Endrigkeit sat silently, looking straight ahead. Once again, an indistinct feeling of irritation was rising in him. How simple things had been in the past, God damn it! Back then, a deserter was a scoundrel, a traitor to the Fatherland who could be dealt with summarily. But now, all of a sudden, things weren't so straightforward any more. Loyalty, justice, honour, duty, obedience – this all suddenly appeared in a very questionable light. And even love of the Fatherland had now instantly taken on an ambiguity. Why had this set of concepts, once so rock-solid, suddenly become so shaky? Were the Nazis to blame for this as well? Or was it Stalingrad? Endrigkeit liked simplicity and clarity. He'd lost his bearings in this new landscape. And that appalled him.

Faced with the captain's ominous silence, Lakosch had also stopped talking. He held out a grubby envelope to Endrigkeit.

'If I might be so bold as to ask the captain for one last thing,' he said hesitantly, 'my mother's address is on this envelope. If the captain would be so good as to write and tell her that... well, that I got back on the right track after all.'

Endrigkeit turned slowly to face the little driver and gave him a wide stare. His broad chest rose and fell with the deep breaths he was taking. Without warning, he sprang to his feet. 'Get out!' he roared, his whole body shaking. 'Out! Get lost, you wretch! And be quick about it, or I'll kick you up the backside, d'you hear, you wastrel? And don't show your face round here ever again, you miserable specimen!'

Lakosch stared at the captain in astonishment. Had he suddenly taken leave of his senses? But then it began to dawn on him. A look of amazed disbelief crossed his face. He approached the captain, searching for some appropriate words of thanks. But Endrigkeit had already flung the door open and gave Lakosch such a terrifying look that the driver, cowed into silence again, simply squeezed quickly past him and rushed up the steps and dashed past the baffled sentry into the gathering darkness.

Captain Endrigkeit sat down on the bench and wiped the sweat from his brow. He was perfectly well aware – as both an officer and a policeman – of what he had just done. And of the consequences. But despite that, he felt an enormous sense of relief. Let them put him up in front of a court martial, let them shoot him – what did he care now? Final sentence had already been passed on all of them here in the Cauldron, including those who still took it upon themselves to judge others. In the face of certain death, the judgement of men counted for very little; all that really mattered now was the verdict of one's own conscience. And his conscience had just acquitted him – just as he had decided to acquit the deserter Lakosch.

Endrigkeit stood up and stretched his limbs. As he did so, he chuckled softly to himself. He was now so far beyond caring about what would happen to him that he could raise a smile, even at a time like this, at the prospect of Unold's dumbstruck expression tomorrow when he learned of what had happened. Yet there was one thing that Endrigkeit couldn't see, nor could he possibly have been expected to realize it: that his judgement on Lakosch was at the same time a judgement on his own entire, long life and on the world in which that life had been led – and that he had effectively burned all the bridges to that world.

He went over to the door and called the sentry in – Senior Sergeant Kleinke, a man he'd fought alongside since day one of the war, and who was still standing outside at his post wondering what the hell had just happened. He put his arm round Kleinke's shoulder.

'Take the weight off your feet, why don't you, Heinrich?' he said. 'Let's you and I chew the fat for a bit…'

The candle had long since burned down. But the two men were still sitting there in the darkness. They talked about Lakosch, who wanted to desert to the Russians to try to save the Sixth Army, and about the war and justice and dying. And as always happens when people take stock of their lives, the captain found himself delving further and further into his past. He told Kleinke about his childhood, and the vastness and the silence of the Masurian forests. And he fell to describing the picture that hung in the little log cabin his family called home, showing the knight riding steadfast and upright flanked by Death and the Devil and making his way inexorably to his destination, the strong fortress on the hill.

The stretcher-bearers are dashing about, distraught. The surgeons' hands shake, and instruments clatter to the ground. Agitated voices, shouts and curses fill the room, and even the delirious ramblings, wheezes and moans of the seriously wounded sound more restless than normal. What has happened? What did that murderous artillery barrage last night portend?

The day brings new streams of wounded men. They recount

what they've been through, their eyes full of sheer horror. The front has been smashed. The Russians are coming!

In the afternoon, the first tank shells slam into the gorge from the surrounding high ground. By the evening, the chief surgeon of the Corps is on the field telephone:

'Evacuate immediately!'

The staff doctor's hand is trembling so violently he can hardly hold the receiver.

'Evacuate? Yes, but how? And where to?'

'Anywhere behind our lines. No, not to Pitomnik; that's pointless… To Gumrak! There's still room there!'

'To Gumrak… But what about vehicles, Colonel? And petrol… No, we don't have any left! Twenty lorries, Colonel… or fifteen at a pinch… or ten at the very least! Ten lorries, Colonel!'

'My dear fellow, what are you thinking of? Where am I supposed to get hold of ten trucks? No, you'll have to fend for yourselves! Besides, you've got a better overview of the situation from where you are. You'll manage it somehow, I'm sure!'

'But… Colonel… Colonel!'

The line goes dead. He's hung up!

The doctor jumps into a VW *Kübelwagen* and roars off into the snowy night, taking the road to Karpovka, before climbing up to the burning town of Bolshaya Rossoshka, pockmarked by bomb impacts. There, he drives around visiting divisional and regimental staffs, logistics units and supply depots. Almost everywhere he goes, he is shunned and ignored. And even in the few places where he's given a hearing, they quickly tell him they're very sorry but they can't help him. They've got their own problems to worry about.

As he's driving along, he falls foul of a Russian 'U2' on its bombing run. Thirty metres ahead, it sets a radio van ablaze. Together with the driver, he pulls two wounded men from the burning vehicle. Two new casualties to add to the six hundred – that's all he returns with from his nocturnal foray.

But then, the next morning, things unexpectedly fall into place. Twelve lorries draw up, hissing and steaming, outside the field hospital. An empty supply column that had been bringing munitions up from behind the lines. Losing no time, orderlies and doctors carry out the moaning, whimpering wounded. They are packed on to the open flat-bed trucks like cigars in a case. Thirty to forty men per vehicle, each wrapped only in a single blanket. Would they ever reach their destination? And where was that, anyhow? Even so, how promising this uncertainty was compared to the awful certainty of remaining behind!

Padre Peters hurries to and fro, helping carry patients and load them up, and offering consoling words and dressing wounds. Despite the cold, the sweat is streaming off his brow. He keeps hard at work to avoid having to think too much.

'Hello, Padre!'

Peters looks up into a wild face.

'We know one another! From the divisional staff. Lieutenant Harras!'

So, this is Harras, is it, the elegant Harras? The padre offers him his hand without a word. Only now does he notice the filthy, blood-soaked rag wrapped round the officer's hand.

'Padre, might you be able… look, could I go on one of the lorries?'

'On a lorry?' the padre echoes. 'Certainly not! You can still walk, can't you? But I'll see if I can do something about that wounded hand of yours. Come and see the doctor with me, maybe he can get you a fresh dressing.'

The lieutenant gives a start and quickly hides his hand behind his back.

'No, no,' he mutters, 'but thanks anyhow! That won't be necessary. It's a clean shot, straight through. No thanks!' Saying this, he steps aside.

The trucks are full. The drivers close up the side flaps and secure the latches. The troops of the escort detail jump to their feet and the lorry engines chug into life. The fat tyres crunch into the snow and the heavy vehicles begin to roll forward slowly. This activity suddenly galvanizes the miserable, shot-up, starving mass of humanity that is milling about or sitting around on the ground. All those who have assembled here in the crazy hope that some miracle might happen leap into action, storming the trucks as they move off, trying to secure a handhold anywhere, on the side panels or the mudguards or the handle of the driver's cab door. They stumble and trip over one another, or kick each other to the ground, or are dragged along for a stretch before they are shaken off and crushed beneath the wheels of the vehicles behind.

But more than two hundred men are still left lying inside the stables! Over two hundred seriously wounded soldiers hear the noise of the departing lorries. And it dawns on them that no one will be coming to fetch them any more. They have been abandoned. The surgeon, who has kept on working tirelessly throughout (though to what purpose, who can say?), is startled by the concentrated animal-like howl that goes up around the room, as if from a single throat, and then dissolves into a cacophony of individual sighs, groans and roars, mounting over and over again. He sees how, in the semi-darkness at the back of the room, the mass of men lying there begins to stir; he sees faces twisted in pain, the whites of men's eyes shining, torsos swaying this way and that, limbs stretching, hands with no strength in them being balled into fists; and he notices how men who have lain there for days as motionless as if they were dead suddenly raise themselves up and fall over one another. He sees the grey mass propel itself slowly and clumsily towards the exit, like a river of lava, and then watches as it subsides and solidifies. The groans and screams tail off into a helpless whimpering.

The stretcher-bearers carry eighteen corpses out of the stables, men who have succumbed during their final, desperate battle to stay alive. But the remainder have been defeated and sit sunk in silent lethargy, having surrendered themselves to the inevitable.

They don't even stir a muscle as the thump of exploding shells grows louder, or when an officer dressed in a white fur overjacket and clutching a machine-pistol enters the room, followed by a handful of soldiers.

'What are you still doing here, doctor?' the man calls. 'Clear out this instant! This is where the main defensive line is now!'

'Are you telling me the main front… runs right through this building?' the surgeon asks, dumbfounded. He unbuttons his blood-spattered rubber apron and lets it fall to the ground.

'That's right! We're going to try to halt the Soviet advance here again.'

'Yes, but…' He glances briefly at the officer and then casts his eyes over to the dark, silent space at the back of the room. The officer follows his gaze. He realizes what the doctor is getting at and says nothing. Then he looks at the doctor once more, shrugs his shoulders, and walks out. Now that he has been wrenched from his numbing surgical procedures, the surgeon's actions take on a nervous haste.

'Finish up!' he shouts. 'We're leaving!'

His assistant packs away the instruments, while medical orderlies drag equipment outside. The last vehicle's engine is fired up. The staff doctor and most of his company have already left. The surgeon stops Padre Peters.

'I'm going to have to prevail upon you, Padre, to assemble all those who are still mobile in some shape or form and walk them down to Gumrak.'

'So who's going to stay back here with those who can't get away?'

'I will,' says a quiet voice. It's the other army chaplain, the Catholic padre. This 'I will' hangs in the room like an omen. It brooks no contradiction.

'I'll leave three days' worth of rations here for you,' says the doctor. He doesn't mean it to sound sarcastic; it's just force of habit.

Padre Peters takes his leave of his fellow chaplain with a silent handshake. What could he say anyhow? And who knows which of them has drawn the shorter straw? The men who await certain death in a building that will shortly be swamped by the tide of battle, or those who have to drag themselves out and face the uncertainty of a twenty-five-kilometre-long march through the snow and the bitter cold? Doesn't this spell the end for all of them, one way or another? Padre Peters dismisses these gloomy thoughts and rushes out. He still has one more task to perform.

The area outside is now deserted. White-clad figures are scrabbling around on the far side of the valley. Infantrymen digging themselves snow holes. An 88-millimetre flak gun is being set up at one corner of the stable block. Tank shells hiss over the escarpment. Where they land, a small yellow cloud of smoke can be seen above the snow. Further to the north, a string of bombers passes undisturbed across the sky. The ground shakes under the impact of the thudding bomb blasts.

Behind the building, the handful of medical orderlies have mustered all the walking wounded. A group of around eighty men so far, though their number is constantly swelled by others emerging from houses, foxholes and gullies. What is it that attracts them all, what drives them on? Is it the conviction that hope still resides at the place they're being led to? Or is it the lure of the legendary field hospital at Gumrak, or the magic word Stalingrad? Out here in the icy wasteland of snow, soldiers' crazed pipe dreams transform Stalingrad, that bombed-out, shot-up pile of ruins, into a Promised Land that holds out the prospect of a roof over one's head, warmth and food. Maybe they are drawn by the little handcart being pulled along by the orderly there, with a few meagre loaves and tins of food on it? Or is it simply the naked animal instinct for survival?

Padre Peters scans the marching column that is just setting off slowly. What a picture of abject misery it presents. Are those figures dragging themselves along there still human? Those figures draped in tarpaulins and blankets, hobbling along and supporting one another, their heads swathed in white bandages, their arms in splints, their legs in lumpy plaster casts, their feet resembling club feet from the straw or pieces of rag they had wrapped around them? Yes, these emaciated bodies, these waxen yellow skulls and these grotesquely swollen faces covered in chilblains belonged to people. And these two soldiers carrying their stricken comrade along in a tarpaulin despite being scarcely able to stand upright themselves – my God, yes, these were all human beings! They had all lived and erred and sinned. But could a person be so guilty that they deserved this fate? No! Padre Peters's innermost being screamed the word. Dear Lord, no, this cannot be Your will! My God, why hast Thou forsaken us?

The sky is overcast. Whirling snow sweeps over the procession as it makes its arduous way down the ice-crusted road. A soldier is dragging himself along between the padre and one of the medical orderlies. He can hardly lift his feet and is tottering about like a drunkard. His head, swaddled in a woollen scarf, is lolling backwards and swinging to and fro. His glassy eyes stare up at the sky. Peters is clinging on to this man for dear life. He is in the grip of an obsession. He must save this one man here, this hopeless case, at all costs. Then everything will be all right.

Just once, he cast a glance back at where they had come from. As he did so, he thought that some horrific apparition was mocking him. The building in the distance, which they had left just an hour before, was in flames… Now he didn't look back any more. What lay behind him was erased for ever. And so he does not notice how, behind his back, the ranks of marching men begin to thin, as every so often a man collapses into the snow, never to rise again.

Hours pass. Littering their route are dead men who have keeled over and been mercifully covered by the falling snow. Vehicles over-take them, rushing past: empty or nearly empty lorries, or buses crammed with wood, crates, furniture and beds. But none of them stop to exchange their senseless, inanimate cargoes for the living.

A village appears, teeming with people. They take a short rest and

shelter from the wind in the lee of the houses. The blast of exploding
bombs nearby forces them to move on. Many remain behind, while
others join their ranks. Onward they march, into the night, which
is closing in from the east, the never-changing night of searchlights,
blackout screens and bombs. In the darkness of a ravine, they come
across a convoy of halted vehicles, heavy three-axled lorries with
their radiators buried deep in wind-blown snowdrifts. The men
rush up to them. These are some of the same trucks that only this
morning… It's so quiet, uncannily quiet. No sign of any drivers or
orderlies. Every shout in this desolate place has an eerie echo. They
climb up onto the trucks. There they all lie, just the same as when
they were loaded up this morning, but now they are dusted with
snow, frozen stiff and dead. And now the living fall upon the dead,
dragging off their blankets, tearing the clothes from their hard-
frozen bodies, screaming, jostling and tussling with one another
to get hold of any warm piece of clothing they can lay their hands
on… Oh God, why hast Thou forsaken us?

The night comes to an end and another day passes. Only a small
band remains under the padre's care now. And the one whom he
was determined to save at all costs has long since frozen to death
and is lying back there somewhere in the snow. Something has
frozen inside Padre Peters, too, over this last dreadful day and a half.
He thinks and feels nothing any more.

Another dawn breaks. Houses come into view, and a railway
embankment. Gumrak, their destination! To their right is the wide
expanse of a cemetery, an immense forest of crosses. Perhaps that's
their destination? Dead on their feet from exhaustion, the men
stumble across the bomb-cratered road and make for a low brick
building. Stepping over bodies lying on the ground, they crowd
around the entrance to the field hospital. A sentry is stationed there.
He holds his rifle at port arms and bars their way.

'For Christ's sake!' he shouts. 'What do you want? It's chock-a-
block here, floor to ceiling! There's no room inside!'

He knows his duty is to defend those who have managed to find refuge here from the importunate, death-bringing world outside. And so he grips his rifle tightly and pushes these spectres of the night back into the darkness. They tumble over one another and sink to the ground, first snivelling and eventually falling silent. They have reached their goal.

A night disrupted by air raids and the distant sounds of fighting was followed by an uneasy day. Columns of vehicles and men came streaming from the west on their way to Dubininsky, bringing with them the hot breath of the front into the tranquil bunker city. Wood fires crackled beneath engines that had been allowed to freeze up; spurred on by superiors barking orders, soldiers dragged mattresses, window frames, planks and pieces of furniture from foxholes and piled them up on lorries in huge heaps. Panic gripped the logistics and supply units that were stationed here away from the front-line fighting and roused them from their hibernation.

Staff officers and the heads of various other units crowded into Unold's bunker; some of them were wrapped in fur greatcoats and carried weapons slung round their chests. There was a strong smell of sweat and stale tobacco smoke. Unold stood leaning against the edge of the table. On this occasion, he exuded an air of almost too-punctilious correctness. However, the hunted look in his eyes belied these outward signs of self-confidence, while the pungent smell on his breath instantly betrayed what he had been seeking solace in (even if one failed to notice the half-empty bottle on the card table).

'Gentlemen,' he began, lowering his voice to a whisper that only served to make the tension in the room unbearable. 'Since yesterday the major Russian offensive has been underway. It has forced a collapse of our western front. The Russians could be here as early as tomorrow. Our orders are to prepare to defend Dubininsky on all sides and to hold... to hold it to the last man! I don't think we need waste any time assessing the importance of this order.'

A look of consternation crossed the officers' faces. All-round defence? Without any fixed positions or any materials for fortification? There'd clearly been a will and a way to construct ostentatious staff bunkers. No shortage of time, materials or manpower for that task, apparently. But no effort had been expended on preparing defensive positions!

Breuer was standing next to Captain Engelhard's desk. His eyes wandered over the map, the pencils all neatly laid out, the fastidiously stacked piles of paperwork and files. On the desk lay a sheet of white paper. Breuer's gaze came to rest on the few oversized letters the page contained, which read:

'They could not prevail, they could only fall in battle! 11.1.1943. Unold.'

In front of the sheet of paper sat Captain Engelhard, bolt upright and very composed. Absent-mindedly, his hand was doodling along the bottom edge of the page. He was drawing a series of little crosses. Disturbed from his reverie by Breuer's attention, the captain glanced up.

'You can write home one more time, you know,' he said quietly. 'Straight after this meeting, we're sending a messenger down to the airfield with the post.'

'Lieutenant Colonel Braun will be in charge of defending the fortified position at Dubininsky,' Unold continued.

As he made this announcement, he pointed to an officer with a ruddy face and watery goggle eyes who was turning a lambskin cap round and round in his hands.

'As of now, all units stationed in and around Dubininsky are under his direct command... and that includes our staff. I need to speak with you presently, Fackelmann, about putting together a special fighting group. First Lieutenant Breuer will serve as Lieutenant Colonel Braun's adjutant and the rest of the staff officers will form an officers' fighting unit at the front under the command of Captain Engelhard.'

The disquiet among those present increased palpably.

'But that's out of the question!' a short captain muffled up like Father Christmas called out nervously. 'We're in the middle of baking... our division has to eat, after all! I can't just drop everything all of a sudden and leave the loaves and the flour standing there. The whole lot'll be nicked in the meantime!'

'And what about my workshop?' shouted another. 'I've got two tanks and about thirty other vehicles under repair.'

'And I...' 'And I...' A cacophony of objections buzzed round the room. It transpired that a large number of those present ruled themselves entirely out of participating in the defence of Dubininsky on the grounds that they had more important tasks to perform.

'Now just hold your horses a minute!' Unold interrupted the hubbub. 'I think you're labouring under some kind of misapprehension. To put it bluntly: we've had it! There aren't any other tasks any more. We're under orders to die here, and that's that! You're aware that the Corps commander is here with his staff, too. Well, he's already chosen the foxhole where he's going to fight till the very last bullet. That's how things stand!'

The room had fallen very quiet. Only the little bakery captain kept muttering: 'My God, my God!'

At the back of the room, the door creaked and someone pushed their way rather roughly to the front. It was Captain Endrigkeit. He gave an awkward salute.

'Lieutenant Colonel, sir, beg to report,' he droned in his deep bass voice, 'that we've seen the last of the prisoner.'

For a moment, Unold looked at him blankly. He'd forgotten completely about Lakosch in the interim. Then he remembered.

'Very good, Endrigkeit!' he replied briefly. 'So that business is settled, then.'

'No, not at all, Lieutenant Colonel,' Endrigkeit persisted. 'It's not settled at all… far from it, in fact. Lakosch is gone, he's done a bunk. When we opened up the bunker first thing this morning, he'd vanished.'

And that was indeed the truth of the matter. For a few moments, the lieutenant colonel's face took on an expression of childlike helplessness.

'Endrigkeit!' he gasped, almost imploringly. 'You're driving me round the bend!' Then he barked, at the top of his lungs: 'Do you take me for a complete fool, you… I hold you fully responsible for what's happened! I'll have you court-martialled for this! Thrown in the glasshouse, and shot! I'll get you sent to the front, you incompetent ass…!'

He broke off suddenly, as he realized how empty his threats were.

'You'll pay for this stunt of yours, Endrigkeit!' he said through gritted teeth, before adding, quite calmly and impersonally: 'You are to place yourself and your squad at Lieutenant Colonel Braun's disposal for the defence of the village.'

No one in the intelligence division had any more time to think about the 'Lakosch case'. First Lieutenant Breuer was immediately requisitioned by the new base commander. Lieutenant Colonel Braun's frenetic activity knew no bounds. He was constantly having new brainwaves, and the orders he issued, in a hoarse croak of a voice, were frequently unintelligible. Breuer was on his feet from dawn to dusk without pause. He had to go round visiting units and brief detachments on defensive techniques; provisions, weapons and entrenching tools had to be found from somewhere. Stubbornness and ill will led to friction and clashes. From the outset, this was particularly the case up at the forward position on the road, where, with the help of the military police, the bands of soldiers streaming back from the breached front were to be intercepted. Men from the most diverse units pitched up there, exhausted, with no officers in charge and in some instances without any weapons. If the accounts they gave – a blend of truth and skittish fantasy – were to be believed, then German forces at the western front of the Cauldron had been wiped out. Two completely distraught medical orderlies recounted how Russian tanks had broken into their dressing station. Total panic had ensued. Stretchers with wounded men on them were simply left out in the open and abandoned. A captured Russian major who had been among the serious casualties had been swiftly 'dispatched'.

'What – you shot the wounded Russian?' those listening cried in horror. 'And left the body next to your German comrades? Are you crazy or what? You know what'll happen to our wounded now, don't you?' The two men fell silent. Finally, one of them said, 'Look, it's all the bloody same now. The Russians are killing everything that moves anyhow!'

Only late in the evening did Breuer finally find the opportunity to request some free time from the lieutenant colonel in order to sort out his own affairs. He was dismissed brusquely. When he got to his bunker he found it empty. The men had already left. The little stove was glowing red-hot, and papers were lying scattered on the floor. Corporal Herbert had evidently burned all the files and dispatches that had accumulated again over the past few weeks. Breuer cast his eyes around the room, over the cracked clay walls, the rough plank table that had served as his and Wiese's bed, the telephone, the little flickering storm lantern, and the slogan on the wall, already rather yellowed and faded. 'I break on through and never look back...' His thoughts were calm and collected. So this was the end. There would be no breakthrough and no future. Now they'd perish here on a distant foreign field, abandoned, forgotten, and with no hope of even a grave... It wasn't death itself that frightened him. But he had a strong sense that he'd lost all faith in the point of his impending demise.

What are we dying for exactly? he asked himself. For the Fatherland? That could scarcely be defended from their position here on the Volga. For metal ores, oil and wheat? No, not for those commodities either. To save the Eastern Front, then? Well, if the twenty-two German divisions had been on the other side of the river, west of the Don, they might have stood a chance of saving the Eastern Front, but not here. So for what? Just because Hitler had once boasted 'Once we're dug in somewhere, there's no shifting us'? Was that the reason they were being cut down here like robbers and bandits?

Breuer sat down at the table and rested his fevered brow in his hands. The only good thing was that they wouldn't have to advance any more, into a witches' cauldron where they would all be wiped out; better that they were making a final stand here, at this spot that he and his comrades had made into a little piece of home. Breuer would never have wanted to wish away the last few weeks he had experienced here. Sometimes, it seemed to him that they had been the most worthwhile part of his entire life. Every song that the men had sung together, every poem that had been read out loud, every word that had been spoken during the long hours of the night had had real resonance and value and depth here and had helped give them all inner strength. At one stage, he had hoped that these six weeks spent in the earth bunker outside Stalingrad might be a fresh start, a first step towards a new land. And no, it turned out not to have been a beginning, but an end after all.

Breuer looked up. There on the wall hung the photograph of his family still. His wife holding the baby on her lap, and their elder child standing beside her, his arm round her shoulders. Her smile radiated out into the room. That had been taken back then, in peacetime… Should he write to her? And what should he write? He knew that she was brave, but would she be strong enough to endure the truth, *this* truth? Might it not be better to leave it to the official Wehrmacht communiqué to report the demise of the Sixth Army? Sure, it wouldn't represent the truth, but it would be the kind of bland statement that would soothe the pain. Breuer pulled a little packet from his map case. The letters that his wife had written to him while he was on campaign. He carefully unfolded the sheets and began reading. He was taking his leave of her. But as he read certain sentences, he pulled up short. They struck him as unfamiliar, somehow new. Puzzled, he looked at the date: 8.12.1940… Oh, right, that was when he'd been in France, luxuriating in peace and quiet. In those circumstances, he could well have skipped over parts of her letters. He read the lines through again:

> You see, I've always taken the view that you can never be said to really love another person unless you allow them to put themselves in harm's way. For in most cases, fearfulness for another person is nothing more than the cowardice of egotism. On the other hand, I honestly believe that true love's preoccupation is to be constantly ready to support your partner wholeheartedly and to the best of your ability in all the dangers that might befall him…

Breuer put down the letter. He felt closer to her again, and he felt he could find the right words now. He started to write:

11.1.1943, OUTSIDE STALINGRAD

DEAR IRMGARD!

I am sorry to be the bearer of painful tidings. What you may already have surmised is true. We are encircled. And there's no prospect of being rescued any more. The end is near. I can't tell you in just a few words what's happening here. A great crime is being committed, and one day our country-men will call the guilty parties to account.

My dear Irmgard, we will surely never see one another again. At this sad time, I want to thank you for all the years of work and the cares and worries we shared and for all the happiness we enjoyed.

Even now I feel your closeness. From now on, you'll have to be both mother and father to our boys, and looking after

them will give you the strength to carry on. Bring them up to
be good and upright men, who will fight for justice and the
truth and for brotherly love one day. And when they're older,
tell them that their father too once believed that he was living
and dying for a noble cause. Irmgard, my darling, farewell!

Your,

BERNHARD

Breuer sealed the envelope and put it in his coat pocket. And once
more he picked up the bundle of letters from his wife. He held them
in his hand, spread out like a fan, and drank in the sight of the familiar
handwriting. Then he shuffled them all back together again and slowly
tore the sheaf of letters into tiny pieces. He also took the photograph
down off the wall and shredded it. He threw the pieces into the stove.
Flames leaped from the glowing red embers and crackled up into the
flue. Then the first lieutenant picked up his machine-pistol, which
was hanging on the wall. He checked it carefully and clipped in the
magazine. Slinging it round his shoulders, he took one last look
around the room, turned out the lantern and walked out.

Colonel von Hermann stood up on the main road, where a stiff
breeze was blowing. He had sent his staff car on ahead, down into
the gorge where the command post was located. He wanted to have
a few minutes alone to collect his thoughts and take stock of what
he had just heard. His gaze wandered past the dome of the church in
Gorodishche out to the grey houses down in the east, beyond which
the ribbon of the Volga could just be made out. Down there somewhere was where the extreme forward positions of the division he was
now in command of were situated. The Volga front had been quiet for
some time now. The only activity was the occasional reconnaissance
party, aerial attacks by night and sporadic disruptive artillery fire

from the far side of the river. Only yesterday the colonel had visited the well-fortified positions out front there and been delighted at the atmosphere of peace and optimism he had encountered. Of course, the effects of the Cauldron were also apparent here, in the reduced rations and the fact that the division had had more and more men 'combed out' of it to reinforce other units elsewhere. Occasionally, an entire cohesive unit of the division would disappear to shore up the defences somewhere in the rear, never to return again. In general, though, they remained relatively unaffected by what was going on in the west. Just like his gaze right now, so the eyes of the whole division were turned eastward. That was where the front was, their front, which the men had contested and held at a huge cost in lives, and which they were determined to continue to hold. And now he was expected to tell them that all their sacrifices had been in vain... Would they believe him, would they be able to grasp the enormity of the present situation? Well, they'd have no choice but to believe it, when in just a few days' time the front rolled up towards their rear, and when the remnants of defeated divisions and columns of marching casualties showed up here. And it would be a good thing if the men were forewarned of this well in advance.

'So, von Hermann? What does the Corps say? Have you broached the question of fuel for the stoves with them yet?'

Colonel von Hermann turned around. In front of him, with the fur collar of his greatcoat turned up against the cold and his hands buried deep in the pockets, stood Major General Calmus, the discharged divisional commander. He waved his hand in the vague direction of the nearby gorge, which was sparsely wooded with alders and poplars. In grateful recognition of this natural wonder, the troops had named this particular *balka* the 'forested ravine'.

'I took another look at the stocks of wood down there,' Calmus continued. 'It's incredible how much timber they've felled in such a short time. There's simply not enough there, old man! There's no way it's going to last us until the new year!'

The colonel looked thoughtfully at the general's frost-reddened, worried face. When the news of the encirclement came through, Major General Calmus had suffered a nervous breakdown. From that point on, he showed not the slightest interest in leadership, but sat in his bunker the whole time calculating when the army would finally starve to death if this or that size of ration was issued daily. Or he spent his time mooning about the staff divisions bemoaning the dreadful situation and seeking reassurance from his colleagues.

In the end, in view of the poor state of his health, the army had relieved him of command of the division. However, he was told in no uncertain terms that he was to remain with the unit, to avoid unsettling the men.

'Pretty soon we won't have any more need of firewood, General, sir,' said the colonel. 'The western front has been overrun by the Russians. In a few days, our fate here will be decided too.'

Any semblance of composure vanished from the general's face. His hands dabbed ineffectually at the fur lapels of his coat.

'Overrun, you say? So, what's going to happen now? My God, it's a catastrophe!'

The major general's expression froze, his mouth gaped and his lower lip trembled slightly. He swung around and ran down the slope, taking short steps as he went. The colonel watched him depart and shook his head. So that was a German officer, one like thousands of others, an educated, refined, cultivated person, a man of spirit, who up till now had in times of both war and peace been the very model of a good soldier. And now a man like him was simply collapsing here, and whining like some old woman. Had Stalingrad changed people so radically? Or was it that they were being revealed in their true colours here, stripped bare of all pretence and fripperies?

Colonel von Hermann mused on all this without any arrogance. After all, what made him any better than this general? A modicum of composure and self-control, that was all. And what lurked behind that façade? Uncertainty, inner turmoil and tortured anguish...

The colonel slowly made his way down the steep path leading to the gorge. He had been weaned on the notions of 'duty' and 'honour'. At the military academy he had taught courses on the honour of an officer and a soldier's duty. These consisted in obedience, courage and being prepared to lay down your life at any time for the Fatherland. That was clear-cut. No open-ended questions, no complications there. The fact that soldiers fell in battle, that units suffered losses or were wiped out, these were painful but self-evident necessities. And the fact that this death often looked so very different from the heroes' deaths celebrated in soldiers' songs and books about war should not... no, really *ought not* to be allowed to override this necessity. The colonel clenched his teeth, and the muscles in his face tensed. He made a conscious effort to suppress that horrific image he had strenuously succeeded in banishing forever from his waking consciousness, but which haunted him every night in his sleep. And this image was always the same: flames, blood-curdling shrieks, the fresh face of a young man twisted in the most ghastly agonies and ultimately a head, small, black, and with bared teeth... No, any individual, personal concerns should not play any role here! Colonel von Hermann was too much of a soldier to cast doubt on things that he had taught countless times and demanded of others when they happened to hit him with full force.

But there was also something else that was eating him up and it was growing stronger with every day that passed. That was the situation here on the Volga, the death of huge numbers of men, hundreds of thousands in fact, with only a small fraction killed as a direct result of enemy action and by far the greater part dying from hunger and the cold. It could all be ended with just a word, a brief command... yet this command was never issued. Instead, a whole army was being ordered to starve and freeze to death! This was completely beyond the normal bounds of a soldier's experience, and nothing to do any more with duty or honour. And that in turn prompted the otherwise strictly taboo question for any military man, namely why they were fighting? The colonel had tormented himself with this question, and after a thorough investigation of all the available documents he needed to come to a judgement on the current military situation, he had become convinced that there was no longer any military necessity for maintaining the siege of Stalingrad that could possibly justify such a huge sacrifice. Hitler had promised that they'd be relieved, but he hadn't been able to keep his promise. Now he needed to take a hands-off approach towards the army, and allow it to act as it saw fit and on its own authority. Yet he wasn't doing so. Why was that? Could it be that three hundred thousand men were dying here just because one man did not want to admit that he was... No, he must stop himself from thinking! It only opened up a yawning abyss.

Colonel von Hermann was walking along the narrow path that ran for a stretch along the face of the escarpment just above the valley bottom, and led to his quarters. The location was quiet and peaceful, and everything was laid out like they were going to live here for all eternity. At the entrance to the well-entrenched bunker, which was built into the cliff side, stood colourful signs decorated with witty slogans and caricatures of the occupants. It was a regular knights' fortress here: drawings of Iron Crosses all around – that was the chief adjutant's section; a picture of a pair of compasses and a ruler – the cartographic unit; while the greyhounds there surely denoted the dispatch riders' unit. At that moment, two soldiers were busy taking down a sign bearing the inscription 'Wholesale Warehouse' and a row of horses' skulls hung above it.

'What's all this, then, Stegen?' said the colonel in passing to the officer who was overseeing the work. 'On the move again?'

'Yes indeed, Colonel, more's the pity! Though pretty soon there'll be nowhere left to go. First it's the quartermaster and all his stores we have to make room for, and now the Eighth Corps comes creeping round here, looking for space. Even their C-in-C was here in person. So now we've got to give over five of our best bunkers to them. Couldn't you lay down the law, Colonel? After all, this is meant to be our area here!'

'Sorry, Stegen, no can do,' replied the colonel, moving on. 'I dare say we'll all be having to bunk up a bit more in the few days we've got left here.' The captain gave him a puzzled look as he went on his way.

The chief of operation's bunker had all the creature comforts of a cosy living room: carpets, a battery-powered desk lamp and separate sleeping alcoves. On the small stove built of red bricks with white pointing stood a set of cast-iron stove tools. It was much the same story with the forward companies, too. They were at a stable front here and had got themselves settled in for the winter as comfortably as possible. The chief of staff was stretched over the map, drawing in troop positions. He straightened up when the colonel walked in. The C-in-C was small and slender, with neatly parted, glossy black hair above a round face. He had a fleshy nose and a somewhat glazed expression in his eyes. This look of his was a legacy of a time-fuse explosion in Kiev, which the lieutenant colonel had been the only person in his unit to survive.

'Colonel Steffen reports that he has just beaten back another attempted breakthrough at his sector, under his personal command,' announced the colonel. 'We'll have to put in for another Knight's Cross for him. And then we're supposed to take over the defence of this group of houses here from the 305th as well. They can't squeeze any more men out of our unit, so now they're just making the sector we have to cover bigger. It's outrageous!'

The colonel had come to a halt by the desk without taking off his coat. 'Listen, Dannemeister,' he said, 'the western front of the Cauldron has collapsed. It's all over! Hube's come back from the Führer's HQ with the suggestion that, as a last resort, we should make a kind of Alcazar in the ruins of Stalingrad.'

The lieutenant colonel flung his pencil down on the table.

'That's sheer insanity!' he roared. 'And are you telling me the

Army High Command's going along with that? Has everyone here gone stark raving mad? How much longer are they going to dance to the tune of this crazy corporal? The Officer Corps, the generals and the field marshals – the whole German general staff is letting itself be led by the nose by this upstart, incompetent, loud-mouthed little thug? It's enough… enough to…'

He stared at the wall and clenched his fists, ready to strike an unseen opponent.

'Pull yourself together, Dannemeister!' the colonel rounded on the chief of operations. 'Don't forget that you're an officer! I won't stand for any criticism of the Führer in my presence, understood? You can think what you like as far as I'm concerned, but keep your thoughts to yourself!'

The lieutenant colonel was startled by the unexpectedly sharp tone of the colonel's rebuke. Cowed into submission, he asked quietly, 'So what do we do now, Colonel?'

'What do we do?' the colonel repeated in astonishment. 'You're asking me that? You're a soldier yourself, man! We'll follow orders, that's what!'

The apathetic mood of indifference that had come over Lieutenant Wiese prevented him from speculating on why the colonel had chosen him, of all people, to be his adjutant. He never took him on inspection tours, gave him no tasks to perform and left him entirely to his own esoteric devices. But Wiese was shaken out of his ivory tower when the colonel summoned him out of the blue one evening.

'There are professional and personal reasons why I've ordered you here,' said von Hermann, pushing one of the two chairs in his room towards Wiese and offering him a cigarette. 'We're in the endgame, Wiese; the Cauldron's falling apart. The final act of the tragedy has begun.'

The lieutenant looked wide-eyed at the colonel, who in the meantime had stood up and was slowly pacing up and down the room.

'No one will want to hear the truth about Stalingrad,' he went on, 'but I honestly believe Germany needs to know about it. There must be men over there with the courage to report what really happened. And that oughtn't to be just a soldier, it needs to be someone who can… well, who can tell the story from a human perspective, if you catch my drift? And I'd also like…' – here his voice gave a slight tremble – 'I'd like it if my wife heard from the right person something that I can't put down on paper – about how we met our end here, and also… how our son died.'

Wiese slowly rose to his feet. He had turned white as a sheet.

'Oh, yes, that's right,' the colonel went on, 'you didn't know, did you? Yes, he's dead. Anyway, the Corps has been ordered to appoint a messenger to the army group. I've nominated you, Wiese. Everyone was in agreement. You'll fly out tomorrow from the airfield at Pitomnik. Here, take this package. My wife's address is on it. You can collect the other officers' letters tomorrow from the adjutant.'

Wiese felt like his legs were made of lead and the room swam before his eyes. The colonel looked at him, seemingly waiting for an answer. Then he placed his hand on his shoulder.

'I quite understand, Wiese,' he said in fatherly tones. 'Just make sure you get on that flight. After this war, Germany's going to need men like you who aren't just soldiers.'

Searching for an adequate response, the lieutenant was tongue-tied. But then he blurted out something really stupid, something every soldier would have laughed at because it was so out of place and old-fashioned, reminiscent of the spiked helmets and shaven heads of the Prussian military:

'At your command, Colonel, sir!'

2

Look What They've Done to Us!

FIRST LIEUTENANT BREUER LAY stretched out on his plank bed with his eyes closed. He could feel the lice crawling slowly up and down his prone form. His body, emaciated by dysentery and hunger, burned and itched all over. But that wasn't the worst of it. There was also corruption that ate away at a person from the inside.

That final night in Dubininsky, he'd drawn a line under everything in the belief that that fateful order – 'The position is to be held to the very last man!' – was going to be carried out to the letter. Like the fool he was. Could he really have thought for one moment that a man like Unold would see it as his solemn duty to be the last man to fall at Dubininsky? Hadn't he known that the 'last man' always meant someone else and never yourself? Well, he knew it now!

What had happened? There had been one icy night full of anticipation, involving a lot of shouting and nervous to-ing and fro-ing and frozen limbs. But the Russians had never appeared. It hadn't come to that quite yet. The front hadn't been destroyed everywhere; in the north, the Russian attempt to break through came to nothing, while at the salient at Marinovka a German division had held a supposedly hopeless position for several days. And even at the place in the west where a breakthrough had been achieved, the enemy were hesitant at driving forces through the gap they had opened up. The Russian military leadership was taking its time. Victory was already assured, and there was no desire to make needless sacrifices just in order to chalk up a high-profile success. This had enabled the Germans to use the remnants of their defeated units to establish another front in the Rossoshka Valley, where favourable terrain facilitated the formation of a shortened defensive line. This line held for four days. What remained of the German artillery fought in the most forward positions there and used up the last of its shells in a direct bombardment. It was a last-ditch effort. On the fifteenth of January, the last of the field guns and the smoke mortars were blown up. Now there was precious little left to hold back the Russian advance.

Breuer only learned all this long after the event. The morning after in Dubininsky, all he'd heard was an order from Unold: 'Get yourselves ready immediately! The divisional staff is relocating to the rear!' Confronted with uncomprehending, questioning faces, Breuer had muttered something about a fresh start. But then his nerves had frayed: 'Any shithead can die!' he'd yelled. 'But it takes a general staff officer to have brains and show some leadership!'

The first lieutenant thrashed about uneasily on his pallet. A choking sense of disgust rose in his gorge. They'd fled twenty kilometres to the east in the last of the serviceable vehicles, trading in their last vestiges of dignity and self-esteem for a few days' delay of the inevitable conclusion. How squalid the whole situation was!

Now they were holed up here in a gully not far from the main road leading from Gumrak to the centre of Stalingrad. On the map, the place was identified as 'Stalingradski'. Once again, they'd escaped from the front. But the frequent impacts from Russian artillery shells, fired across from the east bank of the Volga, must have brought it home even to Unold how pointless it would be to keep on running. They were caught in a trap that was closing tighter with every hour that passed. Up on the plateau above stood the last few vehicles they'd been able to salvage: a crew bus, a few lorries, staff cars and *Kübelwagen*, and last but not least the mess truck with the alcohol supplies (which Unold had commandeered for his personal use). All the rest, which they could not get started or had no more fuel for, they had destroyed at Dubininsky. Nor had they bothered any more to put the vehicles under cover here, in however rudimentary a fashion. The jalopies had done their bit. There was no fuel left for any more retreats.

Dry mud crumbled through the thin plank ceiling of the bunker, which clung to the lip of a secondary branch of the gully like a swallow's nest, while the wind gusted snow through the incessantly flapping door, right up to the tinny stove glowing ostentatiously red-hot but delivering little in the way of warmth. Sergeant Herbert was busy trying to plug the many cracks in the windowpanes and the wide gaps in the external walls of the bunker with paper, while Geibel was dangling his frozen heels in a bowl of hot water. Up until now, Geibel had survived the weeks of gnawing hunger without showing signs of any major ill effects, but just in the last three days had suddenly and quite alarmingly gone to pieces. His round baby face now resembled a partially deflated balloon. The warmth that crept comfortingly up his legs prompted some pensive musings.

'Do you really think the Führer will get us out of this jam? What if we can just manage to hold out here until the spring?'

In reply, Herbert grunted something unintelligible, which could have just as easily had to do with the windowpane, from which another piece of glass had just dropped out.

'Dear me, what's my wife going to do without me!' Geibel continued.

'She'll go and find another husband,' growled Herbert insensitively. 'There's plenty more dimwits like you out there!'

Geibel wasn't put out by this and kept pursuing his line of thought. 'So, d'you reckon the Russians'll butcher the lot of us?'

He cast a cautious eye over to the corner, where Breuer seemed to be napping, and lowered his voice. 'Hey, listen, I found this leaflet that says we get given six hundred grams of bread a day if we're taken prisoner. Imagine that, Herbert, six hundred grams! Maybe it isn't a load of eyewash after all. And Lakosch wouldn't have... Look, what I'm saying is, if the Russians actually take prisoners... well, I don't mind if they keep me banged up for three years, or even longer, ten years, say. Just as long as I can get back to my wife and kid at the end of the day...'

Geibel paddled his feet round in the water, which by this stage was only lukewarm. His moist eyes gazed blissfully into the far distance. In all probability they were already back in the comfort of the family home in Chemnitz, wandering through his cosy front parlour with the moquette-covered armchairs. All of a sudden, he leaned right over to where Herbert was sitting and his voice sank to a secretive whisper.

'Herbert, man, you and me are only small fry – just like all the other enlisted men, for that matter! We're not to blame for this war. Why would they do anything to us? Maybe they'll just bump off the officers... If only *his nibs* down there would put us in the picture!'

Saying this, he shot a pointed look down towards the rear of the bunker.

'But he keeps his trap shut. He must know how things are over there – but will we ever get the truth out of him?'

The person Geibel was referring to was the Intelligence Section's latest guest: a middle-aged man with a broad, good-natured face, who was dressed in a blue-grey French military jacket. He sat silently on a bench at the back of the bunker, staring fixedly at his clasped hands with his small, grey eyes, which were framed by countless little crow's feet. He was twiddling his thumbs incessantly. This was the Russian Lieutenant Colonel Nasarov.

Herbert began to lose his cool.

'Just put a sock in it, will you?' he snapped. 'God help us if *you*'ve started thinking! Leave that to the horses – their heads are bigger than yours!'

'Yeah, yeah,' complained Geibel, 'that's what I always used to do. But when your own life's on the line…'

'Herbert!'

Breuer's alert voice made them both start.

'Lieutenant, sir!'

'Have you finally sorted that business with the lieutenant colonel's food?'

'Yes, sir, Lieutenant! As of today, he'll be getting the normal rations from our canteen.'

Breuer turned over on to his side again. That was all he needed right now, to be saddled with this Russian. Unold had selected him personally at the end of September from an elite camp for captured Red Army officers and requisitioned him to command the Cossack detachment. He'd arrived at Wehrmacht Staff HQ just before the Cauldron had closed, with the highest of commendations from the camp commandant, but had never set eyes on the unit he'd been assigned to lead, and thereafter had sat around uselessly at the quartermaster's division as a silent eyewitness to the unfolding catastrophe. Yesterday, he'd suddenly turned up at the door of the intelligence division bunker. Major Siebel had sent him over. Siebel told them he had no further use for the Russian, and that division Ic was responsible for prisoners of war anyhow! Sonderführer Fröhlich had managed to assuage Breuer's anger and the Russian had remained with them. He proved to be friendly, unassuming and helpful. Most of the time, though, he just sat quietly on his bench. And because he could only speak a few snatches of broken German, he didn't disturb anyone. His relaxed face betrayed no agitation or disquiet, though he could scarcely have been unaware of the general situation and his personal predicament here in Stalingrad. What must he have been thinking? Perhaps the only thing on his mind was that perpetually Russian attitude, that cure-all demeanour expressed in the word *nitchevo!* – no matter! Fröhlich had had a couple of long chats with him, but only gave evasive answers about their outcome.

In the afternoon, Unold called all the staff officers to a meeting in his bunker. On this occasion he was not lying in bed with a bottle of cognac beside him, as he had been wont to do since their arrival in Stalingradski, but received his fellow officers dressed in his grey leather coat, ready to go out. He was even freshly shaven.

'Gentlemen!'

Unold's voice, which was soft to begin with, was muffled so much by the woollen blankets hung up all round the walls as to be virtually inaudible.

'Well, gentlemen, I approached the general staff again and asked them whether they really wanted, in all seriousness, to needlessly sacrifice an entire well-qualified divisional staff, which has no further use here, by sticking its officers in the front line and wasting them as simple pistol shooters. I might as well have banged my head against a brick wall. "No further use here, you say?" Schmidt laughed when I said that. "We've got plenty of tasks lined up for you!"'

Breuer cast his eye over the wall cladding, installed just to spare Unold's nerves when shelling started, and thought of all the men outside freezing for lack of blankets.

'And now I must take my leave of you,' said Unold. 'I've been ordered to go to Army High Command with Captain Engelhard to receive new orders. I've no idea what they are, or whether it's a long- or a short-term assignment. In any event, though… Farewell!'

'So, what do you make of that?' Siebel asked Breuer as they trudged back through the ice-bound gorge to their quarters.

'He just never lets up!' continued the major, 'but you mark my words, one day he'll just up and get a flight out of here!'

When Lieutenant Wiese paid a visit to the commandant of the headquarters, Captain Stegen, to say his goodbyes, a young officer unknown to him was already there, and in the midst of a very animated anecdote. The captain stood up and shook Wiese's hand.

'So, all the best to you, dear Wiese, and please give our best regards to Germany!'

Gesturing towards the unknown officer, who had also stood up, Stegen announced: 'Your replacement is here already. First Lieutenant Tausend has just flown in. He needs to get back to his battery without delay.'

Wiese glanced back and forth between the two officers. He estimated they were around the same age. And yet what a difference! On the one hand the thin, pallid intelligence officer in his threadbare uniform, tired, stooped and with a grey, drained-looking face. And on the other, the fresh-faced artilleryman, bursting with vigour and with the fresh air of home still clinging to him.

'So, you're flying out?' Tausend enquired with a disparaging look.

'That's right, as an army messenger,' replied Wiese.

'Aha, I see. Still, not a very enviable task, eh?'

Wiese shrugged his shoulders and swiftly took his leave. Captain Stegen shook his head sadly as he left. There was a group of staff officers (made up of those who secretly envied Wiese) who expected him to act outraged or at least feign regret at the task he had been assigned. It was only seemly for him to do so. When all was said and done, he was a German officer, after all! Equally, there were many others who would have been delighted if he'd been openly overjoyed at the prospect. But no one could understand the profound, detached indifference that Wiese displayed. This indifference was not put on, it was quite genuine. It arose from the feeling that he would never be able to escape Stalingrad come what may, however long he lived. The terrible events here in the Cauldron, condensed for him in that gruesome experience in Dubininsky (the full horror of which a kind providence had still kept hidden from him), would follow him wherever his path might lead him. And this same indifference was also no doubt to blame for the fact that Lieutenant Wiese, official army messenger, never reached the airfield at Pitomnik – that gateway to the outside world that was the focus of so many fevered fantasies of the dying and so many secret hopes and yearnings of the living. On a road in Gumrak pitted with reddish-brown bomb craters, he failed to heed the alarmed warning shouts of bystanders and the ominous drone overhead and drove straight into the path of a stick of bombs dropped by a Russian plane. The third explosion blew his *Kübelwagen* off the road, hurling it on to the verge and peppering it full of holes like a sieve.

The young first lieutenant, the man by the name of Tausend, is sitting in front of Colonel von Hermann and explaining his circumstances. News reached him of the encirclement of the Sixth Army while he was on an artillery training course in France. He immediately announces his withdrawal; he wants to get back to his regiment. On the return journey, he leaves himself barely any time to visit his young wife. The military authorities in Millerovo order him to take command of a new operational company assembled from soldiers back from leave. However, he refuses to give up his quest, writes countless transfer requests and keeps badgering his superiors. Finally, with a bewildered shrug, he's granted leave to fly back into the Cauldron. So now here he is! His eyes twinkle, and he's laughing like he's just pulled off a schoolboy prank.

The colonel stares earnestly at Tausend's carefree face.

'You do know the predicament we're in here, don't you?'

'Yes, sir, Colonel!' the lieutenant smiles. 'But things could be worse. Everyone back home's full of confidence. Tanks in their droves are underway here. It's an awesome sight! Give it four or five weeks and we'll be liberated. There's no other possible outcome, Colonel!'

The colonel says nothing. Looking into the eyes of the young man, he catches a glimpse of the old world of soldiering in which he was raised. Parades, flags flying, sparkling uniforms, the crunch of marching boots. A lot of this was superficial and hollow, nothing but ossified ritual. But how much genuine enthusiasm and honest belief there was too, and how much pride in German military might and readiness on the part of the country's youth to make sacrifices! Like a reflection of his own earlier life, this all comes shining over to the colonel from the dim and distant past, across an abyss over which hangs a banner with the name 'Stalingrad' – Stalingrad, the graveyard of the German Army. Here it had met its end, dishonoured in body and soul, abused and trampled in the mud by scoundrels. This is how the colonel sees things right now, and it's quite an epiphany for an old soldier. And he continues to hold his peace. He gets up and accompanies the lieutenant to the door.

And the young soldier who does everything by the book is disconcerted to feel the divisional commander put his arm gently around his shoulders.

A clear, bitterly cold January. Across the crackling expanse of snowy wasteland west of Gumrak, shimmering in the glow of the yellowish winter sun, a four-wheel-drive *Kübelwagen* made its laborious way to a distant line of snow ramparts, topped with radio masts. This location was home to the Sixth Army's General Staff.

On the back seat of the car, two officers sat freezing under layers of blankets and coats. First Lieutenant Breuer and Siebel; two days before, aged just twenty-seven, Siebel had been promoted to major.

'What do you think Unold has got us here for, then?' asked Breuer through his woollen balaclava, on which a thick beard of icicles had formed. The major looked bored and shrugged his shoulders.

'Haven't the foggiest! He ordered all the rest of his stuff to be brought over too. Perhaps he's planning to fly out and take us with him.'

Breuer shot Siebel a sideways glance through the balaclava.

'Do you really think so, Major?'

Siebel gave a mirthless laugh.

'Honestly, you're so naive!'

The car came to a halt in a circular parking area surrounded by high snow banks. Breuer struggled free of his blankets and then turned to help the major, who was hampered by his false arm. Siebel was always very reluctant to accept such offers of assistance. An officer in a white fur coat came rushing up.

'Quick, hurry it up!' he began calling from some way away. 'Could you get a move on, please! Get that car clear!'

He cast a worried look up to the clear blue vault of the sky, which was filled with the faint drone of engines. The two newly arrived officers hurried past a blackish bomb crater towards the bunker entrance, on which hung a board with the inscription 'Id'.

In the Army's High Command post, the course of those anxious days of the Russians' major offensive – the speed of which made a mockery of any notion of central command – were almost always the same. The mornings were filled with a sense of confidence shot through with nervous tension. Then, towards midday, a series of alarming reports would begin to come in. An overwhelming assault by the enemy in one place. A serious breakthrough at another. At yet another, two battalions wiped out. Send reserves, urgently! There ensued feverish, nerve-jangling activity by the staff of the chief of operation's division. Pencils dashed across maps and communiqués, telephones jangled, a hubbub of shouting voices arose, and officers clutching papers scurried to and fro. Nonetheless, this bustling activity failed to keep pace with the growing avalanche of the unfolding catastrophe. Orders to lay down curtain fire were issued to artillery batteries whose guns had already been blown up or fallen into enemy hands; fuel that had already been consumed was earmarked for dispatch by transport units that no longer had any trucks, to units that had already abandoned their last-reported positions. Detachments that no longer existed were sent to plug gaps where breakthroughs had occurred, which in the interim had become massive, gaping holes in the line. By the evening, the situation had been brought under control – at least on paper. And the general mood calmed down until the next day, when the cries for help from fronts that had been smashed found their way once more to High Command through official channels or via the roster of regular reporting deadlines.

Unold and Engelhard had found themselves caught up in this hustle and bustle for some days now. The collapse of the Cauldron fronts in the west and the south had, among other things, prompted the army to find out exactly how many tanks it still had at its disposal. To perform this task, Captain Engelhard found himself going around day after day searching – mostly in vain – for tank workshops that still existed on paper. It was also understandable that the army, after eight weeks of encirclement, which it had endured trusting in an ultimate liberation, should now hit upon the idea of expanding the network of rearward defensive lines within the Cauldron. This plan was to blame for a marked deterioration in the state of Unold's nerves.

When Breuer and Siebel walked into the room they'd been told to go to, Unold's seat was empty. A soldier was busy mending the shattered window with a sheet of cellophane, evidently having realized that glass wasn't a suitable material to use given the constant air raids. The only other person present was an elderly artillery officer, a lieutenant colonel, who was standing around waiting. A narrow, heavily lined face with a brush-like moustache and a pince-nez peered out from above a green wool scarf, while on his head he wore a peaked officer's cap customized to the requirements of the winter with makeshift black earmuffs. Beside him was a grained leather suitcase. The man struck Breuer as somehow familiar.

After a few minutes, Unold burst in, carrying several large map rolls under his arm. He nodded curtly to Breuer and Siebel and, after sitting down, began nervously rooting around among his papers. The artillery officer approached and casually tipped his cap in salute.

'I'm trying to find out the whereabouts of my columns at the moment. I last saw them in Karpovka ten weeks ago. I was on leave in the meantime, you see, and I only just got back here by plane early this morning, and because we're an unattached unit, well, as you can imagine, that makes for certain...'

Unold looked up briefly from his papers.

'So... flew in this morning, did you? Very good. Right, as of now you're under the command of the major here. You can stay and listen to the orders I'm about to issue. So, Siebel—'

'Excuse me,' the artillery officer butted in, 'there's clearly been some misunderstanding here. I'm a first lieutenant, in charge of an autonomous division located somewhere in the Cauldron. The only thing I'm concerned with is trying to ascertain where my—'

'Yes, yes, you've explained. I'm perfectly aware of that!' Unold interrupted him. 'Your columns have doubtless been redeployed as infantry, and they've probably long since gone to hell in a handcart, rest assured! So, you see, Siebel...'

The lieutenant colonel took a deep breath.

'Look here... I really must protest in the strongest possible ter—'

'How dare you?' barked Unold, leaping up from his chair. 'Do you know what an order is, sir? We have martial law here!'

Under this onslaught, the old artilleryman's composure dissolved completely. He took his pince-nez from his nose with trembling hands and began polishing it, as though it was at fault for his incomprehension. His shortsighted eyes looked helplessly at his interlocutor and his lips moved, though no sound emerged. Unold paid him no further attention, but called the major – who had enjoyed the whole incident with a malicious smirk on his face – to come over and look at the map with him.

'So, Siebel,' he began, 'you need to prepare this area here on the railway line west of Yeshovka right down to the station at Voroponovo as a holding position for the retreating Fourteenth Panzer Corps. You have the Army High Command's full authority in this matter. It's essential that all the troops streaming in from the west are intercepted here and grouped into work parties that can start digging foxholes without delay. And make sure you include the drivers, too. All vehicles must be left parked off the road – those carrying the wounded and senior staff officers excepted, of course. Primarily, make sure you winkle out some officers with real drive to assist you. You've already got the lieutenant here; Breuer will accompany you as your adjutant. On top of that, the Fifty-First Corps of the military police will be under your direct command. You'll be based at the Talovoy Gorge. Quarters have been prepared for you there. Any questions?

The major bit his lip. Now it was his turn to seethe with fury.

'That's not going to work, Lieutenant Colonel, sir,' he announced with great determination. 'Even assuming we manage to intercept some of the troops there, where am I supposed to find food, accommodation for the men and above all any kind of materials for building defences from?'

Unold's face started to twitch.

'Siebel, please,' he answered, 'don't go asking such stupid questions now! The very reason I'm sending you there is so you can bring some kind of order to the situation on the ground!'

Major Siebel was renowned as someone who always spoke his mind without fear or favour. And that was exactly what he did now.

'Can't be done, sir! It's easy enough resolving impossible situations in a war room. You issue various orders, and if things go pear-shaped later the shit sticks to those who are charged with implementing them. I know all about that… but I'm not prepared to play along with this sham, Lieutenant Colonel, sir!'

The colour drained from Unold's features. For a while, the two officers stood silently, sizing one another up, and even Siebel's face slowly began to blanch. Then the lieutenant colonel spoke quietly through gritted teeth.

'Siebel – you know me. I'm warning you.'

Ssssss – Woom! The bunker reverberated and shook. The cellophane panel was torn from the window as if by some invisible hand. A cloud of snow, chalk and fine soil enveloped everything. In a single bound, Unold had leaped to the wall and pressed himself flat against it. Now he dashed back to the table, pulled the map with the new positions on it from under a heap of rubble and pressed it into the major's hand.

'Go on, get on with it – now! No time to lose!'

And with that, he ushered the three officers from the room.

Anyone stepping into the sweeping Talovoy Gorge, which sliced through the flat land west of Yeshovka, found themselves quite unexpectedly in a valley of peace. The bunkers and sheds there nestled between trees and bushes (a curious miracle of survival) like the huts and chalets on an allotment. Field kitchens steamed away, well-fed horses grazed on long yellow stalks of grass, and fresh laundry fluttered on washing lines strung between lorries and trees. Pink and blood-red cuts of juicy meat could be glimpsed through the flaps of a butchery unit's tent.

While Siebel, with the lieutenant colonel from the artillery in tow, went to announce his arrival to the Corps commander, Breuer sought out the resident intelligence officer.

He found two elegantly dressed officers, who greeted their dishevelled guest with somewhat perturbed civility. Breuer took in the desk and chairs here, the thick-pile carpet and the pictures on the walls. He started to recount his experiences. He talked about the ferocious rearguard actions, the destruction of the division and the miserable hunger they'd endured... His hosts listened to him with the kind of polite interest with which a neurologist listens to the stammerings of a deranged patient. 'Yes, we heard about that... It's been quiet for weeks here on the Volga front... Oh yes, it must have been really bad for you back there.' 'Back there'! They made it sound like he was talking about China. How was it possible that there were still people here in the Cauldron whom the whole Dance of Death of the last two months had left totally unscathed?

'Gentlemen.' Breuer's voice took on an imploring tone. 'Gentlemen! In two days' time, a front line of defence is going to be drawn immediately to your rear, just a few metres away – that is, if a front even exists by then!'

Yes, yes, they were well aware of that. They had taken note of it, like something one hears but doesn't really comprehend.

Where the Talovoy Gorge opened out into a flat depression resembling a broad square – the sides of the ravine were at this point only some three or four metres high – the windows and doors of a line of bunkers with a wooden walkway in front of them, partitioned off by a balustrade, mimicked a row of houses on a street. The scene in some measure reminded Breuer of a corner he knew in the bazaar quarter of Sarajevo. This was the site of the quarters that the Corps had assigned to the 'Fortress Construction Group Siebel'. Breuer and Siebel entered one of the two rooms. Plywood-panelled walls with built-in cupboards and seating recesses, a large cooking range, curtains and some stylish peasant furniture! The officers looked at one another. They opened the door to the second room and stood there, dumbstruck. They found themselves standing in a – bar! Sideboards, bar stools, drinks' cabinets, a pendant light with a red silk shade. On the walls, which were a deep shade of pink, someone had painted a series of racy murals showing young men in tuxedos embracing half-naked girls. In one corner stood an iron stove, a proper heavy old German one with a manufacturer's nameplate.

'I think I'm going crazy!' exclaimed Major Siebel, momentarily distracted from his cares and worries by the unlikely sight before his eyes.

'What on earth is this place?'

'It was the 79th military police division's HQ.'

'Never knew such a place existed. How is it even possible? People are lying out there in the open, and here…'

The only person who found no reason to be amazed was the unfortunate lieutenant colonel. Grumpily, he picked out for himself the best-sprung mattress in the sleeping bay and started complaining about the fact that they hadn't been supplied with any blankets. Other cares were weighing down on him as well, as it turned out. 'I've got to find out what's happened to my columns tomorrow,' he muttered. 'How stupid to deploy gunners as infantrymen – who ever heard of such a thing! Outstanding leadership here, I must say. And who knows where the hell our vehicles have got to by now! If anything's out of order, I'll be the one who carries the can for it later.'

Breuer looked at the lined face sporting the pince-nez, which struck him as so curiously familiar, and shook his head in despair. Did the man have any idea of the situation he was in? On the other hand, how could he? Well, he'd find out soon enough.

Siebel paid not the slightest heed to the lieutenant colonel. He paced up and down the room with long strides, raking his good hand through his tousled hair and nervously plucking at the leather glove on the hand of his false arm. He was struggling with a sense of duty on the one hand and a feeling of outrage on the other. He kept cursing under his breath: 'What total madness! It's all so pointless… fantasies, criminal fantasies, the whole thing!'

All of a sudden, he threw himself into a nervous flurry of activity. Rudely, and none too gently, wrenching the lieutenant colonel from his new-found cosiness, he announced that the two of them were going to go off there and then and inspect the planned defensive line.

Breuer stayed behind to keep an eye on their quarters. A few steps further on there was a supplies bunker, where a friendly and innocent paymaster handed out four days' worth of rations up front: fresh-baked bread, crispbreads, cheese, butter (Breuer wondered where in heaven they'd got that!), tins of potted meat, sardines, dried coffee, and last but not least three pounds of home-made horse sausage. It was like being in a fairy tale. Before long, logs were blazing in the stove and thick slices of sausage were sizzling in billycan lids. Breuer was as happy as a sandboy. If they only had a short while left to live, then they might as well live well! Out of the blue, as if by magic, a reflection of the old comfortable, peaceful feeling of well-being had come to life once more in the midst of chaos and destruction, a final salutation from the past, as it were, before everything finally came to an end.

It was getting dark outside. Breuer drew the curtains and got out the candles they'd brought with them. Just then, the prettily carved wooden candelabra above his head flickered into life and the room was bathed in electric light, courtesy of a quiet and efficient generator nearby. Breuer jumped up and went over to the switch near the door. He switched the light on and off, on and off, over and over again, laughing like a small boy and with tears running down his face.

After several hours, the major and his companion returned. The lieutenant colonel was still unsuspecting, while Siebel's downcast face revealed that no progress had been made on the defences. He brightened up, however, when he saw the cheerfully lit room and all the wonderful food on offer.

'Good heavens!' he cried, 'I'm bowled over! It's a real Land of Plenty here! Okay, let's forget about all the crap for now! Let's just live for once in our lives. In three days, we're all going straight to hell anyhow… Haven't we got anything to drink, though?'

They most certainly did. For a small consideration, and with due deference to the major's Knight's Cross and wooden arm – which the first lieutenant told him about – the paymaster had let Breuer have a couple of bottles of Hennessy cognac.

★

By January 1943 the village of Pitomnik, formerly situated southeast of the aerodrome, only continued to exist on the map. Where rows of wooden farmhouses may once have stood (two or three broken-down shacks and a few charred remains of fireplaces were the only remaining signs of habitation), a huge collection of vehicles had now assembled. Lorries, cars, tractors, buses and self-propelled howitzers of all types were parked up there, camouflaged with whitewash or still asphalt-grey, covered with snow, immobile and dead. All the life of Pitomnik had fled beneath the ground, which was tunnelled through and riddled with excavations like those of giant moles. In the days following the tenth of January, a constant influx of troops arriving from the west boosted the numbers of people living this troglodytic existence.

The scene is one such bunker, identical to countless others; it lies buried deep underground, is warmed by the glow of a small cylindrical stove, and is crammed full of men. They squat on the floor or squeeze together in a standing position, surrendering themselves gratefully to the little bit of warmth and shivering whenever the entrance hatch opens for a moment and the winter night pokes its icy fingers into the room. And the hatch is opened frequently. New figures flow down the steps in a steady stream, and their frozen rigidity slowly melts as the heat radiating from the stove thaws them out.

Jammed between stinking, silent bodies crouches Lieutenant Harras. His head, shrouded in a field-grey balaclava, is leaning against the tacky earth wall, and his fur cap has slipped down over his eyes. He dozes fitfully, and his breathing is laboured in the stuffy miasma produced by damp clothes and boots, frostbitten limbs and suppurating wounds. His wounded hand, which he's rested on his drawn-up knees, is causing him intense stabbing pain under its filthy dressing. Some terrible days lay behind him, since he'd been cut off from the rest of his unit in the wake of the big Russian offensive.

The rightful owner of the bunker, a paymaster who has been

shoved to a corner of the table by this unwelcome invasion of his space, is sitting by candlelight and feverishly totting up long lists of figures with the help of two soldiers. Once again, the sums don't add up. Hardly a day goes by when provisions aren't pilfered from the supplies bunker. His piggy little eyes skim suspiciously over the dull faces all around him before returning to check on the piles of tinned goods, loaves of bread and the large portion of fat that he has piled up in front of himself on the table as a precaution. Every time Harras's gaze lighted on this table, he found himself seized anew by blind fury. The moment he arrived here he'd asked the paymaster for some food. The man had looked him up and down.

'Got your unit with you?'

'Unit… no, I'm on my own.'

'Then I can't give you anything. According to regulations I can only issue rations to entire detachments, not to individuals.'

And he refused to budge from this position, despite all entreaties and threats. Neither Harras nor any of the other solitary soldiers who were milling about here got so much as a bit of bread from him. Harras felt like punching the fat bloke in the face. 'You fucking bastard!' he thought bitterly. 'You stubborn, stupid little pen-pushing arsehole!' And at the same time he felt an anger welling up inside him at his constant ill fortune. During a bombing raid on the airfield, he'd managed to filch some crispbreads and a few packets of glucose from the backpack of a junior doctor, who'd dashed off to attend to some screaming casualties. But immediately afterwards, his little stash had in turn been stolen from him in a bunker… 'You just can't trust anyone any more!' he concluded sadly. 'Time was it would have been unheard of in the German Army for a common soldier to steal from an officer.'

'Lieutenant!'

Harras feels an elbow prodding him tentatively in the side. A pointed little face with round, sharp eyes looks imploringly at him from the white-fringed hood of a camouflage jacket.

'Have you got anything to eat by any chance, Lieutenant, sir?'

Harras turns away. Such an idiotic question doesn't deserve an answer.

'Do you have any idea where the staff is now?' enquires the shrew-like face, undeterred.

'Which staff do you mean?'

'The divisional staff of the Third Motorized Division.'

'No.'

The little fellow carefully rubs the back of his hand along his damp nose.

'Pity,' he replies. 'When someone escapes from the Russians, they're really meant to report to their staff... And when all's said and done, at least there was something to eat over there.'

Harras pricks up his ears.

'Were you captured by the Russians too, then?'

'Yes, sir!' the man in the hood nods eagerly. 'They caught us at Dubinsky or whatever the name of that dump is – me and two others from my unit and a couple of Romanians. They got all matey with the Romanians straight off, but they treated us okay as well.'

Harras perks up all of a sudden. Some of those around him also begin to stir from their half-slumbers.

'Whassat, you were with the Russkis?'

'Come on, mate, spill the beans! What was it like?'

The little man is pleased to find himself suddenly the centre of attention, and really gets into his stride.

'The Russians... well, let me tell you, they're no slouches! Actually they're as smart as whips. So, first of all they took our weapons off us and then our pocket knives and watches and cigarette lighters. Then they gave us something to eat: bread, as much as we wanted, and sausage and bacon and cheese...' The men are hanging on the speaker's every word, like children being told about paradise. '... then this commissar turns up – you know, one of them in the black uniforms – and he speaks perfect German and he asks us whether we'd like to go back to our own side and tell them to end the whole thing right now. Well, one of our lot didn't want to. He was thinking it's a trick and they'll shoot us in the back. So he stayed put there. But me and the other bloke said yes straight away, and they let us go.'

'What, they released you just like that?'

'Yeah, they gave us back all our stuff and packed us off back to our lines… and they stood laughing and waving at us as we left.'

Silence. Then one of the men asks, hesitantly: 'So why didn't you just stay there?'

'Stay there? Pah, what do you know? We were happy to be away from there again! Who's to say they weren't just being friendly for propaganda reasons? And once they start taking more prisoners, they'll do 'em all in!'

'Dead right!' 'Yeah, it's all a big con. Nothing but propaganda!'

'Well, hang on, lads, I'm not so sure about that…'

'Tell me,' asks Harras, 'did you run across any Germans when you were over there? You know, emigrés and the like?'

The little fellow thinks long and hard about this.

'There was this soldier there,' he says at length, 'a little ginger guy. He was only allowed to say a few words to us, and the commissar watched him like a hawk. He said we should say hello from him to our comrades when we got back and tell them they should all defect, and that Hitler's to blame for everything, and the Red Army has only our best interests at heart.'

Hollow laughter breaks out all around.

'Oh yeah, I'm sure that's what they've got planned for us!'

'Us defect? Yeah, right, that'd suit them very nicely, the dozy idiots! Reckon we'd rather wait till Adolf gets us out of here!'

'So this bloke was a German soldier, you say? There's no way!'

'It must have been a Russian in disguise! They'll try anything, those devils!'

'Or maybe a Jew! They can all speak German.'

'Red hair, you say? And bandy legs and jug ears too, right? I knew a bloke like that once. Used to peddle mousetraps round Finkenwerder before '33.'

'Pipe down, will ya! Let him finish his story!'

'So then,' the little soldier continues, 'this guy that looked like a German soldier says we should ask this German sergeant major who's mentioned somewhere in the reports and who'd been over with the Russians once. Says that he knew exactly what the score was with the Russians, but that we'd have to grill him to get the truth out of him… Don't you remember the story, Lieutenant, sir? There was a lot of talk going round about it one time. What was he called again? Had a name like a dog!'

'Will you lot just shut up!' yelled the paymaster over the general hubbub. 'Zip it right now, or I'll chuck you all out! You can't hear yourself think with all this bloody chatter going on!'

Grumbling resentfully, the troops lapsed into silence. At the back, though, someone said in a stage whisper: 'Fat ponce!'

A few of the men keep on whispering, quizzing the extraordinary messenger.

Harras feels a chill run down his spine. Who on earth might that ginger-haired scoundrel be who had such a vivid memory of him? That was all he needed, for stupid rumours about his escapade to become common knowledge here! Nor did it seem like a good idea to fall into the Russians' hands for a second time. He was really up shit creek now! He had always been a conscientious, keen and spirited soldier, exactly the type that officers loved. And it had been solely down to his courage and his resourcefulness that he'd been made an officer and had been personally commended by the CO. In normal times, he'd have been made for life, but here… They couldn't expect him to allow himself to be shot like a dog, or starve or freeze to death for sweet FA! He had to get out of here as quickly as he could… But how? Nothing had come of the fact that, when the Russians launched their big offensive, the initial shock had caused Harras's Luger to go off and the bullet to go right through his left hand, of all the rotten luck (he was far from acknowledging that this had been anything but an unfortunate accident). As if they'd fly someone out with an injury of that kind when they were even keeping people here who'd lost an entire leg! Harras groaned quietly to himself. Perhaps he ought to try going back to the aerodrome once more, despite the constant air raids. He could lend a hand there loading up the severely wounded… maybe one time have a quiet word with one of the pilots… Harras keeps turning the idea over in his mind until he finally lapses from sheer hunger and tiredness into a fitful half-sleep.

Hours pass. A few shells explode outside. Harras's subconsciousness registers 'air raid' but lets his exhausted body sleep on. Suddenly the hatch to the bunker flies open. Along with gusts of icy wind and snow flurries, piercing shouts penetrate the room.

'Alarm! Everybody out! The Russians are coming! Russian tanks!'

The paymaster is the first to leap up.

'Oh Christ,' he shouts. 'The stores!'

He grabs his fur jacket and makes for the exit hatch, but then quickly turns back and crams some tins and loaves into his pockets before clambering out of the bunker.

'Good idea!' thinks Harras, still half-asleep. 'Smart move. That's one way of clearing out the bunker, at least!' So he sits there calmly while everyone stumbles over him, shouting and swearing. But after the yelling and shooting continues for a while outside, he too struggles to his feet. The table has been overturned and the lantern extinguished. In the glow of the overheated stove he can still see some men crouching round the walls.

'Hey! Don't you want to leave? It's not a drill! The Russians are here!'

No one answers, no one moves. Behind the table, a man is crawling on the ground scraping together bits of spilt fat from the dirty puddles on the floor.

Harras struggles out into the cold. A grotesque sight meets his eyes. All round him, people are emerging out of the ground! All of a sudden, he finds himself whisked up in a wild maelstrom of fleeing men and carried away. Images of blind panic flit past him: running and screaming figures carrying pieces of clothing, weapons and equipment or desperately trying to start frozen engines. With a dull roar, some vehicles spring into life and, bumping into one another, roar off, ploughing into the heaving mass of humanity ahead of them. He sees burning lorries glowing white-hot, the wide-open, yelling mouths of officers frantically and fruitlessly trying to stem the tide of retreat, and men grasping at the fleeing vehicles, attempting to get a handhold on radiator grilles, tarpaulin sides or gun barrels as they pass. As some soldiers try to climb on to tracked vehicles, they get trapped in the moving tracks and fall to the ground with lacerated hands. As he listens, the general cacophony of shouting, with some sharp cries repeatedly ringing above it, the rattling and barking of engines that haven't yet warmed up, and the dry chattering of machine-gun bursts, which in the crystal-clear frosty air sound uncannily close at hand, all merge into a single, terrible din. Anti-tank shells come whizzing over their heads in a flattened arc. Beneath their flaming tails, the whimpering huddle of people pause and flinch like they've been whipped before rushing crazily on.

The seething Cauldron is finally boiling over. A single notion, hatched in several desperate individuals' minds, lends the flow a direction and an objective: Stalingrad! Gumrak, Pitomnik, that was all a fraud. Stalingrad, though, that can't possibly be an illusion. There, they'll find thick walls, deep cellars, and warmth, warmth! There they'll finally reach their destination and won't have to keep on running through the night and the snow. There they can crawl into a hole and wait for either a miracle or the end. So, onward to Stalingrad!

The seething human tide rolls on to the east. It is a bright, clear night beneath a velvet-black sky sprinkled with points of light.

A deadly cold descends from this vastness of space. The air itself seems to solidify, trembling and shimmering in a glittering dance of ice crystals as fine as dust.

The firing has ceased. Gradually the feverish flow begins to cool down into a viscous lava of vehicles and people, flowing on incessantly but now ever more sluggishly, creeping forward metre by metre. The lorries and cars advance several vehicles abreast, bumping and nudging past each other or grinding one another into immobility. The snow squeaks sharply under the pressure of their turning wheels. Heavy tracked vehicles come rumbling and rattling along, turning jerkily and making the hard ground rumble as they pass. Steadily, the clusters of men begin to drop off the canvas sides, mudguards, running boards and bonnets. One by one they fall off, frozen stiff, into the carriageway, where they are run over, mangled and crushed.

Harras trots along between the vehicles. That's the only way of making any headway. On the verges the snow is lying knee-deep. By now his clothes have lost the last vestiges of the warmth from the bunker. An icy band of cold grips him ever tighter. The frost creeps up his arms, seeps through his felt boots and up his legs and gnaws at his entrails. He feels like his eyeballs are embedded in dishes of ice, that his nostrils are clogged up with frozen threads, and that every breath he takes is laced with sharp needles. A walrus moustache of ice is slowly forming on his balaclava. His brain feels like it has been paralysed. He hardly notices the people who are creeping along beside him, the horde of lost souls who have no more energy or willpower left to clamber on to a vehicle. Wrapped in blankets, their hands buried in their coat pockets and their heads shrouded in cloths and scarves, they haul themselves onward, supporting their wounded or frostbitten limbs on sticks and crutches or taking painful, staggering steps, one at a time, on feet wrapped in formless bundles of rags or straw overshoes. As they go, they leave elephants' tracks behind them in the slushy snow. Hardly anyone is carrying a weapon any more; even through gloves, hands would freeze hard to metal barrels on a night like this. One or two of them are pulling along little sleds piled with bags or equipment, and paying no heed to anything that falls off. Cold and hunger have killed stone dead all thoughts and feelings, any glimmer of obedience or sense of duty or camaraderie, any last vestiges of helpfulness or even of pity. Somewhere deep within them there still glows a tiny spark of life, which drives them on. It is just enough to sustain the naked urge for self-preservation, and the impulse to find food and warmth. They creep along mechanically and ghostlike, on the edge of dying of exposure. Here and there, one of them topples over this edge, falling down silently. He makes one final effort to lift his torso from the snow, and falls back; slowly his hand tries to support his heavy head, but slips off. Then his body moves no more. The others stumble over him and go on their way.

Vehicles are also giving up the ghost during this night, dying of lack of fuel and of the snow, in which they stick fast. Three five-ton tractor units pulling light howitzers have stopped dead in the middle of the road. Several men are busy removing the breechblocks from the guns and fetching their few belongings down from the trucks. A lieutenant stands and supervises them; he should have blown up the guns back in Dubininsky. But he hadn't been able to bring himself to do it; instead he'd secretly siphoned off fuel from the tanks of some fully laden staff trucks. It has taken him and his guns as far as this, but now the games's up... He stands there staring vacantly, his arm resting on one of the gun barrels. Staff cars sway past him, along with lorries piled high with crates, mattresses and bed frames. The transport section of a staff corps. One of the lorries is towing a car with a dismantled engine... The driver of a three-ton Opel truck stands beside his vehicle, clutching two loaves of army bread.

'Bread for petrol!' he whispers to the drivers of passing vehicles. 'Anyone swap some fuel for a loaf?' Someone knocks the bread from his hand as they drive by. With a cry of rage, the man leaps forward to retrieve it, but slips over and gets caught in the tracks of a self-propelled gun. The heavy vehicle rocks slightly as it lumbers over the obstacle. A short death scream is drowned out by the grinding rattle of the broad tracks. In the meantime, men have clambered into the back of the abandoned Opel and are silently rifling through its cargo for anything edible or for warm clothing. Crates are tipped out, presently followed by suitcases, items of uniform, boots, radio equipment and bundles of official documents. Down below, others are standing around, sorting through the plunder, rejecting some items but pointlessly encumbering themselves with others, only to cast them off, one by one, after just a few steps.

A VW *Kübelwagen* that was trying to get past the truck sticks fast in the verge. Its tyres, wrapped with snow chains, spin wildly, kicking up dirty snow behind it. An officer paces back and forth beside the car. His long fur coat is unbuttoned and his sheepskin cap has tipped back on his head. It is Colonel Steigmann.

'Stop!' he shouts. 'Lend a hand here, will you? Come on, someone give us a push!'

He shouts himself hoarse. No one is listening to him. He leaps over to the line of figures shambling past, tugging at their sleeves and staring into their expressionless faces. They casually shrug him off, push him aside. He shrinks visibly, all the determination drains from his face and his eyes narrow and moisten. The giant of a man shivers with impotent rage.

Harras lets himself be carried onward. Mechanically he moves his stiff feet: one – two, one – two. The road appears endless to him, and time infinite. He is bemused by the unreality of this grim night. It is as though he has been transported to some dead planet in the outer realms of the universe. Is this still the Earth, then, this awful, silent, icy wasteland surrounding him here? Are these still human beings, these grimacing, unfeeling wraiths? In his state of utter exhaustion, tantalizing images start to swim before his consciousness, images full of light, warmth and life. Spring meadows full of flowers, sunshine, the scent of lilac, and soft music...

Once more the column grinds to a halt. Half-frozen bodies slip down from the lorries and try to instil some warmth into frozen limbs by shaking their arms jerkily and stamping up and down. Meantime, others on foot who still have some energy and hope left crowd around the trucks to see if they can find themselves a free space, but are pushed away fiercely by those sitting up back. Harras gropes his way along the line of stationary vehicles. He knows he could keel over at any moment and he doesn't even fight against it any longer. He is brought up with a jolt as he walks into the back of another person. A pair of eyes looks at him from above a heavily frosted scarf. From their depths there suddenly comes a flicker of recognition.

'Is that you, Lieutenant, sir?' says the figure. 'Are you still alive?'

Saying this, he tugs aside the scarf. It is his batman.

'Hey, Franz, Karl! Give me a hand here! It's our lieutenant!'

Hands are extended towards Harras, hauling him up into the back of a lorry. He sinks down between crates and barrels and densely packed figures dusted with snow. Men from his company are among them. The truck is one from the battalion's transport unit. Someone pulls a sheepskin from the back of the lorry and blankets are thrown over him. The truck moves slowly forward.

Somewhere further back in the stream of vehicles, Colonel Steigmann's VW is on the move again. A colonel without a regiment – a head without a body. Can a head keep on living when the body has been torn to pieces? At one point, there's a bang somewhere at the rear. Damn it, thinks the driver, a puncture! But the car trundles on at the same slow tempo. Just a backfire!

Harras is unable to provide any answers to the brief questions his men ask him. An overpowering feeling is welling up within him and stifling his ability to speak. He looks up to the pitch-black night sky, where the bright stars once more seem close and familiar to him.

People! This is the one thought that comes into his head: these are people, after all! He drags the sheepskin over his head and nestles his frost-stiffened face in the woolly pelt. He feels small and safe, like a child back in the arms of his mother. Her deep voice is ringing in his ears. 'My boy, my boy!' That's what she always used to say to him. She'd been so proud of him, and had shown such faith in him. Tears are running down his face. 'What have they done to us?' he thinks. 'My God, what have they done to us?'

Colonel Steigmann's car finally noses its way into the mayhem of the Talovoy Gorge. The divisional staff must be somewhere around here! The driver switches off the engine. There's no movement in the back of the car. The driver turns round and sees that the colonel is lying dead, his pistol still clutched in his hand. The blood on his face is frozen. So, it hadn't been the car backfiring after all…

That was the night of the sixteenth of January, 1943. For some time thereafter, long lines of abandoned, looted vehicles, discarded clothes, scattered papers, weapons and equipment, frozen-stiff bodies crouching down in the lee of cars or crushed and splattered to an unrecognizable pulp on the carriageway scarred the route from Pitomnik to Talovoy. In the event, it turned out that all this chaos and panic, and all the many deaths that ensued, had been triggered by nothing more than a Russian raiding party, supported by two or three tanks, which had probed as far as the village of Pitomnik and, after a few firefights, had promptly withdrawn again.

The lieutenant colonel had made himself comfortable at the quarters. Major Siebel had gone out early that morning with Breuer, so he was hoping to spend a pleasant day with no disturbances. A search of their new quarters had turned up a well-thumbed volume bound in linen. Stretched out contentedly on a bench, he carefully polished his pince-nez and then, with raised eyebrows, opened the book. In large red letters on the title page he read the word 'Bread!' and underneath it the subtitle 'The Defence of Tsaritsyn'. What was this – the author's name was Tolstoy? That was that old Russian count with delusional ideas on religion and social reform! But that Tolstoy's Christian name was Leo, if memory served, whereas this writer was called Alexei. Ah well, probably a son of the old Tolstoy. Sometimes becoming a writer was a hereditary thing... He started leafing through the book. It was all about this dump here, Stalingrad! The city had once been called Tsaritsyn, had it? Aha... And it turned out that German troops had been here before in numbers, in 1918. Well, well, you learn something new every day! Seems it had been a do-or-die affair for the Bolsheviks back then, too. Well, hadn't he been saying all along that what happened at Stalingrad would decide the outcome of the war! If the Germans were to succeed this time around, then it'd finally be curtains for Stalin and his comrades. He put the book down and picked at his teeth reflectively. All the same, it had to be said that things weren't going too well right now. After what he'd witnessed in the past couple of days... The German Army High Command seemed to have no overall grasp of the situation! And there was no order, no discipline! Things wouldn't have been like that in the '14–'18 war...

The lieutenant colonel threw the book onto the table and jumped up. Wouldn't this infernal noise ever cease? A badly tuned engine had been left rattling away outside the bunker for quite some time; every now and then the sound was interrupted by the engine backfiring. The lieutenant colonel flung open the door. Christ Almighty, it was cold out there! From the ridge opposite, a long column was snaking down into the gorge, an unbroken line of lorries and cars. Vehicles were already beginning to crowd into the broad square in front of the bunkers. Immediately outside the door stood an open-topped *Kübelwagen*, snorting and shuddering like an exhausted horse. A man was looking inside the open bonnet. In his fur greatcoat, which reached almost to the ground and had a broad turned-up collar, he looked like a polar bear.

'Hey, you! Are you out of your mind, or what? Turn the engine off, will you, or clear off!'

The frost in the air deadened the words to virtual silence. The man didn't even bother turning round. The cold appeared to have robbed him of all capacity of hearing and speech. It also dissuaded the lieutenant colonel from investigating the matter any further. Coughing, he turned away and slammed the door behind him. He switched the light on, threw a couple more logs into the stove and immersed himself in his book once more. But he was not to be granted any peace. Outside he heard the sound of clumping footsteps. The door flew open and a group of soldiers barged their way into the room. Their bluish-yellow faces, frozen-stiff coats and jackets, and snow-encrusted bundles of rags wrapped around their feet instantly turned the atmosphere into the inside of a refrigerator. The men at the front stopped and blinked stupidly at the unaccustomed brightness. The lieutenant colonel furrowed his brow and peered over his pince-nez at the interlopers.

'What's the meaning of this?' Silence. The lieutenant colonel got to his feet. 'What do you want?' he asked sharply. The soldier right at the front took off his cap like a supplicant. Tousled hair was poking out of his balaclava. The left side of his face grimaced in an incessant twitch; it made him look as though someone was constantly jabbing him with a needle. 'Just wanted to warm up a bit, sir. We're—'

'So you thought you'd just burst in here without so much as a by-your-leave, eh? Without knocking? Unbelievable. This is a staff billet, understood? A staff billet! So, about-turn now and out you go!'

The troops hesitated, staring in disbelief at the officer. The lieutenant colonel's face flushed.

'Never heard of such a lack of discipline!' he muttered. He went and stood right in front of the men. 'Are you hard of hearing or something? Don't you understand? Make yourselves scarce!'

The men didn't understand. All they understood was that they had spent weeks on end lying in snow holes with frozen limbs and one hundred and fifty grams a day bread ration each; and that, deserted by the High Command and hounded by the enemy, they'd dragged themselves for hour after hour through terrible cold; and that here was a bunker, a bunker such as they had never set eyes on since they'd begun the siege of Stalingrad, with electric light and a warm stove and benches and tables and beds with mattresses; and that this bunker was virtually unoccupied. That was what they understood. But in ten years of military service, they'd had it dinned into them that the only way of expressing their wishes was to keep shtum and that, when asked, the only reply that was expected of them was 'Yes, sir!' And they'd learned that lesson well. The most terrible war of all time had been started with lies and betrayal. They'd kept quiet about that. They had been used as instruments for the oppression and abuse of foreign peoples. They'd kept quiet about that. Foreign countries had been pillaged through their efforts and finally they'd been led deep into the heartland of Russia, as far as Stalingrad, where they'd been ordered to fight, starve and freeze and where, if they'd fallen sick or were wounded, they were left to die in conditions you wouldn't even leave an animal to die in. They'd kept quiet about that. And when someone who was unsettled by the unspoken questions in their faces spoke to them, they simply replied 'Yes, sir!' like they'd been told to. And so it was that they kept quiet again when they were expected to understand that this warm bunker hadn't been prepared for the likes of them, but for the others – those who had the power to decide over life and death – and that they were destined to die. And even if they didn't understand that, they still said 'Yes, sir!' to it, albeit not in as many words. So, slowly and exhaustedly, they shuffled backwards towards the door, casting a last stolen glance at the wonderful pleasures of this room as they went.

Even so, the lieutenant colonel was not left to savour his victory. The door kept opening time and again, and finally it remained open the whole time. The lieutenant colonel was at his wits' end. He telephoned the Corps and asked for a military policeman to be

dispatched on an urgent service assignment involving the establish-
ment of a new front. And one duly arrived, put on his steel helmet,
hung his shiny breastplate round his neck, and with the help of
these symbols of authority shooed the unwanted guests out into
the darkness.

Meanwhile, it had grown cold in the bunker. In addition, the lights
had gone out.

'Oh, that's just great!' the lieutenant colonel muttered to himself.
'Just great! And that's how we're hoping to win this war, is it?'

He pulled out his slippers from his leather suitcase, lit a candle
and sat down in front of the rekindled stove. That was how Siebel
and Breuer found him when they returned in the late evening, dog-
tired and frozen through. Major Siebel had thrown himself into the
pointless task he'd been assigned with a zeal that would have been
worthy of a far better enterprise. He had really sunk his teeth into
the task, as if the outcome of the whole war depended on its success.
The Corps' military policemen and their commander had vanished,
one by one. Only at the railway crossing where Breuer and Siebel set
up their checkpoint did they manage, with some difficulty, to scrape
together a force of around fifty men. They were standing around
there starving and with their teeth chattering; some collapsed there
and then. But food and accommodation proved impossible to find,
let alone any materials for constructing defences. And so the major
was forced to send them away again. And when, as the evening
drew on, the ever-increasing stream of retreating soldiers made
any further effort impossible, Siebel drove to the High Command.
There, they could scarcely even recall what the assignment was.
Unold had already disappeared. 'So, right,' he was finally instructed,
'fair enough: your role in the operation is complete. The Fourteenth
Corps, which was due to occupy that sector, is now in place. It will
take over the task of building the defensive line.'

★

The task of building the defensive line! Recalling this phrase, Siebel chuckled grimly to himself as he gathered up his things at the bunker.

'What's going on, then?' asked the lieutenant colonel uneasily.

'We're shipping out, back to our unit.'

'What about me, then? What are my orders?'

'You? You're free to do as you please. Maybe you can even look for your artillery columns. You'd better start right here in the gorge, though! It's crammed full of vehicles. Some of your lot are bound to be among them.'

The lieutenant colonel jumped up.

'That's outrageous! Simply turfing an officer out on the street like this, quite outrageous… I'll file a formal complaint! I'll go straight to High Command with this!'

He flung his slippers and washing kit into his suitcase and threw on his fur coat.

'With this fantastic level of organization,' he grumbled, 'I wouldn't be at all surprised if we lost the war. But at least in this case there's no doubt who's to blame. The top brass, that's who, this bloody idiotic top brass!'

Breuer sat down at the table and laid his head on his arms. The impressions of this day, the dreadful, pitiable scenes of the German army in retreat and the chaotic scenes back at the railway crossing, all this had shaken his mental equilibrium to the core. He would have liked nothing better than to just crawl away somewhere and hide, and not to hear or see anything any more. Couldn't this old man just shut his trap for once? He shot the lieutenant colonel a furious glance – and suddenly he remembered where he knew this face from. The pince-nez, the centre parting, the little moustache – and that expression…

'So,' said the lieutenant colonel in parting, 'I hope I'll eventually see you all in my machine-gun company!'

Gripped by an insane fury, Breuer leaped up and launched himself at the lieutenant colonel. 'Who's to blame?' he screamed.

'The top brass? No, I'll tell you who's really to blame. *You* are – yes, you! You and all your bloody kind! With all your jingoism and the warmongering you use to poison children's minds – all your fine talk of steel helmets and swagger sticks and the red-white-and-black flag and "Let's March to Victory Over France". *You* are to blame, you and no one else – Mister Schoolmaster Strackwitz!'

He'd grabbed the lieutenant colonel by the lapels of his fur coat and was shaking him like a bundle of straw. The old officer's eyes were bulging out of their sockets, and beads of sweat were forming on his brow. He thought he'd been transported to a madhouse and began to doubt his own sanity. With a sudden strength born of desperation, he wrenched himself free of Breuer's grip, snatched up his suitcase and ran out. Only when he was safely outside did he pull out his pay-book to check for himself whether he wasn't actually the schoolteacher Strackwitz, instead of the same old Lieutenant Colonel Friedrich Sauer from Breslau, a Great War veteran drafted back into military service in 1936, and before that a successful travelling salesman dealing in vacuum cleaners.

The engine made a deep growling sound, and even the rattling of the doors and the bodywork sounded more muffled than usual. The intense cold of this night seemed even to have altered the structure of metal. Breuer sat jammed in a corner of the car. His teeth were chattering and not just from the appalling cold. The dreadful images of disorganization floated before his eyes. He thought back to his conversations with Wiese. 'He was right,' he said to himself, 'we're losing the war. Right here at Stalingrad. What will become of Germany? Of our homeland?'

The car came to a halt with screeching brakes. The railway crossing at Gumrak was blocked by a tangle of vehicles. The night was lit by the glow of flames. Major Siebel got out and directed the four-wheel-drive Horch limousine next to them through the snow.

When, with some difficulty, they finally made it to the open road to Stalingradski, the major announced quietly: 'So, this is my wedding night—'

Breuer turned his head.

'How come?' he said in a tired voice.

'First thing this morning I dispatched a telegram,' the major replied, 'from High Command to Gleiwitz, addressed to my fiancée… proposing long-distance marriage by proxy. At first they didn't want to send it, told me the telegraph lines were too busy. But Paulus himself sanctioned it. Said he could understand my position. And this evening the adjutant told me that a message had come through. It's from my fiancée, confirming that she's willing to go ahead.'

When the two officers arrived at the CO's bunker to send a reply, Captain Engelhard was already sitting there, reading in the light of an oil lamp. He sat up and, casting a cautious look into the corner of the bunker, put his finger to his lips. Unold lay on a camp bed there, under a blanket. His eyes were closed and his gaunt, white head stood out against the darkness. He wasn't moving, but it was hard to tell if he was asleep. Next to him, on a crate, lay his gun. The major pulled a bottle of cognac from the depths of his greatcoat, and Engelhard placed two glasses and a china beaker on the table. Siebel poured. He slapped the captain on the shoulder.

'You'll laugh yourself sick at this, man, but I'm getting married!' he said. 'So let's drink to my wedding night!' He emptied his glass in one and then started telling Engelhard quietly about the events of the past two days. The captain listened with an earnest and calm look on his face. Now and then he glanced into the corner, to see if Unold was listening to their conversation, but everything remained quiet there.

'Yeah,' Engelhard said when he'd finished, 'looks like it's the end. All over and done with, I reckon. All that remains is for us to quit the scene with as much decency as we possibly can.'

'Decency?' Siebel scoffed. 'There's no decency here! The gentlemen from High Command should crawl out from their holes some time! Paulus ought to go out onto the streets just for once and see if what's happening there warrants the name of a decent death! He thinks he's still got soldiers he can lead, and who can build defensive lines? He really ought to get out more! There's never been anything like it in the whole of history!'

He ran his hand through his unruly hair, which kept falling into his eyes.

'But of course the "Greatest Commander of All Time"* must also accomplish a defeat the like of which the world has never seen!'

He reached for the bottle to refill the glasses. Captain Engelhard signalled that he had had enough. His strict code of correctness was scandalized at seeing a fellow officer drop his inhibitions like this.

'Major, I beg you,' he said in deliberately measured tones, 'you've really overstepped the mark there! I just don't understand how you can cast aspersions on the Führer. Mistakes have been made all down the line, especially by minions who aren't remotely a match for the genius of the great man. None of this will have the slightest effect on Hitler's rightful place in history, let alone tarnish it. Hitler stands far above us; he's a unique secular phenomenon who's immune to any criticism. He is "beyond Good and Evil"; there's something of the Nietzschean "superman" about him!'

Again he cast an expectant eye at the camp bed in the corner. Surely if the lieutenant colonel had been asleep then this heated conversation would have woken him by now. But Unold made not the slightest sound; he was far away from all discussions of supermen.

---

* 'Greatest Commander of All Time' – German: *Größter Feldherr aller Zeiten*, abbreviation *GröFaZ*. A term of adulation for Adolf Hitler, coined by the obsequious Field Marshal Wilhelm Keitel, supreme commander of German forces, after the triumphant *Blitzkrieg* of 1940 against the Low Countries and France. Later in the war, as defeats mounted for the Nazis, and especially in the aftermath of Stalingrad, the abbreviation began to be used ironically, particularly by opponents within the armed forces.

Also, Siebel had barely listened to Engelhard's rant. His eyes were already glazing over.

'Oh Christ,' he said, clutching at Breuer's shoulder, 'when I think of my fiancée it's enough to give me the screaming abdabs. We've sacrificed the best years of our lives to that criminal shit, and now he's letting us go to the dogs... Come on, let's drink! It's the only thing that makes any sense any more!'

Breuer drank. He could feel the alcohol going to his head. Engelhard stared fixedly ahead, his fingers drumming on the table.

'Tell me honestly, Captain,' asked Breuer. 'How do you think this will all end here?'

Engelhard took a deep breath.

'Well, we're going to hold out until the bitter end. And maybe we'll be lucky enough to be picked off in the process. But if not, there's always our own pistols... Or would you rather be force-marched to Siberia, and eat raw flesh from corpses along the way?'

Siebel, his face red from exasperation and alcohol, slammed down his hand, which had been propping up his head, hard on the table. 'Even if I'm forced to work for ten years in a lead mine and have to eat dirt!' he shouted, 'I'm telling you, Engelhard, that I've done my duty as a soldier, d'you hear me! I earned my Knight's Cross honestly, not like some people! I sacrificed my arm and never complained – but I'm not putting a bullet through my own head! I want to get back home! And then, Engelhard, there'll be a reckoning. Payback for what those bastards have done to us!'

He got to his feet unsteadily and reached for his coat. Engelhard waved his hand at Breuer, in whose befuddled brain Siebel's words had coalesced into spectral visions, and pulled his own fur coat on to accompany the two of them outside. Unold was still lying prone on his bed. He didn't move a muscle, but his breath was now coming in heavy pants, while his wide-open eyes stared sightlessly at the ceiling.

★

Not far from the parking lot in the snow-covered valley bottom of the 'forested ravine' stood a group of soldiers. Men from Colonel von Hermann's staff and some of those who in the past few days had entered the gorge from the west and infested its villages like a swarm of locusts. Only a few of them noticed the lieutenant colonel who had just stepped out of a rattling *Kübelwagen*; they bestirred their tired limbs to give him a salute. The others were hanging, full of desperate hope, on the words of an anti-aircraft gunner who was addressing them, and gesticulating wildly as he spoke:

'What if I tell you that German tanks are on the high road above the Don? Only thirty kilometres from here!'

Lieutenant Colonel Dannemeister stopped in his tracks.

'What's that you're saying?'

The men around the speaker nudged him and he turned round. Shocked at the sight of an officer, he snapped to attention and saluted. 'Begging your pardon, Lieutenant Colonel, sir!' he stammered. 'I didn't see you—'

'Who told you this nonsense about tanks, I'd like to know!'

'The tanks? Um, our CO announced it. This morning, in front of the whole battery!'

'Well, it's rubbish!' barked the lieutenant colonel. 'Complete drivel! Don't you dare go spreading rumours like that here!' As he went on his way, the officer cursed under his breath: 'Brilliant! Another bloody leak!'

'Yes, sir, Lieutenant Colonel!' the gunner shouted after him. Then, with a sly grin, he turned to the men around him and whispered: 'Hear that? There you have it – "another leak"! See, the whole thing's still top secret!'

In the divisional CO's bunker the lieutenant colonel found the regimental commanders and leaders of the independent units already gathered, around ten officers in all. They were standing around, murmuring and whispering to one another. Colonel von Hermann had only been waiting for the arrival of his adjutant to begin proceedings. His clean-shaven face and crisp uniform stood out among the stubble beards and the grubby fur jackets, in an underground space that reeked of sweat and damp leather.

'Gentlemen,' began the colonel, 'you're all aware of the current situation. Pitomnik is lost, and we'll only be able to hold Gumrak for a few more days. That's the end of the Cauldron. In these circumstances the High Command is toying with the idea of a "breakout on all sides". In other words: each of the divisions that are still capable of fighting needs to muster its entire operational strength and use it to achieve a surprise breakthrough of the enemy sector facing it, and then drive deep into their heartland. For our division, that would mean breaking out east across the Volga, then swinging round to the south to attack the Russian artillery positions from the rear before crossing the Volga again south of Stalingrad. Somewhere around there we can expect to link up with the Fourth Corps.' The colonel shot a swift glance at the uncomprehending faces of his officers. His pale-blue eyes had a dusty look. Then he went on. Restrained tension resonated alongside the cool objectivity of his voice.

'The military purpose of this operation is to sow confusion behind enemy lines. In addition, the hope is that large numbers of their forces will be tied down in giving pursuit.'

The officers looked at one another and then at the colonel. His face was impassive. A wave of indignation and derision arose.

'What's the meaning of this?' – 'To the east of all places, across the Volga… why don't we just keep going until we get to Japan?' – 'What utter nonsense!'

The colonel raised his hand.

'Gentlemen, please! The first thing we must do is to find out how the men will react to such a plan.'

The CO of the artillery regiment, a major in the reserves, who was a small, bustling man with a florid alcoholic complexion, took out of his mouth the cigar stub he'd been busily sucking on throughout the meeting.

'Well, I reckon the plan isn't at all bad,' he announced. 'Only trouble is, it's come far too late! We've already spiked our guns and our ammunition's all gone. But if there's a real chance of breaking through to our lines, even if only some of the units make it, then that's a pretty good plan to my mind.'

He looked around the room, waiting in vain for agreement from his fellow officers, and lapsed into silence. Colonel von Hermann closed his eyes for a moment.

'I'm afraid that's out of the question,' he said. 'The front is almost three hundred kilometres from here. Our troops are half-starved and exhausted, and our transport units are dispersed. We can't now undo the mistakes that were made when the Cauldron was first created; that's not the intention anyhow. The whole operation is meant to be a kind of suicide mission – nothing more, nothing less. It's a way of short-circuiting the business of "fighting on to the last bullet", speeding up our annihilation while inflicting as much damage on the enemy as we possibly can. That's its sole purpose. There's no longer any question of saving the Sixth Army.'

Colonel Steffen nodded in agreement. Downy hair grew profusely from the back of his neck at the base of his bald head, like a cockatoo's crest. He was a General Staff officer. Differences of opinion with his CO had led to his transfer to the regular forces. In the hope of being reappointed to a staff soon, he led his infantry regiment with élan, strict discipline and ambition.

'A heroic death – good idea!' he said huskily; his Adam's apple bounced up and down above the collar of his camouflage jacket. 'It's the only proper way to go now that the game's up. In any event, far better than sitting around here waiting to be cut down. The Sixth Army'll go out in one last blaze of glory!'

The hubbub of dissent in the room grew louder. A clear voice suddenly rang out from the back.

'What's going to happen to the wounded?'

Colonel von Hermann looked intently at the speaker's gaunt face, framed in a soft Christ-like beard. He had a lot of time for the young major, who had taken command of an infantry regiment just a fortnight previously. He repeated his question, this time with even greater urgency.

'What will happen to the wounded? We've got thousands of untended wounded and sick here in the Cauldron. It's a state of affairs that casts a shadow over the "glory" of the Sixth Army, if you ask me.'

'The plan doesn't say anything about the severely wounded,' replied the colonel, laying out his words carefully like coins on a table. 'We're going to have to abandon them to their fate. For men with less severe wounds, or those suffering from battle fatigue or frostbite – in short, for anyone who's no longer capable of marching, the following is envisaged: the rapid Russian advance from the west could put the plan in jeopardy. So the idea is to set up a defensive line on the railway embankment between Gumrak and Voroponovo, comprising all those wounded and sick men who can still fight...'

The colonel took a single deep breath before continuing with his address in a rapid and almost offhand delivery.

'There's a worry that those concerned won't be able to summon up enough enthusiasm for the task. As a result, it's been recommended that they be told that... that a thousand German tanks are en route from the west to liberate us, that they have already reached the high road above the Don, and that until they arrive the position must be held at all costs. While they're busy fighting in this expectation, the rest will effect a breakthrough at another location.'

Only the busy ticking of the pocket alarm clock on the table broke the silence that followed. Colonel Steffen gasped for air a couple of times, but after looking at the frozen faces of his colleagues refrained from voicing his thoughts on the matter. Without warning, the major who had spoken up before pushed his way to the front. He took two paces forward, composed himself and raised his hand to speak. His voice cut through the air like a sword.

'In the name of my regiment, I hereby declare that the men would not be prepared to go along with… with a "plan" like that!'

That broke the spell of silence. The room erupted in shouts of agreement and indignation.

'Quite right!' – 'Yes, it's out of the question!' – 'Sheer impertinence!' – 'It's a disgrace!'

Even the little artillery officer became animated. 'The whole thing's a fool's errand, in my view. To try to bamboozle those poor blokes who are at death's door by building castles in the air like that and use them to try to win glory for yourself – I say it's a fool's errand!'

Colonel von Hermann gestured with his hand to quell the mounting tide of noise.

'Very well, Meyer,' he said curtly. 'Your objection is duly noted… What about you, Steffen?'

The colonel's piercing gaze swivelled round the room. It met with an icy wall of hostility.

'Look, if only we could at least give them a chance of success… if only we could tell them…'

He struggled to finish his answer. No one came to his aid. Finally, he gave it up.

'So, it looks like a heroic last stand is very doubtful, very doubtful indeed. Seems as though there isn't enough support for it.'

'Anyone here take a different view?' Hermann asked finally. No one responded. The colonel gave a sigh and his face relaxed.

'Thank you, gentlemen,' he said, a little less formally. 'I wouldn't have expected you to do otherwise. If we have to die, then we want to do so as upstanding soldiers – in so far as that's in our hands.'

He bade farewell with a handshake to each of the officers in turn. The last one to come up was a captain, one of the adjutants.

'Permission to ask the Colonel a question? Does this… this plan come directly from the Führer's HQ?'

The colonel grasped straight away what the captain was driving at. 'No, Winter,' he replied. 'Not this time – more's the pity!

He went over to the window and looked at the sparkling, radiating pattern of the frost on the glass. From outside came the sound of the departing officers talking excitedly among themselves. No, this plan, this crazy mishmash of desperate bravery and criminal wickedness, hadn't come from Hitler. No one knew in what deranged minds here in the Cauldron this scheme had been hatched. But the army chief of staff had – without the knowledge of the commander-in-chief – latched on to it and, through soliciting his commanders' input, elevated it into the realms of the feasible. Under his breath, the colonel began murmuring to himself, 'The times are changing… it'll be a grisly end. Ah, we'll need to turn it all on its head, start afresh, wipe the slate completely clean…' He turned away from the window. His face wore an embarrassed smile that made him look oddly younger. His gaze met that of Dannemeister, who was looking at him stupidly through red-rimmed eyes.

'It's so insane,' he said hoarsely. 'The crazy things you find yourself thinking… just absurd!' Saying this, he picked up the receiver and briefly informed the chief of staff that his officers had unanimously rejected the plan for a 'breakout on all sides'.

'Very well, I thought as much,' replied the voice at the other end of the line; it sounded calm, almost indifferent. 'The other divisions report the same. That means the matter's settled for us. By the by, my warmest congratulations, dear Hermann! I've just spoken with the C-in-C; your promotion to Major General's been confirmed!'

Von Hermann gave the customary bow in front of the telephone and politely expressed his thanks. He slowly replaced the receiver. He was a general! The dream he'd had since he was young had finally come true, much faster than he could ever have expected. Stalingrad was to thank for that, too—

But he took no pleasure in it.

★

Breuer could only shake his head in bewilderment at the behaviour of the Sonderführer over this period. Fröhlich seemed to be gripped by a zealousness that was impossible to fathom. He spent almost the entire day on the move or having long conversations in Russian with Nasarov. He no longer offered any predictions concerning the military and political situation, but his silence was born of a sly optimism. At his instigation, two Russian volunteers he had picked up somewhere were working in the kitchen. He always made a point of giving them something from his own meagre daily rations. One day Breuer caught him giving the Russian lieutenant colonel a long lecture in front of the intelligence division's large-scale map of the front. Breuer blew his top about that. The Sonderführer maintained a haughty silence as the first lieutenant tore him off a strip. But when Breuer's fury refused to abate and he threatened to report him, Fröhlich was moved to speak.

'I didn't want to say anything, actually; but it can't harm, the die is cast now… or pretty much, anyhow. Don't think for a moment that the Führer's abandoned us. He's promised he'll get us out of here. But even so, he might come too late. And in any event, all we need is to start throwing in the towel now!'

'Perhaps you'd be so kind as not to beat about the bush!' the first lieutenant interrupted him.

'I… I've made preparations for a breakout.'

'Whaaat!?'

Breuer's face looked quite dumbstruck for a moment. Then he shrugged and turned away.

'You've lost your mind!' he laughed. His anger had blown over by now. Fröhlich wasn't fazed in the slightest.

'Allow me to explain, Lieutenant,' he continued. 'The moment may come when the whole shooting match here collapses, agreed? – where no one's issuing orders any more – and everyone has to fend for himself. Well, I've made preparations for just such a case. We're going to break out to the west under our own steam!'

Breuer had opened the door and called for his batman to bring him his second pair of trousers, which were generally hung up outside throughout the day to try to delouse them in the winter cold; he cast a careful eye over them when they were handed to him. He knew that many people had started to think like the Sonderführer recently. He regarded their ideas as childish notions, the product of fevered imaginations.

'My dear sir, how do you imagine we're going to do that, then?' he said pityingly. 'The Russians aren't stupid, you know! Do you think they haven't anticipated such desperate moves? And even if you did manage to get through their lines, you're facing a journey of three hundred kilometres through deep snow, at temperatures of minus thirty, on foot, and in the condition we're in. And where do you suppose we'll find food for a week's route march? No, my dear fellow, drop this nonsense and stop putting stupid ideas in our men's heads!'

Fröhlich was not to be dissuaded, however. He rubbed his hands cheerfully.

'I've thought of all that. I've factored in everything like that. All we need is a spot of luck and it simply can't fail to succeed!'

And so he duly set about outlining his plan. As he proceeded, Breuer put down the trousers he was holding and began to listen attentively. So, the idea was to find a hideaway and let the Russians roll right past. And then, with the help of the Russian officer and the two Russian *Hiwis*, to pretend first that they were a party of German POWs under escort. Breuer had to hand it to Fröhlich; that wasn't so stupid after all! He jumped up and started pacing the room. Then, they'd commandeer a lorry somewhere in the depopulated hinterland and drive towards their own lines masquerading as Russian reinforcements. Yes, that could work! It really could! Breuer called to mind the confidential reports on German special forces who had achieved some notable successes behind enemy lines while wearing Russian uniforms. If nothing unforeseen happened, the operation could be wrapped up within twenty-four hours. That meant that there'd be no problems with food supplies or any overtaxing physical hardships. Fröhlich continued laying out his scheme, methodically and carefully. Breuer was amazed at how astutely the Sonderführer had thought through even the minutest details of his plan. He found himself gripped by a feverish excitement.

'What about fuel?' he asked, his voice hoarse with emotion.

'There'll be bound to be enough for a three-hundred-kilometre drive. Every Russian lorry carries a reserve tank.' Breuer's hand was shaking as he traced their route on the map.

'Not directly west, though,' he exclaimed breathlessly. 'That's not a wise move; they'll be watching that sector. We should go south-west – here, look – towards Rostov. No one would expect us to head there. Besides, I know my way around that area!'

Suddenly all the colour drained from his face.

'Oh no,' he gasped, crestfallen, 'I've just realized – it won't work. We've been dreaming… We'd need identity cards, Fröhlich. Papers!'

'I've already discussed that with the lieutenant colonel,' replied Fröhlich, unperturbed. 'He'll prepare them for us. He knows what they have to look like. One set for the POW escort to the Russian Staff GHQ on the Don front, and another for the reinforcement order. We'll fake the official stamps with indelible pencil.'

Breuer looked mistrustfully at Nasarov, who was sitting on his bench as unconcerned as ever and staring at his hands.

'What does *he* reckon to all this? Is he willing to go along with it?'

'Of course he is! After all, he's got nothing to lose and everything to gain… And he thinks it'll work.'

The first lieutenant was growing more exhilarated by the minute. The room started spinning around him, and he could scarcely get his words out. The thought of the world beyond, which he'd already renounced for ever, assailed him again like a turbulent current that swept away all misgivings, all inhibitions, and all obligations of duty and comradeship. He seized the Sonderführer by the shoulders.

'Fröhlich,' he stammered, 'Oh, Fröhlich… Freedom, getting out of this hellhole… Living again… Yes, we're going to live again!'

Only one thing still troubled him – that they wouldn't get the preparations done in time. So he immediately set to work with an indelible pencil, mocking up a Russian stamp. As a template he used the reverse of a Russian coin. Then he transferred the design to a piece of moistened blotting paper. The test printings from this 'negative' looked extremely genuine.

Geibel and Herbert returned and were informed of the plan. They listened to it with uncomprehending credulity. When Geibel heard that it would mean ambushing and killing people and robbing them of their weapons and clothes, his childish eyes grew large and round and his whole body started shaking. Major Siebel, who was also going to be part of the group and whom Fröhlich had already apprised of the plan, put in an appearance too.

'Gentlemen,' he announced, 'if we pull this off, I'll give this fellow' – here he pointed at Nasarov – 'a job for life on my estate. Tell him that, will you, Fröhlich!'

Siebel went over and clapped the Russian heartily on the shoulder with his real hand. Nasarov gave the major a look of devoted loyalty, like a Newfoundland dog, and smiled mutely.

3

Guilty in the Eyes of His People

THE DAYS PASSED AT breakneck speed. The men's faces became ashen grey and their eyes large and sunken, like people facing the executioner's axe.

Lieutenant Colonel Unold, whose secondment to Army High Command was now at an end, was occasionally seized by a fit of nervous energy that saw him rush from bunker to bunker, treating all and sundry to a vitriolic and wholly undeserved tongue-lashing. For the most part, though, he lay dozing on his camp bed, with his pistol next to him, along with the inevitable bottle of brandy and a photograph of his wife, which he gazed at adoringly and moist-eyed. For a while he experienced a resurgence of hope. A miracle had occurred. A front had once more been established in the west, running along the Gontchara Gorge and the railway embankment down to Pestshanka. The Cauldron had shrunk by two-thirds of its original total area, but for a brief spell it was at least a cauldron once more, with secure borders. The Russians, who pursued the remnants of the western units as they retreated through Dubininsky and Pitomnik (they conducted this operation at a leisurely pace and were rather surprised at the fierce resistance they encountered in parts from certain scattered detachments), were astonished when, on the seventeenth of January, they came across this new front. In the main, the defenders were elements of divisions from the Volga that had been stood down, and who now felt the enemy breathing down their necks for the first time. There were no fixed positions – Unold's belated mission had come to nought – but the terrain was favourable and the well-equipped and still reasonably well-fed units fought with a courage born of desperation. For two days, they drove back the enemy infantry. Then the Russians lost patience. They brought up armour and artillery in great numbers, sent in squadron upon squadron of ground-attack aircraft, and pounded a gap in the front. Now they were already outside of Yeshovka. Even this brief dream of supremacy had faded for the Germans. Unold knew that, and others on the divisional staff also suspected as much. Only in the Intelligence Section's bunker did a feverish optimism still hold sway, of the kind that is wont to affect consumptives in the final days of their terminal illness.

One morning, the twenty-first of January, Geibel came back from collecting their rations. The customary expression of dumb loyalty on his face had been enlivened by an exciting piece of news.

'The balloon's going up today, Lieutenant, sir! Captain Fackelmann is to assemble a task force from the remnants of the staff! We'll be picked up at midday by lorry. Everyone's coming along; only the cook's staying here along with the lieutenant colonel's batman and Sergeant Schneider.'

This news broke the tension like the first clap of thunder breaking the sultry atmosphere just before an impending storm. Breuer and Fröhlich looked at one another. This was their chance!

'What about the officers?' asked Breuer. 'Are they going along as well?'

'I don't know about that, Lieutenant, sir,' murmured Geibel anxiously.

Breuer rushed out. Discussions were taking place in the chief of staff's bunker. He flung the door open without knocking. At the table, poring over the map, stood Unold, Colonel Dr Steinmeier, Major Kallweit and Siebel. They started up like counterfeiters caught in the act at Breuer's abrupt entrance.

'What? What's the meaning of this?' rasped Unold. 'Is it something urgent? If it isn't, please come back later!'

Breuer elected to go outside and wait. His fingers drummed impatiently on the wooden wall. From the bunker came the sound of agitated whispering. Finally, the door flew open. The tight-fisted divisional medical officer rushed past with a curt nod, followed by Kallweit and Siebel. Kallweit's face had by now lost all trace of its former freshness and nonchalance; he seemed to be deep in thought and failed to acknowledge Breuer's salute, though surely not maliciously. Only Siebel stopped to talk. He was chewing on his top lip and looked up at the lieutenant from the bottom of the bunker steps.

'Well, Breuer,' he said, 'that's just the way it is. Nothing to be done about it, I'm afraid.'

'What's going on exactly, Major?'

'What's going on?' Siebel gave a nervous little laugh. 'We're flying out… that is, the senior MO, Kallweit and myself. On the orders of High Command.'

With trembling lips, he gave a truculent sideways glance, like a boy scolded for being naughty. There he stood, this young soldier, already a major, with his wooden arm and his Knight's Cross. His broad face with a slightly turned-up nose had a faint redness about it, while his unruly mop of hair poked out from beneath his forage cap. In his furious set-to with Engelhard, he had vowed to stage a 'reckoning', to have 'payback' when he returned to Germany. He certainly had the necessary gumption. But would it even occur to him, now that things had turned out so differently for him? Or would he just step up meekly to the microphone and talk about the 'heroic struggle we put up at Stalingrad, confident in our Führer's leadership' and then take command of a battalion and return to the front line somewhere – and forget all about Stalingrad?

'I'm delighted for you… and for your young wife,' said Breuer with a weak smile, offering the major his hand. 'You're going to have it easier than us now… with our breakout. Farewell, then!'

In response Siebel uttered a bitter laugh, tormented and terrible to hear; it seemed to sum up all the insanity of this world. No, he wouldn't forget. At least, he would never forget these few seconds. As if by way of reassurance, he grasped Breuer's hand and gave it a short but firm shake. Then he turned on his heel and walked off.

Unold received his intelligence officer with the cool detachment of a very busy person.

'How can I help you?'

'I just wanted to enquire what's going to happen to me, Lieutenant Colonel?'

'Why?' Unold shot back; his tone was sharp and suspicious.

'Well, will I be staying here with the staff or going out with the task force?'

'Ah yes, of course…' Unold seemed only now to take on board the fact that he still had an intelligence officer. 'I'll think about it. I'll let you know in due course.'

On his way back from the bunker, Breuer ran into his adjutant, Captain Gedig.

Gedig's initial response when the lieutenant quizzed him was unequivocal: 'You want to know what's to become of you, my dear Breuer? You'll be staying with us, naturally! Goes without saying! We have to stand shoulder-to-shoulder over these final few days.'

Then his smile grew distracted. 'That is, I don't know yet for sure… The lieutenant colonel said… Well, anyhow, wait and see. We'll know soon enough.'

Gedig too, it appeared, was much preoccupied with his innermost thoughts about his own situation. The division had fallen apart already and now the rest of the staff was following suit, fragmenting into individual urges and individual destinies. Endrigkeit was dead too, killed at Dubininsky. One of the stragglers had brought the news.

Breuer's mind was made up. He, too, was only thinking of himself now. He could no longer identify any higher principle or point of fixity that he could cling on to or navigate by.

'I'm coming with you, Fröhlich!' he announced to the Sonder-führer. 'This is our chance. We're no use here any more.'

He stuffed the few items that seemed worth taking along – including his mouth organ and the camera that had accompanied him through three and a half years of campaigning – into the deep pockets of his greatcoat. Everything else – his fine riding boots, his second pair of trousers, the contents of his kitbag – he left behind with no regrets. If the plan succeeded, they'd be over behind German lines within two days and would get all their hearts desired issued to them anew. And if it didn't – well, then that was that anyhow. In that event, he wouldn't be needing any socks or shirts either.

As midday approached, the newly formed 'company' assembled on the parade ground above the gorge, where three lorries stood waiting. Including clerks, batmen and drivers, predominantly from the quartermaster's section, a quite respectable band of around sixty men had been scraped together. Dressed in motorcycle jackets or greatcoats, with their heads covered by all manner of caps and balaclavas and hoods, and brandishing a ragbag of weapons, they looked like a band of brigands. Morale was extremely bad. The men were grumbling and swearing quite openly. The batmen and the men from the cookhouse were cutting up especially rough.

'What the fuck's going on, then?'

'They're wanting rid of us! So they can sneak off nice and quietly!'

'Unold should be coming with us!'

'Yeah, that's right. Where is he? Surely we're worth at least a final pep talk, aren't we?'

But there was no sign of Unold. Instead, Captain Fackelmann prowled round the band of grumbling troops like a watchdog.

'Gentlemen, please!' He raised his hands beseechingly. 'The lieuten-ant colonel has no intention of flying out. He has a new assignment from High Command. He's incredibly busy right now. He… he sends you all his very best. He's very proud of you – the last soldiers who will uphold the honour of our division.'

Small groups of unknown, scruffy foot soldiers came sniffing around the division's vehicles, which were parked up there, for the most part unscathed, and were now to be abandoned for ever. Like hyenas, they circled in a wide arc around the doomed little task force. They could scent unoccupied bunkers and booty. Fackelmann mopped his brow and looked imploringly at Breuer, who at that moment appeared with Fröhlich, Nasarov and the two *Hiwis*. But the first lieutenant seemed unwilling to get embroiled in anything that called for leadership. The fact that the three Russians were armed and so were clearly determined to fight alongside the Germans helped defuse the atmosphere.

The countryside was shrouded in dank fog. By the time the three lorries drove on to the broad expanse of the former Russian airfield at Gumrak, it was almost dark. They passed a line of wrecked aircraft and burning vehicles. Red and yellow flares were shooting into the sky and from somewhere high up above the drifting banks of fog came the rumble of unseen aircraft. From time to time a plane would suddenly roar down, large and heavy, into the scene of confusion below and taxi to a halt on the runway. Shouts and whistles rang out, interspersed with the thud of artillery shells landing. Disgorged from the trucks, the band of soldiers stood around aimlessly by the entrance to a bunker, into which Captain Fackelmann had disappeared with an officer from an anti-aircraft battery. They had stopped moaning and cursing by now. The sixty men awaited their fate silently and dutifully. After a while Fackelmann reappeared and the detachment marched off into the damp night. The captain came up to Breuer.

'Unold was in there,' he said, *sotto voce*. 'He's assigned to Colonel Fuchs, who's been given charge of defending the airfield. But not a word to our men about it! Really brilliant that he couldn't even bring himself to say a few words to our lot.'

'What's our mission precisely?' asked Breuer.

'Securing the eastern perimeter of the airfield.'

'Hmm—.' The column was tramping along a muddy track in single file through high banks of snow. There was a light snowfall. A cluster of whitewashed vehicles loomed up out of the fog and, alongside them, the domed roofs of a cluster of earth bunkers. They stumbled on over duckboards and strings of barbed wire. Their guide stopped outside a bunker entrance. They had reached their destination. Muffled gramophone music drifted up from underground. Fackelmann and Breuer went in. In the smoky room, a captain got up as they entered; his jacket was unbuttoned. He sized up the newcomers somewhat disparagingly, his bovine eyes bulging from beneath a low forehead.

'So, you're the reinforcements we were promised. How many of you? Fifty-six men and three officers? Okay, let's see where we can accommodate you.'

A quick discussion with a thickset corporal yielded the intelligence that twenty-five men at most could be shoehorned into the few available bunkers.

'Well,' the captain told Fackelmann, 'up front, about eight hundred metres over there in the gorge, there's supposed to be a pioneer corps. They must have some free bunkers there, for their transport section and so on. Most of them cleared off yesterday like frightened rabbits; you'll be bound to find some space there.'

He cast an eye around his own bunker.

'And one of you gents could doss down here if you fancy it, too.'

Captain Fackelmann, who couldn't square his romantic conception of life at the front, still untainted despite his experiences, with the conditions on the ground here, chanced a few hesitant questions about the lie of the land and the enemy positions. The young captain jovially clapped Fackelmann, who was at least fifteen years his senior, on the shoulder.

'Oh, no need to worry about that now! You can do a bit of poking around first thing tomorrow morning. We're just a kind of holding position here, for all eventualities, you know. The front line's up ahead of us, and the entire Forty-Fourth is dug in there. Apart from the odd spot of artillery fire, we've got it pretty cushy here – isn't that right, Wilhelm?'

He winked at the corporal, stuck his hands in his trouser pockets and stretched contentedly. Captain Fackelmann decided to throw his lot in with the bulk of his men. He asked Breuer to stay put with the Number 1 platoon and to give the platoon leader – a corporal named Klucke from the quartermaster's section, who was a bland pen-pusher – some support. Breuer nodded absent-mindedly. He was worn out by the day's exertions. The breakout plan would have to wait. For the time being, the key thing was to gather his strength, physical and mental. Slowly he peeled off his overcoat and slumped down on the stool that the captain pushed over to him. The captain then reached for a plump smoked sausage, cut off a fat slice four fingers thick and handed it to Breuer.

'First off, have something to eat! You must be famished!'

He shoved a hunk of bread and a knife towards Breuer and poured out some yellowish liquid from a half-empty bottle into a couple of long-stemmed tin goblets. Meanwhile, the corporal had wound up the blue Morocco-leather-covered chest gramophone and put on another record. The tinny sound of a shrill woman's voice emerged, singing a cheesy hit from the Twenties to a ragtime accompaniment which, God alone knew how, had found its way here:

> Now Dolly's doin' good,
> She's livin' in Hollywood…

Breuer bit hungrily into the sausage.

'So where did this come from?' he asked. 'It's great!'

The captain chuckled smugly. 'It's literally manna from heaven round here, dear boy! The air crews chuck the stuff out when they can't make it in to land. A whole crate of this stuff almost dropped on our heads early this morning. We picked up twenty-six salamis!'

'Don't you have to hand over things like that?'

'Who to?' asked the captain, blinking in astonishment. 'Those morons over at the base, so they can eat it all? Since yesterday morning, when we took up position here, they haven't sent us out a single crumb of food. All we need now is to start handing this stuff over! If they want some, they can come out with us and collect it!'

He raised his goblet and toasted with Breuer. The liquid turned out to be a sweet orange liqueur.

'Did this fall from the sky too, then?'

'Nah! We've got other sources for that. Tell you what, if you ever need a silk shirt or some pyjamas or a pair of boots or a new officer's cap, just tip us the wink. We've got the lot here!'

He stretched his legs, resplendent in a pair of top boots, in expansive fashion, slapped his chest a couple of times and addressed the corporal again, chortling as he did so.

'That was a hoot yesterday, wasn't it, eh, Wilhelm? The way they all legged it, those idiots from the Pay Corps. Dear me, we laughed like drains! They skedaddled like a troop of monkeys when they heard the main front was going to run through here. That's their vehicles they left behind out there – well, when we took a gander inside 'em, we were gobsmacked, let me tell you! The stuff they'd salted away! This old gramophone, for instance. It's not without its risks, mind. The Ivans can just see the tops of the lorries poking out above the hill, so now and then they toss over a shell. They caught old Franz back there this morning while he was digging out a bottle of red wine.'

He nodded towards a wide set of bunk beds where some men lay snoring beneath furs and blankets. One of the men was flat on his back, staring at the ceiling. He wasn't snoring but struggling to catch his breath. His hands clutched convulsively at his chest.

'Was he badly wounded?' asked Breuer.

'Shrapnel in his side. We don't have a doctor here. The medical orderly's given him till tomorrow morning. He's dying from internal bleeding. Oh, well… Care for some cigars?'

He handed the lieutenant a little box of fine sand-leaf cigars decorated with elaborate banderoles. The song's chorus squawked from the gramophone for the third time:

> Now Dolly's doin' good,
> She's livin' in Hollywood.
> She's doin' fine,
> And she's mine, all mine!

The encircled army's situation had become hopeless. It was no secret any longer to anyone who had managed to retain even a modicum of common sense. In these critical days, many high-ranking officers attempted to gain access to the supreme commanders and bring their influence to bear. One of these was Colonel Kniffke. It was with very mixed feelings that Kniffke had flown into the Stalingrad Cauldron at the beginning of January.

His orders had been to 'establish the communications ground-work for the Sixth Army to break out or for an external rescue mission'. Some assignment! Particularly when no one at Army High Command was making any bones about the fact that no more help would be forthcoming for the men trapped at Stalingrad – either inside the Cauldron or from outside. He was under no illusions, then: flying into Stalingrad was like being given a free pass to view the mortuary.

Up till now, the colonel had only seen the war from the perspective of a high-ranking staff officer. He was cock of the walk among the young women reservists who staffed the Wehrmacht's signals network from the Bay of Biscay to the River Don. The outward sign of his key role glittered on his chest in the shape of the 'German Cross', a gaudy Nazi decoration that ordinary soldiers nicknamed the 'Fried Egg' or the 'Party Insignia for the Shortsighted'*. Under these circumstances, however, he did not feel much inclination to die a heroic death for Hitler. And who could blame him? Even so, if the colonel had still embarked on his journey with any hope at all, then it was because he was flying to an army staff headquarters. They would surely find some way out before the worst happened. It was inconceivable that the country's leaders would allow an entire staff of top brass simply to be snuffed out!

Yet what he subsequently saw and heard when he was with the Sixth Army shocked him to the core. People there were sticking their heads in the sand or seeing things through rose-tinted spectacles. 'A breakout!' they laughed when he told them about his assignment. 'Surely someone's coming to bail us out of here, aren't they?' But all his pleas and entreaties (He was sure a rescue mission was planned! He knew how things stood over there!) fell on deaf ears. No one took him seriously. And then came the collapse of the Cauldron from the tenth of January onwards. That was a fine mess, to be sure! Hadn't he always predicted just that? But even now, nothing was happening, absolutely nothing. It almost seemed as though they were wanting to do Hitler a favour and fight to the very last man standing, including the last member of the armed forces staff.

Colonel Kniffke grew increasingly nervous. And that was the reason he was standing here now, having a private meeting with the C-in-C without the Führer's knowledge. Overnight he had felt renewed hope when he thought about how persuasive a speaker he could be. And he was more than a little flattered by the thought that he might, setting aside all questions of personal vanity, become the saviour of the entire Sixth Army. The colonel had thought the whole matter through very carefully. He made no mention of

---

* 'German Cross' (German: *Deutsches Kreuz in Gold*) – the German Cross in Gold was a Nazi Party decoration showing a black swastika on a large white disc and surrounding golden sunburst design. Its size and gaudiness prompted its nicknames *Spiegelei* ('fried egg') and *Ochsenauge* ('bullseye').

'signals girls' or of his mission (which had long since ceased to be realistic). Instead, he talked about all the things he'd experienced here, through speaking to commanders in the field on the 'phone: the troops' hunger, the hopelessly unequal struggle in the absence of heavy weapons with dwindling supplies of ammunition and lacking properly fortified positions and adequate winter clothing. And about the abject failure of the Luftwaffe, which at the time was only managing to fly in around forty tons of supplies daily (barely one-seventh of what was needed); about the increasing signs of disintegration and the growing numbers of wounded and sick that could not be cared for. He spoke eloquently – perhaps too eloquently.

'In the west, there's no longer a watertight front to speak of. We can hold out for ten days more at the most. But ten days' worth of desperate, if heroic, fighting isn't going to help anyone any more. I would respectfully ask the Colonel General to consider what these ten days might mean for us. The breakup of the army, the chaos and the senseless slaughter of us all! The Russians are still standing by their offer of an honourable surrender. That couldn't possibly compromise any larger military strategies now. And there's no help to be expected from outside any more. I'm giving the Colonel General my solemn word of honour: I can assure you no help will be arriving! I pride myself on knowing how things stand over there. I've seen it with my own eyes, after all! They've written us off. That's why – and I'm sure the Colonel General will forgive the forwardness of an honest German concerned about the welfare of his compatriots – I'm begging and imploring you to take this step! The Colonel General holds all our fates in his strong hands... please capitulate now!'

Colonel General Friedrich Paulus sat calmly and collectedly at the table, his slender hands folded in front of him and resting on the tabletop. His head, with its wispy hair flecked with strands of grey, was slightly bowed, and his face displayed a quiet courteousness. His eyelids, though, were afflicted by an unsettling and uncontrollable blinking and twitching. Nothing in his demeanour gave any sign of the deep distaste he felt for this garrulous colonel they'd saddled him with, this windbag who was speaking so glibly about the most difficult topic of all, these terrible matters that tormented him day and night. He reached over to a side table and picked up a note, which he passed to Knippke with his fingertips.

'Read this, please!'

The colonel jammed his rimmed monocle into his eye and read the note. The red slip of paper, printed on both sides with smudged ink, was a leaflet produced by the Red Army. It gave an exhaustive overview of the situation, which was accurate on all points and really quite restrained in its presentation of the facts. It came to the conclusion that further German resistance was fruitless. The colonel looked up.

'What do you have to say to that?' enquired Paulus.

'It… Well, every word of it's true, Colonel General.'

'It's also virtually word for word what you just said. Have you seen this pamphlet before?'

'Colonel General, I really must protest!' The colonel's tone was one of polite indignation. He genuinely didn't know the pamphlet.

'Then how is it that you're saying exactly the same thing?'

'Because…' Groping for a reply, the colonel pulled a face like a constipated sheepdog. Then the answer suddenly came to him. 'Because it's the truth!' he blurted out vehemently. 'There is only the one truth, Colonel General!'

The commander-in-chief stood up, his bushy eyebrows raised.

'If I were to follow your advice, I'd be doing exactly what the enemy wants. It's out of the question for that reason. True or not, it's quite impossible!'

Faced with this irrefutable soldierly logic that made no sense at all, the colonel blanched. Impossible? He could feel the ground swaying beneath his feet. He tried just one more tentative approach, but already knew it would all be to no avail.

'Should we hesitate to do the right thing,' he said weakly, 'just because—?'

'How do I know if it's the right thing?' Paulus broke in. 'Can I second-guess what's being planned at the Führer's HQ? Do I know what preparations I might be stymieing? No, I cannot and will not disobey my orders!'

The colonel took the slender hand that was extended to him, tired and limp, and bowed without a word. He couldn't understand the C-in-C. All he needed to do was... It all seemed so straightforward to him, so laughably straightforward, just as every load seems light to the person who isn't having to carry it on his own shoulders. The colonel departed, leaving the commander alone. He propped his chin in his hands. He was tired, immeasurably tired. The last two months had weighed down heavily upon him. During peacetime, he had headed an intelligence division. That had been his last operational command. Then, in quick succession, he had been appointed chief of staff of the Sixteenth Panzer Corps, of Army Groups Command and of the Sixth Army under the strong and inflexible Field Marshal von Reichenau, before becoming deputy chief of the German Army General Staff. Always a second in command, always in the shadow of someone stronger... And then he was given command of the Sixth Army. And found himself at Stalingrad – he, who had never learned to stand on his own two feet! And so he let himself be carried along, and looked on meekly while his own chief of staff was promoted over his head.

What was now being asked of him was an act of salvation, an open revolt against Hitler. That called for either great courage or great cowardice. Paulus possessed neither. He was neither a hero nor a scoundrel, perhaps in the end not even a soldier. All he was was weak, weak like other men: too weak to bear the burden of responsibility that a merciless fate had heaped upon him. Under this crushing weight, he dragged himself on day by day, and closed his eyes. And he also no doubt convinced himself that it wasn't he who was carrying this weight but that terrible man in Berlin who issued the orders. He clung to these orders, they were the stick on which he supported himself, and they saved him from having to take action on his own initiative, a prospect he frankly dreaded. So he shut his eyes, failed to notice how his flaccid weakness turned to cruel harshness all around him, refused to see how this corrosive weakness condemned hundreds of thousands to a senseless death, and did not realize that his duty did not lie in the place where he sought it.

And so he became guilty, guilty before his peers.

Breuer had crawled over onto the pallet bed beside the groaning wounded man. As the new day dawned, loud voices roused him from a deep sleep. He sat up. Grey light penetrated the dirty glass of the windowpane. He cast an eye over the man next to him. During the night, his hands had stopped moving and his stertorous breathing had ceased. Glassy eyes stared past a pointed, waxen nose. The captain was already up and about. He was listening with a bleary face to the agitated report of his sentries. 'They've been marching the whole night… and there's still some arriving now! All from the Forty-Fourth!'

Breuer went outside with the captain. The Russian artillery was still firing. Cautiously they picked their way out onto the road that ran close by the bunkers. Larger and smaller groups of men were trudging along it, tired and apathetic, and seemingly oblivious to the shell bursts landing slap in the middle of the road and tearing great craters in its surface. There were no vehicles in evidence. The men were carrying only small arms; a few had machine guns, while others were dragging sleds laden with wounded comrades. A lone anti-tank gun trundled by, pulled by a team of soldiers. The captain asked the men where they'd come from. Nobody replied. Eventually a small column of men came into view; they looked fresher than the rest. Their leader, a lieutenant, gave the captain all the answers he was seeking.

'We're from the Forty-Fourth. We're the Bicycle Squadron!'

'Where are you headed?'

The lieutenant shrugged his shoulders.

'Somewhere or other... I've no idea. Most likely all the way to Stalingrad – into the city.'

'Right, but what about the front?'

'The front? There's no one else following on behind us. We're the rearguard!'

The procession moved on to the east. Its route was lined with dead and wounded, to whom no one paid any attention. A few stragglers brought up the rear, then emptiness and silence closed in once more. The captain's face had turned pale.

'Fuck it all!' he muttered. 'This fucking shit!'

Breuer thought this an opportune moment to go and search out his men who had decamped the night before with Captain Fackelmann.

Fackelmann had indeed discovered a line of bunkers at the head of the gorge that ran perpendicularly ahead of the main front and which, after about eight hundred metres, joined a larger crossing gully. They were occupied by pioneers from a bridge-building unit, who were in a state of considerable uproar. After some initial difficulties, Fackelmann was able to find enough space for half of his men. The rest, along with troops from the pioneer battalion, took up front-line positions in hastily dug snow holes along the lip of the gorge. These men were relieved every two hours, so that everyone managed to get at least a couple of hours' shut-eye that night.

The commander of the pioneer battalion, a major in the reserves, was a dignified gent with grey hair and distinguished features (Fackelmann learned later that he was a professor at a technical college). He received the captain with a mixture of relief and indignation.

'Just look at my battalion!' he groused, polishing his gold-rimmed spectacles. 'We were six companies at one time… almost a thousand men. And all of them experienced specialists, excellent and irreplaceable men worth their weight in gold. And now look what they've done to us! At the beginning of January we were deployed as infantry for the first time. All my old crew fighting as infantrymen! Seventeen of them froze to death in the first night alone. And when we got back to our base – I only managed to bring half of them back – all our trucks and equipment had been blown to pieces by bombs. Our priceless kit and our special vehicles – all gone! My adjutant, an architect from Vienna, an Austrian with a really sunny disposition, well, he couldn't take it any more and shot himself.'

The old man wiped his eyes with a trembling hand.

'And now we're here, and we've been detailed to dig defences… just eighty of us. That's all I have left. All the rest are either dispersed, or dead, wounded, starved or frozen to death or have been drafted into other units… And the day before yesterday this first lieutenant appears, some lah-di-dah little jackass, you know the type, I'm sure. Tells us the front has been breached! And that we've got to hold this position to the last man! Of course, he promptly clears off himself. And we're left sitting here, seeing nothing, hearing nothing and not knowing our right hand from our left. No doctor, no telephone, no food… but all the same, we're supposed to hold our position! To the last man! I ask you, what kind of madness is that? Is there any rhyme or reason to it? Is that any way to treat people? Oh, that devil, that bloody devil!'

Fackelmann got to hear this last exclamation from the old man many times, without ever knowing who he meant by it.

The night passed peacefully. From first light, though, mortars began landing in the gorge. Every now and then, a burst of machine-gun fire, from some distance away, whistled over their heads. Later that morning, Fackelmann went in search of the lieutenant colonel of the Pioneer Corps, who was reputed to be encamped with the rest of his unit around the corner in the larger gully. He was met by a wizened figure with a malevolent expression and short, bandy legs. His stature had earned him the nickname 'radish-dragger' among his men ('if you stuck a radish in his arse, the top'd drag along the ground'). He greeted Fackelmann in his comfortable bunker in the foulest of moods.

'What news have you got about the situation, then?'

The captain said he regretted he knew nothing.

'Nothing? What are you doing here, in that case? Why have you come here at all, in fact? Oh, reinforcements for the defensive front, are you? Great, then you can start by taking over the first two hundred metres of my sector here! I've got to shift further to the right. I've got no support down there.'

The captain's timid reply that he wasn't actually under the lieutenant colonel's command went unheard by the little gnome's malformed ears.

'You keep a civil tongue in your head, understood? I'm not leaving this bunker here come hell or high water! Wouldn't dream of it!'

Fackelmann was relieved when Breuer appeared. But the lieutenant didn't bring him any cheer either. Taciturn and indifferent to the captain's loud complaints, he soon moved on to try to track down Fröhlich. He found him in a remote bunker with no heating, which he had picked out as a hidey-hole. Breuer then went to find his men. The first person he came across, behind a snow rampart, was First Lieutenant Nasarov, with his two *Hiwis* in tow. They were all carrying captured Russian weapons. Nasarov had put on Breuer's motorcycle jacket over his Russian greatcoat. He smiled at Breuer from beneath his fur cap and slyly showed him the red collar flashes and the enamel Soviet star that he'd got hold of somewhere to lend the finishing touches to his uniform when they put their escape plan into action.

'Goot, goot, Lyevtenant, sir,' he said in broken German. 'All will go very goot!'

Geibel and Corporal Herbert sat crouched over a machine gun. They were frozen stiff, from the wet snow soaking them to the skin through their clothes, but otherwise in good spirits.

'Look over there, Lieutenant!' said Herbert, pointing over the bank of snow. A long column of vehicles could be seen moving in the far distance. Breuer reached for his field glasses.

'Well I never!' he exclaimed in a puzzled tone. 'Could those be ours?'

Herbert couldn't suppress a laugh.

'Ours? No, it's the Russians! They've been dashing about there since first light.'

Breuer put his binoculars down.

'Damn and blast it!' he said through gritted teeth. 'It's come to that already, has it? If only we could lob a few shells in among them! But with what, eh? Oh well, no matter.'

He turned back to his men.

'OK, as you were; we're going to stay back here as planned, come what may! Everything's disintegrating, and it'll all fall apart here soon as well. If the retreat is sounded or the position's overrun, we'll assemble individually in the bunker over there and wait until the coast is clear.'

He clapped them both on the shoulders.

'Our scheme's got to work – just as long as our side doesn't go and ruin it by breaking out themselves!'

The two men nodded and laughed.

Around midday, urgent shouts are heard at the western end of the line.

'The Russians! The Russians are here!' A Soviet patrol on snowshoes has pushed forward into the corner between the main German defensive line and the gorge. The men up front start shooting; some of them have got up out of their snow holes and are shouting and waving excitedly. Captain Fackelmann is no infantryman, but he realizes straight away that the men standing up over there on the ridge are blocking the line of fire from the main defensive line, where the Russian patrol was spotted some time ago.

'Lie down!' he yells. 'Are you crazy? Lie down!'

All the yelling and shooting had lured the 'radish-dragger' out of his lair.

'Unbelievable!' he screeched. 'That's what passes for soldiers nowadays!'

Saying this, he sets off up the slope without more ado, his little dachshund's legs pounding away furiously.

'Everyone listen to my commands! Follow me! Chaaaaarge!!!'

And he dashes off across the open expanse. Some of the men follow him.

'Chaaaaarge!' His battle cry sounds hoarse and rather constricted at first, but then rises to a clear, furious pitch, transcending all fear. The cooks, office clerks and drivers following in his wake must be uttering this cry for the first time in their lives. They put all their pent-up frustration into it. Up to now, all they've been required to do is to suffer, suffer and hold out. Now at last they can see some action – finally! And however futile this action might be, it brings them a sense of release.

From behind the charging men comes the staccato bark of a machine gun. The Russians are laying down covering fire for their men. Here and there, some of the attackers fall down, while the rest, quickly brought to their senses, stop running and stand frozen between fear and doubt, helplessly exposed to the bursts of fire from the machine gun. Breuer has also set off up the incline. He recognizes the folly of the initial assault and can see the danger the men are in.

'Stop!' he bellows at the top of his lungs. 'Turn around! Lie down! Stop!!'

Suddenly something knocks him to the ground. A searing pain

centred on his left eye bores into his skull. He feels something warm
running down his face. Then he slips into unconsciousness.

When, not long after his discussion with Knittke, the commander-
in-chief of the army summoned the heads of the various corps to a
meeting, the colonel's hopes were raised again. He was tempted to
chalk this up as a success for himself. But he was wrong in this. The
meeting had been arranged some time beforehand. The Eighth and
the Eleventh Corps were only represented by their respective chiefs
of staff. No one at all from the Fourteenth Panzer Corps attended.
The one-armed general who had intended to fight to the death in a
foxhole in Dubininsky had just flown in a few days ago, fresh from
attending his daughter's wedding, and was present, resplendent in
his Knight's Cross with Oak Leaves. On the orders of Army High
Command he had left the celebrations in a tearing rush, without even
saying goodbye. 'To bring some order to the air supplies,' was the
official reason. It seemed an operational general from the Stalingrad
Cauldron was needed to make sure that no more old newspapers,
jam and private parcels were flown in for the top brass! Schmidt had
suggested his old regimental comrade; he was to become the rope
with whose help he would be able to extricate himself from the trap
at the very last moment. The only commanders to put in a personal
appearance were those from the Fourth and the Fifty-First, generals
Jaenecke and Von Seydlitz.

Under the frosty gaze of General Schmidt, discussion at the
meeting was weary and sluggish. The chiefs of staff hardly dared
to open their mouths. General Jaenecke showed not the slightest
interest any more in proceedings. He was wearing a dressing on
a head wound. During an air raid, a beam from the ceiling of his
bunker had come loose and cut a nasty gash in his head. Army
High Command had been informed about this injury. And he
had friends in high places, so he could count on being flown out.

For good measure, he had already brought his successor along to the meeting. This was the old white-bearded general whom the Russians had harried so relentlessly at Zybenko. He delivered a morose account of the situation in their sector. Yes, he reported, lots of complaints were being made, and there had even been a few instances of open rebellion. His division scarcely existed any longer. It had disintegrated and dispersed. Yet he had little inclination to admit this in front of his own division.

The only person at the meeting who was loud and bullish was General von Seydlitz.

'This so-called "fight to the last bullet" is insanity: complete and utter insanity!' he boomed, emphasizing his words by rapping with his knuckles on the tabletop. 'It's easy to issue such an order from a conference room two thousand kilometres from the action. But I notice that none of the gentlemen responsible have ever come to see the situation on the ground here for themselves, not one of them! – What do we have left now? Let's see – no artillery, no pilots, no ammunition and no fuel… just half-starved, exhausted troops and wounded men in their thousands, not to mention all the fatalities! So what are we supposed to fight with? With pistols, rifles and machine guns against tanks and Stalin organs and massed artillery?'

He cast his eye around those present in the room. It encountered faces that displayed either defeat or boredom. They were used to General von Seydlitz getting on his high horse every now and then, and knew all his arguments by heart. They were always the same. Schmidt's eyes twinkled in an almost friendly manner at the general. The usual flare-up from this blowhard, he thought contemptuously. Von Seydlitz's face was glowing with rage; he was lost for words. How many times had he said the same thing in this forum, always the same message and always to no purpose? They'd got him pegged as a troublemaker, which made it easy for them not to take him seriously. But that wouldn't prevent him from saying it over and over again, from proclaiming his message about the atrocity that was taking place here to the world at large, now and for all time. His hand hammered down on the table. Once again his voice cut through the air with its high pitch and clipped delivery.

'A battle of this kind, which apart from anything else is completely senseless and pointless, is – and this must be said loud and clear, because there's no getting away from it – is nothing short of immoral and criminal! What's happening here can never be the ultimate meaning of a soldier's honour!'

Paulus looked up with a pained expression.

'Thank you, gentlemen!' he said. 'I trust…' – here he cast a questioning glance at the inscrutable face of his superior, Schmidt – 'I trust I will be acting in the best interests of you all if I make representations to the Führer one more time, present him with the unvarnished truth and request that I be given a completely free hand.'

No one made any response to this, not even General von Seydlitz. He was relieved to have got things off his chest. Once again his anger had been dissipated through the safety valve of thunderous protest. This safety valve, which General Schmidt prudently refrained from blocking, guaranteed that this influential Corps commander's recurrent outbursts of rage never became dangerous, never built up until the pressure was such as to cause a massive explosion, or to prompt any cathartic action on the general's part. General von Seydlitz did what the others dared not do: he protested, valiantly and openly. But crucially, even he did not back up his words with action.

Colonel Knittke read the radio message that Schmidt had given him to encrypt and to transmit as a matter of the utmost urgency to the Army High Command. It began with a report of the current situation: shortages of everything – that had been said many times already, it really ought to have been expressed in stronger terms! Sixteen thousand untended wounded – that was good, and arresting.

Incipient signs of serious disintegration – not bad either. Then came the conclusion: 'Requesting freedom of action either to continue fighting, in so far as this is still feasible, or to capitulate, should further resistance prove impossible, so as to prevent complete annihilation and to ensure the welfare of our wounded and starving men.'

The colonel was bitterly disappointed. How could there be any talk of capitulation? That nullified the effect of all the other arguments: it torpedoed their own decision. Freedom of action – that would have sufficed! That left all possibilities open. But this unfortunate word 'capitulate' – one could of course contemplate such a thing and even do it when it became inevitable. But actually to utter the word, to a man like Hitler? Never! There could only be one reply.

The 70-watt transmitter quickly dispatched the message to the Führer's headquarters. After little more than a couple of hours, the reply was already there. A long-winded answer, which began with unstinting praise. But what followed exceeded their worst expectations.

'Freedom of action and capitulation refused! ... All measures for large-scale supply already in train... Through its heroic struggle the Sixth Army will fulfil the historic mission of facilitating the formation of a new front close to and north of the city of Rostov.'

How clear, how dreadfully clear the whole situation now was. Large-scale supply – when the final airfield had just fallen to the Russians? Formation of a new front? The whole thing was total nonsense, nothing but shadow-boxing! The order that was being issued here – dressed up in nauseating stock phrases and shameless lies – was the cold-blooded sacrifice of an entire army. Three hundred thousand men – slaughtered to the last man... an act of mass murder that made the ghastly sacrificial killings of the Aztecs look like child's play. And to what end? Because a heroic myth was required for the greater glory of the madman back in Germany! That was the real 'historic mission'! The colonel groaned. So, they were to die a heroic death! His knees grew unsteady. All his hopes lay in ruins. And the pity of it all was he loved heroism, albeit only at one remove and not at the cost of his own skin.

But if Colonel Knittke had expected this brazen reply to spark open revolt among the commanders of the Sixth Army, he was to be sorely disappointed. The mood remained calm, suspiciously calm. Did they go in such great fear of the tyrant, even thousands of kilometres away here, well beyond his sphere of power? Or – or had Schmidt actually wanted Hitler to send the reply he did? The colonel couldn't fathom things any more. He could see how the cards were dealt but didn't understand the rules of the game.

When Paulus retired with the message into the adjoining room, General Schmidt took the colonel by the arm and steered him aside.

'Tell me, Knittke, do you have any way of contacting the Russian front along the Don?'

The colonel could not believe his ears. So it really was happening! Finally, things had come to a head! Of course, this was the inevitable outcome. And he, Knittke, and no one else had been the catalyst. He was the saviour of the Sixth Army!

'Indeed, General, sir! Of course!' he said eagerly, already savouring a growing feeling of his own importance. In a trice, the deceptively cheerful expression of his interlocutor changed to a face like a thundercloud. And without warning the storm broke over the colonel.

'How the devil can that be?'

The blood drained from the colonel's face as he was brought down to earth with a bump.

'I… I don't understand the General's question. There are always ways and means of establishing contact!'

'So you've tried it already, have you?'

'No, General, sir!'

'So how can you know such a possibility even exists?'

In an instant, the colonel spotted the deadly danger he was in.

'We know all the frequencies and the call signs the Russians use,

General!' he said as calmly as he could. 'If we were to broadcast on those, we'd be picked up over there. There's no need to try to make contact in advance.'

A good feint and parry, he thought to himself. But overconfidence got the better of him and he added, 'Actually, even someone who isn't a signals expert ought to be able to grasp the principle of that, General, sir!'

'Aha, I see...' General Schmidt studied his fingernails. 'Well, Colonel, I'd strongly advise you against such an attempt. Any contact with the enemy is an act of high treason. It will cost you your head!'

Paulus returned. He seemed relaxed and content. When he noticed the colonel's stricken face, he looked embarrassed.

'You see, I tried everything,' he said, as if to excuse himself, 'but I'm only just another link in the chain. I can't break the chain.'

That same day, Schmidt presented the C-in-C with an order of the day to the troops that he had drafted. Paulus gave it a cursory look and signed it.

The order was dated the twentieth of January, 1943.

4

Horror at Gumrak

THE SENSELESS ATTACK BY the Russian reconnaissance party had cost Fackelmann's company three wounded and one dead. Breuer was taken to the old major's bunker. The medical orderly had not been able to do anything more than apply an emergency dressing. It was by no means clear exactly what had happened. It appeared that, as Breuer fell to the ground after being wounded, something sharp had jabbed itself into his eye. Moreover, he must have suffered some sort of brain concussion, because he was still unconscious. Fröhlich was by his side almost constantly, and even Herbert and Geibel came and stood around helplessly. The incident had thrown all their calculations into disarray. The whole escape plan was now in doubt.

Night closed in. It had stopped snowing and the temperature had dropped again. The moon shone full and sickly green through veils of fleeting grey clouds. Beyond the German front line the Russians, in carefree abandon, had lit blazing campfires all around. Black figures stood out in sharp relief against the bright flames. Snatches of laughter and singing drifted over, engines stuttered into life and vehicles cast dazzling headlight beams across the snowy landscape. They knew that their prey, which they now held in a choking grip, was no longer to be feared. Now and then, a low-flying 'sewing machine' came puttering along and circled over the gorge. The dark bird-like silhouette of the machine was clearly visible against the milky moonlit sky and its red and green navigation lights looked down like the eyes of a raptor. But it didn't strafe them or drop any bombs. It wasn't worth it any more! Despite their miserable predicament, the men crouched behind the snow ramparts, clenched their teeth grimly and clutched their rifles tightly. This shameful lack of respect shown by the enemy was worse than any pitched battle.

Breuer tossed and turned on his camp bed. Glaring lights pierced the darkness of his unconsciousness. He moaned in feverish dreams. It was high summer. He was stretched out on a beach somewhere on the Baltic Sea, with the sun beating down out of an unbroken expanse of azure sky. The white sand stretched out as far as the eye could see, silent and soothing. The sea lapped softly at the shoreline, while behind him, improbably far away, the white humps of shifting sand dunes shimmered in the heat haze. But now the sun was burning, glowing red-hot, scorching his flesh! Its searing heat gnawed ever more ferociously into his defenceless body. Pain… pain… and then darkness once more. And now another image floated before him. A lake, in the shadow of a black wood. Straw-roofed buildings nestling in a green forest clearing. The sound of bells pealing across the water from an isolated church tower. On a distant hill, three black crucifixes loom over the dead from the Battle of the Masurian Lakes. Little by little, the boat rocks through the lapping waves. Two brown eyes are shining with happiness. Irmgard – there is a sharp hiss as the boat noses its way through tall reeds and its bow slices deep into the mossy bank. Redness flows instantly from the wound it has made, spreading out over the shoreline and the lake. Help, help! The earth is drowning in blood…

When Sonderführer Fröhlich arrived at the bunker the next morning, he met Breuer staggering out of the doorway towards him. He looked dreadful. His flowing greatcoat was covered with large, rust-brown stains and beneath his misshapen head bandage the lieutenant's stubbly, blood-caked face looked ghostly thin. His good eye flitted about restlessly.

'B-But Lieutenant, sir!' Fröhlich stammered.

'Ah, it's you, Fröhlich… Yes, I'm off now. I'm leaving.'

'Leaving, Lieutenant? You can't leave now! Where will you go? And besides, we're still planning. I mean, what'll happen to our breakout, sir!'

'Breakout? Ah yes, breakout… You'll have to go it alone now. What day is it today exactly, Fröhlich?'

All the while, Breuer's hand pawed aimlessly at his head bandage.

'The twenty-third, sir. But you've got to—'

'The twenty-third! Right, right… That's okay, Fröhlich. All fine and good. I've just got to learn to see. Learn to see, Fröhlich, even with no eyes… If you get lucky and make it through, say hello to my wife from me!'

The Sonderführer called Herbert and Geibel over to help him deal with this delicate situation. But Breuer had a childish obstinacy about him.

'No, no, I've had enough… I'm going to Gumrak… or back to the Staff HQ.'

'Then at least let one of us come with you! You can't go out on your own like that!'

'Nonsense! You just make sure you manage to escape! Go on now, best of luck to you. Break a leg!' Breuer attempted to crack a smile but only succeeded in producing a pained grimace. Then he stumbled off. The three men watched him leave in silence until he disappeared round a bend in the path. Geibel swallowed hard a couple of times and sniffed theatrically.

Over the course of the morning, the Russian mortar bombardment increases in intensity. Occasionally, nervous bursts of machine-gun fire sweep the gorge, or a tank round punches a blackish hole in the steep side of the *balka* facing the enemy line. High up above, heavy artillery shells whine over to the rearward positions. Otherwise, though, nothing happens. Now and then the noise of moving columns and the faint sound of fighting drifts over from the right. No one knows what's going on there, as the pioneer battalion has no telephone contact with that sector. Captain Fackelmann also finds the failure of any orders to materialize and the absence of any communications with the rear deeply unsettling. He still sweats profusely, despite having lost all his former corpulence.

Around midday, the man who he's sent over to the positions occupied by the anti-aircraft battery and its captain comes back. Even from a distance, he starts waving his arms in agitation.

'There's no one there any more! They've all cleared off – along with our first platoon!'

He tells the captain that he found every last bunker abandoned. The radio telephone equipment was still in place. But all attempts on his part to call the command post on the airfield were in vain; no one was answering.

As fast as his weakened legs will carry him, the captain runs over to the major's position to confer about the situation. All of a sudden there comes a terrified shout from the gorge:

'Tanks! Tanks!'

Fackelmann climbs up and peeks over the snow ramparts. It's true! Up ahead there, barely a thousand metres away, three tanks are advancing like turtles towards the mouth of the gorge. My God, what can they do now? All they've got are their rifles and two malfunctioning machine guns! And no one in proper command... There he stands now, Alois Fackelmann, the proprietor of a furniture shop, with cold sweat breaking out on his jaundiced brow. There he stands, with sole responsibility for almost sixty of his compatriots, ignored, abandoned and betrayed by the High Command and the Corps and the division and the officers in command of the airfield.

And this Captain Fackelmann – who up to this point has only been responsible for matters pertaining to the canteen menu, and who is now utterly alone and left to his own devices as a military commander, and is in complete possession of his mental faculties and fully conscious of the painfully limited options open to him – takes a decision in this instant that no Paulus and no Seydlitz and none of the corps commanders have had the courage or the force of will to take: namely, to lay down his arms and to cross the line into the unknown, in order to save his men from reeling headlong into a senseless massacre. And in order to save himself, he's not ashamed to admit. Because living to run a furniture store seems to him more sensible than dying for nothing. Yet this man Fackelmann, who is only a temporary officer and wholly inexperienced in infantry matters, has no idea how to put his momentous decision into action. And in the search for urgent advice, he scrambles down the slope and makes for Fröhlich's bunker, which is on the other side of the gully.

The Sonderführer, meanwhile, has summoned Corporal Herbert in order to go through all the details of the escape plan with him one more time. He senses that the time for a decision is close at hand. Suddenly the door flies open and the captain is standing on the threshold, with his spindly legs and his praying hands, yet he seems larger than usual, almost like Breuer. He yells something, but as the words leave his mouth they are drowned out by an ear-splitting crash. A fearful blast shakes the room, hurling Fröhlich into a corner. Beams splinter and a fog of thick dust fills every nook and cranny. There is a smell of burning, of scorched flesh…

After quite some time, Fröhlich struggles to his feet. Gingerly he pats himself down to see if he's been wounded. The skin has been torn from his hands, his face has been blasted with grains of sand, and he can feel one of his eyes beginning to swell up and close.

'Hey, anyone here still alive?' he asks, noticing how strange his voice sounds.

'Yes, I am,' Herbert's voice replies tearfully from somewhere. 'Pass me a cigarette, will you?' The captain has collapsed in the doorway. The tank shell has torn right through his chest. He lies there like an empty sack. His face is frozen mid-scream in a waxen rictus of terror. Fröhlich and Herbert lift his body out of the pool of blood it's lying in and lay it on a camp bed. Without thinking, the corporal starts to tug off Fackelmann's felt boots as Fröhlich looks on numbly. Suddenly he snaps out of his shocked daze.

'Get out!' he shouts. 'Over to the shelter! I'll get Nasarov!'

But the Russian is nowhere to be found. He's vanished, as if the ground has swallowed him up. Fröhlich runs around all the forward positions and through every bunker. He is beside himself with frenzy and fear. But the three Russians have disappeared without a trace. No one has seen hide nor hair of them. Fröhlich pauses for a moment in his fruitless search. He begins to realize what's happened... Mad with despair, he reaches for his holster to end it all. But then he comes to his senses. And in this moment, Sonderführer Fröhlich suddenly transcends his former self. For the first and only time in his life, this foolish fantasist sees the truth. He sees the awful plight of the men here and he realizes that he has to lead them now. In a flash, he is calm and clear-sighted.

'Attention, everybody!' he shouts into the general confusion. 'I'm in command now! All the men of the divisional staff – assemble and get ready to decamp!'

A few minutes later, what remains of Fackelmann's task force winds its way in a long line back through the gorge, under intensified Russian bombardment, towards the airfield at Gumrak.

Gumrak! What a hideous word, how far from the soft-sounding, lilting, caressing names of the Russian villages. What a torturous consonance of dull hopelessness and cruel destruction. Gum – rak! Don't you feel the hunger in your guts at the sound of this word?

Or the tearing, nagging ache of your suppurating wounds? The groaning death rattle of a tormented life? Can't you hear in it the crunching of the snow, the crackle of the frost in the walls of houses, the roar and blast of bombs, the splintering of planks and beams, the cawing of the black birds that fly up from frozen-stiff bundles of human flesh? Gum – rak! Gum – rak!

Around fifteen kilometres west of Stalingrad, sprinkled on the huge white platter of the steppe, a handful of gloomy wooden houses and dilapidated shacks cowered by the side of the railway tracks running north. The presence there of buildings providing shelter and of track-mending materials (still in use until recently), plus the proximity to the headquarters of German Army High Command, was reason enough for the place to have drawn the diligent attention of long-range Russian artillery and repeated visits by Soviet Air Force bombers. They used a water tower to help them to spot and home in on their target. Anyone who knew the hamlet tried to give it a wide berth. Vehicles sped along the streets here like they were being hounded.

In this dismal place, surrounded by the constant stench of death, stood the Sixth Army's only field hospital. This was the main assembly point for the huge numbers of crippled men who, bewildered and disorientated, streamed in from all corners of the Cauldron seeking help and salvation. Here, unable to go any further, they holed up in unprotected nooks and crannies, at first overcome by sheer desperation. Little by little, though, they increasingly resigned themselves to their fate, a fate the vast mass graves of the cemetery here left them in no doubt about.

Padre Peters had remained in Gumrak. This terrible place held him fast in its grip. The army pastor stationed there, who over several weeks had tried to bring help and solace, had been buried when his bunker took a direct hit from a bomb. Peters took his place. His regular beat took in the densely packed wooden houses along the road; often one or other of these would be razed to the ground overnight by bombing or shelling. He crawled into the few unlit bunkers that remained in a landscape pitted with craters or stumbled over the train tracks to lines of railway carriages on sidings. These were home to the so-called 'lightly wounded'. Often he would spend minutes crouched between the iron wheels, with bomb splinters humming around him, before the sliding doors were pushed open to let him in. Not infrequently one of the carriages took a hit and each time, as if by some miracle, out of the twenty or thirty occupants some six to ten got out alive. To keep the carriages warm, they burned the wooden crates that shells came packed in, stacks of which were piled up at the entrance to the village. The wounded men had to fetch them themselves. They also had to forage for their own food. Because the daily ration of sixty grams of bread that the army had once set aside for the wounded had long since dried up, they would wait for sick horses to keel over or hobble to the abattoir three kilometres away, where, if they got lucky, they could pick up a bloody chunk of horsemeat or a handful of oats. Apart from that, all they had to eat were the scrapings from empty cans of tinned meat and snow.

In the ten days he had been there, Padre Peters had celebrated communion twice in the larger of the two stone station buildings. This was no easy task; the stairs and corridors were crammed with men who were either wounded or dead. It was hard to tell which, because, as the shockwave of exploding bombs smashed the windows, one after the other the resulting gaps were bricked up, cutting out what little natural light was available. At least this made the building slightly warmer. Finally, one morning, when a bomb fell no more than a couple of feet away from the outer wall of the building into the cesspit of the latrine and blew out all the remaining glass, without causing any other damage, the interior was plunged into an airless total darkness. Thoroughly demoralized, the doctors at the field hospital suspended almost all their operations.

Holding a lit candle and treading on silent, yielding bodies, the padre pushed his way through to the door that separated the building's two rooms. In the sooty smoke rising from the brick fireplaces he read a few passages from the Bible and delivered a brief sermon about the only path left open now: the path to heaven. His words fluttered bashfully into the oppressive silence. His face burned from the concentrated gaze of the eyes that stared at him from out of the gloom, wide-open eyes that had seen the truth. He couldn't help them any more. He was scraping the bottom of the barrel. In a numb stupor, Peters was wading through a thick mire of misery, from which individual images rose up now and then like toxic bubbles. Only rarely did one of these – and not even always one of the most terrible – remain with him. One that did was the picture of the two dead Romanians left lying on the street in Gumrak not far from the circular stone fountain basin where corpses had been piled up like logs. Every day, their rigid bodies were mutilated a bit more by passing traffic until finally they were squashed flat, steamrollered like the two naughty boys under the philosopher Diogenes' barrel in a picture-story by Wilhelm Busch.* Or the image of the bodies that had been heaped up to make a set of steps into the tall cattle trucks on the sidings and which he had to climb every day. Also etched indelibly on his memory was the face of a young soldier who had sunk to his knees in front of the sentry outside the station building and begged to be let in. The next morning he was still there, bent double and slumped over to one side. The last tears he had cried still clung to his frozen, dead cheeks like pearls of ice.

---

* 'picture-story by Wilhelm Busch' – the cautionary tale 'Diogenes and the Naughty Boys of Corinth' (*Diogenes und die bösen Buben von Korinth*) by the nineteenth-century German illustrator Wilhelm Busch. In it, the boys decide to play a joke on Diogenes, the Greek philosopher who was famous for living in a barrel, by setting his home rolling down a hill. They get their comeuppance when they are flattened by it.

Through the houses and the foxholes, through the bunkers of the POW camp on the outskirts of the village and through the barracks and tents attached to the field hospital out there in the *balka*, Padre Peters wandered wraithlike, a shadow of his former self. Time and time again, he encountered individuals who were eager to open up to him and who clung to his paltry words with desperate faith and hope. But this was nothing but a crazed hope for the earthly miracle that Hitler had failed to deliver, and which God was now expected to perform. By now Peters was already too weak to try to disabuse them of this blasphemous misconception. His conscience barely even registered a twinge of shock as he heard himself promising them that the miracle would come to pass. He lied like a doctor telling a dying patient that he'll rally and recover. And as he did so, Peters preached and prayed and baptized. Yes, incredibly he was still baptizing people! One soldier lay there with a wound in the small of his back that refused to heal. He asked Peters to baptize him. He also requested that his father should not be told about it, or he'd be angry. Peters baptized him with the full panoply of religious ritual, including a candlestick with a baptismal candle. But his heart remained dark. The other soldiers looked on with a mixture of emotion, embarrassment and solicitousness. After several days, when he found the soldier again in a hole somewhere (the house where he had been convalescing had collapsed one night), he was dead. The stub of the candle was still by his head.

As the few healthy men remaining increasingly took refuge in camaraderie, instilling courage into one another through the dreadful hours of the night with songs and stories and dirty jokes, all to hide their dread of dying, Peters retired to his bunker, which was covered with pieces of railway line and never saw so much as a glimmer of daylight, and which rocked like a little boat on the open sea whenever bombs rained down. There he would idle away his time in daydreams, undisturbed by the frequent comings and goings of others. They'd feel their way down the clay steps and acclimatize themselves to the darkness before sinking down in a corner, where they'd lie exhausted; after several hours, they would either leave or remain lying there, dead. Peters, too, would doubtless have wasted away here had it not been for Corporal Brezel.

Corporal Brezel – now there was a real character! The very first day after his arrival in Gumrak, Peters had screwed up his courage and climbed the freestanding, wobbly ladder to the top floor of the station building. After proceeding through a dark passageway filled with axes and severed horses' legs, he emerged into a small, improbably clean attic room. A wizened little man with a crumpled face and a flowing mane of hair rose from behind a table strewn with papers and photographs and, with a mixture of soldierly stiffness and urbane politeness, bade him take a seat. That was Corporal Brezel, a poet in civilian life, but for the time being the custodian of a small group of Russian prisoners whose duties included cleaning-up operations and foraging dead horses for the field kitchen. In return, the Russians were given the horses' legs, their only source of food, while the men at the abattoir sometimes put by a bit of tongue or liver for the corporal. As a sideline, though, sitting up here in his lofty perch while bombs and shells exploded all around, the corporal was also, at the behest of his staff officers, writing the history of his division. This was a commendable task, in so far as the division in question was clearly about to become extinct. Brezel proudly showed the padre his draft chapters and the photographs he'd collected: snaps of exercises and inspections, head-and-shoulders portraits of officers in full dress uniform, and bathing scenes from beaches on the Bay of Biscay. In addition, oblivious to everything that was going on down below, he penned verses about whatever took his poetic fancy: the nerve-jangling drone of the 'sewing machines', the searchlights playing in the night sky above the airfield, the riot of colour unleashed by the rising sun. And all the while he was so happy and positive that even Peters found himself momentarily jolted from his state of lethargy by the sight of this bizarre poetic idyll, like that famous painting by Spitzweg seen through a distorting lens.*

Two days after their first encounter, Brezel appeared in Peters's bunker with a cheery 'Top of the morning to you, Padre!' While the corporal had still been in bed, a shell fired from across the Volga had smashed through the window of his attic room, pierced the wall close to where he lay sleeping and exploded somewhere down on the street. 'God gave a merciful sign and his servant heeded the warning,' said Brezel when wrapping up his story. After this incident, he had brought his divisional history to an abrupt conclusion, summarily released his Russian prisoners, for whom there was no more food anyhow, and, furnished with the material for a new poem, had left his room to take a stroll.

From that day forward, he lived in Peters's bunker, gladly performing the duties of a sacristan and making sure the place was neat and tidy. He foraged wood for the little stove, carried out the dead and cadged petrol from passing lorries for the thirsty home-made lamp he had fashioned out of a tin can and a piece of rag. They would use its dim, guttering flame to eat by (when they had some food), to melt snow with and to catch lice. And Padre Peters took refuge from the horror that skulked in the dark corners of the bunker by reading the white pages of his Bible in the small circle of light it cast. The words flickered before his eyes. His strength was at an end.

Brezel was the person who ensured that they didn't starve to death.

He was always on the alert. He kept an eye out when the Russian auxiliaries came to the tower with their horse-drawn sleigh to

---

* 'that famous painting by Spitzweg' – *The Poor Poet* (*Der arme Poet*; 1839), by the nineteenth-century German painter Carl Spitzweg, is one of the most famous examples of the Biedermeier period of art, characterized by its choice of homely, sentimental themes. It shows a struggling poet living in a rundown garret and composing his works under an umbrella to protect himself from a leaking roof.

collect water. Wounded men and shady freebooters tended to gather there, hanging around in the hope that one of the emaciated nags might keel over and die. And when the Russians weren't looking they'd even help things along a bit, toppling the horse and falling upon it like wolves. Brezel, who despite his highly strung artist's temperament stood his ground manfully, emerged triumphant, his blood-stained sidearm still in his hand and waving a hunk of meat covered with shaggy horsehair, which he braised for hours on the stove. As he did so, he composed poems on the faithful look in horses' brown eyes.

The equilibrium of Brezel's sunny disposition was never disturbed. Only one thing bothered him: the state of mind of the padre, who couldn't even summon up the energy to be grumpy any more. That was a bad sign for sure! In addition, he'd got such strange bees in his bonnet of late, one might well have imagined he'd gone insane… For instance, one time Peters returned clutching beneath his arm a pair of shapeless straw overshoes that he'd found tucked away under the seat of an abandoned vehicle from the baggage train. No one thought anything of it. But Peters spent the whole of that evening sitting muttering to himself. And in the middle of the night – as usual, bombs were raining down – he got up abruptly and took the shoes back. Brezel shook his head. 'He's losing his mind,' he thought to himself, with touching concern. The next morning, he went to see what Peters had been up to. The lorry was still standing there, in the middle of nowhere. A soldier had just discovered the shoes and was feeding them to his horse.

On another occasion the padre came back from one of his perambulations laden with ammunition belts and a machine gun, which he had salvaged from a wrecked aircraft. The corporal shook with laughter at the sight.

'What on earth do you want with that, Padre? Honestly – dragging a thing like that round with you!'

Peters shot him a dirty look.

'Don't stay here on my account! Go on, clear off, go and hole up in Stalingrad for all I care! I at least mean to stay and fight here, yes sir... to the last bullet... to the last man standing!'

The machine gun had to be stowed under the camp bed. Once it was out of sight, the padre promptly forgot all about it.

Also, in the middle of reading something, Peters would suddenly give a violent start. 'Listen, can't you hear those monsters grinding their teeth? All their screaming and groaning?'

Brezel could hear nothing but the regular heavy breathing of someone sleeping in the corner.

'That's my domain,' the padre whispered. 'I'm the King of the Dead of Gumrak!'

As Peters was returning one day from the nearby airfield, where he'd gone to deliver the post, he passed two soldiers dragging behind them a tarpaulin full of loaves of bread. Peters hadn't seen any bread for days. He swooped down on the men like a hawk.

'Hey, where do you think you're going with that?'

The two men, a sergeant and a corporal, stopped in their tracks, uncertain what to do. They clearly had a guilty conscience.

'Planning to eat the lot yourselves, were you, eh? Unbelievable! That's just not on—'

Peters was shaking with hunger and greed. He dug his hands into the pile of frozen loaves and rummaged around.

'How old are you?' he suddenly asked the nonplussed sergeant. 'Thirty-six, eh? Right, give me three of those loaves! And you too. Three loaves apiece, that's not asking too much! That's just behaving like decent human beings.'

And before they could stop him, he'd stuck six loaves under his arms and made off with them. He did some sums in his head as he walked: six loaves between two men at the rate of half a loaf per man per day – that meant they'd last six days all told! For six whole days he and Brezel could stuff themselves, really eat till their bellies were bursting. He was whistling to himself as he walked down the bunker steps. Brezel's eyes almost popped out of his head when he caught sight of the loaves. His respect for the padre suddenly shot up, though he also felt a twinge of something like envy that he hadn't managed to pull off such a coup himself. Peters was more cheerful than he'd ever seen him.

'How about that, then?' he crowed. 'Daddy's brought home the bacon! Pass me a knife!'

As they were tucking in, with bulging cheeks, one of the medical NCOs came in, a small, inoffensive man with an ascetic face that looked like it had been transplanted to this war zone from a monastery. Normally he was welcome in Peters's bunker, but today that was clearly far from the case. He immediately twigged to the hostile atmosphere. He went and sat down quietly in a corner and tactfully refrained from noticing the loaf on the table. All at once, Peters lost his appetite. He pulled out a loaf from under the camp bed and pushed it over to the corporal.

'There, that's for you!'

The corporal thanked him sheepishly; he stroked the loaf lovingly and sniffed it but then left it be. With studied insouciance, Brezel explained how they'd come by this unexpected cornucopia. The Franciscan monk was incurious to a degree and so the conversation dried up. After a while he stood up to go.

'So… can I take this loaf with me?'

'No, you've got to eat it here!' said Peters gruffly. 'If you take it away with you, you'll be left with…' He broke off, transfixed by the long, serious and not remotely reproachful stare the corporal was directing at him.

'You've no idea how much I'll enjoy that, Padre,' he said quietly. Peters's pale face became so drained of blood that it took on a sickly greenish hue. He began shaking uncontrollably. He reached under the bed again and pulled out another loaf – and a second, and a third, and eventually a fourth, all the remaining loaves.

'There… there! Take the lot… just take them!'

It was like a sudden attack of self-destructiveness. He even threw in the rest of his own half-loaf.

'Go on, take it! And clear off!'

Without a word, the medical NCO gathered up the dark loaves and disappeared. His eyes were shining. Five loaves! With a bit of adroit cutting, they could get twenty slices out of each loaf. That meant two hundred men, two hundred hungry, wounded men would get an extra half slice of bread today!

The poet Brezel slunk around Peters's bunker like a whipped dog. He didn't dare speak to the padre. But Peters had retreated far back into the shadow of his corner. He was weeping.

A heavy grey pall hangs above the ground. The harsh frost has disappeared. The dry snow still makes a noise when you tread on it, but it no longer emits a sharp, tormented squeak; now it sounds more like the lazy croaking of disgruntled frogs. First Lieutenant Breuer is making his way through the scattered foothills of the gorge to the airfield at Gumrak. He is trudging along the winding footpath, often sinking up to his knees in the deep snow and stumbling over abandoned foxholes. Behind him, the voices of his comrades and the sound of sporadic gunfire grow ever fainter. He steps out on to the open plain. A light wind playfully whips up little eddies of snow. In the distance, the blurred outlines of stationary vehicles begin to emerge from the surrounding gloom. He heads towards them. Under his frozen, brown-stained head dressing, a blinding headache is raging in his skull, pulsating right through to the roots of his hair and rendering his thoughts dull and confused. Thousands of men are being torn to pieces by shells, he thinks, thousands bleed to death or die of their festering wounds, or of the cold... And one man who's remained hale and hearty and unscathed then goes and falls over and pokes his eye out. Like he wasn't in Stalingrad at all, but somewhere in Berlin, or Königsberg! For that, he won't even get a badge identifying him as one of the war wounded. How stupid it would be, he thinks, how ignominious if he were now to die from this injury!

Abruptly, he finds himself in an abandoned town, walking past ransacked, wrecked vehicles, past burned-out aircraft fuselages, bent radio antennae, and blasted concrete bunker roofs. No people, no smoke, no signs of life at all. Everything lies extinct in an abyss of solitude. Now and then a shell fired from somewhere or other and heading for who knows where whines over his head with an evil *zisssch* sound. An overpowering urge takes hold of him simply to crawl into a hole in this forsaken place, to avoid seeing or hearing anything more and slowly drift into sleep. Tomorrow is the twenty-fourth of the month. Tomorrow it will all be over and done with…

Breuer stops dead. He is breathing heavily. His gaze fixes on a figure he suddenly sees standing there, grey and sunken-eyed, by the entrance to a bunker.

'Hey! Hey, you there!'

He is shocked at the sound of his own voice. The man doesn't move. He looks across at Breuer like a timid deer. Then, all of a sudden, he gives a start and disappears in a single bound into the bowels of the earth.

This place gives Breuer the creeps. He moves on, quickening his pace. Eventually he comes upon a road that bends off to the left, which he takes without thinking. Signs of a village appear some-where off in the distance. *Whooo-sh-sh* comes a tearing sound high above his head. Up ahead, three large sulphurous mushroom clouds billow into the sky. The ground quakes slightly, followed by the dull rumble of the heavy explosions. They must have hit Gumrak… Breuer breaks his stride for a moment. He wonders whether he ought in fact to avoid the place. But he baulks at the thought of wading through deep snow. It's all of no account anyway. Tomorrow is the twenty-fourth.

Gradually, the village takes shape against the snowy backdrop.

White-roofed sheds, a stone building with several floors, a sturdy, round tower with a swollen head, and then some railway carriages and stationary locomotives. The scene changes radically on both sides of the road. The snow looks scorched here, and all kinds of debris are lying scattered around – splintered pieces of wood from barns, fences and farm carts, along with rocks and steel rails. In between, circular bomb craters yawn, and the black holes of exposed cellars and bunkers with their roofs blown apart. From the innards of this devastated landscape, thin blackish wafts of smoke rise and drift along the ground. Mingled with this haze, which has an acrid smell of burning, is a hint of that sickly sweet stench that had lain like a nightmarish miasma over the sites of the battles fought during the hot summer of '42. A smell of cadavers. Off to one side, more shells fizz by. Violent impacts shake the ground. The fire is concentrated on the southern exit of the village. A figure is poking around in the debris to one side of the road. It looks like a very old woman, but is actually a soldier. Once again, Breuer is hit by a paralysing feeling of exhaustion. Where should he head for now? The Staff HQ in Stalingradski will have long gone. They'll have taken cover somewhere, waiting for the end to come!

The figure has vanished underground. At the point where he disappeared, a light plume of smoke is twisting up, suggesting human life. Breuer totters over piles of rubble and makes for the spot. He slips down into a hole in the ground. It is a small, dark opening, covered in makeshift fashion with a piece of concealed corrugated iron. Chinks of daylight coming through the gaps at the edges of this ramshackle cover illuminate dirty puddles on the floor. Breuer ducks down. He presses his back against the wall, his hands groping along the damp clay. His good eye struggles to make out any details in the semi-darkness. Are those figures cowering silently against the walls or lying prone on the floor dead bodies? They're certainly not moving or speaking... No, they're not dead – there's the man he'd spotted outside squatting in front of the small doorless stove!

He's feeding damp pieces of wood into the fire. Stolidly, and oblivious to any interruption, he stares with dead eyes into the blaze; his mouth hangs open and his lower jaw trembles like a dotard's. But there really are some corpses here too! The terrible smell that he smelled outside gives the game away, this disgusting stench of sweat, pus, human excrement and... decaying flesh! Breuer can feel his whole body beginning to shake. He's seized by an urge to get away from this place – anywhere but here! Frost, snow and loneliness suddenly seem inviting compared to this ghastly mixture of the decomposing dead and the decaying living. But he still hesitates to leave. He's just heard someone call his name, surely! Is he feverish, hallucinating? Is his pain-wracked head mocking him? There it is again, more clearly now, but still sounding like it's coming through a wall:

'Breuer!'

Breuer winces in fear. He holds his breath and listens... Yes, there it is again.

'Breuer... I'm here!'

The first lieutenant stumbles over a tangle of limbs to a bundle of rags in the far corner. The grey light filtering through the bunker cover falls on a yellowed face, with what looks like parchment stretched over it; the contours of the man's skull shimmer through his taut skin. A downy beard covers a pointed chin. Two unnaturally large eyes sunk in deeply shadowed sockets are trained squarely on him. Breuer feels his knees buckle.

'Wiese – is that you?'

The man's mouth, no more than a thin line, opens in a feeble smile, revealing the exposed roots of his top teeth.

'Yes, Breuer, I... to think it's come to this!'

There's another thump of falling shells, very near this time. The corrugated iron rattles loudly, and snow and earth crumble down into the bunker. The tangled heap of bodies shifts and groans. Someone mutters prayers, hurried and fearful. Breuer has stooped over the sick man, as if to shield him. 'My God, Wiese,' he stammers, 'how did you end up here – in this awful dump?'

Wiese had closed his eyes momentarily. Now they open, large and clear, once more. It is as though his failing body has redirected its last vestiges of energy into these eyes.

'You can't mock God's justice!'* he proclaims earnestly, showing wisdom beyond his years. Breuer still can't understand what's going on. He presses his comrade for answers. Wiese doesn't appear to hear him. He keeps talking all the while, quietly and calmly.

'It's so hard to die... like this.'

And he tells Breuer, haltingly and incoherently, about his feelings of guilt.

'I saw it all coming and didn't do anything to stop it. I thought I could choose my own path, just for myself, aside from the mainstream... And I've been punished for that.' Sometimes, his train of thought gets muddled and his eyes glaze over; but he always rallies and becomes lucid again. He talks about his life, his parents' house in a small town in the Rhineland, and his schooldays. His father had wanted him to go to university and become a teacher. But he didn't want that and had joined the German railways instead, so he'd have the freedom and leisure to devote himself entirely to music and his beloved books when the working day was over. And fate was kind to him, even in this conflict. He'd come through the war unscathed, untainted. And then came the incident with the burning plane...

Breuer has heard all of that before. But today it is bathed in a new light, under the merciless glare of a clear-sighted self-awareness. It makes Breuer forget all his pain and his own hopeless position.

'I'll stick by you, Wiese! I'll get a doctor and find us something to eat... you just wait, you'll make it through all right!'

---

* 'You can't mock God's justice' – quotation from St Paul's Epistle to the Galatians, chapter 6 verse 7.

Wiese dismisses Breuer's words with a wave of his hand.

'At night the faces of all the dead crowd round me, looking at me... You didn't know anything... But I did, I knew everything, Breuer. And I said and did nothing! I wanted to be the only righteous person among all the lost souls. And I've paid the price for it. God cannot be mocked!'

Tiredness forces Lieutenant Wiese to pause. Breuer is shaking, all too painfully aware of his own impotence. What's going on here cannot be happening; it's blasphemous folly! He wants to help but has no idea what he should do. In the gloom, he tries to make out if Wiese has a dressing, or any signs of a wound. But all he can see is a ragged, sticky, brown-stained greatcoat. A hand is pushed towards him.

'It's good that you've come, Breuer. It makes things so much easier now... Here, have a look through my coat pockets, will you, the right one? I've got papers, letters and my pay-book. Be a good chap and take all that stuff with you? For my parents, my fiancée.'

Breuer's hand searches tentatively through the coat until it finds the inside pocket and feels inside. He recoils in horror. His fingers have encountered a warm, sticky mass. He looks aghast at the motionless eyes that hold him with their wide and knowing gaze... Slowly he withdraws a filthy packet of papers. He's tongue-tied and can barely get his words out.

'My God, Wiese, I don't even know if I'm going to—'

'You're right: there's no way back now. I'm sure you'll make it home, though – someday. A different person in a different world... I just know it. Now go, will you? This is no place for you, Breuer. Please go now. Please!'

Breuer leaves the bunker...

He wanders out on to the main road with its hard-packed surface of snow, where a cordite-smelling haze of shellfire still hangs in the air. Strewn across the roadway are mutilated bodies, scraps of flesh and severed limbs. The pools of blood are still fresh and red and gently steaming. Lorries roar past like hunted animals. Breuer takes none of this in. In his mind, he's still talking to his dying friend. Guilt! The word burns in his soul. 'Yes, we're all guilty!'

A figure approaches him and makes to pass by without a word of greeting. Breuer does a double-take.

'Padre Peters!'

A dead-eyed face turns to look at him.

'Padre, please, come over here, quick! Wiese's lying in a bunker out there. Lieutenant Wiese: you know who I mean! He's at death's door!'

The padre passes a weary hand over his sunken face.

'Wiese – the little lieutenant… Yes, there's lots of men dying here. But I must get to the station now… What's the matter with you, by the way? An eye injury? Why don't you walk with me, maybe the doctor might be able… There's not much for him to do round here any more. Anyone who can still walk has moved on already.'

Breuer staggers after the padre in a daze. His thoughts are far away. He trips over dead bodies and wounded men, and eventually finds himself facing a doctor.

'What's the problem? Eye injury? You know this man, Padre? Oh, shi… look, with an eye injury you can get flown out, as a priority case even! I'll write you a note here. You don't need the army's authorization any longer. At least you can still walk fine. Get yourself over to Stalingradski and see if you can still get a plane out.'

Saying this, the doctor presses an exemption note into his hand. He seems pleased that he can still make a difference here on something that matters.

Breuer stands outside the station. He looks blankly at the card he's holding, with its red border and little attached ribbon. Funny, it looks like a parcel dispatch note. So, it's as simple as that… And a sudden realization hits him. My God, he's free! This is his passport back to life! Everything else fades into irrelevance… Fröhlich's risky escape plan, his comrades, the grisly Dance of Death going on around him, his dying friend… it all begins to fade away like a bad dream. But taking its place in his pain-filled head there comes a resurgence of the distant, long-vanished past, stretching out a thousand arms to him and taking on gigantic proportions. Irmgard, the children, the daffodils in the garden, the lilac hedge, the bookcase full of books, the little library he'd built up and so loved – he'd see all that again, in just a few days' time! Just for the loss of one eye, he thinks, a small price to pay for everything to be back the way it used to be! But somewhere in a recess in his brain there also lurks a dark thought: the twenty-fourth… God cannot be mocked! But it's of no consequence any more; it's lost all the power it once had.

And so, with death all around him but now gripped by an ardent desire to live, he who was already marked to meet his maker hurries on towards the airfield at Stalingradski.

5

No Way Back

FOLLOWING THE LOSS OF Pitomnik and the abandonment of Gumrak, Stalingradski is the last operational airfield still open to the Sixth Army. If it, too, were to fall to the Russians, the last thread of a connection to the outside world would be cut. Admittedly, there is talk of a runway being built in the city of Stalingrad itself, and army commanders have sent in construction units to do the preparatory earth-moving operations. But that's only to boost the troops' morale, in the full knowledge that such a plan is in fact wholly unfeasible.

Stalingradski's 'Flight Control' is situated in a bunker in a gorge just off the main road. Breuer pushes his way through the half-open door into the room, which is full to bursting. His euphoric mood of earlier has not subsided. The first things that meet his ear are the clatter of a typewriter and the raised voice of a medical officer.

'No, I'm telling you, you're wasting your time! If you don't have a valid sick pass there's nothing to be done. Get out! Jesus Christ Almighty, we're not running a bloody shop here!'

Breuer pushes forward and hands over his card. The doctor gives it a cursory look.

'There's no authorization from the army here,' he says.

Breuer has to lean on the table to stop himself from fainting. It's like someone has slammed a door in his face. 'But I thought… I was told—'

'Then you were told wrong!' snaps the MO. And without more ado, he addresses all the waiting men. 'Right, hand me your cards! I've got to go over and see the army surgeon anyhow. Maybe he'll sign them off.'

Surrender his sick pass? Breuer wavers between fear and hope. The doctor loses his temper.

'For God's sake, do you want to give me that or not?! It's all the same to me!'

Breuer reluctantly parts with the valuable, or possibly worthless, card. He and the others make their way outside. With some effort, he climbs back up the slope out of the gorge and crosses the busy road, which is lined with hedges. His thoughts have become a blur by now.

A few hundred metres beyond the road is the edge of the airfield, an expanse of white that stretches into the distance. The green-grey fuselages of three or four transport planes are clearly visible, along with several grey trucks and various knots of people milling around and being shepherded by a handful of black-clothed figures. A plane is slowly lifting off the runway. At least they're still flying out of here, then. And the prospects for those due to depart are looking good. In these overcast conditions, there's no danger of encountering enemy fighters, so in a couple of hours' time the passengers in the plane that's just taken off will be touching down safe and sound at the airfield at Shakhty or Stalino.*

With a mad haste, quite uncalled for given the circumstances, Breuer races ahead towards the aerodrome. Keeping pace alongside him, with long, loping strides, is a fellow officer.

'This stupid countersignature rigmarole,' he grumbles. 'Total

---

* Stalino – former name of the city of Donetsk, Ukraine.

bloody shambles! Wonder if we'll even see that MO again? Of course, a bastard like him who has to stay here come what may doesn't have the slightest interest in... Anyhow, I reckon we should keep our beady eyes on him... Look out for one another, what?'

He is a major, tall and slim, and with a rather rakish air.

His cap is set at a jaunty angle above black earmuffs. His left arm is in splints and heavily bandaged. A camouflage jacket is draped across his shoulders like a hussar's fur cape.

A keen easterly wind has got up, and is blowing powdery snow across the airfield. It seems that Stalingradski is only a temporary airstrip. A really quite restricted area of relative flatness, but pretty uneven for all that, with some treacherous dips in the surface and lots of small man-made hummocks dotted about. Breuer can't make out what they are: piles of corpses, no doubt, or perhaps discarded equipment. As testament to the hidden dangers here, several wrecked aircraft are scattered around the airfield's perimeter. These are the planes that Breuer spotted from the road. The tail of one is sticking out of the ravine that lies at the airfield's southern end. Nearby, an ill-defined black mass of something is moving, jelly-like. As Breuer draws closer, the details become clearer. A mass of people is milling about there. People? Distorted reflections of human misery, more like – sick and wounded soldiers and men gone to rack and ruin, crippled, hobbling around using sticks, propping themselves up on home-made crutches or leaning on one another for support. These had once been men – Germans, Romanians, soldiers and officers alike, as revealed by their tattered uniforms. And now? Now they have become a bellowing, seething, hate-filled mob. Nor does the melee show any signs of abating; instead, it forms a self-contained mass, swirling round some unseen focal point, as everyone fights to ensure they get the elusive, illusory 'first seat on the plane'. Standing to one side is the flight dispatch officer, his legs apart like a ringmaster, tense and ready to spring forward at a moment's notice. The pistol in his hand guarantees he is shown respect. Everyone knows he'll open fire without hesitation if the violence and chaos spill over from the jostling mass. His voice is hoarse from shouting; it sounds like rusty tin.

'For the last time – if you lot don't fall in line this instant, I'll pull the plug on the whole show! That's right – I'll radio all the incoming pilots to return to base, I'm telling you!'

Various figures are circling like jackals around the periphery of the group. These are the wounded, starving and freezing men who couldn't get to see a doctor anywhere and who haven't been fortunate enough to secure a sick pass home. Yet they still live in hope. And bodies are lying in the snow, not all of them dead. Some are still crawling around while others are trying to get back up. One man is lying there with his kitbag under his head. He's not moving a muscle. His eyes are all skew-whiff, like a broken doll's. His mouth is hanging open and out of it, from deep within his chest, there comes a gurgling, sobbing, unintelligible scream of anguish...

Breuer holds his hand in front of his face. Only one eye, he thinks crazily. How good that only one eye is witnessing all this! He realizes that he must fight here, fight for his life, ruthlessly and brutally, that he must turn into an animal before he can become a human being again. And yet he feels like he's paralysed. So that's that! Hadn't he always suspected it would come to this? Had he ever seriously imagined... Exhausted, he slumps down in the lee of a wrecked aircraft fuselage to get out of the biting wind. The major sits down beside him, fishes out a pack of cigarettes and offers one to Breuer.

'Sheer lunacy, eh? Stuffing these planes full of chaps like that!' he witters. 'I mean to say – I'm wounded myself,' he continues, cheerfully waving his bandaged arm, 'but let's face it: what the devil are they going to do with cripples like that back home? There's no question of returning them to front-line duties. And just think of the effect blokes like that will have on people's morale. Don't get me wrong; I'm only saying this from the point of view of how to wage a war rationally... but priority really ought to be given to general staff officers, and competent commanders, and specialists and healthy infantrymen... They're always going on about being ruthless but when the chips are down, it's a different story...'

'Yes, yes,' mutters Breuer distractedly. His attention has been caught by a droning noise that's growing louder by the minute. A dark shape emerges from the uniform grey blanket of cloud; as it descends and gets larger, its markings become clearer. At a low altitude, it executes a careful turn over the airfield to check out the terrain before coming in to a bumpy landing and taxiing to the end of the strip.

A new spasm of unrest convulses the heaving mass of those who have been thrown together here from all over the place, men who have been wrenched from their final moorings and stripped of their last bit of security. But no one makes a dash for the aircraft; order hasn't yet broken down to that extent. The dispatch officer has shot down two men already today. There's a tussle among the group to try to form an orderly queue, and to secure a place at the head of it. One man has detached himself from the crowd. Egotism impels him to appoint himself leader. 'Line up in ranks of three!' he shouts. 'There are more planes coming! Either we all get out of here or none of us will!' But it's all to no avail. The men are beyond the reach of reason. They start pushing forward again on the right – five, six, ten abreast. This enrages those on the left. 'Shove off! Get back in line!' they yell.

Pandemonium ensues. 'What? Whaaat?... I was here long before you...' – 'I'm a colonel, sir! A colonel!' – 'Smack the bastard in the mouth!' A flurry of punches are thrown. Yells of fury and pain. The sounds of splintering wood and of groaning bodies thudding into the snow. 'Ow! Ow! ... Aaaargh...!' Boot heels stamp on the fallen as they lie on the ground, crushing the life out of them.

Stalingradski airfield has become an arena for combat between wild beasts. What price humanity now? Or comradeship, discipline and honour? Or sympathy or brotherly love? Are people nothing but animals? Though even animals have a sense of loyalty and gratitude. What is man?

Surreptitiously, meanwhile, another phalanx of men, three abreast, has formed to one side. The dispatch officer selects a dozen or more soldiers from their ranks. They can't believe their luck. They run pell-mell like some deranged mob for the plane, which has started to rev its engines. They tug, shove, tumble and scramble their way up the ladder. The radio operator, who is standing in the cabin door, lays into the knot of men with his fists.

'Get back there, you pack of filthy swine! You'll tear this old crate apart if you're not careful! The pilots are officers, I'll have you know…'

The dispatch officer has rushed up too. Swearing volubly, he tugs apart the tangle of men at the aircraft steps. Breuer gives a sudden start. The person in the leather coat there, isn't that…? But by now all twelve of the men have vanished into the aircraft cabin. Their faces appear, one by one, in the murky windows. Two soldiers from the unit detailed to pick up air-dropped food deliveries trot up. The dispatch officer points to the man lying in the snow with his head on his kitbag. By now, he's stopped screaming. They lift him up and carry him over to the aircraft. The radio operator bends down.

'What's all this then?' he asks, nonplussed. 'Since when do we fly corpses out?' Only now do the soldiers take a closer look at their burden. Then they glance up at one another. 'Oh shit!' one of them murmurs. The dead man arcs through the air into the snow as they fling him aside. He doesn't need to fly out; he's gone home already.

The plane's engines roar, its propellers whipping up clouds of snow as the big machine shudders and starts to roll forward on its splayed undercarriage. Suddenly a man bursts out from the crowd and bounds forward. What's his game? Has he lost his mind? At full stretch, he lunges desperately at the departing aircraft's tail end, and somehow finds a handhold. His legs flail wildly in the air. The dispatch officer's hoarse cry of rage mingles with the howl of the engines. He chases after the lumbering machine, which hasn't lifted off yet, stops and raises his pistol, and then fires – once, twice. Up ahead, a soldier on the back of a truck unshoulders his rifle and shoots… The man falls from the aircraft and is hit by the passing tailplane; his body somersaults a couple of times and then comes to rest, motionless.

Even though he's still sitting down, Breuer feels his legs starting to shake. And that's not just the result of the frost that's slowly creeping up his body. The euphoric feeling of hope he once had has fallen away, flaked off him like a substandard paint job. Had he really imagined that he'd simply be able to board a plane here like he was getting on a train? That he'd be able to walk out of the catastrophe at Stalingrad like he was leaving a bad play? He can feel all the energy draining out of his limbs. But behind this impotence, he has the first inkling, albeit still only slight, that 'Stalingrad' has already transcended space and time, that there's no longer any escape from it even if one went to the ends of the earth, and that unbreakable bonds now tie him to the hundreds of thousands still here – those who are still alive and suffering, the mistreated and the betrayed, and the dead. Anyone who survives these gruesome events unfolding on the snowy fields beside the Volga will henceforth carry Stalingrad with them throughout their entire lives. Minutes spent in the arms of their beloved wife – Stalingrad! The sight of their children's sparkling eyes – Stalingrad! There'll be no happiness and no tears without Stalingrad; no achievements, no work and no striving without Stalingrad. No rest, no sleep, no more dreams that don't involve Stalingrad! And when this life finally comes to be weighed in the balance at the End of Days, the dead of Stalingrad will also pass judgement. And every thought and every deed that was not aimed at overcoming that ludicrous, destructive spirit that insisted upon the mass slaughter of Stalingrad as some ghastly ritual of a barbarian cult of idolatry would be repudiated.

As yet, Breuer only has a faint inkling of all this. And he struggles to fight back this thought and summon up his strength for the fight that still awaits him.

'Total bloody shambles!' says the major next to him again. 'This morning about twenty planes took off from here. Almost all of them empty. There was hardly anyone here for them to take. But still the idiots wouldn't let you through without a countersigned chit.'

'Is that a bad injury?' Breuer enquires absent-mindedly, keeping a lookout all the while for the doctor. If only he'd come back! Assuming he was planning on returning at all, that is. What would happen if he didn't? There are hundreds of men massing there now.

'Oh, it's still just about working,' replies the major, smiling complacently. 'Whole arm got ripped open. Real bloody mess, I can tell you!'

Wheeeeuw—whumm! Jesus, what was that? Artillery fire! That's all they need! The sky grows ever more dull and grey. Snowflakes drift over the airfield. Another droning noise overhead. An aircraft looms up, large and grey, out of the mist, and banks several times over the landing strip, tighter and tighter each time… Everyone is staring up at it intently. Is it going to land? Breuer leaps to his feet. Where the hell has that bloke with the passes got to? There, the plane has lowered its landing gear and is coming in to land! With its engines roaring, it thunders low over their heads. The marshals on the ground wave their flags to direct it in. Up ahead, one of the 'bodies' lying in the snow suddenly raises himself up and staggers across the airfield, waving his arms. The aircraft, which is seconds from touching down, hurtles towards him. Everyone on the airfield is yelling in horror. One of the plane's main wheels clips the man; he spins round a couple of times before slamming to the ground. The aircraft, thrown off course by the impact, makes far too heavy a landing, breaking off its undercarriage. It pancakes onto the landing strip, its fuselage screeching as it ploughs into the snow. A crash-landing. End of story.

★

Gumrak's days are numbered. Now that artillery fire is raining down on the area from the west as well, and columns of men and vehicles are streaming out of the village, there can be little doubt on the matter. Anyone who still has the use of his legs, even if only very approximately, has set off on the hopeless journey to Stalingrad. The rest have no choice but to stay behind. In the final days, some thirty to forty men have still been flown out daily. Yet fifteen hundred troops remain holed up in the bunkers, railway carriages and houses there, as well as in the POW camp on the outskirts and the barracks and tents in the nearby *balka*. What will become of them when the medical personnel also pull out someday soon? The doctors shrug their shoulders and say nothing. Their silence is answer enough.

Padre Peters is no longer with the wounded men, not even in his thoughts. He sits in his bunker and stares at the fire in the stove. In his hand, he weighs a small-format Bible, printed on India paper. It has travelled with him from the altar of the Church of St Andrew in Braunschweig to military cemeteries in Poland and the Ukraine, through field hospitals, bunkers and trenches, and finally found its way here, to Stalingrad. The black Morocco leather binding is as soft as velvet and the pages are like silk to the touch. He's not about to let the Reds tear it to pieces with mocking laughter before his very eyes! He drops the Bible into the flames and sits and watches it curl up and its pages fan out as it is slowly consumed by the fierce, red-hot glow... Muddled thoughts keep skating over the surface of his consciousness. He's lost any capacity to control them. What a hard road Padre Peters has had to travel! Cocooned in the robust armour of his faith, he has struggled and fought against the overwhelming horror like no one else. He has prayed for strength, found an inner strength, and inspired others to be strong. He has shone a light into hell. At least, that was once the case... but Stalingrad has shredded him, torn him to pieces, ground him down both physically and mentally; it has squeezed the last drop of strength out of him. What remains is a wreck, a floundering, helpless, rudderless wreck of a human being.

Peters is no longer master of his own fate. He has immolated himself.

Corporal Brezel bursts into the bunker.

'Time we were off, I reckon, Padre! The doctors have left in the car, and the rest over there are getting ready to clear out. There's already some shooting going on, down over on the far left – small-arms fire!' He plonks a salami down on the table.

'From the food stores. The men have just ransacked it.'

Padre Peters gets to his feet like an old man. He breaks the sausage in two, takes a bite of his piece and then pours himself a mug of communion wine from a canteen. Vacantly, he passes the canteen to Brezel, who takes a swig. Thank God, the corporal thinks. He's coming to his senses again! He anxiously gathers up his few belongings. His history of the division is not among them. All the while, Peters sits on the camp bed, chewing the salami. He has no thoughts or feelings any more. Brezel, who is preoccupied with his own worries, eventually drags him to his feet, drapes his greatcoat round him, shoves a blanket and haversack under his arm, and takes him outside. The street is totally deserted. Deep silence still looms like a nightmare over the place, and everything seems to have perished. Yet this silence is deceptive; secretly, life goes on in a thousand different ways, albeit a forsaken, doomed kind of life. Peters feels nothing; aimlessly and passively he staggers along beside Brezel into the grey gloom. He has forgotten everything: the past, the present – and he has no conception of any future.

By the side of the road, a man is lying in the snow, covered with a coat, with a pillow under his head and a loaf and his wash bag beside him. He lies there motionless in the wintry solitude, with only his eyes showing any signs of animation in his bluish face. 'Take me with you!' he begs them quietly. 'Take me with you!'

Peters sees the man but trots on mindlessly, utterly oblivious to his plight. He has seen too much, and experienced too much suffering… Even so, it is as though the solitary man by the roadside has surreptitiously planted a seed in his heart, which now starts to germinate vigorously. Thoughts begin to stir in his addled head, generating an unsettling humming and circling sensation that grows stronger by the second. One phrase above all starts to form from the background of white noise and push itself to the fore: 'He saw the man and passed by on the other side.' The biblical reference jolts Peters out of his stupor. Without warning, he stops dead in his tracks. He seizes Brezel by the forearm and stares wide-eyed into his startled face.

'Saw the man and passed by on the other side,' he mutters.

Brezel is alarmed. 'Come on, we've got to keep moving!' he urges, tugging at the padre's arm.

But Peters stands his ground like a stubborn mule.

'Saw the man and passed by on the other side,' he repeats, turning aside. Stiff-legged, he starts to walk back the way they've come.

'Padre!' Brezel calls after him. 'Padre!' He really has gone mad, he thinks despairingly. He's gone out of his mind; there's no helping him any more. He doesn't dare follow. His strength, too, is at an end. And now the crackle of gunfire resumes behind them.

Peters kneels down beside the wounded soldier. He wonders how on earth he got here. Some exhausted comrades may have left him here and put the pillow under his head as a final mark of their impotent concern.

'Take me with you,' he murmurs, over and over. 'To Stalingrad!'

Peters lays a hand on his brow. It's as cold as ice.

'No, no, lad!' he says quietly. 'We're not going to Stalingrad. What would the two of us want with Stalingrad? We've got our Dear Lord, and the only path we'll take leads to him.' His own words strike him as new. The crippled man looks up at him, silent and attentive. His eyes probe unknown realms. Peters takes off the silver crucifix that he wears round his neck and, holding it fast, prays with the man and gives him communion. He still has some altar wine left in his canteen and some wafers in his pocket.

Time drifts by silently. After slipping imperceptibly into the arms of death, the invalid by the roadside has gone into rigor mortis. Padre Peters stands beside the dead man, contemplating his calm, relaxed and peaceful face. A sense of profound loneliness suddenly folds him into its stifling embrace. His gaze falls on the crucifix in his hand... 'And surely I am with you always...' It is as if he is waking from a state of deep unconsciousness. Peters breathes a heavy sigh. What a Doubting Thomas he was! He can feel strength flowing into his body from the crucifix in his hand and from the dead man's transfigured features. With a great upsurge of joy, he realizes that he can still help. And, isolated as he is, abandoned by everyone else and all alone with his crucifix, he comes to a momentous decision.

Peters covers the dead man with his coat and departs. But not in the direction of Stalingrad. He walks back through the abandoned town of Gumrak. But now he sees it through waking eyes. To his left is the cemetery. There, the bodies lie cheek-by-jowl, from a time when it was still possible to bury corpses. Each grave has its own cross. And there's the house where the lieutenant lies dead, whose eyes they shot out. How often he'd come away from there feeling enriched and humbled by the young lieutenant's confidence.

'And surely I am with you always, to the very end of time.'

The frozen bodies of men still lie outside the door to the railway station. But there is no sentry there now, barring their entrance. No one outside *wants* to get in any more, while no one inside *can* now leave. The silent, desperate plight of the four hundred or so men lying in the darkness there screams out into the hush of the village. Peters moves on, towards the advancing Russians. He's not thinking of himself. He senses that he, a priest, can't hope for much leniency from the enemy. But death, whose gruesome presence he has now felt beside him a thousand times over, no longer frightens him. He thinks of the others, of this or that soldier in their fox-holes and the men in the sepulchral station house. And he also calls to mind the blind lieutenant... Perhaps things aren't as bad as he's always imagined them, timid soul that he is? Maybe there are human beings on the other side too? He'd encountered genuine human beings many times in the farmhouses of the Ukraine, wherever he went.

The padre leaves the bounds of the village and makes for the POW camp up ahead in the gorge. The grey wilderness is wreathed in silence as dusk falls. There comes the sound of a single shot, somewhere in the distance. All is light now within Padre Paters, though; the darkness of the past weeks has lifted.

Suddenly, the calm is broken. Silent figures step forward out of the mist, white-clad figures wearing fur *ushankas** and with their rifles at the ready... Red Army troops! Peters stands still – he can feel his heart racing, while his hand tightly grips the crucifix in his pocket. Yet his agitation is in no way tinged with fear. Slowly, hesitantly, the strange figures approach him. Peters takes out the crucifix and raises it to heaven:

'*Christos voskresty!*'† he cries. His voice rings out clear as a bell across the snowy landscape.

'*Ya svyashchennik!*'‡ Dear Lord, Peters prays to himself, if this be Thy will, then Thy will be done! But what happens next takes the padre completely by surprise. The Russians stop. One man who was ahead of the others, scouting out the terrain, lowers his weapon and his face cracks into a smile – and he laughs, a deep and hearty laugh. He lumbers up to Peters, places his hands on his shoulders and gives him an affable shake.

'*Batyushka!*' he says, and for a moment this little, friendly word entirely eclipses the war. The other soldiers stand around, seven small figures with snub-nosed, childlike, Ukrainian faces that appear somehow unfinished. They stare inquisitively at this curious saint. But in the background, three of them silently and bashfully make

---

* *ushankas* – Russian army hat with fur-lined earflaps.
† *Christos voskresty!* – 'Christ is risen!'
‡ *Ya svyashchennik!* – 'I'm a priest!'

the sign of the Cross. Padre Peters falls to his knees and buries his face in his hands.

Back at the airfield, time passes excruciatingly slowly for the waiting First Lieutenant Breuer. Suddenly, though, the major tugs at his sleeve.

'Hey, look over there! I think that's him!'

'Where? Who?'

'The bloke with the passes!'

It is indeed the MO from Flight Control. Breuer and the major rush forward to speak to him. Has he got their sick passes, they want to know. Yes, he has them, and they have the requisite counter-signatures. They urge him to hand them over without delay. Already, another aircraft is circling overhead. But the doctor is determined to take his time. He makes great play of deciphering their names, mistrustfully scrutinizing the recipients to make sure they are bona fide and asking to see their pay-books to confirm their identity. Finally, though, Breuer gets his hands on his sick pass. A signature has been hastily scrawled on it in ink – 'Approved, Dr Rinoldi'. Above them, the plane keeps banking over the field. Breuer sprints over to the dispatch officer, who is busy selecting passengers from the seething crowd of soldiers.

'Hey, hey, over here!' he shouts 'I've got an eye injury! Look here… here's my authorization!'

By now the harassed officer is a bundle of nerves.

'Shit on your eye injury!' he yells. Even so, he gives Breuer a shove that propels him into the midst of the little cluster of chosen ones. The major's approach, on the other hand, is to have a word on the q.t. with the officer. He must have a silver tongue, because he too finds himself joining the select ranks of passengers. The crowd of men who have been passed over seethe and yell angrily.

Darkness starts to fall. To the north, artillery fire lights up the milky sky with red flashes. The plane is still circling overhead. The pilot has switched on his navigation lights. He seems to be having second thoughts about landing. Little wonder; if he crash-lands, then he and his crew will be caught in the mousetrap, too. Suddenly, a small parachute drops from the fuselage and begins its slow, rocking descent. A few solid objects also plummet to earth, where the guard detail immediately pounces on them. The aircraft makes one final turn before disappearing into the gathering gloom.

Anger, disappointment and rancour seep through the waiting crowd. Their pent-up fury threatens to break over the head of the dispatch officer. He spots the danger in time and seeks to head it off.

'Hey, just hold your horses there!' he croaks. 'There'll be plenty more planes along! Lots more are on their way! See? There's another one already!'

It's true; somewhere in the sea of grey cloud a new droning noise can be heard. The aircraft begins to corkscrew down. Is this one going to land? Yes, it's dropping all the time – no, wait a minute – yes, yes, it's touched down, a textbook landing on the rapidly darkening airfield. The engines are throttled back and tick over lazily; the big bird waits there, shuddering, ready to take off again and depart at any moment. The doors fly open and the ladder shoots down; a few provisions are unloaded, and then the crew, like cats on a hot tin roof, are urging everyone to hurry it up. To a man, the twelve chosen ones are seized by a terror of being left behind. They lunge forward to the plane like shipwrecked men grasping at lifeboats, pushing and shoving to be the first to board. Reason dictates that every one of them is certain of a seat. But reason flies out of the window at times like this! The dispatch officer couldn't care less about the mayhem; he's done his duty, and the ones left behind are causing him enough headaches as it is.

Breuer finds himself trapped in a tangle of shouting people and is crushed against the short set of steps up to the plane.

'Go on, go on!' urges the major from behind. He can already see into the plane's cabin through the legs of the man who's gone before him, and looks directly into the face of the radio operator…

Then something unforeseen occurs. Something truly absurd, a horrible twist of fate. It happens so fast, in a split second, that, even when he looks back on it later, Breuer can never fully fathom quite what happened. With his impaired vision, did he perhaps miss his footing on the smooth metal steps of the ladder? Or was the furious red face of the radio operator to blame for the whole incident – that face whose passing resemblance to Wiese's caused him to hesitate momentarily? And did that brief hesitation of his prompt the swearing major to shove him in the side? Or was he simply overcome by a fit of giddiness? Or maybe his nerves failed him in the final, critical moment? Perhaps his body had somehow instinctively refused to carry out the instructions it was being given by a none-too-certain will?

By the time the slipstream from the propellers rouses him from where he is lying on the ground – he had fallen hard, hitting his chin on the metal steps and presumably knocking himself out for a few moments – it is too late. No one takes any notice of him. The ladder has long since been pulled up, the door closed, and the plane is lumbering off down the airstrip, clumsy as a fleeing chicken. Off to one side, the crowd of men left behind are still roaring and bellowing.

Unnoticed by them (their self-interest leaves them no time or inclination for mockery or scorn), Breuer stands there and watches the plane recede into the distance. Dazed, he feels his bruised limbs. His sick pass is lying at his feet. And as he bends down to pick it up, he suddenly realizes that there's no point now. There was no repairing the damage. No more planes were going to land in Stalingrad. A decision had been made, and it was irrevocable…

Despair rages through Breuer's brain like a centrifuge that threatens any minute to reduce his body to atoms. Hot blood surges through his head and limbs, and the dizzying whirl forces clear thoughts and feelings to the surface once more. And suddenly an image reappears that had been erased during the last few hours of high emotion. This image grows ever clearer and firmer and becomes, so to speak, the axis around which everything else rotates: it is the picture of his dying friend in a snow hole in Gumrak. And he knows now for sure that there is no way back!

Little by little he calms down, until finally there is nothing left except an infinite expanse of emptiness. It is as if all the hopes and yearnings that were rekindled over the preceding hours – indeed, as if everything that once existed – have flown away for ever with that last aircraft. What does he actually want? He knows the truth – yes, deep in his heart he's known it for a long time: there's no way back now! The only way is forward. Who can say where that road leads? Into darkness, into the unknown. And maybe also into humiliation and self-sacrifice. And perhaps also – no, definitely – to death. But what did that matter? Let the twenty-fourth of the month claim its victim after all! To him that's not the bogeyman it once was; its sting has been drawn. And even his death here in the killing fields around Stalingrad will ultimately have a point: a fitting conclusion to a misguided life. And what if he doesn't die? Well, that would also have a purpose that would one day become apparent… Breuer firmly believes that his fate will have a meaning one way or another.

Darkness is already falling. Shells are falling on the airfield with increasing frequency. To the north, the reddish glow of the barrage, shot through every now and then with bright flashes and accompanied by the faint noise of fighting, swells up ever more clearly and ominously. The dispatch officer is nowhere to be seen. Yet the throng of waiting men keeps pushing and shoving amid sporadic yells and outbreaks of violent anger. Breuer stumbles over a kitbag half-buried in the snow. He picks it up. It contains nothing edible, only socks and some other clothes. Breuer takes it all the same. These things have a purpose once more. He walks unconcernedly past the seething mob. As he passes, he picks up snatches of conversation.

'Of course!' – 'He said so!' – 'Nothing else is coming! It's a load of bollocks, as usual!' – 'What if I tell you fifty Ju 52s are supposed to be arriving this evening?' – 'Then you don't need to keep pushing like that, do you?'

Someone tumbles over in front of Breuer. He grabs hold of the fallen man to pull him to his feet. Someone else comes over to help.

'Lieutenant, sir!' the other soldier urges the man who's tripped. 'Don't give up, Lieutenant! Not now we've made it so far!'

Breuer's gaze is transfixed by the lieutenant's felt boots; slowly he raises his eyes to the man's face. My God, yes, it really is him!

'Dierk!' he shouts, grabbing the officer's shoulders.

'Dierk, lad, it's me!

But his young comrade is all in. His head is lolling helplessly this way and that and he seems incapable of speaking. 'Come on!' Breuer quietly tells the man who seems to know the lieutenant. 'There's no point hanging round here any more… We need to get to Stalingrad!'

The man looks at him, dumbfounded.

'But… you mean…'

'See for yourself!' Breuer jerks his head in the direction of the red glow of the artillery barrage to the north.

They carry the lieutenant under his armpits and drag him towards the road. On the right stands the truck with the airdropped supplies. At that moment, someone rushes up and whispers something to the two sentries guarding it. They shoulder their rifles and disappear at the double, leaving the lorry and its cargo unattended.

The other soldier assisting Dierk wastes no time in clambering up into the lorry, where he starts throwing down tins of food and wrapped loaves of bread. Breuer stuffs the kitbag and his wide greatcoat pockets full of provisions. It's clear that Dierk is really out of it. He's dragging his legs like a cripple. The main road lies just ahead; they can hear the sound of passing cars and lorries. Breuer casts one final glance back at the airfield. It has vanished, swallowed up in the darkness. The only thing still visible, in the far distance, is the noisy, churning mob of waiting men, sharply silhouetted against the blood-red, flickering skyline. What are they waiting for? For a miracle! Their own personal miracle – the fifty Ju 52s that are rumoured to be on their way.

It's less of a troop detachment and more of a ragtag bunch of helpless, destitute individuals that has found its way to the village of Gumrak from the abandoned airfield there. Anyone still motivated by fear or hope has tagged along – men from the pioneer battalion, from Fackelmann's task force and various other troops who have become separated from their units or been wounded. The others have stayed behind, including the old major who'd once been a technical college professor.

'No, no, you go on!' he'd told Fröhlich, on the verge of tears. 'Anyone who's able to should get out now. I'm stopping here. I've had enough, come what may. It's a damned disgrace! To go and betray us like that! Oh, that devil, that bloody devil!'

The little group disperses in Gumrak, merging into the general stream of retreating troops. Fröhlich's sense of responsibility and leadership urge have quickly evaporated, and only a grim, unfocused rage drives him on. With his collar turned up, Breuer's machine-pistol slung over his back, and his head lowered like a bull's against the driving snowflakes, he tramps ahead; scarcely noticed by him, Herbert and Geibel trot along in his wake like loyal dogs. In his determined stride they can scent a purpose that he himself is unaware of.

Muzzle flares from artillery fire can be seen all around. Mysterious shadows flit sideways through the grey mist. Occasionally there comes the sound of gunfire; no one knows who's shooting, or at whom. Here and there, one of the retreating troops drops silently and unnoticed into the snow. Sometimes shells land nearby, spraying out blood and flame, and with each impact a handful of men are swept from the road. Stolidly, the rest press on through the screaming, moaning and gurgling of the mortally wounded. No one bothers throwing themselves to the ground any more as the projectiles come whistling in. It's no longer worth the trouble.

Geibel has been limping for a while. He stops and clings on to Herbert's arm. His face is a dirty yellow hue.

'Herbert, mate... I think I've copped one!'

He wipes his hand on his trousers, and looks at the blood on his fingers with childlike wonder. His lower lip trembles. Together they squat down at the roadside and Fröhlich takes a look at the private's injuries. A bullet wound in the upper thigh. Herbert pulls out a grubby handkerchief and ties it round the wound with a bootlace. There's nothing more he can do.

After just a few steps, it's obvious that he can't continue on foot any more. Just ahead of them are the trailers of a signals unit. Maybe he can hitch a ride with them. Suddenly, very close at hand, thunderous blasts rend the air. 'Tanks! Tanks!' Vehicles sound their horns in alarm and crash into one another as a crazy chorus of shouts goes up. Everyone is energized by the warning cry of 'Tanks!' The road becomes a raging, roaring, tumbling torrent. The signals troops, their faces frozen in fear, throw away their rifles and ammunition belts, tear off their bulky fur jackets and run for all they're worth. Their CO shouts himself hoarse trying to call them back, but all in vain.

Clanking shadows appear in the foggy dusk. Fröhlich has crawled beneath one of the abandoned trucks on the road. He is beside himself with fury. He'd like nothing better than to settle scores with Nasarov and with the Russians in general. He's a Baltic German, after all...

A tank rumbles up, a T-34. It doesn't open fire. A figure in white winter camouflage is standing up in the turret, waving his cap and calling, 'Churman soldier, come, come!'

Fröhlich yanks the machine-pistol into firing position, takes careful aim and with gritted teeth pulls the trigger. *Bratatatatat…* the man in the turret stiffens, his voice dies in his throat and he sinks slowly down through the hatch. As the tank rattles by, only his limp hand is still sticking out, waving to and fro as if in farewell. The cap falls from his hand and rolls into the road.

'Got you, you fucking dog!' growls Fröhlich, completely unmoved by the Russian's apparently friendly intentions. Cautiously he pokes his head out from under the lorry. The tanks have veered off to the left. They have forced the fleeing Germans to leave the road and are driving them across the steppe into the thickening fog. Fröhlich crawls out from his hiding place. He kicks the Russian's cap aside and strides over to the signals vehicles. A driver is trying to get the coughing engine of one of the lorries to turn over. A knot of distraught men has gathered round. Herbert is just helping the shaking Geibel up onto the truck. Fröhlich climbs aboard too. His good mood has returned.

'Ha, we really stuck it to 'em, eh?' he brags. 'Pack of bloody filthy swine! Thought they had us in the bag here, didn't they? Ha! We can still show 'em a thing or two! Specially when we're properly dug in in Stalingrad, right?'

The others don't respond. They've found a sack of wheat on the lorry and are busy chewing the hard grains with grinding teeth. Finally the engine roars into life. The driver steps on the accelerator and crashes through the gears, sending the heavy vehicle on a wild, hurtling course down the highway.

The fog grew ever denser as the night set in. The route along which the long column of fleeing men was slowly and haltingly making its way through powdery snow entered uncharted territory. Again, for the umpteenth time, Breuer stopped to wipe the sweat from his burning face. A raging fever was thumping and hammering away in his head and sending black waves of migraine across his field of vision. The bulging pockets of his army greatcoat tugged down on his shoulders like lead weights. Would this march never end? They must have been underway for an eternity already and put countless kilometres behind them. With no destination in sight, nowhere to call home (even a foxhole would do!) and cast adrift from everything that had gone before, if he had been alone in the hostile winter night he would probably have thrown himself down in the snow, never to rise again. But he wasn't alone. He and the corporal were supporting the wounded, listless Lieutenant Dierk. Breuer himself had no idea what possessed him, at this desperate time when every man scarcely had enough strength to save his own skin, to drag this broken and clearly half-dead man through the night. Perhaps it was just the dread of loneliness that drew living creatures to one another.

'Come on, Lieutenant, sir!' urged Corporal Görz (he had, in the meantime, introduced himself to Breuer). 'It can't be far now. And we'll be bound to find somewhere we can doss down. Especially with our bag of goodies…'

He triumphantly brandished the kitbag of provisions he was carrying. The two men took a firmer grip under the lieutenant's armpits and pressed on.

A procession of vehicles – three or four cars and a lorry, all keeping a sensible distance and in good order – was inching its way past others that had ground to a halt and got wedged against one another. An officer was supervising the tricky and dangerous operation.

'Steer left! … Left, I said! I suggest you stick your nose out of the car so you can see where you're going, you halfwit!'

Breuer stopped. The voice struck him as familiar.

'Von Horn?'

The man he'd addressed turned round and walked over, bringing his blond-bearded face close to that of the questioner. A monocle flashed at Breuer. He couldn't suppress a smile. A monocle – amid all this chaos? Oh well, why not! It was some people's way of keeping things in order.

'Ah, Breuer, it's you!' The officer's voice sounded clear and fresh. 'This is all a bit of a closing-down sale, eh?'

'Where are you off to?'

'Why, to the municipal theatre of Stalingrad, of course! It's where all the best people are headed, don't you know? The curtain's about to go up on the final performance there!'

'Can you take us with you?' Breuer asked.

But the Tank Corps adjutant had already leaped onto the running board of the last car and vanished like a shadow in the night.

They must have struggled on about another kilometre when Breuer stopped again. He tried to peer through the fog that was shrouding the road and growing denser by the minute. 'Look over there!' he shouted. 'Aren't those houses?'

Corporal Görz cast a sceptical glance over at the vague dark shapes in the grey wall of fog. 'Come on, Lieutenant, sir!' he replied. 'The city can't be far off now, honestly!'

'No, we can't go on – it's too much. Just look at him, will you?'

Dierk was hanging limply from the shoulders of his helpers. His breath was coming in choking gasps. They wouldn't get much further with him in that condition. The corporal recognized that too. They turned off the road and made for the dark something, which began to emerge more clearly from the surrounding grey as they drew nearer. Indeed, it was a house – actually, more of an unprepossessing log cabin whose windows and doors were boarded up. The corporal knocked, but the house remained lifeless and silent. Should they break in? – A short way off, there seemed to be another house. It was dark and shuttered like the first. But here they could smell smoke and feel some warmth, and through the gaps in the boarded windows they made out chinks of light. Breuer tugged at the door, which was bolted from the inside. 'Open up!' he shouted.

Nothing stirred. He banged his fists against the boarded windows and kicked so hard at the door that the wood began to splinter.

'Open up! Open up!!'

Inside, a door banged. There came the sound of whispering voices and faint footsteps were heard approaching the front door. In the freezing air, the mist of someone's breath came out through the gaps in the boards.

'Open up, God damn it! We're German officers! … Open up or we'll blow the place to pieces!'

Hesitantly, the bolt was slid back. Breuer pushed open the door. In the darkness, he could discern what looked like the figure of a woman, and behind her another person; stumbling over clutter, he entered a kitchen. Behind him, the corporal dragged the lieutenant in.

The kitchen was bright and full of soldiers – men just like the thousands who were roaming around the fields out there. Some were sitting there still wearing their greatcoats or with bandages wrapped round their heads, while others were busy unwinding the stinking rags from round their feet or warming themselves and brewing tea at the hot cooking range. In among them were some others, clean-shaven, with clean clothes and the pale faces of people who spent their time indoors – evidently the occupants of the house. A wizened *babushka* was pottering about at the stove. She was the first woman Breuer had set eyes on in the Cauldron, just as this was the first house in it that he had stepped inside. Seeing that they were officers, she obligingly pushed open the door to the adjoining room. Görz and Breuer stared open-mouthed at the brightly lit scene that met their eyes. A table laid with a blue woollen cloth, a red plush sofa, two beds piled high with cushions, some dusty pot plants and walls covered with faded framed photographs and matt-gold icons. As they entered the parlour, a girl, barely twenty, with shining black hair and a broad, fresh face, flitted past them with an anxious yet inquisitive expression, trailing behind her a waft of cheap perfume. The whole scene was as improbable as an absurd dream, but at the same time exhilarating in its unquestionable reality.

A corporal, clearly taken aback by their intrusion, got up from the sofa.

'These are staff quarters!' he said, in an unmistakably Slavic accent. Breuer flopped down on the sofa.

'Sorry, old chap! Looks like you're going to have to make room for the three of us.'

All of a sudden, he felt unburdened and relieved. But he was also well aware of how deceptive this enchanted picture of cosiness and security really was.

The corporal did not get up again to make any further trouble; he could see that he was outranked. Breuer set about piling up the contents of his pockets on the table, while Görz, without more ado, laid the semi-conscious lieutenant down on one of the beds. At the sight of the cans of food and the loaves, the corporal's face brightened considerably. He was visibly relieved. As Breuer was getting comfortable on the sofa, a rosy-cheeked NCO came in with another girl. They were chatting away intimately in some Slavic language or other. The mystery of this place and its occupants was soon explained. They had stumbled upon the staff office of a Croatian artillery regiment, which was attached to a German infantry division fighting on the Volga front. Breuer now recalled having seen a lorry out on the road with the familiar insignia of that division: a stylized fir tree with a line through the crown and an 'S' beside it. The troops had reinterpreted this ingenious rebus* – which was meant to represent the name of the division's commanding officer, General Sanne – in their own inimitable way: the division was commonly known as 'Shit in the Woods'.

'You're in clover here, aren't you?' Breuer said to the newcomer, as he took one of the pre-sliced loaves from its tinfoil wrapping. The Croatian NCO smiled sheepishly but dismissively at the suggestion. Görz emptied out some braised tinned meat into a billycan lid. They tucked in and talked about the day's events.

---

* 'this ingenious rebus' – the German word for a fir tree is *Tanne*; replacing the first letter with an 'S' gives 'Sanne', the commander's name.

'Things are going to get pretty nasty here too, and fast!' reckoned Breuer. 'The Russians aren't far away. The airfield at Stalingradski's already been evacuated.'

The Croatian's eyes widened. They clearly had no idea what was coming. His conversation dried up and after a short while he got up and left. The old woman brought in a steaming samovar. Görz gave the lieutenant, who was awake but clearly unaware of where he was, a few sips of tea, talking comfortingly like a mother to him as he did so.

'Hit in the arm by a shell burst,' he explained in response to Breuer's enquiry. 'Plus he got shot clean through the upper right thigh – and the frostbite on his feet is really bad… And now it looks like he's got brain damage as well…'

He tucked the lieutenant in and then went to make up a bed for himself on the floor, where the Croatian NCO was also planning to bunk down. Breuer took the sofa, while the Croatian corporal occupied the second bed. After the light had been turned out, one of the girls came in and joined him, whispering and giggling. Despite being dog-tired, Breuer slept fitfully on his strangely soft bed. He was repeatedly disturbed by the couple's canoodlings and by Dierk's heavy breathing. At length, he sank into a leaden state of oblivion.

After several hours, at around four in the morning, he was rudely awoken by the sound of people crashing about and agitated voices. The Croatians had put all their boxes of paperwork on the ground and were rummaging through them by candlelight. The girls were standing over them, crying.

'Hey, what's going on?' The corporal raised his worried face.

'General alarm,' he replied in a subdued tone. 'All combat units to the front, and the staffs and clerical units to central Stalingrad!'

'Right, we should hit the road again then, too!' said Breuer briskly, pulling on his boots.

Görz had already brewed coffee and made up some sandwiches. Now he went to rouse Dierk. The rest had clearly done the lieutenant good; he was able to sit up at table and eat something. After nodding briefly to Breuer, he stared ahead with an expressionless face. It wasn't clear whether he had actually recognized him.

After a generous breakfast, the three men set off, rested and fortified, and with the girls' laments and the muted oaths of the busily packing Croatians ringing in their ears. The farce was at an end and the tragedy was about to unfold.

6

Die – And Rise Again!

THE TRACK THEY WERE on turned into a road. Through its patchy shroud of snow shone the steely sheen of ice. The group of fleeing soldiers had become ragged and strung out. Here and there, an exhausted cluster of stragglers limped along, as the odd vehicle sped by, heading for the city. To the side of the road stood signposted bunkers, silent and abandoned, along with the roofless ruins of humble little dwellings and overgrown gardens with black trees whose shredded crowns were lost in the fog.

Pulling the small toboggan that he'd scrounged from the Croatians, Corporal Görz was always some way ahead of his two companions. Of the three of them, he was the most robust. Breuer could feel the exertions of the past few days in his limbs. His injury was also hurting badly again. After their abrupt departure from the Croatians' house, the feeling that they had been abandoned hit him once more with redoubled force. Things had become rather different since yesterday. His surroundings, which the vision through his one good eye made into a surface lacking any depth, appeared strangely altered. Sure, he was still in the midst of the same wretched figures, but the connections between people and things seemed to have changed. It was all different, totally different…

Breuer shot a sideways glance at the lieutenant, who was tottering along next to him on his frostbitten legs with a gait that looked like he was walking on stilts. He had rallied overnight and with mute determination had refused all offers of help. He was still refusing to speak, maintaining a horribly frosty silence.

Nothing about him recalled the enthusiastic young officer of former times. His face resembled a cratered field after a battle. Suddenly overcome with emotion, Breuer caught hold of Dierk's arm.

'Dierk, old son! What's got into you? Talk to us, for God's sake!'

And at the same time, he was thinking: What's got into all of us, for that matter? The lieutenant turned his face towards Breuer for a fleeting instant. His blank expression dismissed the query out of hand. What's got into us…? Breuer tried to summon up images from the past: his study at home, the green chair with the standard lamp beside it, in whose warm light he used to sit and read; the faces of his wife and children; that last pleasure-boat trip to the sand dunes of the Curonian Spit, just a few days before he'd been called up to take part in a 'short-term exercise', which in the event had turned out to be endless. It was no good. Everything had become pallid and blurry in his memory. The world as it existed before the war had been extinguished; he could only dimly discern its outlines like he was peering through a veil. He could not understand how, just a short while ago (had it been the day before yesterday? Or yesterday?), he had been looking forward so excitedly to breaking free and flying out of the Cauldron. Where had he planned to go? There was no going back now. How had it come to this? Had that Breuer from the past, whose death date Schoolmaster Strackwitz had foretold, actually died in the night before the twenty-fourth? It almost seemed to be so. Maybe that upstanding, amenable Breuer, who was so well grounded in considerate middle-class respectability, really had perished along with everything that he thought, believed in, held dear and longed for. What remained was an empty vessel devoid of hope, inured to pain, and containing nothing but a hollow, boundless emptiness.

'I do not dream of past happiness…' No, he didn't dream of anything any more. Had it even warranted the name of happiness, that complacent, superficial day-to-day existence, only disturbed now and then by the mild irritation of childish worries, where you just let yourself drift along like you were immersed in a warm, soporific stream? Hadn't it all been just self-deception, a grand illusion whose inevitable and logical conclusion was the dreadful unmasking of Stalingrad? A cruel hand had swept across the board and in a stroke wiped away the cheerful signs of a false happiness. All that was left behind was the empty blackboard. Would new signs ever appear on it one day, pointing towards a new future?

'Nice of them to let us know, eh?' said Corporal Görz, pointing at a large sign by the side of the road. On it was the warning: 'Attention! Road under enemy surveillance! Don't drive in groups!' The road into Stalingrad they were on was situated on high ground. In clear conditions it must have been visible from the far bank of the Volga. Now only the odd shell whistled aimlessly overhead. The few small houses on the city outskirts here that still offered any kind of shelter were crammed with people, while thousands of others still roamed the streets, leaderless and milling about in all directions. If the Russians had been in a position to send over a squadron of bombers…

The three of them found themselves standing on the lip of the Zariza Gorge. In among the snow and the debris and rubbish scattered about, the entrances to caves yawned blackly in its steep slopes. Crowds of men had gathered there too. Where could they find some shelter? Or were they fated to die out in the open, like so many before them? Clambering over the ruins of a wooden shack that had been knocked down, Breuer came across a flight of steps leading underground. A murmur of voices was coming from below. They descended the winding steps cut into the earth to a barricaded plank door. The corporal started kicking it.

'Open up!' he bellowed. 'German officers!'

The voices fell silent within. Then they heard, clearly and unmistakably, someone respond with the infamous line from *Götz von Berlichingen*.* This stung Görz into a fit of fury.

'You bunch of fuckers!' he yelled. 'Open up right now or I'll—'

Breuer restrained him.

'Come on!' he said. 'Just leave it. None of that stuff cuts any ice any more.'

Weary and despondent, they dragged themselves back to the main road that led to the city centre. As the day had progressed, more and more people had joined the throng there. Now, in between the wooden houses, the odd tall stone building had begun to appear. Yet on closer inspection these turned out to be nothing more than the façades of houses, behind which stood huge piles of rubble. And the specimens of humanity wandering about there over the bomb debris, through the tangles of barbed wire and past burned-out tramcars – they, too, were nothing but ghostly reflections of people: masks, façades hiding piles of wreckage…

'Where… where's the ho-… ho-… hospital, then?' said a beaky figure, thrusting his bird-like face at Breuer. He was hobbling along, propping himself up on a home-made cudgel, and with huge bundles of rags tied round his feet. A greatcoat that was far too large for him hung off him like a sack. Hunched over, with twisted limbs and convulsed by an uncontrollable shaking, he looked like a witch from a fairy tale.

'A hospital? Sorry, I don't know if there is such a thing round here,' Breuer answered.

And while he was still mulling over this strange encounter, someone in the crowd said something about the 'District Commander's Office'. Of course. How could he have forgotten? The

---

* 'the infamous line from *Götz von Berlichingen*' – the line in question comes from Act 3 of Goethe's 1773 debut play, when the eponymous hero says: '*Er aber, sag's ihm er kann mich im Arsche lecken!*' ('As for him, tell him he can kiss my arse!')

headquarters of the commander of the Central Stalingrad district! The phrase, which immediately conjured up images of German order and efficiency, had a magic effect on those who heard it. Their faces lit up. Of course, the Stalingrad DCO was the responsible authority here. It'd do something to help them, surely!

As a lorry towing a flak-gun limber passed, Breuer and Görz hoisted the lieutenant onto it and swung themselves up after him. No one shooed them off. The truck trundled down the street into the city. When it halted briefly at a road junction, they hopped off. A sign with the letters DCO on it pointed them to the left. Yes indeed, order evidently still prevailed here, thank goodness! From a way off they could make out an imposing building, which must have been about five storeys tall, standing out from the ruins around it and looking remarkably intact.

Two soldiers were walking towards them. Their eyes were shining.

'Have you heard, Lieutenant, sir?' one of them called. 'The advance guard of our tank divisions has entered Karpovka!'

'Yes, yes, we heard about that!' replied Breuer, waving them aside.

There was no point trying to reason with madmen. But that went against the grain with the corporal. 'Hey, you two, hold it right there!' he ordered, beckoning them to approach. 'You blokes lost your tiny minds or something? Don't you dare go spreading rumours like that around, d'you hear?'

'But it's true!' wailed the man who'd spoken, incensed by the corporal's harsh tone and lack of faith. 'We just heard about it at the District Commander's Office, ain't that right, Georgie boy? Straight from the captain's mouth! The news just came through!'

In no time at all, a circle of stupid, credulous faces had formed round the little group. The second soldier nodded in affirmation.

'Two SS Panzer divisions have broken through!' he went on, waving his hands about in excitement.

'It'll only be a matter of hours before they get here! We ought to spread the news round town!'

For a few moments, Breuer felt his heart beating faster. Could it be true? They hadn't heard anything from the front for days… But then he laughed inwardly at his own foolishness. What did he care?

A crowd of hundreds was gathered outside the commander's office. The rumour was doing the rounds there too. Groups of men began peeling off in all directions. Over the entrance to the courtyard hung neatly painted signs with instructions for men going on leave and men looking for their quarters. Oh yes, order still reigned here, all right! The three men squeezed their way into the overcrowded inner courtyard. The entrance to the building proper was cordoned off with wooden barriers, and guarded by military police with steel helmets, gorgets and rifles. Breuer pushed his way through to ask one of the policemen if they were taking in wounded men.

'Not now – come back in about two hours!' came the brisk, indifferent answer. 'We're just in the process of, ah… reorganizing.'

'Reorganizing, eh?' Breuer glanced up at the windows of the building.

'There's word that tanks have reached Karpovka. You heard anything about that?'

The man looked askance at the lieutenant.

'Yeah, rumour has it!' he growled.

'From what I hear, that rumour started right here!'

'Well, don't go looking at us, mate! We don't know anything about it!'

Breuer turned away in disgust. So that was how it was, was it? Some people were being fobbed off with talk of 'reorganization' while others were being fed the line about 'tanks in Karpovka'. Their sole concern was to get people off their backs by telling them what they wanted to hear. No, there really was nothing to beat German efficiency!

★

The multistorey stone edifice of the Central Stalingrad District Commander's Office, a modern apartment and office block with central heating and toilets that was visible for miles around, had in all probability once been intended to be the proud seat of a powerful regional administration. But that had never come to pass.

The institution of the District Commander's Office, which in fact consisted of nothing more than a handful of military police, a general heading the outfit who was no longer fit for any other duties, and a few officers, had set up operations in the basement of the building, safe from bombardment. The far less secure storeys above ground, however, had been swamped – long before the great flood of troops retreating to the city had begun – by wounded, sick and displaced soldiers seeking a final refuge there.

It is night. Huddled up close together, Herbert and Geibel are hunkered down on the stone floor of a gloomy corridor. The signals lorry set them down outside the DCO building. They were turned away by the guards but managed to gain access through a badly secured back door. The cold is preventing them from sleeping. Geibel is moaning from the pain of his wounded leg.

As soon as it gets light, Herbert goes off to explore their new surroundings. The corridors and stairs of the building are filthy and full of rubbish, while the icy toilets are stalactite caves of frozen excrement and urine. The pungent stench of a wild animal's cage wafts towards him out of the dark, crowded rooms… Herbert realizes that he has a lot to learn about Stalingrad. A whirling sensation in his head threatens to overpower him. His knees buckle and he has to lean against a doorpost. 'Oh my God,' he stammers to himself. 'Oh my God…'

'What's up with you, then, eh?'

Herbert looks up. To his right, squatting against the wall of the dimly lit room amid a tangle of sleeping men and blankets, is a soldier. On his head is a Romanian lambskin hat, pulled so low it squashes his ears down. He looks like some venerable gnome who's been sitting there for a hundred years. He looks at Herbert through a pair of curiously lively squirrel's eyes.

'What's wrong?' the gnome persists. 'Got the collywobbles, have you? Or the runs?'

'What, me?' mutters Herbert, peering into the room. 'Nothing wrong with me. But…'

'What, nothing?' says the man. 'Nothing at all? A picture of health, eh?'

His little eyes widen with astonishment as he says this. Herbert imagines it's how Red Indians must have looked at the first white people.

'Then you can stay here!' the gnome blurts out, clapping his hands like a delighted child. No sooner has he said it, though, than his voice becomes tearful.

'There's no one here to look after us! We haven't had anything to drink since yesterday… We had one bloke here, he was almost completely healthy like you. Just his left hand and his ears lost to frostbite. He used to go down and bring us up some snow. But yesterday he went out and never came back…'

Herbert drags Geibel up the two floors and deposits him, for the time being, by the door. The cold night spent on the flagstones has just about done for him. His teeth are chattering incessantly.

'Herbert, mate,' he moans, 'I think the bone's broken after all!'

Herbert takes a look at the wound. Geibel's heavily bloodstained, encrusted trousers are stuck fast to his leg. It proves impossible to pull them down. The gnome looks on with interest. He seems contented that at least one of the newcomers has 'copped one'.

'You could do with a bit more light on the subject,' he says. 'All you need to do is take those two planks off the window over there and we'll make a fire to keep the place warm… We've had fires going here a few times before. But then they start to smoke the place out. Look, we just need to get those boards down… I'll give you a hand. But I can't be bending down.'

Herbert creates 'a bit more light'. Cold, fresh air rushes through the opening into the miasma in the room. Only now does he have a clear view of his surroundings. There are around fifteen men lying in the two-windowed room. On the other hand, it's quiet, uncannily quiet. Just that one guy over there… he's lying on his back, with his ivory-coloured face, tinged with bluish shadows, looking up at the ceiling. His large, black-rimmed eyes are rolled up into his head, showing the whites. The only thing moving – incessantly – is his spittle-wet mouth. He's babbling away incoherently to himself, apparently having a heated conversation with someone, and between whiles he utters a fleeting laugh or hums snatches of songs. Then there's a lieutenant with his left arm missing, who's sitting with his back against the wall. His right hand keeps a tight hold on the stump, which is wrapped in bloody rags, like he's fearful that even this pitiful remnant might also fall off. His upper body sways back and forth in a regular pendulum motion. Every time he rocks forward, his thick mop of hair flops into his face, and he moans softly and wheezily through his mouth and nose. Whenever the chirpy gnome pipes down, these are the only sounds in the room. In any event, the man over by the window wearing an *Organisation Todt** uniform keeps working away in silence. He looks to be in his fifties; the stubble on his lined face has already turned white. He's stretched his legs out in front of himself and his naked feet are blue with cold. On his knees is a coat, which he's busy cutting up into strips of a hand's width each with a small pair of scissors; he works away industriously, sunk in thought. Every so often he stops and

---

* *Organisation Todt* – a civil and military engineering organization in Nazi Germany. It was responsible for large-scale civil engineering projects in pre-war Germany, such as the construction of the early autobahns. It became notorious for the use of slave labour during the Second World War. When it is mentioned later in this chapter with the comment in parenthesis 'the name says it all!', this is a pun on the name of the organization; it was named after its founder Fritz Todt, but *Tod* in German also means 'death'.

holds up one of the strips to the light with a satisfied smile... The rest of the men lie there motionless, only distinguishable from the three dead bodies in the room by the fact that they are no longer covered by blankets or coats. The whole scene is one of gruesome unreality. Even the gnome perched on his pile of coats like an overseer doesn't seem to regard his comrades in the room as living beings any more. He follows Herbert's horrified gaze with the unassuming pride of a fairground sideshow proprietor presenting his freaks. Yet his face suddenly grows sharp and tense when Herbert turns to a soldier who is lying a little apart from the others. He's still a boy, around nineteen or twenty years old perhaps. He's lying there with his hands folded on his chest and smiling so sweetly that he could be dreaming on a summer meadow in the sunshine. In actual fact, what he's lying on is a grey blanket; but it's a strange, coarse-grained grey. It looks like a thick sheet of waterproofing. As Herbert bends down to take a closer look, the realization suddenly hits him: the grey surface is alive! Lice – hundreds and thousands of lice! 'Remarkable, eh?' says the gnome. 'There's not a single one left on him or his clothes. And when he arrived here, he was teeming with the things. Made him look like he had mildew... Then in the blink of an eye, they all migrated. Did you ever see such a thing!'

Herbert feels his gorge rising.

'There was a time when they could all walk,' the gnome continues. 'But then they started bringing up a few invalids, too. And then the ones that were still mobile cleared off 'cos there was no food left. So, the first thing we need to do now is get those three out of here. Then you can go and fetch some snow! I can't bend down, see...'

Propping himself against the wall, he painfully straightens up and with stiff legs gingerly extricates himself from the coats and blankets. He really is very small, a whole head shorter than Herbert even with the fur hat on. Herbert doesn't notice that, though. He's transfixed by the man's feet. They're in a pair of black jackboots that have had the toecaps neatly cut off, and his toes are sticking out.

No, wait a minute, it's not his toes, but a row of white bones framed in a blue-black mass of something! … The gnome follows Herbert's gaze, looking lovingly and wistfully at his putrefying feet. Even they, it seems, are part of his cabinet of curiosities.

'Before,' he says, nodding down at them, 'when they still hurt, I kept rags tied round 'em and bundles of straw. But now they don't hurt at all, not in the slightest in fact. Only my legs and knees are giving me gyp now. So I don't need to keep changing the rags on my feet any more. Quite practical really, eh?'

They drag the three dead men out by their feet into the corridor. The gnome says he reckons they won't decay in the cold out there. Then Herbert goes down to collect some snow. In the meantime, the gnome lights an open fire in the middle of the room. Acrid smoke billows out of the door.

'I… I've got… some wheat grains here,' coughs Herbert. 'But it's… it's not enough to go around everybody.'

'No problem,' says the gnome. 'All they want is water.'

They sit round the smoking fire, using one hand to dangle mess tins with the wheat in them on sticks over the flames while wiping their streaming eyes with the other.

There's another dreadful incident during the night. A shot rings out. Herbert gives a start, and then feels something warm dripping on him and trickling down. He shouts in alarm and struggles free from where he was wedged sleeping, lashing out all around in fear as he does so. But there's nothing to be seen. So he curls up in a ball and lies there trembling and wide awake until dawn breaks. Then he sees what happened. The lieutenant with the stump of an arm has blown his brains out by putting a gun in his mouth. He's lying slumped forward on his face. The back of his head is missing.

Lieutenant Dierk was asleep on the ground in a free corner. The other two were sitting against the wall. They, too, were exhausted by the hours they'd spent roaming around. One of the tins of meat had gained them entry to the little house where they now found themselves. It was unbearably hot in the building. The stink of unwashed bodies lay on their chests like a stifling blanket. Around ten Romanians – enlisted men and officers – had spread themselves out in the room. They sat around, lolled over the bare wooden table, and lay or cowered on the floor. Only their eyes were still animated in their otherwise expressionless, dreadfully emaciated faces. Large and black, they smouldered with bitter resentment and hatred. One man was poking the wood fire that had been lit in a tiled stove. A sultry tension hung over the room. Whenever anyone spoke, his words, underscored by jabbing hand gestures, stabbed home like sharp pecks from a bird's beak. Surreptitiously, they kept casting looks of undisguised greed at the bread and tins of food that Görz unpacked from the kitbag.

'We can't stay here,' the corporal told Breuer under his breath. 'In the night, they'll finally work up the courage to do us in.'

From an adjoining room came the sound of someone crying. When the door opened, they could see that the room was full of civilians – men and women of all ages, and children. Children, thought Breuer. How could children be living in this hellhole!

'There's something I've been meaning to ask you all along,' he said to Görz. 'How on earth did Dierk get into that state?'

The corporal shrugged his shoulders and stared at the ground.

'Yeah, I've no idea what's got into him,' he replied. 'I mean, I've only known him for a few days, but in the beginning he was quite different.'

Breuer was astonished.

'What – you mean to say you're not from his platoon?'

'No, I'm from a heavy flak unit. We were stationed at Pitomnik, then later we were transferred to Gumrak. Finally we got involved in the ground fighting there, defending the airfield with our two 88-millimetre guns.'

'You were at Gumrak airfield?' cried Breuer. 'We were there too, in the Gontchara Gorge!'

'Oh, right, we were over on the west side, right out in the open on that flat area, a few hundred metres behind that shot-down Focke-Wulf Condor, if you can remember. That's when Lieutenant Dierk came to us. He'd reported in person to the colonel with his handful of men and their 20-millimetre flak guns. Said he'd come from the west and that his unit had been badly mauled at somewhere-or-other, and so on. Well, of course, the colonel was only too happy to have him on board. Two four-barrelled AA guns, that's not to be sneezed at! … That was on, now let me think … On, hmm… yeah, it was on the nineteenth… That's right, just five days ago… Everything went haywire for us in Gumrak. We were having to deal with up to thirty air raids a day, and that was no easy task with our knackered old guns. And on top of that, there was nothing to eat! The food store was being looted like nobody's business. And there were drumhead courts-martial and firing squads… And then our commanding general just pisses off on a plane one day… You must have heard about that, right? No? Well, I'll tell you all about it some other time.… And then when everyone could see that the game was up, they go and throw us into fighting on the ground. The sighting mechanism on one of our eighty-eights was up the swanny, so the colonel told us to just aim along the barrel. "Doesn't matter," he said. "We've all had it anyway!" That's how desperate things were with us. Everyone was sick to death of the whole business… Anyhow, when the lieutenant turns up – bear in mind he'd already been shot in the arm and contracted frostbite by then – first thing he tries to do is give us a pep talk, going on about "fighting to the last man" and "the whole of Germany's looking at us" and "unswerving loyalty to the Führer" and such. You can imagine, that immediately got him in hot water – "Knight's Cross hunter" and "cheeky little twerp" were some of the politer insults that came his way, sometimes to his face. And in all honesty, it was pretty naive of him to arrive and start strutting around like that. Even so, I dunno what it was, but somehow I couldn't be angry with him. He was different from those standard-issue tub-thumpers, and it was clear he wasn't after medals or personal glory. I saw straight away that he genuinely believed what he said. It was like… yes, like a child who believes in Father Christmas. And even when it slowly dawns on the kid that it's all a fake, he still goes on believing, just because it was such a lovely dream. I'm sure that's how it was with Lieutenant Dierk. And I felt truly sorry for him, 'cos I could see how much it got him down that the lads wanted nothing to do with him. And his own men, who were still minded to defend him, clearly also thought of him as a bit of a dreamer, as a big kid…'

Corporal Görz turned to look at the lieutenant, who was moaning every so often in his fitful sleep. An elderly man dressed in respectable clothing and a girl had come in from the next-door room. Preoccupied with his thoughts, Breuer watched as they leaned against an old sideboard and ate a few seeds from a bowl and spoke quietly to one another. The girl had a black ponytail. Carelessly, she spat out the husks onto the soldiers sleeping on the floor. From time to time, a loud explosion shook the damaged windows. Sporadic disruptive mortar fire – evidently the Russians weren't particularly straining themselves. They knew what the outcome would be.

'So, two days later,' Görz picked up the thread of his story again, 'the Russians advanced on the airfield, about three or four battalions I guess, coming down from the escarpment in march formation. And there we were, with just our two eighty-eights behind a snow bank, right out in the open! Plus a company of infantry in front of us. And they weren't even proper infantry, just blokes from the transport division with a reserve officer in command… At eighteen hundred metres, the Russians fanned out. Three tanks push forward ahead of them to about fifteen hundred metres. Well, we get one of them with the first shot. And the second takes a direct hit as well, from our gun with the buggered sights, what's more! With the second shot, it explodes in flames. But then all hell broke loose! The third tank had got wise to us. Certainly, it was total madness to go taking potshots at armour when you've got no cover or camouflage! Suddenly there's an almighty bang and the barrel flies up and the gun base splits open like… well, like a rosette. The captain of the gun crew and one of the men were killed instantly. And the rest hit in the stomach by shrapnel; they were reeling round the thing like crazy spinning tops, yelling in pain.… Even so, for some reason the attack ground to a halt, and we got a bit of peace and quiet overnight, except for one of the transport boys' machine-gun positions up front, which the Russkis hit three times in succession with anti-tank rounds. The tank we'd hit kept burning all night… When it got light, we could see the enemy were still out there, lying in the same positions. They'd stayed there out in the open the whole night, in freezing temperatures! All these little figures in brown uniforms in the snow, just like on the parade ground. The officers were standing upright behind the lines and using hand signals to point out targets. With the one gun we had left, we destroyed two more tanks. But they still had around eight or ten in total. All of a sudden, there's a massive explosion again. A shell had punched right through the eighty-eight's gun shield, blowing the hands off the man in the direction-finder's seat. He rushes around screaming and flailing about with the bloody stumps. A second shell scores a direct hit on the ammunition pile… So, that was the end of us. And then the cry goes up "Russian breakthrough on the left!" That was where Dierk's second gun was positioned. And it turned out that his crew had gone, just legged it without firing a single shot! I'll never forget the look on the lieutenant's face… But he quickly recovered his composure and shouted "Counter-attack! Follow me!" And he started charging towards the Russians on his knackered legs, with a machine-pistol in his hands. And no one followed, not a single man… It had begun snowing again by this stage, pretty heavily too. I saw him fall flat on his face once. And then we heard him shouting: "Hurra, hurra, hurra…" like some lunatic. The Russians scarcely fired a shot; they must have been too astonished. The rest of our men simply shrugged their shoulders and said "Stupid bastard!" We were really fed up to the back teeth with the whole affair… But it didn't sit right with me. We can't just leave him to die like a dog out there, I thought to myself. I couldn't get that image of his face out of my mind when he learned that his men had just done a bunk. So when night fell I set out with a couple of other men to try to find him, in driving snow. It was no easy task, let me tell you… But finally we tracked him down in one of our old bunkers. He was sitting in a corner with his face buried in his hands. There was a dead Russian in the other corner. On the way back, a sniper got him in the leg and me in the arm. Since then, we haven't been able to get a sensible word out of him… So now' – here the corporal blushed like a schoolgirl – 'I'm hitched to him for keeps. I know it's all nonsense, but… well, I was the one who got him out of there… and he's not much more than a boy, in all honesty… plus it makes things a bit easier for me not to be all on my tod.'

The light was already fading. A Romanian brought in a steaming cauldron with a huge, meatless bone sticking out of it. The others immediately cheered up. With a hoarse cry of joy, they all crowded round the pot, served themselves and then sat cradling mess tins and plates and eagerly slurping down the warm, meaty broth. Breuer's gaze was fixed on the lieutenant, who'd slept undisturbed through all the kerfuffle. In his mind's eye, he could still see the florid face he knew so well of old, glowing with enthusiasm after one of their heated debates. What a terrible change there'd been since then! The poor lad's world must have simply imploded when he saw the truth stripped of the veil of illusion…

What was it that the corporal had also said, though? That it was better not to be all alone at times like this? But what help were people? You could be lonely even in a crowd. Breuer felt alone, quite alone…

★

Sonderführer Fröhlich has been roaming around the city for two days now. He's separated from his comrades. He's not in search of peace and quiet, he's looking for a fight. He wants to engage in a large-scale, heroic battle. The Alcazar* all over again! The Führer's miracle would act as a call to arms to worthy warriors. But Fröhlich never encounters them. All he finds are helpless, nervous superiors yelling at exhausted officers and men, artillery fire from out of the blue, and general disintegration. It's no longer a question of grim hand-to-hand combat and 'seeing the whites of the enemy's eyes'. And looming over everything is this terrible hunger.

Yesterday he hooked up with a captain who'd been trying to find his way back to his division to fight again, with eight other men from his battalion. But in the meantime the battalion had got cut off and was stuck in the northern sector of the Cauldron. And the task force he'd been sent to join instead...

'You want to go into combat? Fine,' the colonel he'd spoken to had told him, 'but I don't have any food for you or your men. You'll have to fend for yourselves.'

Fröhlich certainly had fended for himself. He'd filched a can of fish (though not the last one!) and half a loaf of army bread from the captain and vanished into the night. Hunger is a bad business. You can't be a hero with hunger gnawing at your vitals. Now at least he's over the worst of it. He fetched up with a flak battery, all well-fed, well-equipped lads. And they had food to spare, thank goodness. They're stationed on the outskirts of Stalingrad, protecting the town from the west. Their captain, a square-bashing type, decided

---

* The Alcazar – in a speech on 30 January 1943 in the Sports Palace in Berlin, Hitler made the following statement on Stalingrad: 'Every German will one day speak in solemn awe of this battle, and will recall that, in spite of everything, the foundation of Germany's victory was laid here. They will speak of a Langemarck of daring, *an Alcazar of tenacity*, a Narvik of courage, and a Stalingrad of sacrifice.' The allusion was to the defence of the Alcazar in Toledo by Franco's Nationalist forces during the Spanish Civil War.

to let Fröhlich stay. He can't stand special officers, but when all's said and done a machine-pistol's not to be sneezed at. Weapons are in short supply.

The flak-battery captain has billeted himself in a wooden hut with civilians, after turfing out a couple of soldiers who'd been living there. When he came in they were sitting there, with no weapons, grinding coffee and muttering something about frozen feet. He turned them loose but only in exchange for half their supply of coffee. All sorts of riff-raff were washing about the place, it seemed!

There's an occasional burst of gunfire. But on the whole it's quiet. Somewhere up ahead there's rumoured to be a front. Confusing reports come from the regional Staff HQ, which is located in a flying school. So for the time being all they can do is wait, eat and kill time.

Suddenly the door opens and two men walk in, wearing fur hats and felt boots. The captain gives a start and reaches for his pistol. 'Soldiers?' '*Nyet, nyet!*' The two civilians disappear. 'Dammit, though,' says the captain, 'what a stink they've left behind!' It's clear that Russians are starting to infiltrate the city.

From the darkness, another person stumbles through the door, a rifle slung over his shoulder. A Russian! He's lost his way. They relieve him of his gun and send him on his way. 'The whites of the enemy's eyes!' Ha!

'What are you planning to do?' Fröhlich asks the captain. He'd pictured the last stand of the Sixth Army quite differently.

'The top brass are still attempting to issue orders,' replies the captain. 'But when that dries up, we're out of here. I've got a lorry waiting, loaded with a fortnight's supplies. We'll get all the men in and head west. If we make it through, well and good. And if we don't, there's nothing lost.'

Fröhlich asks if he can come along, but the captain refuses.

'You've got more of a chance with your Russian!' he tells him. He doesn't like special officers.

In the morning, the corporal comes in.

'We've got him at last, Captain! The bastard who's been stealing from us the whole time!'

Two of the flak gunners drag in a scruffy-looking man. His eyes are deeply sunken and he's smeared with filth. His parchment-like face is fringed with a shaggy growth of beard an inch or so long. His eyes dart about fearfully. The captain looks him up and down, and his gaze comes to rest on the shoulders of his ragged coat. The epaulettes have been torn off. A few light threads can still be seen poking out of the seams.

'You're an officer?' shouts the captain. 'And yet you come round here nicking stuff?'

He strides up to the tramp-like figure and tears open his greatcoat. He's wearing a brown waist belt.

'Your pay-book!'

A trembling hand fishes in a pocket for the grubby book. The captain leafs through it. 'So, you're a lieutenant! Aren't you ashamed of yourself, man, disgracing the Officer Corps like this?' The soldiers standing around grin maliciously.

'I don't know,' mumbles the man, picking nervously at his face. 'I'm so confused. I was hungry…'

The captain gives him a frosty look.

'I hope you realize what's expected of you now!' he says, handing the man back his pistol.

'I'll give you five minutes. Then…'

The scruffy man nods silently. The men take him out, their faces suffused with sneaky pleasure at the lieutenant's misfortune. Fucking officers! 'He donned his coat of many colours and thought himself better than his brothers.' Good that they'd caught one of the bastards for once!

'Put him in the bunker over there!' the captain calls after them. 'No more than five minutes, you hear me? Marvellous, isn't it?' he says, turning to the Sonderführer. 'A German officer stealing! Absolute bloody disgrace!'

Fröhlich can't find any words. Presently, one of the men returns.

'Captain, sir, nothing's happened yet!'

'Right, then, give him a helping hand!' the captain tells the man. Fröhlich comes over to the table, picks up the pay-book and opens it at the first page.

'NCO,' he reads. And below, bordered in black, is the man's service record: '1 October 1939: promoted to corporal.' Then on the following line: '1 November 1942: promoted to lieutenant.' Finally, beneath this information, there is an extravagant signature: 'Günther Harras'...

The man comes back.

'It's done!' he grins.

'Good,' says the captain.

With some effort, Breuer climbed up through an icy gorge behind the Romanians, crossed a railway line and crawled between goods wagons. It turned out to be a long way to the Romanian staff headquarters. He'd spent an uncomfortable night, with his head resting on all his belongings and his pistol readily to hand. Their little stock of food was on the wane by now. Maybe he and the others would be able to find accommodation with the staff of the Romanian cavalry division, where the affable First Lieutenant Schulz was acting as liaison officer. At least they could give it a go. It was worth six cigarettes for his guide and this rather onerous journey on foot.

They came to the city suburbs. Broad streets full of ragged soldiers drifting about aimlessly. To the right and left stood the dead, windowless façades of five- and six-storey apartment blocks. That was how Warsaw had looked in the winter of '39. War left the same traces of death and destruction everywhere. The street was cordoned off by a barricade of sandbags, behind which stood sentries with steel helmets and rifles, a very odd sight in the midst of the general confusion. The circular building off to the right here, with people in front of it, was the theatre. Okay, if need be they could try to find some space in there. Breuer's Romanian guide, a good-natured man with a broad peasant face, turned off into a side street jammed with columns of army vehicles. A ramshackle gateway, the small courtyard of a joinery, piles of rubble, the close-packed remains of vehicles. It was also damned difficult, Breuer found, judging the depth and distance of deep ruts and holes with his one eye. In front of a partially destroyed wall, a set of dangerously rickety wooden steps led down into a second courtyard set on a lower level, surrounded by the ruins of tall, red-brick buildings.

The Romanian disappeared through a cellar entrance half hidden by a heap of debris. After a while he returned, followed by a German officer wearing a sleeveless lambskin jerkin over his uniform jacket.

'Ah, Herr Breuer – yes, of course I remember! Back in Kletskaya, wasn't it? Take a seat? If only you'd come yesterday! Everywhere's jam-packed today. We're even having to constantly bunk up to make room. The general's sharing a hole with five others…'

Breuer was bitterly disappointed. Merely in order to say something else, he enquired: 'So what does your general reckon to the situation? What's he planning on doing?'

First Lieutenant Schulz shrugged his shoulders.

'His plan? He's going to shoot himself! What else are we supposed to do? Hang on, though, something's just occurred to me – the tank destroyer company that was billeted here yesterday; I think they're from your division!

He proceeded to lead Breuer down a long corridor to a dimly lit and crowded cellar room. Men with bare torsos or lower bodies were attending to their wounds, getting bandaged up or warming their frostbitten limbs by the glow of a stove. An adjoining room was a little brighter. Here, too, a fire had been lit amid the rubble. Officers were sitting round a table, almost all with visible injuries. From a faded armchair that some staff must have left behind rose a familiar figure – Captain Eichert. He seemed to have aged many years. His face was even more angular than before, while his mop of dull blond hair had grown even more unruly above his bulbous forehead. A brief glimmer of pleasure flashed in his grey eyes.

'Oh, Breuer, it's you! Of course, there's always room for you! I haven't forgotten how you rescued me from the clutches of the pen-pushers. The gentlemen from the military court'll be mightily pissed off now, I'll bet!'

He chuckled mirthlessly, but his laughter soon dissolved into a hacking cough. He then introduced the other officers. There was a junior doctor by the name of Korn, an animated chap with dark hair; Breuer clocked him as a sound-looking bloke. And Chief Paymaster Jankuhn – who, it later transpired, came from Danzig – cut an impressive figure with his clear gaze and firm handshake. Breuer already knew the adjutant, Lieutenant Bonte, from before. As for First Lieutenant Schmid, one of the company commanders, there wasn't much of him to be seen, since his face was disfigured by several large scabs, the legacy of hand-grenade shrapnel. He couldn't lie down and could barely sit. The other company commander, First Lieutenant Findeisen, was regarded as some kind of legendary figure. He had been wounded five times in quick succession, and every time he had avoided damage to any vital organs by a whisker. Most recently, a machine-gun bullet had knocked out six of his teeth; his head had swollen to the size of a pumpkin. When he spoke, it looked like he was trying to blow the words out through a straw.

Breuer thanked First Lieutenant Schulz, sent his Romanian guide back to fetch his two companions, threw his belongings into a corner and sat down on the bench-end that was offered to him. When he told them about Dierk, a loud 'hurrah' went up; they'd all thought he was dead.

'You shee!' Findeisen slurred through his smashed teeth. 'What am I olways sayig? Bad weeds grow tall!'

And he ought to know, if anyone did. He'd fought his way through from Gumrak single-handed, on foot through the Russian armoured advance, with shrapnel and a bullet lodged in his leg.

'So, tell us, Breuer,' said Captain Eichert. 'What's your take on all the shit that's going down here, you old staff warhorse?'

Breuer gave a sketchy account of the events of the past few days. 'You see, I probably know less than you do,' he concluded, 'but for what it's worth, my opinion is: we're finished. The game's up.'

Captain Eichert had rested his chin on his hands.

'Well, *we're* definitely done for, no question about that,' he said. 'You can't imagine what we've been through! The cellars round here are full of our people. Old and new, seriously wounded, lightly wounded, and the rest. But they're all done in. None of them have any fight left in them. Even so, Breuer, I still can't quite believe it. It's unheard of for more than an entire army to fall to pieces like this! We hear the official army communiqués on the radio every day. Right now, they keep going on about successful counter-attacks. You just wait, they might well still pull it off! Don't you remember some of the amazing things we managed back in the day in Belgium and France? If they could only drop one or two airborne divisions back on the River Chir, then we'd have our bridgehead! Look at this: surely Paulus wouldn't write stuff like this if all hope was lost!'

Breuer took the slip of paper that the captain proffered him. It read:

> We all know the threat that looms if the Sixth Army should cease its campaign of resistance. Certain death awaits most of us, either from an enemy bullet or from the hunger and cold and cruel mistreatment in Siberian POW camps. There is only one course open to us, therefore: to fight to the last bullet. We shall continue to hope for our imminent liberation, and operations to this effect are already underway.

Breuer glanced up questioningly and then looked again at the message. The army communiqué was dated the twentieth of January 1943.

'If there was no truth in that,' said First Lieutenant Schmid, 'then surely Paulus would have surrendered long ago, I'm sure of it. Hitler himself would order capitulation – yes, the Führer himself! He's concerned about the life of every individual. Remember after the Polish campaign, and the war against France, too, how relieved he was that there had been so few German casualties? He wouldn't go and sacrifice an entire army to complete annihilation. It's completely out of the question!'

Eichert nodded. 'Just wait and see,' he said. 'Something's going to happen, right at the eleventh hour: some miracle!'

The others sat around despondently. Breuer did not know what to say in response. He heard their words as if from far away. How alien these people had become to him, with all their fanciful thoughts! Couldn't they see that a whole world was coming to an end here?

It was getting dark by the time Görz and Dierk finally arrived. The doctor examined the lieutenant and re-dressed his wounds and searched out a quiet sleeping place for him somewhere on the flagstones. Finally, he wanted to take a look at Breuer's eye injury. He carefully loosened the blood-encrusted emergency dressing.

'Close your right eye, please!' he told the lieutenant.

Groggy from the pain, Breuer complied. The wall of darkness descended once more. But it was no longer unrelieved blackness. Bright spots floated up and down in it and coalesced into circular patterns that increased steadily in size. And all of a sudden he saw before him Wiese's face, looking just as it had the last time he'd seen him, in the semi-darkness of the bunker at Gumrak. Slowly the face began to change, becoming broader and coarser, while the hair above the slyly twinkling eyes turned ginger. It wasn't Wiese any more, it was his driver, Lakosch. Lakosch the deserter – what was it he'd said back then? 'I wanted to see if I could save my comrades!'

The doctor gave a smart tug and pulled off the last corner of the eye bandage adhering to Breuer's skin. Breuer gritted his teeth against the sharp pain that stabbed right to the back of his head. Saving his comrades, that was it! Escorting them to pastures new after the apocalypse…

'Christ, man, you were incredibly lucky!' said the doctor. 'Instead of draining out of the eye, the aqueous humour has gone viscous and formed a crust. For the time being there's nothing we can do. Turn your head to the light, will you? Can you see anything?'

'Yes, I can see something,' said Breuer quietly. 'A very faint shimmering pattern… I think – yes, it's getting brighter!'

General von Hermann had come to terms with himself. He knew now what he had to do. There was only one solution.

His decision had not been reached without some deep soul-searching. The question he was wrestling with was the same one that had been troubling all the senior staff officers of the Sixth Army since the tenth of January – namely, what should they do when the end came? There had been long discussions on the subject. At the beginning, when the situation hadn't been quite so grave and the question was more in the realms of theory, the general consensus had been that they were duty-bound as officers to shoot themselves. The idea of suicide suddenly became all the rage – in theory, at least. And von Hermann, who as a Christian had spoken out against it right from the outset, had been subjected to some very disparaging looks, which carried more than a hint of an accusation of cowardice. But now that the subject had taken on a deadly earnest, no one spoke about shooting themselves any more.

A truly oracular directive had been issued from on high: 'The officers commanding the Sixth Army will share the fate of the troops until the bitter end!' This gave rise to long and heated debates, until eventually most people came to the view that it meant that the staffs would *lead* right to the last in order to facilitate an ordered surrender.

Facilitate surrender? Such a sudden about-turn! There was a standing order that ran: 'Fight to the last man and the last bullet!' Up till now, every order and directive issued by Army High Command had dismissed out of hand any thought of going into captivity. Soldiers who even mentioned surrendering were summarily shot. And now – out of the blue – this? Now, when the staffs ought to have been sticking firmly to their own orders, there was talk of capitulation?

General von Hermann recalled that Lieutenant Colonel Unold of the General Staff in particular had been a strong advocate of doing the decent thing when the time came. 'The very idea of a general or General Staff officer standing in the trenches with his rifle like Private Dogsbody is quite preposterous!' he'd said, for instance. 'We didn't undergo our training at the military academy to do that sort of thing!' And General Schmidt, the Sixth Army's chief of staff, had only recently offered the view that the world should be spared the undignified spectacle of a German Army staff being routed on the battlefield by the Russians.

Undignified? What was there about the whole escapade at Stalingrad that wasn't undignified? It was undignified that thousands of wounded men should have died in filthy holes in the ground, that thousands had starved to death, and that soldiers who were half dead already were being hounded into battle!

Two days before, he'd been at the front. He'd seen a field hospital full of wounded men – a long, two-storey building that was some kind of former warehouse – set ablaze by shellfire. A few men on the upper floor had saved themselves by climbing out of the windows onto trees. But the flames from below steadily licked up to where they were perched. The men in the trees started screaming, 'Shoot us, shoot us!' And the soldiers below opened fire, and one after the other the trapped men plunged into the flames...

That had all been undignified, shameless and criminal. 'Stalingrad began as an assault, became a defensive action, and ended up as a crime!' he had written in a letter to his wife. The German Wehr-macht, he claimed, 'had lost face'.

But was it really so undignified for General Staff officers to engage in combat? Maybe that would have been one way for them to save 'face'. They certainly had a duty to do so, he felt.

That was General von Hermann's view of things, at least. No doubt he was the only one to think this way. But as far as he was concerned there was only one way out. He'd thought it through with unerring consistency. Orders were orders. And they applied to everyone. To the common soldier and commander alike, without exception. Every soldier's duty and honour required it, as did his oath. It was terrible that this oath of loyalty was sworn to a criminal... but it remained an oath nonetheless. Such were the thoughts of General von Hermann as he dispassionately received one piece of bad news after another during the cold days of January, and as he succinctly and unequivocally issued his orders. He had become hardened, so desensitized that his officers were alarmed when they looked into his stony face. He showed no pity any more, least of all to himself.

It was different at night when he lay sleepless on his camp bed, shrouded in darkness and staring into the black void. It was then that the searching and questioning began. Was an oath really still binding on someone when they'd sworn it to a criminal? Weren't there obligations that overtrumped this? For instance, a person's loyalty to their family, or their fellow countrymen – or to God? Was he really acting as a Christian? He felt, alarmingly, that the ground had suddenly been cut from beneath his feet. Yes, there genuinely was another way: to refuse to carry out the criminal order, to counter it with a firm 'No' and suffer the consequences, to make a clean break with everything that had gone before. And yet that was mutiny, revolution! The general shuddered at the thought. Revolution: that was something for people who wore flat caps – it was the guttersnipes who stirred up revolution. He, on the other hand, was from an old military family, an aristocrat. He couldn't possibly have anything to do with revolution! That would mean declaring war on the world that he belonged to by dint of birth and education, severing his own roots and sawing off the very branch he was sitting on. It was tantamount to self-sacrifice, a moral self-annihilation.

Yet at the same time he could see how the aristocratic, militaristic world in which he was rooted was crumbling before his eyes. Every day brought new evidence of its demise in a series of horrifying images. Nor was it just being destroyed from outside – from within, too, it was disintegrating into meaningless phrase-making, hypocrisy and cowardice, and bursting open like a plague boil. The wretchedness of its exponents was causing it to break apart, to spiral into terminal decline in the same way the proud Age of Chivalry had degenerated into tawdry exploitation by robber barons and eventually collapsed in disgrace and dishonour.

And he recognized that a new dawn was breaking, an age he did not understand, with ideals and values that were alien to him and inhabited by a new breed of person. He could see them all around him already, even within his own Officer Corps, these young men who still wore the same uniform and who observed the outward forms of military life to the letter, and yet in whose eyes there was a curious gleam whenever they answered 'Yes, sir!' It was almost as if they were laughing inwardly at this whole world. What was going on in their heads? No, let these other people go their new way – he certainly wasn't capable of doing so. He was too old – and his son, for whom it might have been worthwhile to make a completely fresh start, was dead…

And besides, it was too late now. Too many men had perished in Stalingrad for anyone to try to abdicate responsibility for their deaths now through some Damascene conversion. No, only one course of action remained open to him: to pursue the path he had set out on to the bitter end, with his head held high. He looked down on the others with unutterable contempt, those wavering figures using a cowardly compromise to try to find an ignominious way out for themselves. The old world was dying, and he would die with it. He was determined to save face and to die as the last representative of the old order – the last true knight.

Among the officers sitting in their rotten cellar like they were in a molehill, the mood veered between crazy momentary hopefulness and bleak despair. Breuer was the only one who had been overcome by a great sense of calm. Things became progressively brighter and clearer to him. His thoughts kept returning to Lieutenant Wiese and the little ginger-haired bloke. Wiese, whose words he only now began to truly understand, had foreseen the course this German tragedy would take and its likely outcome more clearly than anyone else; but he had lacked the strength to convert his awareness into action. That was what had broken him. And what about Lakosch? The little corporal surely only had a very vague appreciation of the bigger picture. Yet he had had the courage to act, quite unilaterally, off his own bat and on his own authority, in defiance of all the rules and conventions. New signs were appearing on the dark wall, and the script was becoming more legible by the minute.

The entrance to the house wasn't easy to find. You'd scarcely have imagined that an undamaged cellar lay beneath the badly damaged storeys above. Nevertheless, in the corridor and the rooms underground, especially in the vestibule, where Dr Korn had set up an observation room, there were constant comings and goings. No one was especially bothered by all this activity. The only surprise came when Captain Gedig, the divisional adjutant, suddenly appeared in the basement and announced his intention of moving in.

'Heavens above, what an honour!' Captain Eichert greeted him with dry sarcasm. 'The entire divisional staff assembled in our modest little abode!'

But when he took a closer look at the new arrival, his desire to mock suddenly evaporated. Something wasn't right!

'No offence, Gedig,' he said seriously. 'Of course you're welcome. Where are the others, though? Isn't Unold coming too?'

The captain took a long draught of the hot coffee that First Lieutenant Schmid handed him. His eyes looked in bewilderment over the rim of the billycan lid. But at first all he did was drink. Then, taking a deep breath, he set down his makeshift cup.

'The others?' he asked. 'Which others? Seems you're well behind the times here. Unold did a bunk ages ago!'

'Damn and blast it!' Breuer blurted. He recalled the leather coat he'd spotted that time at Stalingradski airfield.

'What? How come?' the others all asked at once, clearly stunned at the news.

'Unold's gone? So he managed it then, eh?'

'What do you mean, "managed"?' Gedig broke in testily. 'He didn't manage to do anything. It's a crazy business. I'm not even sure I should be telling you about it—'

'Come off it, will you! We're entitled to hear what happened to our divisional commander!'

Gedig dropped his coy attitude and launched into his account. As he spoke, the reticence he'd cultivated as an adjutant fell away.

'Okay, you heard he was promoted to full colonel on the twenty-second... Oh, you didn't? Yeah, supposedly for service beyond the call of duty in defending the Cauldron. He also swung it for Engelhard to be promoted to major. Hey, wouldn't you like to be a major too, Eichert? I tell you, right now's your best chance. You can all get a promotion! And a German Cross, a Knight's Cross, whatever you want. All you need to do is go over to High Command and tell them about your heroic deeds. Business is booming over there – a fire sale at knockdown prices!'

'Get on with it!' the men urged. 'What happened with Unold?'

'Unold, yeah, right… So, the next day he's vanished into thin air. Snuck off to the airfield and flew out!'

'What? Pissed off, just like that? Impossible!'

'Without any orders? But that's… that means…'

'Yeah, we didn't want to believe it at first either. When it came out what had happened, the shit really hit the fan at High Command. Schmidt immediately radioed the Army Group. They were just as astonished at their end. For a colonel on the General Staff charged with the special task of organizing supplies to behave like that, just before the balloon went up, seemed like insanity even to them. In any event, they hauled him up in front of a court martial, charged with desertion. Yesterday we heard that he'd been shot. Engelhard was completely devastated at the news; he blew his brains out yesterday evening in our bunker.'

The gaggle of men had fallen silent. All of them had got to know the lieutenant colonel personally at some stage, and for the most part not from his best side. And no doubt everyone was thinking the same thing at this moment: Unold – a workaholic, bursting with ambition; heartless, but with a sharp, caustic intellect and a brutal, unbending will. A General Staff officer with a future. And yet men of his stripe always failed miserably when the chips were down…

Captain Eichert had buried his head in his hands.

'I could never stand the bloke,' he said at length. 'A smarmy bastard who stopped at nothing to get what he wanted. But flying out like that… My God, I just don't understand what's going on any more!'

'Really? Don't you?' Captain Gedig gave a forced laugh. By now, his adjutant's smooth veneer was entirely gone. 'Surely you've had enough object lessons by now! Look at Hube and Jaenecke* – what

---

* Hube and Jaenecke – for Hube, see note on page 265; General Erwin Jaenecke was, like Hube, one of the last high-ranking officers to be flown out Stalingrad before the final German defeat.

about them? Or that big cheese of a flak general, whatever his name was… Pliquet,* I think. Come on, gentlemen, open your eyes! Then you'll see what's going on!'

'Pliquet? Don't know him. Who's he then?'

'He was in charge of air operations here for a while. He flew out too, as far as I know.'

'*You* must know him, surely, Görz!'

'Yes, I do,' muttered the corporal. 'Better than I'd like to, in fact.'

And Görz proceeded to tell them things that most of them had only heard about through rumours. Major General Pliquet had been the commander of the only flak division in the Cauldron and was put in charge of all air force units caught within the encirclement. He was a *bon vivant* and was insistent on maintaining a lifestyle befitting his status. That was why, last Christmas, when it was decreed that no more parcels should be sent to troops in the Cauldron because of lack of space on aircraft, he still had a batch of turkeys flown in for his staff officers' dinner table. Mind you, that wasn't to say that the general had no concern for the troops' welfare! Every so often, he'd generously donate to the men a bottle of the cognac that he had his batman bring in by the crateload via the air bridge. On the fourteenth of January, when things began to get dicey, he flew out of the Cauldron with a fighter escort to 'present his report'. And because he was travelling 'on official business', he refused to take any wounded men with him. He was duly awarded the Knight's Cross by none other than Hermann Göring himself, and never returned. Instead, a radio message was received to the effect that he had come back on a plane and spent ages circling over the airfield at night but had been unable to land due to 'heavy ground fighting' and 'the presence of enemy fighters'. On the night in question, around

---

* 'Pliquet' – a thinly disguised allusion by Gerlach to General Wolfgang Pickert, commander of the Ninth Flak Division, who flew out of the Stalingrad Cauldron on 13 January 1943.

fifteen transport planes carrying supplies had landed successfully at the Pitomnik aerodrome and flown out again with casualties on board.

Captain Gedig was able to add his own anecdote. 'Yesterday, Colonel Fuchs received a radio message from Pliquet. In it, he said the division should continue fighting courageously – to the bitter end. The creation of a new flak division with the same illustrious title was already underway, "in a spirit of revenge for Stalingrad".'

'Jesus Christ,' announced Lieutenant Bonte. 'The man's got all the sensitivity of an attack dog!'

'For God's sake!' groaned Captain Eichert. 'These are the people who were our tutors at military academy. Tell me Gedig, is that the gospel truth?'

'Eichert, please; would I lie to you? Colonel Fuchs reacted much like you when he got the message. And his reply didn't mince any words, I can tell you: "As a new flak division is already being assembled," he wired, "I should like to know what those sections of the old division that are still fighting in Stalingrad should call themselves from now on." Just wait till this whole shebang is over! Then you'll really see some fireworks!'

'God fucking damn it all to hell!' yelled Eichert, slamming his fist down on the table. 'Fourteen years I've been soldiering, body and soul. Things were never like this in the old days! Back then, we believed in things like loyalty, doing one's duty and honour – has that all gone out the window now?'

A violent coughing fit robbed him of breath and turned his face blue. Breuer had grown more and more furious listening to this account, too. He thought of Wiese, who'd had to die like an animal in a foxhole, his spirit broken; of the orderly from the records office who'd shot himself; of Fackelmann and Endrigkeit and of all the misery they'd endured over the past few months. And of the general who, not long after the encirclement and despite much fighting talk, had taken himself off to a sanatorium in Vienna. That had been the start of this exodus of top brass. A surge of blind fury welled up in him.

'Loyalty, doing your duty, honour!' he shouted. 'That's still true of the poor trusting bastards out there. But it's long since ceased to hold good for their lords and masters! To them, they're just cheap words: clichés they use to keep us all stupefied and turn us into willing tools for their grubby plans. And what about us? We went along with it all like the idiots we were, just played along meekly and unthinkingly! Everything in the garden was rosy! We hid behind the broad backs of others... And now that it's our necks on the line and those others are laughing up their sleeves, we finally wake up and look all dumb and innocent and start wailing and complaining... Some soldiers we are! We've been nothing but mercenaries – stupid bought-and-paid-for mercenaries – for far too long, ten years now! It's high time we came to our senses!'

The others maintained a shamefaced silence; they were clearly moved and embarrassed by what Breuer had said. Eventually, First Lieutenant Schmid said frostily: 'Why are you subjecting us to these unfair and tactless outbursts, Breuer? We're in the shit, too, you know. Ultimately it's all about the Wehrmacht, which we're all members of. People like Unold and this flak general are still the exceptions, thank God. There are still plenty of decent officers and generals around!'

Breuer had recovered his composure.

'Look, I don't want to hurt anyone's feelings,' he said quietly, 'but if we were to survive Stalingrad and yet still learned nothing from the experience, then we wouldn't have deserved to go on living... It's not about the individual here; it's about the system, about the very Wehrmacht you've just mentioned. Colonel von Hermann once said that the German Army had lost face at Stalingrad. There's some truth in that, except... maybe it's just that its true face is emerging from behind a mask of tradition and empty forms. At least, the face it's been forced to wear over the last ten years.

Just think of Beck, Fritsch, Blaskowitz, Hoepner* and all the others! Anyone who showed a bit of gumption and fight either had their spirit broken or were forced to quit. What's left isn't the Wehrmacht of old times. As far as its leadership goes, it's rotten to the core. As long as everything was going well, that was all papered over with grandiose rhetoric. It took Stalingrad to open our eyes. It tore the mask off our face, of us and our ideals! Now it's clear for all to see: nothing we believed in is valid any more – not the people or their ideas! It's no good clinging to the old ways in times like this. You can't prop up something that's already collapsing.'

A massive explosion rocked the cellar. Snow and dirt blew in through the shattered window. The officers leaped to their feet.

'God damn it!' cursed First Lieutenant Schmid when he saw that the coffee pot on the stove had been covered with a layer of plaster dust. First Lieutenant Findeisen cast a wary eye up at the ceiling. 'Seems to moy,' he muttered through his swollen cheeks, 'if thot lot came down, wuh wouldn't hove much chance of holding it up.'

Everyone laughed.

'Tell me, Breuer,' Captain Eichert said a little later, attempting a smile, 'you were always such a quiet, unassuming young man. I hope you won't mind me saying, but there was a time when you scarcely opened your mouth. I know that Unold thought very highly of you for that. And now, all of a sudden, you're sounding off like some rabble-rouser. What's happened to you?'

'There was also a time,' Breuer replied, rubbing his forehead, 'when you were different too, Captain! If I'd said to you then what I've said today, you'd have had me arrested, no question! None of us are like our former selves any more. And that's a good thing.'

---

* 'Beck, Fritsch, Blaskowitz, etc. – the names of German Wehrmacht generals who were openly critical of the Nazi leadership, and in some cases of atrocities carried out by the SS, but who were sidelined, killed or forced to recant their position.

★

On the orders of the Army High Command, the building that formerly housed the Divisional Commander, Central Stalingrad is to be made ready to receive and provide care for the countless casualties of the battle. A senior doctor is charged with organizing this. In no time, he finds himself despairing at this impossible task.

The morning of the twenty-sixth of January sees the arrival of various remnants of medical companies. Some of them are leading long crocodiles of wounded men. They descend like a swarm of locusts on the already overstuffed building, increasing its population at a stroke to around seventeen or eighteen hundred men. They lie beside and on top of one another in the rooms and on the ice-cold corridors and staircases: the wounded, the emaciated, the dead, the yellow-fever patients, all lumped together with no rhyme or reason. There is a constant coming and going in the building, a hustle and bustle and push and shove like on a station concourse – aimless and ceaseless.

The medical personnel set up shop in the basement. The military police have moved out; they have been ordered to defend the city's Red Square. They appear to have departed in haste and in some anxiety, as their quarters have been left in a state of total chaos. Field caps, suitcases, police badges, and rolls of fabric lie all over the place, together with packages with addresses already written on them, which they were meaning to send home. Some of these contain wheat flour. The floor is strewn with torn-off sleeve insignia. In addition, the general appointed as the city commandant of Stalingrad has remained behind. He has barricaded himself in his suite of rooms and later announces that he wishes to be taken into custody under the protection of the Red Cross. The doctors throw him out.

When the medical staff first set foot in the building and start making their way through the rooms, they are horrified by what they find. They have been used to many terrible things, but have never seen anything like this. What can they do? Is there anything to be done?

'Clear out the dead first off!' the staff doctor urgently orders. The corpses are duly removed. The first day's body count alone is one hundred and fifty. Out in the courtyard is a large open wooden shed. The dead men are stacked in there like logs. This task goes on seemingly without end. Men are dying on an hourly basis from fever or starvation or cold, or shoot themselves or slash their wrists.

'Then I want all the riff-raff out of here!'

All kinds of people, it's true, are still washing about the large building, especially its upper floors. There, for quite some time, shadowy figures have been leading a wild, gypsy-like existence. Soldiers from all manner of units, and Croatians and Romanians, plus two completely feral German women and railway employees. The open camp fires they keep alight up there all the while, with the windows closed, are endangering the fabric of the building. Several hundred of them are turned out onto the street. But like mice they keep sneaking back in, day and night. Keeping them out also proves an unending task.

One medical company still has a couple of horses, and these are now slaughtered. Violent clashes break out around the field kitchen. Armed orderlies end up having to protect it. In the twinkling of an eye, the entrails and feet of the butchered horses are stolen.

Herbert goes downstairs armed with mess tins. He's not heading for the field kitchen. You get nothing there unless it's your turn. He's after some snow, as Geibel's contracted a fever and needs cold compresses. And they must have something to drink. But it's becoming harder and harder to find the stuff. All the snow around the building has been collected and eaten, despite having been trampled by boots and sullied by all and sundry relieving themselves there. As Herbert makes to cross the road, a lorry draws up. It stops. It has been loaded up with provisions. Suddenly, there comes a whistling sound, followed by an explosion and a sheet of flame.

People standing around the truck are scythed to the ground. The driver slumps from his cab into the road. A piece of shrapnel has clearly sliced through his thighs, as his legs are bent backwards up to his neck. A steaming pool of blood is forming underneath him. He's still alive, gasping for air like a landed fish. His co-driver has jumped down from the other side. He catches holds of the gurgling man, spins him round, and claps him on the shoulder. 'Where are the keys, Otto? ... Hey, Otto!'

While this is going on, other men start ransacking the cargo. By the time the co-driver turns round to see what's going on, the lorry is empty. Herbert didn't have his wits about him. He's standing with his back pressed against the wall. His whole body is shaking...

When he's filled the mess tins with snow and tries to get back into the building, a corporal from the Medical Corps bars his way. 'What do you think you're doing skulking about here, eh?'

'I wanted... I've... My comrade in there...'

'Comrade, comrade... You'll feel the sole of my boot up your arse, you bloody vagrant! Make yourself scarce, d'you hear? Go on – scram!'

Herbert is wearing his coat. But he's left his blanket and his kitbag of clothes upstairs. And Geibel's lying up there too. But he can't get back into the building now.

'So, what else should we be doing?' asks the senior doctor.

'Triage. We should be laying out the hopeless cases in the corridors. That'll make more room for the rest,' replies the staff doctor.

Seeing the shocked face of his colleague, he adds, under his breath: 'Freezing to death is a kind way to go.'

That afternoon, Herbert manages to get back to his room by sneaking through the back entrance of the building. Geibel isn't there any more. His things have gone too. The babbling man and the lad with the lice have disappeared as well. Others have taken their place, in some cases men with dreadful mutilations.

'They're from the floor above!' says the gnome, who's still there on his pile of coats; he points at the ceiling. 'Hit by a shell burst… What's that, you want to know what's happened to the others?' He shrugs his shoulders. 'No idea. They came and took them away round noon today.'

Herbert wanders round the rooms and corridors. He finds the delirious man in a freezing-cold passageway where all the windows have been blown out. He's still alive, singing and chuckling to himself. He also tracks down the young soldier; they've taken away his lice-ridden blanket, along with his boots and greatcoat. He's already frozen to death. But Geibel's nowhere to be seen.

Cold, clear weather set in again. Every now and then, a pallid reflection of the winter sun shone through the window of the cellar room, which was fitted with bars and made opaque by a dirty pane of glass. Someone always had to be ready to cushion this windowpane against the blast whenever heavy mortar rounds exploded outside. With stubborn regularity, the mortars targeted the same spots: the road outside the house and the courtyard. After suffering a number of shrapnel injuries and two fatalities (one of whom was Corporal Görz, who'd been searching for food in a derelict car) from these insidious munitions, which made no noise as they came in, they only dared to venture outside in extremis. Eichert and the junior doctor now dreaded doing their daily rounds of the surrounding basements to tend to the wounded. The men relieved themselves right outside the door; as a result, a mirror-smooth sheet of ice formed, on which two men slipped and broke their legs at night. Whenever Breuer stuck his nose out into the courtyard, an eerie feeling crept over him. Each time, the silhouette of the red-brick ruins of houses had changed noticeably. Here a new hole now gaped, and there yet another entire floor was missing. Way up high, the interior of a room was suddenly exposed, suspended in mid-air with all its furniture, beds, and pictures on the walls like a theatre set. But not for long! Pretty soon, all that remained there were some jagged stumps of masonry. Down in the courtyard, the brick- and plaster-dust lay inches thick and the piles of rubble grew and grew. A city was gradually being levelled. It was as if the decay of all man-made objects, a process normally concealed from mortal eyes by the slow passage of the years, was here being made visible by some merciless time-lapse camera.

The sun brought the planes with it. They moved across the back-drop of a light-blue sky, tiny and distant and detached, as pale and transparent as the lice you picked off your shirt. But down below, the bombs they dropped whistled and wailed and tore new wounds in the bleeding city. The crump and roar of their detonations, magnified a hundred times over by the bare walls and the rickety rafters and the corrugated iron roofs of blasted factory buildings, shook at the ruins of the houses and the shattered hearts of men with a dreadful rumbling reverberation. At night it was quieter. Then the air was filled with the rumble of transport aircraft circling at low altitude; their shadows flitted beneath the stars like the outlines of enormous bats. All around, colourful flares shot up, and hidden faces scanned the sky anxiously for the hazy shapes of parachutes floating down and listened out for the near or distant impact of air-dropped supplies hitting the ground – authorized search parties and desperate marauders always found themselves in a race to get to these first. For provisions were now only being distributed to those who were able and willing to fight. The wounded officers sat in their cellar, not speaking to one another. Each of them was far away in his thoughts, mentally taking leave of the past and quietly asking himself the question: 'What now?' There was more than enough wood here in the ruins, so the stove was kept fully stoked. A pot of coffee always sat steaming there. Enough coffee was still to be had – it was pretty much *all* they had to sustain and fortify them. Occasionally Jankuhn, the popular paymaster, would produce some tinned meat. Bread was a very scarce commodity now. Everything was shared between everyone.

'Help yourselves for as long as our little stock of food lasts,' Eichert told his guests. 'What's ours is yours.'

Breuer thanked him. But not in the customary manner, by saying: 'Permit me, Captain, sir, to humbly express my gratitude.' Instead he simply said: 'Many thanks, Herr Eichert!' No one batted an eyelid. Everything had changed.

Lieutenant Dierk, who was well looked after by the others, especially the junior doctor, began to take a little more interest in his surroundings. Yet his scant replies remained mechanical and empty and discouraged questioners. He slept for the most part. Deprived of rest for weeks, his ravaged body demanded its rights. When Corporal Görz, lacerated by shrapnel, was fighting his losing battle to stay alive in the next room, Dierk sat with him and stroked his hand. One time, he clutched at Breuer's sleeve as the lieutenant was about to leave and looked up at him with fear in his face.

'The Führer…,' he whispered, 'a whole army… and he can't help! What a blow for him…'

When the first rumours began to circulate about the Cauldron splitting in two and the southern section collapsing, a lively debate was rekindled. The divisions south of the Zariza River had supposedly taken matters into their own hands and laid down their arms. No more orders were coming from above. The High Command was wreathed in silence. It did not countermand the order to 'fight to the last bullet' but nor did it insist that it be carried out. Did a command structure even exist any longer?

'This is the end,' declared Captain Eichert. 'Anyone who wants to clear off, break out or whatever… please, be my guest, I won't try to stop you. As for me, I'm going to end it all. I'm not going to be taken prisoner.'

'End it all? No, don't even think of it!' said Jankuhn. 'The Russians aren't going to eat us! And Siberia's supposed to be a very pretty place. Lots of prisoners were housed there during the last war and are still living there now. And if need be, there's an escape route to Manchuria or even India. As long as there's still a chance, you can always "end it all" later if you want to!'

'Captivity means death, we know that!' interjected Lieutenant Bonte. 'Why let ourselves be butchered when we can choose our own way to go?'

He and a group of friends were determined to try to fight their way through to the German lines. Since only his lower arm was shot up, he reckoned he stood a good chance.

'What Paulus has written there is a lie,' said Breuer firmly. 'This whole order is one big, miserable lie! Believe me, I've interrogated any number of Russians, many of them senior staff officers. The Russians treat their prisoners well. Whether we can survive captivity after all these weeks of starvation is another matter. But no one's going to be mistreated or killed, that's for sure.'

There was great excitement during the night. Findeisen, who had gone outside on a 'call of nature', rushed back in, breathless.

'Outside… quock, quock… Roight here across the street, it londed roight over there!'

He'd spotted a parachute supply drop. A search party was sent out. After just a few minutes they returned dragging a sack of bread.

'Oho, that'll keep the wolf from the door all right!' cried Eichert. 'We can really live high on the hog in our final hours. The men'll be amazed!'

Air-dropped supplies had to be handed in. The penalty for disobeying this order was death.

The fifty loaves in the sack were distributed. Every man under Eichert's command received a quarter-loaf. Shortly afterwards – they'd indulged in a night-time feast and were still chewing away with full cheeks – a furious paymaster appeared, in the company of two military policemen.

'You've recovered a supply drop!' he said, eyeing their masticating faces suspiciously.

'That's right,' replied Eichert, 'so what?'

'The drop landed in the zone controlled by our division. I demand you hand it over right now!'

'The food stays here,' responded Eichert calmly. There was a dangerous glint in his eyes, however. 'It tastes just as good to our men as it would to yours.'

The paymaster was quivering with indignant rage.

'So you're refusing?' he shouted. 'Then I'll have you arrested! And you know what'll happen to you then!'

Eichert had stood up. He reached for his machine-pistol.

'Arrested?' he growled. 'We'll see about that! We've decided not to fire another shot in anger. But I'm willing to make an exception where these last few bits of bread are concerned. Now get out of here!'

He raised his gun.

'I'll count to three. If you aren't gone by then, you're dead meat!'

The others had risen to their feet too. The paymaster struggled for words.

'One…' Eichert began counting and cocked the gun. 'Two…'

The paymaster turned abruptly on his heel and disappeared with his two companions. Hoots of derision followed him out of the door.

The Russians advanced from the west, forcing the exhausted division to defend its own rear. Bombs and artillery shells rained down, destroying what little was left of the city. And one day it was clear: this was definitively the end…

General von Hermann searched out his best uniform tunic and pinned on all of his medals, including the Knight's Cross he'd not yet worn here in Stalingrad. A stickler for correctness, he pinned it on back to front. There was no swastika on the reverse, only the date 1813. Then he summoned the divisional chaplain. He handed him his signet ring, his wedding ring and a letter to his wife. Tersely and objectively, with an expression that quashed any contradiction, he told the padre:

'Please tell my wife that I have discharged my duty as a soldier and a staunch Christian to the best of my ability. My life has always been guided by the principle: *"He who sets the direction, course and path of the clouds, air and winds will also guide me on my way."** Stay with the wounded, padre, and don't be afraid!'

As he did every day, he bade farewell to his chief of staff and departed. He left a slip of paper behind on his desk. On it was printed the latest 'watchword' from the top brass: 'It is not dishonourable to be taken prisoner. It is not dishonourable to turn one's weapon on oneself. It is not dishonourable to break out!' Diagonally across this note, the general had written, in capital letters: 'It is not dishonourable to consider one's duty and honour!'

He walked out towards the western front of the Cauldron. His batman followed him, carrying two carbines. He passed lines of soldiers streaming away from the front.

The army was disintegrating. He didn't attempt to halt the flow. Let them run and save themselves any way they could. He had just one account to settle, namely his own. What came after that was not his concern.

The sound of rifle fire drifted over from the railway embankment, along with the asthmatic chattering of a machine gun. Craters made by mortars and shells lay all about. On the road stood a short, stockily built general, the commander of the neighbouring division. He was shouting and waving his arms and trying in vain

---

* 'He who sets the direction, course and path of the clouds...' – a line from the hymn *'Befiehl du deine Wege...'* (1653) by Paul Gebhardt.

to hold back his fleeing men. His voice was already hoarse from the effort. 'What are you doing here?' von Hermann asked. 'Come with me!'

The little general took off his fur cap and wiped the beads of sweat off his bald pate.

'Where to?' he asked in astonishment.

Von Hermann did not reply, but kept on walking. And now the other man understood. Carrying rifles to the front line… right, of course! Setting a good example to the men! Not a bad idea at that, even if it was downright dangerous. But because he was curious to see whether it would work, he set off in pursuit. Cautiously he climbed the embankment. At the top, a few soldiers and officers were strung out at some considerable distance from one another. They were firing without pause. Ahead of them the Russians were advancing, walking tall and oblivious to the danger, as they always did during these attacks.

'Bravo, lads!' yelled the little general. 'Let 'em have it!'

He gesticulated wildly, but a bullet that whistled close by caused him to duck. Warily, he looked around to see if he could spot his erstwhile companion. With a sudden shock, he saw General von Hermann standing upright on the crest of the embankment, with his carbine raised to his shoulder, bold as brass like he was at a country house shooting party. He was loosing off shot after shot. As soon as he emptied one magazine, his batman lying behind him passed him a newly loaded gun.

'Have you lost your mind?' bellowed the little general. 'Lie down, for God's sake, or you're a goner!'

But his words fell on deaf ears. He realized with horror that the general was on a suicide mission. Appalled, he buried his head in the snow to avoid seeing any more.

General von Hermann stayed on his feet and kept firing. He stood on the embankment for what seemed like an eternity. It was as though death was intent on mocking him. But then, as if some unseen hand had shoved him over, he was abruptly poleaxed onto his back, straight as a die, and slipped without a sound down the steep bank.

When they retrieved his body, they found a single bullet hole right in the middle of his forehead.

'A hero!' sobbed the little general. He found it deeply upsetting that a general should have suffered the same fate that had befallen hundreds of thousands of ordinary soldiers, like it was the most natural thing in the world. 'A hero!' he lamented, drunk on his own emotion, as General von Hermann's batman silently closed his superior's eyes. 'The Hero of Stalingrad!'

And doubtless only the dead man, lying there on his back with his marble-white face, knew that this 'heroism' was nothing but the hopeless despair of a broken heart.

One morning, a young officer dressed in a fur cap and coat appeared in Eichert's bunker, with a machine-pistol slung across his shoulders. He'd come to pick up Lieutenant Bonte. He was the son of a general who was commanding an infantry division in the southern sector of Stalingrad. On being asked about his father, he shrugged his shoulders and his face registered no emotion.

'No idea. He said goodbye to me yesterday,' he said. 'I expect he's already dead by now.'

'Dead?'

'Yes, he's either shot himself or swallowed poison. I don't know which. Half his staff have taken their own lives: the regimental commanders, the head doctor… The others were planning on breaking out. There's nothing else to be done in the current circumstances.'

'And what about his division?'

'I'm sure it's still fighting – well, part of it, at least. But I can't say for sure. It's one big ball of confusion there.'

In the meantime, Captain Gedig had also collected his belongings.

'Don't tell me you're going too?' a shocked Breuer asked him.
'It's utter insanity!'

'I have to, Breuer! I must do something! I can't just sit around here
and wait. I can't stand it any longer. And then… well, I've got a girl
back home waiting for me. Perhaps we'll strike lucky and make it
through.'

'The whole of Germany's waiting for us, Gedig. But we won't get
to see it the way you're planning!'

'It has to be this way, Breuer! Goodbye – and good luck!'

The captain was a changed man. His eyes shone with a spirit
of enterprise and youthful exuberance. He was also harbouring a
secret. Engelhard had confided it to him shortly before his death.
A radio message had come from General Hube, which had secretly
been shown to a chosen few at the Army High Command. It said
that Stalingrad was now a lost cause. Troops attempting to break
out should lie on the ground and make signs for planes to spot; they
would be supplied with air-drops. So that was the extent of Hitler's
help for the Sixth Army! And relying on this assistance, the captain
was preparing to embark on a journey of almost three hundred
kilometres through the Russian winter.

When the three officers went to take their leave of Eichert, the
captain sprang to his feet. 'Hang it all, lads!' he exclaimed. 'I'm
coming with you! Who knows? We might just pull it off! But there's
nothing lost even if we don't. At least it'll be a soldierly way to go.
Paymaster, let's have some of those tins of yours, enough to last us
a fortnight!'

'Bravo, Captain, sir!' cried Lieutenant Bonte. 'At last! With you on
board, I'd be surprised if we don't make it!'

'If only I could move a bit better,' snarled First Lieutenant Schmid,
'I'd come with you, no question!'

The rest stood as if rooted to the spot. Lieutenant Dierk stared,
silently and with expressionless eyes.

'You're really going?' asked Breuer, distraught. 'What… What about your men? Only yesterday you were willing to lay your life down for them, and now… Is that what you call responsibility?'

'Responsibility, my arse!' snapped the captain, reaching for his coat. 'You said yourself that all bets are now off!'

'Unfortunately, that's true, right enough… even so, some things are still sacrosanct, surely! These gentlemen here can do what they like. They're free agents. But *you* aren't! You can't just leave your men in the lurch now!'

'What utter bilge – you and your qualms, Breuer! Come on, Paymaster, break out those tins, will you!'

Jankuhn was reluctant to oblige, however.

'No, Captain, sir, I can't give you anything!' he said adamantly. 'You do what you like. But these supplies are for the men!'

Eichert put down his coat. Nothing like this had ever happened to him before.

'Do you really want to desert your post like Unold?' Breuer pressed him. 'Leave your men up shit creek like that general who abandoned his front-line division? Look, no one would ever hold you to account if you tried breaking out, you can be sure! On the contrary, you'll be a hero if you pull it off. But you'd still be a deserter – nothing more, nothing less. And you're better than that, Eichert!'

Eichert sank back into his chair.

'You're right,' he said in a flat voice. 'You're dead right. There's more to life than written orders… Damn it, the lessons you're forced to learn in this shithole. Okay. Off you go, lads!'

He gave the departing men one final wave. Frustrated and crestfallen, they went on their way. An embarrassed silence settled over the rest. It was as though their final hope had now been dashed. But there was no more talk of people shooting themselves. Even the Romanian general had given up that idea, it seemed. In any event, First Lieutenant Schulz, who looked in on them now and again, reacted with astonishment when he was asked about it. 'Shoot himself? Why on earth would he do that? He's going to be taken prisoner – like the rest of us.'

Because the divisional staff no longer existed and no orders were being received from elsewhere either, Eichert decided to place himself and his men under the command of the Romanian general, who was the ranking officer in the building. Deserted by their own top brass, German soldiers chose a Romanian to be their commander. The foxholes and cellars of the apartment block were home to five hundred severely wounded men and around three hundred with more minor injuries. And the general had the courage to do the right thing. He ordered his men not to defend the block and instructed that Red Cross flags should be flown when the Russians approached. Acting on his own authority, this Romanian commander, who had been abused and betrayed by the Germans and whose downtrodden troops had been left to starve in misery in the Cauldron after their horses were requisitioned and eaten, took it upon himself to save the lives of hundreds of Wehrmacht soldiers. His name was General Brătescu, commander of the First Romanian Cavalry Division.

In silent accord, they began to prepare for captivity. Only by way of catering for all eventualities, naturally! For on the quiet many of them still believed that the 'great miracle' would happen.

'Whereabouts are you going to sew your wedding ring for safe-keeping?' Schmid asked the paymaster, who was busy pulling on a double layer of underclothes.

'I think I'll sew it into the waistband of my trousers, under a button. That'd be the safest place.'

Captain Eichert sewed Russian banknotes into the lining of his greatcoat. Jankuhn rummaged in a small suitcase and offered the others all the pullovers and other garments he could not manage to squeeze into himself. Everyone went through their kitbags and carefully picked out the most essential items, discarding many things that they had long cherished. Diaries, letters and photographs were all consigned to the flames. Breuer was spared this agony; his only possessions were what he stood up in or carried about his person. He felt his camera in his greatcoat pocket. He weighed it in his hand for a long time. It was a Zeiss 'Ikonta' that had cost him a hundred and five Reichsmarks. When his first son was born, he had sold his typewriter and bought this instead. It had accompanied him through his first years of marriage and on the highways and byways of this crazy conflict. There was a length of iron piping on the stove. He picked it up and began laying into the camera, once, twice, a third time – the little camera refused to die; it wasn't how it was meant to meet its end. Finally, Breuer gave up and tossed it into the fire. He then took a long, hard look at his mouth organ before eventually slipping it back into his pocket.

'You'd best ditch your felt boots right now,' said the paymaster. 'They won't last five minutes, then you'll have to walk barefoot all the way to Siberia!'

He went outside and returned with a pair of brand-new brown jackboots. 'Hey, will you look at all the stuff he's still got!' the others exclaimed. 'Come on then, paymaster, turn all your clobber out this instant! You must have cases and cases of tinned food left!'

'Wouldn't dream of it,' replied Jankuhn, visibly irritated. 'Say we still find ourselves sitting here for a fortnight or more – what do you plan on eating then?'

These were their preparations for when the end came.

Sonderführer Fröhlich wanders through the ruins of Stalingrad. He has no idea any more where the front line is, or where his comrades are. He couldn't stick it out with the flak battery; they'd started to give him the creeps. And he hadn't dared purloin any food. Now hunger is gnawing at him once more.

He's a Baltic German. He wears the blue-and-white cross of the Baltic Territorial Force with pride. He's determined not to fall into the hands of the Russians. 'Anyone else,' he says to himself, 'but not that filthy rabble!' The innate arrogance of the Baltic 'master race' is in the blood of this small fishmonger. Yet he remains hopeful. What was that he'd heard that time at the Staff HQ where he'd spent the night? 'Gentlemen, I saw it with my own eyes,' the colonel surgeon had whispered. 'He smiled. The Führer actually smiled! Mark my words: something's afoot!' Fröhlich feels sure that something's about to happen, too. The Führer keeps his word. The thirtieth of the month is still to come, the tenth anniversary of the 'national revolution'. That's the day it'll happen! That's when Hitler will reveal himself in all his glory, to the shame and disgrace of the unbelievers.

A courtyard in the vicinity of the Central Stalingrad commandant's headquarters. The house next door is home to a food depot. The courtyard is full of people. They're skulking around there, shifty and unarmed, waiting for an opportunity to storm the depot and overpower the paymaster there. In a corner is a large heap of weapons, including rifles and machine guns. An officer is standing next to it, recruiting men for a last stand. 'Two hundred grams of bread for everyone who takes a gun!' His face is flushed from shouting. Every so often, someone comes up, to shouts of derision or hatred from the crowd, sullenly picks up a gun and reaches out to take one of the hunks of bread. But things aren't that simple, it transpires. The officer picks out various people and checks whether they can hold the gun properly and know how to shoot it. Not many of them can.

Fröhlich receives his portion of bread and is assigned to an officers' patrol that's detailed to 'comb through' cellars and bunkers. The squad comprises himself and two NCOs. A lieutenant's in charge, a very young fellow with flashing eyes.

All the underground lairs they visit are crammed with people. In one, they're playing cards ('Hey, what's happening? Has anything happened yet?'). In others, they're burning banknotes, or stuffing themselves pointlessly full on stolen provisions, wolfing sardines and letting the oil run down over their stubbly chins. They're waiting, starving, or dying in these holes in the ground. Germans, trembling Russian girls, Romanians, Croatians, and Italians as well (what are Italians doing here?). In one basement, they encounter a sea of black faces. Yellow, blue, grey and green faces aren't uncommon. But black faces? It turns out that they've been lighting camp fires down there using car tyres!

Poking out from the entrance to one cellar is a stick with a scrap of white cloth tied to it. Inside, a group of uncommunicative old men are sitting round the walls. 'OT' – *Organisation Todt* (the name says it all!). They look like they've been turned to marble. None of them even turn their head.

'You gone crazy or something?' the lieutenant yells. 'Take down that shameful rag outside this instant! Come on, clear out of here, you lot!'

He fires a shot into the ceiling from his carbine. A ripple of muffled grumbling breaks out, softly at first, but growing louder all the while. A voice rises above the hubbub, shrill and piercing: 'Do the bastard in!'

One of them gets up. He approaches, a tall, stocky figure. His face is like a block of wood.

'Piss off, sonny!' he says quietly. 'Go outside and take a pop at someone if it'll amuse you. But leave us in peace! We've had a skinful of you lot!'

With a deft movement, he whips the carbine out of the officer's hand, turns it upside-down and jabs the butt up under his chin. There's a wooden thud, and the lieutenant keels over, flailing with his hands. Fröhlich gets out as fast as he can.

Outside, explosions are going off left and right. Mortars! The two NCOs have disappeared. Fröhlich flings himself into a house doorway. A blast hurls him to the ground before he has a chance to find his feet. Beams are splintering all around him. 'Wood's nothing!' he thinks. 'The fish smokery is tiled. A Horch six-cylinder limo. Sunday on the Wannsee and in the Spreewald…' After some minutes, he struggles to his feet and stumbles into an adjoining room. Piles of rubble cover dead soldiers, one with his torso slumped across a table. Fröhlich wrenches open a door. A woman is lying on the floor, her face a bloody lump of flesh. Beside her an old man is kneeling, stammering out prayers and weeping. But in the middle of the room there stands a child, a little girl of about three years perhaps. Just standing there, rigid and mute. Her small mouth is open a fraction, and her big bloodshot eyes stare unblinking at the intruder. Her tiny hand is clutching a rag doll…

Fröhlich narrows his burning eyes. He recovers from the initial shock and runs out. Shooting is coming from all sides now – rifle fire and machine-gun bursts whipping down the street. Some people are cowering in the shelter of a wall; they brace themselves to make a run for it and then dash across the road. In mid-sprint, one of them suddenly leaps up like a rubber ball, flings his arms into the air and then swings them down between his legs and pitches forward like he's doubling up with laughter. 'Aieeeee!' comes his shrill scream, 'aiieeeee!' Suddenly he straightens up, falls silent, and topples over like a felled tree.

Fröhlich is screaming too. He doesn't know why, but he's scream-ing all the same, wild as an animal. Swinging the machine-pistol in his hand, he bounds through the hail of bullets in long strides, falls over, picks himself up again and heads off, leaping over fences and through gardens until he finally pitches up, gasping for breath, in the lee of a wall.

Three walls without a roof, the ruins of a shed or a garage. Fröhlich suddenly registers that he's not alone. They're lying all around him in the rubble and snow. Ten, fifteen people. They fled here or were brought here some days ago, clearly. The house has collapsed on top of them. Now they lie here, abused and mutilated, struck down but not yet dead. Limbs bruised black and blue, a gangrenous or bloody pulp of fabric, flesh and bones. Heads drained of life like mouldering skulls or shapelessly swollen and looking like they have been eaten by leprosy. There's a babel of slurring, whimpering, gurgling and moaning. One man's laughing crazily to himself. Another has stood up. Two burning irises, framed in white, blaze at Fröhlich, and a skeleton's hand reaches out to him.

'Out there...' – the words sound like they're coming through a crackly tannoy – 'round the corner... the Führer, with my wife... Tell them I'll be along soon... Get going, will you!'

He sinks back with a gurgling sound. There's a greenish froth around his mouth. Fröhlich feels someone tugging at his sleeve.

'Please,' comes a whisper, 'please!' He spins round and finds himself staring into an ivory-white face, grotesquely distorted like a carved carnival mask. A hand gropes at his pistol holster.

'Have mercy!' the voice whispers again. Fröhlich's troubled gaze scans the body writhing in front of him. It's incomplete, with nothing below the knees. The splintered bones poke out white from the tattered, blood-soaked, frozen trouser legs. Something inside Fröhlich snaps.

'Help!' he shrieks, reeling away. 'Heeelp – Heeeelp – Heeeeeelp!!'

The air is crystal-clear and bitterly cold. A flak battery has taken up position beside the District Commander's building. The commander of the battery is urged to take his unit elsewhere. He refuses indignantly. Orders are orders! The light from open fires flickers through the blind windows of the upper storeys and their sooty smoke rises steeply skywards. The visibility is good. The Russians concentrate their fire on the building, which is visible for miles around. All around it, bomb-bursts erupt, while artillery and tank shells and mortar rounds scar and pockmark the walls. Whole rooms and their occupants are blasted into the air. Fires break out repeatedly and are only extinguished with much effort. District Command Central Stalingrad is no longer a peaceful place, most definitely not! Alongside clouds of acrid smoke and a sulphurous yellow mist, the noise of moaning and screaming permeates the rooms and the icy corridors. In the long wooden shed in the court-yard, the bodies are now piled a metre and a half high.

Geibel lies in a room on the first floor. He's running a fever and is delirious. He's barely noticed that his dressings have been changed and that he's getting regular meals: a thin broth of horsemeat, and one time a kind of porridge made from wheat and corn syrup. He has no inkling that he is one of the 'chosen ones', those fortunate few on whom the doctors (simply in order to have something to do and to displace their own fears) are still bothering to operate. With feverish eyes, he looks about in confusion and babbles incoherently when the orderlies come to take him down to the room where the surgeon has set up a makeshift operating theatre. He lies on a wooden table, anaesthetized by ether. And so he fails to notice the massive blast that suddenly rips the wall away and showers the room with fragments of brick and shards of glass. He's also oblivious to the plaster and mortar dust that covers his body, to the piercing cries of the wounded and to the surgeon collapsing beside him, moaning in pain.

When he comes around, he's lying somewhere out in the corridor. Instead of having the bullet that was lodged in his femur removed, he's now picked up some more injuries: a large piece of shell has torn his hip, while his face and arms are peppered with some smaller shrapnel. He's now no longer one of those 'with good prospects'. In fact, things aren't looking too rosy even for them any more. For the surgeon has lost both of his hands in the explosion. With his bleeding stumps of arms, he has himself now unexpectedly joined the category of hopeless cases. No one sees this as clearly as he does. He begs to be injected with an overdose of morphine to end it all. The other doctors discuss the matter but come to no firm conclusion. And eventually the disabled doctor who cannot even dispatch himself is forgotten about. They've got other worries.

For the Russians are now only just a few hundred metres away.

Red Cross flags are hung out. Will the Russians take any notice of the symbol? The whole place is alive with feverish tension. Red Army soldiers have occupied the building opposite, and are firing across the courtyard with a heavy machine gun. But they aren't shooting at the building or at the people who have gathered in front of it in a state of high anxiety.

Then they advance up the street in their white winter camouflage suits. But as they draw near, the colonel surgeon is nowhere to be found. The Russians demand that the building be cleared. With the help of the lightly wounded, the orderlies get everyone out who is still mobile to some extent. There are only a few such patients left. Those in the densely packed corridors who get trampled to death by them as they make their way out are the lucky ones, as soon becomes clear.

Down on the street, the prisoners are being herded in lines to make their way into captivity. They are medical orderlies for the most part.

Corporal Herbert, who has hidden himself in a nearby cellar, emerges and runs along the crocodiles of men. He is looking for Geibel. He doesn't find him. A Russian sentry forces him into line with the others. The only people left in the building now are those who can't move. How many of them are there – five hundred, eight hundred, a thousand even? No one has any idea. In the cellars of Stalingrad, the paymasters are sitting burning banknotes, as per their orders. As they do so, they punctiliously strike through the relevant serial numbers on their lists. But no one is keeping tally of the numbers of wounded here.

Slowly the procession of prisoners begins to move. Herbert keeps looking around him. They've only marched a few hundred metres when bright flames suddenly leap from the building. Herbert lets out a scream and presses his fist to his mouth to stifle it.

The former commander's headquarters was razed to the ground with all the severely wounded men inside.

Among the dead was Private Walter Geibel from Chemnitz.

He hadn't wanted to go to war. In fact, he'd never wanted to leave his little shop in Chemnitz at all. At the front, he'd only had a single goal in life – to see his wife again and his baby son, who'd been born during his absence. This one wish had also flitted through the feverish dreams and ramblings of his final days. But no one had enquired after his dreams. He'd just been a pawn in the hands of others. And quietly, dutifully and trustingly he'd died a horrific death, without ever knowing why.

It almost seemed as though Paymaster Jankuhn was to be proved right: the end still refused to come. In the sector around the Zariza Gorge, it was rumoured that a new front had opened up. The name of one Colonel Rostek was mentioned. New hope flickered into life with this news. Only Captain Eichert no longer wavered.

'Don't be foolish, gentlemen,' he said, 'it's all pointless! The handful of men they've cobbled together there can't hold out for more than two or three days at most, and they'll be annihilated in the process. It's a crime! And all just because some nutter's still got a point to prove!'

But it seemed there were more such 'nutters' around. Without warning, a general appeared in the cellar. They could hear him storming down the corridor even before he entered the room. Wearing a peaked cap with earmuffs, carrying a knotted stick in his hands and accompanied by two helmeted officers with carbines, he burst in, cursing and yelling.

'No preparations… no barricades… not a single man with a rifle to be seen! And there's someone waiting out there in the corridor with a white flag! What's the meaning of this, eh?'

The officers had stood to attention when he came in. They did not recognize this tigerish face, which was currently as dark as a thundercloud. They had no idea who they were dealing with. Having gone for days without any orders or news, they knew nothing of the changes that had taken place in the interim in the leadership of the Sixth Army. So they were unaware that General von Seydlitz, commander-in-chief of the eastern front of the Cauldron, had finally decided, after one last fruitless appeal to Paulus, to take matters into his own hands.

'Since the High Command has given up issuing orders, I'll give them instead!' he'd informed his commanders. 'And my orders are these: to prevent scattered units engaging in senseless fights to the death and incurring pointless casualties, I'm giving the commanders of individual detachments the authority to cease hostilities locally once they've exhausted all their ammunition.'

This very sensible new autonomy had succeeded in stirring the top brass from their lethargy once more. Very gently and carefully, von Seydlitz had been relieved of his command, though in secret Schmidt had even weighed up the option of having him arrested. Command of the eastern front, now only some two kilometres long, was transferred to the 'Tiger', who had found himself separated from his corps and displaced to the central sector by the surprise splitting of the Cauldron. The draconian orders of the last few days had been his doing: anyone touching a supply drop without authorization to be shot on sight. Likewise anyone who attempted to make contact with the enemy. And so on, and so forth… summary execution for a whole range of misdemeanours.

And here he was in the flesh. Uninformed and innocent, yet somehow in thrall to the aura of death and destruction that this figure exuded, the assembled officers stared into the poisonous face of the old general. No one could find anything to say in reply. Only Dr Korn, who was just in the process of replacing Lieutenant Dierk's bandages, mumbled something about the number of wounded men.

'Wounded? What do you mean, "wounded"?' roared the general. 'You've been ordered to fight to the last man! Anyone who's still able to hold a rifle should be out there, this instant! Understood?' He turned to the officers who'd come in with him.

'No matter where you go, you find these slackers loafing about without any sign of get-up-and-go in 'em! What do you reckon to that, eh?' he hissed at the men, who stood there like statues.

'Do you even know where the front line is right now?' he asked, turning back to the room.

Breuer was standing in the corner. He struck himself as being somewhat detached from proceedings. His thoughts were turning somersaults in his head. What did this general want with them? Fighting to the last man, huh? Yeah, that's right: 'man' was the operative word here! There was a world of difference between 'man' and 'general'. After the last man had fallen the general would pack his bag and head off into captivity in the comforting knowledge that he'd carried out his orders to the letter. Lakosch, he was just such a 'man'. But he'd chosen not to fight to the last. He'd done more, he'd tried saving his comrades, 'men' like him. Now he was over with the Russians, and the general, this slave-driver whipping them up for one last Dance of Death, was here. Yes, where was the front line?

As if in a dream, Breuer heard his own voice fill the ominous silence and felt all eyes glued on him: 'The front line runs between Justice and Injustice, General, sir! And you – you're on the wrong side.'

The general looked at his interlocutor with piercing eyes. Then he shrugged his shoulders faintly and turned away. 'Some kind of lunatic!' he thought to himself, comfortingly. You ran across this kind of thing a lot now. In the meantime, though, Captain Eichert had regained his composure. He fought to suppress a coughing fit.

'There are five hundred wounded men in this building, General,' he said with studied calm, though his voice sounded hoarse. 'Five hundred severely wounded men. We're not firing another shot here – unless it's to protect these wounded men from lunatics!'

The two men's gazes locked. And in this instant it dawned on Captain Eichert what he'd just done. It amounted to insubordination, refusal to obey an order, insulting a superior – the worst crimes a soldier could commit! But he held his ground. He thought of his division and the three defeats it had suffered, and the wrecks of men that were lying around here now. He had fought on the western front of the Cauldron from day one, constantly at hotspots, fighting courageously and successfully over and over again without ever questioning the point and the purpose or the number of casualties – as he'd been ordered to. He'd led the poor wretches from the Fortress Construction Battalion to their deaths when all was already lost – as he'd been ordered to. They'd held out on the railway embankment for three long days, had taken out twelve Russian tanks and had slowly bled to death – as they'd been ordered to. They'd blown up their last heavy guns – as they'd been ordered to. They'd done everything they believed it was their duty to do, they and thousands of brave soldiers and officers from other units, all of them loyal and courageous. They'd carried out every order bar none, even the most senseless. Without them, the Cauldron would never have survived for so long, and the criminal game of the top brass could never have been played out to the final act. But there was a limit that no order could overcome. And that limit had now been reached.

Through narrowed eyes, Eichert calmly took the measure of the general. The right corner of his mouth had curled up slightly, forming a sharp vertical crease in his cheek. He knew what had to happen now. He knew from fourteen years' experience the mechanisms of military discipline that would now kick automatically into action. But he was ready for anything.

And then the Tiger lost his nerve and looked away. All of a sudden his face slumped and he looked old and grey. He turned to his companions.

'Very well, then, this building's a field hospital,' he said dully. 'Okay, let's be on our way. Time's short.'

And turning up the collar of his coat, he stomped out. And those who remained behind realized: it wasn't simply a general who had just climbed down.

7

Twilight of the Gods

THE THIRTIETH OF JANUARY 1943 – ten years since the Nazi 'takeover of power'! Everyone's thoughts turn around this date. What had things been like back then? Ten years ago…*

Germany Awake! Torchlight processions… 'Hail to our Leader!' The National Awakening!

'Give me four years!' The Reichstag fire. 'The SA is on the march…' Book burnings, Certificate of Aryan descent, 'When Jewish blood flows under the knife…' *'Germany Has Become More Beautiful.'*

Nuremberg, the rallies: flags, sunshine, the Badenweiler March, Coca-Cola, the fairground in Fürth… *'We will tear up the shameful treaty!'* … 'Hitler weather'…

Rearmament! Cannon instead of butter! … *'not in order to deprive*

---

* The following list comprises a mixture of Nazi slogans and names of policy initiatives, snatches of nationalistic and popular songs of the period, and excerpts from speeches predominantly by Adolf Hitler but also by Joseph Goebbels and Hermann Göring. Where Gerlach has quoted a line of the popular wartime song 'Lili Marleen' – as performed by the German singer Lale Andersen (*'aus der Erde Grund – grüßt dich im Traume…'*) – rather than offer a literal translation, I have taken the liberty of substituting a line from Vera Lynn's contemporaneous version of the song, which will be more familiar to English readers.

other peoples of their liberty...' The Winter Aid Programme, 'One-Pot Meal Sunday', Marriage loans, the Cross of Honour of the German Mother, occupation of the Rhineland... Military service! 'I swear... unconditional loyalty to the Führer' – 'People – To Arms!'

The Anti-Comintern Pact – the Spanish Civil War... 'a training ground for our troops – with live rounds!' – 'Back home to the Reich!' 'The Saar is German...' The annexation of Austria: 'I proclaim before history...' The Sudetenland, Munich... 'no further territorial demands... from now on things will get better and better...' Protectorate – A thousand years of Greater Germany – 'Ein Volk, ein Reich, ein Führer!'

'...and tomorrow, the whole world!' Lebensraum! Lebensraum! Blood and Soil! 'Hoist the flags in the east wind...' '... for me, the war has not ended since 1914...' Danzig. Poland: 'I trust some swine won't come running to me suggesting mediation...' War!! 'Since five forty-five this morning, we have been returning fire... with a joyous heart... I am your conscience!'

Denmark, Norway: 'Aryan blood shall never perish!' – Holland, Belgium – Fanfares – 'We march triumphantly into France!' Fanfares, fanfares!

'... only one enemy remaining...' 'For we sail to take on the English, the English!' Eight hundred thousand tons, a million tons! 'If Mr Churchill thinks... Rest assured, he is coming! ... we will wipe out their cities!' 'Even if everything shatters...'

Yugoslavia, Greece: 'German retribution in the Balkans! – 'The New European Order!

Twenty-second of June 1941... against Russia? Against Russia! '... I have signed a Non-Aggression and consultative pact .., scrap of paper ... Where I have placed my signature...' 'Command us, Führer – and we will follow you!'

'Animals... Asiatic hordes' Crusade against Bolshevism! '...we will switch to the land policy of the future...' Commissar decree... 'Take weakness and bestiality equally into account! ...language that only he understands. Kill, kill, kill! Have no conscience. I am your conscience!'

Smolensk, Odessa, Kiev, Vyasma-Bryansk… *'already broken and will never rise again! … for the final mighty blow … before the onset of winter.'*

Rommel the Desert Fox… Bombs on Berlin! … *'you can call me Meier'*… War against America! … *'Mr Roosevelt without ships… all just nobodies…'*

Winter battle outside Moscow – Retreat from Moscow! *'*… gave his life for the cause of Greater Germany… With faith in the Führer…' 'I'd hold you tight, We'd kiss goodnight, My Lili of the lamplight…' The Cross of Honour of the German Mother! *'Never again will my actions cause a German mother to weep.'* 'We give thanks to our Führer!'

'We have managed to avert the looming catastrophe… worse cannot and will not follow.'

Summer 1942: Voronezh, the Caucasus – 'Our work in the east is paying dividends… for oil and iron, for waving fields of wheat! That's what motivates our soldiers and gives them a cause to die for!'

Stalingrad – 'a few small combat patrols… no second Verdun … Let's just wait and see whether that was a strategic mistake…'

Stalingrad! 'You can be sure that no one will ever dislodge us from this place!' And that is what they are dying for, dying… Never again will a German mother… 'There's an end to it all, There's an end to it okaaay…'

Stalingrad! To the last bullet… 'You can rely on me with rock-like confidence!'… 'No sacrifice too great… everything shattered…'

The thirtieth of January 1943 – ten years of the 'Third Reich'… 'We give thanks to our Führer!'

The officers were still asleep. The first pink-tinged reflections of the morning sun were just glinting through the ruins opposite onto the cellar window when the moaning of wounded men in the adjoining room was interrupted by the slamming of doors, running steps, and a loud, staccato voice. They could hear snatches like 'divisional staff' and 'deployment'. Someone answered lethargically.

Breuer woke from his slumbers with a violent start. He knew that voice. Before he had time to think, the door was flung open and in stumbled a figure clutching a machine-pistol.

'Fröhlich!' cried Breuer, getting to his feet. 'Good God, man, where on earth did you get to? I'm amazed you're still alive!'

The Sonderführer's face underneath his fur-trimmed cap looked frightful. Dark shadows had appeared beneath his angular cheek-bones, and a pair of jaundiced-looking eyes goggled glassily from black sockets. His pupils stared hard past the rims of weak eyelids. His mouth stood open in a gesture of dumb expectation, and wisps of straggly beard hung down from his protruding chin.

'Like Don Quixote,' thought Breuer in shock. 'He looks just like Don Quixote!'

'Where have you been? What about the others? Sit down, tell us what's happened!'

The Sonderführer opened his eyes wide and furrowed his brow.

'Today,' he whispered hoarsely, 'the thirtieth... ten years! He waited till today...'

He paused, cowered slightly, hunched up his shoulders and held up his left forefinger. He seemed to be listening for something.

'We have to go,' he hissed, 'right now... a counter-attack... if they come! German planes, three of them – just spotted 'em! Quite high up... It's a sign!'

Breuer put his hand on Fröhlich's shoulder. 'Come on, why don't you start by putting down your gun... that's it. Now take your coat off and get comfortable! There's coffee on the go and we've still got something to eat.'

Meanwhile, the others had perked up at the news.

'Hey, that's right, lads! Today's the thirtieth of January – the ten-year anniversary!'

'Do you remember how it was back then?'

'Yeah, it was a right old shindig... A torchlight procession through the Brandenburg Gate... and the Reich Chancellery... Hitler and

Hindenburg at the window… everyone thinking things were going to be rosy from then on.'

'I couldn't have imagined then that in ten years' time I'd be up to my neck in this shit here…'

'Anyhow, I'm all ears to hear what they're planning to celebrate back there today. Is Adolf going to speak?'

'I think Göring's meant to give a speech,' said Captain Eichert. 'We should listen to it. Maybe he'll sort this mess out for us, eh?'

As Breuer tried to pump the Sonderführer for information on the fate of Fackelmann's task force, Jankuhn took a look at the radio set. Over the last few days, they'd had sporadic reception on it. When the customary mortar-round reveille had passed, the paymaster crawled out of the cellar. A new antenna was rigged up, a still-usable battery cannibalized from a shot-up car, and after a bit of tinkering they managed to find some music, quite clearly, on the short wave. Anticipation rose. 'What's he going to talk about? Wonder if he'll mention Stalingrad?' Hitherto, the regular army bulletin had never mentioned Stalingrad by name and had only spoken in vague terms about 'heroic defensive actions in the east.'

'Course he'll mention Stalingrad! He can't keep avoiding the subject, especially not today. He's bound to say something.'

The announcer's voice came on the wireless. 'Unfortunately, the start of our broadcast from the banqueting hall of the Reich Air Ministry to celebrate the tenth anniversary of the accession to power has had to be postponed for about an hour for technical reasons. Until then, some marching-band music.'

There came the strains of the 'Finnish Cavalryman' followed by the Hohenfriedberger March. Despite some atmospheric interference, the transmission was pretty good. Fröhlich sat against the wall with his knees drawn up to his chest. He had closed his eyes and was beating out time to the music with his hand.

'Well, they seem pretty cheerful about things over there, I must say!' said First Lieutenant Schmid. 'I can't wait to hear Göring's speech. Listen here, lads, how about if he says something like this: "You've kept on fighting, believing in the Führer. And now your faith has been rewarded. The Führer hasn't left you in the lurch. We've kept quiet for so long because we wanted to wait for a happy outcome. Today, on the tenth anniversary of our coming to power, we have succeeded in liberating you. Airborne divisions have made contact with the forces that were encircled. Loyalty in return for loyalty!" That'd really be something, wouldn't it?'

'Loyalty for loyalty!' screeched Fröhlich like a parrot.

The others laughed nervously.

'I'll be happy,' said Eichert, 'if he just tells it like it is. If he says: "We've made mistakes—"'

'He'll nover soy that!' interjected Findeisen.

'"—made some serious mistakes, as a result of which the Russians have managed to encircle three hundred thousand men at Stalingrad. They have fought valiantly, above all against hunger and cold, and in the process have tied down a large part of the Russian forces. In doing this, they have discharged the last unglamorous duty they could be called upon to perform, and have incurred heavy losses. They have achieved more and endured more than any German troops have done before. And they have suffered all this hardship because of our stupidity and shortsightedness (Okay, he doesn't need to say that!). Now all that remains in Stalingrad are wounded, starving and half-frozen men who are incapable of fighting. As a result, the Führer has today decided to order the remnants of the Sixth Army to seek an honourable surrender. Through this order he has saved around a hundred thousand German men – fathers and sons – for our nation. This is the Führer's gift to the German people to mark the tenth anniversary of his accession to power…"'

Captain Eichert paused and took a deep breath.

'He could say something like that, for instance.'

The others kept silent. 'Yes,' they thought to themselves, 'he certainly could!'

At that moment, a soldier rushed into the room.

'Captain, sir!' he called. 'The Russians! They're already three blocks beyond us!'

'The Russians? How come? Why?'

'They couldn't go through the square and the streets; there's too much shooting going on there still. So they smashed their way from house to house through the cellar walls! Some guys came from the neighbouring block and said...'

Eichert stood up.

'Okay,' he said, 'the sentries with the white flags should get ready! Corporal Kunze will organize it! As soon as the Russians appear anywhere, put out the flags and report back! Gentlemen, I think this is it! Seems like we won't get to hear what Herr Göring has to say after all... I think I can safely say we've made all the necessary preparations.'

Chief Paymaster Jankuhn had turned pale. He hesitated for a moment, then left the room. After a while he came back with seven tins of preserved meat and a case of cigars.

'I'll share out the remaining supplies,' he said sheepishly. 'No point hoarding them now.'

He handed each of them a tin.

'Hey, Paymaster, you must take the prize for klutz of the century!' cried Schmid. 'For days, we haven't had so much as a blade of straw to smoke, and now you turn up with these great big coffin nails!'

Everyone pounced on the cigars. Jankuhn ceremoniously produced a bundle of banknotes, crisp new fifty-mark bills issued by the Reich Credit Bank.

'So, gentlemen, if you'd care to use these notes as firelighters!' he said, waving the wad of money around. 'Let's see out the end of the world in style, at least!'

'Oi'm losig moi mind!' exclaimed Findeisen. 'Oi've only read about this sort of thig in dime-store novels before!'

He rolled up a note, crossed his legs expansively and lit up his cigar like some bigwig. Presently, the room was shrouded in a dense fug of cigar smoke. Breuer spooned pinkish liver sausage into his mouth out of the kilogram tin he'd opened. There was no bread left. After ten minutes, he belched like he'd been consuming rotten eggs. But he carried on eating manfully. Who knew when they'd next get food? The men's attention turned once more to the radio set. It was still playing marching tunes. The start of the transmission had already been delayed twice.

'What's the problem there?'

'Maybe Hermann's mislaid his medals!'

'Or the RAF have laid a couple of eggs over Berlin to wish him many happy returns! I wouldn't put it past them!'

But finally, the start of the Reichsmarschall's speech was announced. Over the radio came the murmur of a hall full of expectantly waiting people. The presenter, his voice hushed with studied reverence, described the scene:

> ...representatives from each of the three branches of the armed forces plus the Waffen-SS are in attendance... all young soldiers, adjutants... and now in comes the Reichsmarschall...

The muted sound of military commands and the click of heels. The radio presenter's voice sinks to a whisper. In shrill and excited tones, a master of ceremonies announces Göring's speech. The room falls silent...

And then comes the voice of Göring, plump and jovial like some cheerful 'mine host'. The officers huddle closer round the receiver. From outside, soldiers filter in, with gaunt faces, darting eyes and open mouths. Everyone listens intently. Göring waxes lyrical about the supposed causes of the war, the evil attacks by World Jewry and envious plutocrats, and of Germany's military triumphs. How often they'd heard all that stuff, how sickeningly often. Gradually the Reichsmarschall works his way round to the present:

> … And then began the second harsh winter… bitter enough to
> cast its icy spell over everything – rivers, lakes and marshes…
> making the whole terrain traversable by the enemy again.

'It's common knowledge every winter's like that here,' observed Jankuhn drily. 'We were taught it at school!' Saying this, he lit his fourth cigar. The things had to be smoked. It'd be a shame if the Russians…

> … this enemy is tough, make no mistake. Their leadership
> is barbarically harsh …they've never been afraid of using
> the whip to mobilize their troops. If anyone collapsed from
> exhaustion, they got a bullet in the head. Anyone governing a
> people like that is going to be a tough adversary!

'Oh, now he admits it! Last year, the Russians were on their last legs, supposedly!'

> … yet right now we are witnessing one last effort – admittedly,
> a gigantic one – on the part of the enemy. New divisions
> have been formed and others replenished; but it's not fresh
> recruits, oh no – instead, weary old men and boys of sixteen
> are being pressed into combat… And behind these front-line
> battalions, the machine guns of the commissars have been
> tripled, quadrupled, and Russians soldiers are being driven…

Bitter laughter ripples round the cellar. 'It's like an idiot's guide to the war against Russia! Maybe that lot back home really believe the crap he's talking!'

'Shut your mouth, will you?'

… convinced that this is their final roll of the dice – they're trying to squeeze the very last drop from their reserves… Their commanders are brutal in the extreme, but in spite of that we've beaten them up till now and we'll keep on beating them… we'll drive them back, all along the line! … Germany will fight and bleed but it will emerge victorious!

'Emerge victorious, ha ha! "Emerge victorious" – that's a good one! "All along the line"…'

'If he's talking about victory, I don't reckon he'll be mentioning Stalingrad!'

'Shhh! Will you pipe down?'

The speaker's voice reached a crescendo of sublime pathos:

… and now Stalingrad, the struggle for Stalingrad, rises up like some gigantic, monumental edifice! One day, this will go down in legend as the greatest heroic struggle in our history… and anyone who is in this city, from the general down to the last man, anyone who is fighting there for every stone, every hole and every trench will be a hero… a powerful heroic epic about a battle without equal, like the Song of the Nibelungs… men who fought on relentlessly to the bitter end… Even in a thousand years from now, every German will utter the name Stalingrad with a reverential shudder and recall that it was there that the Wehrmacht laid the foundations of Germany's ultimate victory.

Silence had descended, so completely that you could hear quite distinctly through the walls the sounds of distant banging and hammering and of collapsing rubble.

'What the hell is this?' asked Eichert, looking at his fellow officers. 'It's a bloody funeral oration. He's not speaking to us any more!' His voice rose to a scream. 'We're already dead! Like lambs to the slaughter... slaughtered for propaganda!' He grabbed Breuer by the arm and shook him. 'Breuer, what's going on? What does this mean? It – it's just terrible!'

A horrible fit of coughing cut him short. Breuer had no time to reply. He cast a concerned eye at Lieutenant Dierk. He was sitting against the wall. His eyes were wide open and his chest was heaving as he gasped and wheezed for air. Sounding far-off and broken up across two thousand kilometres of ether, the solemn, bombastic words of the eccentric guest speaker still resonated clearly enough from the vibrating metallic box:

> ...my young soldiers, your hearts must surely be beating all the more proudly and joyfully in your breasts in the knowledge that you are part of a nation and an army like ours. It is a wonderful feeling, a regal feeling... to fight and fight again as heroes on the ruins of this city. Despite being so few in number...

'Three hundred thousand,' whispered Jankuhn, 'only three hundred thousand of us!'

> ... your resistance is still a towering achievement. My soldiers, most of you will have heard of a similar example from history... When you consider that many thousands of years have gone by since Leonidas stood with three hundred fellow Spartans at a narrow pass in Greece... the sky grew dark from the number of arrows unleashed against them... the Persian ruler Xerxes had a force of thousands at his disposal, yet the three hundred men did not waver or yield; they kept fighting a hopeless battle... until the last man had fallen. And in this narrow pass there now stands an inscription: 'Stranger, when you find us lying here, go and tell the Spartans we obeyed their orders.' They were a mere three hundred, my comrades!

Millennia have passed and today... this sacrifice of yours is just as heroic... one day, men will say: 'Stranger, bear this message to Germany, that you saw us lying in Stalingrad...'

'Saw us lying? Saw us lying?' yelled Fröhlich, stretching out his hand as if reaching for something that no one else could see. A shiver ran down the others' spines. Buried alive – defenceless, they were to be entombed here and condemned into the bargain to listen to these hypocritical eulogies to the great crime! It seemed that the speaker could sense the wave of bitterness rising up against him from the distant mass grave; he became ever more agitated and began to scream and curse:

...duty of the whole German nation! No one should start bleating and quibbling about whether this or that action was necessary, or whether our soldiers should have been defending Stalingrad or not. They were ordered to defend it, plain and simple! The law required it – the law of honour, but first and foremost the law of warfare...

'The law of incompetence and megalomania and obstinacy!' yelled Schmid at the blameless metal box. He tried to get up, but sank back in his chair with a sigh, overcome by the pointlessness of his protest. Göring's voice went on pitilessly:

... in the final analysis, though this may sound callous, it is all the same to a soldier whether he falls in battle in Stalingrad, in Rzhev, in the deserts of North Africa or in the icy wastelands of the North; the main thing is that he has offered up his life...

'Oh yeah, of course it's all the same to us...,' thought Breuer, shaking with rage at what he was hearing. 'All the same to us whether we're defending our homeland on its borders or two thousand miles away in the middle of nowhere, all the same whether we're doing it for justice and freedom or for minerals, oil and wheat or whether our sacrifice is for our fellow Germans or for a bunch of criminals! All the same, all the fucking same…'

> …or think of the Goths at the Battle of Mount Vesuvius. The same principle applies there too! They made the final sacrifice when they realized there was no hope left for them…

No hope left! For the tens of thousands of wounded and sick, no hope left… And this sack of shit dared to say that!

Captain Eichert had jumped to his feet.

'Enough of this!' he shouted. 'Enough, I say!'

He grabbed the iron bar that lay on the stove and set about the radio like a madman. Göring's voice fell silent. The radio crashed to the floor, dragging the battery with it. There was a tinkle of glass as the valves shattered. Eichert dropped the iron bar and mopped his brow with the back of his hand.

'Betrayed and sold down the river,' he said quietly, in a surprised tone as if he'd just had a fresh insight. 'Abandoned, just abandoned… Naturally, so no one will be left to tell how things really were…' Then his rage bubbled to the surface again: 'They're fabricating a new heroic epic so they can convince a new generation of hundreds and thousands… that miserable bunch of lying bastards!'

Breuer had not taken his eyes off Dierk the whole time. All of a sudden, he launched himself at the lieutenant and took a swing at his arm. A shot rang out and a bullet embedded itself somewhere in the ceiling. Breuer wrestled the pistol from Dierk's hand.

'Not you, Dierk!' he gasped. 'Not you, lad! I know where you're coming from, but you can't do that!'

After a few minutes, once the excitement had died down, and the soldiers had filed out, cursing under their breath, and the rest were sitting round drained and shattered, the captain leaned over and said to Breuer: 'Why didn't you let Dierk have his way? He's right, you know – it's better to put a bullet through your own… oh Christ, it's all so desperate, so awful…'

'You really want to do the Russian bandits' dirty work for them, Eichert?' Jankuhn asked bitterly. 'That's exactly what they want, for us all to do ourselves in… so no one ever gets back home! We've seen too much, we know too much! What's the betting they're still afraid of us, even now?'

Eichert wearily dismissed the paymaster's objections. 'What's the point in anything now! The war's lost, I see that now. This madman's going to make sure that the whole of Germany goes up in flames – And you still talk about going back and confronting these criminals with what we've gone through here? Breuer, I don't think I have the strength to laugh any more—'

Breuer grasped the captain's hand.

'Yes, we've got to make it back!' he said. 'To ensure that what's happened here can never, ever happen again! And to bring those responsible to book – that's worth living for! Germany's not going to perish. As sure as day follows night. And one day, maybe, we'll learn to laugh again too… Hitler wants us to die. If we stay alive, then we've struck the first blow against him, the first blow for a new world of the future!'

In the cellar of the large, semicircular building on the southwestern corner of Stalingrad's Red Square sat Colonel Lunitz, surrounded by his officers. His tanned, leathery face was scored with countless wrinkles and deep folds of skin, and the close-cropped curly hair on his angular skull shone as white as snow on a field in April. The colonel was not in the best of moods. After the divisional staff had been transformed overnight into the opaque 'Unold Staff' and then vanished without trace somewhere in the general collapse of the Sixth Army, Colonel Lunitz, commander of the artillery regiment, had faithfully led the remnants of the tank division (that is, the handful of men and vehicles that remained after the almost total 'combing-out' exercise had depleted it) through all the many perils of the Cauldron to Red Square in Stalingrad to await the end of hostilities. But in the event, his little band was not to be left to rest in peace. Colonel Rostek, the 'strong man' who, after the collapse in the southern sector of the city, went on to shore up resistance in the Zariza Gorge – for three days, at least – had assigned Colonel Lunitz the task of combing through the cellars of the bombed-out buildings and assembling fighting units from the soldiers he managed to winkle out there and his own men. These sad little detachments, cobbled together only through the prospect of getting something to eat, had been severely mauled by the first Russian assault on the Zariza front. The last dregs of this force were now stationed on the southern perimeter of Red Square – facing the Russians. The Gorky Theatre opposite, which had been full to the rafters with wounded men, had been cleared. And here on the street, directly in front of his command post, three Russian tanks had been standing immobile for over an hour, with their guns trained on the building. They surely wouldn't remain there doing nothing for much longer. They couldn't destroy them, as they had no armour-piercing rounds left. If only First Lieutenant von Horn were here with his last serviceable tank! But he was up at the railway station, to which Russian units had also advanced... And if that wasn't all bad enough, Army High Command had to come along and saddle him with this impossible assignment! For several days, the army staff had been occupying the department store on the northern side of the square, under the command of Colonel Rostek (correction: his successful organizing of resistance on the Zariza had seen him promoted to general in the interim). And the Russians were positioned here on the southern side! Little wonder, then, that they'd started to get a bit jumpy over there. In any event, Lunitz had suddenly received a call from General Schmidt, chief of staff of the Sixth Army, in person.

'Listen here, Lunitz,' Schmidt had said, 'the southern perimeter of Red Square must be held at all costs – at all costs, do you understand? I'm making you personally responsible for ensuring that we don't all get hauled out of our beds and taken prisoner in the middle of the night.'

'Yes, General, sir, but I'd like to know what forces—'

'At all costs, whatever it takes! Understood?'

And with that, he'd hung up. It was a deuced easy business, issuing such an order – but quite another matter carrying it out.

'What a heap of crap!' said the colonel, looking round his assembled officers. In their faces, he could see they completely agreed with this assessment of their situation. All politeness had by now gone out the window. But that made it easier for them to communicate. A soldier came in. After making something of a meal of knocking the snow off his boots, he gave a perfunctory salute.

'Colonel,' he announced, 'there was someone over at the theatre shouting across to us. Said we should clear the building immediately, or the tanks'll open fire on us.'

'There you go!' said the colonel. 'Nice of them to warn us in advance, mind. Well, if they're so polite, they'll be bound to contact us again. Very well, then,' he said, turning to the soldier, 'the next time anyone appears, call me!'

The soldier shuffled out.

'So, what do we do now?' the colonel mused, rubbing his nose. 'We can't evacuate the building. That'd be flouting High Command's orders. But can we risk being bombarded? How many wounded do we have here?'

'Four or five hundred, Colonel, sir,' replied his adjutant, Captain Schulte.

'Out of the question, then. So, what's to be done?'

After a quarter of an hour, the colonel was called up to ground level. From a blasted window, he looked out over the three tanks towards the theatre. There, making no attempt to take cover, a

German officer stood cupping his hands round his mouth like a megaphone.

'Attention!' he shouted. 'Ultimatum from the Red Army to Colonel Lunitz! Attention! The Red Army orders you to clear the building opposite within ten minutes! Otherwise it will be blown to bits.'

The officer repeated this demand twice before withdrawing. By now, nothing fazed Colonel Lunitz – not the sight of a German officer acting as a mouthpiece for the Red Army, nor the fact that the man knew his name. Living in this madhouse had taught him not to be surprised by anything.

'In ten minutes? You must be off your rocker!' he muttered to himself.

'Go over there, would you, Schulte, and persuade them to desist from this bloody nonsense. There's just no point any more!'

Captain Schulte pulled out his handkerchief, but after giving it a quick once-over stuck it back in his pocket. Its indeterminate colour might be misleading, he decided. Instead, he held up a sheet of paper as a makeshift white flag and made his way across the street past the three stationary tanks to the theatre.

Twenty minutes later he reappeared.

'There's no talking to them! You'll have to come and have a word with them yourself, Colonel, sir!'

'Hmm – very well, then!' said the colonel, and set off across the square with two of his staff officers. In the theatre foyer, they were received by Russians, who led them further into the building. They didn't even think it necessary to blindfold them. The place was teeming with Red Army soldiers, sitting cosily round open wood fires like there wasn't a war going on. And he and his pathetic handful of men were supposed to defend the Sixth Army High Command against this horde! Then a brainwave suddenly struck him – a truly Solomonic inspiration. Yes, he thought, if he could pull that off, everything would be hunky-dory!'

A Russian major received the German officers in a little wooden house that was still occupied by civilians. He switched on a radio transmitter, spoke a few words and then passed the handset to the colonel. Lunitz cleared his throat.

'Colonel Lunitz here, commander of a tank division!' he announced. 'Putting on airs is half the battle,' he thought to himself.

'Colonel Lossev here, commanding officer 29th Division!' came the reply from the other end, in impeccable German.

'Colonel, you've threatened to blow my command post to smithereens. I would ask you to refrain from doing so! There are hundreds of wounded men in the building, and it's not practicable to evacuate them in so short a time frame. In addition, I'm requesting a ceasefire be put in place until 0400 hours tomorrow morning for my entire sector.'

There was silence at the other end of the line for a moment. Then the voice, clearly that of an interpreter, came on again. The speaker did not address the colonel's request at all, but instead began reading out the official Red Army conditions of surrender. Midway through a sentence there was a loud click and the connection was broken... Now of all times, damn it to hell! The major tinkered with the radio set, but to no avail! It proved impossible to establish any further communication. What now? Colonel Lunitz had no choice but to try to continue negotiations with the major, at least. But all he did was insist that the Germans lay down their arms straight away, and refused to discuss any other option.

'You know what?' said the colonel finally. 'Let's do a deal! You grant me a ceasefire until four o' clock tomorrow morning, and at that point my men and I will let you take us prisoner!'

The Russian major was in agreement. They parted on the best of terms.

Colonel Lunitz was pleased with himself. The building was saved and at the same time he'd be able to carry out his orders from High Command. The chiefs of staff could sleep safe in their beds that evening. He'd like to see someone do any better! What happened afterwards was no concern of his. Orders were orders!

Even so, he was somewhat ill at ease. He ate his evening bread ration silently and morosely.

'The Russians!' someone shouts in panic into the room. Everyone leaps up. Breuer throws on his coat.

'Quick, come with me!'

He drags Fröhlich to his feet and rushes outside. The Sonderführer follows hard on his heels, holding his machine-pistol.

They stumble up the wooden stairs. Bullets ping over their heads, making a pattering sound as they thud into the brickwork. A sentry is cowering beside one of the pillars at the entrance to the courtyard, waving his white flag. He gestures to them to hurry up. Breuer sticks his head around the corner in time to see two small brown-coated figures come running across the square, crouching low and carrying machine guns. The ear flaps of their *ushankas* waggle like elephants' ears.

'Come, come!' they call from some distance away, beckoning to them.

Fröhlich stands rooted to the spot, gazing at them. Breuer feels his heart pounding so hard it seems to have risen to the back of his throat.

The Russians steadily advance, chattering excitedly and shouting over one another. Over and over, in broken German, they keep calling:

'Come, all come!'

Fröhlich leans against the wall. He is shaking all over.

'Why don't you open your mouth, for Christ's sake!' Breuer yells at the interpreter. 'Tell them we want to speak to an officer, and that we've got wounded men…'

Fröhlich's body is shaken by a sudden violent spasm.

'No!' he roars. 'Noooooo…!'

Abruptly, he lurches out from his cover and makes off with long strides across the street and out into the square. The two Russians stare at him in astonishment. His head thrown back, he gallops away, his legs kicking out to the side like a startled colt. His coat tails billow out behind him. His bellowing echoes spookily across the square:

'Noooo… nooooo… No-oo-ooo!!'

There comes the hollow rattle of a machine gun. Fröhlich leaps high into the air, flings his arms wide, and hops from one leg to the other like some demented elf before clutching at his midriff and sinking to his knees. His torso slumps forward and he lies still. At the sound of the machine gun, Breuer has thrown himself to the ground. One of the Russians has disappeared somewhere and the other is rolling on the ground, moaning. He has dropped his machine-pistol. He shoots Breuer a look of pure hatred and reaches for his pistol. He clearly thinks they've been tricked. The machine gun is still spitting murderous volleys from the far side of the square. By crawling round the injured Russian, Breuer is finally able to make it to the safety of the courtyard gate.

The passageway leading to the cellar is thronged with soldiers. The Romanian general is there too, with his officers.

'It isn't quite time yet,' Breuer tells them. 'The surrender didn't work. We'll have to wait a bit!'

Later, not without difficulty, they rescue the wounded Russian from the courtyard. He's been shot through the thigh. Dr Korn dresses the wound. When he realizes that he is being treated well and even allowed to keep hold of his weapons, he calms down and gets chummy.

'Nu shto?'* he asks them, a broad grin breaking across his round face, 'Gitler kaputt, yes?

---

* *Nu shto?* – 'What do you think?'

The officers say nothing in response.

Hitler kaputt!

The night is exceptionally quiet. Transport aircraft still circle in the clear sky above. None of the officers gets a wink of sleep. They sit around, sunk in their thoughts. There's nothing more to be said.

It was around seven-thirty in the evening when an unknown officer appeared at Colonel Lunitz's command post. With his steel helmet, his carbine in his hand and grenades clipped to his belt, he looked very martial. The man gave a stiff salute.

'The Colonel is to accompany me forthwith to the High Command!' he announced formally. The colonel blanched. So, they'd listened in to his conversation with the Russian officer, had they? He knew what that meant. After all, hadn't Schmidt wanted to court-martial the army's head of signals on the mere suspicion that he might have tried to make contact with the enemy? Without a word, he stood up and put on his fur coat. Captain Schulte sprang to his feet.

'I'm coming with you, Colonel!'

'No, you stay here,' the colonel declined. 'Make sure everything stays shipshape here – in the event I don't come back.'

Colonel Lunitz had trodden the path to High Command many times, certainly far more often than his weapon-encumbered escort, as it turned out. For even after just a few metres, as they picked their way over piles of rubble and round bomb craters, he'd managed to lose him somewhere in the darkness. Lunitz turned off to the right, heading for the front-line positions. He'd negotiated with the enemy, acted on his own initiative. He knew what awaited him. Far better to end it all on his own terms! He was so heartily fed up with the whole business, sick to the back teeth. He felt for his pistol. But an inner feeling of outrage, a nagging resentment, stayed his hand. Had he done something so very terrible? No, he'd taken the only course of action left to him! If that was such a grotesque transgression against tradition and protocol, was that his fault? Was there anything about Stalingrad that wasn't grotesque?

The night was bitterly cold. The Ju 52s were still droning overhead. Off to one side, some bright beads of tracer fire shot up into the sky, and here and there a red or a white flare. That was the Russians; they were firing off captured German signal flares in the hope of seizing supply drops. Hitler was supplying the Red Army. 'One Führer, One People, One Theatre!' someone had chalked on the entrance portal to the Gorky Theatre.

The colonel walked slowly along the southern side of the square, where his men were crouching, at intervals of some twenty to thirty metres, on heaps of rubble or behind the remnants of walls. This was the 'front'. And these were his defences protecting the High Command against artillery and tanks! In truth, it was just a string of sentries too weak even to cordon off the square against a mob of unarmed protestors. He spoke with a few of the men, jollying them along and handing out the last of his cigarettes.

'Go ahead and smoke!' he said. 'Nothing'll happen tonight, and tomorrow you'll have lived to tell the tale.'

Then he turned away and headed diagonally across the square towards the High Command bunker. No, he wasn't going to shoot himself. He'd defend his modus operandi and pull no punches. He'd give full vent to his anger. Then they could do what they wanted to him for all he cared. Let them shoot him. He really couldn't give a shit any more.

The chief of staff's room was ablaze with light. Schmidt and General Rostek were sitting at a card table. Rostek had stretched out his legs and he blinked lazily at the newcomer. Schmidt rose and with a friendly smile extended his hand to the colonel.

'Please take a seat, my dear Lunitz!' he said with superficial suaveness. Only his vulpine eyes told a different story.

'Glass of wine? Cigar? Hmm, now – you made radio contact with the Russians from your command post, I believe?'

'No, General, sir, that's not true!' said the colonel sharply.

He was on his guard. He knew from experience that this suspect friendliness was often just a trap. In the blink of an eye it could flip over into the ice-cold sharpness of a razor blade or the violent uncontrollability of a street-fighting yob. Calmly, lucidly and succinctly, he recounted the events of the last few hours. He spoke about the German delegation to the Russians, about the impossibility of fulfilling his assignment, and finally – his heart was beating thirteen to the dozen as he broached this – his agreement with the Russians. He concealed nothing. Yet the explosion occurred nonetheless. The general leaped up from his chair, his face a puce colour.

'I've no idea what's going on!' he shouted, slamming his fist down on to the table. 'Delegations always come to you... but no one ever comes to speak to us!'

The colonel's jaw dropped. For a moment he thought he'd misheard the general. It took a little while for him to regain his composure.

'What, General, sir,' he finally managed to say, 'that's the issue that's concerning you? Well, if *that*'s the problem, then I guarantee that a Russian delegation will be waiting outside the department store here at eight o'clock sharp tomorrow morning!'

General Rostek chewed on his lower lip and shot occasional glances up at the ceiling. Schmidt, seemingly bored, studied his fingernails intently.

'Very well, agreed!' he said curtly.

The colonel still couldn't fully grasp the situation. It made no sense! Schmidt's previous orders had been unequivocal: 'Fight to the bitter end... delegations are to be shot at...' He'd read that with his own eyes! Yet now... What had happened to change matters? Unbeknown to the colonel, on the twenty-fourth of January General Schmidt had finally received the order he'd been longing to hear with every fibre of his being, instructing him to report to the Führer's headquarters and to bring all the relevant documentation with him. Trouble was, the order had come twenty-four hours too late. By then, the last airfield had fallen into Russian hands. Nothing was getting out of the Stalingrad Cauldron any more, not even so much as a mouse, let alone an army commander. And from that point on, things took on a very different complexion. Yet, knowing nothing of all this, Lunitz could only interpret the general's extraordinary behaviour as a ruse, some as yet unfathomable attempt to entrap him.

'General, sir, I reiterate,' he said slowly, stressing every word, 'just to avoid any misunderstanding – I plan to cease hostilities at four o'clock tomorrow morning and to lead my men into Russian captivity! And at eight o'clock a Russian delegation will be outside this building.'

The general nodded almost imperceptibly.

'Yes, yes, right you are!' he said. 'Agreed!'

Colonel Lunitz thought he saw the ghost of a scornful smile play around the corners of Schmidt's mouth.

'Right you are!' How wonderfully clear and simple and self-evident everything was… now! All of a sudden! And for that, hundreds of thousands of men had to…? The colonel felt his head start to spin. Like a drunkard, he tottered over debris and past shell holes back to his command post. He tripped and fell to his knees but picked himself up. 'One Führer, One People, One Theatre!' Step right this way, ladies and gentlemen, for a once-in-a-lifetime experience! A farce the like of which you've never seen! A cynical, shameless, bloody farce! But no cause for alarm, ladies and gentlemen, you won't faint at the sight! Only the bit-part players will come to grief, the poor little cheap extras! The leading lights will survive, rest assured! They are indispensable, we still need them for the next show!

'Ha ha ha…' laughed the colonel into the cold, clear night, and the sound, now multiplied, reverberated from the hollow walls of the ruined buildings: 'Ha ha ha ha ha… ha ha ha ha ha ha.'

That same night, the officers in the building on the corner of the square packed up their belongings and slept soundly and peacefully in a way they had not done for months.

On the thirty-first of January, at around seven in the morning, when the Sixth Army's chief of staff General Schmidt entered the room of the supreme commander, he was still asleep. The general approached the camp bed, looked at the sleeping C-in-C for a few seconds and then shook his shoulder. Paulus woke with a start.

'Yes?' he stammered. 'Yes, what's up? Is it time?'

General Schmidt gave a slight bow.

'Good morning, Field Marshal, sir!' he said, stressing the rank. 'Permit me to offer my congratulations on your promotion. The news just came through from the Führer's HQ!'

With some effort, Paulus raised his eyebrows to try to banish the last vestiges of sleepiness from his face. He had sat up long into the night.

'Ah,' he said, shaking his chief of staff's proffered hand, 'many thanks! Any other news?'

General Schmidt's face remained inscrutable.

'At the same time, I have to report that the Russians are at the door!'

'Mm, hmm,' replied the field marshal, rubbing his forehead. He gave Schmidt an uncertain look. A smile flitted across the latter's face. Distrusting Lunitz's promises and not being one to take half measures, he had sent his interpreter out at first light with the instruction: 'Make sure no fighting breaks out around Paulus's command post!'

And so his interpreter, a former ensign in the Tsar's army, asked the first Red Army officer he came across: 'Do you want to earn yourself the Order of Lenin? Or maybe even be made a Hero of the Soviet Union? Then come with me, and you'll be able to take Field Marshal Paulus prisoner!'

This Russian officer was currently waiting outside, alongside the negotiators whom Colonel Lunitz's message had set in motion.

'In ten minutes, we'll commence negotiations for the handover,' said Schmidt with brisk formality. 'Does the Field Marshal wish to personally conduct…?'

Almost in shock, Paulus waved his hand dismissively.

'No, no, my dear Schmidt, spare me that, please! You can conduct the negotiations on my behalf. You can do that better on your own!'

Once more, the ghost of a smile crossed Schmidt's face. Hadn't he been doing everything on his own for weeks now? Shortly before, he had sent a final radio message to the outside world:

'Russians at the gate! Will destroy everything!'

That had been a very diplomatic transmission. It remained unclear what precisely was going to be destroyed: the Wehrmacht's confidential files, the Sixth Army's equipment, or the last remaining men? Or maybe even the Russians? Or had the top brass of the Sixth Army fallen on their swords by heroically blowing themselves up on the ruins of Stalingrad? Everything remained open-ended, all things were possible. Hitler could use this message as he saw fit. General Schmidt was content he'd done his part.

'Can I do anything more for the Field Marshal?' enquired Schmidt, like a nurse addressing a patient.

'No, I don't think so… thank you! Perhaps you might see to it that we're allowed to keep our cars? And my batman, too, if possible, I'd like to keep hold of him.'

The handover negotiations did not last long. Throughout, General Schmidt retained what he referred to as his 'dignified bearing'. After all, he wasn't the supreme commander who was putting the ruins of a defeated army at the mercy of a victorious enemy. He was merely playing at being a king signing away his realm.

★

Two officers emerged from the cellar of the department store. They were Colonel Kniffke, who was carrying a large black suitcase, and an even younger captain with a rucksack on his shoulders. On the square in front of the building, German soldiers and Red Army troops were standing round in a jumble and cheerfully chatting to one another in broken German and Russian. Some of the Germans were still carrying their weapons. It would have been easy to forget what had just happened here. The army staff cars had just drawn up. Troops loaded private luggage on to the back of a lorry, which at Schmidt's request the Russians had provided specially for this purpose.

The captain surveyed the scene in front of him with some embarrassment.

'I'm really not sure about this, Colonel, sir,' he said, shaking his head. 'I don't know... whatever happened to "fighting to the very end"?'

'What's your problem?' exclaimed the colonel, spitting out the stub of the cigarette he'd been smoking. 'Haven't we done just that? I'd say we have! And today *is* "the end"!'

Eichert has also made all his preparations. It has all passed off very quickly and undramatically. On learning that the Russians have finally arrived, the officers stand up, silently collect their paltry belongings, including their kitbags, blankets and knapsacks, chuck their pistols into the flue of the stove and walk out. Breuer pushes his way through the knot of men gathered by the door. Outside, the Romanian general is already in conversation with a Russian officer escorted by armed soldiers.

Breuer introduces himself. 'We've got about two hundred walking wounded and around five hundred with serious injuries in the building. What's going to happen to them?'

The Russian officer looks at him calmly and dispassionately.

'Do you have a doctor with you?' he asks in German. 'Very well, then, you should leave him behind here. We'll see! Those of your men who can still walk should form up in four columns, with the officers at the head. All weapons are to be deposited in front of the building! Hurry up now, time is pressing!'

Captain Eichert is standing on a chair in the crowded corridor of the cellar.

'Comrades!' he says in a hoarse voice. 'We've marched together for many years now, obeying our orders, never questioning our superiors and always believing that our cause was a just one. Many of our number, so very many, have given their lives for it. And now we know that we've been lied to and betrayed.'

Breuer stands leaning against the wall. He looks at the faces around him, faces upon which the three-month ordeal of the Stalingrad Cauldron – which has weighed down so much more heavily than the three and a half years of war and the decades of peace before it – has left its indelible scars. These faces are a world away from those of the young, fresh soldiers who would have stood in front of the primped-up Reichsmarschall in Berlin the day before. The soldiers here had seen more than other men; they'd stared into the abyss of hell.

And now an eerie transformation comes over these faces. In their crazed desperation, they must surely have still nurtured some belief and hope in spite of everything – even in spite of the funeral oration they'd been treated to yesterday. But now they realize: it's over, really and truly over. And their faces turn to stone, and their feeble hands form fists. And suddenly one of them shouts:

'We give thanks to our Führer! – Heiiiil Hitler!'

Others take up the chant. The cellar resounds to the drone of their voices: 'Heiiiil Hitler! … Heiiiiiiiil Hitler!' This cry, once uttered over and over again by millions in hysterical rapture, has never sounded like it does here now. It's not mockery, it's not ridicule, it's a cold, clear, terrible reckoning. It's like an executioner's axe falling.

Breuer can feel his eyes growing moist.

'Did it have to end this way?' he thinks. 'Yes, there was no alternative!'

'So this is the end,' the captain continues. 'We didn't want this to happen. But we followed in blind obedience all the same. We're not blameless… And now I'll do everything in my power to ensure that we go down this last difficult road together. We don't know what the future holds for us. But whatever it brings, we should see as an atonement… Anyone who's still got a weapon should dispose of it by the door in the courtyard! We were soldiers of the Führer – but from here on in, let us be human beings. Break step – Quick… March!'

The Final Reckoning

THE GERMAN FORCES TRAPPED in the northern sector of the city – who had been cut off from all communication with Sixth Army High Command since 26 January – held out for a further two days, during which time they came under massive artillery bombardment and heavy attacks from the air.

The divisional commanders begged the CO of the XI Corps, who had supreme command over the northern end of the Cauldron, to put an end to this senseless slaughter. Regimental and squadron commanders lost all composure and went down on bended knee, imploring him to surrender. Unable to free himself from the stone labyrinth of conventions and prejudices in which he had been confined during more than forty years of military service, the old bullet-headed East Prussian general refused to heed their pleas.

'No. I could never look the German people in the face again!'

On the night of 31 January–1 February, he had heard on the radio a 'report from the front', actually fabricated in Berlin, which spoke of the 'heroic last stand being taken by Army Group Paulus', which went on to claim that 'Field Marshal Paulus has personally burned all confidential documents in his cellar. The officers and soldiers of his unit have fought to the last man and the last bullet!'

From this, he got the impression that Paulus himself had perished.

On 2 February, sometime between three and four in the morning, a radio message from Hitler came in:

'Every day, every hour that you go on fighting facilitates the formation of a new front. I expect Army Group North to discharge its duty with the same heroism displayed by Army Group Centre!'

Yet by this stage, the northern sector of the Cauldron was already collapsing. Troops were surrendering in droves to the Russians, regimental and divisional commanders took it upon themselves to make contact with the enemy, and entire units laid down their arms. When, on 2 February 1943 at 11 a.m. German Standard Time, the general signed the order to surrender, he had no troops left to command.

The Battle of Stalingrad was over.

Twenty-two crack German divisions plus elements of other units were wiped out. It was the greatest military disaster in German history.

According to Soviet reports, the bodies of 147,200 German officers and men were recovered from the battlefield and laid to rest.

Over 91,000 men went into captivity, including 2,500 officers and clerical staff. That figure represented less than a third of the Sixth Army's original complement of men and around half its officers. Of the thirty-two German generals in the Cauldron, seven had been flown out, one died in battle, one shot himself and one was posted as missing after 2 February 1943; this left twenty-two generals taken prisoner, foremost among them a field marshal.

Four-fifths of the soldiers and half of the officers who went into captivity subsequently died as a result of the trauma they had suffered. Of the twenty-two generals, one succumbed to stomach cancer.

In the spring of 1943, Field Marshal Freiherr von Weichs, C-in-C of the disbanded Army Group 'B' (of which the Sixth Army had been part up to November 1942) and his chief of staff, General von Sodenstern, were paying a visit to the Führer's headquarters. The first letters from the troops captured at Stalingrad had just begun to filter through to Germany. Over lunch, the two officers voiced their opinion that these letters – evidence that many of the men who had fought at Stalingrad were still alive – must have come as a great relief and comfort to their relatives.

Hitler looked up with a glowering expression on his face that dumfounded the two men. Then he said: 'The duty of those who fought at Stalingrad is to be dead!'

Afterword

THIS BOOK IS A work of fiction. Any attempt to identify real historical personages in certain of the protagonists (unless, of course, they are well-known figures like Field Marshal Paulus or General von Seydlitz) would be unjust and could potentially do a great disservice both to the dead and to people who are still alive. Yet at the same time, nothing in this book is 'fabricated'. All the incidents recounted in the action of the novel actually took place sometime and somewhere, either on the snowbound fields outside Stalingrad or in the ruins of the city itself. The author has exercised poetic licence only where certain details of place, time and dramatis personae are concerned. He has taken the subject matter of his book both from the experiences he himself underwent in and around Stalingrad and from accounts given to him by survivors of the battle – soldiers, officers and generals – during the three years he spent in captivity. It is incumbent upon him to thank here all his former comrades for their invaluable assistance and cooperation.

Appendix

BY CARSTEN GANSEL

I. Seventy years in captivity –
The remarkable story of Heinrich Gerlach's novel
Breakout at Stalingrad

My quest to find the original manuscript of Heinrich Gerlach's 1957 bestseller about the siege of Stalingrad (*Die verratene Armee*, translated into English by Richard Graves in 1958 as *The Forsaken Army*) has a personal preamble that goes back to German reunification in 1989–90 and to the archives in East Berlin that were opened up for the first time during that period. The Aufbau-Verlag, the foremost literary publisher in the German Democratic Republic, had commissioned me to edit a forthcoming work on Johannes R. Becher. In that momentous autumn of change in 1989, Becher – who had been one of the co-founders of Aufbau in August 1945 and was appointed as the GDR's first minister of culture in January 1954 – was emblematic like no other writer of the 'rise and fall' of East Germany and of a part of its literature. What becomes of a state's 'poet laureate' when that state no longer exists? And what remains of his literary output? These were questions that were not just being asked at Aufbau, which held the rights to Becher's estate and had published an eighteen-volume edition of his works. They were now planning one further volume containing previously unpublished poems and letters of his, together with other documents. I was particularly drawn to this project because researching in the archives would give me an opportunity to fill in certain 'blind spots' in my knowledge of the writer. Becher was something of an unknown quantity, and not just to the younger generation, largely because of the way he had been enshrined uncritically in the collective cultural memory of the GDR. His pathos from the pioneering years immediately after the war, his simple stanza forms and rhyme schemes and his outmoded lyricism were clearly at odds with the apprehensive 'waiting-room feeling' (Heiner Müller) experienced by people in the GDR in the 1980s and with the increasingly critical questioning that was going on, not just in literary texts. Hans Mayer, one of the most eminent German scholars of the postwar period, who knew Becher personally and thought highly of him, believed that he had been a 'godsend' to the GDR as minister of culture, but also pointed out that 'the contradictions in his life and work ... are too many to enumerate'. And it was precisely the contradictions in Becher's life and work that would be highlighted in the work I was about to edit, since, prior to 1989, all the details that didn't fit with the image of an exemplary (communist) writer had been hushed up.

So it was that in the spring of 1990 I found myself in a large room in the Central Party Archives of the Socialist Unity Party (SED), poring over the hitherto secret files on Johannes R. Becher. Behind me, I recognized Walter Janka, one of the most popular figures in the GDR during reunification. In the autumn of 1989, his essay 'Difficulties with the Truth' had been published by Rowohlt in Hamburg; when Aufbau reprinted it in January 1990, it reached a wide audience in the East and was read out in public, including at universities. Janka, sitting there now hunched up with his wife on a school bench and reading the SED's secret files on him, which elicited a groan from him now and then, had been head of the Aufbau publishing house in 1956, when he and a number of others – Wolfgang Harich, Gustav Just, Heinz Zöger and Erich Loest – had been sentenced to long prison terms in show trials. 'Participating in a counter-revolutionary group' read the charge sheet at the time, an accusation that went unchallenged by such authors as Anna Seghers and Johannes R. Becher – both of whom attended the trial – despite the fact that they knew it was a lie. Walter Janka gave a detailed account of this in his essay, remarking on Becher: 'If we ever get a chance to examine the state and party archives, scholars of literature will find it hard giving an assessment of so prominent a literary figure.'

At the time when he was writing his memoir, Walter Janka could surely never have imagined that this would actually come to pass, but things moved at a breakneck pace in the autumn of 1989; the state and party archives were indeed opened, and files long kept secret suddenly became accessible! Among the documents on Johannes R. Becher that I had now unearthed I found secret character appraisals by Wilhelm Pieck and Walter Ulbricht from the time when they were all living in exile in Moscow, along with confidential letters that Becher wrote to the Central Committee of the German Communist Party (KPD) after attempting suicide at the 'Hotel Lux', the haunt of exiles in Moscow. Suddenly, I also found myself in possession of the secret 'Medical Dossier on Comrade Becher', containing information that I thought would be out of place in any edition of his writings. But I also came across written reports by Becher of fifty-one interviews that he had conducted in June 1943 with German officers of the Sixth Army who had been taken prisoner by the Soviets after the Battle of Stalingrad in January and February of that year and who were being held at POW Camp 160 in Susdal. Like the camps at Krasnogorsk, Yelabuga, Oranki and Voikovo, Susdal was reserved for German officers. In the course of his conversations in June 1943, Becher was forced to conclude that only a handful of the officers were prepared 'to work for the cause of peace'. Most were unwilling to commit themselves, describing themselves as apolitical and bound by their oath of military allegiance, and fearing that any anti-fascist activity on their part might count against them at the war's end. From his comments, one got a sense of how disappointed Becher was that no real change of heart had set in, even after Stalingrad. For instance, he noted on one of his conversations:

> Lieutenant Colonel von Sass, whom I'd met at Krasnogorsk, was again sporting the Knight's Cross that he'd taken off there, along with all his other medals. Friendly and polite. Very content with the camp food, etc. No grounds for complaint. Waxes lyrical about how pleasant life is in the

camp, and that they were kept busy from dawn to dusk with all kinds of tasks.

Becher summed up his attempt to recruit Von Sass for the planned National Committee for a Free Germany (NKFD), an action group formed by officers and other exiles to fight against the Nazi regime, in the following terms: 'He avoids taking any kind of political stance, just like that time in Krasnogorsk, but now he also appears to have "composed" himself again. He plans to go down with Hitler. That will be his fate, he says, if it comes to it. He swore his oath to the Führer and that was that.' But Becher's conversations with Colonel Luitpold Steidle, a fellow Bavarian who some years later ended up in the same swimming club as the writer, took a quite different turn. 'Cuts a very impressive figure,' noted Becher. 'Insists that he's proud to have belonged to the division (Daniels) that surrendered at Stalingrad in time to avoid unnecessary bloodshed. Like Major Seffke, he's keen to point out that he's being treated well as a POW.' Becher had a second talk with Colonel Steidle, in which he tried to sound out his political views. 'Quizzed on his attitudes as a Catholic to National Socialism, he sidesteps the question by saying that its ideological contradictions made little impression on him as an individual,' the author reported. And to Becher's question 'What did the men of the officers' corps think about anti-Semitism?', Steidle was at pains to stress that the officers 'never subscribed to many of the more extreme National Socialist views' and that 'anti-Semitism had never been rife in the officers' corps or in the Army of the Reich'. The two conversations with Steidle were, according to Becher, so promising that they were joined for a third by the Soviet academic Professor Arnold. Arnold, whose real name was Abraham Guralski, and who had a chair at a Soviet university, was appointed as a political instructor for German prisoners of war, and had been engaged in discussions primarily with officers since the autumn of 1941. In the process, he had managed to persuade one officer to work with him: Dr Ernst Hadermann, whom Gerlach later got to know. Between 1943 and the end of the war, Arnold became one of the most important figures liaising with the captured officers, who rated his intellect and breadth of knowledge very highly. Like Becher, Professor Arnold came to the view that Colonel Steidle was an 'easy-going and sincere officer' who was 'civilized and measured' and 'intellectually a cut above the general run of German colonels'. In conversation, Steidle gave the impression of being fully prepared to 'fight for the cause of freedom', but also of being 'unwilling to make a commitment in his present circumstances, where he did not have access to the full facts'. Following this assessment by Johannes R. Becher and Professor Arnold, it comes as no surprise to learn that, a few weeks later, Colonel Steidle was among those who formed an action group that led to the formation of the League of German Officers (BDO).

The importance that the Soviet leadership attached to convincing German officers, and especially the generals who had fought at Stalingrad under Field Marshal Paulus, the commander in chief of the defeated Sixth Army, to join the struggle against Hitler may be gauged from an incident just three weeks later. High-ranking Soviet military personnel accompanied the leadership of the exiled KPD in a delegation to Susdal to try to persuade officers to work with them in setting up the National Committee for a Free Germany. At this juncture, the generals refused to engage in any discussions, meaning that the delegation was forced to focus its efforts once more on the lower ranks up to colonel.

Reading through Becher's extensive notes on these conversations in the archive in the spring of 1990, I had no inkling that over the following years I would repeatedly encounter several of the personalities mentioned there – and not just in the archive files but also, in one instance, even face-to-face. I experienced something of a feeling of déjà vu when I discovered that Heinrich Gerlach, whose trail I began to follow only several years later, had been in Susdal at exactly the same time as Becher and the German communist exiles had been recruiting there for the NKFD. Gerlach arrived at the Susdal camp on 23 June 1943 after four months in solitary confinement. Soon after his arrival he became acquainted with prominent German communist exiles like Wilhelm Pieck and Johannes R. Becher, and also Professor Arnold, with whom Colonel Steidle had already had dealings. Twenty years later, in his autobiographical work *Odyssey in Red*, he – or, more precisely, his fictional alter ego, First Lieutenant Breuer – recalls how he met German émigrés in the camp and was introduced to Johannes R. Becher. The picture that he paints here of Becher is less than flattering:

> Breuer grasped the soft, childlike hand that was extended limply to him. He gazed into a weary face that was lent an expression of ill-temper by a permanently drooping lower lip. He noticed the thin hair that had turned grey at the temples and was already very wispy on the crown, and searched in vain for the man's eyes, which were hidden behind the heavily reflective lenses of a pair of horn-rimmed spectacles. So this was Becher, the communist poet with the poncy Christian name; the man whom homesickness had inspired to create artworks, and hatred driven to pen angry pamphlets. The dark-grey single-breasted suit, the carefully knotted tie… A proletarian? A communist? Breuer was taken aback. The man just didn't fit any of his preconceptions.

The following day Breuer attended a meeting at which Becher reported on the situation in Germany after Stalingrad. Yet he delivered it in a language 'that bandied about terms like "the Hitler cabal" and "the Nazi clique" so liberally' that the officers '[felt] forced back into a sense of fellow feeling with the person being abused, an allegiance they'd only just begun to detach themselves from'. Their response was correspondingly lukewarm. Only the man sitting next to Breuer, 'a plumpish man in a light-grey suit', seemed to be really enthused by the speaker. 'White hair, badly cut on the sides, with a squat neck and a broad face in the middle of which a bulbous nose glowed red as a strawberry' is Gerlach's vivid description. It turned out later that the man with the bulbous nose was Wilhelm Pieck, formerly a Communist Party representative in the Reichstag. Pieck, who returned from exile to Berlin along with other leading KPD members on 1 July 1945 and served as the GDR's first and only president from 1949 to 1960 (after which the office was replaced by a collective head of state, the State Council), was sixty-seven years old in 1943 and chairman of the illegal KPD. The captured officers in Susdal only realized later who they were dealing with. 'My goodness, so he's the top dog! It'd be really good to bend his ear, then...' was one reaction.

In complete contrast to his jovial appearance, in evaluating the various meetings with the officers in Susdal – the delegation was in the camp for a total of ten days, from 18 to 28 July – Wilhelm Pieck gave a sharply astute summary of the situation that corroborated Becher's assessment. The officers, in Pieck's view, 'see it as tactless of us to try to force them into a decision with such haste'. All in all, he continued, in the short time available it had not been possible to impress on the prisoners that the National Committee 'was meant to help the German people bring the war to an end'. Becher and Pieck also believed that the anti-fascist newspaper for prisoners of war, *The Free Word (Das freie Wort)*, had largely failed because its editors, lieutenants Bernt von Kügelgen and Heinrich Graf von Einsiedel (the great-grandson of the first Imperial German Chancellor, Otto von Bismarck), were regarded as too young and inexperienced and that the tone of the paper was too stridently polemical and 'un-German'. Heinrich Gerlach ran into Bismarck's great-grandson just a few weeks after first getting to know the exiled German communists. But what made the greatest impression on Gerlach during his time in Susdal was a lecture by a German captain whom Arnold had managed to recruit early on to the anti-fascist cause, Dr Ernst Hadermann.

'He was one of them, and he was using their language. And the ideas he was expressing were theirs, but they'd been given order and structure by a superior intellect,' as Gerlach later recalled. At Hadermann's urging, Gerlach started using the camp library, which, in addition to light fiction, contained the works of some of the great storytellers of the nineteenth century, as well as German writers like Lion Feuchtwanger, Franz Werfel, Arnold Zweig, Leonhard Frank, Thomas and Heinrich Mann, Hermann Hesse and Ernst Wiechert, Rudolf Georg Binding, and even Hans Carossa. Another book that he found in the library was Johannes R. Becher's semi-autobiographical novel *Farewell* (*Abschied*), published in Moscow in 1940, which he read with great interest. His commitment did not go unnoticed; Professor Arnold invited him for a chat and intimated that he could see Gerlach being called to higher things during his captivity: 'You'll go to another camp. There, you'll learn and study and talk to proper people.' What Gerlach refers to here was not a case of his memory playing tricks. Seventy years later – something I'll discuss presently – I was to discover notes of this conversation in a Russian archive. Professor Arnold really had submitted a very positive assessment of Heinrich Gerlach, which laid the foundations of the subsequent stations in his captivity. In this report, dated 14 July, we read:

> Character sketch of the prisoner-of-war First Lieutenant in the German Army Gerlach, Heinrich. Gerlach, Heinrich, Lt. is one of the most active, clever and able officers in Camp No. 160. He assists us in our work, and has undertaken a series of tasks involving communicating with and processing fellow officers. Appears to be an opponent of the Hitler regime. He presumably had something to do with military intelligence in the Wehrmacht and was responsible for carrying out particular political duties. Where the political aspirations and objectives of the USSR are concerned, Gerlach still harbours

many prejudices. Aspires to learn (further education). Could
be useful, and enjoys a good deal of authority among senior
officers. Professor Arnold. 14 July 1943.

Just before this appraisal, on 12–13 July 1943, the NKFD was founded
at Krasnogorsk camp near Moscow, despite a flat refusal on the part
of the Stalingrad generals to extend it any cooperation. Gerlach
learned of its inception from a newspaper called *Free Germany* (*Freies
Deutschland*) that was left on tables in the camp. This provoked a
great deal of outrage among the inmates, especially as the banner
at the foot of the front page was printed in black, white and red,
namely the colours of the flag of the Second German Empire from
1871, and again from 1933 onwards. The founding manifesto of the
National Committee, Gerlach read in *Free Germany*, had been signed
by twelve communist exiles and twenty-one prisoners of war,
whose membership was authenticated in each case by a facsimile
signature. The most senior of the eleven officers on the committee
– Karl Hetz, Herbert Stößlein and Heinrich Homann – only had
the rank of major. Gerlach did not know these officers, though
he had spoken with Captain Cramer and Captain Dr Hadermann,
two of the other founder members, in the camp just a few days
before. Gerlach recalled the name of another signatory solely
because of his prominence: 'There was a count among them as
well. Breuer pondered for a moment. Yes, that's right, it was that
bald great-grandson of Bismarck, who was a flight lieutenant with
three confirmed kills and a Knight's Cross. Back in Stalingrad, in the
Cauldron [the encircled pocket where German forces were trapped],
they'd seen a Soviet propaganda pamphlet with a picture of him and
thought it was a fake.' Just two months later, Gerlach would get to
meet Bismarck's descendant in person – who actually had a tally
of thirty-five downed enemy planes and was highly decorated and
who'd been shot down on 30 August 1942 near Stalingrad – at the
founding of the League of German Officers.

Almost fifty years later, at the beginning of the 1990s and shortly after publication of my two volumes on Johannes R. Becher for Aufbau, I, too, would get to know this Heinrich Graf von Einsiedel. In May 1991, at the inaugural congress of the German Writers' Association for the whole of the reunified country, a history commission was established and charged with the task of researching the history of the two parallel associations that had existed when Germany was divided. I was elected to the commission and Heinrich Graf von Einsiedel joined a little later. As the count had known Johannes R. Becher from his time in the NKFD, we compared notes on several occasions. For him, Becher was an ambiguous person who was no longer of interest to him. Stalingrad and the period he spent in captivity in the Soviet Union, however, remained his abiding theme. He referred me to his *Diary of a Temptation: 1942–1950*, which had been published back in 1950 by Pontes Verlag. In our discussions, which also touched on literature about the siege of Stalingrad, Von Einsiedel drew my attention to a documentary novel entitled *Die verratene Armee*. He told me it had been written by a first lieutenant whom he'd got to know in Krasnogorsk camp at the inauguration of the League of German Officers; the man's name was Heinrich Gerlach. Einsiedel only ever referred to him as 'the teacher', and recounted how the book had been very successful in the Federal Republic. According to him, it had none of the sort of macabre scenes of death and destruction that appeared in, say, Theodor Plievier's bestseller *Stalingrad*, which Aufbau had published in 1946. Recently, in the new edition of their co-edited book entitled *Stalingrad and the Individual Soldier's Culpability* (1993), he and Joachim Wieder had reiterated their high opinion of Gerlach's work. He recommended both books to me unreservedly. At that stage, I had a good knowledge of all the novels about the war that had been published in the GDR, beginning with Erich Loest's *Jungen, die übrig blieben* (*The Boys Who Survived*, 1950) and running through those novels that came in for harsh criticism from the GDR Writers' Association for their allegedly 'hard-bitten writing style', written by authors who were then still young, like Harry Thürk's *Stunde der toten Augen* (*Hour of the Dead Eyes*, 1957) and Egon Günther's *Dem Erdboden gleich* (*Razed to the Ground*, 1957). While the novels of the 'hard-bitten' school had meanwhile been erased from the collective consciousness of the GDR, the epic novels of character development that appeared in the 1960s were still much in evidence. Principal among these was Dieter Noll's *Die Abenteuer des Werner Holt* (*The Adventures of Werner Holt*, 1960), which for many years was on the GDR's school curriculum. Likewise, the appeal of the novels *Wir sind nicht Staub in Wind* (*We Are Not Dust in the Wind*, 1962) by Max Walter Schulz and *Der Hohlweg* (*The Defile*, 1963) by Günter de Bruyn went far beyond just literary specialists. By contrast, the Second World War novels that had come out in the Federal Republic were largely unknown to me, nor was I sufficiently well versed in the secondary literature on Stalingrad. The events that Von Einsiedel had witnessed at first hand and reported to me were, by and large, uncharted territory for me. All I knew about the NKFD were the familiar accounts in GDR literary histories, and I'd never heard of the League of German Officers, which had been founded in Soviet captivity. Ultimately, I took Von Einsiedel's advice and read his diary and – albeit rather cursorily – Heinrich Gerlach's *Die verratene Armee*. I had to agree with him: Gerlach's novel really was, as he and Wieder had claimed, 'a book with no prejudice or resentment, which avoids painting things in black and white and shuns ideological distortion'. It was also a novel that presented an unsparing picture of the horrors of war – an example of a 'hard-bitten writing style', if ever there was one. This tone was sustained throughout, but was most in evidence in the episode when Gerlach described the 'Bone Road':

> Then he caught sight of something that made him screw up his eyes and lean further forward. By the side of the road, the leg of a horse was sticking out of the snow. And another, and another. On the left a pyramid of bones had been erected, and

a little further on a horse's skull had been stuck on top of a pole. Further on he saw a man with his head and shoulders buried and his legs sticking through the snow like a pair of candles. A light coating of snow covered the yellow soles of his bare feet. The driver had noticed Eichert fidgeting and said, 'The Bone Road. We had to mark it somehow, because it's always disappearing under the snow. If we put up wooden signposts, they grab them for firewood. They even collect the bones of the horses.' Captain Eichert had been in the army for thirteen years and had become extremely tough, but the Bone Road gave him the creeps.

Our conversation about Heinrich Gerlach's novel – which, with a view to the novels written about the Second World War in the East and West and Stalingrad, fitted precisely into the history commission's discussions – remained a private one. Subsequently, Heinrich Graf von Einsiedel and I took different positions on how to set about relating East and West German biographies, destinies, codes and experiences to one another. After the Twelfth Congress of the German Writers' Association in 1994, he resigned from the history commission, put himself up for election and entered the German parliament in October 1994 on the Democratic Socialist Party ticket as a member for Saxony, a role he performed until 1998.

Though I'd lost touch with Count von Einsiedel, after the 1994 Congress in Aachen I developed a close relationship with another author who had also made his debut with a war novel, namely Erich Loest, whom I'd known since 1990. His novel *Jungen, die übrig blieben* was first published in 1950, when the author was only twenty-three years old. As with Gerlach, it was a recollection of the war, of the fear experienced by the ordinary soldier and of the hopeless predicament of those who found themselves condemned to kill or be killed. It recounted in great detail the passage to manhood of a group of schoolboys during the final years of the war: the inhuman square-bashing and constant humiliation during training, followed by the horror of combat, disillusion and despair. Loest's novel, which came out at Christmas 1950, was savaged in the *Tägliche Rundschau* (*Daily Review*), the newspaper of the Soviet Military Administration (SMAD):

> Loest's attitude may have been typical of hundreds of thousands of soldiers. If he really did think at the time that such a pathetic stance was the only one open to him, that might to some extent be excused by his youth. But five years have passed since then, and today it's no longer appropriate to write in such an 'objective' and disengaged way about the war. Nowadays, every German must know how wrong and disastrous his spineless attitude was back then towards the Nazi military machine.

Similar arguments – which I will touch on later – were also used in the Soviet Union to substantiate the supposed danger posed by Gerlach's Stalingrad novel. Following this criticism of his novel, Erich Loest lost his job at the newspaper where he worked (the *Leipziger Zeitung*) and embarked on a freelance career. 'All water under the bridge now,' Loest told me when I met him. I grew even closer to him after he was elected as chairman of the German Writers' Association. Naturally, we also swapped notes on both his own debut novel and Gerlach's *Die verratene Armee*, which Loest knew. He shared Von Einsiedel's high opinion of it, while adding the mild caveat that Gerlach had, after all, been thirty-three years old and a qualified teacher at the start of the war, whereas he was still a secondary school pupil at the time. But it was really important, he stressed, that we should now revisit these war novels from the East and the West. A short time later, in 1995, after I'd been invited to take up a professorship in Gießen, Loest and I (Loest on behalf of the German Writers' Association and myself for my university) signed an agreement to collaborate on a joint project that would examine the literary history of the two Germanys between 1945 and 1989, including comparing the war novels written in both countries during the Fifties and Sixties. We arranged special access facilities to the archive of the (East) German Writers' Association (DSV), which the history commission had voted should now be housed at the Academy of the Arts. I had already been working in the archive since the early 1990s. I now found myself wading through a pile of hitherto unseen documents relating to the history of the two Germanys. In the process, I also chanced upon an audio recording of a meeting of the executive board of the DSV, which took place in the East German government's official guesthouse on 11–12 June 1959. The topic under discussion was: 'Reality is harsh – but what are we to make of the hard-bitten writing style?' These disputes about the 'hard-bitten' style of writing in the GDR concerned the war novels of young authors who, from the mid-1950s on, began writing about the Second World War and about life and death at the front, taking their cue from American role models like Norman Mailer and Ernest Hemingway. Official criticism of these writers was scathing, with the novels of Harry Thürk, Egon Günther and Hans Pfeiffer that I'd talked about earlier with Heinrich Graf von Einsiedel being shunned as 'decadent' and 'objectifying'. The discussion on the tape also turned to the question of how to distance war fiction in the GDR from that of West Germany, which was regarded as revanchist. Heinrich Gerlach's Stalingrad novel supposedly belonged in this category! For the project examining German literature post-1945 and the role played by the Writers' Association, I had such a mass of material to work through that I decided to restrict myself to the years immediately after 1945 and the hopes of authors at that time for a 'parliament of the intellect' (a slogan coined by the writer Günther Weisenborn to describe the first postwar congress of German writers, held in Berlin in October 1947). For the time being, my work on the 'hard-bitten' war novels and also on Heinrich Gerlach's Stalingrad novel took a back seat.

II. 'It's all come back to me...' –
Using hypnosis to release locked-away memories

After repeatedly touching upon questions of the depiction of war in connection with my work on the literary canon and censorship, on the formation of literary groups and on the publications of the proceedings of the second and third writers' congresses held in the GDR in 1950 and 1952, it was only in the spring of 2007, while working on the topic of 'literature and memory' with my fellow researcher, Norman Ächtler, that I encountered Heinrich Gerlach's Stalingrad novel once more. When we studied the book more closely, we quickly recognized that the story of Gerlach's novel is unique in German literature. Our investigation led us inevitably to a sensational report published in the magazine *Quick* on 26 August 1951. The banner headline ran: 'It's All Come Back To Me...' The subtitle then went on to reveal the sensational secret: 'Returnee from Russia regains his memory through hypnosis.' The report began with a summary of Gerlach's capture at Stalingrad, his odyssey through POW camps and the amnesia brought on by these traumatic events:

> Finally, eight years after being taken prisoner at Stalingrad, and with many long, demoralizing years in Soviet POW camps behind him, he returns to his home town on the River Weser. The years of captivity are like a grey veil to him, with the images blurring and growing ever more indistinct. All the events and years and landscapes begin to merge into one. And then dissolve. What was it really like? He doesn't know any more. Then, out of the blue, he gets a letter from an old army mate telling him about a manuscript that Gerlach had handed to him when he, the friend, was released. In the event, he continued, he hadn't been able to hand it over to Gerlach's wife. At the border, the novel – a package containing several

hundred handwritten pages – had been confiscated. Now it all starts coming back to Gerlach. That's right – a manuscript about his time in Stalingrad, which he'd got off his chest during his time as a POW. But what on earth had he written?

Granted, this was something of an exaggeration; Gerlach hadn't forgotten his years in captivity or even the existence of his Stalingrad novel. But what he could no longer recall was the structure of his novel and the chronology of events. It was in this situation that Gerlach came across an article in *Quick* on 13 October 1950. It was written by a Munich physician called Dr Karl Schmitz and was entitled 'The Unconscious Assignment'. In it, Schmitz described the possibility of retrieving repressed memories through hypnosis. The article raised Gerlach's hopes that he might, after all, be able to remember his lost war novel. The manuscript had been confiscated by the Soviet secret services in 1949, shortly before his own release in April 1950. Accordingly, in January 1951 Gerlach wrote to Dr Schmitz, asking him if he could help him reconstruct his novel. He went on to describe what happened whenever he tried to recall what he'd written:

> I've tried reconstructing it, but failed. At each attempt, a mist seems to descend. I just can't do it! The only thing I've managed to retrieve is a section that was particularly important to me – my description of Christmas 1942. Over Christmas last year (1950), in a state of high emotion, I was able to get this down on paper in just half an hour, and with no corrections.

Heinrich Gerlach now asked Schmitz if he thought it might be possible 'to summon up through hypnosis a "content of consciousness" like the one he'd just described so vividly that it could be written down'. Schmitz showed an immediate interest in treating Gerlach. He was just about to publish his book *Hypnosis – Its Nature, Scope, and Purpose*, and saw an opportunity to generate publicity for hypnosis as a cure – and naturally also for himself – by conducting a high-profile experiment. After Sigmund Freud had ultimately distanced himself somewhat from hypnosis as a therapeutic method, it was only just beginning to gain in popularity once more in Germany at the start of the 1950s. Even so, Schmitz cautioned Gerlach not to invest too much hope in the procedure. This would, after all, be a 'hypnotic experiment on a grand scale'. All the same, he continued, he still thought it quite possible that he might be able to get Gerlach 'to relive the events, perhaps even in their entirety', and hence was keen to chance the experiment. But because Gerlach did not have the necessary funds to pay for the procedure at the time, he was forced to shelve the plan. Initially, Gerlach was very disappointed, but then – at Dr Schmitz's instigation – he hit upon a new scheme. On 6 July 1951, he wrote to seven leading news magazines, offering them exclusive rights to the story if they would agree to fund the experiment. Within just a few days he received a reply from *Quick*, inviting him to come to Munich. Gerlach arrived in the city on 15 July, went straight to the magazine's offices and signed a contract that had been drawn up in advance. It contained the following clause:

> You are undergoing a course of treatment by the Munich physician Dr K. Schmitz of No. 20 Jahnstraße with the aim of being able to reconstruct the manuscript you have mentioned … The extent of our obligation to Dr Schmitz shall be entirely at our discretion…

Years later, Heinrich Gerlach recalled that he had regarded the offer by *Quick* in 1951 as a unique opportunity for everyone involved:

> All in all I considered this contract as very fair and advantageous to those concerned. The magazine could be sure

of a good story come what may. Dr Schmitz would receive what would surely be a handsome fee for his treatment and his subsequent report [he got 1,750 Deutschmarks from the magazine], and besides he also had the possibility of having the experiment scientifically evaluated. As for me, this procedure gave me the hope that I might soon retrieve my lost manuscript.

So, a classic 'win–win' situation, from which all parties could only benefit. The plan was set in motion and the result of the experiment duly appeared in the 26 August 1951 issue of *Quick*:

> At the invitation of *Quick*, he [Heinrich Gerlach] travels to Munich, and in a course of treatment lasting three weeks, the miracle actually happens: all the years that have been sunk in the abyss of oblivion rise to the surface once more. In agitated outbursts, recorded by the doctor or his assistant, as well as in the notes that Gerlach himself scribbles down while under hypnosis, his experiences come flooding back, and the individual scenes and chapters of the book are brought to life for a second time. Once again, the bridge of consciousness spans the dark chasm of those lost years. After three weeks Heinrich Gerlach returns home and get all his experiences from Stalingrad off his chest and down on paper once more.

As reported in *Quick*, Gerlach's 'treatment' commenced in mid-July 1951 at Dr Schmitz's practice. Gerlach, who had only recently moved from Berlin to take up a position as a German and Latin teacher in a grammar school at Brake on the Lower Weser and had just completed his first semester there, was on his summer holidays, giving him the leisure to travel to Munich. Straight away, Schmitz explained to Gerlach that it wouldn't be possible for him to simply 'hallucinate' the novel, as it were, and then write it down in one hit.

Nonetheless, they embarked on the experiment on 15 July 1951. To start the ball rolling, in the first hypnosis session Schmitz induced Heinrich Gerlach to cast his mind back to the first chapter of the novel and instructed him to write it down. At this first attempt it immediately became apparent how slim the pickings were, as Gerlach only got a single sentence down on paper – and, what's more, in a woeful hand that was virtually illegible. Confronted with the result when he was woken from his hypnotized state, he remembered that the sentence he'd scrawled was the first draft of the beginning of the novel, which he'd written in the summer of 1943 before reworking it several times. The sentence read as follows: 'Winter had sent out a reconnaissance party into the area between the Volga and the Don. The roads were covered with a snowless frost...' But this outcome also demonstrated that it would be impossible to recreate a manuscript of more than six hundred pages using this method. Schmitz therefore tried putting his test subject Gerlach into a state of hypnosis and getting him to recall one specific event, to which he would then return in the next session. In this way, the plan was to call the course of events around Stalingrad and their fictional depiction to life once more. In the process, Gerlach was woken from hypnosis every ten minutes. In most cases, he was then able fluently to reproduce what he had remembered up to the point where the recollection broke off again. Thereafter, he was put back under hypnosis. The sessions, each of which lasted for around two and a half hours, thus generated a succession of sequels that were also taken down in shorthand by Dr Schmitz's secretary. A photo of one session, in which Heinrich Gerlach – in the company of Dr Schmitz and his secretary – is seen recalling episodes from his memory was printed in the *Quick* report, alongside examples of Gerlach's handwriting.

Heinrich Gerlach himself summarized his observations while under hypnosis two days before the end of the experiment, on 28 July 1951. The preservation of these notes is on the one hand down to the fact that this spectacular experiment was ideally suited for Schmitz to underline the importance of hypnosis. At the same time, the doctor was intent upon drawing conclusions from it regarding the function of memory. However, we are by no means solely reliant upon Schmitz's account of proceedings, since some years later the working relationship between Gerlach and Schmitz became the subject of an extremely high-profile legal battle that once more caught the public eye. While this was going on, Heinrich Gerlach's own observations again came under discussion. He had jotted down the following impressions in 1951:

> At the beginning of the experiments I was deeply sceptical. During hypnosis, my doubts manifested themselves in the form of snippets of thought that flickered like coloured flashes on the margins of my state of unconsciousness, and on one occasion even took the shape of a giggling goblin, who called out from the back of my head: 'Serves you right, this is all a load of nonsense!' When I'm under hypnosis, I'm in a state of split consciousness. I know that I'm sitting in Dr Schmitz's practice and that he's talking to me, but at the same time I'm reliving the past in any given situation that has been evoked by the hypnosis. The intensity of these two perceptions changes according to how deeply I am asleep. Mostly I relive the same mental images that came into my head at the time when I was writing the book. In scenes that rely heavily on personal experiences, these experiences also come vividly to life once more, and sometimes make me very emotional. These experiences continue immediately after I've been woken from hypnosis, and can even gain in clarity as I'm recounting them. My description of the images I see after waking is very halting and awkward, and I generally have no recollection of my original stylistic formulation of them. Everything just unwinds out of me like a very slow film.

However, this description by Gerlach has certain gaps; notably he says nothing here about the lost manuscript. In the documents I discovered in a Munich archive – of which more later – I also found a copy of Gerlach's observations:

> One time, during a very deep sleep, I got the feeling that I'd become detached from myself and was floating in the air about 50 centimetres above my sleeping body. At the same time I had the impression that it would only take a little push to send me down into total darkness. The experience was pleasant and gentle. [...] Sometimes, I'm leafing through the manuscript and can see the exact colour and weave of the paper and read entire lines off the page and see on precisely which pages a particular scene is described.

Gerlach's notes paint a picture of how his memory was stimulated by being placed in a hypnotic state, causing parts of the manuscript to resurface. Admittedly, the triggers provided by Dr Schmitz during hypnosis and Heinrich Gerlach's own notes prompt even more far-reaching suppositions about the psychic processes that occur when writing. The writer Uwe Johnson, whose debut novel *Speculations about Jakob* was published in 1959, exactly two years after Gerlach's Stalingrad novel, saw novel writing as an attempt to create a 'social model'. 'Yet this model consists of people,' Johnson maintained. 'These people are invented, assembled from many of my own personal impressions. In this sense, the act of inventing is actually a process of remembering.' Here, Uwe Johnson is highlighting the role of experience that lies at the root of all storytelling. And this was exactly what came into play during Heinrich Gerlach's attempts to reconstruct his work, since ultimately his thoughts were consciously recalled in a slow process that involved evoking sensory experiences or events. In addition, the much-quoted 'madeleine' episode from Marcel Proust's epochal novel *In Search of*

Lost Time – which one cannot help but call to mind here – showed the kind of things that can act as the key to the past.

For Proust's narrator, Marcel, it is the taste of a kind of cake called a 'petite madeleine' dunked in lime-blossom tea that suddenly opens the floodgates to his childhood. Barely has the cake melted on his tongue when a feeling of 'exquisite pleasure' washes over him. And a moment later the narrator notes: 'And suddenly the memory returns.' It is not the sight of the madeleines that sets the process of remembering in motion here but that single second when 'the warm liquid, and the crumbs with it, touched my palate'. For Heinrich Gerlach, the recollections of the act of writing in the POW camp, prompted by the trigger of hypnosis, mingle with his actual experiences in Stalingrad.

The experiment in reconstructing parts of a novel through hypnosis became an important basis over the following years for Dr Schmitz to draw conclusions about the function of memory and recollection in general. He speculated, for instance, that 'everything that we have learned consists of "sensory impressions of situations"', such as 'read, heard or felt experiences… the vast majority of which have long since faded from our conscious mind'. 'However,' Schmitz went on, 'in secret all these unconscious impressions continue to operate and to govern all our attitudes, thoughts and deeds.' These insights of Schmitz's should be regarded as serious and significant, given the general state of psychology in the 1950s. Hans Markowitsch, a distinguished physiological psychologist who has specialized in the field of memory and recollection and was head of the memory clinic at Bielefeld University Hospital, maintains that hypnosis remains a difficult topic even today, even though a great deal of research has been done in this area over the past few years. In the context of what is known as retrograde amnesia, in which people are unable to recall particular events after a given point in time, Markowitsch points to experiments that succeeded in reactivating a patient's memory by means of hypnosis. Researchers nowadays work from the premise that hypnosis employs 'the powerful effects of attention and suggestion… to generate, alter and corroborate a broad spectrum of experiences and behaviours that are subjectively evaluated as compulsive'. Today, hypnosis has undergone an upswing in interest as part of the research programme of the cognitive neurosciences. Recent studies have demonstrated that the 'manipulation of the subjective consciousness through hypnosis under laboratory conditions can provide insights into those mechanisms of the brain that are involved in attention, in motor skills, in the perception of pain, in beliefs and in volition (willpower)'.

In this regard, Dr Schmitz's efforts to reactivate Heinrich Gerlach's memories through hypnosis also represent a thoroughly innovative experiment even from a modern perspective. When Schmitz later remarks that Gerlach was an easy subject to hypnotize, this is a sign of a possible connection between personality traits and memory. Although, to date, no psychological correlates have yet been found for a so-called 'divergent suggestibility' among people, despite numerous attempts to establish one over the past few decades, the latest research seems to confirm that 'connections between suggestibility and mental preoccupation' on the one hand and 'a mental constitution inclined to fantasy, creativity and empathy' on the other do nevertheless exist. This is certainly true in spades of Heinrich Gerlach. Furthermore, we may assume that the attempt to reconstruct the novel was only successful because what Gerlach had previously gone through had imprinted itself forcibly on his stored memory and was in each case linked to concrete experiences in Stalingrad.

The attempt to reconstruct the lost novel came to an end on 30 July 1951. In twenty-three extended sessions, Schmitz and Gerlach had gathered together an extensive body of material. Schmitz estimated that they now had to hand 'the contents of two major sections of the former manuscript'. As the original manuscript comprised three parts, this meant that 'two-thirds of the work had been rescued from oblivion'. He assumed that the methods they had employed had 'given a powerful impetus to recollection and that the remainder of the work would duly emerge in the course of processing the material, as generally happens in the case of memories'.

The *Quick* story, the first part of which gave a graphic impression of how the sessions had gone in the accompanying photos, was rounded off with a report by Dr Schmitz giving a suspenseful account of certain selected episodes from the experiment. He followed this with a summary of the overall result for the readers of *Quick*:

> The lost manuscript began to emerge once more from a thousand individual details, and its forgotten structure likewise became clear once more. So, the strenuous work of this treatment was not in vain. The darkness was illuminated better than we could have hoped. One report on the whole process confirms that the faculty of memory has automatically been strengthened by it. As a result, we are confident that everything will re-emerge, perhaps even in a better and clearer form than it had been before.

It was with this prospect in mind also that Heinrich Gerlach returned to Brake on the Weser and began piecing together his novel on Stalingrad. Even so, his hopes of now being able to get on rapidly with preparing the text for publication were not realized. This was one reason why, six months later, on 11 January 1952, Gerlach wrote once more to Dr Schmitz seeking his help. He told the psychiatrist that he would send him large parts of the reconstructed manuscript in order to satisfy the doctor's 'strong personal interest in the outcome'. At the same time, he also asked Schmitz to show this completed section of the novel to *Quick*. In fact, Gerlach himself had already sent the first chapter to the magazine in October, while admitting that he did so 'only very reluctantly, as people won't be able to make head or tail of it as it stands'. Unfortunately, he told Schmitz, he hadn't yet received a reply. He presumed that Schmitz's good offices would make more headway:

> It's always better to pester people in person, and because you have a direct intellectual and material interest in the book, I am trusting that you won't find my request unreasonable.

This letter, which came to light during the subsequent dispute between the two former partners, allows us to draw conclusions about Gerlach's situation at the time and his plan on how to proceed with work on the manuscript. It is also interesting that Gerlach clearly thought about soliciting *Quick*'s interest for a second time in supporting the undertaking. His letter to Schmitz continues very much in this vein:

> I hope to complete the second section in the period from March to June. This will have the added advantage of furnishing *Quick* with enough material to decide whether they'd be willing to finance another trip by me to Munich. Provided your schedule allows, we could then work together in July on the third – and by far the most important – section (where many things are still very unclear to me), and by August or September or at the latest October, everything would then be cut and dried. Anyhow, those are my hopes and plans; let's hope fate conspires to make it so!

In addition, Gerlach asked Schmitz to send him the transcript of the sessions, claiming that it would 'help me greatly in my work by prompting my rejuvenated memory'. Sadly, only a portion of the records would ever come to light, breaking off after page seventeen. He also asked about the date of manufacture, delivery address and price of the 'small typewriter' he'd seen at Schmitz's practice and which he'd been very taken with. Gerlach's letter ends with a commitment to their continuing collaboration and the positively autosuggestive confession that the novel had to be published at all costs:

> My dear Herr Schmitz, I should like to assure you that since working together I feel very close to you on a personal level. I promise you that I will do everything in my power to ensure that we bring our collaboration to a successful conclusion. Money matters are the very least of my concerns here, given that I've got a steady job and income and no pressing needs. But I am obsessed with the thought that this book *must* see the light of day, all the more so in this current age, which seems hell-bent on preparing for another war and forgetting the horrors of the one just past.

In the event, this further collaboration would never come about. Similarly, Gerlach's plan to finish reconstruction of the novel manuscript by the end of 1952 also came to nothing. By the end of April 1952, he had only written ninety pages; the complete reconstruction of his book would ultimately take him another four years. In a long conversation with me and an extensive letter of July 2012, his daughter, Dorothee Wagner, recalled her father's working methods in the years following his hypnosis: 'From the outset,' she told me, 'my father would involve other people in his writing. He asked them to recount things to them, quizzed them, and gave public readings of his work. He was happy to receive suggestions and criticism. [...] He got our family engaged in the new edition of the novel and maintained close contact with friends and former fellow camp inmates. Many of them came to stay with us, and the talk then was invariably of Stalingrad and life as a POW. My father eagerly followed everything that was published on the subject and studied historical sources on the war, in so far as that was possible back then.'

The delay in work on the new novel was also due to the fact that after eleven years of military service and as a prisoner, Gerlach had to work his way back into the business of being a schoolteacher. Following his return from captivity, he first found employment at a secondary school in Berlin. From 1951, he occupied a senior master's post at a grammar school in Brake on the Weser. He taught German and Latin to pupils in the upper school – both subjects that called for a great deal of preparation and correcting of scripts. Over and above this, he also had to deal with the sort of problems that faced all late returnees from the war. 'My father first had to find his way back into family life,' recalled his daughter. 'That hardly left any time for writing, so he used the school holidays for that.'

III. *The Forsaken Army* –
A surprise bestseller

Finally, in the autumn of 1956 Heinrich Gerlach was in a position to send the completed manuscript to the Nymphenburg publishing house in Munich, which replaced the original title *Durchbruch bei Stalingrad* (*Breakout at Stalingrad*) with *Die verratene Armee* (*The Forsaken Army*), feeling it was more in keeping with the spirit of the 1950s. The new title not only sounded better, but also chimed in with the myth of 'lambs to the slaughter' that had worked its way into the public consciousness since the start of the new decade. The publisher put the Stalingrad novel on its forthcoming list for autumn 1957. And so a radical experiment that was unique in the annals of German literature came to its successful conclusion. Nymphenburg did not expend a lot of effort on promoting *The Forsaken Army*; the sensational story of its genesis generated enough publicity of its own. The large print run of ten thousand for the first edition of the book sold out within weeks in November 1957. Curt Vinz, who had founded the publishing house with Berthold Spangenberg and Gerhard Weiss in 1946, was ecstatic about the book's impact:

> We've also got firm contracts with publishers in New York, London, Milan, Stockholm and Holland, plus options for French, Spanish, Norwegian, Finnish and Danish co-editions. We've even received an enquiry from Poland – a first for us – and the radio station in the Soviet zone of Germany has requested an excerpt for broadcast. We've never experienced anything like this!

Indeed, the 'Novel of Stalingrad' (as the subtitle dubbed it) really did capture the mood of the age, giving a voice to those who had survived Stalingrad and Soviet captivity. Although Hans Schwab-Felisch, one of the most renowned literary critics associated with the *Gruppe 47* ('Group 47') circle of writers, placed a caveat on Gerlach's literary achievement by pointing to the novel's documentary character, he was still full of praise: 'Even so, one must give credit to the author, who gives evidence in this work of a remarkable ability to impose a tight and consistent order on an immense mass of material, but most of all for his consummate skill in squaring and blending the chance events of his personal experience with the general run of events, and his objective recounting of military matters with the demands of a novel.' Ultimately, the critic maintained, in its portrayal of the 'common soldier' as well as various 'washed-up types' among the ranks of the officers, the novel came across as far more 'immediate and true to life' than Theodor Plievier's *Stalingrad*. Above all, Schwab-Felisch continued, Gerlach offered an authentic account of what those who had been soldiers in the Third Reich had gone through, from gnawing hunger to being ordered to defend their positions 'to the last man', which amounted to a death sentence. The reviewer of the *Stuttgarter Zeitung* also heaped praise on the author's achievement. Heinrich Gerlach, who unlike Theodor Plievier had 'been through hell' and who 'had been trapped in the Cauldron at Stalingrad from the first to the last day', had 'not been able to attain the kind of distance that a novel about the "forsaken army", about that historical event, requires'. The fact that the enterprise succeeded nevertheless and that the book 'had such a shocking emotional impact' on the reader 'must be attributed above all to his careful planning and his unflinching honesty'. With regard to the lost manuscript, Gerlach's use of hypnotism and the recreation of the novel, the reviewer stressed:

> This fact alone demonstrates the urgency that drove the author to put pen to paper. It was the urgency of a man who feels a compelling need to write about his terrible experiences and the unimaginable suffering of almost three hundred

thousand soldiers, lest the slaughter of Leviathan appear a wholly senseless undertaking.

It was astonishing, he claimed, how Heinrich Gerlach had managed not to lose sight of this mission despite the huge cast of characters in his novel. Although he set it in various locations – the army's supply train, field hospitals, airstrips, field HQs and forward positions on the main front – the different strands of the narrative never got tangled: 'On the contrary: before long, they start to form a tight network consisting of countless snapshots evoking anger and pain and bitter lament, each of them displaying an immediacy that is often compelling.' This reviewer was evidently deeply moved and made no attempt to hide it when discussing the war and the fate of the Sixth Army at Stalingrad:

> Because Heinrich Gerlach gives the reader a detailed insight into the Führer's direct orders, into Colonel General Paulus's decisions and into the discussions of the situation that took place in the divisional headquarters, and shows that the lower ranks, all those starving, freezing, emaciated poor wretches, knew nothing or next to nothing about the hopeless predicament they were in, you find yourself gripped time and again by a sense of impotent rage. You know that every day will be more horrific than the last, yet you can do nothing to help. Here, in order to sustain the myth of the promised 'imminent final victory', an entire army was knowingly and without the slightest scruple put to the sword.

Both of these reviewers drew comparisons with Theodor Plievier's bestseller on Stalingrad. That was understandable, since Gerlach also restricts narrated time to the decisive phase in Stalingrad, namely the months from November 1942 to January 1943. As well as this compressed time frame, both novels also went in for minutely detailed depiction of selected events. In addition, a stylistic trait they both shared with the novels being criticized in the GDR at around the same time for their 'hard-bitten writing style' was the absence of any commentary on events by a sovereign narrator. Instead they are predominantly a personal account, in which events are seen through the eyes of the protagonists themselves. An impression of immediacy is also heightened by extensive passages of discourse and dialogue. What was not mentioned in reviews at the time, however, was Gerlach's use of certain features of modern narration. As in Plievier's work, frequent shifts in pacing, a multiplicity of narrative voices and the use of flashback sequences all serve to disrupt the closed epic form. This said, though, Gerlach clearly links the course of the unfolding tragedy at Stalingrad to his central character, First Lieutenant Breuer, who can be seen as an autobiographical sketch and who in the final analysis functions as the author's alter ego.

As the hypnosis sessions with Dr Schmitz had already shown, Gerlach had structured his novel in three major sections that chronologically followed the most important phases of the battle for Stalingrad. The first part, which he gave the heading 'Storm on the Horizon', portrays the Red Army offensive up to the closing of the encircled pocket called the Cauldron. The second ('Between Night and Morning') runs from the immediate aftermath of the encirclement to the rejection of the Soviet offer to accept a German surrender, while the third part ('The Moment of Truth') covers the final phase of the Battle of Stalingrad up to the ultimate catastrophe. Like Plievier, Heinrich Gerlach lends events at Stalingrad an eschatological dimension by importing motifs of biblical destruction and downfall, which anticipate the end even at the start of the text, for example when he talks about a 'huge mushroom cloud' and a 'blood-red pillar of fire':

> A few days later all their hopes of seeing the mountains of the Caucasus and the palm groves of the Black Sea coast were

shattered. The division was diverted to the northeast and it was then for the first time that they heard the name, never to be forgotten, of Stalingrad. They marched on over the Kalmyk steppe with sand, as fine as dust, filtering into their pores and into the motors of the cars. Squadrons of Stukas pointed the way. A huge mushroom cloud of smoke reached up to the sky, silver-grey and solid as a monument by day, a blood-red pillar of fire by night.

This passage conveys the hopeless, inescapable fate of the troops as the catastrophe of Stalingrad unfolds. As an example, Gerlach shows how social order breaks down in the course of the battle of annihilation, leaving individuals helplessly exposed to the tragedy that is about to be visited upon them. Mercilessly, he shows how especially those figures he has set up as role models are not immune from the ravages of death and destruction. From the perspective of the central character Breuer – and not some commentating narrator – the reader can accompany the protagonist through to the point where he finally realizes that war inevitably leads to the dissolution of the community and the destruction of the individual:

Breuer began to understand what was happening. The people were struggling for priority – everyone wanted to get the first place – a senseless, hopeless, lunatic struggle, Breuer thought despairingly. Were they even human beings any more? He saw oddments of different uniforms, and various badges of rank and decorations underneath bulky winter clothing, officers' caps with silver braid and the dirty yellow-coloured Romanian 'sugar-loaf' helmets. These men had once been Germans, Austrians, Luxemburgers, Croatians and Romanians. Superiors and subordinates, all comrades at one time. Workers, peasants and townspeople, Protestants and Catholics, fathers and sons... People perhaps formed and shaped by the nurturing atmosphere of a loving family home, and maybe by the humanist education they received at school, by the church they attended where they were enjoined to love their fellow man, by the communitarian ideals of National Socialist organizations or by the iron discipline of a German army steeped in tradition. People who had once set great store by such things as love and loyalty, camaraderie and duty, or who had at least had a veneer of so-called bourgeois 'respectability'. And now? No trace of any of this. All the many and varied manifestations of two thousand years of human culture and civilization swept away, with the time-honoured norms now counting for nothing. Everything sloughed off like a crumbling, dried skin. Not even the herd instinct of primitive man, of animals, not even that! Just nothing, nothing…

What is true for Breuer also goes for all of the other characters without exception, who are bound together by the chain of military command and their oath of allegiance. Their lot is hopeless and their sacrifice senseless. Even Corporal Lakosch is forced to concede this. Looking back, the life and death situation they find themselves in suddenly dawns on him:

> He saw now that the road he had followed so far was a false one but he could no longer go back. He saw himself caught like a mouse in a trap. This was the end, without sense or consolation, like a criminal's end upon the electric chair.

If Lakosch and the other characters have no alternative and ineluctably become the victims of a war machine, then Heinrich Gerlach is following here a basic narrative trope successfully put in place by representatives of the younger generation of writers around Group 47 after 1945, namely that of the young generation as victims of tyrannical rule and war. After returning from military service and captivity, Hans Werner Richter, Alfred Andersch, Walter Kolbenhoff, Wolfdietrich Schnurre, Günter Eich, Wolfgang Weyrauch, together with Heinz Friedrich and Walter Mannzen, all harked back, initially in newspaper and magazine pieces, to a 'common core of experience' and presented the younger generation as tragic victims. It was Hans Werner Richter who first described this arc of shared experience, which stretched 'from the inquisition to life at the front, and from the concentration camp to the gallows'. Undoubtedly, the dissemination of this kind of 'narrative of soldierly victimhood' was aimed at establishing a stabilizing frame of identity and was instrumental in forging a literary group mentality. It was therefore no coincidence that Alfred Andersch, in his 1946 essay 'The Face of Young Europe is Starting to Emerge', defined the younger generation as 'men and women between the ages of eighteen and thirty-five'. According to Andersch, 'they are distinguished from older people by their lack of responsibility for the Hitler regime, and from younger people by their experience of the front and prison, in other words by their "inserted life"'. Andersch thus demarcated them (by virtue of their 'experience of the front and prison') just as sharply from authors who had gone into exile as from those successful writers who had chosen to remain in Germany after the Nazis came to power. Andersch's upper age limit of thirty-five exonerated those young men who, in 1933, had been under the age of twenty-three and therefore not liable for military service. In this way, the narrative of victimhood furnished a collective symbol that became the basis of a community of (young) former German soldiers who had become the victims of Nazism and who were bound together by shared experiences and memories. Principally in novels and short stories, a quintessential figure emblematic of his whole generation came into existence, representing the common soldier as the victim of a totalitarian regime. Heinrich Gerlach's *The Forsaken Army* had a clear affinity with novels such as Theodor Plievier's *Stalingrad*,

Hans Werner Richter's *Die Geschlagenen* (*The Defeated*, 1949), Heinrich Böll's *Wo warst du, Adam?* (*And Where Were You, Adam?*, 1951) or Alfred Andersch's *Die Kirschen der Freiheit* (*The Cherries of Freedom*, 1952). Even in instances where Stalingrad did not – as with Gerlach – become the chronotope of the narration, the 'narrative of soldierly victimhood' provided a ready-made 'master narrative' that was capable of reorganizing experiences for a large part of the war generation and of gathering together in a common history the 'disturbances' they had suffered in the 'service of generating social cohesion and shaping identity'. It became common public knowledge in the 1950s that only 91,000 German soldiers from the 300,000 originally trapped in the Stalingrad Cauldron had survived and been taken prisoner. Of these, a mere 6,000 returned to Germany in the years up to 1956. Heinrich Gerlach was one of this handful of men, and for that very reason wanted to 'bear witness in the name of the dead'.

Ultimately then, literary texts like Gerlach's novel played a key part in shaping the collective memory of the German people. These texts were well received by readers because they told a story that met with general consensus, which was recounted 'in the service of creating a national identity'. According to the historians Konrad Jarausch and Martin Sabrow, the collective memory, and hence the groups or authorities promoting it, are all aimed at establishing 'macro-histories' or 'master narratives'. The 'narrative of soldierly victimhood' was one such 'coherent account of history, told from an unambiguous perspective [...]', whose shaping force not only had the effect of 'creating a whole genre of literature' but also attained 'public pre-eminence'. The 'master narrative' of the ordinary soldier as the sufferer and victim acquired validity throughout the whole of society in the Federal Republic only after it had been 'given concrete shape, disseminated and institutionalized'. The 'narrative of soldierly victimhood' became common currency in the 1950s because it reflected 'cultural trends of the age', caught 'the tenor of the times' and deployed 'appropriate ways and means... of making itself heard both within its specialist field and in the wider world'. For the reasons outlined, that also applied specifically to Heinrich Gerlach's Stalingrad novel, which over time became a bestseller. After just three months, it had sold more than 30,000 copies. In 1959 Gerlach's *The Forsaken Army* was awarded the Premio Bancarella, an Italian literary prize established in 1953; previous winners included Ernest Hemingway's *The Old Man and the Sea* (1953) and Boris Pasternak's *Doctor Zhivago* (1958). While Gerlach had initially considered the loss of his manuscript in captivity as the price he'd had to pay for his life and freedom, when it came to it he wasn't prepared to pay it. 'I'd expended too much effort and nervous energy on that book to give it up for lost without a fight,' he asserted. Ultimately, it appeared, he'd won his fight. But another was soon to follow.

IV.   A novel on trial –
A first in legal and medical history

In my first attempts to piece together the story of Heinrich Gerlach's bestseller about Stalingrad, I naturally found myself drawn to the spectacular hypnosis experiment, since it had to do with questions touching on certain aspects of our research into memory. But on closer investigation, it turned out that the story of the genesis of *The Forsaken Army* did not end with the runaway success of the published novel. I uncovered a report in the news magazine *Der Spiegel* on an unusual dispute that was without precedent in the history of German jurisprudence and medicine. It appeared on 29 January 1958 and began:

> Senior teacher Dr Heinrich Gerlach, 49, from Brake, near Bremen, has unexpectedly found himself at the centre of an astonishing controversy unprecedented in the history of German literature. It has generated so much publicity for his first work – the Stalingrad novel *The Forsaken Army* – that the Nymphenburg publishing house only needed to make a few standard promotional statements when it announced the imminent publication of the sixth edition of the novel (26,000th–30,000th copies) to booksellers last week. This publicity-generating controversy is being fought out between the writer Gerlach and the Munich psychotherapist Dr Karl Schmitz, 69. Wide-ranging legal briefs prepared by the lawyers for both parties in the dispute are further inflaming the dispute, which goes back to a curious experiment: Dr Schmitz, who recently published a book on his 'completely new insights into hypnosis' (with the title *Healing Through Hypnosis*), claims that Heinrich Gerlach was only able to get his novel on Stalingrad down on paper in the first place

thanks to his skill in the art of hypnotism. On the basis of this conviction and various select pieces of evidence, the physician Schmitz is hoping that the court will recognize his claim to 20 per cent of the author's earnings from the bestseller as his rightful share of the profits.

The article went on to recount the curious story of the manuscript lost in Soviet captivity, the hypnosis experiment in Munich and the unexpected success of the book. Following the novel's success, after an interval of seven years Dr Schmitz once again entered the picture:

> Meanwhile, hypnosis specialist Schmitz found himself obliged to refresh his former patient's memory for a second time, by sending him a copy of the participation agreement from 1951. Taken aback, the author Gerlach acknowledged that the signature on this unorthodox contract was indeed his, but pointed out that he may well have signed the document at a time when he was not in full possession of his mental faculties.

Subsequently – according to *Der Spiegel* – Heinrich Gerlach sent an enquiry through his solicitor to the 'Regional Medical Association of the City and District of Munich', asking whether such a contract between a doctor and his patient did not in fact infringe against the professional code of physicians and should therefore be deemed unethical. Dr Schmitz, who learned of this enquiry, in turn approached his professional body, requesting that it confirm to him the rectitude of his position on the basis of the law as it pertained to doctors. However, the president of the doctor's professional organization could not be persuaded by either Heinrich Gerlach or Dr Schmitz to deliver an unequivocal opinion on the matter. In the meantime, Gerlach had offered to pay Dr Schmitz a commensurate fee for his medical treatment. Dr Schmitz had turned this down, though, insisting on the legality of his 'private literary agreement'. His words were quoted verbatim in *Der Spiegel*:

> For the German edition of 30,000 copies at 17.80 Deutsch-marks apiece, Gerlach (who earns 10 per cent of the retail price) has pocketed a total of DM 53,400! On a rough calculation, according to this I should have received around 10,000 Marks. Not to mention foreign and film and other rights, which bring in even more revenue!

For his part, Dr Schmitz suggested to Gerlach that they agree to submit themselves to an arbitration ruling by the Munich Medical Practitioners' Association. The *Spiegel* report ended with some fighting talk by the doctor: 'If Gerlach won't agree to this, I'll see him in court. Who knows, otherwise people might start claiming I'd tricked him into signing the contract while he was under hypnosis.'

Two days later, the *Süddeutsche Zeitung* also reported on the legal dispute. The journalist who wrote the piece, Ernst Bäumler, followed *Der Spiegel* in sketching out the story of the novel. In order to give the reader an idea of the positions of the two parties in the dispute, he had interviewed them both. Dr Schmitz argued that Gerlach had not approached him as a 'normal patient'. 'He wasn't ill,' said Schmitz, 'rather, he clearly intended that I should help him create a transcription of his book. That's why I didn't demand a single penny in fees from him for the countless experiments we conducted, but instead a share of the profits.' Furthermore, Schmitz pointed to letters from Gerlach that seemed to confirm him in his belief that he, Gerlach, had also understood their arrangement to be a 'business partnership'. Gerlach, on the other hand, maintained that he had no recollection of entering into any agreement with Dr Schmitz. The first thing he knew of the existence of the contract, he claimed, was when Schmitz sent him a copy. Asked whether Dr Schmitz might possibly have extracted a signature from him while he was under hypnosis, Gerlach gave a very cagey response: 'I'd be wary of drawing such an inference. All I would say is that the course of treatment put me in a position of some dependence upon the doctor.' Heinrich Gerlach also had different memories of the actual experiments:

> The sessions did not last for three weeks, but two. On only one occasion was his secretary present. Before each session I sketched out the particular scene to Schmitz that I hoped we might be able to reconstruct while I was hypnotized. After Schmitz had put me in a state of half-sleep, he sat beside me and whispered certain words to me that I'd given him in advance, whereupon I would recount the scene to him in full while under hypnosis.

In retrospect, Heinrich Gerlach took a less euphoric view of the sessions than he had done in the letters he had written to Schmitz at the time. During the treatment, he claimed, they hadn't managed to reconstruct two-thirds of the plot of the novel, but only about a quarter. His summary was correspondingly downbeat:

> We're talking about some 150 pages of the 614 pages of the original manuscript. Schmitz sent the transcript to me at Brake. There, using the 150 pages that Schmitz had coaxed out of me, I wrote the first and second parts of my novel. The missing 450 pages or so of my old manuscript I conceived afresh over the next four years, via a combination of memory research, conversations with friends and studying historical sources.

Heinrich Gerlach's account here accords with the statements that his daughter, Dorothee Wagner, made more than fifty years later, without any knowledge of the documents concerning the legal dispute.

Gerlach's indication that hypnosis had yielded only 150 pages and that it had taken another five years to write the remaining 450 pages still rings true today.

Finally, the Hamburg edition of the popular tabloid newspaper *Bild-Zeitung* also picked up on the court battle. On 31 January 1958, the *Bild*'s chief reporters, Dr Hermann Harster and Max Pierre Schaefer, ran a full-page story with the headline: 'The Horror of Stalingrad – Relived in the Psychiatrist's Chair'. Here, too, the story of the recreation of the novel was recounted. However, *Bild* put more emphasis on the legal side of the contract and asked: 'Is a doctor entitled to demand a financial stake in the intellectual property of his patient instead of his customary fee? That is the key question at the centre of an odd legal dispute that has no precedent in the history of jurisprudence and medicine in Germany.' Once again, both sides were interviewed for the article. The war, Gerlach's time in captivity, the loss of the manuscript and the attempts to piece it together again were all graphically described. *Bild* also printed a facsimile of the agreement, which did indeed carry Gerlach's signature. The text of the document, which was dated 30.7.1951 and certified with the signatures of both Heinrich Gerlach and Dr Schmitz, ran as follows:

> The first signatory, Herr H. Gerlach of Hunterstrasse 6 in Brake, and Dr K. Schmitz of Jahnstrasse 20 in Munich have on this day come to the following agreement. In the event that Herr Gerlach should, as a result of hypnosis by Dr Schmitz, manage to reconstruct his manuscript 'Breakout at Stalingrad', which he has forgotten, Herr Gerlach hereby undertakes to pay Dr Schmitz by way of a contingent fee 20 (twenty) per cent of the anticipated gross receipts accruing from publication of the manuscript, or of parts thereof. Dr Schmitz hereby signals his willingness to take the course of treatment through to a successful conclusion.

Alongside the facsimile of the contract, Hermann Harster and Max Pierre Schaefer placed a feature panel in which two legal experts laid out the provisions of current contract law. They explained that, according to paragraph 138 of the German Civil Code, any contract that was morally objectionable should be deemed invalid. In line with this, all gross violations of professional duty were to be regarded 'as unethical and as rendering null and void any legal transaction (German High Court ruling 153/260)'. However, it was incumbent upon the professional code for German doctors to pronounce on whether an agreement involving a contingent fee constituted a violation of a physician's professional duty of care. Their conclusion was that, in the present case, particular note should be taken of the statement (in paragraph 1 of the code) that 'services to health' was not a business. Furthermore, the fee charged by a doctor must be commensurate with the treatment; the official schedule of fees should serve as a guide here (Paragraph 10). In other words, the legal evaluation of the case in hand was contentious. Doctors whose opinions on the dispute were solicited by *Bild* were quoted as taking the following stance:

> An obstetrician might just as well demand a share of the royalties earned by a child he'd helped bring into the world and who later became a writer.

It was evident that the sympathies of the doctors questioned tended to lie with Heinrich Gerlach. Two months after the first reports of the clash between the writer and Dr Schmitz, the *Frankfurter Illustrierte* also took up the topic, headlining its story 'Did He Write "Stalingrad" Under Hypnosis?' The extensive report included testimony from someone who, in the magazine's view, had not yet had sufficient opportunity to state his case: Heinrich Gerlach. Alongside an outline of the history and the genesis of the novel, the piece also included an interview, in which the author answered a series of questions. Among the areas covered were the 'mysterious and incomprehensible' circumstances of the contract with Dr Schmitz. On this point, Heinrich Gerlach noted in conclusion:

> The 'contract' was dated 30.7.1951. By that stage I had been hypnotized 23 times by Dr Schmitz and was in such an unstable frame of mind that I'd have sold him my grandmother. Why hadn't Dr Schmitz presented me with such an agreement at the start of the treatment programme? Isn't this at the very least a case of medical malpractice?

The article, which also carried a photograph of Heinrich Gerlach in the offices of the *Frankfurter Illustrierte*, concluded with an excerpt from the novel, which it then went on to print in full, in instalments.

For all the extensive reporting in the press of the legal dispute at the beginning of January 1958, there was no information at that juncture about the outcome. Had the Munich Medical Association issued an arbitration ruling or did the matter come to trial? I resolved to examine Dr Schmitz's papers to find the answer. Sixty years was a long time, to be sure, but considering the uniqueness of either of these outcomes, it seemed fair to assume that there would probably be a paper trail somewhere in the form of archived material. After numerous attempts, however, I was forced to abandon this hope. My last chance at finding information was scotched by the Munich district court, where I'd enquired after Dr Schmitz's death date. I was informed that the doctor had died on 15 March 1967. In the public records, his wife was given as the sole heiress, along with a note that she, too, must have passed on in the interim. The court records office could tell me nothing about the doctor's son, who had been resident in Munich in 1967. However, a series of enquiries led me to the Munich Association of Statutory Health Insurance Physicians, which also had a small archive. Several requests on my part finally yielded the information that they did indeed hold microfilm archive material of the Schmitz–Gerlach case. I was really keen to see what transpired from this source, but my hope of being able to use this material to piece together a complete picture of the dispute was immediately frustrated when I sat down at the microfiche reader in the Association's library. The documents that had been preserved on film were incredibly difficult to decipher, and in parts completely illegible. Nevertheless, I was able to reconstruct the route Dr Schmitz had taken to try to corroborate his claim. Among the documents, alongside Heinrich Gerlach's 'Observations During Hypnosis' I also found the agreement that he and the doctor had signed.

This archive material confirmed that no definitive ruling had been forthcoming, and that as a result the matter had gone to court. In this forum, the dispute excited media interest nationwide. For instance, a brief note appeared in *Der Spiegel* on 12 March 1958, referring back to the magazine's earlier report on 29 January of that year and announcing:

> The documentary filmmaker Wilfried H. Achterfeld from Essen has asserted copyright of the title 'Dictated Under Hypnosis' by entering it on the list of film titles in the German movie industry's voluntary registration scheme. The subject of the planned film 'will be closely based on the current legal dispute between the psychotherapist Dr Schmitz and the bestselling author Dr Gerlach'.

The fact that the idea for the film never came to fruition almost certainly had to do with the length of the trial, which dragged out over several years and only ended on 29 January 1961 with a settlement between the parties. A newspaper report on the long-running case reported the outcome thus:

> The question of the validity of the signature on the contract played a decisive role in the case. For instance, was it obtained

during hypnosis or under the after-effects of the procedure, as Gerlach implied? The matter was finally resolved by a handwriting expert's report prepared by the Niedersachsen Criminal Police Bureau. According to this, there could be no doubt that Gerlach signed the agreement of 30.7.1951 while in a fully conscious state. The matter thus became subject to settlement. Schmitz accepted the sum of 9,500 Marks, and the author indicated that he was willing to pay that sum.

According to the Oldenburg district court, in compliance with the ordinance governing such matters, the records of this civil action were subsequently destroyed. The same went for the graphologist's report, which was prepared in the context of the trial and which formed the basis for the settlement between the two disputants. I hoped I might still find a copy of the report in the state police bureau in Hanover, but was disappointed. In any event, the resident graphologist there told me that the kind of report that had been drafted back then would no longer be admissible, since in the interim it had been shown that even signatures written in trance-like states do not necessarily display the slightest deviation from the norm!

V.   A spectacular discovery –
Breakout at Stalingrad

And with that, I considered my involvement with Heinrich Gerlach to be at an end. Notwithstanding the book's genesis, unique in the history of German literature – which, astonishingly, even literary scholars of the older generation did not know about or had forgotten – the fact remained that the original draft of the novel was lost and the only extant version was the successful new one. In his foreword to *The Forsaken Army*, Gerlach had explained the very special circumstances of the novel's emergence in captivity, the seizure of the manuscript and his eventual recreation of the novel:

> In 1944–45, when everything that had happened was still fresh in my mind, I wrote this book while I was a prisoner of the Russians. My fellow prisoners, from all ranks and walks of life, helped me with their recollections and constructive criticism. In December 1949, the manuscript that I'd carefully guarded for so long was confiscated by the Soviet Ministry of Internal Affairs (MVD). The brave attempt by a friend of mine to smuggle a miniature transcript written on twenty sheets of paper to Germany also failed... In the period from 1951 to 1955 I rewrote the manuscript after my return to Germany. I saw it as my duty towards my dead and living comrades.

In the Cold War period of confrontation between East and West, it seemed a hopeless endeavour to try to track down the manuscript seized by the MVD. But on rereading Gerlach's preface, I couldn't help but speculate on how the two versions might compare. Given that many commentators saw the key achievement of Gerlach's reconstruction of his Stalingrad novel as being its authenticity, what must the original have been like, written as it was in the immediate aftermath of the military catastrophe at Stalingrad? I wondered whether the manuscript had been destroyed after being confiscated, or was languishing in some secret Russian archive. But I could see no possible way of finding out.

As it happened, just such an opportunity did arise in October 2011, albeit completely fortuitously. I was swapping notes with Manfred Görtemaker, a leading scholar of modern history who taught at the University of Potsdam and the author of such titles as *History of the Federal Republic of Germany* (1999) and *Thomas Mann and Politics* (2005). During our conversation about the projects we were currently working on, Görtemaker mentioned some recent research that had taken him to Moscow. In response to my question whether it was now possible to work in Russian archives again, he replied that, although not exactly straightforward, it wasn't out of the question either. I kept thinking about our discussion after I got home, so I sent him an email telling him about the material in the Russian archives that particularly interested me. It didn't just concern Heinrich Gerlach, but more generally cultural activity among German prisoners of war and attempts to harness this for the purposes of Soviet re-education in writers' workshops. I cited exiled German writers like Erich Weinert or Johannes R. Becher. Görtemaker responded straight away and put me in contact with Moscow. The documentation I got back raised my hopes, with the result that on 14 February 2012, we – namely I and my colleague Norman Ächtler – found ourselves standing outside the Russian State Military Archive (RGVA) in Moscow, a plain, functional two-storey building on Admiral Makarov Street. In the rear section of the building, not visible from the street, there is a silo-like tower containing a series of Russian archives. I was aware that the Russian State Military Archive had had several names throughout its history, and was founded in 1918 as the 'Archive of the Red Army'. It had been given its present name in 1992 following the collapse of the Soviet Union. The enormous body of documentation relating to all the different branches of the Soviet armed forces, including special forces, from the time of the Civil War to the Second World War is held here, including all relevant files on individuals. I also knew that, since 1999, the military archive also included a so-called 'special archive' containing the bulk of records in German.

Access to the special archive, which was established in August 1945 by the Soviet secret service to house all the papers seized from the Germans, was at first the sole preserve of the People's Commissariat for Internal Affairs (NKVD), which after 1954 changed its name to the Committee for State Security, or KGB. The records kept there also served post-1945 as evidence in war crimes trials and to assist the KGB's activities, both internally and abroad. Up to the 1970s the holdings of this archive had been catalogued on a card-index system, though this work had not followed a consistent logic. As a result, even today not all the documents have been registered or made accessible. This can mean that you find none of the documents you're looking for, but also that you sometimes unearth wonderful chance discoveries. We not only knew exactly what we were looking for in the archive but had also thought long and hard about where best to commence our search. We were fully aware that, although the documents housed in the military archive were in principle accessible to foreign academics as well, in practice the restrictions on making copies meant that it was virtually impossible to cast one's net very wide.

In addition, all the papers in the archives that had long been kept secret have to go through a complicated declassification process before they are made available to the public. In other words, a special commission has to release the documents, and in cases where they only exist in German, translations have to be provided in the archive before the decision on whether to sanction them for public use can be taken. Add to this the fact that it is almost impossible even to begin to use the 'holdings' – as these resources are called in Russia – and to get remotely close to what you're searching for without a good knowledge of Russian. Fortunately, I'd read Slavonic Studies at university; this was to prove crucial to our ability to continue, since it greatly facilitated swift communication with the authorities about the documents we were examining.

When we finally pushed open the heavy wooden door to the Russian State Military Archive for the first time, we were confronted with a barrier behind which Russian guards were carrying out security checks. Registration took an eternity, but finally we were issued with our passes and granted entry to the archive, which was located on the second floor. We soon realized that the research facilities here were in no way comparable to those we were used to in Berlin or Marbach. This was only to be expected; I knew that Russian archives received very limited state funding. We were also informed that we could sign out a maximum of five documents a day. So, we needed to examine what we called up from the stacks very thoroughly to avoid losing entire days of work. The archive room itself was furnished with three long rows of tables equipped with two-seat benches, like in school. Distributed across the benches were a number of large, heavy instruments for reading documents on microfiche. Eventually we were given a kind of User's Guide in Russian and could begin our search. After some considerable time spent sifting through the seemingly endless catalogue, we hit upon some interesting-looking records, which included talks given by captured German officers, letters from trainees from the anti-fascist schools, documentation from Camp 27, where the League of German Officers was founded and which Count von Einsiedel had told me something about already, messages of greeting from Stalin to students on anti-fascist courses, and letters of thanks to Stalin from prisoners of war from various camps. Finally, though, we came across an entry with details of cultural work in the camps. And that was where we found what we'd been looking for all along. Written in Russian, it wasn't instantly recognizable, but even so there was the heading: Gerlach, Heinrich: Novel 'Breakout at Stalingrad'! Norman and I stared at one another, maintaining a calm exterior. We couldn't order up the relevant files quickly enough, and the time spent waiting seemed interminable, but finally we were handed all the five documents we'd requested. We were really worried that Heinrich Gerlach might not turn out to be there after all, but that wasn't the case: on the desk in front of us lay the novel *Breakout at Stalingrad*! In response to our tentative question how often the manuscript had been requested by previous readers, we were told that we were the first to look at it.

Looking at the manuscript, we could only wonder at how Heinrich Gerlach had carried this weighty tome in his rucksack from camp to camp, and how he had managed to keep this treasure safe. It was, after all, over six hundred pages long. Nevertheless, this original manuscript was in remarkably good condition. Gerlach had presumably bound it together himself with shoemakers' twine. Even so, it looked different to how we'd imagined it. Heinrich Gerlach had once described the single-volume work that he'd written in prison thus: 'On the cover I stuck a cutting from a newspaper showing a field of corpses with a cross in the background. Above it I wrote "Breakout at Stalingrad" in red letters. But the manuscript in front of us had no image of a field of corpses or any red lettering. On the yellowish cardboard cover, in blue handwritten Gothic script resembling the 'Tannenberg' font developed in the 1930s, stood the title *Durchbruch bei Stalingrad*. Signs that it had been impounded by the Ministry of the Interior were also immediately apparent, in the form of a stamp with the manuscript's registration number. A handwritten slip alongside the manuscript contained a note in Russian about a decision that – though I couldn't have known it at the time – was the outcome of an elaborate procedure involving the highest echelons of the Soviet Communist Party. The text of the note ran:

> This book was sent back on 18.05.1951 with the submission number 8/09/3196 (N/27) by the operational directorate of the GUPVI-Office of the Interior Ministry; the decision has been made that it should not be returned to Gerlach.

On the inside title page, beneath the author's name in red, stood the title once more and the date 1944. If that was meant to signify the date the novel was completed, it was surprising, since Gerlach himself had stated that he only finished writing it in May 1945. On the right-hand bottom edge of the page, two stamps in red ink could be made out, indicating the submission date of the confiscated manuscript. On closer inspection, the following words could be read on the top stamp: Secretariat OB (organizational bureau) of the Central Committee WKP (b) Communist Party of the Soviet Union, supplement to 1065.

On the following page, before the Table of Contents, Gerlach had written a dedication in Latin: *Mortuis et Vivis* and below it, in pencil, 'To the Dead and the Living'. The next double-page spread was then occupied by the Table of Contents: the first part originally carried the title 'The Escape', but this had been crossed out and replaced by the handwritten correction 'The Gathering Storm', as in the new version of the novel. The second part was entitled 'Between Night and Morning' and the third 'The Moment of Truth', exactly as in the 1957 edition.

At the bottom of the page, another typewritten slip in Russian had been pasted into the book, giving the following information:

> Gerlach, Heinrich, born 1908, originally from Königsberg, graduated from the Philological Faculty of the University of Königsberg, secondary school teacher by profession, First Lieutenant, head of the intelligence unit of the 14th Tank Regiment. Taken prisoner at Stalingrad. Member of the National Committee for a 'Free Germany' from 14 September 1943.

There was no indication of who the author of this typewritten slip was, nor when it had been stuck into the book. Looking at the kind of typewriter used led us to surmise that the note was added when the novel was confiscated in 1950, as the characters clearly came from a make of machine that was used in the Soviet Union at that time. A cursory first leaf through the original manuscript showed clearly that Heinrich Gerlach had worked constantly on improving the manuscript. There were corrections on almost every page.

There were also some pages that had been edited with hand-written corrections and then struck out entirely. Conversely, there were pages in the manuscript for which Gerlach had typed out a clean version and pasted over the original. It was immediately apparent how much effort he had expended in copying out this text and painstakingly taking in all the corrections.

The author had kept polishing and correcting his Stalingrad novel right to the very end. By the time Gerlach completed his text, on 8 May 1945, the day Nazi Germany signed an unconditional surrender, he already knew the number of soldiers and officers taken prisoner by the Soviets, and also how many had survived. These statistics are reported soberly and without emotion by the narrator in the 'Final Reckoning':

> Over 91,000 men went into captivity, including 2,500 officers and clerical staff. That figure represented less than a third of the Sixth Army's original complement of men and around half its officers. Of the thirty-two German generals in the Cauldron, seven had been flown out, one died in battle, one shot himself and one was posted as missing after 2 February 1943; this left twenty-two generals taken prisoner, foremost among them a field marshal.
>
> Four-fifths of the soldiers and half of the officers who went into captivity subsequently died as a result of the trauma they

had suffered. Of the twenty-two generals, one succumbed to stomach cancer.

The original manuscript ends with an episode in the headquarters of the Führer:

> In the spring of 1943, Field Marshal Freiherr von Weichs, C-in-C of the disbanded Army Group 'B' (of which the Sixth Army had been part up to November 1942) and his chief of staff, General von Soderstern, were paying a visit to the Führer's headquarters. The first letters from the troops captured at Stalingrad had just begun to filter through to Germany. Over lunch, the two officers voiced their opinion that these letters – evidence that many of the men who had fought at Stalingrad were still alive – must have come as a great relief and comfort to their relatives.
>
> Hitler looked up with a glowering expression on his face that dumbfounded the two men. Then he said: 'The duty of those who fought at Stalingrad is to be dead!'

However, unlike the new version of the text, in which Hitler has the last word and condemns himself out of his own mouth without any commentary by a narrator, Gerlach ends the original version with an afterword, which, while expressly claiming the foregoing text to be a novel, nevertheless maintains that 'nothing in this book is "fabricated"'. The manuscript ends with a pointer to the factual basis of the book and an expression of thanks to the 'surviving Stalingrad veterans':

> [The author] has taken the subject matter of his book both from the experiences he himself underwent in and around Stalingrad and from accounts given to him by survivors of the battle – soldiers, officers and generals – during the three

years he spent in captivity. It is incumbent upon him to thank
here all his former comrades for their invaluable assistance
and cooperation.

On an initial skim-read, it quickly became apparent what a complicated task it would be to compare the original manuscript with
the version that Heinrich Gerlach had reconstructed and the new
text he had written. But in order to even begin this task, it would
be necessary to obtain a copy of the manuscript held in the archive
here. We knew that there would be no possibility of copying the
614 pages of the original in the special archive. We still had a few days
at our disposal there, however, especially since we were planning
to look at some more material on cultural activities in the Soviet
POW camps. Furthermore, other documents were available with
information on the work of the League of German Officers, whose
founder members included Heinrich Gerlach. Over the ensuing
days, we discovered numerous wall newspapers, poems, songs and
stories that would help us build up a picture of cultural activity in
the camps, and which later formed the basis of an exhibition on
German POWs in the Soviet Union. But by the time we left Moscow,
we also had something else in our luggage, which had been the
real reason for our trip there: Heinrich Gerlach's novel *Breakout at
Stalingrad*. In the form of 614 individually photographed pages.

VI. All in the past –
Memoirs of a Königsberg man

Back in Germany, we realized that the real work was now about to begin. In any event, we needed to produce a printed version – an unusually complicated, time-consuming and laborious process in view of the many corrections and reworkings made by the author. In addition, the question of copyright had to be resolved. We were greatly aided in our work on the novel by the fact that in 1966 – almost ten years after the publication of *The Forsaken Army*, which by then had become a huge bestseller – Heinrich Gerlach had picked up where the novel left off and, in his work *Odyssey in Red* (*Odyssee in Rot*), given an account of the long spell that he and his fellow German soldiers and officers had spent in Soviet captivity. As in his novel, Gerlach once again 'encoded' his own fate in this autobiographical work in the figure of First Lieutenant Breuer. In the Lunyovo camp near Moscow, where the founding of the League of German Officers was due to take place in September 1943, Gerlach's alter ego, Breuer, recalls his home town of Königsberg and his tutor, Ernst Wiechert:

> Breuer closed his eyes. How warm the sunshine still was! What a lovely day! Scraps of thoughts floated like clouds across the sky of his drowsy consciousness. [...] The words of Ernst Wiechert, his teacher in Königsberg, came back to him: 'I urge you all never to stay silent when your conscience bids you speak.' Too many people had kept silent for too long, and wasted too many opportunities. And look at the dreadful price they'd paid. First Stalingrad...

The reference to Ernst Wiechert was no coincidence. In the early 1930s, Wiechert was one of the most popular writers in Germany. His novels and short stories like *The Wolf of the Dead* (1924), *The*

Silver Coach (1928), *The Small Passion* (1929) and *Jürgen Doskocil's Maid* (1932) were reprinted many times and his place in the German literary canon was ensured by his inclusion on the grammar-school curriculum. On 29 March 1929, Wiechert gave a famous valedictory address to a group of pupils whom he had tutored for four years in preparation for their school-leaving exam, though this was never published. It was a quite different story, however, with his famous 'Address to German Youth' of 6 July 1933, which he delivered in the main auditorium at the University of Munich. It was this speech, which invoked values like conscience and civil courage, that Breuer was quoting off the top of his head. Yet Heinrich Gerlach was not actually, as his memoir suggests, a student of Ernst Wiechert. Although Wiechert had indeed worked in Königsberg between 1920 and 1930 as a grammar-school teacher, he had taught at the *Hufengymnasium* in the city, whereas Gerlach had attended the *Wilhelmsgymnasium* throughout his time at school. He took his school-leaving exam there in February 1926 aged seventeen, the youngest in his class. In an unpublished memoir entitled 'All Things Must Pass – Memoirs of a Königsberg Man', which he wrote for his children and grandchildren at Christmas in 1987, he recalled his childhood and youth and gave a sketch of his family's life. On beginning his studies at Königsberg University, he noted:

> In the meantime, I'd made up my mind to study philology. After a rather tentative first semester at our venerable Albertina [a nickname for the Albertus-Universität Königsberg], at the tender age of eighteen I left the family home for the first extended period of my life. To study abroad! I resolved that if I was going to go at all, then it should be as far away as possible – to Vienna.

Although the subsequent biographical details of Heinrich Gerlach's life, from his army call-up in August 1939 to Stalingrad, have hitherto been a closed book, they can in part be reconstructed on the basis of this unpublished family memoir. After embarking on his studies in Königsberg followed by two semesters in Vienna, he completed his fourth semester at the University of Freiburg. In fact, after Vienna his family's finances could not stretch to another semester's study away from his home town, but like some 'Deus ex machina' his mother's younger brother, Bruno Kördl, who was engaged at the Freiburg Municipal Theatre as a much-vaunted heroic tenor, suddenly stepped in. Gerlach's uncle offered to provide Heinrich with board, lodging and free theatre tickets if his parents would undertake to pay his university fees and send him 50 Reichsmarks a month as pocket money. So it was that Gerlach came to enrol at the University of Freiburg for the winter semester of 1927–28, where he attended an undergraduate seminar run by the Latinist Wolfgang Aly. Aly, who taught at Freiburg as an associate professor, was a specialist in Greek literature as well as various Latin authors such as Livy. While attending his seminar, Gerlach wrote a paper for Aly on the 'Civis', a short epic written in hexameters, whose provenance was unknown at the time. The student Gerlach, too, was unable to solve this mystery, but in the Latin exam at the end of his coursework, he did manage to show that the philologists of humanism had each, at various intervals, arrived at very similar theses and arguments on the work. This essay of Gerlach's so impressed the then still young Königsberg ancient philologist Harald Fuchs – who at twenty-nine had been appointed to the chair in philology at the Albertina as Wolfgang Schadewaldt's successor – that he offered to accept the work from Gerlach as a doctoral dissertation. Gerlach refused, because he had promised Josef Nadler that he would join his group of doctoral students, who were preparing a wide-ranging research project on Johan Georg Hamann. Yet Josef Nadler, who was well known at the time for his *Literary History of the Germanic Tribes and Landscapes*, and who had been a lecturer at Königsberg University since 1925, then suddenly and quite unexpectedly took up an invitation to work at the University of Vienna. This effectively ended Heinrich Gerlach's ambitions to take a doctorate. He duly finished his undergraduate degree course in Königsberg and in 1931 took the first state examination to become a teacher. From the autumn of that year he did a year's internship at a grammar school at Tilsit before returning to his former alma mater, the *Wilhelmsgymnasium* in Königsberg, where in the autumn of 1933 he passed the second state teaching exam. However, as Gerlach recalled, job prospects at that time were fairly bleak:

> The education authorities sent out hectographed notes en bloc to all of us fresh-faced and newly qualified teachers, informing us that permanent or even temporary posts were out of the question for the foreseeable future. So, what were we to do now? In the end, I got very lucky and secured a temporary position at the military academy in Osterode, which was really hard work and involved lots of burning the midnight oil. I survived on a diet of bread rolls spread with liver-sausage and maté tea, and diligently saved my money.

On 20 April 1934 Gerlach married his girlfriend of many years, Ilse Kordl, in Königsberg. Shortly after the wedding the young couple moved to Lyck, in Masuria, where Gerlach had obtained a position 'for a maximum of six weeks' at the High School for Boys. As things turned out, the family's six-week sojourn in the picturesque little town on Lake Lyck was to turn into a ten-year residence. Five years in, however, Heinrich Gerlach was called up as an army reservist on 17 August 1939:

> It was one of the last days of August in that fateful year of 1939. Thirty degrees in the shade. The sun was blazing down on the sports field of the little town of Freystadt, not far from the Polish border. We had been encamped here for two days, eating pea

soup from the field kitchen wagon. When I say 'we', I mean the horse-drawn 228th Intelligence Division, a Territorial Army outfit that had been newly re-formed in the middle of the month, mainly with reservists from the Elbing region. It was clear bad things were about to happen; the previous day live rounds had been handed out to us. As a junior officer and commander of a telephone line construction unit, I applied myself strenuously in this period to learning about horses and picking up at least a few riding skills. Dressed in fatigue bottoms, our bare torsos burned red by the sun, we loafed about in intense boredom on the treeless sports field, cooling the horses every few minutes by hosing them down with water.

No further precise locations in Heinrich Gerlach's 'war biography' are given in his personal memoir. All we learn is that he came to be stationed in Paris in the winter of 1940–41, a place he had already visited as a student. Yet in his recollection, he found the atmosphere in occupied Paris oppressive:

The city centre was off-limits to German soldiers and could only be accessed with a special pass. Our division was issued with three such passes, which the officers used in rotation. In this way, I got to see the city once more, and everything was totally different. There were no visible signs of war damage, but the buildings were dreary and grey, and the streets were covered in slush and shrouded in mist in this dank winter. The people were glum, hungry and freezing, and still evidently in a state of shock after their country's terrible lightning defeat [...] There was no mention of de Gaulle or the Resistance at this stage. There was tentative talk of collaboration, of Marcel Déat and a new form of socialism, and the populace looked hopefully to Marshal Pétain, the grand old man in Vichy, who had prevented the very worst from happening. People dealt

politely with the equally polite and correct occupation force.
No one lifted the veil on what the SS and the Gestapo might
be getting up to somewhere in the dark recesses—.

Gerlach then fast-forwarded to describe what transpired after the
occupation of Paris:

> Then, one day in March, we suddenly received orders to pack
> up and ship out. And so we plunged head over heels into
> the escapade in Yugoslavia and shortly thereafter into the
> crazy war against the Soviet Union, in which well-meaning
> Frenchmen, who were more far-sighted than us, had already
> cautiously warned us not to become embroiled.

But how had Heinrich Gerlach subsequently risen through the ranks
to become a first lieutenant? However paradoxical it may sound,
information on this aspect of his life only came to light through the
Soviet POW records, in which Gerlach meticulously listed where he
saw action and on what date he was elevated to what rank. From
February to April 1940, he attended the officer cadet school in Halle,
passing out successfully with the rank of sergeant. In April Gerlach
was transferred to Königsberg to join the 1st Intelligence Battalion.
From August 1940, we find him attached once more to the 228th
Intelligence Battalion in Westphalia. On 1 September he was promoted to a lieutenant in the reserves and from December 1940 to
April 1941 he served as a platoon leader in the occupation of France.
He then spent a month (April 1941) in Yugoslavia, and in June was
attached as an officer to the 16th Motorized Rifle Division. On 22
June, the so-called Russian campaign began for Gerlach. On 24 July
1941 he was appointed as a staff officer to the 48th Armoured Corps,
and on 1 July 1942 promoted to first lieutenant. From 24 October
1942 onwards, Heinrich Gerlach was a General Staff Intelligence
Officer Third Class (Ic) for the 14th Armoured Division.

Gerlach was engaged in the Stalingrad campaign right from the outset, right up to the murderous battle when German forces were encircled in the Cauldron and the final capitulation at the end of January 1943. With other survivors of the defeated Sixth Army, he spent days huddled in foxholes, cellars and abandoned bunkers. For Gerlach there now began a seven-year-long odyssey through prisoner-of-war camps. His first place of incarceration was the town gaol in Beketovka, 15 kilometres south of Stalingrad. Just a day after the cessation of hostilities on 3 February 1943, the acting People's Commissar for Internal Affairs, Ivan Serov – who many years later, in 1950, would be the person dealing with Gerlach's impounded manuscript – ordered that the required number of POW camps should immediately be set up in the area around Stalingrad. However, the Soviets had underestimated the numbers of captured German troops by tens of thousands. Beketovka was chosen as an assembly point because here the level of destruction was less than in other places, though even in this town 90 per cent of the housing stock had been destroyed. According to an NKVD report of the time, the 'assembly points and distribution camps at which the prisoners arrived, either in a state of total apathy or in constant fear of being summarily "finished off", after gruelling marches around the outskirts of Stalingrad, in severe subzero temperatures and without any food or overnight accommodation, […] had only "rudimentary facilities" at best'. Unlike many of his compatriots, who were utterly exhausted and frozen half to death, Gerlach was in good enough shape to take stock of his surroundings on his arrival at Beketovka:

> BEKETOVKA. Lots of people out on the streets, largely women
> and children. Odd to find so much life in a place not far from
> the City of Death! Taciturn expressions with a searching
> look. Very occasionally an open threat, either verbally or in
> a person's demeanour. Adolescents jump out and make as
> if to land a punch. The guards shoo them away, calmly but

firmly. All without any fuss, and almost without a sound. Breuer can feel their gaze on his skin, scanning his face, and sometimes he's amazed to see a hint of pity in their eyes. Of course, it was the head bandage he was wearing! That filthy, blood-encrusted dressing must look frightful. On the plus side, the wound to his left eye seemed to have healed well, and he could hardly feel any pain there any more. Head bandages have an extraordinary effect on people. They embody picture-book notions of heroism. A hero with a stomach wound or frostbitten feet, say, would be unthinkable!

In the camp at Beretovka alone, more than 27,000 prisoners died between 3 February and 10 June 1943, putting the mortality rate of the survivors of Stalingrad at over 90 per cent. As the war progressed, around three thousand POW camps would be set up in the Soviet Union, split between main and subsidiary camps. These facilities each housed anything between a hundred and several thousand inmates. The camp administration was situated in each main camp. But in the subsidiary camps, too, there was an independent array of amenities, comprising a hospital, kitchen, laundry, barber's shop and shoe-repair workshop. In sum, from the first day of captivity to the last, the camps were 'total institutions' that radically restricted the individual's freedom of movement and subordinated him to an inflexible system. This began with early-morning sports or PT and continued with work assignments and increasing possibilities of regulated leisure-time activities. In this respect, for every soldier who underwent the experience, being a prisoner of war was a highly unusual situation. It was particularly difficult for those soldiers who were taken into captivity individually rather than in groups. Mass capitulations, such as happened at Stalingrad, were a different matter. Initially, Heinrich Gerlach also found that being taken prisoner was almost an 'anonymous act'; he was just one among thousands. He was extremely fortunate, since he was among a group of hand-picked officers who were driven to the camp in lorries. Gerlach noted the exact date in his memoirs: 24 February 1943, barely three weeks after his capture. Although the situation in the camps was chaotic at first, care was taken to register the details of all POWs when they first arrived. During interrogation, they were required to fill out a questionnaire, which gave them a registration number and was filed in their personal dossier. The questionnaire contained other information such as surname, Christian name, date of birth, home address, nationality, education history and occupation in civilian life, together with the date and place of capture or of transfer from another camp. Precisely this first Soviet record of Heinrich Gerlach came to light in the material from the special archive, thus enabling us to document the first important stage in his odyssey through the camps. His first destination was the famous Camp 27 at Krasnogorsk, near Moscow.

Just a few days after arriving there, however, Gerlach was singled out and transferred to the notorious 'Lefortovskaya' military prison in Moscow. The undoubted reason for this was that, as part of his designated role as a Third General Staff Intelligence Officer, Gerlach would have been responsible for gathering information on the enemy and for counter-intelligence. The authorization to this effect, which was also included in the documents on Gerlach, confirmed his transfer from Camp 27 of the NKVD to the military prison.

Gerlach spent four months in solitary confinement and was interrogated repeatedly by NKVD officers. He was released from the military prison in June 1943 and taken to POW camp 160 at Susdal, 200 kilometres from Moscow. The camp was reserved for officers and was administered by the Soviet secret service, the NKVD. This stage in his captivity is precisely attested too, by another interrogation or questionnaire form on Heinrich Gerlach with the code number 1050.

Fellow inmates at Camp 160 included Field Marshal Paulus and other generals of the defeated Sixth Army. On 22 July 1943, Gerlach was again ordered to decamp and put on a Ford V3000S lorry heading towards Moscow. Once again, his destination was Camp 27 in Krasnogorsk. Attached to this facility was the Lunyovo special camp, which was under the control of the Soviet Military Secret Service, the GRU. A working party in Lunyovo was already planning the formation of the League of German Officers (BDO), which would work against the Hitler regime from captivity; Gerlach was assigned to this group. At its head was Lieutenant Colonel Bredt, the former chief of the logistics division supplying the Sixth Army. At this stage, Gerlach still did not know that officers had been brought from several different camps to Lunyovo. Colonels Luitpold Steidle and Hans-Günther van Hooven also joined the group. Against their will, the Soviet secret service had also transported the renowned Stalingrad generals Walther von Seydlitz-Kurzbach, Dr Otto Korfes and Martin Lattmann to Lunyovo in ZIS limousines. Major General Walther von Seydlitz-Kurzbach, the most well-known of them, had fought his way out of encirclement by Soviet forces in the Demyansk Pocket in the spring of 1942, saving six divisions. Thereafter, Hitler took to calling him 'the toughest man in an encirclement'.

Seydlitz had gone into captivity with the rest of the Sixth Army at Stalingrad, after having tried in vain to persuade the commander-in-chief of the Sixth Army, Field Marshal Paulus, to defy Hitler's orders and break out of the Cauldron. Major General Martin Lattmann headed the 389th infantry division, while prior to his capture Dr Otto Korfes had been in command of the 295th infantry division. Colonel Steidle, who was a regimental commander when he was taken prisoner at Stalingrad, tried to convince the generals that they should collaborate with the BDO by pointing to a historical parallel, the Convention of Tauroggen, which Prussian general Ludwig von Yorck signed with the Russians on 30 December 1812, without prior authorization by his king, Frederick William III. For Steidle, the Sixth Army, which had been written off, needed to make its voice heard in order to bring about a swift end to the war and prevent the total destruction of Germany. Yet the generals initially turned down any collaboration, because they felt bound by their oath of allegiance and believed that any activities conducted from captivity amounted to an act of treason against the troops who were still fighting. The group of officers around Steidle were deeply disappointed. Ultimately, though, General Melnikov of the NKVD managed to win round the generals by conveying to them assurances from Stalin: if anti-fascist forces managed to bring about the fall of the Hitler regime and an end to the war against the Soviet Union, Germany would remain intact with her borders as at 1937. The three generals grasped at this straw of hope. After a further night of mulling over the situation, they agreed to join the League of German Officers. Some decades later, Walther von Seydlitz described the decisive moment in his memoirs:

> The thing that finally tipped the scales for me was the thought that if we managed through our involvement to make even a small part of the Russian assurances a reality, we should not hold back from collaborating. Hitler's madness was leading Germany so surely to destruction that unconventional action on our part was required to salvage what we could. My two comrades, Dr Korfes and Lattmann, came to the same conclusion and decision quite independently, without any urging from me.

This account outlining the dilemma faced by the three generals and the outcome they arrived at was attested by the memoirs of other officers such as Dr Korfes, Steidle and von Einsiedel.

The decision taken by the generals around von Seydlitz at the founding of the BDO to stake everything on Hitler's downfall and to work for a prompt peace settlement met with a hostile rejection from a section of the officers. Then again, as early as 1977, Bodo Scheurig, who edited Walther von Seydlitz's memoirs posthumously, correctly pointed out: 'We now know, however, that the situation at the time fully vindicated Seydlitz's decision.'

Following the generals' agreement, it still took some time for the BDO finally to be established. A preparatory conference took place at the end of August, at which the agenda for the inaugural meeting was sketched out, the next steps were planned, and the BDO's relationship with the National Committee for a Free Germany was discussed. An agreement was also reached on the composition of the future executive committee, with Major General von Seydlitz as its president. As a member of the working party, Heinrich Gerlach was part of the inner circle of the BDO's leadership.

VII. Heinrich Gerlach in Lunyovo special camp – The founding of the BDO – Lost documentary footage

The summer of 1943 came and went in the Lunyovo special camp without any firm deadline being set for the founding of the organization. Then everything happened very suddenly. On 10 September, news came that the founding of the League of German Officers would take place the very next day. Frantically, the necessary arrangements were made. On 11 September, at around 10.00 a.m., the attendees at the inaugural meeting of the organization finally filed into the festively decorated dining room of the special camp. Heinrich Gerlach was impressed. But what surprised him even more were the 'bundles of cables, the enormous spotlights, the microphones and the huge film camera'. The Soviet Interior Ministry had given instructions for the event to be filmed. Great store was set by this initiative by German officers, who were convinced that their involvement in trying to oust Hitler would help avert the worst outcome for Germany.

Heinrich Gerlach's comment set me wondering what had become of the documentary footage recorded by the Soviet film crew in Lunyovo in 1943. It was widely thought to have been lost. But after a painstaking search, we managed not only to find the film stock in one of the Soviet archives but also – no easy task – to make a copy of it. The footage confirmed the account of proceedings written by Gerlach, who is clearly identifiable in various sequences.

Gerlach took his place in the middle of a row on the right-hand side at the front, from where he had a view of the entire hall. In the far-right corner, he spotted the lectern, draped with the black, white and red flag. The future members of the committee of the BDO had seated themselves up front on a separate table. As chairman by seniority, sixty-two-year-old Lieutenant Colonel Alfred Bredt opened proceedings. Spotlights and the camera were trained in turn on the committee and the prominent speakers, including Erich Weinert, who, as president of the National Committee for a Free Germany, welcomed the foundation of the officers' association.

The tenor of all the contributions was the same: the officer's league was seen as a way of forcing the Hitler regime's resignation, demonstrating the German people's readiness for peace and bringing about a ceasefire as swiftly as possible. The address given by Colonel Hans-Günther van Hooven particularly impressed all those present. Van Hooven, who had only been airlifted into the Cauldron at Stalingrad at the end of December 1942 as the Sixth Army's new head of signals, gave a forensic analysis of the military, political and economic situation after Stalingrad, and asked:

> Are we not compelled by a moral imperative, by human compassion and by a love of the German people and homeland to take decisive action before it is too late? You all know the answer to this. I have come to the conclusion that as a military commander Hitler has already lost this war. He unequivocally assumed the role of C-in-C when he dismissed Field Marshal von Brauchitsch. The failed Winter Campaign of 1941–42, undertaken without proper winter clothing, the risky offensives against Stalingrad and the Caucasus, and the loss of North Africa are all the result of his volatile nature and lack of military know-how. And as a statesman, Hitler has lost this war politically too. He has managed to bring together a coalition of countries against Germany, while the measures taken by him and his regime have ensured that not only other nations' military might is now ranged against us but also the immeasurable hatred of their people. As an economic strategist, Hitler only reckoned on lightning wars and lightning victories. As in the First World War, time and space – whose effects, in the face of all experience, he tried to

claim as his own – have now turned against us. Total war has become totally hopeless, and so to continue with it would be both pointless and immoral.

Like all the speakers who came after him, Colonel van Hooven's aim was to underline the huge significance of the German Army in bringing about an end to hostilities and in securing postwar stability in Germany. 'Reason and humanity therefore dictate,' he argued, 'that we end this war and sue for peace before it is too late.' The colonel alluded to the end of the First World War and painted a clear-sighted picture of what they could look forward to if they failed to conclude a timely peace:

> It is tempting to draw a comparison with 1918, but history does not repeat itself. This time, if the Wehrmacht is defeated things will be far worse, because this war was fought not just on the basis of economic and political questions of power arising from National Socialist Party doctrine, but also on ideological grounds, like the wars of religion in the Middle Ages. And because the hatred of the entire world is now directed against Germany. This time there is no German parliament, no political parties and no organs of the state such as existed in 1918. Once the Wehrmacht is smashed, nobody will be able to prevent the worst from happening or vouchsafe order and security. In such an outcome Germany would be nothing but an object with no weight of its own.

Looking at the current situation, van Hooven could only draw one conclusion:

> Only a timely peace might avert this likely fate, inasmuch as it would preserve the only instrument that can safeguard order and prevent chaos, namely the German Army.

Following van Hooven's speech, Colonel Luitpold Steidle spoke about the moral circumstances in Nazi Germany, pillorying the coercion exerted on people's consciences and beliefs and the twisting of justice and the law. He, too, came to the same conclusion:

> There is therefore only one hope of salvation. A clean break with Hitler! In this sense, in view of the total war that is being waged in an unprecedented way, we demand that we, as captured German officers, be heard, despite the fact that we have already been written off back home.

General von Seydlitz emphasized the necessity of toppling Hitler and his regime, once again on the basis of what the Sixth Army had experienced at Stalingrad. Their 'bitter realization' of what had happened there should become a springboard for an 'act of salvation'. Von Seydlitz made an emotional plea to the people and the army:

> We're talking primarily about the commanders, the generals and other officers of the Wehrmacht. You are facing a huge decision. Germany expects you to have the courage to see the truth and on the strength of that to act boldly and swiftly. Do all that is necessary. [...] The National Socialist regime will never be prepared to take the only path that leads to peace. This insight demands that you declare war on this corrupting regime and take up arms to install a government supported by the trust of the people. Only such an administration can create the conditions for our Fatherland to make an honourable exit from the war [...] Do not refuse this historical mission; take the initiative [...] and demand the immediate resignation of Hitler and his government. Fight side by side with the people to get rid of Hitler and his regime and save Germany from chaos and collapse.

To the applause of those present, General von Seydlitz ended his speech with the rousing slogan: 'Long live a free, peaceful and independent Germany!' Von Seydlitz was elected president of the BDO, with colonels Van Hooven and Steidle as vice-presidents. Generals Martin Lattmann, Dr Otto Korfes and Alexander Edler von Daniels were appointed to the executive committee. As we have seen, by dint of his place on the working party Heinrich Gerlach was also among the leading lights of the BDO.

The events surrounding the founding of the league, of which Gerlach gave a lively account more than twenty years later in his book *Odyssey in Red: My Time in the Wilderness*, became the subject of a documentary entitled *The House at Lunyovo*, directed for German television by Franz Peter Wirth in January 1970, four years after publication of the author's memoirs. Gerlach's book formed the basis of the script, which was written by Peter Adler. This was the first time that the 'renegade officers', who, according to the commentary, 'realized after the defeat at Stalingrad that Hitler was leading the German people to disaster', were not – in the words of a review of the programme in *Der Spiegel* – portrayed as 'simple Soviet stooges … but rather as true German patriots'.

The activities of the BDO and the National Committee, in both of which organizations Heinrich Gerlach played an active part until their disbandment in 1945, were the subject of much controversy right up to the 1990s. A fairer evaluation of the BDO only became possible after the opening of the archives in 1989 enabled new research into the organization. In common with other publications, Bodo Scheurig, in the introduction to his edition of Walther von Seydlitz's memoirs, highlights the military and political situation in the Soviet Union after Stalingrad. In 1943 Stalin found himself in a complicated position. His Western allies had still not launched a 'Second Front' against the Nazis, which left the Red Army bearing the brunt of the fighting. The only operation that the Allies had thus far undertaken – the landings in North Africa – brought no military relief to the Soviet Union. For this reason, too, Stalin secretly began to sound out the possibility of opening negotiations with the Third Reich. The National Committee and the League of German Officers were charged with the task of airing certain negotiating positions in public, including the assurance that the peace could be concluded provided Hitler's troops withdrew to within Germany's borders. In summary, Scheurig conjectures that 1943 had presented a very real opportunity to 'save Germany from the worst' and pointedly notes:

> The Wehrmacht, a force numbering in the millions, was still deep within Russian territory. The Red Army was still facing a long campaign that would cost untold numbers of lives before final victory was – possibly – secured. No final decisions had yet been taken regarding the future of the Reich [...] Stalin shunned any talk of 'unconditional surrender'. But the feelers he put out in Stockholm showed that he did not discount doing a deal, even with Hitler.

These suppositions continue to be disputed among historians even nowadays. They are, however, relatively unanimous regarding the situation facing the Soviet leadership in the summer of 1943. Despite the defeat of German forces at Stalingrad and Kursk, militarily the Soviet Union had still not achieved anything more than a stalemate with the Third Reich. Accordingly, the Germans still had a brief window in which to act. The circle of officers around Seydlitz in the BDO recognized that there was still a chance of averting total defeat for Germany, with all the consequences that would entail. In this respect, the contributions by the officers regarding Germany's situation at the inaugural meeting of the BDO are very acute, sounding out the existing possibilities, making concrete suggestions, and anticipating what might happen if the war could not be brought to an end. Yet the calls to the army's commanders, generals and other officers to act got no response. This had to do with the fact that the leadership of the Wehrmacht, though fully aware of the hopelessness of the war, was neither prepared nor in a position to think in political terms and banked on a diplomatic solution being found. The time window for action closed again with the Tehran Conference and the meeting of the Allied leaders from November to December 1943. Stalin was reassured by the imminent prospect of the Normandy invasions and the opening of a 'Second Front', while Churchill and Roosevelt accepted his plans for the postwar redrawing of borders. Henceforth, the sole aim was Germany's unconditional capitulation, a decision that had major implications for the National Committee and the BDO. The proposed withdrawal to the borders of the Reich and the conclusion of a peace treaty was now supplanted by the defensive solution of 'joining forces with the "Free Germany" movement'.

Von Seydlitz and the officers of the BDO fought tooth and nail against this new strategy, since at root it meant accepting precisely what they had tried to prevent by founding the BDO in the first place: namely the destruction and surrender of the Wehrmacht! But even when the situation of the German forces became even more hopeless, attempts by the National Committee and the League of Officers to persuade troops on the Ukrainian front who, at the beginning of February 1944, found themselves trapped in the Cherkassy Pocket to surrender likewise met with no success. The Soviet leadership had brought General von Seydlitz, General Korfes and Major Lewerenz right up to the front on this occasion. Yet their appeals via propaganda pamphlets, personal letters and tannoy announcements all fell on deaf ears. Instead, so great was their fear of Russian captivity that the encircled German troops tried on several occasions to break out, sustaining heavy losses in the process.

The ultimate failure of the BDO's activities – in which, as a member of the editorial staff of the paper *Free Germany*, Heinrich

Gerlach was also involved – did nothing to alter the fact that its founding had been an honourable attempt, in view of the worsening military situation, to save the German people from the worst losses and complete destruction of their country. In Scheurig's estimation, 'Seydlitz acted according to the same clear, irrefutable logic to which the German High Command was also party. He only acted "wrongly" insofar as the army and the people did nothing to liberate themselves from their corrupters.' What was true of General von Seydlitz could also be said of most of the officers in the BDO and the National Committee. In the opinion of military historian Gerd R. Ueberschär: 'The ranks of those who resisted National Socialism also included those members, officers and men alike, of the National Committee for a Free Germany and the League of German Officers. Despite being behind the barbed wire of POW camps and finding themselves in an extreme situation – not least in having to make common cause with Germany's arch-enemy – they felt driven by a moral imperative, a sense of humanity and a love for their country and its people to join the fight against Hitler's rule.'

Like most of his fellow captured officers, Heinrich Gerlach hoped that their founding of the BDO might allow them to intervene in the course of history. The traumatic after-effects of his experiences in the Cauldron at Stalingrad were still a vivid memory that gave him the impetus to do something. He could not rid his mind of terrible images of the battle. He remembered how divisional commanders had begged the commander-in-chief to 'put an end to the senseless slaughter'. He knew that 'twenty-two of the best German divisions and parts of other units' had been wiped out. He'd learned that 'the bodies of 147,200 dead German soldiers and officers were collected by the Russians and buried in mass graves on the battlefield'. And he'd heard about the judgement that Hitler would pass on the survivors of Stalingrad over the dining table: 'The duty of those who fought at Stalingrad is to be dead!' In his memoirs, written more than twenty years later, Gerlach would recall his feelings after General von Seydlitz's closing address and the League's rousing appeal to German officers ('Calling all German generals and officers! Calling the people and the army!'):

> Once again, images welled up of the sombre events on the Volga, in all their monstrous gravity and enormity. The appalling sacrifice ordered by a madman, unparalleled in its savagery. This was the answer. One by one, the delegates filed forward and added their signatures to the document.

VIII. Heinrich Gerlach in Lunyovo special camp and the German communist exiles – A 'Who's Who' of the future GDR

The founding charter of the League of German Officers was also signed by captured soldiers and German exiles from the 'National Committee for a Free Germany'. Even in the course of the inaugural meeting, there had been spontaneous fraternization between the BDO and the National Committee. Looking back, Count von Einsiedel took a very different view from Heinrich Gerlach, believing that with its incorporation into the National Committee the BDO had 'fulfilled its task, so rendering its continued existence pointless'. Of course, this was not a view that the captive officers could take in 1943. The National Committee and the BDO, both of which were based in Lunyovo, were responsible for producing the paper *Free Germany* and running the radio station of the same name, which was headed by the communist Anton Ackermann. Alongside Heinrich Gerlach, the POWs from Lunyovo who made up the newspaper's editorial staff were Major Homann, Major General von Lenski, First Lieutenant von Kügelgen and Corporal Kertzscher.

Gerlach already had experience of editorial work; prior to the founding of the BDO, as a member of the working party he was obligated to work on the *Free Word*, the forerunner of *Free Germany*. Unlike the *Free Word*, the aim of the newspaper of the National Committee was to win round officers and men to the anti-fascist cause through articles combining analysis with political argument. The large-format paper appeared weekly and was produced by the planographic process, which in this case meant that every single copy was printed by hand. The first edition of *Free Germany* had already appeared on 19 July 1943, containing the manifesto of the National Committee, which Rudolf Herrnstadt had played a principal part in drafting. Heinrich Gerlach was still in Susdal at that time. During

632

his spell on the paper's editorial staff, he was one of its most active contributors. Between 19 July 1943 and 3 November 1945, he would write twenty-one articles for the weekly paper, which ran for a total of 120 issues. This made the teacher from Elbing, as he styled himself several times in his pieces, one of the key shaping voices of the newspaper. From the executive committee of the BDO, only General von Seydlitz (with forty-two articles), Dr Korfes (twenty-seven) and Lattmann (twenty-five) were more frequent contributors. The involvement of Colonel Luitpold Steidle (twenty-one articles), Major Hetz (ditto) and First Lieutenant Bernt von Kügelgen (twenty-eight) was also decisive in giving the paper its particular character. Ultimately, however, final editorial control over the paper was wielded by another branch based in 'Institute 99' in Moscow.

Following the dissolution by Stalin of the Third Communist International (Comintern) in 1943, Institute 99 took over responsibility for the political education of POWs. To fill the most important posts in this organization, the Soviet leadership turned primarily to 'tried and tested' KPD (Communist Party of Germany) functionaries, all of whom Heinrich Gerlach got to know in Lunyovo. Walter Ulbricht played a key role, and it was he who would determine Gerlach's fate. After 1945, Ulbricht came to occupy decisive positions of power, first in the Soviet Occupation Zone and then (after its inception in 1949) in the German Democratic Republic, as first secretary of the Socialist Unity Party (SED) from 1950 to 1973 and later as head of state (1960–73). All the other communist exiles whom Gerlach had dealings with were also appointed to senior posts in the Occupation Zone and the GDR post-1945.

Rudolf Herrnstadt, Anton Ackermann and Karl Maron were responsible for print media and radio broadcasting. The *Free Germany* radio station transmitted between fifteen and ninety minutes of programmes each day on various wavelengths. A typical day's broadcasting comprised fifteen minutes of news, fifteen minutes reading out the names of those taken prisoner, and thirty minutes of original programming. Somewhat surprisingly for a communist broadcaster, the intermission signal followed the melody of an old patriotic student fraternity song from 1812 known as the *Vaterlands-lied* ('Song of the Fatherland').

The editorial staff of the identically named newspaper, with Rudolf Herrnstadt as editor-in-chief, had much more work to do. Herrnstadt, an experienced journalist, had excellent contacts with the Soviet leadership. Before 1933, he had been a correspondent in Warsaw and Moscow for the *Berliner Tageblatt*, and in 1941 he emigrated to the Soviet Union, where from 1943 onwards, like so many other communist exiles, he lived at the Hotel Lux in Moscow. Karl Maron, Lothar Bolz and Alfred Kurella were also on the editorial staff of *Free Germany*. Gerlach subsequently worked with these communist exiles, clearly finding some of them more sympathetic than others. After his first meeting with Herrnstadt, he wrote that he exhibited 'the aloof chilliness of a block of ice'. This was probably an accurate summation of the editor-in-chief's emotional state at this time.

It must have been hard for someone like Herrnstadt, who had been involved in the resistance against Hitler from the outset, to now have to work alongside captured Wehrmacht officers. In her biography of her father, Herrnstadt's daughter, Irina Liebmann, speculates how he must have felt: 'If you look at photos from this period and see the German officers standing there in their jackboots and their military insignia – well, Herrnstadt knew full well what the outcome would have been if they'd encountered him on the other side of the front.' In addition, like many other communist émigrés, Herrnstadt had undergone experiences in Soviet exile that he couldn't talk about. Irina Liebmann quotes the photographer Eva Kemlein, who tells of her disappointment at meeting the German 'émigrés from Moscow, whose arrival I'd keenly anticipated': 'When they arrived, they were like blocks of ice.' But there was something else about Herrnstadt: in the Soviet Union, he couldn't say anything about the 'murder of his own group, the worst of all possible outcomes': when they met, Gerlach had no idea that Herrnstadt had been the handler of the Berlin anti-Nazi resistance group known as the 'Red Orchestra' (*Rote Kapelle*), whose members were sentenced to death and hanged, along with the spy Ilse Stöbe, by a German war tribunal in December 1942. Gerlach took a very different view of Alfred Kurella, who proved to be 'an educated and open-minded individual, who was prepared to discuss all aspects of life without the slightest prejudice'. Kurella could speak seventeen languages, translated Central Asian poetry into Russian and German, and was a great admirer of the writings of Romain Rolland, whose secretary he had once been.

Yet for all the distance between himself and his editor-in-chief, Gerlach found the atmosphere at *Free Germany* intensely stimulating. He wrote prodigiously, edited, and mapped out ideas for broadcasts. His first article, published in the 5 September 1943 edition of *Free Germany*, carried the title 'War without People' and examined the 'campaign' against the Soviet Union. The topics for articles in *Free Germany* were set by the editorial board and the contributions were discussed once they had been written. Gerlach gained great satisfaction from writing. After studying her father's papers on the enforced collaboration between officers and communist exiles, Irina Liebmann wrote very appositely: 'Under laboratory conditions, a rapprochement took place that was deeply absurd, but a rapprochement for all that. Herrnstadt's memoirs contain remarkable vignettes of German officers in these exceptional circumstances. What bound them all together was a shared concern for Germany.' If one examines the contributions to *Free Germany* in their entirety, which were the work of 274 authors in all, inmates of Lunyovo and of the officers' camps at Krasnogorsk, Yelabuga, Oranki, Voikovo and Susdal, one finds oneself agreeing with Irina Liebmann's impression: 'How sad they are [...] This comes across in the absence of rhetoric in all the articles, and in the welter of surprising details – a descriptive style that vanishes once the war is over.'

The staff of the newspaper were shocked when they were confronted with evidence of war crimes committed by the Wehrmacht. As early as 1943 – before the founding of the BDO – the Red Army, as it advanced west, was known to have found in Krasnodar vans that had been converted into mobile gas chambers. This was very disturbing news to the officers, who had not wanted to acknowledge systematic atrocities hitherto, preferring to regard them as exceptions. This conviction was seriously undermined when Major Karl Hetz, vice-president of the National Committee, told a group of officers at Lunyovo how such gas vans worked. Rudolf Herrnstadt was shocked to learn of this. After the BDO was formed, the editorial board decided that Hetz should be called upon to explain how he came to know about the gas vans. Accordingly, on 15 September 1943, just a few days after the formation of the League, an article by Major Hetz appeared in the paper under the headline 'The Gas Van'. As Irina Liebmann noted: 'This was the very first German newspaper article anywhere in the world on this form of crime.' A few months later, the newspaper received a report by Lieutenant Bernt von Kügelgen about mass murders perpetrated against the civilian populace of Kiev. Cracks also began to appear in Heinrich Gerlach's conviction that the German forces were 'clean'. He recalled the winter of 1939–40 in Warsaw, when he saw SS officers mistreating a young girl who was selling stockings on the street. His driver had also once related to him an incident at a transit camp in Dubno, when five hundred Soviet officers were gunned down one night under floodlights. Gerlach was aware of how he had tried to assuage his conscience at the time by telling himself such things were exceptions, excesses committed in the heat of the moment. But after reading Kügelgen's report he was forced to admit to himself: 'It was organized from above, it was systematic.' Finally, fifty years and more after the end of the Second World War, two travelling exhibitions organized by the Hamburg Institute for Social Research (in 1995–99 and 2001–4) brought public acknowledgement at last of the war crimes carried out by the Wehrmacht during the invasion of the Soviet Union.

The twenty-one articles that Heinrich Gerlach wrote while working on the editorial staff of *Free Germany* analyse the catastrophe at Stalingrad and the current military situation; he also reported on meetings of the National Committee and tried to put across a more objective image of the Soviet Union to counter the clichéd view of Bolshevism that was peddled in Germany. He also gave authentic accounts of life in the Cauldron, culled from the novel he was working on. His article of 26 March 1944, recalling the German capitulation at Stalingrad a little more than a year after the actual event, begins thus:

> Fourteen months ago, the Sixth Army was wiped out at Stalingrad. Hundreds of thousands died, not for their home-land – since that could hardly be defended there on the Volga – nor for oil, metal ores or wheat – they couldn't be obtained by seizing others' territory – nor even to save the endangered Eastern Front – the mass killing at Stalingrad couldn't achieve that; no, the sole reason for their cold and brutal sacrifice was Adolf Hitler's dogmatism and self-regard. And because the men knew that they had to die for nothing, they didn't go to their deaths with a victorious smile on their faces, with flashing eyes and singing the national anthem, but instead, dressed in rags, emaciated by hunger, filled with all the pain of tormented animals, they died a miserable death in frost and snow, and with a curse on their lips against the man whom they'd once trusted. *That was Stalingrad.*

The rest of the piece is an unsparing reckoning with Hitler and with German propaganda, which made 'out of the senseless, criminal sacrifice of hundreds of thousands of men a new heroic epic to rival the *Nibelungenlied*'. Gerlach's acute and bitter account climaxed in a call that he believed would presently grow ever more insistent on the home front too: 'Hitler must be toppled if Germany is to survive!'

In July 1944 – with the front moving inexorably closer to Germany – he invoked a nightmarish vision of the death and destruction that was about to be visited upon the country. Harking back to his last home leave at the end of April 1942, he conjured up a picture of Lyck in East Prussia, which was situated around 150 kilometres from Gerlach's birthplace of Königsberg and was still untouched by the war – 'My home town – what a charming little place!' He described the island on the lake, the marketplace, the church, the water tower and the Ernst-Moritz-Arndt School, for many years his residence and place of work. 'What's about to happen?' Gerlach asked, before delivering a sobering and positively chilling answer: 'It's not *about* to happen, it's *happening* right now! Today, Hitler ordered the alarm bells rung throughout Lyck! Evacuation! Assemble on the market square, women, children and pensioners with hand luggage, handcarts are permitted.' Gerlach foresaw destruction: total destruction. 'Hitler is setting out his killing zone in Germany! Blowing up buildings! Setting light to houses! No stone is to be left standing!' And he saw what would be left after a fight to the death: 'All that remains is a heap of stones, a pile of smoking, smouldering rubble. A smell of burning wafts far and wide across the countryside. That was Lyck!' Confronting any illusions people might have, he noted: 'It's impossible to imagine – but this is how it will turn out, this is the only possible outcome if we let Hitler continue with his war. For wherever Hitler wages war, he recognizes no mothers, no children, no home towns and no schools. All he sees is "defensive terrain" that is to be left as scorched earth when German forces withdraw.' In the desperate hope that such a dreadful scene might still be averted, Gerlach positively implores his countrymen not to submit to this fate but to rise up against the dictator:

This must not be allowed to happen! My East Prussian countrymen, my fellow Germans all, whom Hitler has consigned to the same fate: now, finally, you must refuse to obey this lunatic, you must now stay the hand of the executioner of Germany.

Heinrich Gerlach's terrifying vision would become reality, and even his own family was forced to leave Lyck, but not because of the advance of the Red Army; instead, like other families of BDO members, they were rounded up and taken into custody in July 1944. Six months after Gerlach's article, in late January 1945, Elbing was besieged by the Red Army and doggedly defended by the German garrison. Five thousand German troops died in this pointless action. By the time the siege was over, 60 per cent of the town lay in ruins, with only six houses left standing in the old town. In sum, it is fair to say that all of Heinrich Gerlach's journalistic contributions show him to be a perceptive analyst of current affairs and a firm opponent of Hitler.

IX.   'They'd stared into the abyss of hell' – Writing as an act of liberation

Heinrich Gerlach's involvement with the BDO and the newspaper *Free Germany* could do nothing to dispel his repeated flashbacks of the traumatic experiences he had gone through during the catastrophe at Stalingrad. Yet he saw an opportunity to rid himself of them through the act of writing. He began with a series of diary entries, but did not get very far, because the events began to coalesce in his mind and to become ever more monstrous with the passage of time, while the urgent necessity of processing his experiences constantly increased. At the end of 1943 he decided to switch from diary entries to an epic form of narrative. For that, he needed characters, plus locations and a time frame within which the action could unfold.

Gerlach had all that at his fingertips, given that Stalingrad and the annihilation of the Sixth Army provided him with a ready-made storyline, so to speak. In the spirit of Uwe Johnson, Gerlach could therefore hold fast to the maxim that 'the narrative begins once the story is complete'. He spent a long time agonizing over how to begin the text and formulate his opening sentence, which would, after all, set the tone for everything that came after. With his thorough grounding in German literature, Gerlach knew full well how crucial the start of a narrative had been to a novelist he greatly admired, Theodor Fontane, who wrote to his friend Gustav Karpeles in 1880: 'The first chapter is always the most important thing, and within that first chapter the first page, in fact pretty much the first sentence, is key. If you've structured your novel properly, then the first page should contain the germ of the whole narrative. That's why I'm forever fussing and tinkering. What comes after is plain sailing by comparison.'

In order to finally put pen to paper, Gerlach began by giving his first chapter the title 'Home On Leave?' The question mark was quite deliberate; the German forces dug in outside Stalingrad kept hoping that they would be relieved by fresh troops and might still make it home for Christmas. After several reworkings, Gerlach settled on the following opening sentences:

> Winter had sent out its reconnaissance parties into the brown steppe between the Volga and the Don. The unseasonal warmth of the first days of November had, by the sixth, given way to a snowless frost that froze the mud on the endless tracks as hard as asphalt. Along this pleasingly smooth, firm new surface sped a small grey car, lively as a colt that had bolted from its stable.

These lines, which at first glance depict an almost idyllic winter landscape, lead the reader into the actual story. The very next sentence steers us towards the heart of the action: 'It was coming from the great depression to the south, where the general staffs and the supply trains for the German units fighting to take Stalingrad had dug in, and heading for the railway station at Kotluban.' Only after this descriptive passage does Gerlach introduce the first of his characters, namely the car driver 'so heavily muffled in winter clothing that all that one could see of him were a pair of crafty eyes gazing out at the world and a red snub nose'. In the version that the author pieced together from memory and rewrote fifteen years later, Gerlach opted for a different, more direct lead-in. For the start of the narrative, he chose some unspecified point *in medias res* and began with a snippet of dialogue, with an unnamed character exclaiming: 'Hell, it's cold!' The second sentence then goes on to identify the speaker as Lieutenant Breuer, the alter ego of the author.

However, these finer points of narrative construction were as yet of no concern to Gerlach when he embarked on his novel project at Lunyovo in the summer of 1943. Other, more practical, concerns preoccupied him then. He was in need of paper, a commodity in short supply in a prison camp, and above all a typewriter. Alfred Kurella and the émigré actor and writer Fritz Erpenbeck, whose novel *Emigrants* (1939) was a favourite book among the inmates of Lunyovo, not only came to the rescue with paper, but also gave this literary novice the benefit of their experience. Eventually, Gerlach also acquired an old Remington typewriter, which he used on an almost daily basis. He would sit typing in the conference room until late at night.

At the same time as Gerlach was writing, another occupant of Lunyovo was also busy assembling material for a novel, with the provisional title *Hitler's Soldier*. This was the exiled German author Theodor Plievier, who was known both in Germany and beyond for his anti-war novel of 1930, *Des Kaisers Kuli* (*The Kaiser's Coolies*). Most of the officers held at Lunyovo had read it. Plievier had gone into exile in 1933, journeying to Moscow via Prague, Zurich, Paris and Oslo. When Hitler invaded the Soviet Union in 1941 and threatened to capture Moscow, he had been evacuated to Tashkent along with other German writers like Johannes R. Becher, Gustav von Wangenheim, Adam Scharrer and Anton Gábor. Plievier returned to Moscow in 1942, where he was active on the NKFD. He used his visits to Lunyovo to find out how the military campaign was proceeding. Having neither served in the Wehrmacht nor experienced the Cauldron of Stalingrad at first hand, he would invite some of the surviving officers who had served there to come over for evenings and tell him about the battle. An added inducement for the officers were the cigars that Plievier handed out, and in this way he got to learn of the day-to-day progress of the war. He took notes at these meetings and would reappear a few days later with his first attempts at fictionalizing them. This time, roles were reversed and it was Plievier reading to the officers and enquiring after the factual accuracy of his account.

Gerlach did not want to have his confidence shaken, especially not by such a successful author, and so avoided participating in these soirées with Plievier. He felt more at ease among his fellow newspaper editors and chose this forum instead to present some completed excerpts from his novel. These included an episode depicting the desperate situation facing the encircled troops in the Zybenko sector. This piece was praised by Alfred Kurella and discussed in approving terms by the editorial board. It duly appeared in the 16 January 1944 edition of *Free Germany*, under the heading 'What For?' By this stage – only six months had passed since Gerlach embarked on his novel – he was already working on the second part and had completed 300 pages. It was an astonishing work rate. The published excerpt recounts how the central character, First Lieutenant Breuer, and his fellow officer Captain Gedig, who had returned voluntarily to the Stalingrad Cauldron, witness the sacrifice of two hundred men, who, acting on superior orders, make a futile attempt to defend a piece of high ground. Gradually the fate that awaits them dawns on the two men. The piece printed in *Free Germany* ends thus:

> The commander makes a vague forward motion with his hand. There's the hill, the position they've got to defend. The men's faces, haggard from sickness and hunger, stare into the distant blackness, which is lit only by the muzzle-flare of the Russian artillery. But there are no trenches or pillboxes up there! The white expanse stretches out endlessly all around them, with clouds of powdery snow gusting across it. There's no retreating that way. Anyone who isn't struck by an enemy bullet will simply die of the bitter cold this icy January night. The unit fans out and disperses across the open ground. One by one, the men take up a prone position and are slowly enveloped by the white death shroud, as tracer bullets from Russian machine gun positions whistle overhead. No one calls out or asks a question, there's not a sound. Only those who have given up all hope can be that dreadfully still. But this appalling silence ascends to heaven like one great painfully

pressing question to which there is no answer from any quarter: What is this sacrifice for, in God's name, for what?

At Kurella's suggestion, though, Gerlach cut something from the excerpt. Originally, we learn that even the commanding general cannot contain himself when he receives the senseless order to hold the hill. At first, in the face of objections from his officers, he angrily implements the order while at the same time imploring them with tears in his eyes to appreciate his position. That was too much for Kurella. One of Hitler's generals crying, he told Gerlach, struck him as too much of a cliché and as something that readers would find implausible. Even so, the author retained the emotional depiction in the novel itself. The full passage read: 'He [i.e. the general] comes up to the silent captain and takes both of his hands in his. There are tears in his eyes again. He whispers, "It's dreadful, I know. But there's nothing I can do to help you!"' The episode is also significant for the later plot progression and for Gerlach's work on the manuscript in so far as it is at this point that the officers begin to realize how hopeless the Sixth Army's predicament is:

> In a blinding insight born of all that he has experienced over the past few days, the truth now dawns on Captain Gedig: the High Command… Army Group Manstein… No, these two hundred sacrificial lambs won't save the Sixth Army. No one can save it now. It too is going to be put to the sword, pointlessly, senselessly… It's all over!

Gerlach has the figure of Colonel von Hermann express what Breuer and Gerlach are feeling about the loss of the two hundred men:

> 'It's nothing short of criminal!'
> The two officers sitting at the back of the bunker give a start. What was that? Did someone speak? Or are some

thoughts so distressing and urgent that they can miraculously express themselves? The colonel up front there can't possibly have said anything so outrageous. It's just not possible! But then the two of them hear quite clearly what Colonel von Hermann says next:

'And the worst thing is, there's no way out... and woe betide anyone who tries to save his own skin after he's had to demand this of his men!'

'So, there's no escape from here?' thinks Breuer desperately. 'Is there such a thing as a "must"? Is there really and truly no way out?'

Three months later, by Easter 1944, Gerlach had made significant progress on the manuscript. Conditions in the camp allowed him to write late into the night. Alfred Kurella supplied him with more paper and enquired every so often how the novel was proceeding. Gerlach, though, remained tight-lipped and read the pages he produced to just a small group of trusted officers, whom he encouraged to offer criticism. An authentic portrayal of what had occurred at Stalingrad was his top priority, and for that he needed feedback from other veterans of the battle.

While he was writing the novel, certain events took place that impinged particularly on Gerlach. A conspiracy against the National Committee in April 1944 unfairly made him the target of suspicion on the part of Walter Ulbricht. Ulbricht took Gerlach to task for waiting too long before informing General Lattmann about the plot. His criticism culminated in the accusation: 'You're not a good anti-fascist yet.' A few weeks later, Ulbricht analysed what had happened in front of the executive council of the committee and summed up the situation thus, as Gerlach recalled:

The question this raises is whether some comrades still aren't proper anti-fascists, right? I submit that they'll have plenty of opportunity to become real anti-fascists back in the camps!

Walter Ulbricht, who became the foremost politician in the Soviet Occupation Zone after 1945 and thereafter in the GDR until the early 1970s, comes across in Heinrich Gerlach's memoirs as almost a stereotypical figure: 'Walter Ulbricht. With his small, strangely unfinished and yet at other times somehow ancient-looking head. Those floating, restless eyes and that lilting, mollifying, garbled way he has of speaking that mangles everything he utters...' This was Gerlach's unflattering description of the man who pulled the strings at Institute 99 in Moscow and who played a key role in setting the agenda for the National Committee for a Free Germany.

It is a well-known fact that memoirs cannot create a faithful representation of the past. All that can ever be achieved is a partial, incomplete and even sometimes distorted piecing together of past occurrences. For the time lapse between the 'real past' and the contemporary moment in which it is recalled necessarily means that the earlier events are seen and evaluated from the perspective of the present. This therefore entails a kind of reconstruction right from the start. When Gerlach wrote his memoirs, Ulbricht had already been General Secretary of the Central Committee of the Socialist Unity Party since 1950, and was the most powerful man in the GDR. At the same time, he was the most hated politician, and not just in West Germany. During the Workers' Uprising of 17 June 1953 in East Germany, demonstrating construction workers marched along the Stalinallee in Berlin chanting 'Goatee Beard Must Go!' In 1956, Ulbricht was responsible for bringing trumped-up charges of 'conspiratorial counter-revolutionary activity' against the writers Wolfgang Harich, Walter Janka and Erich Loest, and in 1961 he ordered the building of the Berlin Wall. So, did Heinrich Gerlach perhaps superimpose the image of Ulbricht from the postwar period on the situation back at the camp in Lunyovo? Did 'external elements' retrospectively creep into his recollections and combine with his own experiences to produce a distorted picture of Ulbricht as a person?

Documents from the Russian special archive, which I have been able to locate and study over the past few years, help to throw light on this and other questions concerning Heinrich Gerlach. These files show that he had a remarkable memory for even the tiniest details and gave a very precise assessment of all the people in Lunyovo. There was also another document about Gerlach in the archive, containing a brief character sketch, which confirms the feeling of dread that assailed him after his dressing-down by Ulbricht. The appraisal of First Lieutenant Gerlach was signed by Walter Ulbricht and Rudolf Herrnstadt.

Translated into English, the original Russian typescript reads:

> Gerlach, Helmut [sic!], First Lieutenant.
>
> A typical representative [illegible] of Hitler's army, talented but not honest. Attempts to hide his real opinions by providing information to Soviet organizations. He can be employed for manufacturing work in the Soviet Union.
>
> Ulbricht, Herrnstadt

This assessment, which must have been written sometime in 1944, was totally at variance with the one written by Professor Arnold on 14 July 1943, who described Gerlach as 'one of the most active, clever and able officers in Camp No. 160'. This new appraisal by Ulbricht and Herrnstadt would have disastrous consequences for Gerlach! But in April 1944 he still had no inkling of this. Rather, he was shocked by a piece of news that Erich Weinert brought from Moscow when he visited Lunyovo. According to this, on 26 April 1944 the Supreme Military Court in Germany had sentenced the president of the League of German Officers, General Walther von Seydlitz, and the other members of the executive committee to death for alleged high treason. Heinrich Gerlach was now in no doubt what fate awaited him in Germany, and he was deeply worried about his family.

The claim that Heinrich Gerlach was condemned to death in absentia alongside other officers of the BDO is still made even today. I researched this in various archives including the German Federal Military Archives in Freiburg, but found no trace of any files on Gerlach. Nor were there any trial papers on General von Seydlitz, though I did come across appraisals from March and May 1940, as well as from July 1942, noting that Walther von Seydlitz was a natural leader and stressing his 'first-rate qualities both as a soldier and as a person'. A dispatch of 18 January 1944 from the 'Sixth Army Processing Unit' concerning 'notification of officers missing in action' disclosed that Artillery General Walther von Seydlitz-Kurzbach had been missing since 23 January 1943 while serving at Stalingrad. The hint at a possible court martial is contained in a telegram from the Supreme Imperial War Attorney's office (Torgau division) ordering the 'immediate transfer' of General Seydlitz's personnel file.

My search for the trial papers likewise drew a blank at the Federal Archives in Berlin. However, certain files relating to Lieutenant Heinrich Graf von Einsiedel in the military archive did corroborate the fact that proceedings had been instituted against members of the BDO, including Heinrich Gerlach. As early as 23 September 1942, the Air Force personnel department raised suspicions of treason. The basis for proceedings against Lieutenant von Einsiedel was a report on Russian radio claiming that the lieutenant, now a prisoner of war, had made the following statement: 'My great-grandfather was right when he told me that Germany should never attack Russia. Our invasion has cost us dear!' The files on Von Einsiedel testify to the intensity of proceedings against the League of German Officers. The bundle of documents on him contained a letter dated 15 December 1944, in which the State Military Attorney informed the High Command of the Air Force that 'legal proceedings on the grounds of treason' were being initiated against the officers Major Lewerenz, First Lieutenant Charisius and Lieutenant Graf von Einsiedel. According to this letter, the case against Charisius and von Einsiedel had already, following preliminary investigation, been referred to the People's Court. Since August 1943, First Lieutenant Charisius had been the official representative of the National Committee for a Free Germany on the Third Ukrainian front. This allows us to conclude that members of the BDO had evidently not been condemned to death before December 1944.

But what had become of the documents concerning the case against General von Seydlitz, and had he really been handed a death sentence? I did finally get an answer to this question, albeit not the one I had imagined. In the State Archive at Stade, I came across papers relating to a trial of 1955–6, again involving Walther von Seydlitz. A month after his release from Russian captivity on 6 October 1955 and his return to Verden, he had instructed a lawyer named Von Hugo to represent his interests by challenging the verdict of the Supreme Military Court against him, of which his family was unaware, in a court of law. This test case examining the soundness of his conviction for treason was a matter of life and death for Von Seydlitz, as he had received neither his military pension since his release nor any payment of the state allowance to which POWs were entitled. And so, in November 1955, the Verden state public prosecutor's office, represented by Attorney-General Bollmann, instituted preliminary proceedings 'against the former General von Seydlitz' with the intention of 'testing the legality of the death sentence handed down to Seydlitz by the Supreme Military Court in 1944, on the basis of the directive of 2.6.1947'. Bollmann noted: 'Since the records of the military court have been destroyed, the bases for this judgement need to be reconstructed.'

The documents of which I had sight, which also allow us to draw inferences concerning the official attitude towards the BDO and

Seydlitz in the Federal Republic from the mid-1950s on, confirm the following: on 26 April 1944, the Supreme German Military Court, with its senate chairman General Staff Judge Schmauser presiding, sentenced General von Seydlitz alone to death in absentia, declaring him 'ineligible for military service' and ordering that his property be seized. As the highest military tribunal of the Third Reich, the Supreme Military Court cited as grounds for its verdict General von Seydlitz's activities as president of the BDO and vice-president of the National Committee for a Free Germany. Evidence of the cited offence came in the form of several copies of the newspaper *Free Germany*, pamphlets signed by Seydlitz and personal letters. The Supreme Military Court had instituted proceedings against the BDO and the National Committee as early as the end of 1943 on Hitler's orders. Generals Korfes, Edler von Daniels, Lattmann, Hofmeister and Vincenz Müller were also targeted in this indictment. Other officers who were identified as being especially active within the BDO were Captain Hadermann and Major Bechler, but also First Lieutenant Heinrich Gerlach. However, at that time the incriminating evidence available was only sufficient to put General von Seydlitz on trial. The instruction to proceed with the prosecution came directly from Hitler via the head of the High Command of the Wehrmacht. The legal basis for the charge against General von Seydlitz was the amendment made during the war to Paragraph 59 Section 2 of the Wartime Penal Code (*Kriegsstrafverfahrensordnung*; KstVO), which stipulated that it was still possible to proceed against a defendant whose whereabouts were unknown if the gravity of the charge warranted it. The prosecution in the case against General von Seydlitz was conducted by Alexander Kraell, who as president of the Second Senate of the Supreme Military Court had already been the presiding judge in the trial of the 'Red Orchestra' resistance group. In November 1955 Kraell appeared as a witness in the preliminary proceedings against Seydlitz, where he gave evidence concerning the circumstances surrounding the death sentence passed in April 1944. Under cross-examination on 30 November 1955, Kraell described the original trial, and emphasized that the most damning evidence had been four to six letters that General von Seydlitz had sent to front-line commanders whom he knew. Kraell made the following statement for the record:

> In these letters, after referring to his former acquaintance with the addressees, Seydlitz launched into a long disquisition promoting his ideas and concluded, as I recall, by demanding that the Sixth Army should retreat and surrender. The letters were examined by both handwriting experts and psychiatrists – the latter because we had to entertain the possibility that his handwriting might reveal that he had been under the influence of drugs, or duress or something of the sort when he wrote it. The experts' reports vindicated the original charge.

In the course of the 1944 trial of General von Seydlitz, Kraell continued, alongside the many newspaper articles and pamphlets, the Supreme Military Court also adduced as evidence a number of photographs showing Seydlitz 'in the company of Weinert, Pieck and others'. Ultimately, he said, the total body of evidence 'was easily sufficient to ensure the conviction of General von Seydlitz'. In his capacity as a witness ten years after the end of the war, Kraell summed up the outcome of the 1944 prosecution thus: 'In response to my application, on the charge of military treason in conjunction with that of high treason Seydlitz was sentenced to death, pronounced unfit for military service and stripped of all his human rights.' According to Kraell's statement, 'on Hitler's orders' proceedings continued 'against the rest of those accused, yet with no satisfactory outcome in the shape of formal charges being brought'. As a result of the assassination attempt against Hitler on 20 July 1944, the case was transferred (again by order of the Führer) from the Supreme Military Court to the Reich Attorney General at the People's Court. In the end, despite more evidential material being gathered, no prosecution was ever brought against other members of the BDO and the National Committee.

Admittedly, going on what Erich Weinert told him in April 1944, Heinrich Gerlach could only assume that he, too, had been sentenced to death. His fears on this score appeared to be borne out a couple of months later, after it transpired that the families of prominent figures in the BDO had been taken into custody under Hitler's orders. Yet at that stage, Gerlach had no idea that his own family was among them. The Gerlach family's ordeal began in July 1944 and only ended on 30 April 1945, when American troops entered Neuschwanstein near the town on Füssen in Bavaria, where they had been interned, and the war came to an end.

Instead, some months later another report prompted an outbreak of positive euphoria in Lunyovo. Four days after publication of Gerlach's dystopian vision of his home town of Lyck, Erich Weinert was once again the bearer of momentous tidings, bursting into the camp on 20 July 1944 with news of the attempt on Hitler's life. The officers and other members of the National Committee thought their moment had come at last; finally, they hoped, senior Wehrmacht officers had seized the reins of power in Germany. The euphoria only lasted for a few hours. Later that day, Greater German Radio announced that Hitler had survived. Over the weeks that followed, the members of the BDO, Gerlach included, felt paralysed, as reports came in of the arrests and executions of the group of conspirators around Claus von Stauffenberg, scotching all hope of Hitler being toppled from power. Not even the declaration on 8 August by Field Marshal Paulus and other Stalingrad generals that they were joining the BDO could alter this mood of despondency. Heinrich Gerlach summed up the hopelessness many members of the BDO now felt regarding their own chances of ever being able to take effective action:

They [i.e. Paulus and the other officers] joined our ranks after realizing that everything had turned out the way the National Committee and the League of German Officers predicted it would. But this realization came too late. They themselves have come too late. A year too late. Now there's no hope of changing or saving anything, and fate has taken its course. The fate of Stalingrad has been visited upon Germany itself.

Even the brief celebration on 22 August 1944 to mark General von Seydlitz's 56th birthday could not halt the creeping demise of the BDO, as Gerlach saw it. While the speeches praising Von Seydlitz and the sight of prominent Wehrmacht generals strolling around in the company of communists like Wilhelm Pieck and Erich Weinert still conveyed the impression of a self-confident group of opponents of Hitler, ultimately the BDO's scope for action continued to dwindle in the light of the ongoing military situation. I found a photograph album in the special archive containing important images of the work of the BDO and its representatives.

As the front crept ever closer to the borders of the German Empire, Heinrich Gerlach felt himself to be in an almost schizophrenic situation. During the day, he would find himself caught up in the infectious optimism generated in Lunyovo by the prospect that the war might soon end. But at the same time, he knew what that meant. Setting aside his personal fears about the way in which the Red Army might conduct itself as it advanced, he wrote several articles attacking the prevailing 'bogey man' image of Bolshevism. For instance, his piece 'Dance of Death Around a Lie', which was published in the 24 September 1944 edition of *Free Germany*, began as follows:

The days of Hitler's rule are numbered. The nearer we come to the moment of final collapse, the more loudly and desperately Goebbels and his henchmen bang the propaganda drum to try

to rouse German people to make one last frantic and pointless
stand. And a key element in this latest propaganda hysteria are
the so-called 'terrors' that the 'Bolshevist domination that will
ensue at war's end' will visit upon Europe and upon Germany
in particular.

Gerlach recounted his experiences as a prisoner of war, and was at
pains to stress that he was neither a communist nor a Marxist. He
told his readers that he did not applaud everything that was done
in Lunyovo, but that he had recognized while in captivity how the
Soviet Union had, within just a few decades, 'achieved centuries'
worth of development'. The Soviet people would '[harbour] no
hatred towards other people, nor any desire for conquest. Having
paid such a heavy price for their own freedom, they would not
dream of enslaving other peoples or imposing on them a political
system they did not want.' Accordingly, it would not be the Soviet
occupation of Germany that plunged the country into an abyss
'but every day that Hitler's war, which is already lost, is allowed to
continue'. Gerlach went on: 'The country's real enemy isn't outside
its borders, but within Germany itself!' Gerlach's next article, which
appeared on 22 October 1944 under the headline 'Oppose Hitler's
Thugs', inveighed against the Third Reich's 'scorched earth' policy:
'Goebbels exhorts the German people to make every home into a
fortress and to raze everything else to the ground. That miserable
armchair general Dittmar [General Kurt Dittmar, the German
general staff radio spokesman] has given official notice of the
bestialization of warfare under the National Socialists. In doing so,
the regime has now finally revealed to its own people the criminal
face it was careful to keep hidden for so long.'

Alongside his continuing role on the editorial staff of *Free Germany*,
in the autumn of 1944 Heinrich Gerlach was already busy writing
the third part of his Stalingrad novel. It was around this time that
he got to know Georg Lukács, who came to Lunyovo to deliver a

series of lectures on German philosophy and literature. Lukács was one of the foremost Marxist intellectuals in exile, and had become embroiled in the Stalinist 'purges' and 'Moscow show trials' of 1936. Though Gerlach found himself deeply irritated by his external appearance – Lukács initially struck him as being something of a caricature of an intellectual – he was nevertheless won over by his outstanding breadth of knowledge. Lukács was a great connoisseur and admirer of German literature and his pronouncements on Thomas Mann, Franz Werfel, Arnold Zweig and Ernst Wiechert chimed in with Gerlach's preferences. Lukács also referred to a novel that he claimed was the best anti-war book ever, Arnold Zweig's *Erziehung vor Verdun* (*Outside Verdun*), which had been released in 1935 by Querido Verlag, the leading publisher of exile writers; all the leading names in German literature who were forced to leave the country after 1933 were published by this house. Gerlach read Zweig's novel over a single night and took inspiration from its title for his own work. He also came across the oft-quoted saying by the German knight and humanist scholar Ulrich von Hutten (1488–1523): *'Ich träume nicht von alter Zeiten Glück, Ich breche durch und schaue nie zurück'* ('I don't waste time dreaming of the good old days, I break through and never look back.'). This novel, which he spent every free moment working on, would be called *Durchbruch bei Stalingrad* (Breakout at Stalingrad).

Because newly captured officers were constantly arriving at Lunyovo, before being transported on to other POW camps, Gerlach was able to glean vital information about the final weeks of the Battle of Stalingrad. He also got to hear of some of the conversations that took place among the general staff of the Sixth Army, to which he of course had not been party. He heard reports, for instance, from Colonel Adam, Field Marshal Paulus's adjutant, about the final hours before they were taken prisoner, while General Vincenz Müller supplied Hitler's notorious statement on the defeat: 'The duty of those who fought at Stalingrad is to be dead!' His novel about

Stalingrad, like the war itself, was now nearing its end. On 21 October 1944, Aachen, the westernmost city in Germany, surrendered to the Allies, and 12,000 men of the Wehrmacht were taken into American captivity. On 31 January 1945, Gerlach's birthplace, Königsberg in East Prussia, which had earlier been largely destroyed by RAF bombing, was surrounded by the Red Army. Gerlach published an article on 4 February 1945, the second anniversary of the capitulation at Stalingrad, which spoke of the endless suffering of the exhausted, starving and wounded men at the front who were still hoping for a miracle, and of Hitler's betrayal of the encircled troops. 'You can rely on me with rock-like confidence!' ran the telegraph message that the Führer had sent to the Cauldron. 'And then,' wrote Gerlach, 'by the beginning of February it was all over. No miracle had happened. We were alone in the ruins of Stalingrad, beneath which tens of thousands of comrades lay buried, along with our faith and our false hopes and wishes. And then the Russians were standing outside our bunkers. Many of our comrades still flung themselves headlong in desperation into the hail of enemy bullets, and many committed suicide. Dying was hard, but it seemed an even harder prospect to go on living.' For Gerlach, the decision to stay alive was his first small and modest act of rebellion against Hitler and for Germany. The hard road to enlightenment after Stalingrad made him realize the absolute necessity of a 'pitiless struggle against Hitler and his entire system'.

On 2 May 1945, the Red Army completed its conquest of Berlin. The Russian troops had advanced on the heart of the city from all directions and the German commander charged with the defence of the capital, General Weidling, surrendered with the rest of the garrison. Seventy thousand German soldiers and officers were taken prisoner. A few hours later, another 64,000 were added to this figure. And with the surrender of the encircled Ninth Army southeast of the city, 60,000 of whose troops had already died in a week of fighting, a further 120,000 officers and men entered captivity. Two days later, on 4 May, *Free Germany* printed something akin to a leader by Heinrich Gerlach, which gave an unsparing account of current circumstances in Germany and called for immediate action in response: 'The situation we now find ourselves in – in a country largely destroyed by war and occupied by the victors – is of necessity our starting point. No one is able or willing to change or alleviate this situation – *we alone* can bring this about.' Alluding to the monologue delivered by the title character of Goethe's *Faust* in his study, Gerlach noted: 'Nothing will happen unless we set it in motion ourselves! We are at a beginning. And in the beginning was the deed. We will only go on living if we *act*. And we have it in our power to act *straight away*. With everyone fulfilling his or her own particular role, however modest it may be.'

Admittedly, Gerlach omitted to mention what impelled him to deliver this impassioned plea, namely his awareness of how limited was his own scope for action, incarcerated as he still was in a POW camp, albeit a rather more comfortable one than previously. What was really oppressing him was the fact that Lunyovo was steadily emptying. Several members of the BDO and the national committee – principally the leadership of the German Communist Party in exile – had returned to Germany; the first to leave, on 30 April 1945, had been the 'Ulbricht Group'. In the camp, no one was sorry to see Ulbricht go. But others who had left for Berlin at the same time included Fritz Erpenbeck, who had lent constant support to Gerlach's plan to write a novel, as well as Karl Maron and Wolfgang Leonhard. Soon after, Maron was appointed First Deputy Mayor of Berlin. Rudolf Herrnstadt, who was also to have been part of the Ulbricht Group, was vetoed by the Soviets for fear he would become the target of anti-Semitic violence in Germany. Even so, before long he was editor-in-chief of the *Tägliche Rundschau* (*Daily Review*) in Berlin, which from 15 May 1945 on was distributed by the Red Army as a 'front newspaper for the German people'. He would presently be instrumental in the founding of the Berlin Verlag publishing house and the newspaper *Free Germany*. He eventually became editor-in-chief of the central organ of the Socialist Unity Party (SED), and from 1950 to 1953 served as an alternate member of both the Politburo and the Central Committee of the SED.

Heinrich Gerlach's involvement in the editorial department of the newspaper became ever more intensive during this period of upheaval: he wrote, edited, and chaired discussions. And with good reason: after more than two years, his ultimate goal was within sight: his Stalingrad novel was finished, a weighty tome of 616 pages! With the end of the war coinciding with the completion of his novel, a great weight was lifted from his shoulders. But he couldn't tell anyone about it or show his manuscript to anyone. Instead, he hid it under his pillow.

X. 'He's trying to cover up his past' – Heinrich Gerlach's odyssey through POW camps

Following Rudolf Herrnstadt's return to Berlin, Alfred Kurella took over as chief editor of *Free Germany*. Yet among the editorial staff, it was not only Heinrich Gerlach who began to question the purpose of the paper now that Hitler's dictatorship had collapsed. It had lost its whole raison d'être: the struggle against Hitler. Who was their target readership? Who were they to write for now? The editorial staff tried to counter this by harking back to the past, to the war and to German guilt and emphasizing the need for change. After completion of the course on anti-fascism, Colonel Adam and generals Vincenz Müller, Lattmann and Lenski all wrote articles in which, in their newly enlightened state, they examined their own guilty involvement with Nazism. Despite its best efforts to remain up to date, the *Free Germany* newspaper increasingly became a 'black box', a closed system with no connections to the outside world.

The editors had no idea what was actually going on in Germany at the time. And as prisoners of war, they had no way of forming an impression of conditions in the Soviet Union, either. They tried to counter this isolation by introducing a new regular feature on the last page of the paper: headed 'News from the Soviet Union', it reprinted reports on what life was like in the Soviet Union. This attempt to find new subject matter was doomed to failure, as Gerlach was well aware. Even so, he made every effort to do what was asked of him. In his piece of 23 August 1945, entitled 'The old school year draws to a close', he tried to cast a spotlight on the day-to-day life of a school in the Soviet Union, an everyday existence of which he knew nothing from personal experience. This article was little short of political kitsch, but Gerlach was still mindful of Walter Ulbricht's warning: those comrades who had not yet gained enough political insight 'would be given ample opportunity in the camps to become proper anti-fascists, you mark my words!' The fact that Gerlach went about his task with conviction, and that he was consequently viewed as a progressive spirit, is evident from a letter that Erich Weinert wrote to Wilhelm Pieck and the head of Institute 99, Mikhail W. Kozlov, in July 1945. In it, Weinert proposed that twenty members of the National Committee, including Heinrich Gerlach, should be dispatched immediately to Germany. However, as it turned out, unlike Captain Hadermann, Gerlach was not among the group sent back to Germany. Understandably, having had no knowledge of Weinert's deliberations, Gerlach himself did not question why this should have been so. With hindsight, though, it is tempting to ask why Gerlach remained behind at the camp. Once again, the documents we found in the Special Archive in Moscow provide an answer, in the form of a one-page report on the person of Heinrich Gerlach, marked 'top secret'. This sheet, which dates from before Weinert's letter of July 1945, bears the signature of Mikhail W. Kozlov. After a quick resumé of Gerlach's biographical details, including his service record in the Wehrmacht until his capture, his membership of the National Committee and the editorial board of the newspaper *Free Germany* is noted. Then, however, comes the following observation:

> Comrades Ulbricht and Herrnstadt report that Gerlach is a typical representative of the German Army, who is trying to cover up his past.

After some notes about Gerlach's closest relatives and his wife, under the heading 'Grounds for refusal', reference is made to the attached documents, which are identified as follows: 'A copy of the personal dossier plus the character witness statement by Ulbricht and Herrnstadt.'

At this stage, this top-secret information still had no impact on Gerlach's fate. While he was not repatriated or sent to work in the

Soviet Occupation Zone, he did remain on the staff of *Free Germany*. His last article appeared on 6 September 1945 under the headline 'The People's Court'. In it, the editor provided a commentary on the start of the War Crimes Trials in Nuremberg, where the first twenty-four defendants appeared in November of that year. In addition to a final reckoning with the leading figures of the Nazi Third Reich, Gerlach also exhorted every individual German to 'put yourself on trial, honestly and openly!' For 'only through this kind of serious and honest self-examination do we earn the right to judge others!' Two days later, on 8 September 1945, the *Free Germany* radio station ceased broadcasting. This deprived the National Committee and the BDO of an important channel of influence, since the newspaper only had a very small circulation within the POW camps. It was hardly surprising, then, when two months later the National Committee and the BDO also applied to wind themselves up.

Eventually, permission to do so was granted by the NKVD, the Soviet Interior Ministry, with the personal blessing of Stalin and the secret police chief, Lavrenti Beria. In the final edition of *Free Germany*, which appeared the following day, 3 November 1945, a statement was printed, explaining that 'after the complete annihilation of the Hitler state and now that a democratic bloc of anti-fascist parties has begun operating in Germany', there was no longer any reason for them to continue their work in the Soviet Union. Henceforth the planning of political activity would be solely the responsibility of Soviet agencies, namely the 'Department for POW and Internees' Affairs' (UPVI) of the NKVD.

Towards the end of the war, then, the emphasis in the POW camps was on enacting an educational concept that was designed to turn the prisoners of war into 'friends of the Soviet Union' and provide an ideological spur for a 'duty to make reparations'. Ultimately, this amounted to nothing more than putting prisoners to work on reconstruction projects in the Soviet Union. According to regulations drawn up by the State Defence Committee of the Soviet

Union as early as December 1944 and February 1945, an increasing number of POWs were to be formed into work battalions numbering 750, 1,000 or even 1,500 men apiece. The prisoners were employed primarily in the construction industry, in coal mining and forestry, and in the rebuilding of ruined Soviet cities. And so, until the great wave of repatriation in 1949, POWs and internees found themselves employed as labourers on all the major building projects in the USSR. These ranged from the construction of collective farms in the Ukraine, coal mining in the Donbass region and the building of the world's largest hydroelectric power station, through repairing and enlarging the Moscow underground system, to the erection of the building that housed the Moscow Special Archive. However, at this early stage, the camp at Lunyovo remained unaffected by these developments. Even so, the situation grew tenser following the dissolution of the National Committee and the BDO. The NKVD conducted repeated interrogations of German officers. Not just the files we found on Heinrich Gerlach, but others too, verify that the Soviet security services had been conducting surveillance on a group of officers from the two organizations with an eye to recruiting them to work for the Soviet Union. To this end, information was gathered on the relevant candidates. In a top-secret communication dated 20 February 1945, the UPVI departmental head and major in the state security service, Klaussen, sent a strictly confidential list to the head of the Operational Department 15-B, Captain Shulchenko. The list, which took the form of a confidential personalized data collection file, contained the names of those members of the National Committee for a Free Germany who were of interest to the security services. Heinrich Gerlach appears right at the top, under the code name 'Teacher'. Major Karl Hetz, Major Heinrich Homann and Colonel Adam were also included.

Christmas 1945 passed without incident. Nor did the following months, up to May, bring any changes. Gerlach took a wryly amused view of the preparations for 1 May 1946, which included decking out the meeting hall with banners printed with typical Soviet slogans like 'Long Live the First of May, the Day of Struggle for All Workers'. Five days later, on 6 May, he was no longer in Lunyovo, but en route to Labor Camp 190 in Vladimir, some 190 kilometres east of Moscow and 25 kilometres away from Camp 160 at Susdal, where he had spent part of 1943. A personal data file for Gerlach, with the registration number 1848 and dated 25 July 1946, confirms his arrival in Vladimir. Before his surprise relocation, Gerlach had passed a rough plan of his Stalingrad novel, outlining its basic structure and chronology, to General von Seydlitz. Gerlach was convinced that Von Seydlitz was about to be released. He could not have known at this point that the general would only return to Germany as one of the last war captives in October 1955, more than five years after his own homecoming.

After his move, Heinrich Gerlach was initially put to work doing heavy labour on a road-building project, during which he stayed at the camp in Susdal. A labour camp was a new experience for him. Up to now, he had lived a privileged life in captivity. He knew that regular prison camps discriminated according to service rank, with the enlisted men receiving the worst treatment where both accommodation and food were concerned. The situation in camps for officers was different, where in observance of the Geneva Convention the inmates were not obliged to work, at least at first. The 'generals' camps', such as that at Voikovo, were the exception, not the rule. In Vladimir, it became abundantly clear to Heinrich Gerlach that most POWs' lives were not played out in the sort of facilities he'd known hitherto, but in these hard labour camps. And he registered with alarm that, in the Soviet Union under Stalin, there was a widespread conviction that 'where the organization of these labour camps was concerned, they had created something quite special and progressive. A visiting card from a new world that was rewriting the history of mankind afresh.' A chill ran down Gerlach's spine when he realized that 'these labour camps reflected Soviet reality. That was the thing. That was the worst aspect.'

But once again fate dealt kindly with Gerlach the war captive. When the subsidiary camp was dissolved in the summer of 1946, Gerlach was transferred to the main camp 190/1 at Vladimir. After a few weeks there, he was offered the post of editor of the wall newspaper by the camp's political instructress. She was familiar with several of his contributions to *Free Germany*. And it was a fortunate coincidence that this political instructress at Camp 190/1 in Vladimir just happened to be one Mishket Liebermann, a relative of the renowned German Impressionist painter Max Liebermann. She had been living in the Soviet Union since the late 1920s. After a brief engagement at the Deutsches Theater in Berlin, she had travelled to the Soviet Union for the first time in 1927, where she got to know Sergei Eisenstein, director of the (even then) famous film *Battleship Potemkin* (1925).

In April 1929, Mishket Liebermann made her way to Russia once more, journeying to Minsk in Belorussia via Moscow. She obtained a position at the Jewish Theatre in the city and made her debut in Ernst Toller's drama *Hoppla, Wir leben!* (*Hoppla, We're Alive!*), the play that had marked the opening of the famous German director Erwin Piscator's agitprop theatre on Nollendorfplatz in Berlin two years earlier. Following a brief spell back in Berlin just before the Nazis seized power, she promptly returned to the Soviet Union. Around that time, Erwin Piscator was establishing a collective theatre in Dnepropetrovsk, a kind of itinerant company involving several exiled German actors, among them Erwin Geschonneck and Mishket Liebermann. When the Nazis invaded the Soviet Union in 1941, she began visiting German POW camps, and became responsible for political education.

At first Gerlach gave her a wide berth and shunned any involvement with the camp's wall newspaper; he simply had no desire to trot out political slogans any more. However, Mishket Liebermann reassured him that the anti-fascist bloc politics being enacted in the Soviet Occupation Zone were not about communist agitation.

And when, in October 1946, Gerlach received the first indications that his wife Irmgard was alive and well, his whole outlook changed. Now, all he wanted was to get by as best he could and return home to Germany and his family. Accordingly, from November 1946 he produced the wall newspaper for Camp 190/1 and could build on the support of his German political instructress. And it was she, too, who retrieved the manuscript of Gerlach's Stalingrad novel, which had meanwhile found its way on to the desk of the camp commandant.

Gerlach was thus exempted from having to work outside the camp, which could well have meant hard labour. The major role the wall newspaper played in camp life was due in large measure to the importance that was accorded to the written word, and indeed to art and literature as a whole in the Soviet Union; this was very much in line with the attitude of Stalin, who in 1932 famously called writers 'engineers of the human soul'. Gerlach treated recurrent themes of captivity in his contributions: daily life in the camp, restitution, promotion of high productivity, cultural work, news from the Soviet Occupation Zone, information on the policies of the Socialist Unity Party and its newly established youth wing, the Free German Youth (FDJ), developments in global politics, and experiences within the Soviet Union. While Mishket Liebermann returned to East Berlin in 1947, Heinrich Gerlach still remained behind at the POW camp, despite the fact that a large number of German prisoners and other interned Germans had been repatriated over the course of the year. According to the latest Russian sources, a total of around 221,329 German soldiers and 33,182 internees had been released by that stage. Camp Number 69 in Frankfurt an der Oder acted as a central transit camp.

Despite his privileged position, Gerlach found the situation increasingly unbearable. Secret service men from the Ministry of Internal Affairs ordered him to compile reports on his comrades. In response, Gerlach took the only honourable course of action, divulging everything to those he was required to write about, and submitting innocuous reports in which he praised their efforts for peace and restitution and emphasizing their anti-fascist disposition. It ultimately dawned on him how the rules of the NKVD worked: ideally, everybody was expected to report on everyone else. But the security officers weren't remotely interested in gathering information; rather, they were after something else: ultimately, this was all a grand exercise in betrayal! But Gerlach had established some clear boundaries for himself; in his view, there was a line that one should not cross and where a refusal to cooperate was the only possible answer.

It is hardly surprising that we initially found nothing in Gerlach's personal dossier to indicate that the Soviet secret service agencies made any attempt to influence him. Instead, I came across a postcard from Germany, sent by the regional authority for Berlin Wilmersdorf, whose offices were located in the city's Charlottenburg district, postmarked 3 April 1948 and addressed to Heinrich Gerlach in Camp No. 2989. Why, I asked myself, should a postcard have been sent to Camp 2989? In April of that year, Gerlach was in Camp 190 in Vladimir. The solution to this supposed confusion was simpler than I thought: the number 2989 actually referred to the hospital at Kameshkovo in the Vladimir region, where Gerlach had been admitted after breaking his foot. The postcard contained an important piece of information:

> For the purpose of presenting prima facie evidence to the Russian authorities, this is to certify that Frau Ilse Gerlach and her three children: Jürgen, Maria-Dorothea [sic!] and Heinrich are all recognized victims of fascism (freedom fighters).

The document was verified by the social security office (district office 'Victims of Fascism').

The secret services in Vladimir took no notice of this corroboration of Gerlach's integrity. But because the doctor who treated him – another captured German officer – ordered that his foot should stay in a plaster cast for several weeks, Gerlach was granted some peace and quiet for a while. But then he found himself assailed from another direction, without knowing how this had come about. All of a sudden, after almost two years in the labour camp at Vladimir, on 6 May 1948 Gerlach was ordered to leave the hospital and travel by train to Moscow, with an army sergeant specially detailed to guard him. The Russian military authorities in the capital were already informed about his arrival; two officers flanked him and marched him straight to a waiting ZIM limousine, which drove out of the city. Its destination was Camp 27 (Lunyovo) at Krasnogorsk, a place where Gerlach now found himself for the third time.

XI. 'Unsuitable for repatriation' – Heinrich Gerlach in the clutches of the NKVD secret service

In Camp 27, Heinrich Gerlach encountered a number of officers with whom he had worked in the BDO and the National Committee, and whom he had assumed had long since gone back to Germany. These included: generals Lattmann, Korfes, Von Lenski and Vincenz Müller, colonels Van Hooven and Adam, and majors Lewerenz, Hetz and Homann. Gerlach was one of this group of former inmates of Lunyovo who now found themselves thrown together once more in Krasnogorsk, where they were accorded a special status. He was very uneasy about the privileged treatment he received in comparison with the other prisoners in the camp. But in any event he was happy to see the back of the camp at Vladimir, believing that he'd seen the last of the security services from Camp 190. Yet at the same time, he suspected that his sudden transfer to Krasnogorsk had not come about by chance, especially as no one at the hospital in Kameshkovo had any idea why he was being moved. All he'd been told was that 'we're not authorized here to give you orders'. In other words, the fate of the former member of the editorial board of *Free Germany* was being decided elsewhere, a thought that made Gerlach nervous. 'We can't give you orders … we're not authorized. So who was? You feel the presence of an unseen eye gazing at you, boring into your temples, the back of your neck, all over. Who's looking at you? What do they want? And why now, all these years after the war?'

What Gerlach could not have appreciated in Vladimir began to become clearer in Krasnogorsk. But the first thing that was laid on for the former Lunyovo prisoners was a regular sightseeing programme – the group was taken on a city tour of Moscow, dressed in civvies, given a guided tour of the Tretyakov Gallery and the Lenin

Mausoleum, and attended lectures on such subjects as the history of the Russian Communist Party, socialism in the Soviet Union and recent developments in the Soviet Occupation Zone of Germany. It soon became apparent what was afoot in Lunyovo: the former BDO members were being prepared for repatriation and deployment within the Eastern Zone! In the process, it gradually emerged which particular area the Russian military authorities had earmarked the former German officers for. The chief intention was for them to play an active role in the NDPD, the National Democratic Party of Germany, which had been founded in the Soviet Occupation Zone on 25 May 1948.

Heinrich Gerlach couldn't believe his ears when he heard that someone whom he had dismissed out of hand – Dr Lothar Bolz, the last chief editor of *Free Germany* and a friend of Rudolf Herrnstadt – had been appointed as the NDPD's first leader. He found it astonishing that the communist Bolz should be made chairman of a party that was a repository for lower-ranking fellow travellers and members of the Nazi Party, plus former Wehrmacht officers. However, these developments in the Soviet Occupation Zone were fully in line with Stalin's policies on Germany and Europe. Stalin, who was actually aiming for Russian hegemony over Europe and the whole of Germany, was seeking initially to manipulate the part of Germany that came under his direct influence. Accordingly, he was fully prepared to go along with the SED in bringing the denazification process to an end in 1948. But of course, in the incipient Cold War, Stalin and the Soviet authorities wanted to have some kind of safeguard and so, as well as ensuring that their informants were installed in all the political and state institutions, also began gradually to build up a network of agents in Germany.

As early as March 1944 a report was presented to the head of the People's Commissariat for Internal Affairs, the secret service chief Lavrenti Beria, which had been prepared by the acting head of the Administration for Affairs of Prisoners of War and Internees (UPVI) at the NKVD, Major General Petrov. The twenty-five-page-long report concerned the 'secret service operational work of the Soviet NKVD administration regarding the affairs of prisoners of war and other detainees'. It began by pointing out that the UPVI conducted no security operations prior to March 1942, because another NKVD department was responsible for such matters at the time. Then, as the number of POWs increased, NKVD order number 002707 authorized the formation of an operational department within the UPVI. But because a number of different agencies within the UPVI were already responsible for the supervision and monitoring of prisoners of war and for processing any intelligence gathered, there was no systematic collating of this data. In addition, the prolif-eration of authorities entrusted with this task violated the very principle of secrecy. The report noted that secret service operations had only been reorganized in August 1943 at Beria's instigation. Consequently, an operational Cheka department was created within the framework of the UPVI, comprising eleven subsections. The principal task of the new department was to organize intelligence gathering and to recruit agents for the postwar period. Suitable stations were set up, mainly in the suburbs of Moscow, for the purpose of conducting surveillance operations among POWs. Lunyovo was seen as especially important in this regard and was given the designation No.15-B by the secret services. Its significance was due to the presence there of the League of German Officers and the National Committee. Because the secret service agents had their eye on influential, well-connected and well-educated personalities and on their potential careers in postwar Germany, they set their sights especially on members of the BDO. As of 1 March 1944, the report records that 3,239 agents had been successfully recruited, 956 of whom were Germans.

Heinrich Gerlach had no way of objectively gauging the extent of the Soviet secret service's activities, and so had no inkling of how this agency was directing his odyssey through the POW camps.

The documents we found in the Special Archive indicate that the Cheka took a marked interest in Gerlach. Alongside the negative character assessment by Ulbricht and Herrnstadt, this was the reason he was not repatriated and fetched up in Lunyovo once more. The central Cheka department in Moscow had plans for Gerlach: the secret service agents in the camps were only required to exert the necessary pressure. Gerlach's personal dossier indicates that, even while he was still recuperating in the hospital at Kameshkovo, his case had been re-examined once more. A handwritten note appears in one of the documents:

> This general review was conducted by First Lieutenant [illegible] on 11 April 1948.

After this entry comes another handwritten observation, again signed by a secret service operative and giving notice of a momentous decision:

> Unsuitable for repatriation. Employee of Department Ic. 14.
> Captain [signature illegible] 25.x.48.

No comments are attached, but the Cheka appear to justify their decision by highlighting Gerlach's role as the head of Department Ic on the staff of the 14th German tank division. The security agents assumed that, in this capacity, Gerlach had been responsible for monitoring the enemy's position, and that in consequence he was the head of a department dedicated to gathering intelligence on the enemy, which had specialized in interrogating captured Russian soldiers to try to gauge the military situation. At the same time, the Russian military secret service understood 'Ic' to mean that they were dealing with a counter-espionage officer who may have commanded a detachment of secret field police. As far as the Russian secret service was concerned, therefore, Gerlach was in military intelligence, in other words a 'colleague'. The MVD officers had no idea that Gerlach had only been deputized to fill the 'Ic' post in the Stalingrad Cauldron, and that counter-espionage had played no further part at that stage. All the same, the order was confirmed on 24 December 1948, by which time Gerlach had been moved to another camp. An official stamp in the corner of the document reads: 'This personnel matter has been correctly dealt with. 24 December 1948.'

Heinrich Gerlach, though, knew nothing of this decision. His signature in the dossier dates from 5 May 1948. This means that Gerlach must have signed it in either Vladimir or Kameshkovo, one day before his transfer to the Lunyovo camp. In Lunyovo, the Cheka decided that the time had now come to recruit Gerlach for the NKVD. He had been under surveillance for years, and the GRU took the view that he was well worth cultivating in view of his role as a former Ic. Gerlach was offered the chance of becoming editor-in-chief of a magazine on art and literature in the Soviet Occupation Zone. In this role, he would be expected to forge links with intellectuals throughout Germany and to compile reports on these connections. Gerlach asked to be given time to consider. Around four weeks later, at the end of July 1948, the time came for him to put his cards on the table. To the astonishment of the secret service men, he turned the offer down, maintaining that he could not and would not cross this line.

His decision had consequences: not long after, on 14 August 1948, he was transported from Lunyovo, together with a number of others who had also refused to sign their personal dossiers. He was taken to Camp No. 435/14, a labour camp located on one of Moscow's main roads, Tverskaya Street. The camp was housed in an unfinished high-rise building whose office space was used by the Interior Ministry (MVD). The POWs were penned in behind a wooden fence topped with barbed wire in various parts of the building. Heinrich Gerlach was first put to work on a nearby building site, and later became a machine operator in a foundry.

On 12 September 1948, an extraordinary event took place. At this stage, hundreds of thousands of POWs were still being held in the Soviet Union. It was announced that a delegation from the German Democratic Women's League, based in the Eastern Zone, would be visiting Central Camp 435. With this in mind, 'Potemkin villages', a ploy typical of the Soviet Union, were put in place to try to disguise the miserable conditions: in this case, the barracks were given a fresh coat of whitewash and the assembled prisoners kitted out in new suits. The idea was that the women's delegation should see well-scrubbed, happy prisoners. Gerlach himself wasn't present at this spectacle, but two other former Lunyovo inmates gave him a detailed account of proceedings:

> The camp gates were opened, buses drove up and disgorged Russian officers in a seemingly endless flow. The orchestra played 'Entry of the Guests' from Wagner's *Tannhäuser*. And suddenly we caught sight of a small group of women, surrounded by Russian uniforms. One of our comrades, a nicely turned-out lad, stepped forward with an enormous bunch of flowers and – no word of a lie – recited a poem. The eight women sat on a podium, looking a bit lost amid all the uniforms. Someone from the anti-fascist education programme said a few political words in greeting. Then a Soviet officer introduced the SPD delegate Käthe Kern, who stepped up to the microphone.

Working in archives – especially in secret and special archives – isn't easy to plan. But my researches unearthed another discovery, in the form of a photograph album documenting the visit of the women's delegation to Camp 435, which corroborates Gerlach's recollection down to the smallest detail. The delegation did indeed visit the camp on 12 September 1948, while the 'nicely turned-out lad' was identified on a picture caption as being the 'Labour Champion Hoppe'.

The man from the anti-fascist programme, who like the rest is sporting a new suit, was a POW by the name of Caspari; it was he who also presented the women's delegation with an album documenting the achievements in re-educating the prisoners.

A few months later, at the beginning of January 1949, Gerlach and his fellow prisoners learned of a report by the Soviet news agency TASS, claiming that over the course of 1949 all the remaining prisoners of war would be released from Soviet captivity. This gave Gerlach new hope and prompted him to make another attempt to safeguard his manuscript. For several weeks, he sat awake on his plank bed, copying out his Stalingrad novel, using an ordinary arithmetic book and a pencil. Gerlach developed a method like that used by Hans Fallada in the diary that he kept during 1944, when he was being held by the Nazis. Falllada wrote on both sides of every sheet and also used 'Sütterlin' script, a historical form of German handwriting that was hard for others to decipher. When he had filled all the pages, he would invert them and use the gaps between the individual lines to continue his diary. In addition, Fallada devised a sophisticated system of abbreviations.

Gerlach didn't make things quite so complicated, though he, too, developed a minuscule form of handwriting and his own system of abbreviations. In the end, he managed to condense a manuscript of at least 614 pages into ten double sheets of the arithmetic book. He then hid this mini-transcript of his novel in a specially prepared false bottom of a wooden chest. At the same time, he approached Professor Janzen, who visited the camp around 1 May 1949, and whom he knew in his capacity as the head of the anti-fascist school in Krasnogorsk. Gerlach asked Janzen which Soviet agency might be responsible for scrutinizing his Stalingrad manuscript and in a position to issue an endorsement testifying to its harmlessness. Professor Janzen told Gerlach that the decision lay with him, and took the manuscript with him when he left the camp. After a few months had elapsed – by this time it was October 1949 – Gerlach enquired after the manuscript and received a note back from Janzen saying that, although he personally had had no concerns, the manuscript had nevertheless been confiscated. He advised Gerlach, once he had been repatriated (which was imminent), to submit a request to the Interior Ministry in Moscow to have the papers returned to him.

This reply shocked Gerlach, but he told himself that the miniature copy of the novel was safely concealed in the false bottom of his chest. Besides, his hopes of being repatriated had been raised. Camp 435 had been placed on the list of facilities that were to be closed down by the end of the year. But when the time came, Heinrich Gerlach once again found that his name was not on the list of those to be repatriated. Worse was to follow: on 16 December 1949, Gerlach was arrested; just before this happened, he was able to shuffle off his chest with the hidden manuscript onto a young fellow prisoner. Soon after, he found himself under arrest and packed off to the MVD's transit gaol. At this point, Gerlach had no idea what he was accused of, but soon found out why he had been detained.

Though Stalin had given an assurance that the last prisoners of war would be released from the Soviet Union by 1949, and indeed had formally honoured this pledge, POWs who had committed war crimes, or were suspected of having done so, were exempted from repatriation. A directive to this effect was issued by the Soviet Foreign Minister Andrei Vyshinsky, Molotov's successor and the man responsible for drawing up the scenario for the show trials of the 1930s in the Soviet Union. The 30,000 or so POWs who were accused of war crimes were dealt with in swift trials beginning at the end of 1949. They included members of the Waffen-SS, police battalions, or security units. Yet a large proportion of those condemned had nothing to do with the crimes of which they were accused. The trials were conducted according to a principle that was valid for all totalitarian systems, which the historian Lev Besymenski has summarized as follows: 'Ultimately, the system at that time had an automatism about it, and if an order went out to find war criminals, then war criminals were duly found.' POWs who had been members of the BDO and interned at Lunyovo, including Heinrich Gerlach, also found themselves caught up in the process of mass sentencing. The reason for this, apart from the negative character assessment by Ulbricht and Herrnstadt in his prisoner dossier, was very simple: his refusal to cooperate with the Soviet security services. Gerlach was released from captivity as a POW and immediately charged, in his role as an Ic, with having deployed agents and saboteurs within the Soviet Union and mistreated and murdered Soviet prisoners. These were trumped-up charges.

A document that for decades was locked away and marked 'top secret' gives us an insight into Heinrich Gerlach's situation in December 1949. The file in question is a two-page detention order dating from 6 December 1948. The order was signed by the military prosecutor Colonel Gasin and by the acting head of department at the Interior Ministry in Moscow, Colonel Gerashenko, on 10 December 1948. This directive furnishes us with proof that at this juncture Gerlach's interrogation by an investigating officer and preliminary proceedings against him had been concluded. Following his arrest, Gerlach himself added his signature on 17 December 1948, acknowledging this order. In line with this, a handwritten note appears on the document stating that 'this order has been read out in German to the accused Gerlach with the assistance of the interpreter First Lieutenant Judaison'. This order truly sealed Gerlach's fate, since the mandatory sentence for the crimes of which he was accused was twenty-five years' hard labour.

The detention order proves that the legal proceedings against Gerlach and his co-accused followed the pattern of the Great Terror of the 1930s. There was no possibility of raising objections, and the twenty-five-year sentence was set in advance. The accused individual's lack of rights was not some exceptional ruling reserved for German POWs; it was common practice in Stalin's Russia to deny even Soviet citizens any right to defend themselves against accusations and to have access to legal representation for their defence at trial. In the Interior Ministry's gaol, Heinrich Gerlach realized that even the former inmates of Lunyovo, whom the Soviet authorities had courted, were not immune from despotism and terror. The fate of Konrad Freiherr von Wangenheim, a cousin of the author Gustav von Wangenheim, who provided him with material for his Stalingrad novel, shocked him to the core. Konrad von Wangenheim, who had taken part in the eventing competition at the 1936 Berlin Olympics as part of the German equestrian team, was sentenced to twenty-five years. When Gerlach realized that the same fate awaited him, he knew what he had to do: simply say 'yes!' to the GRU's requests and survive.

Up to this point, Gerlach had not crossed the boundary he had set for himself, and had remained true to himself. His experiences at Stalingrad had turned him into an opponent of the Hitler regime, but in the interim he had also come to appreciate what mechanisms were used in the Soviet Union in order to transform the ideal of the 'new man' into social reality. Where collectivism was invoked at any price, there was no place for the personality of the individual; indeed, it was a positive hindrance and had, where necessary, to be broken through the sanctions of the state. In the late 1920s, Johannes R. Becher, whose lectures Gerlach remembered well, outlined a set of principles that intellectuals needed to adopt if they were to throw in their lot with the communist movement: 'The intellectual who wants to make common cause with the proletariat must make a bonfire of almost everything he owes to his bourgeois upbringing before he can join the ranks of proletarian freedom fighters.' And with regard not just to the artistic personality, he wrote: 'The much-vaunted, the sacred and hallowed "personality" must die. Likewise the artistic conceit of the internal and external life, the habit of exaggeration and paradox and all the emphasis on individual mood and temperament that the "personality" uses to flaunt its own self-importance. And we also need to put an end to idleness, however brilliant, and irresponsibility, however highbrow. Only if we do away with all this will the true "personality" emerge.' At this stage, Gerlach was not familiar with Hannah Arendt's analysis of the Soviet system in her work *Origins of Totalitarianism*, which does not confine itself to the so-called Stalinist 'purges' to which those German communist exiles that Gerlach had had dealings with were also forced to submit, people such as Johannes R. Becher, Friedrich Wolf, Alfred Kurella, Gustav von Wangenheim, Willi Bredel, Erich Weinert, and Georg Lukács. Hannah Arendt describes how denunciation came to play such a major role in the system of the 'Red Terror':

> No sooner was a person accused than his friends were transformed into his bitterest enemies overnight, since it was only through denouncing him and helping to build the police's and public prosecutor's case against him that they could save their own skin. Because, generally speaking, the crimes for which the accused was standing trial were non-existent, the state was reliant precisely on these people to provide circumstantial evidence against him. During the great waves of purges, there was only one way of proving one's own reliability. And that was by denouncing one's friends. And in turn, where totalitarian rule and membership of a totalitarian movement were concerned, this acted as a completely logical yardstick: in such a situation, truly the only reliable person is the one who is prepared to betray his friends. Conversely, friendship and any other form of attachment were highly suspect.

Within the exceptional circumstances that prevailed in the 'totalitarian institution' (Albrecht Lehmann) of a POW camp, friendship and integrity were precisely what provided a moral yardstick for

Heinrich Gerlach. He admitted to himself that although he had made certain compromises during his years in captivity and executed some tactical manoeuvres, he had thus far been incapable of signing up to cooperate with the Soviet secret services. Now it dawned on him that twenty-five years of hard labour would be the price for him continuing to say 'No'. And so Gerlach wrote a letter to the MVD general who in July 1948 had advised him to take up the secret service's suggestion that he collaborate with them. He announced that he had changed his position and was now ready to cooperate. Things moved quickly over the next few days. On Christmas Eve 1949, Gerlach was taken from his cell and brought with other inmates before a state prosecutor. At first, he did not understand what was required of him, but then signed a log of his detention, which was dated to the day he was sent to gaol, 16 December 1949. With this, his eight days of incarceration in the special prison were effectively struck from the record! All the charges against him were dropped. And indeed, in Gerlach's 'normal' prison record there is no indication whatsoever that he was transferred to an MVD gaol on 16 December 1949. Yet a handwritten entry marking the first lieutenant's transition through various institutions of the Soviet penal system confirms that he really was there. This reads: 'Arrived at Camp 27 on 24 December 1949 from the transit prison of the Interior Ministry, Moscow District.'

Soon after, he was sitting in a 'Black Maria' and being driven out beyond the Moscow city limits. When he stepped out of the van, he found himself in Camp 27 at Krasnogorsk for the fourth time. Here, Gerlach met the last of those who had once belonged to the leadership of the League of German Officers. In the main, these were people who had cooperated with the secret services. Others, like generals Martin Lattmann or Vincenz Müller, Colonel Steidle, majors Homann and Bechler, Military Court Justice Major Schumann or Lieutenant von Kügelgen, had already long since taken up senior positions within the German Democratic Republic.

Gerlach suspected that they had all agreed to work for the Soviet secret service during their time at Camp 27 at Krasnogorsk. The confidential files of the MVD and the KGB confirmed this suspicion.

As for Gerlach himself, a new personal dossier was created for him in Camp 27, dated 28 December 1949, which charted the final stages in his odyssey through the camps. Its reference number (PU-No. 01834838) was the one under which all the material on Gerlach was ultimately filed in the Moscow Secret Archive.

Once again, however, Gerlach found himself in a perilous situation at Krasnogorsk. In January 1950, a first lieutenant from Moscow confronted him with the miniature transcript of his Stalingrad novel, which had been discovered in the false bottom of his chest. Gerlach was deeply distressed; fearing that he would be rearrested, his first reaction was to deny everything. But then, suddenly, a great sense of calm overcame him. He had nothing to lose, so he mentioned his fear of losing the original manuscript and pointed to the fact that, despite having been a member of the National Committee, he had been accused of being a war criminal. The Russian officer knew nothing of this and expressed his sympathy. The manuscript was spirited away and Gerlach was free to go. But ultimately the day came when he was summoned by the secret service; by this time, it was April 1950. Gerlach knew what this meant. He signed his name in the knowledge that paper doesn't blush and that he ultimately had no intention of being made into a Soviet agent. His signature was his ticket from captivity to freedom.

Gerlach's prison dossier indicates that, in accordance with Protocol 582, he was released from Camp 27 on 21 April 1950 and transferred to Repatriation Camp 69. Together with the last of the Lunyovo prisoners, including Colonel van Hooven, he travelled via Moscow, Brest-Litovsk and Frankfurt an der Oder to Berlin. On 22 April 1950, he changed trains at Westkreuz and travelled one stop to Halensee, in the west of the city. He described his arrival there in *Odyssey in Red*:

Slowly he climbed the steps up to the ticket barrier. His air-force rucksack hung from his shoulders [...] His legs grew heavier and heavier. There was the barrier now, beneath the large station clock. And behind it, huddled in a corner by the ticket booths as if in fear, stood a woman [...] [He] went up to her. A boy was standing beside her, as tall as her. A child's drawing, showing a tree and a house and two yellow suns above. Two suns illuminating a bunker in Stalingrad... 'He's going to be confirmed,' said Irmgard, putting her arm round the boy and squeezing him tight. 'It's his confirmation tomorrow!' And she started to weep. It was 23.04...

XII. New-found freedom and fear of abduction – Heinrich Gerlach in the sights of the Soviet secret service

Heinrich Gerlach's prison release papers had actually been issued for travel to East Berlin. But because the train carrying the returnees arrived at Berlin Friedrichstraße station an hour early, no one from the East German authorities was there to meet it. So Gerlach simply got on the local S-Bahn train waiting on the opposite platform and travelled to the western sector of the city. The next few weeks were extremely difficult for him as a late homecomer from Russian captivity. He had joined the Wehrmacht way back in the summer of 1939 and had been separated from his family for eleven years. When his wife, his three children and his mother had been taken into 'kin custody' by the Nazis in the summer of 1944, they had been forced to leave Lyck in East Prussia with just a few suitcases. Following their release by the Americans, they made it to Berlin via Thuringia, because Gerlach's uncle lived in the capital – the opera singer he had lodged with during his semester in Freiburg.

Although his family had been officially designated as 'people persecuted by the Nazi regime', Gerlach was at first refused permission to resume teaching in higher education. Only in October 1950 did he manage to secure a badly paid post at a Berlin primary school. Despite knowing nothing about life in postwar Germany, he was immediately thrown into teaching the higher grades. This was problematic for him, as he found initially that he could not get on with the children in his charge, who had not attended school for several years. But even worse were the shadows of the past. It was not long before the comrades from the East came calling. He refused to collaborate with them and made it clear that he had no intention of pursuing the career that had been mapped out for him in East Germany. Thereafter, he came under increasing pressure.

Gerlach's daughter, Dorothee Wagner, who at the time was thirteen years old, recalled decades later how the children would come and tell their father, 'they're out in the street again' – men 'who really did look like they appeared in the movies, with leather coats and sunglasses'. Gerlach's younger son, too, who was eleven when he returned, remembered how his father had once come home from school in a distraught state and told them what he'd seen: 'At first it was just suspicions, but soon it became clear that those shadowy figures in slouch hats really were following Dad. We needed to be on the lookout, because those guys were loitering around every day at the same time but always at different places around the area, watching the family.' Gerlach warned his wife and children never to leave the house on their own. He was scared because he knew that a number of people had already been abducted. Things came to a head when the secret service men confronted him on the street in broad daylight. Passers-by came to his aid. Gerlach reported the incident to the police, hoping for their help. The eleven-year-old Heinrich Gerlach Jr remembered the response:

> The police said they couldn't do anything. My father had gone to see them on several occasions and told them about these unpleasant types. However, he couldn't even prove that he was their intended victim, and so the police patrol that had occasionally cruised specially down the otherwise quiet Lützenstraße was withdrawn when it failed to find any culprits. Whenever the police showed up, it seemed the black car with the leather coated men inside was never there.

Heinrich Gerlach was finding the situation increasingly threatening and so decided 'to look around for another position in the West'. He spotted a job advertisement in the *Deutsches Lehrblatt* (German Teachers' Journal): the humanist grammar school at Friesoythe in the Oldenburg Münsterland region of Lower Saxony was seeking to appoint a teacher of German and Latin. Gerlach applied and sent in a meticulously prepared CV and other material in support of his application. He received an immediate reply inviting him to come for an interview. Having written back to arrange a date, the next communication he received was a job offer from the headmaster of a grammar school in Brake. No one in the family had heard of this small town on the Lower Weser, which was situated about 70 kilometres from Bremen. Gerlach accepted on the spot. In order not to run the risk of travelling by train through the GDR, it was decided that they should fly from West Berlin to Hamburg. This meant that the family could only take absolute necessities with them in a few suitcases.

By March 1951, just before Easter, everything was ready: the Gerlachs boarded the plane and landed in Hamburg. They then took the train on to Brake. Their furniture was due to be brought to them by a removals firm. In the event, though, it never arrived. The Gerlach family was informed that all their worldly possessions had been destroyed in a fire. They suspected that the Soviet secret service was behind this. This assumption cannot be corroborated, although something else can be proved beyond all doubt by classified documents that have recently come to light: there was a long-standing plan to turn Heinrich Gerlach into a Soviet agent. An appraisal by the Soviet secret service of the spying activities of agents who had been successfully recruited from the ranks of captured German officers contains, alongside information on several other members of the BDO, a relatively extensive report on Gerlach. Their attempt to recruit him is noted as having been a mistake, and a failure on the part of the security services.

This report is the sole instance of Gerlach being referred to by the code name of 'Kurt'. It begins by going into his family background, his army call-up, and ends with an account of his final posting as a supposed military intelligence officer and head of an Ic department. Subsequently, it notes that Gerlach was a member of the action group that founded the BDO and that he worked on the editorial board of *Free Germany*. The report then goes on to deliver a damning criticism of the agent the Soviets thought they had been grooming: 'Kurt'. It claimed that, in the National Committee, Kurt had been 'playing a double game, spreading rumours designed to sow confusion and mocking the German communists'. It went on: 'Though fully aware of the existence of fascist underground groups within the National Committee, he failed to report them, preferring to make anti-Soviet statements himself.' This secret report maintained that it had been the National Committee leadership that had instigated Gerlach's transfer to Camp 190 at Vladimir. It was only after the National Committee had been dissolved that 'Kurt' was recruited.

In 1948, when the Council of Ministers of the USSR resolved that most former members of the National Committee should be repatriated, it was decided that Kurt should also be sent back to Germany, where he could work for the Soviet secret service. But Kurt's refusal to cooperate led to his planned repatriation being rescinded. Nevertheless, the following year the decision was taken to finally release Kurt from prison, since it had been discovered he had been sentenced to death by the Nazis for his involvement with the BDO and the National Committee. The secret service report then noted: 'In the light of this, negotiations were reopened with "Kurt" to try to get him to engage in clandestine work after his repatriation, and "Kurt" agreed to this once more. Secret passwords and methods of contacting the Soviet authorities were all agreed.' However, Kurt had then attempted to smuggle a manuscript he had written about the Battle of Stalingrad to Germany with the help of another returnee. At the border, the book had been found and impounded. This secret report, a unique example of an appraisal of the performance of clandestine agents in the field, sums up Heinrich Gerlach's subsequent activities and the failed attempt to bring pressure to bear on him, as follows:

In the Western zones of occupation, 'Kurt' wrote to a German writer, asking for his assistance in trying to retrieve his impounded book on the 'Battle of Stalingrad'. In this letter, he cast aspersions on the glorious Soviet press organs and claimed that he had been forced to agree to work with our secret services, and that he had no intention of keeping to the agreements he'd made and so would not set foot on the territory of the GDR. It has become evident that 'Kurt' is a sworn enemy of our country and an agent provocateur, whom we failed to uncover until it was too late.

We have decided not to return the impounded book, because a careful reading of the contents revealed its anti-Soviet character and the lack of evidence of any anti-fascist attitudes.

It was a major failure on our part to have tried to recruit 'Kurt' and to have repatriated him.

This report by the Soviet secret service confirmed all of Heinrich Gerlach's suspicions and also reveals the reason he was not repatriated until 1950. Furthermore, after reading these documents, his fear of being abducted by the Soviet secret police does not appear to be remotely unfounded.

XIII. Heinrich Gerlach's 'Breakout at Stalingrad' under scrutiny by the Soviet leadership – Malenkov, Beria, Suslov, Kruglov, Grigorian, Serov and Kobulov

In Brake, Heinrich Gerlach started out by renting two rooms, with shared use of the bathroom, from a widow living at Huntestraße 6. When the summer holidays of 1951 finished, the family moved into a larger flat at Breite Straße 117. Now, at the beginning of July 1951, Gerlach began trying to interest the press in his reconstruction of his Stalingrad novel. As we have already seen, he had already embarked on his first major attempt to recall his novel at Christmas 1950, after he realized that he was never going to get his original manuscript of the work back from the Soviet Union. His attempt to get to the manuscript by approaching the interior ministry through Professor Janzen had come to nothing. Gerlach could not have known that, as of December 1950, some very high-ranking Soviet officials had begun to take a keen interest in his Stalingrad novel.

Once again, earlier secret documents show how 'Breakout at Stalingrad' became an issue of such burning concern to the confidential intelligence community in the Soviet Union. Gerlach's request to the Soviet Ministry of the Interior to return his manuscript had been the catalyst for a great deal of discombobulation within the Russian party and state apparatus. On 29 December 1950, the secret police chief, Lavrenti Beria, aside from Stalin and jointly with Deputy Premier Georgy Malenkov, the most important man in the political hierarchy of the USSR at the time, received a letter, which reads as follows:

> To Comrade L.P. Beria,
>
> Pursuant to the order of the Politburo of the Central Committee of the Communist Party issued on 9 December 1950,

> please find attached information on the content of the book
> written by the former Lieutenant Colonel [sic!] of the German
> Army H. Gerlach, 'Breakout at Stalingrad'.

The letter was signed by Mikhail Suslov and Vagan Grigorian and dated 28 December 1950. According to the distribution list, a copy was also sent to Georgy Maximilianovitch Malenkov. This suggests that in December 1950, the entire governing elite of the USSR was concerned with Heinrich Gerlach and his Stalingrad novel. In 1950, as acting chairman of the Council of Ministers and Secretary of the Central Committee of the Communist Party, Malenkov was second only to Stalin. At that time, Mikhail Andreyevitch Suslov was Secretary of the Central Committee and likewise one of the most powerful politicians in the Soviet Union. Finally, at the time of this matter involving Heinrich Gerlach, Vagan Grigorian was active in foreign affairs. From 1949 to 1953, he was the chairman of the influential Foreign Policy Commission of the Central Committee of the Communist Party of the Soviet Union.

Grigorian was also the first person to deal with the issue concerning Gerlach's novel, and commissioned a report on its contents. He then forwarded this to the Secretary of the Central Committee of the Communist Party, Suslov. Then, in January 1951, three other leading party officials became involved in scrutinizing 'Breakout at Stalingrad'. On 23 January, the following 'top secret' communication was sent to Comrade Kruglov:

> As instructed by Comrade G.M. Malenkov, we are sending
> herewith for your information the report on the content of
> the book 'Breakout at Stalingrad' by the first lieutenant of the
> former German army Heinrich Gerlach.
> The attached four-page report is to be returned after reading.

This letter was signed by an assistant to the Secretary of the Central

Committee. It was also countersigned and dated 25.01.1951 by Ivan Serov and Amayak Kobulov. These three top functionaries – Kruglov, Serov and Kobulov – complete the cast list of Soviet officials dealing with the case of Heinrich Gerlach's novel. Sergei Kruglov was the USSR's interior minister, and Ivan Serov a first deputy of the Ministry of the Interior. Amayak Kobulov was, from April 1950 on, the acting head and later head of the operational directorate of GUPVI (the Main Administration for Affairs of Prisoners of War and Internees). The fact that Ivan Serov was involved in this matter once again prompts us to speculate that Heinrich Gerlach's fear of being abducted was thoroughly justified. After the war, Serov became second head of state security and in this capacity was civil director of the Soviet Military Administration in Germany (SMAD). His duties included tracking down spies, saboteurs and other hostile elements, and neutralizing those who were opposed to the institutions that were then being put in place within the Soviet Zone of Occupation. From 1945, Serov also built up an extensive network of agents within the Zone.

The report primarily went into the content of the Stalingrad novel and the author's standpoint. It stressed that the manuscript 'has as its subject one of the most significant events of the Great Patriotic War, namely the encirclement and crushing of Hitler's forces at Stalingrad in the winter of 1942–43', and that the writer, a former Wehrmacht officer, pointed out in the afterword that 'nothing was fabricated' in his novel but that it was based on 'personal experiences and conversations with German enlisted men and officers who fought at Stalingrad'. Consequently, the author would doubtless claim that he was giving a 'true account of events'. But, the appraisal contended, even the most cursory of readings revealed that the book was not only 'far from being an accurate description of the Battle of Stalingrad', but also 'a pack of lies from start to finish'. The reason for this, the report claimed, was that the author 'was not viewing and portraying the war from the perspective of a progressive anti-fascist mode of writing, but instead from the standpoint of the decadent bourgeois intelligentsia, which sympathizes with fascism'. The report then went on to list reasons why the novel should be dismissed out of hand. Firstly, the author 'seldom expresses his own opinion of Hitler's war'. Rather, fully consonant with his own 'method of bourgeois objectivism', Gerlach had preferred to 'let countless figures in the novel speak, and express a variety of different viewpoints'. Some of them 'timidly criticized the Führer, while others conversely engaged in long and openly fascist diatribes'. Secondly, the report maintained, Gerlach had depicted 'only one side in the conflict, namely the German army and principally German officers at that'. In doing so, the author had 'grossly distorted the real state of affairs', for Gerlach had presented the well-known moral standpoint of the officers of Hitler's army 'in a false light'. In Gerlach's portrayal, then, these officers had 'high ideals' and were 'noble-minded and honourable people'.

Moreover, the author had been at pains to stress the 'steadfastness and tenacity of German officers in combat'. As a result, the novel was full of 'German officers waxing lyrical about their sense of duty towards their homeland and about their loyalty and honour as officers'. The author's intention was clearly to lead his readers to conclude that, if only the kind of steadfastness and tenacity as shown by the officers in his novel had been present throughout the Wehrmacht, Hitler's army might have triumphed over the Russians. Such a biased perspective, 'which is very skilfully presented in Gerlach's novel, can only have one aim, namely to strengthen revanchist sentiment and to promote the planning of a new war against the Soviet Union'. 'It is especially enlightening,' the report added, 'to note the author's attitude to fascist leaders like Hitler and Göring.' To be sure, the novel contained a few statements by officers and generals who thought that Hitler was an 'upstart and adventurer'. But at the same time, there are other passages where the writer 'openly praises the Führer'. For instance, in describing a meeting between Hitler and his generals, Gerlach allegedly emphasized 'the Führer's humanity', while at the end of the novel, the soldiers shout: 'We give thanks to our Führer! Heil Hitler!' The author made every effort to conceal his 'hostile attitude' towards the Soviet Union. Craftily, he had 'put his owns thoughts in the mouths of his characters'. The appraisal ended with the following disparaging conclusion:

> In general, we may say of Gerlach's novel that he grossly falsifies actual events. The author skilfully promotes revanch-ist tendencies and slanders the Soviet Union. In the present climate, a book like this could prove very useful to the Anglo-American warmongers in shoring up revanchist attitudes within West Germany.

The judgement of the report was clear; in addition, it was confirmed by two further negative assessments. These are simply variations on the principal report, with the addition of a few extra quotations from Gerlach's text translated into Russian. Even the earlier, shorter appraisal that Grigorian sent Suslov on 20 December 1950 concluded with a wildly inaccurate character sketch of Heinrich Gerlach:

> It is abundantly clear from the novel that the writer was a dyed-in-the-wool SS man, and has remained so. Returning this manuscript, which represents a calumny of the Soviet people and a hymn of praise to Hitler, would be highly inadvisable. Even without a thorough edit, the book could be used in West Germany for the propagandistic aims of revanchism and remilitarization.

Studying the report on Heinrich Gerlach, one thing immediately becomes apparent: statements by his characters are equated with the alleged views of the author. In addition, the writers of the report were concerned that the writer should have stood back from the wartime events and considered them from a distance. In other words, the report writers wanted to see a sovereign authority imposed on the literary portrayal – that is, a narrator who would explicitly condemn the National Socialist system, the war against the Soviet Union, Hitler and all the officers involved, and obtrude upon the action at various points to give ideological assessments of the situation. Heinrich Gerlach's approach was quite different: through his use of immediacy and unsparing realism, he was attempting to show what the war and Stalingrad meant for the individual. The Soviet assessors were also hamstrung by another problem, namely the translation from German to Russian. As a result, a central episode at the end of the novel is not taken in the sense in which it was intended – that is, as a sarcastic and cynical judgement on Hitler and the Nazi regime. The things that Heinrich Gerlach had experienced and suffered and witnessed induced him to create a concluding episode that is meant to be read symbolically and which largely encapsulates the message of his Stalingrad novel:

> Breuer stands leaning against the wall. He looks at the faces around him, faces upon which the three-month ordeal of the Stalingrad Cauldron – which has weighed down so much more heavily than the three and a half years of war and the decades of peace before it – has left its indelible scars. These faces are a world away from those of the young, fresh soldiers who would have stood in front of the primped-up Reichsmarschall in Berlin the day before. The soldier here had seen more than other men; they'd stared into the abyss of hell.
>
> And now an eerie transformation comes over these faces. In their crazed desperation, they must surely have still nurtured some belief and hope in spite of everything – even in spite of the funeral oration they'd been treated to yesterday.

But now they realize: it's over, really and truly over. And their faces turn to stone, and their feeble hands form fists. And suddenly one of them shouts:

'We give thanks to our Führer! Heiiiil Hitler!'

Others take up the chant. The cellar resounds to the drone of their voices: 'Heiiiil Hitler! … Heiiiiiiiil Hitler!' This cry, once uttered over and over again by millions in hysterical rapture, has never sounded like it does here now. It's not mockery, it's not ridicule; it's a cold, clear, terrible reckoning. It's like an executioner's axe falling.

Breuer can feel his eyes growing moist.

'Did it have to end this way?' he thinks. 'Yes, there was no alternative!'

'So this is the end,' the captain continues. 'We didn't want this to happen. But we followed in blind obedience all the same.'

Admittedly, it appears to be more than just a translation problem that led the Russian assessor to lift the soldiers' chorus of 'We give thanks to our Führer! Heil Hitler!' out of the context of this episode and to completely ignore the subsequent comments by the narrator, which culminate in a moment of realization by the central character. For the 'Heil Hitler!' is, as the narrator says, 'not mockery, it's not ridicule; it's a cold, clear, terrible reckoning'.

This report comprehensively sealed the fate of Heinrich's Gerlach's 'Breakout at Stalingrad'. It promptly vanished into the secret archives of the Ministry of the Interior.

XIV. The original manuscript

In the book of reminiscences that he compiled for his own children, Heinrich Gerlach's younger son, Heinrich Jr, notes how his father, from 1951 onwards, alongside his work as a grammar-school teacher, found himself faced with another, far greater challenge: the reconstruction of his lost Stalingrad novel. According to his daughter, Dorothee Wagner, Gerlach had something akin to a feeling of guilt. Time and again he asked himself why he had survived. The lesson he drew from this for himself was an obligation to bear witness to the catastrophe at Stalingrad. According to Heinrich Gerlach Jr, once the family's circumstances had slowly begun to return to an even keel, his father decided to 'rewrite the novel about the Battle of Stalingrad'. Disappointed by the results of the hypnotism experiments with the magazine *Quick*, the only way forward he could see was 'to rewrite the work from the beginning, relying on some fragments he'd pieced together and his recollection of the novel'. And so, over the following years, and with the family's help, the novel re-emerged, chapter by chapter. 'The sole topic of conversation in the house was Stalingrad,' Gerlach's daughter recalled.

Gerlach involved the whole family in the business of recreating the novel; whenever he completed a chapter, he would 'always read it out in front of us and invite us to criticize it'. Every reading was followed by a lively discussion, in which Heinrich Jr's older siblings stated their opinions very forthrightly, finding as they did 'a lot of the material too "corny" or "long-winded"'. Looking back, Dorothee Wagner has identified two things that resulted from Gerlach's constant work on restoring his novel. On the one hand, as his daughter she felt that she was being taken seriously for the first time, all the more so since Gerlach took the criticisms levelled by his family audience on board and made changes to the manuscript as a result. On the other hand, the whole affair was rather stressful.

'It brought back memories of the war, and in truth that was very taxing for us as children,' she recollected. Even so, after sixty years she still saw that time in a positive light: 'In retrospect, I wouldn't have missed it for the world.'

Even the Gerlachs' younger son, whom his sister assumed might not be able to handle hearing about the events at Stalingrad, regards the reconstruction of his father's novel as a really exciting moment in his own childhood. By his own account, he had 'secretly admired his father for his ability to write such things, and listened with rapt attention to his readings'. Even as a boy, he said, it was clear to him how much effort it must have cost. 'The book didn't write itself,' he acknowledged. As observers during the process of its genesis, the Gerlach children had experienced how 'the writer really had to grapple with the individual sentences, and for days on end the head of the Garlich household [the fictional name Heinrich Jr uses for the family in his memoirs] would go around with a vertical furrow of worry creasing his brow, and nobody dared to talk to him'. In much the same vein as his older sister, Heinrich Gerlach Jr summarized the situation during the process of recreating the novel, which lasted until 1956, thus: 'Stalingrad moved into our back room in Brake and dominated the life of the Gerlach household for years, albeit at one remove.'

These reminiscences by the Gerlach children, as well as the complex genesis of the novel, corroborate the argument that Heinrich Gerlach put forward in his legal dispute with the hypnotist Dr Schmitz. He laid out the facts of the case as he saw it most convincingly in an interview with the *Frankfurter Illustrierte* magazine in March 1958:

> I know exactly [...] what I have to thank Schmitz for. He gave me a strong initial impetus and provided me with the building blocks that enabled me to reconstruct around 150 pages of my confiscated manuscript relatively quickly. But that's as far as it went. Claims that I could never have got my story down on

paper again without Schmitz's help are nonsense. Granted, it
might have taken a bit longer.

Because the original manuscript had either been lost without trace
or disappeared into a Russian archive, Heinrich Gerlach had no idea
whether his attempt to reconstruct the work was close to the original
or if, in the course of the various reworkings he had undertaken up to
1957, he had inadvertently introduced some major changes. Only a
side-by-side comparison of the two versions almost sixty years later
made it possible to solve another mystery in this curious tale. The
question remains as to how such a comparison turned out.

The first thing to say is that the conditions for a reconstruction
of the Stalingrad novel – notwithstanding the time it took and the
psychological stress – were favourable. This was due to a number of
reasons: Heinrich Gerlach had worked out the chronological course
of the Stalingrad catastrophe, and so was able to recall from the
outset the stages of the battle for the city that tied in with his personal
experiences. The key thing, therefore, was to connect all the events,
incidents and occurrences and the people and places involved
and to incorporate them into the flow of the narrative. Moreover,
because Gerlach had, during his time in prison, continued to revise
his novel even after completion, changing and correcting certain
passages, several of the details must have imprinted themselves
firmly on his memory. Add to this the fact that, in preparing
his miniature transcription of the novel in early 1949, he must of
necessity had to vividly recall not only the 614 pages of the original
manuscript but also the actual events in Stalingrad. The task that
he was now faced with thus resembled what would nowadays be
called a mental journey back through time to the past. What was
required was for him to retrieve his Stalingrad experiences piece by
piece from his autobiographical memory. In the process, he needed
to weld together a mass of individual episodes, which in turn were
connected with one another in a variety of different ways, into a

single great storyline. We should therefore not be surprised that, in recreating *The Forsaken Army*, Heinrich Gerlach appeared on the face of things to have succeeded in vividly reconstructing in all its fundamental stages the tragedy that unfolded at Stalingrad. In a nutshell, key elements of the plot are identical in both versions. Likewise, 70 per cent of the chapter headings, written in capital letters, are identical to those in the original manuscript.

Yet common wisdom maintains that the same story can be told in a number of different ways. And that's precisely what emerges from a comparison of the two versions of the Stalingrad novel, which tally with one another only at first glance. On closer inspection, a whole series of differences become apparent, which it would be no exaggeration to call highly significant. Basically, the following points emerge: Heinrich Gerlach's new version/ reworking accords with the new attitude to Stalingrad hinted at in the title. *The Forsaken Army*, with its clear connotations of treachery and abandonment, places the emphasis on what the catastrophe at Stalingrad represented – the deliberate act of betrayal by Hitler and the Nazi leadership, who abandoned 300,000 men to their fate by ordering them to hold the Stalingrad Cauldron at all costs. The original was quite different in this regard. There, Gerlach used the idea of the 'breakout' in the title to make greater play of the military situation and the life-or-death predicament of the German troops caught in the Cauldron at Stalingrad.

The different beginning to the text of each version then goes on to make clear how Gerlach structured his new version. Whereas the original text leads the reader into the story and, by mentioning the precise location of Kotluban, immediately sets the scene for the winter battle for Stalingrad, the new version begins *in medias res* with direct speech and the introduction of the central character of First Lieutenant Breuer. This may seem unimportant, but it actually broaches a fundamental principle that distinguishes the two texts from one another: the original version, with its treatment of military operations between October 1942 and the end of hostilities in Stalingrad at the beginning of 1943, is consistently more precise. Like in a report, exact place names that were of significance to the battle of encirclement around Stalingrad are mentioned repeatedly. The reference to the station at Kotluban right at the start of the text, for example, hints at the actual military state of affairs at the time, for it was around there that the Red Army launched a second offensive in September 1942, which would turn out to be decisive for the fate of the German army at Stalingrad over the ensuing months.

In the original version, Gerlach captures more successfully the increasing hopelessness of the military plight of the Sixth Army, and builds up an atmospherically denser picture of the desperate situation facing the enlisted men and officers. This greater precision, which becomes apparent the further one reads, is evident even in the minutest linguistic details, which seem inconsequential at first. While the original version talks about a 'rapid march' (across the Kalmyk Steppe), in the new version this term was replaced by the synonym 'quick march', more accessible to a 1950s readership. But this alteration sacrifices a rich seam of allusion, since 'rapid march' (*Geschwindmarsch*) was not only a current military term at the time when the action takes place in the autumn of 1942, and formed part of the common vocabulary of the German *Landser* (general infantryman), but was also the term for a Prussian marching style, based on motifs from the composer Johann Strauss the Elder's quadrilles. In general, the protagonists' speech in *Breakout* adheres more closely than the new version to the soldiers' argot with which Gerlach was so familiar – language that often comes across as terse and banal, but which conveys the prevailing tense situation all the more accurately.

It is clear that both versions of the Stalingrad novel are ultimately based on Heinrich Gerlach's own episodic and autobiographical reminiscences. Yet when Gerlach wrote the original version, the disastrous defeat was still fresh in his mind, for he began jotting down his first notes as early as the autumn of 1943, just a few months after the surrender of the Sixth Army. In view of the trauma that Stalingrad represented to Gerlach and his fellow soldiers, this was a very short time span, which inevitably was not without implications for the process of recollection and of necessity impacted on the way the story was told. In consequence, Gerlach tellingly did not choose a mode of narration that created any kind of distance to the events being described, but on the contrary opted for a style that one might term 'dramatic', and he largely narrates the tale with no distancing whatever. Precisely at those points where the horrors of war overtake the desperate soldiers, the narrator's presence recedes into the background, giving the events being portrayed a raw immediacy. For example, when he describes the situation of the exhausted Romanian divisions that are supposed to be providing support for the German troops, catastrophe irrupts in the form of a Russian assault:

> There! Suddenly the air fills with a sinister and eerie hissing and whizzing sound. Cries of fear and shouts of alarm ring out. And then, in an instant, the storm is upon them. All of a sudden, a forest of flames erupts from the rumbling ground, and a hailstorm of shrapnel comes whistling towards them, as clouds of sulphurous smoke billow across the plain. So sudden is this attack, and so unexpected in the sluggish stillness of the morning, that even the front-line troops' keen antennae for trouble are of no use. Only a handful of the men, standing around with no inkling of what's about to happen, heed the threatening hum and dive for cover in time. The rest are scythed down even before they realize what's happening.
>
> The bombardment grows in intensity, with the countless Stalin organs being joined by weapons of every calibre. Fountains of earth burst upwards, forming a wall that then comes crashing down on the minefield in front of their position, setting off the charges, shredding the barbed-wire

entanglements, burying trenches and machine-gun nests, and whipping up a maelstrom of pieces of wood, weapons and human body parts, before rolling on to the rearward artillery positions. All to the accompaniment of a terrible seething, roaring, howling and cracking sound… The very ground on which they are standing, torn and lacerated, flinches under the hellish onslaught of material. What a piece of work is man…!

The description of the same scene in *The Forsaken Army* is very different; there, chaos does not suddenly erupt out of the blue, but instead a narrator guides the reader to the event from his sovereign perspective ('Suddenly the air was full of an odd, sinister humming…'). The chosen tempo of narration, recounted in the past tense, loses the immediacy of the original version and ultimately creates a distance to the events being narrated. Even leaving that aside, however, the account of the Russian attack in the new version is noticeably shorter. A similar situation arises in the description of another military action preceding the encirclement of the Sixth Army, which once more recounts an attack by the Red Army. This assault causes panic among the German men and officers and causes the divisional staff to retreat in the aftermath. In the middle of the night, a stranger bursts into the house where the staff officers have billeted themselves and collapses in a state of near-exhaustion. He is a young sergeant, 'not wearing a coat or helmet, dishevelled and covered in filth. His lank hair is plastered to his forehead, and he is bleeding from a gaping head wound.' All he can say at first is 'The Russians, First Lieutenant, sir, the Russians!' His following description of the events he witnessed then gives readers an authentic impression of what unfolded, drawing them directly into the life-and-death situation, so to speak:

'We're lying in bed, totally unsuspecting… Suddenly, there's a massive bang, and the whole roof comes crashing down on our heads… and the place is on fire… first thing I do is run to the window and climb out into the open! There, all hell has broken loose. Half the village in flames. Explosions all around, everyone running about like crazy. In the midst of all this, Russian tanks… they were firing into the houses… Our horses from the veterinary hospital were racing past in blind terror… some of them hadn't made it out of the blazing stables. They were screaming… literally screaming… It was terrible.'

Then the man shrinks back into his shell once more.

The immediacy of this description derives not least from the sentence fragments, which look like they have been cut off, and whose elliptical form dispenses with finite verbs – a really apposite way of conveying the flustered state of the young soldier. Here, too, the new version treats the incident differently, depicting the situation in a more measured tone in the form of the protagonist's speech and weakening the overall effect through the use of such narrative formulations as 'must have been' ('Well, in any event we must have been pretty fast asleep […] It was as bright as day, half the village must have been on fire.').

Noting these patent differences between the two versions prompts the question as to whether, and if so in what way, the author's particular situation at the time of writing influenced his portrayal. Was it the case that the 'total institution' of the camp caused Gerlach willingly or even subconsciously to adopt the ideological premises of Soviet propaganda? Jochen Hellbeck certainly takes this view, assuming that Gerlach must have been an almost perfect pupil of the Soviet re-education programme in the POW camps. I take the opposite position. While it is beyond question that Heinrich Gerlach, after his experiences at Stalingrad, would have found himself in agreement with certain arguments put forward by the National Committee for a Free Germany, this was in no way the result of didactic influence, but rather the consequence of what Gerlach had gone through in the Cauldron. In addition – as the concluding assessments of his character by the Soviet secret service show – Gerlach had constantly kept his distance from the ideological opinions of the German communists and from Soviet policies.

Another factor also came into play here: by his own admission, Heinrich Gerlach considered the act of writing his Stalingrad novel as an attempt to 'heal his own psyche, in order that he might "finally rid himself of the nightmare visions of what had happened at Stalingrad"' (Paul Kühne). Hence, modulation and self-censorship played no role in the writing of his account. Rather, Gerlach was far more concerned to get as close as possible to the actual experiences. Only by doing so could he ensure that his writing became a 'screen memory' that would perform the role of 'healing him psychologically'. The way in which Heinrich Gerlach then went about configuring his Stalingrad experiences confirms this thesis. Thus, the original text is dominated by a mixture of epic narration and dialogue, with little room left for critical reflection. There are good reasons for that: in terms of cognitive psychology, the original version of the novel acts out so-called 'field memories'. Such recollections are characterized by their tendency to reconstruct past events 'from the original perspective of the subject as they experienced it at the time'. This is quite a different process from that which occurs in 'observer memories'. These are memories in which we primarily behave like 'detached observers' and in this way produce 'modified versions of the original event' which we 'first perceived from a field perspective'. The fact that field memories predominate in Breakout at Stalingrad, whereas The Forsaken Army is overwhelmingly characterized by observer memories, is also evidenced by the greater emphasis on personal narration in the original version, which places front and centre the experiences of the individual as these events unfold around him on the field of action.

The degree to which the discourse of the 1950s obtrudes upon the newly created text of The Forsaken Army and overlays the field memories is also apparent from a chapter that was remarkably sensitive for the period, given that it treated the question of whether and to what extent the Wehrmacht was involved in war crimes. I disagree with German historian Hannes Heer's otherwise very nuanced book *Vom Verschwinden der Täter* ('On the Disappearance of the Perpetrators') about the war of extermination in the East in one key regard: namely his conclusion that works of fiction never portray the soldiers of the German army as having anything to do with such crimes. According to Heer, 'no novel has ever recounted the crimes that were committed in the occupied territories in the East or the Southeast... and there is no literary character who ever admits to these acts or who condemns himself out of his own mouth'. Norman Ächtler has proved that this is not the case, and that the crimes of the Wehrmacht most definitely were treated in literature. Yet in cases where novels did indeed touch on crimes committed by the Wehrmacht, this fact did not gain much prominence in the public's perception, with the result that these episodes were marginalized and pushed to the fringes of the collective consciousness. Heinrich Gerlach therefore belongs – alongside Theodor Plievier, Heinrich Böll, Gerd Gaiser, Hans Werner Richter, Franz Wohlgemuth, Fritz Wöss, Willi Heinrich or Rudolf Krämer-Badoni – to that group of authors who unequivocally do thematize the crimes of the Wehrmacht. Thus, just before he decides to desert, Lakosch, the driver of Gerlach's central character, First Lieutenant Breuer, recalls the crimes of the German army that he was involved in. In the original version of the novel that Gerlach wrote in Soviet prison camps, Lakosch calls to mind 'an incident from the summer of '41'. In the 'Ukrainian village of Talnoye, at the northeastern corner of the Uman Pocket', Lakosch comes across a 'jeering crowd of soldiers, who were herding a bunch of small figures dressed in strange black garb ahead of them down the street. "What's going on here then?" he asked. – "They were firing at us from a basement!" – "What, this lot here?" – "No idea! Someone was, at any rate!" – "So what now?" – "What now? We're gonna do 'em in, that's what! It's all their fault, the swine!" Lakosch joined the procession.' Later, we are told very briefly from Lakosch's viewpoint how a group of fifty Jewish men of middle age, who had already been grievously maltreated, was about to be put to death by boys on fatigue duty, anti-aircraft gunners and soldiers from 'every conceivable unit'. An NCO from the flak battery, whose voice was 'hoarse from shouting' and 'now produced only an animal-like bellow' and who was beside himself with rage, had appointed himself leader of the lynch mob. The escalating situation was finally nipped in the bud by an officer:

> 'What's the meaning of this?'
> The troops flinched, instantly brought to their senses. The NCO approached, swearing and gesticulating wildly.
> 'Get a grip on yourself, man!' the officer barked at him. 'Who gave you orders to do this?'
> Suddenly waking from his frenzy, the NCO stood there silently gaping before slumping down, a broken man. Taking a furious swing, the officer batted the pistol out of his hand.
> 'Get out of my sight, you animal!' The NCO slunk off there and then, without a word. 'And the rest of you, disperse this instant!'
> Muttering among themselves, the soldiers retreated, but stayed loitering around the scene.

This shocking scene ends with the Jewish men trying to express their gratitude, which the officer curtly rebuffs, telling them: 'Just piss off […] and don't show your faces here again!' The direct speech then switches to a passage of internal focalization, giving us Lakosch's reflections on the incident:

> Lakosch also found himself seized with rage at the time, because the officer's intervention had deprived him of a ghoulish spectacle. Even so, he could never rid himself of

the memory of this incident. And this recollection changed his outlook. Now, whenever he thought of the faces of the seventeen-year-old boys on fatigue duty, predatory children's faces distorted with bloodlust – all he felt was disgust and shame.

'That isn't war any more,' he would recall with a shudder, 'it's...'

But he couldn't even find the words to express what was troubling him.

In *Breakout at Stalingrad*, this episode is conveyed in an extremely condensed form through the rapid shift between dialogue and terse narration. Here, too, *The Forsaken Army* does things very differently, interposing comments by the narrator into both elements. Thus, the flak NCO is described in the following terms: 'He had a face of the sort you come across all over the place behind counters and perched on office stools. But the devil seemed to have taken possession of this bland countenance.' While there are no indications in the original version as to why the Jewish men are going to be executed, so expressing the casual matter-of-factness of this act of murder, the new version provides a reason for the soldiers' lack of inhibition. Lakosch, who asks why they are intending to put the men to death, receives the reply they are 'to blame for everything', whereupon the narrator intervenes to comment:

> Lakosch felt ashamed at his question; after all, he'd been given any amount of information about the Jews from pamphlets and lectures. He lifted his carbine off his shoulder and pushed to the front of the crowd. He was filled with a grim satisfaction at finally being able to settle personal scores with those who were really responsible for this war.

This intervention by the narrator refers explicitly to the role of

Nazi propaganda, which was largely responsible for corrupting the young men. Following on from this, the conflict situation, in comparison with the original version, is staged in a far more dramatic way and evolves into a full-blown standoff between a bestial common soldier and a humane officer. The officer is clearly put centre stage as the antagonist of the out-of-control infantryman and the significance of his courageous intervention is emphasized by the thrust and counter-thrust of his exchanges with the soldier. In order to prevent the situation from getting totally out of hand, he is even forced to brandish his pistol. In line with this, his reaction to the gratitude shown by the Jewish men is also more friendly than in the manuscript of *Breakout*, as he tells them: 'Quickly, quickly! Get out of here!' Surreptitiously, through the pointed dialogue the episode turns into an exceptional situation and a clash between a Wehrmacht officer following proper procedure on the one hand and bloodthirsty troops on the other. The subsequent reflection on the part of Lakosch underscores the uniqueness of the incident and the clear effort to direct our sympathies.

The episode outlined above is just one example of how the prevailing discourse of the 1950s was written into *The Forsaken Army*. The existential isolation of the individual is presented much more powerfully in the new version. The situations in which the individual is called upon to make crucial decisions are charged with an atmosphere of existentialism. In tune with the kind of 'big history' that was predominant in the 1950s, the generation who fought at the front are portrayed as the victims of tyranny and war. *The Forsaken Army* thus follows the basic template of a whole generation of works, including essays and especially novels and short stories, that made the German foot soldier into the victim of a dictatorial system.

In summary, we may draw following conclusions: the original manuscript, which was written when Gerlach was still in a POW camp, differs markedly from the reconstructed version, which was created during the period after Gerlach's return to Germany

(1950–56) and in which the tenor of the narrative is unmistakably a vehicle for the postwar discourses of the 1950s. This novel, published in 1957, has acquired the status of an authentic piece of documentation that compares and evaluates in such a way as to make the language appear more weighty, polished and smooth. Furthermore, the device of the narrator acts as a vehicle for putting across the characteristic 1950s' narrative of the soldier as victim.

The author of the original manuscript does not expound problems, and comments on the action to a far lesser extent. Through the 'hard-bitten writing style' of his portrayal, he is therefore able more authentically to form a kaleidoscopic impression not only of the German soldier during a campaign but also of the 'individual' caught in the Stalingrad Cauldron between illusion, hope and inhuman suffering without paying any attention to concerns beyond the story he is narrating. His unvarnished but nevertheless sympathetic gaze adopts the cause of humanity. The depiction gets underneath the grubby uniform of the soldier and reveals his miserable craving for tinned meat rations, cigarettes, firewood and imitation Christmas trees, as well as his loneliness, vulnerability, despair and destitution in the icy bunkers of the battlefield. For all its moral and narrative detachment from any background political or ideological concerns, this uncompromising account nonetheless most definitely succeeds in generating a certain sympathy, not for the German soldier as a fighter, but certainly for the human being in all his weaknesses and strengths. As a consequence of this, the phenomenon called 'comradeship' plays an immeasurably more central role in Gerlach's original manuscript than is the case in the reconstructed and rewritten new version. This obvious compassion for the 'soldier as human being' is the result of the immediate impressions and traumatic experiences of the former officer and eyewitness to the Battle of Stalingrad, Heinrich Gerlach, who, during his long incarceration as a prisoner of war, sought to break the bonds of his captivity through the act of writing.